About the Editor

AL SARRANTONIO'S twenty-five books include the horror novels *Moonbane*, *House Haunted*, *Skeletons*, and *Totentanz*, as well as the critically acclaimed science fiction trilogy *Five Worlds*. He has been an editor, reviewer, and columnist, and has been nominated for the Horror Writers Association's Bram Stoker Award and the Private Eye Writers of America's Shamus Award. His short stories have appeared in magazines such as *Heavy Metal*, *Twilight Zone*, and *Realms of Fantasy*, as well as in anthologies including *The Year's Best Horror Stories*, *Great Ghost Stories*, and *The Best of Shadows*. A collection of his best horror tales, *Toybox*, has just been published. His official website is located at www.members.aol.com/alsarran.

999

*Twenty-nine Original Tales of
Horror and Suspense*

edited by

AL SARRANTONIO

Perennial

An Imprint of HarperCollins*Publishers*

Individual copyright notices can be found on pages 665–666, which serve as a continuation of this copyright page.

A hardcover edition of this book was published in 1999 by Avon Books, Inc.

HarperCollins books may be purchased for educational, business, or sales promotional use. For information please write: Special Markets Department, HarperCollins Publishers Inc., 10 East 53rd Street, New York, NY 10022.

First Perennial edition published 2001.

Designed by Kellan Peck

The Library of Congress has catalogued the hardcover edition as follows:

999 : new stories of horror and suspense / edited by Al Sarrantonio.—
  1st ed.
    p.   cm.
  1. Horror tales, American. 2. Detective and mystery stories,
American. I. Sarrantonio, Al. II. Title: Nine hundred ninety-nine.
PS648.H6A16 1999   99-20895
813'.08738—dc21   CIP

ISBN 0-380-80518-9 (pbk.)

01 02 03 04 05 JT/RRD 10 9 8 7 6 5 4 3 2 1

For
The Editors:
Harlan Ellison,
Kirby McCauley:
Lewis and Clark of no less daunting territories.

Acknowledgments

No book is an island, and this one, especially, owes its form and being to some very special people.

My thanks to:

David G. Hartwell, F. Paul Wilson, Dave Hinchberger, Rich Chizmar, and Matt Schwartz, for pointing me in fruitful directions;

Pete Schneider, who was there from the beginning;

Jennifer Brehl, who let me borrow her writers, and (even when the shovel was broken) dug for gold;

Ralph Vicinanza, who piloted the agent's ship;

Tom Dupree, Avon editor supreme;

Marsha DeFilippo, Angel of Mercy;

And Stephen King—from one writer to another.

Contents

Introduction

What you now hold in your lap (yes, I *know* it's heavy) is a feast.

Quite simply, it's the biggest, the most lavishly appointed, and (we think, hope, and pray) the finest collection of brand-new horror and suspense stories ever published.

Part One: Reasons

In 1996 I set myself the goal to put together, by the end of the millennium, a huge original horror and suspense anthology. My initial inspiration was Kirby McCauley's groundbreaking 1980 book *Dark Forces,* which for many became, and remains, the best collection of new stories in the genre. In turn, McCauley's inspiration was Harlan Ellison's *Dangerous Visions,* which had, almost single-handedly, changed the way readers thought about science fiction. Since Ellison had been at least partially successful in redefining sf as a literary rather than a "ghetto" genre, McCauley decided, at the end of the 1970s, that it was time to do the same thing for the horror field, which was just gaining, due to the trickle-down effect of the best-selling efforts of Ira Levin, William Peter Blatty, and a Young Turk named Stephen King, "ghetto" status of its own. The time was ripe, McCauley reasoned, to elevate the burgeoning horror genre to literary status.

There were successors to McCauley, notably Douglas E. Winter, whose *Prime Evil* gave a booster shot to the idea of horror's literary viability in 1989. But I came to believe that the horror field, here at the end of the millennium, was still to a great extent stigmatized with the ghetto label and that there was more work to do in gaining for it the literary respect it deserves.

So, twenty years after McCauley's effort, I concluded that it was time to prove, once and for all, that the horror and suspense genre is a serious literary one.

I had other reasons for tackling the project. One was my abhorrence of the fact that there are, as I write this, literally no professional markets for good horror fiction. While on the face of it this might prove that the genre has indeed gained literary acceptance—moved out of its ghetto, so to speak—the truth is exactly the opposite: it has been squeezed even tighter into its niche and nearly smothered there. While an occasional story by Stephen King or Joyce Carol Oates might appear in one of the slick literary magazines like *The New Yorker,* these are aberrations, more a consequence of their authors' prominence and individual talent than a widening of the genre's influence. Despite the continuing success of a few semiprofessional magazines, the most prominent of which remains Richard Chizmar's *Cemetery Dance,* there is, today, almost no place where well-written horror stories are allowed to appear with regularity. When I was making my bones in the business in the late 1970s and early 1980s, there were dozens of outlets for fiction, many of them professional—if *Shadows* didn't want a particular piece, then *The Twilight Zone* or *Night Cry* or *Whispers* might surely accept it. Today, a young writer with talent trying to break in has nowhere above the semipro level to go. This is both heartbreaking and infuriating.

Such a book as the one I envisioned would at least give some of these new Young Turks a shot at a market paying more than three cents a word.

Another reason, as one of my recurring pipe dreams went: if such a book were successful, it might even start in the genre a third Golden Age (the first having occurred in the 1930s, covering the heyday of *Weird Tales* under the editorship of Farnsworth Wright; the second covering the fifteen years from 1975 to 1990); then, perhaps, some of those lucrative professional short story markets of the 1980s would return, assuring the continued literary health of the genre.

A final reason was just to do it—to see if a massive original anthology, without a theme and displaying great work, was still possible in the field at the end of the millennium.

Part Two: Definitions

What you will find in this book are stories of both supernatural horror and nonsupernatural suspense. For the purposes of this project, and in order to present the genre at its widest and most representative, my definition of the terms *horror* and *suspense* is the broadest possible one: if it scares you, that's it. There may or may not be a bogeyman. The bogeyman might be nothing more than the human mind (to me, the scariest place of all). The important thing is the scare itself.

(For better, more descriptive, deeper, and more entertaining discussions of what horror, terror, suspense, fear, and all that is, I direct you with enthusiasm to three sources: H. P. Lovecraft's seminal essay "Supernatural Horror in Literature"; the introduction to the best single collection of classic, reprint horror stories ever assembled, Phyllis Cerf Wagner's and Herbert Wise's Modern Library volume *Great Tales of Terror and the Supernatural;* and Stephen King's various writings on the subject—especially *Danse Macabre*.)

Part Three: Reality

I've given my reasons for persuing this project in 1996—how did things turn out?

That I was able to do the book is idiotically self-evident: the damned thing is weighing down your lap at this moment. At more than a quarter of a million new words, and containing one novel, three novellas, eight novellettes, and a whole bunch of short stories, it is the fattest volume of its kind ever assembled; and we were able to pay the authors a very healthy rate—as far as I know, the highest that has ever been paid for an original horror anthology. (They all got the same rate, by the way.)

And, twenty years after *Dark Forces,* I had no trouble collecting quality work with high literary standards.★ Even if the field at this point is horribly contracted (it is) and the markets stink (they do), there is still a hell of a lot of good, well-written stuff out there, much more than I could use. I raised the bar, and the writers, bless 'em all, never brushed it as they vaulted over. Even with all the room I had in this book, I had to turn away top-notch stories.

And I've been able to publish some newer writers who've never been exposed to this kind of venue.

That covers three of my reasons for doing this book.

But what about my fourth reason: to inspire a third Golden Age in the field?

Well . . . that remains to be seen.

It might prove instructive to examine the past before predicting the future.

★To be fair, and with the comfort of retrospection, I think McCauley's precursor, Harlan Ellison, had the tougher row to hoe: wrenching the reins of science fiction from the philistines and hacks who had dominated the sf genre from the beginning (indeed, had invented it) was much more difficult than Kirby's (and, by extension, my own) goal of establishment—after all, horror already had a much more definite literary heritage to draw on. See Hawthorne and Poe for appropriate examples.

Part Four: You Guessed It, the Past

By the early 1980s, the horror field seemed to be driving a steamroller over every other form of imaginative fiction. The number of science fiction, fantasy, and mystery writers who climbed up into the steamroller's cab—not to mention the occasional mainstream or romance writer such as Anne Rivers Siddons, author of the brilliant (if clunkily written) novel of haunting *The House Next Door*—only proved the field's sudden viability (not only was it exciting, there was money to be made). The newly ghettoed genre became a repository for stories that couldn't be published anywhere else (a very good thing, and I'm not the first one to notice this). It coalesced out of nearly nothing into something vibrant, exciting, and controversial—remember the heated arguments over "quiet horror" and "splatterpunk"?—and then ultimately, by the end of the decade, began to deflate and nearly disappear.

Why?

It's tempting to blame the mindless, self-destructive, and boneheaded policies of a publishing industry that never understood the field to begin with, didn't know poop from popcorn as far as what belonged therein, never gave a thought to anything beyond the bottom line, and then crap-published the genre nearly out of existence.

But that's way too easy—publishers *always* follow trends and fads, *always* overpublish, and *always,* because of their inherent wish to make a profit (publishing is, after all, a business—and always was, despite what some of us remember as a kinder, gentler industry before the corporations took over), tend to kill the goose that laid the golden egg.

Let's look deeper.

There is a theory that the core readership of the horror field was always small, and that it ballooned in the 1980s with faddists: these were readers (and even those who don't read very much) brought in by the promise of thrills like those given them by the horror bestsellers: books like *'Salem's Lot, The Shining,* and *Ghost Story.* These clowns were on the roller coaster only so long as it gave 'em a good ride, and then they took their big feet elsewhere.

The definition of the end of a fad is, of course: death.

Or it may be that the visual entertainment industry—television, the movies, video games, more recently CD-ROM and other computer technology—did what it always does to something hot: chewed it up, spit it out, then lapped up the regurgitation and repeated the exercise—and, in the process, co-opted the field.

(Despite all of Harlan Ellison's good and great efforts, isn't this what happened in the science fiction field? Anyone remember *Star Wars,* which was released within five years of *Again, Dangerous Visions?*)

And then there is also flight to the suburbs to consider: many of the most successful writers in the horror ghetto moved out of it into the mainstream as fast as possible, leaving mainly the junk behind (there is no blame involved here; remember, we're talking about a *ghetto*); couple this with the fact that the so-called mid-list in publishing (traditionally the industry's AAA farm system, readying the next generation of sluggers for the big leagues) was in the process of being killed off at the same time, and it ain't hard to figure out what might have happened.

Part Five: The Future

Are we headed for the Great Third Golden Age of Horror Fiction?

There are signs and portents, lately.

For one thing, the small press phenomenon—in particular, the limited edition business, which had constricted a few years ago nearly to the point of winking out of existence—has shown a robustness lately that is encouraging. Since small presses are a mixture of labor of love and moneymaking operation, this is indicative. The same thing happened at the beginning of the second Golden Age. The small publishers are jackals (I don't use this term pejoratively); they come in at sharp angles and snap at the meal until the lions (the big publishers) amble over and put their jaws into it. The small publishers now are making bucks on projects the lions wouldn't touch, but there are signs (this book is one of them) that the lions are beginning to get hungry again.

And though there still might be no professional magazines devoted to horror fiction, there are now numerous smaller journals dedicated to the field, as well as an explosion of on-line magazines publishing the fiction of new and established writers.

Finally, and most important, there seems to be a new generation of readers, growing now beyond the core audience,* clamoring for

---

*Faddists, anyone?—though I'm not completely at ease with the faddist theory, which might actually put the cart before the horse. There might be a core audience that will read *anything,* but I think there is a much larger one that will read quality work, *literature,* when it's given to them.

this stuff. These readers were kids or fetuses during the last boom; they discovered the writers of the 1970s and 1980s in reprints and secondhand editions and now want more—and *new*.

We might, actually, be on the rising crest of a new boom.

Part Six: This Book

As for me, I can't lose. If this book turns out to be revolutionary, helps to revive the field, kills the ghetto, and starts a third Golden Age, so be it. If it doesn't, my backup story is that *999★★* is merely a celebration of the success the field has already achieved—final proof, between two covers, that it *is* a literary genre.

Actually, I'll be the happiest editor in the world if you see fit to put this volume on your shelf between *Dark Forces* and *Great Tales of Terror and the Supernatural.*

Revolution or celebration? You choose.

But as I said at the top of this screed, this book *is* a feast.

Time to dive in.

Al Sarrantonio
May 1999

★★If you haven't figured it out already, the title's meaning is twofold: a contraction of the year the book was originally published, at the cusp of the millennium; and 666 inverted—which means that the title makes sense even if the booksellers stack it upside-down!

999

Kim Newman

AMERIKANSKI DEAD AT THE MOSCOW MORGUE

When I casually contacted Kim Newman by E-mail to ask if he had anything he'd be interested in showing me for 999, *he politely wrote back, almost instantly, that most of what he was working on these days was in a longer length than what I seemed to be looking for. When I gently persisted, asking him to show me something longer, I almost instantly received the following tale, about American "invaders" in Communist Russia, by return E-mail.*

I was flabbergasted at how good it was—not because Kim Newman, the vampire-expert author of Anno Dracula *and* The Bloody Red Baron, *wrote it, since I already knew that he's quietly and systematically become one of the best writers in the field, but because I just couldn't believe that something so wonderful could instantly appear on my computer screen just because I asked for it. Ask and ye shall receive, indeed!*

Kim Newman is also known as a sometime actor, film critic, and broadcaster; more of his fictive magic can be found in such work as Bad Dreams, The Night Mayor, *and, with Eugene Byrne,* Back in the USSA.

At the railway station in Borodino, Evgeny Chirkov was separated from his unit. As the locomotive slowed, he hopped from their carriage to the platform, under orders to secure, at any price, cigarettes and chocolate. Another unknown crisis intervened and the steam-driven antique never truly stopped. Tripping over his rifle, he was unable to reach the outstretched hands of his comrades. The rest of the unit, jammed halfway through windows or hanging out of doors, laughed and waved. A jet of steam from a train passing the other way put salt on his tail, and he dodged, tripping again. Sergeant Trauberg found the pratfall hilarious, forgetting he had pressed a thousand rubles on the private. Chirkov ran and ran but the locomotive gained speed.

When he emerged from the canopied platform, seconds after the last carriage, white sky poured down. Looking at the black-shingled track-bed, he saw a flattened outline in what was once a uniform, wrists and ankles wired together, neck against a gleaming rail, head long gone under sharp wheels. The method, known as "making sleepers," was favored along railway lines. Away from stations, twenty or thirty were dealt with at one time. Without heads, Amerikans did no harm.

Legs boiled from steam, face and hands frozen from winter, he wandered through the station. The cavernous space was subdivided by sandbags. Families huddled like pioneers expecting an attack by Red Indians, luggage drawn about in a circle, last bullets saved for women and children. Chirkov spat mentally; America had invaded his imagination, just as his political officers warned. Some refugees were coming from Moscow, others fleeing to the city. There was no rule. A wall-sized poster of the New First Secretary was disfigured with a blotch, red gone to black. The splash of dried blood suggested something had been finished against the wall. There were Amerikans in Borodino. Seventy miles from Moscow, the station was a museum to resisted invasions. Plaques, statues and paintings honored the victories of 1812 and 1944. A poster listed those local officials executed after being implicated in the latest counter-revolution. The air was tangy with ash, a reminder of past scorched earth policies. There were big fires nearby. An army unit was on duty, but no one knew anything about a time-table. An officer told him to queue and wait. More trains were coming from Moscow than going to, which meant the capital would eventually have none left.

He ventured out of the station. The snow cleared from the fore-court was banked a dozen yards away. Sunlight glared off muddy white. It was colder and brighter than he was used to in the Ukraine. A trio of Chinese-featured soldiers, a continent away from home, offered to share cigarettes and tried to practice Russian on him. He understood they were from Amgu; from the highest point in that port, you could see Japan. He asked if they knew where he could find an official. As they chirruped among themselves in an alien tongue, Chirkov saw his first Amerikan. Emerging from between snow banks and limping towards the guard post, the dead man looked as if he might actually be an American. Barefoot, he waded spastically through slush, jeans legs shredded over thin shins. His shirt was a bright picture of a parrot in a jungle. Sunglasses hung around his neck on a thin string. Chirkov made the Amerikan's presence known to the guards. Fasci-nated, he watched the dead man walk. With every step, the Amerikan crackled: there were deep, ice-threaded rifts in his skin. He was slow and brittle and blind, crystal eyes frozen open, arms stiff by his sides.

Cautiously, the corporal circled around and rammed his rifle-butt into a knee. The guards were under orders not to waste ammunition; there was a shortage. Bone cracked and the Amerikan went down like a devotee before an icon. The corporal prodded a colorful back with his boot-toe and pushed the Amerikan onto his face. As he wriggled, ice shards worked through his flesh. Chirkov had assumed the dead would stink but this one was frozen and odorless. The skin was pink and unperished, the rips in it red and glittery. An arm reached out for the corporal and something snapped in the shoulder. The corporal's boot pinned the Amerikan to the concrete. One of his comrades produced a foot-long spike and worked the point into the back of the dead man's skull. Scalp flaked around the dimple. The other guard took an iron mallet from his belt and struck a professional blow.

It was important, apparently, that the spike entirely transfix the skull and break ground, binding the dead to the earth, allowing the last of the spirit to leave the carcass. Not official knowledge, this was something every soldier was told at some point by a comrade. Always, the tale-teller was from Moldavia or had learned from someone who was. Moldavians claimed to be used to the dead. The Amerikan's head came apart like a rock split along fault lines. Five solid chunks rolled away from the spike. Diamond-sparkles of ice glinted in reddish gray inner surfaces. The thing stopped moving at once. The hammerer began to unbutton the gaudy shirt and detach it from the sunken chest, careful as a butcher skinning a horse. The jeans were too deeply melded with meat to remove, which was a shame; with the ragged legs cut away, they would have made fine shorts for a pretty girl at the beach. The corporal wanted Chirkov to have the sunglasses. One lens was gone or he might not have been so generous with a stranger. In the end, Chirkov accepted out of courtesy, resolving to throw away the trophy as soon as he was out of Borodino.

Three days later, when Chirkov reached Moscow, locating his unit was not possible. A dispatcher at the central station thought his comrades might be reassigned to Orekhovo Zuevo, but her superior was of the opinion the unit had been disbanded nine months earlier. Because the dispatcher was not disposed to contradict an eminent Party member, Chirkov was forced to accept the ruling that he was without a unit. As such, he was detailed to the Spa. They had in a permanent request for personnel and always took precedence. The posting involved light guard duties and manual labor; there was little fight left in Amerikans who ended up at the Spa. The dispatcher gave Chirkov a sheaf of papers the size of a Frenchman's sandwich and complicated travel directions. By then, the rest of the queue was getting testy and he was obliged to venture out on his own. He remembered to fix his mobility permit, a blue luggage tag with a smudged stamp, on the outside of his uniform. Technically, failure to display the permit was punishable by summary execution.

Streetcars ran intermittently; after waiting an hour in the street outside the central station, he decided to walk to the Spa. It was a question of negotiating dunes of uncleared snow and straggles of undisciplined queue. Teams of firemen dug methodically through depths of snow, side-by-side with teams of soldiers who were burning down buildings. Areas were cleared and raked, ground still warm enough to melt snow that drifted onto it. Everywhere, posters warned of the Amerikans. The Party line was still that the United States was responsible. It was air-carried biological warfare, the Ministry announced with authority, originated by a secret laboratory and disseminated in the Soviet Union by suicidal infectees posing as tourists. The germ galvanized the nervous systems of the recently deceased, triggering the lizard stems of their brains, inculcating in the Amerikans a disgusting hunger for human meat. The "news" footage the Voice of America put out of their own dead was staged and doctored, footage from the sadistic motion pictures that were a symptom of the West's utter decadence. But everyone had a different line: it was . . . creeping radiation from Chernobyl . . . a judgment from a bitter and long-ignored God . . . a project Stalin abandoned during the Great Patriotic War . . . brought back from *Novy Mir* by cosmonauts . . . a plot by the fomenters of the Counter-Revolution . . . a curse the Moldavians had always known.

Fortunately, the Spa was off Red Square. Even a Ukrainian sapling like Evgeny Chirkov had an idea how to get to Red Square. He had carried his rifle for so long the strap had worn through his epaulette. He imagined the outline of the buckle was stamped into his collarbone. His single round of ammunition was in his inside breast pocket, wrapped in newspaper. They said Moscow was the most exciting city in the world, but it was not at its best under twin siege from winter and the Amerikans. Helicopters swooped overhead, broadcasting official warnings and announcements: comrades were advised to stay at their workplaces and continue with their duly delegated tasks; victory in the struggle against the American octopus was inevitable; the crisis was nearly at an end and the master strategists would soon announce a devastating counter-attack; the dead were to be disabled and placed in the proper collection points; another exposed pocket of traitors would go on trial tomorrow.

In an onion-domed church, soldiers dealt with Amerikans. Brought in covered lorries, the shuffling dead were shifted inside in ragged coffles. As Chirkov passed, a dead woman, bear-like in a fur coat over forbidden undergarments, broke the line. Soldiers efficiently cornered her and stuck a bayonet into her head. The remains were hauled into the church. When the building was full, it would be burned: an offering. In Red Square, loudspeakers shouted martial music at the queues. John Reed at the Barricades. Lenin's tomb was no longer open for tourists. Sergeant Trauberg was fond of telling the story about what had happened in the tomb when the Amerikans started to rise. Everyone guessed it was true. The Spa was off the Square. Before the Revolution of 1918, it had been an exclusive health club for the Royal Family. Now it was a morgue.

He presented his papers to a thin officer he met on the broad steps of the Spa and stood frozen in stiff-backed salute while the man looked over the wedge of documentation. He was told to go inside smartly and look for Lyubashevski. The officer proceeded, step by step, down to the Square. Under the dusting of snow, the stone steps were gilded with ice: a natural defense. Chirkov understood Amerikans were forever slipping and falling on ice; many were so damaged they couldn't regain their footing and were consequently easy to deal with. The doors of the Spa, three times a man's height, were pocked with bullet holes new and old. Unlocked and unoiled, they creaked alarmingly as he pushed inside. The foyer boasted marble floors, and ceilings painted with classical scenes of romping nymphs and athletes. Busts of Marx and Lenin flanked the main staircase; a portrait of the New First Secretary, significantly less faded than neighboring pictures, was proudly displayed behind the main desk.

A civilian he took to be Lyubashevski squatted by the desk reading a pamphlet. A half-empty vodka bottle was nestled like a baby in the crook of his arm. He looked up awkwardly at the new arrival and explained that last week all the chairs in the building had been taken away by the Health Committee. Chirkov presented papers and admitted he had been sent by the dispatcher at the railway station, which elicited a shrug. The civilian mused that the central station was always sending stray soldiers for an unknown reason. Lyubashevski had three days of stubble and mismatched eyes. He offered Chirkov a swallow of vodka—pure and strong, not diluted with melted snow like the rat poison he had been sold in Borodino—and opened up the lump of papers, searching for a particular signature. In the end, he decided it best Chirkov stay at the Spa. Unlocking a cabinet, he found a long white coat, muddied at the bottom. Chirkov was reluctant to exchange his heavy greatcoat for the flimsy garment but Lyubashevski assured him there was very little pilferage from the Spa. People, even parasites, tended to avoid visiting the place unless there was a pressing reason for their presence. Before relinquishing his coat, Chirkov remembered to retain his mobility permit, pinning it to the breast of the laboratory coat. After taking Chirkov's rifle, complementing him on its cleanliness, and stowing it in the cabinet, Lyubashevski issued him with a revolver. It was dusty and the metal was cold enough to stick to his skin. Breaking the gun open, Chirkov noted three cartridges. In Russian roulette, he would have an even chance. Without a holster, he dropped it into the pocket of his coat; the barrel poked out of a torn corner. He had to sign for the weapon.

Lyubashevski told him to go down into the Pool and report to Director Kozintsev. Chirkov descended in a hand-cranked cage lift and stepped out into a ballroom-sized space. "The Pool" was what people who worked in the spa called the basement where the dead were kept. It had been a swimming bath before the Revolution; there, weary generations of Romanovs plunged through slow waters, the tides of history slowly pulling them under. Supposedly dry since 1916, the Pool was so cold that condensation on the marble floors turned to ice patches. The outer walls were still decorated with gilted plaster friezes, and his bootfalls echoed on the solid floors. He walked around the edge of the pit, looking down at the white-coated toilers and their unmoving clients. The Pool was divided into separate work cubicles and narrow corridors by flimsy wooden partitions that rose above the old water level. A girl caught his eye, blond hair tightly gathered at the back of her neck. She had red lipstick and her coat was rolled up on slender arms as she probed the chest cavity of a corpse, a girl who might once have been her slightly older sister. The dead girl had a neat round hole in her forehead and her hair was fanned over a sludgy discharge Chirkov took to be abandoned brains. He coughed to get the live girl's attention and inquired as to where he could find the Director. She told him to make his way to the Deep End and climb in, then penetrate the warren of partitions. He couldn't miss Kozintsev; the Director was dead center.

At the Deep End, he found a ladder into the pool. It was guarded by a soldier who sat cross-legged, a revolver in his lap, twanging on a Jew's harp. He stopped and told Chirkov the tune was a traditional American folk song about a cowboy killed by a lawyer, "The Man Who Shot Liberty Valance." The guard introduced himself as Corporal Toulbeyev and asked if Chirkov was interested in purchasing tape cassettes of the music of Mr. Edward Cochran or Robert Dylan. Chirkov had no cassette player but Toulbeyev said that for five thousand rubles he could secure one. To be polite, Chirkov said he would consider the acquisition: evidently a great bargain. Toulbeyev further insinuated he could supply other requisites: contraceptive sheaths, chocolate bars, toothpaste, fresh socks, scented soap, suppressed reading matter. Every unit in the Soviet Union had a Toulbeyev, Chirkov knew. There was probably a secretary on the First Committee of the Communist Party who dealt disco records and mint-flavored chewing gum to the High and Mighty. After a decent period of mourning, Chirkov might consider spending some of Sergeant Trauberg's rubles on underwear and soap.

Having clambered into the pool, Chirkov lost the perspective on the layout of the workspaces he had from above. It was a labyrinth and he zigzagged between partitions, asking directions from the occasional absorbed forensic worker. Typically, a shoulder shrug would prompt him to a new pathway. Each of the specialists was absorbed in dissection, wielding whiny and smoky saws or sharp and shiny scalpels. He passed by the girl he had seen from above—her name-tag identified her as Technician Sverdlova, and she introduced herself as Valentina—and found she had entirely exposed the rib cage of her corpse. She was the epitome of sophisticated Moscow girl, Chirkov thought: imperturbable and immaculate even with human remains streaked up to her elbows. A straggle of hair wisped across her face, and she blew it out of the way. She dictated notes into a wire recorder, commenting on certain physiological anomalies of the dead girl. There was a rubbery resilience in the undecayed muscle tissue. He would have liked to stay, but had to report to Kozintsev. Bidding her good-bye, he left her cubicle, thumping a boot against a tin bucket full of watches, wedding rings and eyeglasses. She said he could take anything he wanted but he declined. Remembering, he found the bent and broken sunglasses in his trousers pocket and added them to the contents of the bucket. It was like throwing a kopeck into a wishing well, so he made a wish. As if she were telepathic, Valentina giggled. Blushing, Chirkov continued.

He finally came to a makeshift door with a plaque that red V. A. KOZINTSEV, DIRECTOR. Chirkov knocked and, hearing a grunt from beyond, pushed through. It was as if he had left the morgue for a sculptor's studio. On one table were moist bags of variously colored clays lined up next to a steaming samovar. In the center of the space, in the light cast by a chandelier that hung over the whole pool, a man in a smock worked on a bust of a bald-headed man. Kozintsev had a neatly trimmed beard and round spectacles. He was working one-handed; long fingers delicately pressing hollows into cheeks; a glass of tea in his other hand. He stood back, gulped tea and tutted, extremely dissatisfied with his efforts. Instantly accepting the new-comer, Kozintsev asked Chirkov for help in going back to the beginning. He set his glass down and rolled up his sleeves. They both put their hands in the soft face and pulled. Clays came away in self-contained lumps: some stranded like muscles, others bunched like pockets of fat. A bare skull, blotched with clay, was revealed. Glass eyes stared hypnotically, wedged into sockets with twists of newspaper. Chirkov realized he had heard of the Director: V. A. Kozintsev was one of the leading reconstruction pathologists in the Soviet Union. He had, layering in musculature and covering the results with skin, worked on the skulls tentatively identified as those of the former Royal Family. He had re-created the heads of Paleolithic men, murder victims and Ivan the Terrible.

Chirkov reported for duty and the Director told him to find something useful to do. Kozintsev was depressed to lose three days' work and explained in technical detail that the skull wasn't enough. There had to be some indication of the disposition of muscle and flesh. As he talked, he rolled a cigarette and stuck it in the corner of his mouth, patting his smock pockets for matches. Chirkov understood this was one of Kozintsev's historical projects: high-profile work sanctioned by the Ministry of Culture, unconnected to the main purpose of the Spa—which, just now, was to determine the origins and capabilities of the Amerikans—but useful in attracting attention and funds. While the Director looked over charts of facial anatomy, puffing furiously on his cigarette, Chirkov picked up the discarded clays and piled them in a lump on the table. On a separate stand was a wigmaker's dummy head under a glass dome: it wore a long but neat black wig and facsimile wisps of eyebrows, mustache and beard. Once the skull was covered and painted to the correct skin tone, hair would be applied. He asked Kozintsev to whom the skull belonged and, offhandedly, the Director told him it was Grigory Rasputin. There had been trouble getting glass eyes with the right quality. Contemporary memoirs described the originals as steely blue, with pupils that contracted to pinpoints when their owner was concentrating on exerting his influence. Chirkov looked again at the skull and couldn't see anything special. It was just bare bone.

Each evening at nine, the Director presided over meetings. Attendance was mandatory for the entire staff, down to Chirkov. He was billeted in the Spa itself, in a small room on the top floor where he slept on what had once been a masseur's table. Since food was provided (albeit irregularly) by a cafeteria, there was scarce reason to venture outside. At meetings, Chirkov learned who everyone was: the ranking officer was Captain Zharov, who would rather be put in the streets fighting but suffered from a gimpy knee; under Kozintsev, the chief coroner was Dr. Fedor Dudnikov, a famous forensic scientist often consulted by the police in political murder cases but plainly out of his depth with the Spa's recent change of purpose. The Director affected a lofty disinterest in the current emergency, which left the morgue actually to be run by a conspiracy between Lyubashevski, an administrator seconded from the Ministry of Agriculture, and Toulbeyev, who was far more capable than Captain Zharov of keeping greased the wheels of the military machine.

Chirkov's girl, Valentina, turned out to be very eminent for her years, a specialist in the study of Amerikans; at each meeting, she would report the findings of the day. Her discoveries were frankly incomprehensible, even to her colleagues, but she seemed to believe the Amerikans were not simple reanimated dead bodies. Her dissections and probings demonstrated that the Amerikans functioned in many ways like living beings; in particular, their musculature adapted slowly to their new state even as surplus flesh and skin sloughed off. Those portions of their bodies that rotted away were irrelevant to the functioning of the creatures. She likened the ungainly and stumbling dead creatures to a pupal stage, and expressed a belief that the Amerikans were becoming stronger. Her argument was that they should be categorized not as former human beings but as an entirely new species, with its own strengths and capabilities. At every meeting, Valentina would complain she could only manage so much by examining doubly dead bodies and that the best hope of making progress would be to secure "live" specimens and observe their natural progress. She had sketched her impressions of what the Amerikans would eventually evolve into: thickly muscled skeletons like old anatomical drawings.

Valentina's leading rival, A. Tarkhanov, countered that her theories were a blind alley. In his opinion, the Spa should concentrate on the isolation of the bacteriological agent responsible for the reanimations with a view to the development of a serum cure. Tarkhanov, a Party member, also insisted the phenomenon had been created artificially by American genetic engineers. He complained the monster-makers of the United States were so heavily financed by capitalist cartels that this state-backed bureaucracy could hardly compete. The one common ground Valentina held with Tarkhanov was that the Spa was desperately underfunded. Since everyone at the meetings had to sit on the floor, while Director Kozintsev was elevated cross-legged on a desk, chairs were deemed a priority, though all the scientists also had long lists of medical supplies and instruments without which they could not continue their vital researches. Lyubashevski would always counter these complaints by detailing his repeated requests to appropriate departments, often with precise accounts of the elapsed time since the request had been submitted. At Chirkov's third meeting, there was much excitement when Lyubashevski announced that the Spa had received from the Civil Defense Committee fifty-five child-sized blankets. This was unrelated to any request that had been put in, but Toulbeyev offered to arrange a trade with the Children's Hospital, exchanging the blankets either for vegetables or medical instruments.

At the same meeting, Captain Zharov reported that his men had successfully dealt with an attempted invasion. Two Amerikans had been found at dawn, having negotiated the slippery steps, standing outside the main doors, apparently waiting. One stood exactly outside the doors, the other a step down. They might have been forming a primitive queue. Zharov personally disposed of them both, expending cartridges into their skulls, and arranged for the removal of the remains to a collection point, from which they might well be returned as specimens. Valentina moaned that it would have been better to capture and pen the Amerikans in a secure area—she specified the former steam bath—where they could be observed. Zharov cited standing orders. Kozintsev concluded with a lengthy lecture on Rasputin, elaborating his own theory that the late Tsarina's spiritual advisor was less mad than popularly supposed and that his influence with the Royal Family was ultimately instrumental in bringing about the Revolution.

He spoke with especial interest and enthusiasm of the so-called Mad Monk's powers of healing, the famously ameliorative hands that could ease the symptoms of the Tsarevich's hemophilia. It was his contention that Rasputin had been possessed of a genuine paranormal talent. Even Chirkov thought this beside the point, especially when the Director wound down by admitting another failure in his reconstruction project.

With Toulbeyev, he drew last guard of the night; on duty at three A.M., expected to remain at the post in the foyer until the nine o'clock relief. Captain Zharov and Lyubashevski could not decide whether Chirkov counted as a soldier or an experimental assistant; so he found himself called on to fulfill both functions, occasionally simultaneously. As a soldier, he would be able to sleep away the morning after night duty, but as an experimental assistant, he was required to report to Director Kozintsev at nine sharp. Chirkov didn't mind overmuch; once you got used to corpses, the Spa was a cushy detail. At least corpses here *were* corpses. Although, for personal reasons, he always voted, along with two other scientists and a cook, in support of Technician Sverdlova's request to bring in Amerikans, he was privately grateful she always lost by a wide margin. No matter how secure the steam bath might be, Chirkov was not enthused by the idea of Amerikans inside the building. Toulbeyev, whose grandmother was Moldavian, told stories of *wurdalaks* and *vryolakas* and always had new anecdotes. In life, according to Toulbeyev, Amerikans had all been Party members: that was why so many had good clothes and consumer goods. The latest craze among the dead was for cassette players with attached headphones; not American manufacture, but Japanese. Toulbeyev had a collection of the contraptions, harvested from Amerikans whose heads were so messed up soldiers were squeamish about borrowing from them. It was a shame, said Toulbeyev, that the dead were disinclined to cart video players on their backs. If they picked up that habit, the staff in the Spa would be millionaires; not rouble millionaires, dollar millionaires. Many of the dead had foreign currency. Tarkhanov's pet theory was that the Amerikans impregnated money with a bacteriological agent, the condition spreading through contact with cash. Toulbeyev, who always wore gloves, did not seem unduly disturbed by the thought.

Just as Toulbeyev was elaborating upon the empire he could build with a plague of video players, a knock came at the doors. Not a sustained pounding like someone petitioning for entry, but a thud as if something had accidentally been bumped against the other side of the oak. They both shut up and listened. One of Toulbeyev's tape machines was playing Creedence Clearwater Revival's "It Came Out of the Sky" at a variable speed; he turned off the tape, which scrunched inside the machine as the wheels ground, and swore. Cassettes were harder to come by than players. There was a four-thirty-in-the-morning Moscow quiet. Lots of little noises: wind whining around the slightly warped door, someone having a coughing fit many floors above, distant shots. Chirkov cocked his revolver, hoping there was a round under the hammer, further hoping the round wasn't a dud. There was another knock, like the first. Not purposeful, just a blunder. Toulbeyev ordered Chirkov to take a look through the spyhole. The brass cap was stiff but he managed to work it aside and look through the glass lens.

A dead face was close to the spy-hole. For the first time, it occurred to Chirkov that Amerikans were scary. In the dark, this one had empty eye sockets and a constantly chewing mouth. Around its ragged neck were hung several cameras and a knotted scarf with a naked woman painted on it. Chirkov told Toulbeyev, who showed interest at the mention of photographic equipment and crammed around the spy-hole. He proposed that they open the doors and Chirkov put a bullet into the Amerikan's head. With cameras, Toulbeyev was certain he could secure chairs. With chairs, they would be the heroes of the Spa, entitled to untold privileges. Unsure of his courage, Chirkov agreed to the scheme and Toulbeyev struggled with the several bolts. Finally, the doors were loose, held shut only by Toulbeyev's fists on the handles. Chirkov nodded; his comrade pulled the doors open and stood back. Chirkov advanced, pistol held out and pointed at the Amerikan's forehead.

The dead man was not alone. Toulbeyev cursed and ran for his rifle. Chirkov did not fire, just looked up from one dead face to the others. Four were lined in a crocodile, each on a different step. One wore an officer's uniform, complete with medals; another, a woman, had a severe pin-striped suit and a rakish gangster hat; at the back of the queue was a dead child, a golden-haired, green-faced girl in a baseball cap, trailing a doll. None moved much. Toulbeyev returned, levering a cartridge into the breech, and skidded on the marble floor as he brought his rifle to bear. Taken aback by the apparently unthreatening dead, he didn't fire either. Cold wind wafted in, which explained Chirkov's chill. His understanding was that Amerikans always attacked; these stood as if dozing upright, swaying slightly. The little

girl's eyes moved mechanically back and forth. Chirkov told Toulbeyev to fetch a scientist, preferably Valentina. As his comrade scurried
upstairs, he remembered he had only three rounds to deal with four
Amerikans. He retreated into the doorway, eyes fixed on the dead,
and slammed shut the doors. With the heel of his fist, he rammed a
couple of the bolts home. Looking through the spy-hole, he saw
nothing had changed. The dead still queued.

Valentina wore a floor-length dressing gown over cotton pajamas.
Here bare feet must be frozen on the marble. Toulbeyev had explained
about the night visitors and she was reminding him of Captain Zharov's report. These Amerikans repeated what the Captain had observed:
the queuing behavior pattern. She brushed her hair out of the way
and got an eye to the spy-hole. With an odd squeal of delight, she
summoned Chirkov to take a look, telling him to angle his eye so he
could look beyond the queue. A figure struggled out of the dark, feet
flapping like beached fish. It went down on its face and crawled up
the steps, then stood. It took a place behind the little girl. This one
was naked, so rotted that even its sex was lost, a skeleton held together
by strips of muscle that looked like wet leather. Valentina said she
wanted that Amerikan for observation, but one of the others was
necessary as well. She still thought of capturing and observing specimens. Toulbeyev reminded her of the strangeness of the situation and
asked why the dead were just standing in line, stretching down the
steps away from the Spa. She said something about residual instinct,
the time a citizen must spend in queues, the dead's inbuilt need to
mimic the living, to re-create from trace memories the lives they once
had. Toulbeyev agreed to help her capture the specimens but insisted
they be careful not to damage the cameras. He told her they could
all be millionaires.

Valentina held Toulbeyev's rifle like a soldier would, stock close
to her cheek, barrel straight. She stood by the doorway covering them
as they ventured out on her mission. Toulbeyev assigned himself to
the first in the queue, the dead man with the cameras. That left
Chirkov to deal with the walking skeleton, even if it was last in line
and, in Moscow, queue-jumping was considered a worse crime than
matricide. From somewhere, Toulbeyev had found a supply of canvas
post-bags. The idea was to pop a bag over an Amerikan's head like a
hood, then lead the dead thing indoors. Toulbeyev managed with one
deft maneuver to drop his bag over the photographer's head and
whipped round behind the Amerikan, unravelling twine from a ball.
As Toulbeyev bound dead wrists together, the twine cut through gray

skin and greenish red fluid leaked over his gloves. The rest of the queue stood impassive, ignoring the treatment the photographer was getting. When Toulbeyev had wrestled his catch inside and trussed him like a pig, Chirkov was ready to go for the skeleton.

He stepped lightly down to the skeleton's level, post-bag open as if he were a poacher after rabbit. The Amerikans all swivelled their eyes as he passed and, with a testicles-retracting spasm of panic, he missed his footing. His boot slipped on icy stone and he fell badly, his hip slamming a hard edge. He sledged down the steps, yelping as he went. A shot cracked, and the little girl, who had stepped out of the queue and scrambled towards him, became a limp doll, a chunk of her head dryly gone. Toulbeyev had got her. At the bottom of the steps, Chirkov stood. Hot pain spilled from his hip and his side was numb. His lungs hurt from the frozen air, and he coughed steam. He still held his bag and gun; luckily, the revolver had not discharged. He looked around: there were human shapes in the Square, shambling towards the Spa. Darting up the steps, unmindful of the dangers of ice, he made for the light of the doorway. He paused to grab the skeleton by the elbow and haul it to the entrance. It didn't resist him. The muscles felt like snakes stretched over a bony frame. He shoved the skeleton into the foyer and Toulbeyev was there with his ball of twine. Chirkov turned as Valentina shut the doors. More Amerikans had come: the skeleton's place was taken and the little girl's, and two or three more steps were occupied. Before bolting the doors, Valentina opened them a crack and considered the queue. Again, the dead were still, unexcited. Then, like a drill team, they all moved up a step. The photographer's place was taken by the officer, and the rest of the line similarly advanced. Valentina pushed the doors together and Chirkov shut the bolts. Without pausing for breath, she ordered the specimens be taken to the steam baths.

Breakfast was a half turnip, surprisingly fresh if riddled with ice-chips. He took it away from the cafeteria to chew and descended to the Pool to report to the Director. He assumed Valentina would make mention of her unauthorized acquisition of specimens at the evening meeting. It was not his place to spread gossip. Arriving at the cubicle before the Director, his first duty was to get the samovar going: Kozintsev survived on constant infusions of smoky tea. As Chirkov lit the charcoal, he heard a click, like a saluting heels. He looked around the cubicle and saw no one. All was as usual: clays, wig, shaping tools, skull, samovar, boxes piled to make a stool. There was another click. He looked up at the chandelier and saw nothing unusual. The tea began to bubble and he chewed a mouthful of cold turnip, trying not to think about sleep—or Amerikans.

Kozintsev had begun again on the reconstruction. The skull of Grigory Yefimovich Rasputin was almost buried in clay strips. It looked very much like the head of the Amerikan Chirkov had secured for Valentina: flattened reddish ropes bound the jaws together, winding up into the cavities under the cheekbones; enamel chips replaced the many missing teeth, standing out white against gray-yellow; delicate filaments swarmed around the glass eyes. It was an intriguing process and Chirkov had come to enjoy watching the Director at work. There was a sheaf of photographs of the monk on one stand but Kozintsev disliked consulting them. His process depended on extrapolating from the contours of the bone, not modelling from likenesses. Rasputin's potato-like peasant nose was a knotty problem. The cartilage was long gone, and Kozintsev obsessively built and abandoned noses. Several were trodden flat into the sloping tile floor. After the Revolution, the faith healer had been exhumed by zealots from his tomb in the Imperial Park and, reportedly, burned; there was doubt, fiercely resisted by the Director, as to the provenance of the skull.

As Chirkov looked, Rasputin's jaw sagged, clay muscles stretching; then, suddenly, it clamped shut, teeth clicking. Chirkov jumped and spat out a shocked laugh. Kozintsev arrived, performing a dozen actions at once, removing his frock coat and reaching for his smock, bidding a good morning and calling for his tea. Chirkov was bemused and afraid, questioning what he had seen. The skull bit once more. Kozintsev saw the movement at once and asked again for tea. Chirkov, snapping out of it, provided a cupful and took one for himself. Kozintsev did not comment on the appropriation. He was very interested and peered closely at the barely animated skull. The jaw moved slowly from side to side, as if masticating. Chirkov wondered if Grigory Yefimovich were imitating him, and stopped chewing his turnip. Kozintsev pointed out that the eyes were trying to move, but the clay hadn't the strength of real muscle. He wondered aloud if he should work in strands of string to simulate the texture of human tissue. It might not be cosmetically correct. Rasputin's mouth gaped open, as if in a silent scream. The Director prodded the air near the skull's mouth with his finger and withdrew sharply as the jaws snapped shut. He laughed merrily, and called the monk a cunning fellow.

*   *   *

The queue was still on the steps. Everyone had taken turns at the spy-hole. Now the line stretched down into the Square and along the pavement, curving around the building. Toulbeyev had hourly updates on the riches borne by the Amerikans. He was sure one of the queue harbored a precious video player: Toulbeyev had cassettes of *101 Dalmations* and *New Wave Hookers* but no way of playing them. Captain Zharov favored dealing harshly with the dead, but Kozintsev, still excited by the skull's activity, would issue no orders, and the officer was not about to undertake an action without a direct instruction, preferably in writing. As an experiment, he went out and, halfway down the steps, selected an Amerikan at random. He shot it in the head and the finally dead bag of bones tumbled out of the queue. Zharov kicked the remains, and, coming apart, they rolled down the steps into a snowdrift. After a pause, all the dead behind Zharov's kill took a step up. Valentina was in the steam baths with her specimens: news of her acquisitions spread through the Spa, inciting vigorous debate. Tarkhanov complained to the Director about his colleague's usurpation of authority, but was brushed off with an invitation to examine the miraculous skull. Dr. Dudnikov placed several phone calls to the Kremlin, relaying matters of interest to a junior functionary, who promised imminent decisions. It was Dudnikov's hope the developments could be used as a lever to unloose vital supplies from other institutions. As ever, the rallying cry was "Chairs for the Spa!"

In the afternoon, Chirkov napped standing up as he watched Kozintsev at work. Although the jaw continually made small movements, the skull was cooperative and did not try to nip the Director. He had requisitioned Toulbeyev's Jew's harp and was implanting it among thick neck muscles, hoping it would function as a crude voicebox. To Chirkov's disgust, Rasputin was becoming expert in the movement of its unseeing eyes. He could suck the glass orbs so the painted pupils disappeared in the tops of the sockets, showing only milky white marbles. This was a man who had been hard to kill: his murderers gave him poison enough to fell an elephant, shot him in the back and chest with revolvers, kicked him in the head, battered him with a club and lowered him into the Neva, bound in a curtain, through a hole in the ice. The skull bore an indentation which Kozintsev traced to an aristocrat's boot. In the end, men hadn't killed the seer; the cause of his death was drowning. As he worked, the Director hummed cheerful snatches of Prokofiev. To give the mouth something to do,

Kozintsev stuck a cigarette between the teeth. He promised Grigory Yefimovich lips would come soon, but there was nothing yet he could do about lungs. His secret dream, which he shared with the skull (and, perforce, Chirkov), was to apply his process to a complete skeleton. Regrettably, and as Rasputin had himself predicted while alive, most of the monk had been scattered on the wind.

Lyubashevski barged into the cubicle bearing a telephone whose cord unreeled through the maze of the Pool like Ariadne's thread. There was a call from the Kremlin which Kozintsev was required to take. While Chirkov and Lyubashevski stood, unconsciously at attention, the Director chatted with the First Secretary. Either Dr. Dudnikov had tapped into the proper channels or Tarkhanov was the spy everyone took him for and had reported on the sly to his KGB superior. The First Secretary was briefed about what was going on at the Spa. He handed out a commendation to Kozintsev and insisted extra resources would be channelled to the morgue. Chirkov got the impression the First Secretary was mixing up the projects: Kozintsev was being praised for Valentina's studies. The Director would be only too delighted to employ any funds or supplies in furthering his work with the skull.

Following the telephone call, the Director was in excellent spirits. He told the skull a breakthrough was at hand and insisted to Lyubashevski that he could hear a faint twang from the Jew's harp. Grigory Yefimovich was trying to communicate, the Director claimed. He asked if he remembered eating the poisoned chocolates. After the jaw first moved, Kozintsev had constructed rudimentary clay ears, exaggerated cartoon curls which stuck out ridiculously. Having abandoned any attempt to simulate the appearance in life of the monk, he was attempting instead to provide working features. Since Rasputin's brains must have rotted or burned years before, it was hard to imagine what the Director aspired to communicate with. Then, over the loudspeaker, Dr. Dudnikov reported that there were soldiers outside the Spa setting up explosives and declaring an intention to dynamite the building. Grigory Yefimovich's glass eyes rolled again.

Engineers were packing charges around the foyer. Entering the Spa through the kitchens, they had avoided the Amerikan-infested steps. It appeared a second queue was forming, stretching off in a different direction, still leading to the front doors. The officer in command, a fat man with a facial birthmark that made him look like a spaniel,

introduced himself as Major Andrei Kobylinksi. He strode about, inspecting the work, expressing pride in his unit's ability to demolish a
building with the minimum of explosive matter. As he surveyed, Kobylinksi noted points at which surplus charges should be placed. To
Chirkov's unschooled eye, the Major appeared to contradict himself:
his men were plastering the walls with semtex. Kozintsev and Captain
Zharov were absorbed in a reading of a twelve-page document which
authorized the demolition of the Spa. Dr. Dudnikov protested that
the First Secretary himself had, within the last minute, commended
the Spa and that important work to do with the Amerikan invasion
was being carried out in the Pool, but Kobylinksi was far more interested in which pillars should be knocked out to bring down the deca-
dent painted roof. As they worked, the engineers whistled "Girls Just
Want to Have Fun."

Satisfied that the charges were laid correctly, Major Kobylinksi
could not resist the temptation to lecture the assembled company on
the progress and achievements of his campaign. A three-yard-square
map of Moscow was unfolded on the floor. It was marked with
patches of red as if it were a chessboard pulled out of shape. The red
areas signified buildings and constructions Kobylinksi had blown up.
Chirkov understood the Major would not be happy until the entire
map was shaded in red; then, Kobylinski believed the crisis would be
at an end. He declaimed that this should have been done immediately
when the crisis began and that the Amerikans were to be thanked for
prompting such a visionary enterprise. As the Major lectured, Chirkov
noticed Toulbeyev at the main desk with Lyubashevski, apparently
trying to find a pen that worked. They sorted through a pot of pencils
and chalks and markers, drawing streaks on a piece of blotting paper.
Under the desk were packages wired to detonators. Kobylinksi
checked his watch and mused that he was ahead of his schedule; the
demolition would take place in one half hour. Lyubashevski raised a
hand and ventured the opinion that the explosives placed under the
main staircase were insufficient to the task of bringing down such a
solidly constructed structure. Barking disagreement, Kobylinksi strutted
over and examined the charges in question, finally agreeing that safe
was better than sorry and ordering the application of more explosives.

While Kobylinksi was distracted, Toulbeyev crept to the map and
knelt over Red Square, scribbling furiously with a precious red felt-
tip. He blotched over the Spa, extending an area of devastation to
cover half the Square. When Kobylinksi revisited his map, Toulbeyev
was unsuspiciously on the other side of the room. One of the engi-

neers, a new set of headphones slung around his neck, piped up with an observation of a cartographical anomaly. Kobylinksi applied his concentration to the map and gurgled to himself. According to this chart, the Spa had already been dealt with by his unit: it was not a building but a raked-over patch of rubble. Another engineer, a baseball cap in his back pocket, volunteered a convincing memory of the destruction, three days before, of the Spa. Kobylinksi looked again at the map, getting down on his hands and knees and crawling along the most famous thoroughfares of the city. He scratched his head and blinked in his birthmark. Director Kozintsev, arms folded and head high, said that so far as he was concerned the matter was at an end; he requested the engineers remove their infernal devices from the premises. Kobylinksi had authorization to destroy the Spa but once and had demonstrably already acted on that authorization. The operation could not be repeated without further orders, and if further orders were requested, questions would be asked as to whether the engineers were as efficient as Kobylinksi would like to claim: most units only need to destroy a building once for it to remain destroyed. Almost in tears, the bewildered Major finally commanded the removal of the explosives and, with parental tenderness, folded up his map into its case. With no apologies, the engineers withdrew.

That night, Valentina's Amerikans got out of the steam bath and everyone spent a merry three hours hunting them down. Chirkov and Toulbeyev drew the Pool. The power had failed again, and they had to fall back on oil lamps, which made the business all the more unnerving. Irregular and active shadows were all around, whispering in Moldavian of hungry, unquiet creatures. Their progress was a slow spiral; first, they circled the Pool from above, casting light over the complex, but that left too many darks unprobed; then, they went in at the Deep End and moved methodically through the labyrinth, weaving between the partitions, stumbling against dissected bodies, ready to shoot hat stands in the brain. Under his breath, Toulbeyev recited a litany he claimed was a Japanese prayer against the dead: *"Sanyo, sony, seiko, mitsubishi, panasonic, toshiba . . ."*

They had to penetrate the dead center of the pool. The Amerikans were in Kozintsev's cubicle staring at the bone-and-clay head as if it were a color television set. Rasputin was on his stand under a black protective cloth which hung like long hair. Chirkov found the combination of the Amerikans and Rasputin unnerving and, almost as a reflex, shot the skeleton in the skull. The report was loud and echoing. The skeleton came apart on the floor and, before Chirkov's ears stopped hurting, others had come to investigate. Director Kozintsev was concerned for his precious monk and probed urgently under the cloth for damage. Valentina was annoyed by the loss of her specimen but kept her tongue still, especially when her surviving Amerikan turned nasty. The dead man barged out of the cubicle, shouldering partitions apart, wading through gurneys and tables, roaring and slavering. Tarkhanov, incongruous in a silk dressing gown, got in the way and sustained a nasty bite. Toulbeyev dealt with the Amerikan, tripping him with an ax handle, then straddling his chest and pounding a chisel into the bridge of his nose. He had not done anything to prove Valentina's theories; for its spell in captivity, he simply seemed more decayed, not evolved. Valentina claimed the thing Chirkov had finished was a model of biological efficiency, stripped down to essentials, potentially immortal. Now, it looked like a stack of bones.

Even Kozintsev, occupied in the construction of a set of wooden arms for his reanimated favorite, was alarmed by the size of the queue. There were four distinct lines. The Amerikans shuffled constantly, stamping nerveless feet as if to keep warm. Captain Zharov set up a machine gun emplacement in the foyer, covering the now-barred front doors, although it was strictly for show until he could be supplied with ammunition belts of the same gauge as the gun. Chirkov and Toulbeyev watched the Amerikans from the balcony. The queue was orderly; when, as occasionally happened, a too-far-gone Amerikan collapsed, it was trampled under by the great moving-up as those behind advanced. Toulbeyev sighted on individual dead with binoculars and listed the treasures he could distinguish. Mobile telephones, digital watches, blue jeans, leather jackets, gold bracelets, gold teeth, ballpoint pens. The Square was a purgatory for pickpockets. As night fell, it was notable that no lights burned even in the Kremlin.

When the power came back, the emergency radio frequencies broadcast only soothing music. The meeting was more sparsely attended than usual, and Chirkov realized faces had been disappearing steadily, lost to desertion or wastage. Dr. Dudnikov announced that he had been unable to reach anyone on the telephone. Lyubashevski reported that the threat of demolition had been lifted from the Spa and was unlikely to recur, though there might now prove to be unfortunate official side effects if the institution was formally believed to be a stretch of warm rubble. The kitchens had received a delivery of fresh fish, which was cause for celebration, though the head cook noted as strange the fact that many of the shipment were still flapping and even decapitation seemed not to still them. Valentina, for the hundredth time, requested specimens be secured for study and, after a vote—closer than usual, but still decisive—was disappointed. Tarkhanov's suicide was entered into the record, and the scientists paid tribute to the colleague they fervently believed had repeatedly informed on them, reciting his achievements and honors. Toulbeyev suggested a raiding party to relieve the queuing Amerikans of those goods which could be used for barter, but no one was willing to second the proposal, which sent the corporal into a notable sulk. Finally, as was expected, Kozintsev gave an account of his day's progress with Grigory Yefimovich. He had achieved a certain success with the arms: constructing elementary shoulder joints and nailing them to Rasputin's stand, then layering rope-and-clay muscles which interleaved with the neck he had fashioned. The head was able to control its arms to the extent of stretching out and bunching up muscle strands in the wrists as if clenching fists which did not, as yet, exist. The Director was also pleased to report that the head almost constantly made sounds with the Jew's harp, approximating either speech or music. As if to demonstrate the monk's healing powers, Kozintsev's sinus trouble had cleared up almost entirely.

Two days later, Toulbeyev let the Amerikans in. Chirkov did not know where the Corporal got the idea; he just got up from the gun emplacement, walked across the foyer, and unbarred the doors. Chirkov did not try to stop him, distracted by efforts to jam the wrong type of belt into the machine gun. When all the bolts were loose, Toulbeyev flung the doors back and stood aside. At the front of the queue, ever since the night they had brought in Valentina's specimens, was the officer. As he waited, his face had run, flesh slipping from his cheeks to form jowly bags around his jaw. He stepped forward smartly, entering the foyer. Lyubashevski woke up from his cot behind the desk and wondered aloud what was going on. Toulbeyev took a fistful of medals from the officer and tossed them to the floor after a shrewd assessment. The officer walked purposefully, with a broken-ankled limp, towards the lifts. Next in was the woman in the pin-striped suit. Toulbeyev took her hat and perched it on his head. From the next few, the Corporal harvested a silver chain identity bracelet, a woven leather belt, a pocket calculator, an old brooch. He piled the tokens behind him. Amerikans filled the foyer, wedging through the doorway in a triangle behind the officer.

Chirkov assumed the dead would eat him and wished he had seriously tried to go to bed with Technician Sverdlova. He still had two rounds left in his revolver, which meant he could deal with an Amerikan before ensuring his own everlasting peace. There were so many to choose from and none seemed interested in him. The lift was descending and those who couldn't get into it discovered the stairs. They were all drawn to the basement, to the Pool. Toulbeyev chortled and gasped at each new treasure, sometimes clapping the dead on the shoulders as they yielded their riches, hugging one or two of the more harmless creatures. Lyubashevski was appalled, but did nothing. Finally, the administrator got together the gumption to issue an order: he told Chirkov to inform the Director of this development. Chirkov assumed that since Kozintsev was, as ever, working in the Pool, he would very soon be extremely aware of this development, but he snapped to and barged through the crowd anyway, choking back the instinct to apologize. The Amerikans mainly got out of his way, and he pushed to the front of the wave shuffling down the basement steps. He broke out of the pack and clattered into the Pool, yelling that the Amerikans were coming. Researchers looked up—he saw Valentina's eyes flashing annoyance and wondered if it were not too late to ask her for sex—and the crowd edged behind Chirkov, approaching the lip of the Pool.

He vaulted in and sloshed through the mess towards Kozintsev's cubicle. Many partitions were down already, and there was a clear path to the Director's workspace. Valentina pouted at him, then her eyes widened as she saw the assembled legs surrounding the Pool. The Amerikans began to topple in, crushing furniture and corpses beneath them, many unable to stand once they had fallen. The hardiest of them kept on walking, swarming around and overwhelming the technicians. Cries were strangled and blood ran on the bed of the Pool. Chirkov fired wildly, winging an ear off a bearded dead man in a shabby suit, and pushed on towards Kozintsev. When he reached the center, his first thought was that the cubicle was empty, then he saw what the Director had managed. Combining himself with his work, V. A. Kozintsev had constructed a wooden half skeleton which fit over his shoulders, making his own head the heart of the new body he had fashioned for Grigory Yefimovich Rasputin. The head, built out to giant size with exaggerated clay and rubber muscles, wore its black wig and beard, and even had lips and patches of sprayed-on skin. The upper body was wooden and intricate, the torso of a giant with arms to match, but sticking out at the bottom were the Director's stick-insect legs. Chirkov thought the body would not be able to support itself but, as he looked, the assemblage stood. He looked up at the caricature of Rasputin's face. Blue eyes shone, not glass but living.

Valentina was by his side, gasping. He put an arm around her and vowed to himself that if it were necessary she would have the bullet he had saved for himself. He smelled her perfumed hair. Together, they looked up at the holy maniac who had controlled a woman and, through her, an Empire, ultimately destroying both. Rasputin looked down on them, then turned away to look at the Amerikans. They crowded around in an orderly fashion, limping pilgrims approaching a shrine. A terrible smile disfigured the crude face. An arm extended, the paddle-sized hand stretching out fingers constructed from surgical implements. The hand fell onto the forehead of the first of the Amerikans, the officer. It covered the dead face completely, fingers curling around the head. Grigory Yefimovich seemed powerful enough to crush the Amerikan's skull, but instead he just held firm. His eyes rolled up to the chandelier, and a twanging came from inside the wood-and-clay neck, a vibrating monotone that might have been a hymn. As the noise resounded, the gripped Amerikan shook, slabs of putrid meat falling away like layers of onionskin. At last, Rasputin pushed the creature away. The uniform gone with its flesh, it was like Valentina's skeleton, but leaner, moister, stronger. It stood up and stretched, its infirmities gone, its ankle whole. It clenched and un-clenched teeth in a joke-shop grin and leaped away, eager for meat. The next Amerikan took its place under Rasputin's hand, and was healed too. And the next.

Joyce Carol Oates

THE RUINS OF CONTRACOEUR

Joyce Carol Oates is a publishing phenomenon. Her list of credits is way too long to list here; on any given week you're likely to see a piece in The New Yorker, *a penned review in the* New York Times, *or, perhaps, a new novel, a collection of short stories, an edited anthology, a book on boxing, a play. Even if we restrict ourselves to the horror field the task becomes little easier, though we would do well to mention her collection* Haunted: Tales of the Grotesque, *the anthology* American Gothic Tales, *and the novel* Zombie, *which won the Bram Stoker Award.*

Other recent work outside the horror field includes the family sagas Bellefleur *and* We Were the Mulvaneys.

"The Ruins of Contracoeur" is atmospheric, dense with poetic gloom, touching and unnerving; it was the very first story I received for this book, and even after all this time it continues to haunt me.

I. First Sighting: The Thing-Without-a-Face

It was in June, early in our time of exile in Contracoeur. In the death-stillness of a stonily moonlit night. Not ten days following the upheaval of our lives when Father, disgraced and defeated, uprooted his family from the state capital to live in the ruin of Cross Hill, his grandfather's estate in the foothills of the Chautauqua Mountains. *Bear with me, children. Believe in me! I will be redeemed. I will redeem myself.* My brother Graeme, thirteen years old, restless, insomniac and unhappy prowling the downstairs of the darkened old house like a trapped feral cat. In his pajamas, barefoot, not caring if he stubbed his toes against the shadowy legs of chairs, tables; not caring if, upstairs in the bedroom they shared, his younger brother Neale who whimpered and ground his teeth in his sleep might wake suddenly to see

Graeme's bed empty and be frightened. Not caring how our parents, convalescing from the trauma of the move to Cross Hill and the ignominy of their new life, would be upset by his defiant behavior. For by day as by night Graeme signaled his displeasure in words both spoken and unspoken. *I hate it here! Why are we here? I want to go home.* Graeme was a sallow-skinned, spoiled, petulant child, immature even for his young age: tears of rage and self-pity stung his eyes. He was small-boned, slight; back home, he'd spent much of his time in cyberspace, and had only a few friends from the private school he attended, skilled at computers like himself; he'd never been physically outgoing, or brash, or brave like his older brother Stephen. Now shivering in his thin cotton pajamas prowling the rooms of the vast unfamiliar house that was our father's inheritance; prowling this drafty, high-ceilinged and neglected old house as if it were a tomb in which, his father's son, the child of a man in exile, he was unjustly confined. That evening our mother had come to us in our rooms to kiss us good-night, Mother in a pale silk dressing gown that fitted her loosely, for she'd lost weight, and her beautiful hair that had been so lustrous an ashy-blond now threaded with gray, untidy on her shoulders, touching our faces with her thin fingers and murmuring *Children, please don't be unhappy, remember that we love you, your father and mother love you, try to be happy here at Cross Hill, try to sleep in these strange, new beds for our sake.* Graeme accepted Mother's kiss but lay awake for hours. His thoughts in a turmoil of resentment and fear for Father's safety. At last slipping agitated from his bed which was not (as he told himself bitterly) his bed but one borrowed, uncomfortable and smelling of damp bedclothes and mildew. *I can't sleep! I won't sleep! Never again!*

For not a minute of any hour of any day, nor even night, did we children of a disgraced and defeated man cease to feel the outrage of our predicament.

Why? Why has this happened to us?

Graeme made his way down the staircase that swayed slightly beneath even his modest weight of eighty-nine pounds. He imagined the pupils of his eyes enlarging in the dark, shrewd and luminous as an owl's. The death-stillness of the hours beyond midnight. Moonlight slanting through the latticed windows on the eastern side of the house. In the near distance, the cry of night birds; a screech owl; loons on the lake; the murmurous wind. Graeme shivered—a faint chill wind seemed always to be blowing through the drafty house from the direction of Lake Noir, to the north. *Why was I drawn to see what I had no wish to see? Why I,*

Graeme? For a moment disoriented by the size of the foyer, larger than it seemed by day, and the water-stained marble floor painfully cold against his bare feet; and the vastness of the room beyond the foyer, one of the public rooms, as they were called, only partly furnished and these random items of furniture shrouded in ghostly white sheets; a room with dust-saturated Oriental carpets; and everywhere the sour odors of mildew, rot, the dead, desiccated bodies of mice in the walls. The room's ceiling was so unnaturally high it seemed to be obscured in shadow, from which shrouded chandeliers hung as if floating in the gloom; a room so large as to appear without walls; as if melting out into the shadows of the overgrown grounds. Graeme believed that this room was much smaller by day. Unless he'd wandered into an unfamiliar part of the house? For we were still virtual strangers to Cross Hill, living in only a few rooms of the great old house.

It was then that Graeme saw a movement outside on the lawn.

Certain at first that it was an animal. For Contracoeur was a wild region; everywhere there were deer, raccoons, foxes, even lynxes and black bears—that spring, we'd been told, black bears were sighted in the very city of Contracoeur. By its pronounced upright posture the figure outside on the lawn, moving slowly past the terrace windows, must have been a bear, Graeme thought; his heartbeat quickened. We'd been warned of bears at Cross Hill but had sighted none yet. So Graeme stood at one of the terrace windows watching with excitement the mysterious figure pass at a distance of approximately thirty feet. Beyond the terrace, of broken, crumbled flagstone, was a ragged grove of Chinese elms, storm-damaged from the previous winter; beyond the elms was a lane called Acacia Drive, which split in two to circle a fountain. The upright figure moved along this lane in the moonlight, in the direction of the lake, away from the house; its posture as ramrod-straight, stiff, too straight, Graeme decided, to be a bear. And its gait rhythmic and unhurried, not the shambling, loping gait of a bear.

Graeme then did something not in his character: he quietly un-locked a terrace door and nudged it open and stepped outside breath-less into the chill, fresh air; squatted behind the terrace railing to watch the departing figure. A trespasser at Cross Hill? So far from the city and from the nearest neighbor? A hunter? (But the figure carried no weapon that Graeme could discern.) This figure could not be the white-haired part-time groundskeeper who lived in town. Nor our father—hardly. Nor sixteen-year-old Stephen. The figure was taller and more solidly built than any of these; taller, Graeme had begun to think, with a sensation of dread, than any man he'd ever seen before.

As Graeme stared from his inadequate hiding place behind the railing, the figure halted abruptly as if sensing his presence; seemed to be glancing in Graeme's direction, head tilted, as if it were sniffing the air; in a vivid patch of moonlight revealing itself as—a being without a face.

Not a man, a thing. A thing-without-a-face.

Graeme jammed his knuckles against his mouth to keep from crying out in horror. His knees had gone weak; he had to resist the instinct to turn and run blindly away, which would have called the thing's attention to him.

The figure's head was seemingly human in shape, though larger and more oblong, with a more pronounced jaw, than the average human head. Its hair appeared dark, coarse, unkempt. Its rigid, stiff-backed posture suggested that of a man with an exaggerated military manner. Yet, where a face should have been there was—nothing.

A raw blank expanse of skin like flesh brutally fashioned with a trowel. A suggestion of shallow indentations where eyes should have been, and nostrils, and a mouth; possibly there were tiny orifices in these areas too small for Graeme to see. He dared not look; he'd sunk to the terrace to hide behind the wall like a terrified child.

He was breathing quickly, shallowly. Thinking *No! No! I didn't see anything! I'm just a boy, don't hurt me.*

Waking then sometime later, dazed, still anxious; a sick, sour taste of bile at the back of his mouth. He must have lost consciousness—must have fainted. So frightened he couldn't breathe! And frightened still.

Daring to lift his head—slowly. Cautiously. Wisps of cloud like filmy, darting thoughts were being blown across the moon. The grove of Chinese elms was still; the rutted, weedy lane called Acacia Drive was empty; no movement anywhere except the restless, perpetual stirring of grasses by the wind. All of nature was hushed as in the aftermath of a terrible vision.

The thing-without-a-face had vanished into the night.

2. Exile

At Cross Hill where the perpetual teasing wind from Lake Noir blew southward through our lives.

Where in exile and disgrace and in fear of his life our father had

brought his family, his wife and five children, to live in his late grandfather's ruin of a house; on ninety acres of neglected land in rural
Contracoeur, in the lower eastern range of the Chautauqua Mountains.

Mount Moriah, eleven miles directly due west. Mount Provenance, twenty miles to the south.

Where millions of years ago gigantic ice glaciers pushed southward
like living rapacious creatures from the northern polar cap to gouge
the earth into nightmare shapes: peaks, precipices, drumlins, ridges,
steep ravines and narrow valleys and floodplains. Where as late as
Easter Sunday of mid-May snow might fall and as early as mid-August
the night air might taste of autumn, imminent winter.

At Cross Hill, built in 1909 by Moses Adams Matheson, a wealthy
textile mill owner, positioned on the crest of a glacial incline three
miles south of Lake Noir (so named because its water, though pure
as spring water when examined—in a glass, for instance—irradiated,
in mass, an inexplicably lightless effulgence, opaque as tar) and five
miles east of Contracoeur (a small country town of about 8,500 inhabitants) on the banks of the Black River. Named Cross Hill because
the house, neoclassic in spirit, had been idiosyncratically constructed
in the shape of a truncated cross, of pink limestone and granite; looking now, after decades of neglect (for Moses Adams Matheson's son
and sole heir had never wished to live there) stark and derelict as an
old ship floundering in a sea of unmowed grass, thistles and saplings.

A hundred thousand dollars, minimum, would be required, Father
gloomily estimated, to make Cross Hill "fit for human habitation";
almost as much to restore the grounds to their original beauty. (Which
Father had seen only in photographs.) We didn't have hundreds of
thousands of dollars. We were "reduced to poverty—paupers." We
would have to live "like squatters" in a few rooms of Cross Hill, most
of the enormous house shut up, the rooms vacant. And we would
have to be grateful, Father warned us, for what we had—"Grandfather's legacy to me. A place of sanctuary."

Temporary sanctuary, he meant. For of course Roderick Matheson
meant to clear his name and return to the capital. In time.

Seeing the ruin of Cross Hill that first afternoon in a pelting
rainstorm, our station wagon's wheels stuck and spinning in the grassy-
muddy drive, Mother burst into tears, crying bitterly, "I'll die here!
How can you bring me here? I'll never survive." The younger children, Neale and Ellen, immediately burst into tears too. But Father
quickly reached over to grasp Mother's wrist, to comfort her; or to
quiet her; we heard Mother draw in her breath sharply; Father said

in a lowered, pleasant voice, "No, Veronica. You will not *die*. None of us Mathesons will *die*. That will only please *them*—my enemies."

Enemies: some of them former associates of Father's, even friends of his and Mother's, who'd betrayed him for political reasons; had perjured themselves in a campaign to vilify and destroy his career; had had a part in issuing warrants for his arrest.

Here are facts. We children knew little of them at the time, we had to piece them together afterward. For much was unknown to us. Much was *forbidden knowledge*.

In April of that year, shortly after his forty-fourth birthday, Judge Roderick Matheson, our father, was arrested in his chambers at the State Court of Appeals.

At the time of his much-publicized arrest the youngest of the eleven justices of the court and the one of whom the most brilliant future was predicted.

Roderick Matheson was kept for twelve days in "interrogative detention" in a state facility within a mile of the State Court of Appeals. He was allowed to see only his attorneys and his distraught wife.

Then, abruptly, he was released.

And made to resign his judgeship. And made to surrender to the state most of his accumulated savings and investments. So the family was plunged into debt. Virtually overnight, into debt. So he and Mother were forced to sell their house in the most prestigious suburb of the capital; and their summer cottage on the Atlantic coast in Kennebunkport, Maine; and all but one of their several cars; and their yacht; and Mother's several fur coats; and certain items of jewelry; and other expensive possessions. *Why?* we children asked, and Mother said bitterly, *Because your father's enemies are jealous of him, because they're vicious men who've banded together to destroy him.*

We were forbidden to ask further questions. We were forbidden to see newspapers or newsmagazines, watch TV or listen to the radio. Immediately at the time of Father's arrest we were taken by Mother out of our private schools and forbidden to communicate with even our closest friends by telephone or E-mail. Mother insisted we remain in the house; Mother insisted upon knowing where we were every minute and became hysterical if one of us was missing, furious when we returned. Home, she shut herself away from us to talk on the phone for hours. (To Father? To Father's attorneys? To attorneys of her own? For it seemed for a while that there was a possibility of separation, divorce.) Mother's high shrill plaintive demanding incredulous quavering voice raised as we'd never heard it before. *How can this be happening to me! I deserve better for God's sake! I am innocent for God's sake! And my children—what will their lives be, now?*

We were spoiled, indulged children. We didn't know it at the time, not even Graeme knew it at the time; of course we were spoiled, indulged, the children of rich, powerful, socially ambitious parents. Even the ten-year-old twins Neale and Ellen with their sweet, innocent faces and astonished eyes. Our privileged lives of clothes and computers and private lessons (tennis, ballet, horseback riding), our pride in knowing we were the children of Judge Roderick Matheson of whom so much was said; our lives so like play-lives, and not real lives at all; changed suddenly and irrevocably as the lives of children glimpsed on TV who have suffered natural disasters like earthquakes, famine, war. And so Father himself looked, when he returned to us, the shock of blond-brown hair on his forehead now laced with silver, his cheeks gaunt, his eyes glassy and his once-handsome mouth like something mashed, like one, formerly a prince, who has survived, but only just barely, a natural disaster.

We shrank from him, and from Mother. We were frightened of Mother's changeable moods. For she might stare through us wide-eyed in fear and dismay, her once-beautiful hazel-green eyes swollen from weeping; or she might rush to embrace us, giving a little cry of pain—*Oh, oh! Oh, what will we do?* At such times Mother gave off a scent of sweet perfume commingled with perspiration; her breath smelled of—what? Wine, bourbon? Sometimes it was us, her children, whom she wished to comfort; at other times it seemed to be herself she wished to comfort; sometimes she was angry at Father, and sometimes at Father's enemies; sometimes, for no reason we could comprehend, she was angry at us. Especially Rosalind, who at fourteen and a half, a lanky, long-limbed girl with frowning eyes, had a stubborn way of seeming to be thinking for herself, furrowing her brow and sucking at her lips, brooding silent in that space where even a mother can't follow. So if Rosalind stiffened in Mother's arms, nearly as tall as Mother now, Mother might lean back to stare into her face, gripping Rosalind's shoulders with red-gleaming talon-sharp fingernails and pushing Rosalind from her—*What's wrong with you? Why are you looking at me like that? How dare you look at me, your mother—like that!*

Mother's beautiful face like a mask. A porcelain-cosmetic mask. A mask that might shatter suddenly, like glass, if her blood beat too furiously in her veins.

So Rosalind shrank from her and crept away to hide in a corner of Cross Hill. Thinking *never never never* would she grow up to be so beautiful and so angry a woman.

But it was Father, so changed, who most frightened us. Where once Judge Roderick Matheson had been impeccably groomed, never allowing himself to be glimpsed in other than fresh-laundered clothes, his hair neatly combed, now he often wore rumpled clothes, ran his hands violently through his hair, shaved in such a way (we speculated) as to leave his skin pained, reddened; he was Father, still, and his face was Father's much-photographed face, yet, it almost seemed, something older, rougher, ravaged sought to push its way through. His eyes, liquidy-brown, usually warm and ingratiating, had a dull glassy look; his mouth twisted as if he were arguing with himself.

Father was a hurt, innocent man. A man betrayed, hounded and persecuted by his enemies and by the "ravenous, insatiable, unconscionable media"—the reason we hadn't been allowed to read newspapers or watch TV. Father was an angry man and, sometimes, we had to admit, a dangerous man. For, like Mother, he swung between moods: now distressed, now furious; now optimistic, now enervated; now grieving for his family, now grieving for himself and his blighted career; now youthful, vigorous, now an aging, embittered man.

In his speech-voice, at the dinner table, he might declaim, as if speaking to others, not just us, *Dear wife, dear children! Bear with me! We will return one day soon to our rightful lives. I will redeem the name of Matheson, I will redeem us all—that is my vow. I will seal it with— my blood.*

Face flushed with wine, eyes prankishly narrowed, Father might take up his fork and, before Mother could prevent him, stab it into the back of his hand as if stabbing a small hairless creature that had unaccountably crawled up beside his plate.

We flinched, but dared not cry out. What was required from us was a murmur—*Yes, yes Father.* For crying at such times generally displeased Father for its suggestion that, though we were children quickly murmured *Yes, yes Father* we did not truly believe our own words.

"It's like he died after all, isn't it? In jail. His eyes . . ."

It was after one of Father's strange elated outbursts at the dinner table that Stephen uttered this remark in a drawling voice unlike his normal voice; Stephen whose life had been, until Father's arrest, soccer, football, basketball, sports video games and the intense, rapidly shifting friendships of boy and girl classmates at his school; Stephen, handsome as Roderick Matheson had been as a boy, with his father's broad face and sharply defined cheekbones.

Graeme shrugged and walked away.

Rosalind said something quick and hurtful to Stephen, called him an ignorant asshole, and walked away.

Lying then awake and miserable most of the night. Pressing her damp face into her pillow. Thinking *Can eyes die? A man's eyes—die? And the rest of the man continue to live?* Through the interminable wind-haunted night like each night in this terrible place she hated, so lonely, so far from her friends and the life of Rosalind Matheson she'd loved; waking fitfully to see, as if he were crouched over her bed, the glassy, red-veined eyes of our father glaring at her out of the dark.

Dear God help him to prove his innocence. To clear his good name. Help him to restore himself to all that he has lost. Make us happy again, make us ourselves again, return us to our true home and make the name Matheson a name again of pride.

3. By Crescent Pond

A sunny, wind-blustery morning! One of the grimy-paned windows in the breakfast room was cracked like a cobweb, and scattered tree limbs and debris lay on the terrace rustling like living, wounded things. "Where's Graeme?" we asked one another.

"Where's Graeme?" Mother asked with vexed, worried eyes.

For Graeme had not joined us at breakfast. He'd been awake before us, and dressed, and gone. So little Neale had said, wistfully.

Yet Graeme was somewhere in the house. Stubborn in resistance when we called: "Gra-eme! Where are you?"

Since our move to Cross Hill, his old life left behind, Graeme had been plunged into an angry melancholy. His expensive computer equipment could not function in this ruin of a house: there was inadequate wiring. Our parents' large bedroom at the far front of the second floor, off-limits to us children, was said to contain a lamp with a sixty-watt bulb; and Father's private office on the third floor contained a telephone, a fax, and one or two low-wattage lamps; though the lights frequently wavered and went out, and Father tried to use them sparingly. (Yet often Father worked through the night. He was involved in preparing extensive legal documents refuting the charges and innuendos made against him, to be presented one day to the state attorney's office; he was also on the phone frequently with the single attorney still in his hire.) But Graeme's new-model computer, plugged into one of the crude Cross Hill sockets, displayed a splotched gray screen with virtually no definition. Most of his programs and video games could not be operated. The Cross Hill cyberspace resembled a void; a vacuum; an emptiness like that of the atom, which is said to contain almost nothing; slow-drifting particles like motes in the corner of your eye. It was increasingly difficult to believe, Graeme thought, that such a phenomenon as "cyberspace" existed—anywhere. He'd resumed his E-mail, in defiance of Mother's warning, but the messages he received from his several friends back in the city were strange, scrambled. One morning Stephen came upon Graeme in his room hunched over his computer keyboard, swiftly typing commands that led again and again, and again, as in a nightmare of comic cruelty, to ERROR! SERVER CANNOT BE LOCATED on a shimmering, fading screen. Stephen was shocked by the sorrow in his brother's face. "Hey. Why don't you let that stuff rest for a while? There's other things we can do. Like bicycling. Into town . . ." But Graeme didn't hear. He hunched his thin shoulders farther over the keyboard, rapidly typing out another complex set of commands. The luminous hieroglyphics on the screen floated slowly upward as if channeled from a very great distance through space and time. In the pale clotted light of the overcast June morning, Graeme's adolescent skin had a peevish green cast, like tarnished metal; his eyes glistened with bitter bemusement. In disgust he said to Stephen, "Look." Stephen looked: it was Graeme's E-mail he was scanning, but each of the messages had something wrong with it, as if awkwardly translated from a foreign language, or in code:

```
graememat ± @ poorshit.///
howzit 2b ded!
```

"They think I'm dead," Graeme said, choking back a sob. "The guys are talking about me like I'm dead."

Stephen said quickly, "The message isn't coming through right. Once we get more electricity—"

Graeme stabbed angrily at a key, and the E-mail vanished.

"Maybe I am dead. Maybe we all are, and buried at Cross Hill."

Stephen backed off, shuddering. At such times he didn't want to deal with his brother's moods. He didn't want to think *He knows so much more than I do, he's so much smarter than I am.* He went to announce to the others, "Graeme's getting weird over that computer shit. I think we should pull his plug."

Then there came the morning they couldn't locate Graeme, calling for him up- and downstairs; calling for him out the windows, out the terrace doors overlooking the grove of ragged Chinese elms, and the weedy graveled lane known as Acacia Drive (though most of the acacia trees had sickened and died). Mother, her ashy-silvery hair swinging about her face, her girl's forehead lined with vexation and worry, cupped her hands to her mouth and cried, "Gra-eme! Graeme! Where are you hiding? I insist you come here—at once." As if it was a game of hide-and-seek she might bring to an abrupt end. Yet, like Father, who spent most of his waking hours on the third floor of the house, Mother was reluctant to venture outside; she shaded her eyes to squint toward the outbuildings, the old carriage house and the stable and barns with their rain-rotted, collapsing roofs, and in the direction of murky Crescent Pond, which was at the bottom of the hill, beyond Acacia Drive; but some timidity, or outright fear, prevented her from seeking Graeme in such likely places. After ten days at Cross Hill during which time she'd seen no one outside the family except hired help from Contracoeur, Mother was still wearing expensive, stylish city clothes; dresses, skirts and sweaters, not jeans (perhaps she owned none?) but silk slacks with matching shirts, impractical sling-back Italian sandals with prominent heels. Each morning, on even the most oppressive of mornings, she'd bravely made up her heart-shaped face into that tight, beautiful mask; though the skin of her throat was pallid, beginning to show signs of age. She wore her wedding rings, her square-cut emerald ring on her right hand, her jeweled wristwatch that sparkled on her small-boned wrist. In a breathy, almost coquettish voice Mother complained, "That boy! Graeme! He does these things to spite *me*."

We searched for Graeme all morning. By noon a fierce pale sun dominated the sky. How vast Cross Hill was, this "historic" estate that had gone to ruin; how many hiding places there were out-of-doors in the handsome old barns, in the rotting grape and wisteria arbors, in the evergreens bordering the house, and in the wild grasses, some of them as tall as five feet, in the park surrounding the house; in the derelict greenhouses through whose smashed windows black-feathered birds (starlings, grackles, crows?) rose hastily at our approach, like departing spirits of the dead. "Where is Graeme?" Rosalind shouted after them. "Where is he hiding?"

By chance it was Rosalind who finally found Graeme squatting amid marsh grass and desiccated bamboo shoots on the far side of the Crescent Pond, staring like one hypnotized at the spider-stippled surface of the pond. "Graeme, we've been looking for you everywhere! Didn't you hear us calling?" Rosalind cried in exasperation. She waved to Stephen, to call him over, wading through the thigh-high, sword-like grass. A look in Graeme's pinched, pale face frightened Rosalind and so she continued to chide him. "Making us all look for *you*. Making us all *worry*. I hope you're *satisfied*."

Stephen trotted over, panting. He wore a frayed T-shirt, jeans splashed with mud the color of fresh manure. Rosalind noticed a thinly bleeding scratch above his left eyebrow that must have been made by a sharp branch. "Hey, kid? You okay?" Stephen asked.

Seeing that his hiding place had been found out, Graeme mumbled something evasive. He stood, but not very steadily; he must have been squatting there for a long time. His khaki shorts and T-shirt were covered in burrs. His soft brown, wavy hair, grown unevenly past his ears, looked tangled. He said, swallowing, "I—saw something. Last night."

Yes? What? They waited.

"I don't know. I saw it but I—can't be sure. I mean, if I saw—what it was. Or . . ." Graeme's voice trailed off miserably. It was clear that something had frightened him badly and that he didn't know how to speak of it. He didn't want to risk being laughed at and yet—

Yes? What? Graeme, come *on*.

"It was a—man, I think. Walking along the drive over there. About two o'clock. I couldn't sleep and I came downstairs and I—saw something out the window." Graeme spoke slowly, painfully. He drew his forearm carelessly across his mouth, wiping it. "I came outside onto the terrace. I saw him—it—in the moonlight."

Stephen said, "Someone trespassing on our property?"

Rosalind said, making a joke of it, "You're sure it wasn't one of *us*?" That look in Graeme's eyes spooked her.

Graeme said, choosing his words carefully, "It was a, a thing like a man—a man with no face." He grinned suddenly. "A thing-with-no-face."

Quickly Stephen said, as if he hadn't entirely heard, "A hunter, probably. Trespassing on our property. Someone who lives nearby."

Graeme vehemently shook his head. "No. He—it—didn't have any gun. It was just—walking. But not walking like a normal man. Along the drive there, and into the grass—in that direction. Like it knew where it was going, it wasn't in any hurry. A thing-without-a-face."

"How could it be without a *face?*" Stephen asked skeptically. "Anything in nature, any living thing, has to have a *face.* You must have been asleep and dreaming."

"I wasn't dreaming!" Graeme said agitatedly. "I know what's real, and the thing-without-a-face was *real.*"

Stephen laughed nervously, derisively. He'd begun to back off, pushing the air with the palms of his hands in a dismissive gesture; the thin scratch on his forehead glistened with blood. "How could there be a thing-without-a-face! You dreamt it."

Rosalind said suddenly, stricken, "No. I dreamt it. I saw it—him—too. A man, a thing like a man, without a face—standing over my bed." She covered her eyes with her fingers, remembering, as her brothers stared at her in horror.

Over my bed, in the night; in the moonlight; the shape of a man, a man's head, yet where the face would be—raw blank featureless skin.

4. Other People

Our days at Cross Hill were tense and unpredictable as the sky over Contracoeur. Because of the mountains and the incessant winds that blew across chilly Lake Noir, the sky was forever changing: one minute a clear, pellucid blue like washed glass, the next mottled and roiling with clouds the color of bruised plums. Before an electrical storm, depending upon the direction and velocity of the wind, the temperature could drop as much as twenty-five degrees within a few minutes. Sometimes—this particularly disoriented the younger children—twilight began abruptly at midday, the sun buried in tattered clouds. There were thunderstorms so powerful the earth and sky seemed locked in convulsions; lightning raked the sky, revealed its depths cavernous and sinister as the cellar of Cross Hill (which was officially off-limits for exploration). The moss-rotted roofs and ill-fitting windows of the old house leaked; puddles formed on the once-elegant marble and parquet floors; Mother wept, and cursed our father's enemies—"How can they be so cruel, so vindictive? If only they knew how unhappy we are!" Mother persisted in believing that, if Father's enemies, some of whom were his ex-colleagues and friends, knew how miserable we were in this terrible place, they would take pity on us and exonerate Roderick Matheson completely, and welcome him back to the capital, where he belonged. *If only they knew.*

Father kept to himself, hidden away most of the time in his private quarters on the third floor of the house. On even the hottest, most humid and oppressive midsummer days, Father continued to work; it was said by Mother that he worked never less than twelve hours a day; he would not relent until he was vindicated. We might catch a glimpse of him at a safe distance—tramping through the tall grass, for instance, one of us sometimes glanced up and saw the flash of white of Father's customary shirt at a third-floor window; never did we wave, for Father might misinterpret such a gesture as frivolity, or worse yet, mockery. It was at dinner we saw him, when we saw him at all. When he might appear in our midst, seated at the head of the table before we were called into the dining room by Mother, smiling and hopeful as a convalescent. He ate slowly, with forced appetite, and spoke little, as if to conserve his voice; he didn't like to hear us chatter, but he didn't like us to be absolutely silent, either—"Like mourners." (Though Father seemed tired, he was capable of his old, cutting sarcasm, and outbursts of temper, directed especially at Stephen, whose awkward attempts to appear cheerful were misread by Father as "impertinence.") There were many evenings, however, when Father ate alone upstairs, his food prepared for him by a woman from Contracoeur, Mrs. Dulne, whom Mother had hired as a part-time cook and cleaning woman and whose husband, Mr. Dulne, also helped out as a general handyman and groundskeeper. (The Dulnes were very nice, if reserved and somewhat wary people; old enough to be our grandparents.) It was Mother who carried these meals on an ornate, tarnished-silver tray upstairs to Father, fretting and anxious that he should eat to "keep up his strength." For all of our lives, our very futures, depended upon Father's "strength."

Occasionally, beginning in late June, visitors came to Cross Hill to see Father. Their long, dark, shiny cars seemed to appear out of nowhere, driving hesitantly up the rutted gravel lane. Perhaps these visitors were lawyers. Perhaps they were state investigators. On at least one disturbing occasion, they were a TV camera crew and a woman reporter; Mother barred the reporter from entering the house but was powerless to do much about the TV crew, who simply filmed her as she stood shrinking in the doorway crying angrily, "Go away! Haven't you done enough! Leave us alone!" We were not allowed to speak with these strangers, and we were discouraged from observing them. We were discouraged even from recalling that we'd observed them.

When one of Father's invited visitors left the house late one afternoon, though he'd exchanged greetings with Stephen (who was working alongside Mr. Dulne in the tall grass beside the front walkway, clearing away brambles, bare-chested in the sun), it was Mother's pretext that there hadn't been anyone there at all; at least no one Stephen would have known. In fact, Stephen was sure he'd recognized his father's visitor; he'd seen him at our house in the city several times; one of Stephen's classmates at his old school was the man's son; yet, to Stephen's bewilderment, he couldn't remember the man's name. And when Stephen asked Mother about him, Mother professed ignorance: "Who? I didn't notice. I was napping. This heat . . ." Stephen asked if Father would be presenting his case in court soon, and Mother said nervously, "Stephen, how would I know? I'm not allowed such information. But please don't ask your father, dear. Promise!" As if any of us, particularly Stephen, required such a warning.

So the days, and the nights, were tense and unpredictable. For the first time in our lives, we Matheson children hadn't anything to "do"—no friends to see, no private lessons, no school, no TV, no VCR, no video games, no computers (except for Graeme's increasingly faulty computer), no movies, no malls; some of us were allowed to ride with Mother, and less frequently Father, into Contracoeur to make necessary purchases; but we were forbidden to wander about the town, above all we were forbidden to strike up conversations with strangers. To our surprise, we were assigned chores—as we'd never been assigned chores before in our lives, with our generous allowances and credit cards. Here at Cross Hill, so unjustly, we were given work but no allowances at all! Even ten-year-old Neale and Ellen had chores! Sternly, Mother told us that we must accept the fact that, for the time being, we weren't the people we'd once been. She said, in a lowered voice, as if reciting words she'd been told by another, "We've become, temporarily, other people."

Other people! We were shocked, embarrassed. We knew ourselves cheated. Recalling how Mother used to smile sadly and pityingly when speaking of the "poor"; those who dwelled in ghettos in the United States or in the strangely named Third World; seeing depressing, repetitive footage on television of famine-stricken or war-ravaged people in Africa, India, Bosnia, for instance. Both Father and Mother had been sympathetic with these tragic people but scornful of others, closely resembling ourselves, who had less money and prestige than the Mathesons; men in Father's profession who'd failed to succeed quite as he had, and women who'd failed socially, unlike Mother with her countless friends, clubs, activities; those who'd tried, and failed, to achieve the Mathesons' rank; failed through some moral flaw of their own, and so deserving of scorn.

Except, had we become those loathed *other people* ourselves?

Yet Cross Hill, and the view from the hill of the surrounding country-side, were beautiful, or came, by degrees, to seem so.

When we weren't expecting it. When we turned, suddenly, and our eyes *saw*—before we had time to think.

The mountains were beautiful emerging out of the mist at dawn. Sunsets were beautiful: the western sky beyond the ridge of mountains a vast cauldron of flame that consumed itself, deepening by slow de-grees to night. In the distance, visible on clear days, the buildings and spires of Contracoeur like a toy city on the Black River. And Lake Noir, whose size seemed always to be changing, at its largest and most turbulent when the wind was strong, like a roughened mirror that has sucked all light into it and so appears, an impossibility in nature, sheerly black. Graeme lowered his eyes so he wouldn't be tempted to gaze from his bedroom window; he preferred to think he hated Cross Hill, he wanted only to return home. (But were we home, now that their beautiful suburban house had been sold? Their possessions taken from them? Now that his few friends had forgotten him; no longer sent E-mail to him at all, even to speak of him as dead?) Stephen, resentful of being captive at Cross Hill, and preparing to make a break, had nonetheless come to enjoy working with his hands, at least out-doors in good weather; shrewdly he thought *The other place is lost; this is home*. He'd been popular and much-admired in the city, he hadn't much doubt that he'd be popular and much-admired someday, some-how, in Contracoeur; once he became known.

So dreamlike in beauty! floating in iridescent moisture-laden air!—the view from Rosalind's window looking west to Mount Moriah seemed to pull her eyes toward it; Rosalind couldn't resist. Despite her embittered young heart she found herself thinking *If only we be-longed here! We could be happy*.

5. The Bicycles

Many things, moved with us to Cross Hill, were unaccountably lost. For weeks we'd searched for our bicycles, for instance. And then one day we found them—or what remained of them. Incredulously staring into the debris-cluttered gloom of the carriage house, wondering what had happened to our bicycles. *Our* bicycles, that had been so shiny, so beautiful, so expensive. "God damn! I can't believe this," Stephen said. For Stephen's world-class road bike had been the most prestigious of all.

Not that Stephen had been a serious cyclist, but he'd had to have the best. And our parents had indulged him, of course.

Stephen, Graeme, and Rosalind, fighting back tears of anger and hurt, managed, with difficulty, to extricate the five bicycles from one another and to roll them, or drag them, out into the light. What a surprise! What a shock! There was Stephen's twenty-gear Italian road bike that had cost more than $800, there was Graeme's eleven-gear American Eagle hybrid, there was Rosalind's five-gear Peugeot touring bike that had once been a lovely cool silver-lime color, there were the twins' child-sized matching Schwinns with fat mountain bike tires—all rusted, battered, covered in cobwebs and what appeared to be rodent droppings. You could not have distinguished the quality of Stephen's bicycle from the others; you could not have distinguished little Neale's once shiny-red Schwinn from little Ellen's once robin's-egg blue Schwinn. We started uncomprehendingly, as if our bicycles were a riddle we had to solve, yet could not.

Stephen whispered again, wiping his eyes, "I can't believe this. It's . . . wrong."

Graeme, grown philosophical at Cross Hill, was the first to recover from the shock. He laughed, and thumped the dust-saturated seat of his African Eagle with a fist, and wiped cobwebs from the handlebars, saying, "It's like time has passed. Years. This is what happens to material objects, in time."

"In *time*?" Stephen asked. "But we've only been here for a few weeks."

Rosalind ignored her contentious brothers. She'd felt the hurt of her bicycle's deterioration as she might have felt her own. For this bicycle was *hers* . . . wasn't it? She hadn't ridden it much back home, hadn't had time for it, and, at Cross Hill, had more or less forgotten about it; but now she felt the loss keenly, kneeling to extricate pieces of debris from the spokes, wiping away cobwebs and dust. Except for the corroded Peugeot logo at the front of the frame, she might not have recognized her bicycle at all. She said, uneasily, "Maybe it's a test of some kind. If we don't give in . . ."

Stephen laughed angrily. "*I'm* not giving in. I never will."

If our parents had known we'd been searching for our bicycles with the idea of riding out from Cross Hill toward Lake Noir, or the town of Contracoeur, they would have forbidden us, of course; but neither knew. Unless Father was observing us from his third-floor quarters. (We were partly hidden by the carriage house, or so we believed. In fact, we weren't altogether certain which windows on the third floor were Father's; he might have had access to all, with a three-hundred-sixty-degree view of Cross Hill and its surrroundings.)

All of the bicycle tires were flat. Yet, surprisingly, they didn't appear to be rotted or shredded. Stephen, in a determined mood, located the air pump, also badly rusted, but operable, and energetically pumped air into everyone's tires; so quickly we tried our bicycles in Acacia Drive before the air leaked out again. We were laughing, excited. There was something crazed about our play. We were like children with crude, clumsy, homemade and possibly dangerous toys; toys that might explode in our faces. The twins shouted encouragement to each other, but their Schwinns were so coated in rust they were able to pedal them only a few yards before toppling over into the rutted lane. Lanky, long-limbed Graeme, who'd never been much of a bicyclist, as he'd never been at ease with his body, sat atop his bike and spun the pedals backward; tested the hand brakes (which seemed to work—or did they?); tried without success to straighten his handlebars that tilted comically to one side; and set off, grunting as he strained at the pedals, yet managing to move forward, barely. Rosalind had more success, despite the ravaged condition of her bike; though giggling with apprehension, like a drunken girl laboring to keep her balance as her bicycle wobbled, swayed, lurched and almost fell; yet moved forward. Stephen passed her, fiercely gripping the crooked handlebars of his bicycle; he too was swaying as if drunk, yet determined not to fall; just when you thought his bicycle was going to collapse, bringing him down ignominiously with it, somehow he kept it erect, and moving, by sheer strength. "*I'm* not going in," Stephen cried, laughing. "Never!" We watched as our eldest brother made his way on his wreck of a bike with painstaking effort, the back of his T-shirt soaked in sweat, as if pedaling up a steep incline and not in fact descending a gradual incline, in the direction of the front gate, and the road. A flurry of Monarch butterflies, brilliantly orange and scripted in black, clustered about him like exclamation points.

Stephen was headed for the gate; we'd been forbidden to leave Cross Hill without permission.

The ornate wrought iron gate, of course, was open; permanently open; overgrown with brambles, ivy and moss.

"Hey!" Graeme called after his older brother and sister, who were pedaling away. He hoped to catch up with them but the rusted chain of his bike snapped suddenly, and he was sent sprawling into the grass. Behind him, the twins were whimpering. Ahead of him, Stephen and Rosalind were making their way, with effort, yet steadily forward, without a backward glance. Graeme, panting, his knee aching where he'd fallen, stared after them. He'd ceased smiling. The game was ended. Though the midsummer afternoon was flooded with light, almost blinding with light, he recalled suddenly that the thing-without-a-face had crossed Acacia Drive, in the moonlight, moving in the direction of the gate. Suddenly his knees were weak. There had been rumors of the mutilation-murder of a girl, or a young child, in Contracoeur; a rumor of other incidents, as far away as the village of Lake Noir, which Graeme had never seen; these rumors had been brought to Cross Hill by the Dulnes and never corroborated; Graeme recalled them now, and recalled too that sensation of terror he'd felt seeing the thing-without-a-face in the moonlight, the conviction *This is real! Even if it can't be, it is.* He hadn't seen the thing-without-a-face since that night fifteen days before but he'd had the sense that, somehow, the thing-without-a-face was aware of him; aware of all of them, the Mathesons; it was watching them, always. *And now. Even now: in daylight.* He cupped his hands to his mouth and shouted, suddenly frightened, "Stephen! Rosalind! Come back!"

But they were out of earshot, and recklessly moving away.

Once through the opened gate and onto the country road, Stephen felt remarkably lighter, freer; as if gravity had miraculously lessened; that curious sensation you feel when stepping into water, as it begins to buoy you up. His battered bicycle continued to sway, lurch, shudder beneath him, his seat was unnaturally low, as if for a much shorter boy, there was a staccato *click! click! click!* as if his chain was preparing to snap, yet Stephen persisted; he managed to get the bicycle into a higher gear; by degrees, his speed increased. And Rosalind, trying to keep up with him, experienced much the same sensation of a sudden airiness, lightness, elation, as soon as she found herself out on the road, which was a narrow blacktop road hardly two full lanes. A fragrant wind cooled her heated face and dried the tears of hurt and frustration in her eyes. "See? What did I tell you!" Stephen called to her, grinning. His wonderful sunny smile that lit up her heart. His smile that was like their father's, except its boyishness was sincere, genuine; not lined with irony. They laughed together like careless children. There they were: free! Children of a former justice of the State Court of Appeals, and yet—free!

They were giddy with daring. They knew they might be punished. Yet not thinking of that—their father, punishment—not thinking of anything but the balmy summer air, the exquisite splotched sunlight shining through foliage at the side of the road; in this region of steep and undulating hills that was scarcely known to them, surrounded by dense, shadowy pine forests alternating with open meadows in which wildflowers shimmered with color—the pale blue of hepatica and chicory, the vivid yellow of miniature sunflowers. Close beside the road were shallow, rocky, fast-running brooks; in the near distance, the ever-present, brooding Chautauqua Mountains, covered in pines and misty at their peaks. Rosalind's heart beat with a strange illicit joy. Her flushed, pretty face shone with excitement, her fingers were covered in bright rust from the corroded handlebars. Breathless from the hilly terrain, she called, "Stephen, wait for me!"

They were traveling in the direction of Contracoeur—weren't they? Or was it in the direction of Lake Noir, deeper into the country? They must have bicycled two miles, three miles—yet nothing looked familiar. No houses, no farms, no familiar landmarks. And, oddly, there was no traffic on the road. Rosalind would have called these observations out to Stephen but he was too far ahead, and unconsciously pulling away; the entire back of his shirt was damp with sweat, his sinewy, muscular legs worked powerfully at pedaling. Rosalind felt a stab of apprehension; not fear, exactly, but apprehension; thinking without knowing she'd been thinking of it, of the hideous thing-without-a-face that had appeared in her dream of the other week, and which Graeme had claimed to have seen. Was such a thing possible? On such a summer day, in such surroundings, Rosalind found it difficult to believe.

But, yes: you know it's so.

Another half-mile and there came, returning in her direction, Stephen, concerned that his rear tire was leaking air; so, reluctantly, he and Rosalind pedaled back to Cross Hill, approximately three miles, though it seemed much longer, for the road now ascended almost steadily, and its cracked blacktop surface, apparently unrepaired for years, made their teeth rattle in their heads. By the time the corroded, partly collapsed wrought iron fence that bordered Cross Hill came into view, overgrown with jungle-like vegetation, the sky had gradually darkened with heavy, porous clouds blown by a warm, sulfurous wind from the direction of Lake Noir. Was something wrong? Rosalind tasted alarm, apprehension. Seeing, glimpsed through drooping foliage, the stately old limestone house on its hill, cross-shaped, a somber pink-gray; a storybook dwelling it seemed, surely inhabited by very special people, though whether the house was beautiful, or frankly ugly, Rosalind, panting, dazed with exhaustion, could not have said. What did we children know of the history of Cross Hill, what had we been told of our father's grandfather?—only that the man, deceased for decades, had had a name with a Biblical resonance: Moses Adams Matheson. He'd made a fortune, it was said, as a textile manufacturer in Winterthurn City, forty miles to the south, and had retired to the Chautauqua foothills of Contracoeur. Yet there were no portraits of him at Cross Hill; there were no family portraits at all, and little hanging on the walls except faded silk wallpaper hanging in strips; most of the rooms in the shuttered wings were empty not only of furnishings but of even the memory, the suggestion, of furnishings. *As if history itself had been banished, erased. As if history itself was too painful to be retained.*

As Stephen and Rosalind at last passed through the opened gate of Cross Hill, the first raindrops struck, like hot lead, sizzling and stinging. And what an uphill climb it was: the hill of Cross Hill had never been so steep. And the badly rutted Acacia Drive, leading through the grassy ruin of a park, so arduous to navigate. By the time Stephen and Rosalind arrived at the house, they were breathless and drenched in sweat; there was little that would have seemed attractive about them, for their bodies reeked of perspiration; Rosalind's thin cotton shirt and shorts clung to her slender body, her hard, small breasts, in a way repulsive to her. And there, to their dismay, were both Father and Mother awaiting them in the weedy flagstone square in front of the front entrance; the other children were nowhere in sight, as if banished. Father wore a rumpled off-white linen jacket and sporty trousers; clearly he was angry, yet making an effort to control his anger; some of his old, ironic charm had returned, as if he were addressing the court or speaking on television. His eyes were flat and lusterless but he managed to smile with seeming ease; Mother, just slightly behind him, in pale green silk slacks and a matching kimono-like silk tunic, made no effort to smile at all, for her heavily made-up face was swollen with hurt and anger; her eyes were puffy from crying; for she, who was Mother, had surely been blamed for the bad behavior of her two eldest children. Sternly Father said, "Stephen, Rosalind—how dare you disobey me? You've been gone, without permission, without even informing your mother and me you'd left Cross Hill, for almost eight hours! Such behavior is unconscionable." Eight hours! Stephen and Rosalind exchanged a stricken glance. They protested, "But we haven't been gone more than an hour! We were only just testing our bicycles . . ." Yet it seemed clear that they'd been gone for more, much more, than a single hour. The sky, massed with ugly clouds, had darkened almost to twilight; the temperature had plummeted at least twenty degrees; the harsh, stinging rain began to fall harder, smelling of night. Like a guilty child Rosalind burst into tears—"Father, I'm sorry! So sorry." Father said, incensed, " 'Sorry'! After we've been worried sick about you! You will both go to your rooms now, at once. I'll speak with you privately." Shame-faced, Rosalind hurried into the house; but Stephen remained behind, defiant, saying stubbornly that they hadn't been gone eight hours, he was certain they hadn't been gone eight hours, and anyway they had a right to ride their bicycles—"You can't keep us prisoners, Father, in this place, just because *you're* one."

There was a moment's silence. The only sound was the harsh, hissing sound of rain against the flagstones.

Quickly, yet with dignity, Father took a step forward, and before Mother could clutch at his arm, he struck Stephen a blow with his opened hand on the side of Stephen's glowing, sweaty young face.

6. Poor Mother

Poor Mother—"Veronica Matheson." That melodic name once so frequently uttered, and now so rarely. For to us, of course, our mother was "Mother" and to the Dulnes she was "Mrs. Matheson" or, more often, "ma'am"; of all of the family, only Father had the prerogative of calling her by her lovely given name; yet when he addressed her, at dinner for instance, it was usually in a tone of mild, martyred reproach.

Veronica, what on earth is this food? It tastes of—earth.

Veronica, why do the children persist in coming to the dinner table looking like vagabonds? And smelling as if they haven't bathed in days?

Veronica, why is the air so—heavy in this room? So humid? Or is it our heavy, humid hearts?

Mother sat at Mother's place facing Father at the head of the table smiling her beautiful dazzling smile. Perhaps she heard, perhaps not.

A familiar tale by now, told and retold to us, and to Mrs. Dulne, who only shook her head and made sympathetic *tsking* sounds, how back in the city, as soon as rumors of Judge Roderick Matheson's imminent fall from grace circulated, Mother's telephone ceased to ring. One morning, suddenly—the house was silent. Where once the stylish Veronica Matheson had been dazed by her own popularity, on everyone's guest list, in a fierce round of luncheons, charity functions, museum openings and receptions and formal black-tie dinners, now she, like Judge Matheson, was abruptly dropped, erased. "As if I were in quarantine with some loathsome disease," Mother said bitterly. "All of us Mathesons, even you children—'guilty until proven innocent.'" Her delicate, carefully made-up face began to resemble a smeared watercolor; her eyes, hazel-brown, once so brightly vivacious, were now veined with red from countless bouts of weeping; her breath, breathed accidentally into her children's faces, was sour-smelling as the interior of the old refrigerator in the kitchen. *Is Mother drinking?* we whispered. *Is Mother drunk?* We loved Mother but we hated Mother. We were afraid of Mother. Rosalind said, "I never knew her before, did you?" and Graeme shuddered, and shook his head; and Stephen, who tried to make the best of things even as (we suspected) he was plotting his escape, said, "Mother's just going through a phase. Like a butterfly." Graeme said, smirking, "A butterfly in reverse."

Where in the city Mother had had little time for us, now at Cross Hill, these interminable summer days, where the pale-glowering sun seemed to drag through the sky, and the minute hands of those clocks that functioned seemed sometimes to inch backward, she had too much time. Though Father rose at dawn to resume work on his case, Mother rose late; as late as possible, for she dreaded another day in exile; she bathed in a few grudging inches of rust-flecked lukewarm water in a stained antique tub; she made up her elaborate mask of a face, and tried to do something with her hair; drifted about the house like a ghost in her now rumpled, soiled city clothes, as if waiting for a friend to pick her up to drive her to lunch at the country club or the newest fashionable restaurant. *Is Mother drinking today? Poor Mother.* She grew suspicious, even jealous, of Rosalind, who was growing by swift degrees into a beautiful, physically capable and alert girl, with long wavy-curly red-blond hair bleached by the sun; she was forever interrogating Stephen and Graeme, convinced that they were sneaking away at every opportunity to Contracoeur, or beyond. She assigned chores to her elder children but rarely oversaw them. Where once she'd focused attention on the twins, dressing them with obsessive care as "the last of our babies," now she seemed frankly bored by them, depending upon kindly Mrs. Dulne to take care of them and listen to their anxious, incessant chatter. Little Neale, a bright, articulate child who in the city had been charmingly outspoken, had become morbidly nervous in the country; he flinched and cringed at shadows, even his own; he was forever tugging at Mother's arm in the way of a much younger child, pleading and whimpering. "It's in here, it comes in here when we're not looking and it hides and if you turn on the light it turns into a shadow, if you turn around it turns around with you so *you never see it*—" Neale rambled about someone, or something, he was convinced inhabited Cross Hill with us. Mother laughed irritably, saying, "I don't have time for childish games. I can't be 'Mother' twenty-four hours a day!" Little Ellen, a mirror-image of her brother, though slightly smaller, with wide, ingenuous brown eyes and a habit of sucking at her fingers, believed, too, that someone, or something, lived at Cross Hill with them, except it was invisible during the day. Rarely did Ellen sleep through the night; the poor child whimpered and thrashed in her bed, but Mother refused to allow her to sleep with a lamp burning for not only would it disturb Rosalind, with whom Ellen shared a room on the second floor, but there would be a risk in calling attention to ourselves in the dark—"You can see Cross Hill for miles. We'd be lighting a path to our very beds."

One day, Ellen was whimpering, tears rolled down her flushed cheeks, and Mother, exasperated, knelt before her, gripped her thin shoulders tight and shook her gently—"Darling, please don't cry! There aren't tears enough for us all."

Mother was made especially agitated by the *Contracoeur Valley Weekly,* which Father forbade us, and her, to read, but which Mrs. Dulne smuggled into Cross Hill at Mother's request. Most of the newspaper was devoted to ordinary, domestic news; but the front page had been taken over in recent weeks by ever more disturbing headlines— 6-YEAR-OLD GIRL MISSING, MARSH SEARCHED—GIRL, 17, FOUND MUTILATED AND STRANGLED IN EMPTY GRANARY—CORPSE OF 19-YEAR-OLD MAN DISCOVERED IN ARSON FIRE. Local law enforcement officers were investigating these crimes, and others that may have been related; several suspects were in custody; fascinated and horrified, Mother read through the paper with unwavering concentration, telling us afterward in a faint, thrilled voice, "Now, you see why your father and I don't want you children to go alone into town? Why you mustn't leave Cross Hill at any time, except with us?"

As if our parents left Cross Hill often: never more than once or twice a week. A five-mile journey to Contracoeur! Where, if we were lucky, we might be allowed to accompany Mother, for instance, into the A & P to shop for food specials, or into the ill-smelling drugstore where we were regarded with rude, curious stares, or into Sears or Kmart. We Mathesons, who'd never set foot into such dreary places in our lives until now. Stephen scorned these meager outings, but Graeme and Rosalind, eager for a change of scene, usually went along. They were warned against wandering off—mingling with strangers— but of course they did, as soon as Mother's attention was elsewhere. And they begged, and were grudgingly allowed, to spend some time in the small public library. There, while Graeme avidly browsed book- shelves in the science and mathematics sections, Rosalind, starving for companionship, shyly approached girls her age; daring to introduce herself; explaining that she and her family were new to the area, living at Cross Hill. The Contracoeur girls stared at her in amazement. One of them, with bold crimson lips, toughly attractive, said, "You live at Cross Hill? Nobody lives there."

Midsummer. The warmly sulfurous air, blowing southward from Lake Noir, brought poor Mother migraine headaches of increasing severity.

Midsummer. A throbbing-shrieking of cicadas in the trees, as tem- peratures rose into the nineties, drew poor Mother's nerves taut as wire.

And there were false sounds, as Mother came to call them—"cruel false sounds"—high-pitched vibrations, muffled voices and laughter in distant rooms at Cross Hill; a ringing telephone where there could be neither ringing nor a telephone. *Veronica? Ver-on-ica?* One parched afternoon in late July there came, bouncing along the rutted lane, an elegant silvery-green Mercedes that faded as it drew up the circular drive before the house; throwing poor Mother into a frenzy of excite- ment and panic, for she believed it must be her closest woman friend, from whom she hadn't heard in months, coming to pick her up for a country club luncheon—"And I'm not dressed. I'm not bathed. And look at my hair!"

Mother was so distraught, Mrs. Dulne had to catch her, and hold her in a comforting embrace.

There was no Mercedes at the front of the house, nor had there
been any Mercedes in the drive. Yet Graeme stubbornly insisted he'd
seen it, too. He'd seen something, silvery-green, erratic in motion,
shaped like a car, disappearing by quick degrees as it approached the
house.

Poor Mother. After the false alarm of her friend in the Mercedes, she
was ill, exhausted, for several days. Then rising from her bed abruptly
and filled with energy when Father informed her that important visitors were expected at Cross Hill in a week's time to confer with
him about re-presenting his case to the state attorney general. (He'd
accumulated new data, new evidence, Father said. Proof that his key
informers had perjured themselves in court. Proof that the original
indictments brought against him, by a biased grand jury, had been
fraudulent from the start.) Mother cried, "We can't let them see these
shameful rooms! We must do something." Of course she would have
wished to redecorate those downstairs rooms that were in use—but
there wasn't the money. Instead, her hair tied back gaily in a scarf, in
loose-fitting cotton slacks and an old shirt of Stephen's, Mother led a
housecleaning team of Mrs. Dulne and the children through several
rooms; concentrating, for practical purposes, on the glass-enclosed
breakfast room overlooking Crescent Pond where Father intended to
meet with his colleagues. None of us had seen Mother so girlish and
enthusiastic in months—in years! Her eyes, though slightly bloodshot,
shone. Her complexion, beneath the caked makeup, was fresh, glowing. Within two days, the filth-encrusted lattice windows of the breakfast room were scrubbed so that sunlight rayed through unimpeded;
the parquet floor, long layered in grime, was partway cleaned and
polished; the long antique cherrywood table was polished, and ten
handsome chairs, not precisely matching, but in good condition, were
set about it. The aged, rotted silk curtains were removed, and Mother
and Mrs. Dulne, a skilled seamstress, cleverly refashioned newer curtains from another part of the house, a bright cheerful chintz, to hang
in their place. When Father saw what Mother and the rest of us had
accomplished, he stared in genuine surprise and gratitude. Tears welled
in his eyes. "Veronica, how can I thank you? All of you—you've
worked magic." In boyish delight, he snatched up Mother's hands to
kiss them; hesitating only for an instant when he saw how white they
were, how thin and puckered, like an elderly woman's, from hours
of scrubbing in detergent water.

"Do you love me, then, Roderick?" Mother asked anxiously, in a way mortifying to her children to witness. "Am I a good wife to you, despite all?"

But, poor Mother!—within days, all her labor was undone.

Somehow, particles of dust, dirt, outright grime shifted back into the corners of the breakfast room. A sour odor prevailed of decaying matter. Wild birds, seduced by the cleaned windowpanes into imagining there were no glass barriers, flew into the windows, breaking their necks; in melancholy feather-heaps, they lay on the floor. Rain, blown through the broken windowpanes, had stained and warped the parquet; soaked and stained the chairs' cushioned seats. Even the bright chintz curtains were frayed and grimy as if they'd been hanging there for years. Mother rushed about, tearing at her hair, crying, "But— what has happened? Who has done this? *Who could be so cruel?*" We children too were shocked and dismayed; ten-year-old Neale and Ellen huddled together in terror, convinced that the thing that dwelled in the house with us, invisible, that shifted out of sight when you whirled to see it, had committed this malicious damage. Rosalind was hurt and angry, for she'd worked damned hard; she'd been proud of her effort, helping Mother in good cause. Stephen was silent, thoughtful, gnawing at his lower lip as if he was making a decision. Graeme, his pinched, peevish face smirking in a pretense of satisfaction, said, "Mother, it's the fate of the material universe—to run down, out. Did you think we were special?"

Mother turned upon him and screamed, "I hate you! All of you!" But it was only Graeme she struck, cutting his cheek below his left eye with the sharp edge of her emerald ring.

Mother then staggered and fell. Her eyes swooned back into her head. Her body struck the grimy floor softly, like a cloth bundle that has been tossed negligently down. We children seemed to know, staring at the stricken woman in horror, that Mother would never again be the person she'd been.

7. Victims

Locally, opinion was divided: the marauding killer was a black bear, crazed by having tasted human blood; or, the killer was a human being, himself crazed, simulating the behavior of an aberrant bear.

There was another victim, in late July: an eleven-year-old girl discovered strangled and battered in a desolate wooded area near the village of Lake Noir. And, in early August, a seventeen-year-old boy killed by severe blows to the head, face torn partly away, found at the edge of a cemetery in Contracoeur. Shivering, Mother merely glanced at the newspaper with its lurid headlines—"It's just the same thing over and over. Like the weather." Nor did she show much surprise or interest when, one morning, the local sheriff and two deputies arrived to question us, informally; as, they explained, they were questioning everyone in the area. These men spent most of their time with Father, who impressed them with his intelligence and soft-spoken civility. They must have known something of Roderick Matheson's professional difficulties, yet still they called him "Judge," "Your Honor," and "sir" respectfully; for the state capital was nearly three hundred miles away, and scandals and power struggles there were of little interest in Contracoeur.

On his side, Father was gracious to the police. They had no search warrant, but he gave them permission to search the property outside the house. All of us, even Mother and the twins, who'd been anxiously fretting since the arrival of the police cars, watched from upstairs windows. With the air of one asking an unanswerable question, Mother said, "What do they expect to find? Those poor fools," and Father said, with a trace of a smile, "Well, let them look. It's in my interest to be a good citizen. And then they needn't return, and trouble us ever again."

8. Second Sighting: The Thing-Without-a-Face

What have I lost: my username, my password, my soul.
Where must I flee: not IRL. There is none

This would be Graeme's farewell note, first typed out on his faulty computer, where the words jammed into solid blocks of gibberish, letters, numerals and computer hieroglyphics; then written out, in inch-high headline-letters, with such anger that the point of Graeme's marker pen tore the surface of the paper.

He'd ceased thinking of himself as Graeme Matheson. Both his names had become repugnant to him. "Graeme"-the name *given,* as a gift he'd had no choice but to receive. "Matheson"—the name *inherited,* as a fate he'd had no choice but to receive.

The family believed he'd changed, become brooding, ever more silent and withdrawn, since Mother had slapped him in so public and humiliating a way; since his face, young, stricken, astonished, had bled; since the thin, jagged wound had coagulated into a zipper-like scratch that seemed, so strangely, so perversely, always fresh. (Did Graeme pick at it to assure its freshness? If so, he might have picked at it unconsciously, or in one of his meager, fitful bouts of sleep.) In fact, only Graeme knew that the cause went deeper.

For in the Contracoeur Public Library he'd discovered, in a section titled "Contracoeur Valley History," several aged, leather-bound books whose covers hadn't been opened in decades, and out of curiosity he'd read of the renowned Moses Adams Matheson, the "textile manufacturer–wilderness conservationist" who'd constructed Cross Hill, one of the "distinguished architectural landmarks of the region"; he'd been intrigued to learn that his great-grandfather had crossed the Atlantic Ocean steerage class from Liverpool, England, unaccompanied by any adult, at the age of twelve, in 1873; that he'd been an apprentice to a shipbuilder in Marblehead, Massachusetts, but soon left for upstate New York, where, in Winterthurn City, he built the first of several Matheson textile mills on the Winterhurn River; within a decade, he'd become a wealthy man; by the turn of the century a multimillionaire, in the era in which such aggressive capitalists as J. Pierpont Morgan, John D. Rockefeller, Edward Harriman and Andrew Carnegie made their enormous fortunes through monopolies and trusts; and through the systematic exploitation of unorganized, largely immigrant labor. Moses Adams Matheson was never so rich as these men, nor so notorious; yet, Graeme gathered from his rapid skimming of these texts, his great-grandfather had cruelly exploited his workers; women, young girls, even children had been employed in his mills for as little as $2.50 a week; many of his workers were younger than twelve, and girls as young as six and seven worked thirteen hours a day. Aloud Graeme whispered, "Thirteen hours!" He had never worked at any prolonged task until the folly of the breakfast room, under Mother's guidance; at that, he hadn't worked longer than two hours at a time, and his effort had hardly been uniformly concentrated. He could not imagine working for—thirteen hours! As a young child in clamorous, stifling-hot or freezing conditions.

Graeme read with horror of the "South Winterthurn conflagration of February 8, 1911"—one of the Matheson textile mills had burnt to the ground, killing more than thirty persons including young children; investigation revealed that the mill hadn't been properly equipped with adequate fire exits, and in fact, unaccountably, most of the doors had been locked. He found himself staring at a sepia photograph of a smoldering skeleton of a building; firemen and others stood about, and on the snowy ground were corpses in rows, shrouded in canvas, so many! and some so small! A number of the fire victims had been so badly burnt, their faces so charred, absolute identification was impossible. *Bodies without faces.*

Blindly, Graeme shoved the book back onto the shelf. He'd had enough of family history. How right he'd been to feel a sick sort of shame to be a Matheson and to live at the ruin of Cross Hill; erected, as he was only now discovering, upon the bones of such innocent victims.

He decided not to tell Rosalind or Stephen. Not just yet. The revelation was too ugly, too humiliating. Graeme treasured his own adolescent cynicism but would not have wished his more energetic, more attractive sister and brother to share it. *Someone has to protect the innocent from knowing too much.*

He wondered if Mother knew about Moses Adams Matheson. Probably not. Surely not.

And Father? Surely yes.

To be fated, to be accursed—isn't that also to be special?

Since that June night, early in our summer of exile, when he'd seen the creature he called the thing-without-a-face, Graeme had rarely slept more than an hour or two at a time at night; often he didn't undress and lie down in his bed at all, for it had become to him a place of torment and misery. And so sleep overcame him during the day, in paralytic attacks; helpless to stay awake, he sank into a deep, catatonic sleep, like an infant; spells from which, blinking and gasping for breath, he'd wake with a violent pounding of his heart. (He might find himself on the filthy floor of one of the shut-up rooms at Cross Hill, or in the spear-like grass of the lawn, unable to recall how he'd gotten where he was. Sometimes one of us was stooped over him, crying, "Graeme, wake *up*! Graeme, please wake *up*!") As Graeme's insomnia worsened, his perverse pride in it increased. He could not trust the night for sleep; he could not trust the day. How he wished he could go on-line, to boast to his invisible friends in cyberspace that he, unlike the rest of them, *no longer slept*. He reveled in the fact that Mother, sunk in upon herself, indifferent now to her children, hadn't the slightest awareness of his morbid condition; nor did Father seem to be concerned, except to address him ironically at the dinner table when his head nodded or he failed to reply to a question directed at him. ("Son, I'm speaking to you. Where is your mind?" Father would ask; and Graeme would labor to bring back his mind, his consciousness, as a boy might tug timidly at a favorite kite blown high into the sky by an unpredictable wind with the power to tear it to shreds at any moment. *My mind! My mind! Father, here it is!*)

Yet to be isolated, accursed—that was to know himself special.

Graeme had ceased to believe that our father might be "redeemed"—that "justice" would be executed. He'd ceased to have faith that we would ever be returned to our old lives in the city; he'd ceased to believe that our "old lives" had ever existed, in fact. As cyberspace, in which he'd spent so many hours of his young life, exists everywhere, but also nowhere. *And nowhere must predominate. The final law of nature.*

Now that Mother had been broken by Cross Hill, now that Father had more obsessively retreated to his quarters at the top of the house (forbidden, as the master bedroom was forbidden, for us children to approach), there came to be a prevailing mood of confusion in the household; like that aftermath of shock, yet a silent, undefined shock, following the passage of a powerful jet plane overhead. It was August; a time of intense, sweltering heat; a time of tremulous, quavering heat; and frequent thunderstorms, and lightning; a time of frequent electric failures, when the inadequate wiring at Cross Hill broke down completely and darkness might be protracted for hours. One day we realized that Mr. and Mrs. Dulne had ceased to come to the house; we seemed to know that the couple hadn't been paid in weeks and had given up hoping to be compensated for their work. Mother explained in a blank, indifferent voice, as if she were commenting upon the weather, "They will receive payment. Father will write them a check. In time." But when? we asked. (We were ashamed that this kindly older couple, who'd been so gracious to us, might be cheated.) But Mother merely smiled and shrugged. Since the "betrayal" of the breakfast room, as she'd come to call it, she'd withdrawn from emotion. *Not Mother now,* Graeme thought bitterly. *Then who?*

Ironically, Father's important visitors hadn't shown up that morning. He'd waited through the day for them, and it was one of our longest August days. He'd waited calmly at first, in a newly pressed blue-pinstripe seersucker suit, white shirt and tie, glancing through documents neatly arranged in stacks on the cherrywood table; then with growing agitation he'd waited at the front entrance of Cross Hill, beneath its mossy, discolored neoclassic portico; as the hours passed, and the whitely steaming sun moved lethargically through the sky, he grew calm again, with a look of ironic resignation; staring across the grassy acreage in the direction of the front gate like one who hears distant music inaudible to others and, at last, inaudible to the listener himself.

It was a mid-August night, gauzily moonlit, when Graeme decided to follow his brother Stephen; to lie in wait for Stephen outdoors in the marshy grass at the foot of the drive. He seemed to know that Stephen was slipping away from Cross Hill by night, in secret, on his bicycle; disobeying Father's admonition that no one of us should ever again, on our bicycles or on foot, leave the property without his permission. It thrilled Graeme that his brother was so willfully disobeying our father, yet he was envious too. *Where is he going? Who are his friends? It isn't fair!* Stephen kept his bicycle hidden in one of the barns, surreptitiously oiling it, sanding away the ever-accumulating rust, making repairs; the Italian road bike, though lightweight and graceful in design, was surprisingly sturdy. The chain on Graeme's bike had never been repaired so it couldn't be ridden, but Graeme was thinking he might ride Rosalind's bike; he and Stephen could ride together to— Contracoeur?

So Graeme waited for Stephen, crouched in the tall grass. On all sides, the night was harshly sibilant with nocturnal insects. Some sang in rhythm, others in isolated, piercing, saw-like cries. Graeme's insomnia, he believed, was particularly triggered by moonlight. That moon! A pitiless eye teasing, winking, glowering at him so far below. *Yet it's a talent, never to sleep. Never to be taken by surprise.* Graeme was convinced he'd remained awake but suddenly then he was jolted into consciousness by a sound of footsteps, a vibration of the earth; he sat up, dazed, for a moment confused, and saw then Stephen passing close by, or a figure he took to be Stephen's—noting how tall, how mature Stephen had become; everyone had noticed how muscular Stephen had grown this summer, working outdoors with Mr. Dulne at mowing and tending the enormous lawn, which invariably grew back more lushly within a few days, shoulder-high grasses and brilliantly colored wildflowers in a riot of fecundity. Graeme stammered, "Stephen?— it's me." It came to him in a rush that his brother might reject him:

he, Graeme, had been sulky and sullen for much of the summer, turning from Stephen's frequent overtures of friendship. Graeme said, "Stephen? Wait. Can I come with you? Please—" It seemed strange to him that Stephen, knowing now who he was, had not spoken. Strange that he'd halted so suddenly, approximately ten feet from Graeme, arms raised at his sides, his posture tense, vigilant; his face, shrouded in shadow, showing no animation. "Stephen—?" Graeme blundered forward, unthinking.

Seeing, in that instant, that the figure confronting him wasn't his brother Stephen but—the thing-without-a-face.

Graeme stood paralyzed, transfixed. For it might have seemed to him that this was but a symptom of the insomnia of which he'd grown fatally proud: a nightmare figure standing before him which he'd imagined into being; a dream of his and not "real"; or, if "real," as the atrocities reported in the weekly Contracoeur newspaper were real, in some way not related to him. He hadn't time to cry out for help before the creature lunged at him, swiping with its hands as a maddened bear might swipe savagely and blindly; so much heavier and stronger than Graeme, Graeme was knocked to the ground as if he were a small child and not a thirteen-year-old boy.

Except for the sounds of the nocturnal insects there was silence, for the creature did not speak, nor could Graeme scream, his breath choked off as the thing-without-a-face crouched over him where he'd fallen, raining blows upon his unprotected head, clawing and tearing at his face, tearing away the flesh of his face as Graeme fell, and fell, into the earth beneath the wild grasses of Cross Hill.

9. The Traitorous Son

For the second time that summer, in our exile in Contracoeur, the family woke to discover that our brother Graeme was missing. And again we called his name and searched for him; Rosalind led us immediately to the farther shore of Crescent Pond—which, by August, had shrunken so that it was scarcely more than a black, brackish puddle amid marsh grasses and desiccated bamboo. But of course there was no one there. Nor any footprints in the soft earth. Impatiently we called, "Graeme? Gra-eme!" for we'd come to resent Graeme's childish, self-centered behavior, which upset us all. (With the exception of Mother, who came downstairs late in the morning, in her soiled silk dressing gown, to sit almost motionless in the breakfast room, too lethargic to prepare even tea, as Rosalind customarily did for her; her faded, watery gaze turned unperturbed in our direction.)

At first, Father remained relatively calm, though annoyed that his work schedule had been disturbed; then, as it seemed that Graeme might be truly missing, he joined in our search, awkwardly, with a convalescent's uncertain step, blinking in the harsh sunshine as he waded through the thigh-high grass brushing away gnats from his face. We heard his voice echoing everywhere—"Graeme! I command you to return! Son, this is your father speaking!" He was alternately furious and frightened; his fury didn't surprise us, but his fear began to terrify us, for it was rare that our father betrayed so weak an emotion.

Finally Stephen searched through the things on Graeme's cluttered desk, where he discovered the cryptic message his brother had so conscientiously hand-printed:

What have I lost: my username, my password, my soul.
Where must I flee: not IRL. There is none

Father was astonished by these words, as if he hadn't known that his thirteen-year-old son was capable of such eloquence. In a puzzled voice he asked Stephen what "IRL" meant, and Stephen said, hesitantly, "I think it means 'In Real Life,' Father," and Father said, " 'In Real Life'—but what does that mean?" and Stephen said, reluctantly, " 'IRL' is a cyberspace term referring to—well, all that *is,* that isn't cyberspace." For a long tense moment Father contemplated this disturbing revelation; his pale, wounded mouth worked in silence. Then he said, "So Graeme has left us, then. He has run away. In repudiation of me. He has lost faith in *me.*"

Stephen protested, "But Graeme might be—lost. Even if he ran away, he's only a kid. He might need help; we'd better report him missing," and Father said, with an air of dismissal, "Graeme is a traitorous son. He is no longer my son. I can never forgive him, and I forbid the rest of you to forgive him or get into contact with him. He has repudiated us all—the Mathesons. We must expel him from our hearts."

Before Stephen could prevent him, Father snatched the message from Stephen's fingers and tore it briskly into shreds.

10. The Lost Brother

In that way it happened that our brother Graeme disappeared from
Cross Hill in the late summer of our exile at Cross Hill and was not
reported missing; nor was any trace ever found of him in the old ruin
of a house or on the grounds; though, without knowing what she did,
Rosalind often found herself looking for him, or for someone—hearing
a faint, reproachful voice calling *Rosalind! Stephen!* that, when she paused
to listen more closely, faded into the incessant wind. Rosalind wandered
through distant corridors and rooms in the old house, discovering parts
of it she'd never seen before; ascending narrow, creaking staircases,
poking into closets, peering into the dark, cobwebbed corners where
household debris had accumulated like driftwood. Outdoors, she found
herself drawn to the old, collapsing barns, the rotted grape and wisteria
arbors with their look of bygone romance, the tall, rustling grasses of
the park that extended for acres like an inland sea. *Rosa-lind! Ste-phen!*
Help me! Yet Graeme's features were beginning to fade in her memory,
like a Polaroid photo exposed to overly bright sunshine. And in fact
there seemed to be no photos or snapshots of Graeme in the household;
it was discovered that most of the family memorabilia, kept in scrap-
books once obsessively maintained by Mother, had been lost in the
move from the city. So, if Father had agreed to report his missing son
to the police, there would have been the embarrassment of having not
a single picture of Graeme to give them.

Anxiously, Rosalind examined herself in the murky, lead-spotted
mirrors of Cross Hill. Through the long summer she'd grown an inch
or more, her slender body was filling out, her legs long, beautifully
shaped and subtly muscular; she'd become golden-tan, on the verge
of her fifteenth birthday a striking, increasingly self-reliant girl—yet,
in these antique mirrors, her reflection was wan, tremulous, fearful,
like a reflection in rippling water. Was she, too, disappearing? Or was
it, in fact, but the inadequacy of the mirrors? She'd noticed that Stephen, too, appeared vague and irresolute when glimpsed in certain
mirrors, and the twins, Neale and Ellen, who hadn't grown at all this
summer but seemed, disturbingly, to have shrunk an inch or so,
scarcely appeared at all except as wavering, watery images like poorly
executed watercolors. Scrubbing the grime away from a mirror and
polishing its glass did little good, for the lead backing was seeping
through; as Mrs. Dulne had said, throwing up her hands in genial
exasperation when once she and Rosalind were trying to restore a
mirror, "Cross Hill is *old*."

One night, very late, Rosalind and Stephen were whispering together in the darkened corridor outside their bedrooms, and Rosalind
dared to ask Stephen if he was starting to forget their brother—almost,
Rosalind had forgotten Graeme's name!—quite deliberately pro-
nouncing it, "Graeme." Stephen's reply was an immediate, perhaps
too immediate, "No." Rosalind then asked if Stephen sometimes
heard their names so faintly and teasingly in distance, like the wind,
and Stephen shivered and acknowledged, yes, he sometimes heard
"something—I'm not sure what." "But it sounds like Graeme, doesn't
it?" Rosalind persisted, and Stephen said, as if this were something
he'd been brooding over himself, "If he wants us to join him, how
the hell can we? We don't know where he is." They talked for a
while, in lowered voices, of where Graeme might have gone. Back
home?—to the city? But what would he do there? Live with a friend?
Not very likely. As for relatives, Mother and Father seemed to have
few; Father's parents were long dead, and Mother's widowed mother,
remarried and living in a condominium in Sarasota, Florida, had never
expressed much interest in her grandchildren. Rosalind said, frowning,
"But do you think Graeme could take care of himself, support
himself?" and Stephen said, "We could all take care of ourselves,
if we had to. We could get jobs, we could be independent. We
could go to school but live alone—why not?" Rosalind said in a
thrilled, tremulous voice, "We—could? I'd be afraid, I think," and
Stephen said impatiently, "Our great-grandfather Moses Matheson
came to this country by himself when he was only twelve years
old," and Rosalind said, "Did Father tell you that?" and Stephen
said, "No. I read it in a book in the library in town," and Rosalind
said, "But people were different then! I don't think I would be
that strong or brave," and Stephen said, moving away, a forefinger
to his lips, "Yes, you could."

II. "Immunity"

Stephen whispered aloud, "I can't believe it."

He was too upset to remain seated at the table in the Contracoeur
Public Library and so heaved himself to his feet to continue to read
stooped over the outspread newspapers, a pulse beating in his head,
sweat running in rivulets like tears down his face. Even as he was
thinking, sickened, *I can't believe it; I know it must be true.*

These ugly, damning headlines. In forbidden newspapers dating back to the previous winter. Front-page photographs of Judge Roderick Matheson and a half dozen other men. Arrested on charges of bribery, corruption, conspiracy to interfere with police investigations. These were Albany papers forbidden to us, the children of Roderick Matheson. These documents Stephen had at last sought out in the Contracoeur library, in willful defiance of his father's command.

He wiped tears of angry, hurt shame from his eyes. He hoped no one was watching! Wondering at his naïveté, his stupidity, in having taken so long to seek the evidence when he'd half known, all these months, what it might be.

Should I bring a knife, a weapon to protect myself?

Somehow, Stephen never did. Thinking only of a knife when it was too late, when he was already gone from the house and pedaling his bicycle energetically away.

Those languid summer nights he'd begun to slip away from the ruin of Cross Hill. Too restless to sleep or to lie in his rumpled bed listening to the shrill rhythmic cries of the nocturnal insects. Though in the deep humid heat of mid- and late August there was virtually no wind, yet Stephen heard the faint, whining, reproaching voice calling to him *Ste-phen! Stephen!*

But when he held his breath, to listen intently, the voice was gone as if it had never been.

At last slipping away from the ruin of Cross Hill. In secret!

To ride, defiantly, his spare, lithe bicycle that now hurtled itself along the moonlit road with the hungry energy of a mongrel dog.

The first night, Stephen rode perhaps two miles before, stricken with conscience and worry that Father would have discovered his absence, he turned back. He was fearful, too, of venturing farther in the dark, as clouds like shrapnel obscured the moon. For what of that thing his brother had seen, or had claimed to see—the thing-without-a-face? Stephen didn't believe that such a creature existed but he well believed that a crazed black bear must be preying upon human beings, its appetite whetted by the taste of human blood.

The second night, Stephen bicycled perhaps four miles before turning back. He was breathless, exhilarated. *A weapon, a knife—I should have protection.* How strange that, each time he ventured out on his nighttime journey, Stephen forgot to bring a knife, even a paring knife; only when he was actually on the road, in the stark loneliness

of night, hurtling between somber, darkened, fragrant fields and meadows and wooded hills that quivered with unknown, invisible life, only
then did he remember—*I might be in danger; I should have protection.*

How he yearned never to come back to the ruin of Cross Hill!
His heart beat in an ecstasy of flight. Yet he always returned, of course;
he was a responsible boy; never would he have abandoned his sister,
Rosalind, and the twins, Neale and Ellen; and he was reluctant, too,
to abandon Father and Mother, despite everything. For he yearned to
believe all that Father had vowed—*Bear with me, children. I will be
redeemed. I will redeem us all.* It was true, wasn't it? It had to be true!

So each night in succession, Stephen returned home well before
dawn; his head aching with exhaustion, and yet exhilaration; his shoulder, arm, and leg muscles pleasurably tingling. It was quite an experience now to ride his bicycle: no longer the sleek, elite Italian road
bike that had been a costly birthday present to Stephen from his
parents but this scarred, battered mongrel that fit so comfortably between his legs. Almost, it seemed to him alive. Eager to fly along the
bumpy road into layers of shadow that parted to admit him as if
welcoming him. *Ste-phen! Oh, Stephen!*

And so returning, to hide his bicycle beneath a waterproof tarpaulin in dense cover beside the road. Congratulating himself on his cleverness. Congratulating himself, though he was sweaty and shivering
with nerves, on his fearlessness. He kept his bicycle beside the road
so that he could more readily slip from the house and run stooped
over through the grassy park to push through an opening in the
wrought iron fence, undetected; as he might have been detected had
he pushed or ridden his bike along Acacia Drive.

Stealth had come second nature to Stephen.

He wondered—*Was this Graeme's way, too?*

He wondered—*Am I following my brother's path; will I be reunited
with him?*

Stephen was never detected leaving Cross Hill at night. How
strange then, how unexpected and bold, that he should find himself
daring to slip away during the day.

For by late summer, poor Mother was never vigilant about any
of her children. Rosalind tended the twins, who clung to her like
children of three or four, not nearly eleven. "Poor Neale!—poor
Ellen!" Rosalind hugged them, and kissed them, and tried gently to
extricate herself from their desperate, sticky embraces: "You have got
to find games to play by yourself. Please!" Stephen, though he loved
his baby brother and sister, had even less patience with them than

Rosalind. If they followed him around when he was working out-doors, mowing the ever-lush, ever-fertile lawn, he tolerated them for a while; then sent them indoors, loudly clapping his hands. "Rosalind's calling you!—go *on*." His eye moving slyly to the house, to the blank glittering windows from which, weeks ago, Mother might have gazed to see what he was doing; or lifting to the mysterious third floor, where Father might even now be watching.

But Father was increasingly remote, locked away from us. He rarely appeared downstairs before early evening, and sometimes not even then. No words of chastisement had been heard from him since his outburst of rage at Graeme's traitorous behavior. No words of anger or disgust uttered at Stephen, though sometimes, at the dinner table, he commented sarcastically upon Stephen's "uncouth, dishev-eled" appearance or pointedly asked, "Son, when did you bathe last? Can you recall?"

And so, Stephen began slipping away from Cross Hill during the day. Repairing a barn roof, for instance, he jumped down, ran stooped over toward the road, grinning to himself like a wild, willful child. And there was his bicycle he loved, lying waiting for him beneath the tarpaulin; always, it seemed to Stephen a miracle that the bicycle was there, hidden; he jumped on it, and struck off in the direction of Contracoeur. It seemed the most natural, the most inevitable thing in the world, as if a powerful force were drawing him to that small, ordinary city on the banks of the Black River; a former mill town, no longer economically prospering; yet not so depressed as other, similar towns in the Chautauqua Mountain region, for there was a thriving lumber business. Where once he'd scorned Contracoeur as a hick town, not worthy of a second glance, now he strolled happily about the streets, paved and unpaved; he smiled at strangers and was touched that they should smile at him in return. He was a handsome, tanned, amiable boy with sun-bleached wavy brown hair that grew past his collar, and a frank, direct, warmly brown gaze; yet too lacking in vanity to have a clear sense of how he might appear to others. For when he'd come to Contracoeur with our mother on her strained shopping expeditions, people had stared openly at Stephen; now, alone, he felt their eyes move upon him with pointed curiosity, yet not, so far as he could judge, hostility. One afternoon, seeing boys of high school age playing softball, Stephen was drawn to watch; within an hour he was invited to join the game; before long, he became acquainted with a dozen or more Contracoeur boys and girls. Hesi-tantly he introduced himself as "Steve" at first; only when asked where he lived did he say, "That old stone house about five miles out in the country—Cross Hill." How peculiar the name tasted in his mouth, like tarnish.

Stephen's new friends glanced at one another and at him. A red-haired boy said, smirking, "Cross Hill?—hell, man, no one lives there." Another boy poked this one in the ribs and said, in a quick undertone, "It's lived in now, man. Must be."

Stephen was smiling and did not allow his smile to fade. He asked, "Who lived at Cross Hill before?"

The second boy said, "Before what?"

"Well—five years ago? Ten years ago?"

Frowning, the young people shook their heads. Cross Hill had "always" been empty, they said. For as long as anyone could remember.

On other days, in Contracoeur, Stephen asked for work. Hourly labor hauling furniture, unloading trucks at the Buffalo-Chautauqua railroad yard, sawing and helping to stack planks at McKearny's Lumber. Over the summer he'd grown to a height of almost six feet; his arm and shoulder muscles were filled out and solid; he was unfailingly good-natured, uncomplaining— anywhere that wasn't Cross Hill, and manual labor in isolation, seemed a cheerful, convivial place to him. His Contracoeur employers liked him very much. He seemed to know (for Stephen was as perceptive as any Matheson) that all of Contracoeur was speaking of him; speculating about him; assessing him. *Knowing more about me than I know about myself?* One day in late August Fred McKearny invited Stephen to stay for supper, and soon Stephen found himself befriended by the entire McKearny family, including the golden labrador Rufus, who, while Stephen sat at the dining room table with the McKearnys, rested his head on Stephen's knees. There was Mrs. McKearny, who seemed as fond of Stephen as if she'd known him all of his life, and there was eighteen-year-old Rich, and there was sixteen-year-old Marlena, and there were several younger children; Stephen was giddy with happiness, for he'd forgotten what it was like to sit at a table, relaxed, and eat delicious food, and talk, and laugh as if it was the most natural thing in the world. *This is real life,* Stephen thought.

And how different, too, the semirural neighborhood in which the McKearnys lived, in a large white clapboard house surrounded by similar woodframe houses where homeowners kept gardens, orchards, livestock. Everywhere, friendly dogs like Rufus ran loose. There were roosters and chickens pecking in the dirt by the roadside. And not a mall for miles—many miles. Stephen tried to recall his old home in the city, where no one knew neighbors and where everyone drove cars, rushing from place to place and back again, traffic in snarls on the expressway. How mad that life seemed now. How aberrant, as if seen through a distorting lens.

I never want to return, Stephen thought. *I won't!*

He could attend Contracoeur High School with Marlena. And Rosalind, too, could enroll. Their parents had not said a word about school; perhaps Father expected to be returning to his own life by the time school resumed; how utterly unrealistic, how blind and selfish, for of course that wasn't going to happen; that wasn't going to happen, Stephen realized, for a very long time.

Often, alone, thinking dreamily of Marlena McKearny, who was so different from the girls he'd known in the city, his classmates at his private school; Marlena who was short, freckled, pretty but hardly glamorous—hardly "cool." Her way of hugging Rufus, her sweetly teasing manner of laughing at Stephen as she laughed at her older brother Rick, making both boys blush. Had he fallen in love with Marlena? Stephen wondered. Or with all of the McKearnys. Or with Contracoeur itself.

Stephen wiped angrily at his eyes. Tears embarrassed him!

But he'd been missing it so—*life.*

Stephen, too, had surreptitiously visited the small Contracoeur library to browse through the local history shelves. He, too, had been shocked and disgusted to read about his great-grandfather Moses Adams Matheson. The "most wealthy mill-owner of the Contracoeur Valley"—the "distinguished philantropist-conservationist who had donated thousands of acres of land in the Chautauqua Mountains for free public use." But there was the matter of the South Winterthurn "tragic blaze" of February 1911, killing more than thirty persons and injuring many more. There were striking workers locked out of their mills when they attempted to return, and numerous instances of union organizers "dispersed" by Pinkerton's security police. Stephen read with particular disgust about the construction of "the most ambitious and costly architectural design of the Contrecoeur Valley, Cross Hill." The massive, pretentious limestone house, in emulation of English country houses of a bygone era, had required eight years to build and had cost millions of dollars. Before it was completed, Moses Matheson's wife, Sarah (about whom little information was provided in these texts) had died. Moses Matheson was said to be "estranged" from his single heir, a son, as from most of his family; he lived at Cross Hill in "guarded seclusion" for eighteen years, a recluse who died in 1933, at the age of sixty-five, "under suspicious circumstances, the country coroner not having absolutely ruled out the possibility of a 'self-inflicted fatal injury.'" Suicide! Quickly Stephen turned a page in the crumbling *History of Contracoeur Valley* only to discover that the next several pages had been crudely torn out. Just as well; he didn't want to read further.

Another day, Stephen searched through back newspapers from other cities, primarily the state capital, discovering, again to his shock, information about his father he hadn't known. Beginning in late winter, here were front-page articles with stark, damning headlines: PROMINENT STATE JUDGE NAMED IN BRIBERY–CORRUPTION CONSPIRACY; MATHESON DENIES CHARGES; MATHESON TO TESTIFY BEFORE GRAND JURY; MATHESON, PROSECUTOR WORK OUT IMMUNITY DEAL; MATHESON GRANTED IMMUNITY, GIVES EVIDENCE AGAINST FORMER ASSOCIATES; CONSPIRATORS PLEAD GUILTY IN JUDICIAL CORRUPTION SCANDAL. Stephen was stunned to learn that it hadn't been at all as we were told, that Father had been an innocent victim of others' malevolence and manipulation; instead, Father had initially denied his guilt in numerous instances of bribery (one of the cases involved a $5 billion environmental pollution class action suit brought against one of the state's largest chemical companies), then abruptly admitted it and agreed to inform on his former co-conspirators in exchange for immunity from prosecution. Far from being persecuted by his enemies, as Father had said, he'd been very generously treated. An editorial reeking with sarcasm, in one of the Albany newspapers, put the case succinctly—MATHESON REWARDED FOR RATTING ON HIS FRIENDS.

In a May issue of the newspaper, Stephen read that one of the accomplices named by his father, a high-ranking official in state government who'd been a frequent guest of the Mathesons', had killed himself with a revolver on the morning he'd been scheduled to begin an eight-year prison sentence at Sing Sing.

This knowledge we'd been forbidden, that the rest of the world knew.

Except I'd been too cowardly—too respectful a son—to find out for myself.

Stephen contemplated the rapid succession of photographs in the papers of Roderick Matheson. The earliest was the most familiar—depicting a boyishly handsome man, younger-looking than his age, a lock of hair disingenuously fallen onto his forehead, his gaze direct and forthright at the viewer. After Father's arrest, this image abruptly changed. For here was an angry, resentful, embittered man; once caught in the act of shouting at a television reporter; another time, descending the steps of the state courthouse accompanied by police officers, he was hunched over in guilt and shame, trying to hide his face behind upraised hands, wrists shackled together. Roderick Matheson, in handcuffs! Father, a criminal! For the first time the reality of it swept over Stephen: the enormity of his father's crimes, the shame that accrued to the name Matheson.

Stephen slumped over the library table, hiding his hot, perspiring face in his hands. *I can't believe it! I know it must be true.*

12. The Face

That night returning late to Cross Hill as in one of those dreams of frustrated, impeded progress in which, desperate to move, you seem to be paralyzed; returning far later, past ten o'clock, than he'd ever returned before; for he'd stayed for supper with the McKearnys and lingered at their house as if fearful of leaving until Mrs. McKearny urged him to stay the night and he'd had to stammer that he could not, he had to return home. And Mr. McKearny walked with Stephen outside, and insisted that he take with him a weapon to protect himself, a hunting knife of Mr. McKearny's, a hunting knife with a razor-sharp ten-inch blade; though Stephen protested he didn't need such a weapon, he didn't want such a weapon, Mr. McKearny reminded him of how that evening they'd been talking about the mutilation-murders in the valley, the perpetrator still unknown, a madman, or a maddened bear, and in any case of course Stephen should be armed, and so Stephen agreed, clumsily fitting the knife in its leather sheath into his belt and bicycling off, into the night, a gauzy moonlit night of humidity, droning insects, mosquitoes; and Mr. McKearny called after him, "Good night, Stephen! God be with you!"—so quaint an expression Stephen had to smile, or tried to smile; but he was very nervous.

And so pedaling his bicycle along the streets of Contracoeur, and along the darkened country road that led to Cross Hill, his heartbeat quickening as he left the lights of Contracoeur for the inky featureless night of the country, which was illuminated only dimly, and dreamily, by the moon, through filmy clouds; like the cries of nocturnal insects in his ears *Matheson denies charges! Matheson agrees to testify! Matheson granted immunity! Matheson rewarded for ratting on his friends!* Stephen's eyes misted and stung; he was trying to ignore certain shadowy, indistinct shapes by the roadside that might have been living creatures; except of course they were bushes, small trees; he was trying to ignore his mounting fear; he was trying to ignore the wavering, wobbling sensation of his bicycle on the potholed road; he'd carefully oiled the bicycle that morning, but that morning was now a very long time ago; that morning might have been days, even weeks ago. And how had he dared to stay away so long; what would happen to him now? A voice lifted faintly, reproachfully in the near distance—*Traitorous son! No longer my son! I can never forgive you!*

Stephen realized he'd been seeing, ahead in the road, what appeared to be a human figure—was it? A man? A tall, stiff-poised man? Or was it an upright beast? Along this desolate stretch of road, no houses near and Cross Hill more than a mile away. Stephen swallowed hard, gripped his handlebars tight, felt a stab of fear as he made a swift decision—not to turn back but to increase his speed and pass the mysterious brooding figure, which stood at the left side of the road; Stephen would pedal past him on the right, head lowered, back curved in the classic cyclist's posture; he intended simply to ignore the stranger. Even as he saw out of the corner of his eye that this figure, this man, whatever it was, seemed to be acutely aware of Stephen, as if waiting for him; yet there were no eyes visible in its face, no features at all that Stephen could discern. *The thing-without-a-face!* The thing that Graeme had claimed to see, and Stephen had dismissed as a dream. Touched with horror, yet empowered by it, by a rush of adrenaline like flame through his veins, Stephen didn't slacken his speed, and veered around the thing, which was moving toward him to block his way. But he was past it! He was safe!

Yet somehow falling, a heavy, painful blow catching him on the shoulder, and he was caught beneath the bicycle, the wheels spinning, one of the handgrips in his face; on the ground helpless and flailing as the thing-without-a-face crouched over him, mauling him, striking him, vicious sharp-clawed blows to the chest, the back of the head, his unprotected face. Too terrified to call for help, Stephen rolled from the attack, trying to shield his head and face with his arms; the frenzied creature straddled him; Stephen saw to his horror that it had a face, but without features, smooth-rippled flushed skin like scar tissue, tiny pinpoints for eyes, nostrils, a rudimentary mouth of the kind one might envision in a mollusk, measuring less than an inch. A mouth not for eating but for sucking. Stephen, fighting for his life, had managed to take the hunting knife out of its sheath, somehow the knife was in his hand, tightly gripped in his fingers, he would not be able to recall afterward taking it from its sheath but only the solid weight of it in his fingers, he, Stephen Matheson, a suburban boy who'd never before in his life gripped a knife of this kind, still less in desperation thrusting it at his assailant, driving it up across the creature's collarbone, a slashing, superficial blow, yet so unexpected that the creature could not defend itself; clearly, it was accustomed to overwhelming unarmed victims, smaller than itself. Taken by surprise, the thing-without-a-face was deflected for a moment from its attack, and Stephen thrust the knifeblade up farther, and deeper, with more strength, into the creature's throat; stabbing and slashing at its throat where an artery must have been severed, for, at once, hot dark blood sprang out in a rapid stream onto Stephen's arm, into his face and hair. The creature, so much larger than Stephen, fell to its knees at the roadside as if baffled, uncomprehending; perhaps it felt no pain, but only this profound incomprehension, as of a being who'd imagined itself invulnerable to physical harm, immortal somehow, the delusion now shattered, spiraling away in dark ribbons of blood that could not be stopped. Making a choked, guttural sound, the creature staggered to its feet, hands pressed against the streaming blood, turning away dazed, having forgotten Stephen entirely; at last staggering away, like a drunken man, into the underbrush beside the road. Stephen himself dazed, bleeding, trying to catch his breath, stared after the thing in amazement and elation. He had saved himself! He had cast the thing-without-a-face from him and mortally wounded it, and he had saved himself!

At the ruin of Cross Hill, where stealthily he climbed the stairs to the second floor where Mother and Father slept; at Cross Hill, his heart pounding violently in his chest not in warning, not in caution but urging him on!—on!—for this must be done, this must be accomplished, he dare not turn back, he must push to the very end. And so opening the door of the master bedroom, and so stepping breathless inside that room it was forbidden to him to enter; the sticky, still-warm blood of the thing-without-a-face smeared on his own face, and in his hair, soaked into his clothes and mixed with his own so Stephen knew he must look savage, a terrifying sight. Yet he dared to switch on a light; a dim, yellowed bulb in a dusty bedside lamp; he stood beside his parents' enormous canopied bed; yet only Mother lay there, on her back, unnaturally still and her eyes open; in a satin nightgown so faded it had lost all color; Father's side of the bed was empty, though the bedsheets were rumpled and not very clean. On his pillow was the heavy imprint of his head, a concave shadow. Stephen stared, not certain what he saw. He whispered, "Mother—?" His hand reached out, groping; he dared to touch her—it; pushing gently at the smooth, naked shoulder that, with the attached torso, fell away from the shadowed lower body, and from the neck and head; the head, a mannequin's bald, blank head, rolled to one side on the pillow; one of the limbs, the shapely left leg, had fallen away from the body, as if its joints had become brittle with time, and lay at a grotesque angle perpendicular to the thigh. Again Stephen whispered "Mother . . ." even as he saw clearly that the thing wasn't human and wasn't alive: an elegant department store mannequin, sleekly constructed, rather flat-bodied, with a porcelain-smooth face, beautiful wide-open eyes with absurdly thick lashes. The mannequin's wig—Mother's ashy-blond, now graying and disheveled hair—had been placed, with apparent care, on the bedside table.

Father's handsome face, a molded mask of some exquisitely thin, rubbery material, an ingenious simulation of human skin, had been placed, with equal care, on the other bedside table; it was a mask so lifelike that Stephen winced to see it. It appeared to have been washed, and oiled with a colorless, subtly fragrant cream, fitted to a plaster-of-paris mold of a man's face; these eyes too were starkly open, but more liquidy, human-appearing, than the mannequin's. In horror, and fascination, with the curiosity of a very young child, Stephen reached out to touch the face with his forefinger. How lifelike it felt! How *warm*!

In great urgency then waking Rosalind and the twins, who now slept in her bedroom; though Rosalind, moaning in a nightmare, hardly needed to be wakened, only her name gently spoken—"Rosalind"; and hurrying them out of the ruin of Cross Hill and, on foot, along the road to Contracoeur, only five miles away; there was no time for Stephen to explain to his frightened sisters and brother, and, at this moment, there would have been no words. Rosalind asked in a whisper what had happened to Stephen, had he injured himself, had some-one hurt him, where were they going, and what of Father, and what of Mother, but the twins, sleep-dazed, stifling back sobs, each clutch-ing one of Stephen's hands, did not ask; nor were they ever to ask.

Thomas M. Disch

THE OWL AND THE PUSSYCAT

I've known Tom Disch for twenty-five years; I met him when I was student and he was teacher at the Clarion Science Fiction Writer's Workshop at Michigan State University in 1974. I've been proud to consider him a mentor ever since; his novel Camp Concentration *should be on the shelf of every intelligent reader of imaginative fiction.*

Though never abandoning the science fiction field, he eventually found his way into the horror field with two highly regarded novels, The M.D.: A Horror Story *and* The Businessman: A Tale of Terror. *He is also well known as the author of the children's books* The Brave Little Toaster *and* The Brave Little Toaster Goes to Mars, *as well as the recent critical (and critically acclaimed) study of the sf field,* The Dreams Our Stuff Is Made Of. *He is also a poet and playwright.*

When student humbly asked teacher for a story for this book, student gratefully received this gem.

So when Christopher Robin goes to the Zoo, he goes to where the Polar Bears are, and he whispers something to the third keeper from the left, and doors are unlocked, and we wander through dark passages and up steep stairs, until at last we come to the special cage, and the cage is opened, and out trots something brown and furry, and with a happy cry of "Oh, Bear!" Christopher Robin rushes into its arms.

They liked the mornings best, when Mr. and Mrs. Fairfield were asleep upstairs and the house was quiet and they could snuggle together on the love seat and wait for the train to come rumbling by on the other side of the river. There were other trains at other times of day, but things could get so hectic later on that you might not even realize a train was going by until the windows were rattling.

Those windows should have been fixed years ago, especially the combinations on either side of the TV set. Dampy became anxious whenever there was a storm alert, certain that sooner or later a gusting wind would just suck those old windows out of their aluminum frames. The upstairs windows were more solid, because they were made the old-fashioned way and would probably outlast the roof. Though that wasn't saying much. The roof was in sorry shape, too. One of these days, when he had the cash, Mr. Fairfield was going to fix the roof, but that wouldn't be any day soon, since trying to find a full-time job kept him out of the house so much of the time.

After the train went by, and it started to get brighter, the alarm clock in the upstairs bedroom would go off, and then there'd be noises in the bathroom, and after that from the kitchen the smells of breakfast. Breakfast was their favorite meal of the day, because it was always the same. A little glass of apple juice, and then either puffed rice or cornflakes with milk and sugar and then a crisp piece of toast with butter and jam. They would bow their heads along with Mrs. Fairfield, and Mr. Fairfield too if he were up that early, and thank the Lord for his blessings.

Some Sundays there were even pancakes. Dampy had lived at Grand Junction Day Care before he moved in with the Fairfields (at the time of the *first* Mrs. Fairfield), and once a month there had been a special Pancake Breakfast Benefit in the lunchroom of the day care. The first Mrs. Fairfield had helped make the pancakes on the gas grill, as many as twenty at a time. Wonderful pancakes, sometimes with blueberries in them, sometimes with shredded coconut, and you could have all you could eat for just $2 if you were under the age of six. Later on, the benefits were not so well attended, and only the children came, as though it were just another school day, except with pancakes, and that's when Dampy had the accident that got him called Dampy. The children had a food fight, using the paper plates as Frisbees, even though there was syrup on the plates and Miss Washington said not to. No one paid any attention, they never did with Miss Washington, and one plate hit Dampy and got syrup all over him, so Mrs. Fairfield took him back to the big sink and gave him a sponging off, and when that didn't get off all the syrup, she gave him a real dousing. And he never got entirely dry again.

He didn't mind being called Dampy. Sticks and stones, as they say. But then there was the Terrible Accident (that really was no accident at all), but why talk about that. There is no need to dwell on the dark side of things, and anyhow that was a fine example of a silver lining, since if it hadn't been for the Terrible Accident, Dampy would probably never have come to be adopted by the Fairfields on a permanent basis. And the Fairfields' house despite the arguments was a better place to live than Grand Junction Day Care. Quite lonely, of course, until Hooter had come to live there too, but Dampy had always tended to keep to himself. The new Mrs. Fairfield was the same way. She preferred her solitude and the TV over a lot of friends.

But special friends are different, of course, and from the very start Hooter was to be Dampy's *special* friend. He had come to live with Dampy and the Fairfields when Mr. Fairfield had abducted him from his home at the Grand Junction Reformed Church. There he'd been, sitting in his box, listening to the speaker at the Tuesday night AA meeting, but not listening all that closely, and then Mr. Fairfield grabbed hold of him. Mr. Fairfield was there because he'd been arrested for Driving While Intoxicated, and the judge had said he had to go to AA meetings twice a week. So there he was at the Dutch Reformed Church in the folding chair just beside Hooter's box.

Mr. Fairfield had nervous hands. If he wasn't fiddling with his cigar, he would be cleaning his fingernails with his Swiss Army pocketknife or tearing a piece of paper into the smallest possible shreds. That night, after he'd turned the two-page list of local AA meetings into confetti he began to play with Hooter, not in a rough way exactly, but certainly with no consideration for Hooter's feelings. After the people at the meeting had shared their experience, strength, and hope (except for those, like Mr. Fairfield, who had nothing that needed sharing) everyone joined hands and said the Our Father.

That was when Mr. Fairfield had picked up the young owl and whispered into his black felt ear, "Hooter, I am going to *adopt* you." "Adopt" was what he said, but "abduct" was how it registered on Hooter, who left the church basement concealed beneath Mr. Fairfield's Carhardt jacket with a feeling that his Higher Power had betrayed him. After all the time he'd lived in the church basement he'd come to assume that he *belonged* there, that no one was ever going to take him away, even if he spent every Saturday in the box that said FREE. At first that had been a heartbreaking experience, but the AA meetings had been a consolation in coping with the loneliness and isolation. But Hooter had put his trust in his Higher Power and turned over his will, and he'd learned to *accept* his life as a church owl. And now here he'd been abducted.

Mr. Fairfield pulled open the door of his pickup, and Hooter was astonished to find that someone had been waiting out here in the freezing pickup all through the meeting. Sitting in the dark, wrapped in a blanket, and looking very miffed at having had to spend all this time in the cold.

"Hooter," said Mr. Fairfield. "I want you to meet Dampy. Dampy, this is Hooter. He's going to be your new buddy. So say hello."

Dampy did not respond at once, but at last he breathed out a long, aggrieved sigh. "Hello," he said, and moved sideways to make room for Hooter under the blanket. When they were touching, Dampy whispered into Hooter's ear, "Don't say anything in front of *him*." With a meaningful look in the direction of Mr. Fairfield, who had taken out a brown paper bag from the glove compartment of the pickup.

Hooter knew from his first whiff of the opened bottle that Mr. Fairfield was another secret drinker, like Reverend Drury, the pastor of the Dutch Reformed Church. Hooter had often been the companion of the Reverend's secret libations in the church basement, and when he didn't polish off his half-pint of peppermint schnapps at one go he would often leave it in Hooter's keeping, in the FREE box of broken toys and stained toddler clothes. Now here Hooter was in the same situation again, an enabler.

"Here's to the two of you!" said Mr. Fairfield, starting up the engine of the pickup and lifting the bottle of alcohol towards Dampy and Hooter. They looked at each other with a sense of shame and complicity, and then the pickup moved out onto Route 97.

"I seen you before, you know that," Mr. Fairfield said. "At the Saturday garage sale. I noticed you there on the FREE table. For weeks. They can't give away that ugly little fucker, I thought. So, when I saw you again tonight I thought—I've got just the place for him. The perfect little dork of a buddy. Right, Dampy?"

Dampy was mum. It was a cruel and provoking thing to have said to the poor little owl, who *was* a homely bedraggled creature, to be sure. Dampy was used to having *his* feelings hurt. He was numb to such abuse. But poor Hooter must have been close to tears.

Mr. Fairfield seemed to pick up on that thought. "Hey, I guess I'm no looker myself. You got that beak, I got this gut, and Dampy there is a goddamn basket case. Dampy has got more problems than Dear Abby. But Dampy don't talk about his problems. Not to his family anyhow. But maybe he will to you. What do you say, little fella?"

Neither Dampy nor Hooter said a word.

Mr. Fairfield took another hit from the bottle and they continued the rest of the way in silence.

When they arrived home, it was Mr. Fairfield who introduced

Hooter to the new Mrs. Fairfield. "Look, honey, we got another member of the family." He dropped Hooter into Mrs. Fairfield's lap with a loud but not very owlish *Whoo! Whoo!*

"Isn't he a darling?" said Mrs. Fairfield without much conviction. "Isn't he just the sweetest thing?" She took a puff on her cigarette and asked, "But what *is* he, anyhow?"

"What bird goes *Whoo! Whoo!* He's an owl. Look at him. He's got a beak like an owl, and those big eyes. Got to be an owl. So we called him Hooter."

"But he's got teddy-bear-type ears," Mrs. Fairfield objected.

"So? No one's perfect. He's a fuckin' owl. Give him a kiss. Go ahead."

Mrs. Fairfield put her cigarette in the ashtray, and sighed, and smiled, and planted a delicate kiss on Hooter's beak. Hooter could tell it was a real kiss, with feelings behind it, and so he knew he was a member of the Fairfield family from that point on. He, who'd thought he'd never belong to *any* family but just spend the rest of his life in a box in the basement of the Dutch Reformed Church.

"Okay?" said Mrs. Fairfield, turning to her husband.

"Now tell him you love him."

"I love you," said Mrs. Fairfield, still looking at Mr. Fairfield in an anxious way.

"Okay then," said Mr. Fairfield, rubbing his hand across the fur on his own head, which was the same color brown as Hooter's but much longer. "We got that settled. Now you all better hit the sack. I'm outa here."

Mrs. Fairfield looked disappointed, but she didn't ask where he was off to or whether she could come along.

Mrs. Fairfield was basically a stay-at-home type, and Dampy and Hooter took after her in that respect. They might spend hours at a time on the love seat watching TV with Mrs. Fairfield, or playing Parcheesi by themselves under the dining room table with its great mounds of folded clothes waiting to be ironed. Rarely did they go out of the house, for they knew there was good reason not to. The woods were just behind the house, and Mr. Fairfield told fearful tales about the woods. Most animals that did not have human families to live with had no home but the woods, which could be a dangerous place, even for owls. Owls are predators themselves, and hunt for mice and smaller birds, but they are preyed upon in turn by wolves and bears and snakes. As for young pussycats, Mr. Fairfield said, the woods meant certain death. Dampy must never, never go into the woods by himself, not even with Hooter, or they would certainly be eaten alive by the predators out there.

Dampy would listen to these stories with a shiver of dread. Hooter, however, sometimes wondered if Mr. Fairfield was not exaggerating about the woods. Of course, the woods *were* out there. You could see them through the windows, and you could see the woodland creatures too, if you were patient—the deer and the two nice groundhogs and all the different kinds of birds, some of whom Mrs. Fairfield could identify, the crows and robins and chickadees, but most of the rest she had no name for. At sunset, in the summers, there were even bats, with their squeaky, unpleasant songs. But were all these woodland creatures as unfriendly and dangerous as Mr. Fairfield made them out to be? Hooter was not convinced.

And—another question entirely—was Dampy really a cat? Mrs. Fairfield had said once that he looked to her much more like a koala bear. She pointed out that he had ears like the koala bear in the advertisements for Qantas Airlines. Qantas was based in Australia, where most koala bears live. And Hooter thought she had a point. Even without a nose, Dampy looked more like a koala bear than a cat.

But Mr. Fairfield was adamant. Dampy was a cat. To prove it he sang a song. The song went like this:

> The Owl and the Pussycat went to sea
>   In a beautiful pea-green boat.
> They took some honey and plenty of money,
>   Wrapped up in a five pound note.
> The Owl looked up to the stars above,
>   And sang to a small guitar,
> O lovely Pussy! O Pussy my love,
>   What a beautiful Pussy you are,
>   You are,
>   You are!
>   What a beautiful Pussy you are!

"Dampy is not a girl," Hooter objected. It was the first time he'd ever contradicted anything Mr. Fairfield said, and Mr. Fairfield gave him a sour look and then a swat that knocked him halfway across the room.

"If I say he's a girl, he's a fucking girl. And if I say he's a Pussy, he's a Pussy. You *got* that?"

"Harry, please," said Mrs. Fairfield.

"Harry, please," Mr. Fairfield said in a whining tone meant to mock his wife, though in fact it didn't sound at all like her.

"I guess cats are always females then," said Mrs. Fairfield to Hooter. "Dogs are boys, and cats are girls."

No one went to help Hooter until Mr. Fairfield had left the room, but Dampy exchanged a look of sympathy with him, as sad as could be.

Later, when they could talk without being overheard, Hooter protested (in a whisper, with the sheets over his head): "Is there nothing we can do then? Are we just trapped here, and have to suffer every kind of abuse?"

"He can be very mean," Dampy agreed.

"And just as mean to Mrs. Fairfield as he is to us."

"Meaner, actually. Last year, about a week after New Year's, he sent the *first* Mrs. Fairfield to the hospital emergency room and she had to get seven stitches in her head. You could see them when she took off the bandanna she had to wear."

"Why would he do that?" Hooter asked, aghast. "And what did he do?"

"Well, they'd been singing this song that he likes. Over and over. And finally she said she was too tired to sing anymore, and he just sat there where you're sitting now, staring at her, and then he got up and smashed his guitar right over her head. And do you know what I think?"

"What?"

"I think it was really the guitar he was angry with. 'Cause he never played it very well. But no one ever complained, not with him. But it was a big relief for him not to have people hear how lousy he played his guitar. And he never got another one to replace the one he smashed."

"He's not a nice person," said Hooter gravely.

"He's not," Dampy agreed. "But we should try and get some sleep. Tomorrow is another day." He put his arms round Hooter, and they snuggled.

In such a small household, in a lonely part of the country with no neighbors close by, it was inevitable that Dampy and Hooter would spend much time together and become the closest friends. From Hooter, Dampy learned all about the Dutch Reformed Church and Reverend Drury and the Twelve Steps of Alcoholics Anonymous. Of

Hooter's life before he became a church owl there was not much to be told. He'd been a prize at the ring toss game at the Grand Junction Centennial Street Fair, but the teenage girl who received Hooter from the winner of the ring toss donated him almost at once to the Dutch Reformed's weekly garage sale. Hooter often felt, he confided to Dampy, like one of those Romanian children you hear about on "All Things Considered" (a program that Reverend Drury listened to every day) who have spent their whole childhood in an orphanage and later have trouble relating to their adoptive parents.

To which Dampy had replied, "I'm not so sure that that would be altogether a bad thing. Some parents you might not want to relate to any more than absolutely necessary."

"You mean . . . Mr. Fairfield?"

Dampy nodded. "And not just him. *She* was just as bad, the *first* Mrs. Fairfield. Our life here is actually an improvement over what it used to be, with her."

"You've never said that much about her before. Was it she who . . ." Hooter touched the stub of his wing to the end of his beak to indicate the same area on Dampy's face.

"Who pulled off my nose? No, *that* happened at the Day Care. There was a boy there, Ray McNulty, who kept pulling at my nose, and pulling and pulling. Miss Washington told him not to, but he wouldn't listen. Then one day when everyone was supposed to be napping he just ripped it right off. But that wasn't enough for Ray McNulty! Then he took a pair of scissors and opened the seam at my neck."

"And no one's ever tried to sew it up again?"

Dampy went up to the mirror mounted beside the front door and looked at himself morosely. His neck was slit open from the front to just under his left ear, which gave a sad, sideways tilt to his head and meant that you had to listen very intently when he spoke. "Once, yes. Once, Mrs. Fairfield tried to mend my neck—the new Mrs. Fairfield. She means well, but she's hopeless with a needle and thread. I'm used to it now. I don't mind how it looks."

Hooter went up to him and tried to push the stuffing back inside the wound in his neck. "It's such a shame. You'd look so handsome with just a bit of needlework."

Dampy turned away from the mirror. "That's nice of you to say. Anyhow, I was telling you about the first Mrs. Fairfield."

"Was she like him?" Hooter asked. "I mean, did she drink?"

"Yes, and when she drank, she became violent. They quarreled

'l the time, and she liked to break things. She broke dishes. She
rew an electric skillet through the kitchen window. She poured a
whole bottle of red wine over him when he was lying drunk on the
rug, and when the *ants* got to that, oh boy! And then, if he reacted,
she called the police. She had him sent to jail twice."

"So what finally happened? Did they get a divorce?"

Dampy's reply was almost inaudible. Hooter had to ask him to
repeat what he said. "She died," he said in a hoarse whisper. This
time he added, "And it was no accident either."

He was reluctant to supply any further details, and Hooter knew
better than to pester him with lots of questions. In any case, there
was a more important question pending:

Dampy had asked Hooter if he would marry him!

Hooter had objected that they were the same sex, but Dampy
pointed out that same-sex marriages were discussed all the time on
the news, and while they weren't allowed among Southern Baptists
and Catholics and Orthodox Jews, the two of them were Dutch Reformed if they were anything. Besides which, according to Mr. Fairfield, Dampy was a girl, not a boy, so it wouldn't be same-sex. The
important thing was did they love each other and would they go on
loving each other to the end of time or death did them part. At last,
Hooter had answered, in the words of the song, "O let us be married!
too long we have tarried: but what shall we do for a ring?"

In the poem the owl and the pussycat sail off to a wooded island
where a pig sells them, for a shilling, the ring that's in his nose, but
in real life finding a ring was a lot easier, for Mrs. Fairfield had a
jewel case containing as great a variety of rings as you might find in
a jewelry store. There were rings with rubies and emeralds and two
with amethysts (the new Mrs. Fairfield was an Aquarius, and the ame-
thyst is the birthstone for February), but the ring they finally selected
was a four-carat facsimile zirconium diamond mounted in 14-karat
gold from the Home Shoppers' Club.

They were married in the woods in back of the house on a cloudy
June afternoon, while Mr. and Mrs. Fairfield were away to talk to
their lawyer in Grand Junction. Dampy wore a red-and-white check-
ered kitchen towel that Hooter said made him look like a Palestinian
terrorist. Hooter himself was all in black. It was the first time they'd
been in the woods together so far from the house that you couldn't
even see the roof. For all *they* knew they were lost!

Dampy took the stub of Hooter's wing in his paw and said, "I
thee wed!"

To which the owl replied, "For better or for worse."

"In sickness and in health."

That was as much of the ceremony as they could remember, except for the kissing. Then there was the problem of what to do with the ring now that it was theirs. Dampy wanted to return it to Mrs. Fairfield's jewel case, but Hooter got such a hurt look that Dampy at once came up with an alternate plan. They buried it under a stone out in the woods, marking the very spot where they'd been wed.

When they got back to the house, Mr. and Mrs. Fairfield's lawyer, Mr. Habib, was there with them, as well as two policemen and a lady, Mrs. Yardley, with yellow hair like a movie star's who wanted to talk to them. At first Mr. Habib said she was being ridiculous, the boy was autistic and delusional. Nothing could be gained by speaking with him, and in any case that would be a hopeless task. The boy could not be made to answer questions. Mr. Habib had tried, and so had the police.

"But I understand, from remarks that Mr. Fairfield has made in his deposition, that he *does* speak to, or through, his teddy bears. And I see he has them with him now. I'd like to speak to the teddy bears. Privately."

"You want to speak to a pair of fucking teddy bears!" jeered Mr. Fairfield. "Maybe give 'em the third degree?"

"For the record," said Mrs. Yardley, "we have reason to believe that the child's welfare may be in danger. There has been a history of abuse."

"All those charges had to do with the deceased," Mr. Habib pointed out. "And this boy is surely not fit for a formal interrogation."

Mrs. Yardley smiled a sweet smile and scrunched down beside Hooter. "But I don't want to talk with the boy. It's *this* little fellow I'd like to meet. And his friend." She gave Hooter's beak a gentle tweak and patted Dampy on the head. "If *someone* would introduce me."

Dampy turned his face away, but Hooter was not quite so shy. "I'm Hooter," he confided in a whisper. "And this is Dampy."

Mr. Habib protested vigorously as to the irregularity of Mrs. Yardley's questioning, but she just ignored him and went on talking with Dampy and Hooter, telling them about other teddy bears she knew and respected, an Evangeline, who lived in Twin Forks and was as well-dressed as any fashion model; Dreyfus, who always wore a little bow tie and was knowledgeable about mutual funds; and Jean-Paul-Luc, who spoke French, which made it difficult for Mrs. Yardley to get to know him very well, since she'd only had one year of French in high school, long ago.

She was a really nice lady, but the nicer she was the ruder Mr. Fairfield became, until finally she had to ask the two policemen to escort Mr. Fairfield out to their car. Mr. Habib accompanied Mr. Fairfield to the police car, and Mrs. Fairfield went upstairs.

When they were alone with Mrs. Yardley, she shifted their conversation away from the other teddy bears she knew and wanted to know all sort of things about the Fairfields. Hooter tried to be cooperative, but there wasn't much he could tell her about the first Mrs. Fairfield. Dampy was not as trustful at first, and there were lots of things that he claimed he couldn't remember, especially about the night the first Mrs. Fairfield had died.

Gradually, Hooter realized that Mrs. Yardley thought that Mr. Fairfield had murdered his first wife and was looking for some way to prove it. When she was done asking Dampy questions, Mrs. Yardley asked Hooter the same questions, even after he'd explained to her that he'd been living at the Dutch Reformed Church when Mrs. Fairfield was killed.

"Ah-ha!" said Mrs. Yardley. "Why do you say 'killed'? Is it because you don't believe it was an accident?"

"I don't *know*," Hooter protested, close to tears.

"I guess she must have killed herself," Dampy said unprompted. "That's what Mr. Fairfield says."

"Oh, really? Who did he say that to? To you?"

"No, to me he always says it was an accident and not to think about it. But I heard him say to the *new* Mrs. Fairfield—"

"To Pamela Harper, that is? The lady who just went upstairs?"

"Mm-hm. He told her that no one can take so many sleeping pills by accident. He said he thinks she must of mashed them up in her Rocky Road ice cream. Sometimes she would eat a whole pint of Rocky Road all by herself. Especially if they had got in a fight. He'd apologize by bringing home the ice cream. No one else ever got a bite."

The more Dampy explained to Mrs. Yardley about the ice cream and the liquor and the different arguments there'd been, the clearer it became to Hooter that Mr. Fairfield had probably killed his first wife by mixing up her sleeping pills with the ice cream. Then putting a bottle of whiskey somewhere she'd be sure to find it when he left her by herself. Clearly, Mrs. Yardley suspected the same thing.

Then there was a great ruckus when the new Mrs. Fairfield came storming down the steps and out of the house to accuse her husband of having stolen her four-carat diamond ring from her jewel case.

Hooter looked at Dampy with alarm, and Dampy tilted his head back and stared at the ceiling's intricate pattern of overlapping water stains. Mrs. Yardley could coax nothing more from either of them, so she left them to themselves and went to stand in the front door and watch Mr. and Mrs. Fairfield scream at each other until Mr. Fairfield went from just verbal abuse to a whack across the face, and that was all Mrs. Yardley needed. Dampy and Hooter spent that night in a foster-care residence forty miles away from the Fairfield home, and they remained there all through Mr. Fairfield's trial for the murder of his first wife. They were not qualified, legally, to be witnesses at the trial, and Hooter, for one, was glad to be spared such an unpleasant duty. What could he have said that would be any help to Mr. Fairfield? For all his faults, the man had been like a father to him, and Hooter would not have wanted to be there when the jury brought in their verdict of Guilty of Murder in the First Degree.

At the foster-care residence Dampy and Hooter had been discouraged from seeing much of each other. When they could get together it would have to be in the laundry room when no one was washing clothes or up in the attic, where they weren't supposed to go. Even when they were able to spend a few minutes together, away from the other residents, they were both at a loss for words. Dampy was gradually slipping back into the sullenness and depression that had kept him from talking to everyone at the time before he'd met Hooter. And Hooter for his part spent a lot of his time, as he had in the basement of the Dutch Reformed Church, practicing the multiplication tables.

Neither of them would speak to Mr. Fairfield when he tried to phone, and Mrs. Fairfield never did ring up. Maybe she wasn't really Mr. Fairfield's wife, but just a girlfriend. Anyhow, she moved somewhere that didn't have an address.

"Do you miss her?" Hooter asked Dampy one cold November afternoon when they were sitting behind the clothes dryer in the laundry room.

"Not really. Watching all those programs on the Home Shopping Channel got to be pretty dull. I didn't like the first Mrs. Fairfield that much either, but she was more fun to be with."

Hooter studied one of the big lint balls on the floor with a look of melancholy. "You know what? I miss *him*."

"Oh, we're better off this way," Dampy assured him.

"I suppose so. Will he have to spend a *lot* of time in jail?"

"The newspaper said twenty-five years at a minimum."

"Goodness! He'll be, let me see . . ." Hooter did the arithmetic in his head. ". . . almost fifty-five when he gets out. Well, I suppose it's what he deserves. If you kill someone, you have to pay the price."

Dampy gave Hooter a funny smile. The matron at the residence had sewn up the wound in his neck and now his head tilted in the other direction in a way that was sometimes unnerving. "True," he agreed. "But you know *he* didn't kill Mrs. Fairfield."

"Yes, yes, it's like Mr. Habib says, there was nothing but circumstantial evidence."

"No, that's not what I meant."

"You mean, she really did kill herself?"

"I mean *I* killed her."

Hooter looked shocked. "But you couldn't! You're just—"

"Just a teddy bear?" Dampy asked with a smile. "And do *you* think teddy bears are just stupid cuddly dumb animals?"

Hooter shook his head.

"We may not live in the woods, but we are bears."

"I'm an owl!" Hooter protested.

"And I'm a pussycat. But we're both bears. Don't deny it—look at your ears. Mr. Fairfield is best off right where he is, and as for us, I expect we'll be adopted soon by someone nice. Mrs. Yardley says there have been lots of applications."

And that is just what happened. They were adopted by Curtis and Maeve Bennet and moved to a house on the Jersey shore and there, just as in the poem

> . . . *hand in hand, on the edge of the sand,*
> *They danced by the light of the moon,*
> > *The moon,*
> > *The moon,*
> *They danced by the light of the moon.*

But their wedding ring is still where they left it, under the rock in the woods, marking the spot where they were wed.

Stephen King

THE ROAD VIRUS HEADS NORTH

What can I say about this guy Stephen King? I won't mention his novels, since most of you have already read them all; most of you have also seen the movies made from the books, and listened to the audiotapes, and maybe even own the refrigerator magnets and T-shirts and God knows what other ancillary paraphernalia based on them.

I won't talk about the shorter tales, except to say that some of them (here I'll name names: "Apt Pupil," for example) are still overlooked as some of the finest American stories, period.

I won't talk about the critical writings King has produced, such as the many informative and iconoclastic book introductions, essays, and the collected wisdom of Danse Macabre; *I also won't talk about his basic support of the art of reading, or his boosterism of freedom of thought and expression; and finally, I won't discuss the fact that he virtually invented the modern horror movement out of thin air in the 1970s.*

So what can I say about this guy?

Actually, I think I'll just shut up (no clapping, please) and let Mr. King do what he does best: which is to throw down his own portable campfire in front of you, lean close so the flames dance across his features— and tell you one hell of a story.

Richard Kinnell wasn't frightened when he first saw the picture at the yard sale in Rosewood.

He was fascinated by it, and he felt he'd had the good luck to find something which might be very special, but fright? No. It didn't occur to him until later ("not until it was too late," as he might have written in one of his own numbingly successful novels) that he had felt much the same way about certain illegal drugs as a young man.

He had gone down to Boston to participate in a PEN/New England conference titled "The Threat of Popularity." You could count on PEN to come up with such subjects, Kinnell had found; it was actually sort of comforting. He drove the two hundred and sixty miles from Derry rather than flying because he'd come to a plot impasse on his latest book and wanted some quiet time to try to work it out.

At the conference, he sat on a panel where people who should have known better asked him where he got his ideas and if he ever scared himself. He left the city by way of the Tobin Bridge, then got on Route 1. He never took the turnpike when he was trying to work out problems; the turnpike lulled him into a state that was like dreamless, waking sleep. It was restful, but not very creative. The stop-and-go traffic on the coast road, however, acted like grit inside an oyster—it created a fair amount of mental activity . . . and sometimes even a pearl.

Not, he supposed, that his critics would use that word. In an issue of *Esquire* last year, Bradley Simons had begun his review of *Nightmare City* this way: "Richard Kinnell, who writes like Jeffery Dahmer cooks, has suffered a fresh bout of projectile vomiting. He has titled this most recent mass of ejecta *Nightmare City*."

Route 1 took him through Revere, Malden, Everett, and up the coast to Newburyport. Beyond Newburyport and just south of the Massachusetts–New Hampshire border was the tidy little town of Rosewood. A mile or so beyond the town center, he saw an array of cheap-looking goods spread out on the lawn of a two-story Cape. Propped against an avocado-colored electric stove was a sign reading YARD SALE. Cars were parked on both sides of the road, creating one of those bottlenecks which travelers unaffected by the yard sale mystique curse their way through. Kinnell liked yard sales, particularly the boxes of old books you sometimes found at them. He drove through the bottleneck, parked his Audi at the head of the line of cars pointed toward Maine and New Hampshire, then walked back.

A dozen or so people were circulating on the littered front lawn of the blue-and-gray Cape Cod. A large television stood to the left of the cement walk, its feet planted on four paper ashtrays that were doing absolutely nothing to protect the lawn. On top was a sign reading MAKE AN OFFER—YOU MIGHT BE SURPRISED. An electrical cord, augmented by an extension, trailed back from the TV and through the open front door. A fat woman sat in a lawn chair before it, shaded by an umbrella with CINZANO printed on the colorful scalloped flaps. There was a card table beside her with a cigar box, a pad of paper, and another hand-lettered sign on it. This sign read ALL SALES CASH, ALL SALES FINAL. The TV was on, tuned to an afternoon soap opera where two beautiful young people looked on the verge of having deeply unsafe sex. The fat woman glanced at Kinnell, then back at the TV. She looked at it for a moment, then looked back at him again. This time her mouth was slightly sprung.

Ah, Kinnell thought, looking around for the liquor box filled with paperbacks that was sure to be here someplace, *a fan.*

He didn't see any paperbacks, but he saw the picture, leaning against an ironing board and held in place by a couple of plastic laundry baskets, and his breath stopped in his throat. He wanted it at once.

He walked over with a casualness that felt exaggerated and dropped to one knee in front of it. The painting was a watercolor, and technically very good. Kinnell didn't care about that; technique didn't interest him (a fact the critics of his own work had duly noted). What he liked in works of art was *content,* and the more unsettling the better. This picture scored high in that department. He knelt between the two laundry baskets, which had been filled with a jumble of small appliances, and let his fingers slip over the glass facing of the picture. He glanced around briefly, looking for others like it, and saw none—only the usual yard sale art collection of Little Bo Peeps, praying hands, and gambling dogs.

He looked back at the framed watercolor, and in his mind he was already moving his suitcase into the backseat of the Audi so he could slip the picture comfortably into the trunk.

It showed a young man behind the wheel of a muscle car—maybe a Grand Am, maybe a GTX, something with a T-top, anyway—crossing the Tobin Bridge at sunset. The T-top was off, turning the black car into a half-assed convertible. The young man's left arm was cocked on the door; his right wrist was draped casually over the wheel. Behind him, the sky was a bruise-colored mass of yellows and grays, streaked with veins of pink. The young man had lank blond hair that spilled over his low forehead. He was grinning, and his parted lips revealed teeth which were not teeth at all but fangs.

Or maybe they're filed to points, Kinnell thought. *Maybe he's supposed to be a cannibal.*

He liked that; liked the idea of a cannibal crossing the Tobin Bridge at sunset. In a Grand Am. He knew what most of the audience at the PEN panel discussion would have thought—*Oh, yes, great picture for Rich Kinnell; he probably wants it for inspiration, a feather to tickle his tired old gorge into one more fit of projectile vomiting*—but most of those folks were ignoramuses, at least as far as his work went, and what was more, they treasured their ignorance, cossetted it the way some people inexplicably treasured and cossetted those stupid, mean-spirited little dogs that yapped at visitors and sometimes bit the paperboy's ankles. He hadn't been attracted to this painting because he wrote horror stories; he wrote horror stories because he was attracted to things like this painting. His fans sent him stuff—pictures, mostly—and he threw most of them away, not because they were bad art but because they were tiresome and predictable. One fan from Omaha had sent him a little ceramic sculpture of a screaming, horrified monkey's head poking out of a refrigerator door, however, and that one he had kept. It was unskillfully executed, but there was an unexpected juxtaposition there that lit up his dials. This painting had some of the same quality, but it was even better. *Much* better.

As he was reaching for it, wanting to pick it up right now, this second, wanting to tuck it under his arm and proclaim his intentions, a voice spoke up behind him: "Aren't you Richard Kinnell?"

He jumped, then turned. The fat woman was standing directly behind him, blotting out most of the immediate landscape. She had put on fresh lipstick before approaching, and now her mouth had been transformed into a bleeding grin.

"Yes, I am," he said, smiling back.

Her eyes dropped to the picture. "I should have known you'd go right to that," she said, simpering. "It's so *you*."

"It is, isn't it?" he said, and smiled his best celebrity smile. "How much would you need for it?"

"Forty-five dollars," she said. "I'll be honest with you, I started it at seventy, but nobody likes it, so now it's marked down. If you come back tomorrow, you can probably have it for thirty." The simper had grown to frightening proportions. Kinnell could see little gray spit-buds in the dimples at the corners of her stretched mouth.

"I don't think I want to take that chance," he said. "I'll write you a check right now."

The simper continued to stretch; the woman now looked like some grotesque John Waters parody. Divine does Shirley Temple. "I'm really not supposed to take checks, but *all right,*" she said, her tone that of a teenage girl finally consenting to have sex with her boyfriend. "Only while you have your pen out, could you write an autograph for my daughter? Her name is Michela?"

"What a beautiful name," Kinnell said automatically. He took the picture and followed the fat woman back to the card table. On the TV next to it, the lustful young people had been temporarily displaced by an elderly woman gobbling bran flakes.

"Michela reads all your books," the fat woman said. "Where in the world do you get all those crazy ideas?"

"I don't know," Kinnell said, smiling more widely than ever. "They just come to me. Isn't that amazing?"

The yard sale minder's name was Judy Diment, and she lived in the house next door. When Kinnell asked her if she knew who the artist happened to be, she said she certainly did; Bobby Hastings had done it, and Bobby Hastings was the reason she was selling off the Hastings' things. "That's the only painting he didn't burn," she said. "Poor Iris! She's the one I really feel sorry for. I don't think George cared much, really. And I *know* he didn't understand why she wants to sell the house." She rolled her eyes in her large, sweaty face—the old can-you-imagine-that look. She took Kinnell's check when he tore it off, then gave him the pad where she had written down all the items she'd sold and the prices she'd obtained for them. "Just make it out to Michela," she said. "Pretty please with sugar on it?" The simper reappeared, like an old acquaintance you'd hoped was dead.

"Uh-huh," Kinnell said, and wrote his standard thanks-for-being-a-fan message. He didn't have to watch his hands or even think about it anymore, not after twenty-five years of writing autographs. "Tell me about the picture, and the Hastingses."

Judy Diment folded her pudgy hands in the manner of a woman about to recite a favorite story.

"Bobby was just twenty-three when he killed himself this spring. Can you believe that? He was the tortured genius type, you know, but still living at home." Her eyes rolled, again asking Kinnell if he could imagine it. "He must have had seventy, eighty paintings, plus all his sketchbooks. Down in the basement, they were." She pointed her chin at the Cape Cod, then looked at the picture of the fiendish young man driving across the Tobin Bridge at sunset. "Iris—that's Bobby's mother—said most of them were real bad, lots worse'n this. Stuff that'd curl your hair." She lowered her voice to a whisper, glancing at a woman who was looking at the Hastings' mismatched silverware and a pretty good collection of old McDonald's plastic glasses in a *Honey, I Shrunk the Kids* motif. "Most of them had sex stuff in them."

"Oh no," Kinnell said.

"He did the worst ones after he got on drugs," Judy Diment continued. "After he was dead—he hung himself down in the basement, where he used to paint—they found over a hundred of those little bottles they sell crack cocaine in. Aren't drugs awful, Mr. Kinnell?"

"They sure are."

"Anyway, I guess he finally just got to the end of his rope, no pun intended. He took all of his sketches and paintings out into the back yard—except for that one, I guess—and burned them. Then he hung himself down in the basement. He pinned a note to his shirt. It said, 'I can't stand what's happening to me.' Isn't that awful, Mr. Kinnell? Isn't that just the awfulest thing you ever heard?"

"Yes," Kinnell said, sincerely enough. "It just about is."

"Like I say, I think George would go right on living in the house if he had his druthers," Judy Diment said. She took the sheet of paper with Michela's autograph on it, held it up next to Kinnell's check, and shook her head, as if the similarity of the signatures amazed her. "But men are different."

"Are they?"

"Oh, yes, much less sensitive. By the end of his life, Bobby Hastings was just skin and bone, dirty all the time—you could smell him—and he wore the same T-shirt, day in and day out. It had a picture of the Led Zepplins on it. His eyes were red, he had a scraggle on his cheeks that you couldn't quite call a beard, and his pimples were coming back, like he was a teenager again. But she loved him, because a mother's love sees past all those things."

The woman who had been looking at the silverware and the glasses came over with a set of Star Wars placemats. Mrs. Diment took five dollars for them, wrote the sale carefully down on her pad below "ONE DOZ. ASSORTED POTHOLDERS & HOTPADS," then turned back to Kinnell.

"They went out to Arizona," she said, "to stay with Iris's folks. I know George is looking for work out there in Flagstaff—he's a draftsman—but I don't know if he's found any yet. If he has, I suppose we might not ever see them again here in Rosewood. She marked out all the stuff she wanted me to sell—Iris did—and told me I could keep twenty percent for my trouble. I'll send a check for the rest. There won't be much." She sighed.

"The picture is great," Kinnell said.

"Yeah, too bad he burned the rest, because most of this other stuff is your standard yard sale crap, pardon my French. What's that?"

Kinnell had turned the picture around. There was a length of Dymotape pasted to the back.

"A title, I think."

"What does it say?"

He grabbed the picture by the sides and held it up so she could read it for herself. This put the picture at eye level to him, and he studied it eagerly, once again taken by the simpleminded weirdness of the subject: kid behind the wheel of a muscle car, a kid with a nasty, knowing grin that revealed the filed points of an even nastier set of teeth.

It fits, he thought. *If ever a title fitted a painting, this one does.*

"The Road Virus Heads North," she read. "I never noticed that when my boys were lugging stuff out. *Is* it the title, do you think?"

"Must be." Kinnell couldn't take his eyes off the blond kid's grin. *I know something,* the grin said. *I know something you never will.*

"Well, I guess you'd have to believe the fella who did this was high on drugs," she said, sounding upset—authentically upset, Kinnell thought. "No wonder he could kill himself and break his mamma's heart."

"I've got to be heading north myself," Kinnell said, tucking the picture under his arm. "Thanks for—"

"Mr. Kinnell?"

"Yes?"

"Can I see your driver's license?" She apparently found nothing ironic or even amusing in this request. "I ought to write the number on the back of your check."

Kinnell put the picture down so he could dig for his wallet. "Sure. You bet."

The woman who'd bought the Star Wars placemats had paused on her way back to her car to watch some of the soap opera playing on the lawn TV. Now she glanced at the picture, which Kinnell had propped against his shins.

"Ag," she said. "Who'd want an ugly old thing like that? I'd think about it every time I turned the lights out."

"What's wrong with that?" Kinnell asked.

Kinnell's Aunt Trudy lived in Wells, which is about six miles north of the Maine–New Hampshire border. Kinnell pulled off at the exit which circled the bright green Wells water tower, the one with the comic sign on it (KEEP MAINE GREEN, BRING MONEY in letters four feet high), and five minutes later he was turning into the driveway of her neat little saltbox house. No TV sinking into the lawn on paper ashtrays here, only Aunt Trudy's amiable masses of flowers. Kinnell needed to pee and hadn't wanted to take care of that in a roadside rest stop when he could come here, but he also wanted an update on all the family gossip. Aunt Trudy retailed the best; she was to gossip what Zabar's is to deli. Also, of course, he wanted to show her his new acquisition.

She came out to meet him, gave him a hug, and covered his face with her patented little birdy-kisses, the ones that had made him shiver all over as a kid.

"Want to see something?" he asked her. "It'll blow your panty-hose off."

"What a charming thought," Aunt Trudy said, clasping her elbows in her palms and looking at him with amusement.

He opened the trunk and took out his new picture. It affected her, all right, but not in the way he had expected. The color fell out of her face in a sheet—he had never seen anything quite like it in his entire life. "It's horrible," she said in a tight, controlled voice. "I hate it. I suppose I can see what attracted you to it, Richie, but what you play at, it does for real. Put it back in your trunk, like a good boy. And when you get to the Saco River, why don't you pull over into the breakdown lane and throw it in?"

He gaped at her. Aunt Trudy's lips were pressed tightly together to stop them trembling, and now her long, thin hands were not just clasping her elbows but clutching them, as if to keep her from flying away. At that moment she looked not sixty-one but ninety-one.

"Auntie?" Kinnell spoke tentatively, not sure what was going on here. "Auntie, what's wrong?"

"That," she said, unlocking her right hand and pointing at the picture. "I'm surprised you don't feel it more strongly yourself, an imaginative guy like you."

Well, he felt *something,* obviously he had, or he never would have unlimbered his checkbook in the first place. Aunt Trudy was feeling something else, though . . . or something *more.* He turned the picture around so he could see it (he had been holding it out for her, so the side with the Dymotaped title faced him), and looked at it again. What he saw hit him in the chest and belly like a one-two punch.

The picture had *changed,* that was punch number one. Not much, but it had clearly changed. The young blond man's smile was wider, revealing more of those filed cannibal-teeth. His eyes were squinted down more, too, giving his face a look which was more knowing and nastier than ever.

The degree of a smile . . . the vista of sharpened teeth widening slightly . . . the tilt and squint of the eyes . . . all pretty subjective stuff. A person could be mistaken about things like that, and of course he hadn't really *studied* the painting before buying it. Also, there had been the distraction of Mrs. Diment, who could probably talk the cock off a brass monkey.

But there was also punch number two, and that *wasn't* subjective. In the darkness of the Audi's trunk, the blond young man had turned his left arm, the one cocked on the door, so that Kinnell could now see a tattoo which had been hidden before. It was a vine-wrapped dagger with a bloody tip. Below it were words. Kinnell could make out DEATH BEFORE, and he supposed you didn't have to be a big best-selling novelist to figure out the word that was still hidden. DEATH BEFORE DISHONOR was, after all, just the sort of a thing a hoodoo traveling man like this was apt to have on his arm. *And an ace of spades or a pot plant on the other one,* Kinnell thought.

"You hate it, don't you, Auntie?" he asked.

"Yes," she said, and now he saw an even more amazing thing: she had turned away from him, pretending to look out at the street (which was dozing and deserted in the hot afternoon sunlight), so she wouldn't have to look at the picture. "In fact, Auntie *loathes* it. Now put it away and come on into the house. I'll bet you need to use the bathroom."

Aunt Trudy recovered her savoir faire almost as soon as the watercolor was back in the trunk. They talked about Kinnell's mother (Pasadena), his sister (Baton Rouge), and his ex-wife, Sally (Nashua). Sally was a space-case who ran an animal shelter out of a double-wide trailer and published two newsletters each month. *Survivors* was filled with astral info and supposedly true tales of the spirit world; *Visitors* contained the reports of people who'd had close encounters with space aliens. Kinnell no longer went to fan conventions which specialized in fantasy and horror. One Sally in a lifetime, he sometimes told people, was enough.

When Aunt Trudy walked him back out to the car, it was four-thirty and he'd turned down the obligatory dinner invitation. "I can get most of the way back to Derry in daylight, if I leave now."

"Okay," she said. "And I'm sorry I was so mean about your picture. Of *course* you like it, you've always liked your . . . your oddities. It just hit me the wrong way. That awful *face*." She shuddered. "As if we were looking at him . . . and he was looking right back."

Kinnell grinned and kissed the tip of her nose. "You've got quite an imagination yourself, sweetheart."

"Of course, it runs in the family. Are you sure you don't want to use the facility again before you go?"

He shook his head. "That's not why I stop, anyway, not really."

"Oh? Why do you?"

He grinned. "Because you know who's being naughty and who's being nice. And you're not afraid to share what you know."

"Go on, get going," she said, pushing at his shoulder but clearly pleased. "If I were you, I'd want to get home quick. I wouldn't want that nasty guy riding along behind *me* in the dark, even in the trunk. I mean, did you see his teeth? *Ag!*"

He got on the turnpike, trading scenery for speed, and made it as far as the Gray service area before deciding to have another look at the picture. Some of his aunt's unease had transmitted itself to him like a germ, but he didn't think that was really the problem. The problem was his perception that the picture had changed.

The service area featured the usual gourmet chow—burgers by Roy Rogers, cones by TCBY—and had a small, littered picnic and dog-walking area at the rear. Kinnell parked next to a van with Missouri plates, drew in a deep breath, let it out. He'd driven to Boston in order to kill some plot gremlins in the new book, which was pretty ironic. He'd spent the ride down working out what he'd say on the panel if certain tough questions were tossed at him, but none had been—once they'd found out he didn't *know* where he got his ideas, and yes, he *did* sometimes scare himself, they'd only wanted to know how you got an agent.

And now, heading back, he couldn't think of anything but the damned picture.

Had it changed? If it had, if the blond kid's arm had moved enough so he, Kinnell, could read a tattoo which had been partly hidden before, then he could write a column for one of Sally's magazines. Hell, a four-part series. If, on the other hand, it *wasn't* changing, then . . . what? He was suffering a hallucination? Having a breakdown? That was crap. His life was pretty much in order, and he felt good. *Had,* anyway, until his fascination with the picture had begun to waver into something else, something darker.

"Ah, fuck, you just saw it wrong the first time," he said out loud as he got out of the car. Well, maybe. Maybe. It wouldn't be the first time his head had screwed with his perceptions. That was also a part of what he did. Sometimes his imagination got a little . . . well . . .

"Feisty," Kinnell said, and opened the trunk. He took the picture out of the trunk and looked at it, and it was during the space of the ten seconds when he looked at it without remembering to breathe that he became authentically afraid of the thing, afraid the way you were afraid of a sudden dry rattle in the bushes, afraid the way you were when you saw an insect that would probably sting if you provoked it.

The blond driver was grinning insanely at him now—yes, at *him*, Kinnell was sure of it—with those filed cannibal teeth exposed all the way to the gumlines. His eyes simultaneously glared and laughed. And the Tobin Bridge was gone. So was the Boston skyline. So was the sunset. It was almost dark in the painting now, the car and its wild rider illuminated by a single streetlamp that ran a buttery glow across the road and the car's chrome. It looked to Kinnell as if the car (he was pretty sure it was a Grand Am) was on the edge of a small town on Route 1, and he was pretty sure he knew what town it was—he had driven through it himself only a few hours ago.

"Rosewood," he muttered. "That's Rosewood. I'm pretty sure."

The Road Virus was heading north, all right, coming up Route 1 just as he had. The blond's left arm was still cocked out the window, but it had rotated enough back toward its original position so that Kinnell could no longer see the tattoo. But he knew it was there, didn't he? Yes, you bet.

The blond kid looked like a Metallica fan who had escaped from a mental asylum for the criminally insane.

"Jesus," Kinnell whispered, and the word seemed to come from someplace else, not from him. The strength suddenly ran out of his body, ran out like water from a bucket with a hole in the bottom, and he sat down heavily on the curb separating the parking lot from the dog-walking zone. He suddenly understood that this was the truth he'd missed in all his fiction, this was how people really reacted when they came face-to-face with something which made no rational sense. You felt as if you were bleeding to death, only inside your head.

"No wonder the guy who painted it killed himself," he croaked, still staring at the picture, at the ferocious grin, at the eyes that were both shrewd and stupid.

There was a note pinned to his shirt, Mrs. Diment had said. *"I can't stand what's happening to me." Isn't that awful, Mr. Kinnell?*

Yes, it was awful, all right.

Really awful.

He got up, gripping the picture by its top, and strode across the dog-walking area. He kept his eyes trained strictly in front of him, looking for canine land mines. He did not look down at the picture. His legs felt trembly and untrustworthy, but they seemed to support him all right. Just ahead, close to the belt of trees at the rear of the service area, was a pretty young thing in white shorts and a red halter. She was walking a cocker spaniel. She began to smile at Kinnell, then saw something in his face that straightened her lips out in a hurry. She headed left, and fast. The cocker didn't want to go that fast so she dragged it, coughing, in her wake.

The scrubby pines behind the service area sloped down to a boggy area that stank of plant and animal decomposition. The carpet of pine needles was a road litter fallout zone: burger wrappers, paper soft drink cups, TCBY napkins, beer cans, empty wine-cooler bottles, cigarette butts. He saw a used condom lying like a dead snail next to a torn pair of panties with the word TUESDAY stitched on them in cursive girly-girl script.

Now that he was here, he chanced another look down at the picture. He steeled himself for further changes—even for the possibility that the painting would be in motion, like a movie in a frame—but there was none. There didn't have to be, Kinnell realized; the blond kid's face was enough. That stone-crazy grin. Those pointed teeth. The face said, *Hey, old man, guess what? I'm done fucking with civilization. I'm a representative of the real generation X, the next millennium is right here behind the wheel of this fine, high-steppin' mo-sheen.*

Aunt Trudy's initial reaction to the painting had been to advise Kinnell that he should throw it into the Saco River. Auntie had been right. The Saco was now almost twenty miles behind him, but . . .

"This'll do," he said. "I think this'll do just fine."

He raised the picture over his head like a guy holding up some kind of sports trophy for the postgame photographers and then heaved it down the slope. It flipped over twice, the frame catching winks of hazy late-day sun, then struck a tree. The glass facing shattered. The picture fell to the ground and then slid down the dry, needle-carpeted slope, as if down a chute. It landed in the bog, one corner of the frame protruding from a thick stand of reeds. Otherwise, there was nothing visible but the strew of broken glass, and Kinnell thought that went very well with the rest of the litter.

He turned and went back to his car, already picking up his mental trowel. He would wall this incident off in its own special niche, he thought . . . and it occurred to him that that was probably what *most* people did when they ran into stuff like this. Liars and wannabees (or maybe in this case they were wanna*sees*) wrote up their fantasies for publications like *Survivors* and called them truth; those who blundered into authentic occult phenomena kept their mouths shut and used those trowels. Because when cracks like this appeared in your life, you had to do something about them; if you didn't, they were apt to widen and sooner or later everything would fall in.

Kinnell glanced up and saw the pretty young thing watching him apprehensively from what she probably hoped was a safe distance. When she saw him looking at her, she turned around and started toward the restaurant building, once more dragging the cocker spaniel behind her and trying to keep as much sway out of her hips as possible.

You think I'm crazy, don't you, pretty girl? Kinnell thought. He saw he had left his trunk lid up. It gaped like a mouth. He slammed it shut. *You and half the fiction-reading population of America, I guess. But I'm not crazy. Absolutely not. I just made a little mistake, that's all. Stopped at a yard sale I should have passed up. Anyone could have done it.* You *could have done it. And that picture—*

"*What* picture?" Rich Kinnell asked the hot summer evening, and tried on a smile. "*I* don't see any picture."

He slid behind the wheel of his Audi and started the engine. He looked at the fuel gauge and saw it had dropped under a half. He was going to need gas before he got home, but he thought he'd fill the tank a little further up the line. Right now all he wanted to do was to put a belt of miles—as thick a one as possible—between him and the discarded painting.

Once outside the city limits of Derry, Kansas Street becomes Kansas Road. As it approaches the incorporated town limits (an area that is actually open countryside), it becomes Kansas Lane. Not long after, Kansas Lane passes between two fieldstone posts. Tar gives way to gravel. What is one of Derry's busiest downtown streets eight miles east of here has become a driveway leading up a shallow hill, and on moonlit summer nights it glimmers like something out of an Alfred Noyes poem. At the top of the hill stands an angular, handsome barnboard structure with reflectorized windows, a stable that is actually a garage, and a satellite dish tilted at the stars. A waggish reporter from the *Derry News* once called it the House that Gore Built . . . *not* meaning the vice president of the United States. Richard Kinnell simply called it home, and he parked in front of it that night with a sense of weary satisfaction. He felt as if he had lived through a week's worth of time since getting up in the Boston Harbor hotel that morning at nine o'clock.

No more yard sales, he thought, looking up at the moon. *No more yard sales ever.*

"Amen," he said, and started toward the house. He probably should stick the car in the garage, but the hell with it. What he wanted right now was a drink, a light meal—something microwaveable—and then sleep. Preferably the kind without dreams. He couldn't wait to put this day behind him.

He stuck his key in the lock, turned it, and punched 3817 to silence the warning bleep from the burglar alarm panel. He turned on the front hall light, stepped through the door, pushed it shut behind him, began to turn, saw what was on the wall where his collection of framed book covers had been just two days ago, and screamed. In his *head* he screamed. Nothing actually came out of his mouth but a harsh exhalation of air. He heard a thump and a tuneless little jingle as his keys fell out of his relaxing hand and dropped to the carpet between his feet.

The Road Virus Heads North was no longer in the puckerbrush behind the Gray turnpike service area.

It was mounted on his entry wall.

It had changed yet again. The car was now parked in the driveway of the yard sale yard. The goods were still spread out everywhere—glassware and furniture and ceramic knickknacks (Scottie dogs smoking pipes, bare-assed toddlers, winking fish), but now they gleamed beneath the light of the same skullface moon that rode in the sky above Kinnell's house. The TV was still there, too, and it was still on, casting its own pallid radiance onto the grass, and what lay in front of it, next to an overturned lawn chair. Judy Diment was on her back, and she was no longer all there. After a moment, Kinnell saw the rest. It was on the ironing board, dead eyes glowing like fifty-cent pieces in the moonlight.

The Grand Am's taillights were a blur of red-pink watercolor paint. It was Kinnell's first look at the car's back deck. Written across it in Old English letters were three words: THE ROAD VIRUS.

Makes perfect sense, Kinnell thought numbly. *Not him, his car. Except for a guy like this, there's probably not much difference.*

"This isn't happening," he whispered, except it was. Maybe it *wouldn't* have happened to someone a little less open to such things, but it *was* happening. And as he stared at the painting he found himself remembering the little sign on Judy Diment's card table. ALL SALES CASH, it had said (although she had taken *his* check, only adding his driver's license ID number for safety's sake). And it had said something else, too.

ALL SALES FINAL.

Kinnell walked past the picture and into the living room. He felt like a stranger inside his own body, and he sensed part of his mind groping around for the trowel he had used earlier. He seemed to have misplaced it.

He turned on the TV, then the Toshiba satellite tuner which sat on top of it. He turned to V–14, and all the time he could feel the picture out there in the hall, pushing at the back of his head. The picture that had somehow beaten him here.

"Must have known a shortcut," Kinnell said, and laughed.

He hadn't been able to see much of the blond in this version of the picture, but there had been a blur behind the wheel which Kinnell assumed had been him. The Road Virus had finished his business in Rosewood. It was time to move north. Next stop—

He brought a heavy steel door down on that thought, cutting it off before he could see all of it. "After all, I could still be imagining all this," he told the empty living room. Instead of comforting him, the hoarse, shaky quality of his voice frightened him even more. "This could be . . ." But he couldn't finish. All that came to him was an old song, belted out in the pseudo-hip style of some early '50s Sinatra clone: *This could be the start of something BIG . . .*

The tune oozing from the TV's stereo speakers wasn't Sinatra but Paul Simon, arranged for strings. The white computer type on the blue screen said WELCOME TO NEW ENGLAND NEWSWIRE. There were ordering instructions below this, but Kinnell didn't have to read them; he was a Newswire junkie and knew the drill by heart. He dialed, punched in his Mastercard number, then 508.

"You have ordered Newswire for [slight pause] central and northern Massachusetts," the robot voice said. "Thank you very m—"

Kinnell dropped the phone back into the cradle and stood looking at the New England Newswire logo, snapping his fingers nervously. "Come on," he said. "Come on, come on."

The screen flickered then, and the blue background became green. Words began scrolling up, something about a house fire in Taunton. This was followed by the latest on a dog-racing scandal, then tonight's weather—clear and mild. Kinnell was starting to relax, starting to wonder if he'd really seen what he thought he'd seen on the entryway wall or if it had been a bit of travel-induced fugue, when the TV beeped shrilly and the words BREAKING NEWS appeared. He stood watching the caps scroll up.

NENphAUG19/8:40P A ROSEWOOD WOMAN HAS BEEN BRUTALLY MURDERED WHILE DOING A FAVOR FOR AN ABSENT FRIEND. 38-YEAR-OLD JUDITH DIMENT WAS SAVAGELY HACKED TO DEATH ON THE LAWN OF HER NEIGHBOR'S HOUSE, WHERE SHE HAD BEEN CONDUCTING A YARD SALE. NO SCREAMS WERE HEARD AND MRS. DIMENT WAS NOT FOUND UNTIL EIGHT O'CLOCK, WHEN A NEIGHBOR ACROSS THE STREET CAME OVER TO COMPLAIN ABOUT LOUD TELEVISION NOISE. THE NEIGHBOR, DAVID GRAVES, SAID THAT MRS. DIMENT HAD BEEN DECAPITATED. "HER HEAD WAS ON THE IRONING BOARD," HE SAID. "IT WAS THE MOST AWFUL THING I'VE EVER SEEN IN MY LIFE." GRAVES SAID HE HEARD NO SIGNS OF A STRUGGLE, ONLY THE TV AND, SHORTLY BEFORE FINDING THE BODY, A LOUD CAR, POSSIBLY EQUIPPED WITH A GLASSPACK MUFFLER, ACCELERATING AWAY FROM THE VICINITY ALONG ROUTE ONE. SPECULATION THAT THIS VEHICLE MAY HAVE BELONGED TO THE KILLER—

Except that wasn't speculation; that was a simple fact.

Breathing hard, not quite panting, Kinnell hurried back into the entryway. The picture was still there, but it had changed once more. Now it showed two glaring white circles—headlights—with the dark shape of the car hulking behind them.

He's on the move again, Kinnell thought, and Aunt Trudy *was* on top of his mind now—sweet Aunt Trudy, who always knew who had been naughty and who had been nice. Aunt Trudy, who lived in Wells, no more than forty miles from Rosewood.

"God, please God, please send him by the coast road," Kinnell said, reaching for the picture. Was it his imagination or were the headlights farther apart now, as if the car were actually moving before his eyes . . . but stealthily, the way the minute hand moved on a pocket watch? "Send him by the coast road, please."

He tore the picture off the wall and ran back into the living room with it. The screen was in place before the fireplace, of course; it would be at least two months before a fire was wanted in here. Kinnell batted it aside and threw the painting in, breaking the glass fronting—which he had already broken once, at the Gray service area—against the firedogs. Then he pelted for the kitchen, wondering what he would do if this didn't work either.

It has to, he thought. *It will because it has to, and that's all there is to it.*

He opened the kitchen cabinets and pawed through them, spilling the oatmeal, spilling a canister of salt, spilling the vinegar. The bottle broke open on the counter and assaulted his nose and eyes with the high stink.

Not there. What he wanted wasn't there.

He raced into the pantry, looked behind the door—nothing but a plastic bucket and an O Cedar—and then on the shelf by the dryer. There it was, next to the briquets.

Lighter fluid.

He grabbed it and ran back, glancing at the telephone on the kitchen wall as he hurried by. He wanted to stop, wanted to call Aunt Trudy. Credibility wasn't an issue with her; if her favorite nephew called and told her to get out of the house, to get out *right now,* she would do it . . . but what if the blond kid followed her? Chased her?

And he would. Kinnell *knew* he would.

He hurried across the living room and stopped in front of the fireplace.

"Jesus," he whispered. "Jesus, no."

The picture beneath the splintered glass no longer showed oncoming headlights. Now it showed the Grand Am on a sharply curving piece of road that could only be an exit ramp. Moonlight shone like liquid satin on the car's dark flank. In the background was a water tower, and the words on it were easily readable in the moonlight. KEEP MAINE GREEN, they said. BRING MONEY.

Kinnell didn't hit the picture with the first squeeze of lighter fluid; his hands were shaking badly and the aromatic liquid simply ran down the unbroken part of the glass, blurring the Road Virus's back deck. He took a deep breath, aimed, then squeezed again. This time the lighter fluid squirted in through the jagged hole made by one of the firedogs and ran down the picture, cutting through the paint, making it run, turning a Goodyear Wide Oval into a sooty teardrop.

Kinnell took one of the ornamental matches from the jar on the mantel, struck it on the hearth, and poked it in through the hole in the glass. The painting caught at once, fire billowing up and down across the Grand Am and the water tower. The remaining glass in the frame turned black, then broke outward in a shower of flaming pieces. Kinnell crunched them under his sneakers, putting them out before they could set the rug on fire.

He went to the phone and punched in Aunt Trudy's number, unaware that he was crying. On the third ring, his aunt's answering machine picked up. "Hello," Aunt Trudy said, "I know it encourages the burglars to say things like this, but I've gone up to Kennebunk to watch the new Harrison Ford movie. If you intend to break in, please don't take my china pigs. If you want to leave a message, do so at the beep."

Kinnell waited, then, keeping his voice as steady as possible, he said: "It's Richie, Aunt Trudy. Call me when you get back, okay? No matter how late."

He hung up, looked at the TV, then dialed Newswire again, this time punching in the Maine area code. While the computers on the other end processed his order, he went back and used a poker to jab at the blackened, twisted thing in the fireplace. The stench was ghastly—it made the spilled vinegar smell like a flowerpatch in comparison—but Kinnell found he didn't mind. The picture was entirely gone, reduced to ash, and that made it worthwhile.

What if it comes back again?

"It won't," he said, putting the poker back and returning to the TV. "I'm sure it won't."

But every time the news scroll started to recycle, he got up to check. The picture was just ashes on the hearth . . . and there was no word of elderly women being murdered in the Wells-Saco-Kennebunk area of the state. Kinnell kept watching, almost expecting to see A GRAND AM MOVING AT HIGH SPEED CRASHED INTO A KENNEBUNK MOVIE THEATER TONIGHT, KILLING AT LEAST TEN, but nothing of the sort showed up.

At a quarter of eleven the telephone rang. Kinnell snatched it up. "Hello?"

"It's Trudy, dear. Are you all right?"

"Yes, fine."

"You don't *sound* fine," she said. "Your voice sounds trembly and . . . funny. What's wrong? What is it?" And then, chilling him but not really surprising him: "It's that picture you were so pleased with, isn't it? That goddamned picture!"

It calmed him somehow, that she should guess so much . . . and, of course, there was the relief of knowing she was safe.

"Well, maybe," he said. "I had the heebie-jeebies all the way back here, so I burned it. In the fireplace."

She's going to find out about Judy Diment, you know, a voice inside warned. *She doesn't have a twenty-thousand-dollar satellite hookup, but she does subscribe to the* Union-Leader *and this'll be on the front page. She'll put two and two together. She's far from stupid.*

Yes, that was undoubtedly true, but further explanations could wait until the morning, when he might be a little less freaked . . . when he might've found a way to think about the Road Virus without losing his mind . . . and when he'd begun to be sure it was really over.

"Good!" she said emphatically. "You ought to scatter the ashes, too!" She paused, and when she spoke again, her voice was lower. "You were worried about me, weren't you? Because you showed it to me."

"A little, yes."

"But you feel better now?"

He leaned back and closed his eyes. It was true, he did. "Uh-huh. How was the movie?"

"Good. Harrison Ford looks wonderful in a uniform. Now, if he'd just get rid of that little bump on his chin . . ."

"Good night, Aunt Trudy. We'll talk tomorrow."

"Will we?"

"Yes," he said. "I think so."

He hung up, went over to the fireplace again, and stirred the ashes with the poker. He could see a scrap of fender and a ragged little flap of road, but that was it. Fire was what it had needed all along, apparently. Wasn't that how you usually killed supernatural emissaries of evil? Of course it was. He'd used it a few times himself, most notably in *The Departing,* his haunted train station novel.

"Yes, indeed," he said. "Burn, baby, burn."

He thought about getting the drink he'd promised himself, then remembered the spilled bottle of vinegar (which by now would probably be soaking into the spilled oatmeal—what a thought). He decided he would simply go on upstairs instead. In a book—one by Richard

Kinnell, for instance— sleep would be out of the question after the sort of thing which had just happened to him.

In real life, he thought he might sleep just fine.

He actually dozed off in the shower, leaning against the back wall with his hair full of shampoo and the water beating on his chest. He was at the yard sale again, and the TV standing on the paper ashtrays was broadcasting Judy Diment. Her head was back on, but Kinnell could see the medical examiner's primitive industrial stitchwork; it circled her throat like a grisly necklace. "Now this New England Newswire update," she said, and Kinnell, who had always been a vivid dreamer, could actually see the stitches on her neck stretch and relax as she spoke. "Bobby Hastings took *all* his paintings and burned them, including yours, Mr. Kinnell . . . and it *is* yours, as I'm sure you know. All sales are final, you saw the sign. Why, you just ought to be glad I took your check."

Burned all his paintings, yes, of course he did, Kinnell thought in his watery dream. *He couldn't stand what was happening to him, that's what the note said, and when you get to that point in the festivities, you don't pause to see if you want to except one special piece of work from the bonfire. It's just that you got something special into* The Road Virus Heads North, *didn't you, Bobby? And probably completely by accident. You were talented, I could see that right away, but talent has nothing to do with what's going on in* that *picture.*

"Some things are just good at survival," Judy Diment said on the TV. "They keep coming back no matter *how* hard you try to get rid of them. They keep coming back like viruses."

Kinnell reached out and changed the channel, but apparently there was nothing on all the way around the dial except for *The Judy Diment Show.*

"You might say he opened a hole into the basement of the universe," she was saying now. "Bobby Hastings, I mean. And this is what drove out. Nice, isn't it?"

Kinnell's feet slid then, not enough to go out from under him completely, but enough to snap him to.

He opened his eyes, winced at the immediate sting of the soap (Prell had run down his face in thick white rivulets while he had been dozing), and cupped his hands under the shower-spray to splash it away. He did this once and was reaching out to do it again when he heard something. A ragged rumbling sound.

Don't be stupid, he told himself. *All you hear is the shower. The rest is only imagination.*

Except it wasn't.

Kinnell reached out and turned off the water.

The rumbling sound continued. Low and powerful. Coming from outside.

He got out of the shower and walked, dripping, across his bedroom on the second floor. There was still enough shampoo in his hair to make him look as if it had turned white while he was dozing—as if his dream of Judy Diment had turned it white.

Why did I ever stop at that yard sale? he asked himself, but for this he had no answer. He supposed no one ever did.

The rumbling sound grew louder as he approached the window overlooking the driveway—the driveway that glimmered in the summer moonlight like something out of an Alfred Noyes poem.

As he brushed aside the curtain and looked out, he found himself thinking of his ex-wife, Sally, whom he had met at the World Fantasy Convention in 1978. Sally, who now published two magazines out of her trailer home, one called *Survivors,* one called *Visitors.* Looking down at the driveway, these two titles came together in Kinnell's mind like a double image in a stereopticon.

He had a visitor who was definitely a survivor.

The Grand Am idled in front of the house, the white haze from its twin chromed tailpipes rising in the still night air. The Old English letters on the back deck were perfectly readable. The driver's side door stood open, and that wasn't all; the light spilling down the porch steps suggested that Kinnell's front door was also open.

Forgot to lock it, Kinnell thought, wiping soap off his forehead with a hand he could no longer feel. *Forgot to reset the burglar alarm, too . . . not that it would have made much difference to this guy.*

Well, he might have caused it to detour around Aunt Trudy, and that was something, but just now the thought brought him no comfort.

Survivors.

The soft rumble of the big engine, probably at least a 442 with a four-barrel carb, reground valves, fuel injection.

He turned slowly on legs that had lost all feeling, a naked man with a headful of soap, and saw the picture over his bed, just as he'd known he would. In it, the Grand Am stood in his driveway with the driver's door open and two plumes of exhaust rising from the chromed tailpipes. From this angle he could also see his own front door, standing open, and a long man-shaped shadow stretching down the hall.

Survivors.

Survivors and *visitors*.

Now he could hear feet ascending the stairs. It was a heavy tread, and he knew without having to see that the blond kid was wearing motorcycle boots. People with DEATH BEFORE DISHONOR tattooed on their arms always wore motorcycle boots, just as they always smoked unfiltered Camels. These things were like a national law.

And the knife. He would be carrying a long, sharp knife—more of a machete, actually, the sort of knife that could strike off a person's head in a single sweeping stroke.

And he would be grinning, showing those filed cannibal teeth.

Kinnell *knew* these things. He was an imaginative guy, after all.

He didn't need anyone to draw him a picture.

"No," he whispered, suddenly conscious of his global nakedness, suddenly freezing all the way around his skin. "No, please, go away." But the footfalls kept coming, of course they did. You couldn't tell a guy like this to go away. It didn't work; it wasn't the way the story was supposed to end.

Kinnell could hear him nearing the top of the stairs. Outside the Grand Am went on rumbling in the moonlight.

The feet coming down the hall now, worn bootheels rapping on polished hardwood.

A terrible paralysis had gripped Kinnell. He threw it off with an effort and bolted toward the bedroom door, wanting to lock it before the thing could get in here, but he slipped in a puddle of soapy water and this time he *did* go down, flat on his back on the oak planks, and what he saw as the door clicked open and the motorcycle boots crossed the room toward where he lay, naked and with his hair full of Prell, was the picture hanging on the wall over his bed, the picture of the Road Virus idling in front of his house with the driver's side door open.

The driver's side bucket seat, he saw, was full of blood. *I'm going outside, I think,* Kinnell thought, and closed his eyes.

Neil Gaiman

KEEPSAKES AND TREASURES:
A LOVE STORY

I first met Neil Gaiman in person at a strange and wonderful little duck of a convention, a kind of summer camp for writers at Roger Williams College in Newport, Rhode Island, called NECON. I did enjoy meeting him during a panel we did together on fairy tales, where I distinguished myself with my lack of knowledge (or interest, if you must know) on said subject—but where Neil showed off his own knowledge to marvelous effect. My real reason for attending NECON, to be perfectly honest, was to track down Gaiman (I had been E-mailing him for months, trying to get him to turn in a story for this book).

Neil Gaiman is, of course, author of the wildly successful Sandman *comic book series and the creator of that perky young woman named Death; he is also the prose author of* Neverwhere, Good Omens *(with Terry Pratchett), and the collection* Angels and Visitations, *among many other works.*

In the end, as you can see, my pursuit of Gaiman was successful. Neil did, at the wire, turn in the following story—again, to marvelous effect.

I am his Highness' dog at Kew
Pray tell me, sir, whose dog are you?
ALEXANDER POPE,
On the Collar of a Dog which I Gave to His Royal Highness

You can call me a bastard if you like. It's true, whichever way you want to cut it. My mum had me two years after being locked up "for her own protection"; this was back in 1952, when a couple of wild nights out with the local lads could be diagnosed as clinical nymphomania and you could be put away "to protect yourself and society" on the say-so of any two doctors. One of whom was her father, my grandfather; the other was his partner in the North London medical practice they shared.

So I know who my grandfather was. But my father was just somebody who shagged my mother somewhere in the building or grounds of Saint Andrew's Asylum. That's a nice word, isn't it? *Asylum*. With all its implications of a place of safety: somewhere that shelters you from the bitter and dangerous old world outside. Nothing like the reality of that hole. I went to see it before they knocked it down in the late seventies. It still reeked of piss and pine-scented disinfectant floor-wash. Long, dark, badly lit corridors with clusters of tiny, cell-like rooms off them. If you were looking for Hell and you found St. Andrew's you'd not have been disappointed.

It says on her medical records that she'd spread her legs for anyone, but I doubt it. She was locked up, back then. Anyone who wanted to stick his cock into her would have needed a key to her cell.

When I was eighteen I spent my last summer holiday before I went up to University hunting down the four men who were most likely to have been my father: two psychiatric nurses, the secure ward doctor, and the governor of the asylum.

My mum was only seventeen when she went inside. I've got a little black-and-white wallet photograph of her from just before she was put away. She's leaning against the side of a Morgan sports car parked in a country lane. She's smiling, sort of flirtily, at the photographer. She was a looker, my mum.

I didn't know which one of the four was my dad, so I killed all of them. They had each fucked her, after all: I got them to admit to it before I did them in. The best was the governor, a red-faced fleshy old lech with an honest-to-goodness handlebar mustache, like I haven't seen for twenty years now. I garotted him with his Guards tie. Spit-bubbles came from his mouth, and he went blue as an un-boiled lobster.

There were other men around St. Andrew's who might have been my father, but after those four the joy went out of it. I told myself that I'd killed the four likeliest candidates, and if I knocked off everyone who might have knocked up my mother it would have turned into a massacre. So I stopped.

I was handed over to the local orphanage to bring up. According to her medical records, they sterilized my mum immediately after I was born. Didn't want any more nasty little incidents like me coming along to spoil anybody's fun.

I was ten when she killed herself. This was 1964. I was ten years old, and I was still playing conkers and knocking off sweet shops while she was sitting on the linoleum floor of her cell sawing at her wrists with a bit of broken glass she'd got from heaven-knows-where. Cut her fingers up, too, but she did it all right. They found her in the morning, sticky, red and cold.

Mr. Alice's people ran into me when I was twelve. The deputy head of the orphanage had been using us kids as his personal harem of scabby-kneed love slaves. Go along with him and you got a sore bum and a Bounty bar. Fight back and you got locked down for a couple of days, a really sore bum and concussion. Old Bogey we used to call him, because he picked his nose whenever he thought we weren't looking.

He was found in his blue Morris Minor in his garage, with the doors shut and a length of bright green hosepipe going from the exhaust into the front window. The coroner said it was a suicide and seventy-five young boys breathed a little easier.

But Old Bogey had done a few favors for Mr. Alice over the years, when there was a chief constable or a foreign politician with a penchant for little boys to be taken care of, and he sent a couple of investigators out to make sure everything was on the up-and-up. When they figured out the only possible culprit was a twelve-year-old boy, they almost pissed themselves laughing.

Mr. Alice was intrigued, so he sent for me. This was back when he was a lot more hands-on than today. I suppose he hoped I'd be pretty, but he was in for a sad disappointment. I looked then like I do now: too thin, with a profile like a hatchet-blade, and ears like someone left the car doors open. What I remember of him mostly then is how big he was. Corpulent. I suppose he was still a fairly young man back then, although I didn't see it that way: he was an adult, and so he was the enemy.

A couple of goons came and took me after school, on my way back to the home. I was shitting myself, at first, but the goons didn't smell like the law—I'd had four years of dodging the Old Bill by then, and I could spot a plainclothes copper a hundred yards away. They took me to a little gray office, sparsely furnished, just off the Edgware Road.

It was winter, and it was almost dark outside, but the lights were dim, except for a little desk lamp casting a pool of yellow light on the desk. An enormous man sat at the desk scribbling something in ballpoint pen on the bottom of a telex sheet. Then, when he was done, he looked up at me. He looked me over from head to toe.

"Cigarette?"

I nodded. He extended a Peter Stuyvesant soft pack, and I took a cigarette. He lit it for me with a gold-and-black cigarette lighter. "You killed Ronnie Palmerstone," he told me. There was no question in his voice.

I said nothing.

"Well? Aren't you going to say anything?"

"Got nothing to say," I told him.

"I only sussed it when I heard he was in the passenger seat. He wouldn't have been in the passenger seat if he was going to kill himself. He would have been in the driver's seat. My guess is, you slipped him a mickey, then you got him into the Mini—can't have been easy, he wasn't a little bloke—here, mickey and Mini, that's rich—then you drove him home, drove into the garage, by which point he was sleeping soundly, and you rigged up the suicide. Weren't you scared someone would see you driving? A twelve-year-old boy?"

"It gets dark early," I said. "And I took the back way."

He chuckled. Asked me a few more questions, about school, and the home, and what I was interested in, things like that. Then the goons came back and took me back to the orphanage.

Next week I was adopted by a couple named Jackson. He was an international business law specialist. She was a self-defense expert. I don't think either of them had ever met before Mr. Alice got them together to bring me up.

I wonder what he saw in me at that meeting. It must have been some kind of potential, I suppose. The potential for loyalty. And I'm loyal. Make no mistake about that. I'm Mr. Alice's man, body and soul.

Of course, his name isn't really Mr. Alice, but I could use his real name here just as easily. Doesn't matter. You'd not have heard of him. Mr. Alice is one of the ten richest men in the world. I'll tell you something: you haven't heard of the other nine, either. Their names aren't going to turn up on any lists of the hundred richest men in the world. None of your Bill Gateses or your Sultans of Brunei. I'm talking *real* money here. There are people out there who are being paid more than you will ever see in your life to make sure you never hear a breath about Mr. Alice on the telly or in the papers.

Mr. Alice likes to own things. And, as I've told you, one of the things he owns is me. He's the father I didn't have. It was him that got me the medical files on my mum and the information on the various candidates for my dad.

When I graduated (first-class degrees in business studies and international law), as my graduation present to myself, I went and found my-grandfather-the-doctor. I'd held off on seeing him until then. It had been a sort of incentive.

He was a year away from retirement, a hatchet-faced old man with a tweed jacket. This was in 1978, and a few doctors still made house calls. I followed him to a tower block in Maida Vale. Waited while he dispensed his medical wisdom, and stopped him as he came out, black bag swinging by his side.

"Hullo, Grandpa," I said. Not much point in trying to pretend to be someone else, really. Not with my looks. He was me, forty years on. Same fucking ugly face, but with his hair thinning and sandy gray, not thick and mousy brown like mine. He asked what I wanted.

"Locking mum away like that," I told him. "It wasn't very nice, was it?"

He told me to get away from him, or something like that.

"I've just got my degree," I told him. "You should be proud of me."

He said that he knew who I was and that I had better be off at once or he would have the police down on me and have me locked away.

I put the knife through his left eye and back into his brain, and while he made little choking noises I took his old calf-skin wallet—as a keepsake, really, and to make it look more like a robbery. That was where I found the photo of my mum, in black and white, smiling and flirting with the camera, twenty-five years before. I wonder who owned the Morgan.

I had someone who didn't know me pawn the wallet. I bought it from the pawn shop when it wasn't redeemed. Nice clean trail. There's many a smart man who's been brought down by a keepsake. Sometimes I wonder if I killed my father that day, as well as my grandfather. I don't expect he'd have told me, even if I'd asked. And it doesn't really matter, does it?

After that I went to work full-time for Mr. Alice. I ran the Sri Lanka end of things for a couple of years, then spent a year in Bogotá on import-export, working as a glorified travel agent. I came back home to London as soon as I could. For the last fifteen years I've been working mainly as a troubleshooter and as a smoother-over of problem areas. Troubleshooter. That's rich.

Like I said, it takes real money to make sure nobody's ever heard of you. None of that Rupert Murdoch cap-in-hand to the merchant bankers rubbish. You'll never see Mr. Alice in a glossy magazine, showing a photographer around his glossy new house.

Outside of business, Mr. Alice's main interest is sex, which is why I was standing outside Earl's Court Station with forty million U.S. dollars' worth of blue-white diamonds in the inside pockets of my mackintosh. Specifically, and to be exact, Mr. Alice's interest in sex is confined to relations with attractive young men. No, don't get me wrong here: I don't want you thinking Mr. Alice's some kind of woofter. He's not a nancy or anything. He's a proper man, Mr. Alice. He's just a proper man who likes to fuck other men, that's all. Takes all sorts to make a world, I say, and leaves a lot more of what I like for me. Like at restaurants, where everyone gets to order something different from the menu. *Chacun a son goût*, if you'll pardon my French. So everybody's happy.

This was a couple of years ago, in July. I remember that I was standing in the Earls Court Road, in Earls Court, looking up at the Earl's Court Tube Station sign and wondering why the apostrophe was there in the station when it wasn't in the place, and then staring at the junkies and the winos who hang around on the pavement, and all the time keeping an eye out for Mr. Alice's Jag.

I wasn't worried about having the diamonds in my inside pocket. I don't look like the sort of bloke who's got anything you'd want to mug him for, and I can take care of myself. So I stared at the junkies and winos, killing time till the Jag arrived (stuck behind the road works in Kensington High Street, at a guess) and wondering why junkies and winos congregate on the pavement outside Earl's Court Station.

I suppose I can sort of understand the junkies: they're waiting for a fix. But what the fuck are the winos doing there? Nobody has to slip you a pint of Guinness or a bottle of rubbing alcohol in a plain brown bag. It's not comfortable, sitting on the paving stones or leaning against the wall. If I were a wino, on a lovely day like this, I decided, I'd go down to the park.

Near me a little Pakistani lad in his late teens or early twenties was papering the inside of a glass phone box with hooker cards—CURVY TRANSSEXUAL and REAL BLONDE NURSE, BUSTY SCHOOLGIRL and STERN TEACHER NEEDS BOY TO DISCIPLINE. He glared at me when he noticed I was watching him. Then he finished up and went on to the next booth.

Mr. Alice's Jag drew up at the curb and I walked over to it and got in the back. It's a good car, a couple of years old. Classy but not something you'd look twice at.

The chauffeur and Mr. Alice sat in the front. Sitting in the back seat with me was a pudgy man with a crewcut and a loud check suit. He made me think of the frustrated fiancée in a fifties film; the one who gets dumped for Rock Hudson in the final reel. I nodded at him. He extended his hand, and then, when I didn't seem to notice, he put it away.

Mr. Alice did not introduce us, which was fine by me, as I knew exactly who the man was. I'd found him, and reeled him in, in fact, although he'd never know that. He was a professor of ancient languages at a North Carolina university. He thought he was on loan to British Intelligence from the U.S. State Department. He thought this because this was what he had been told by someone at the U.S. State Department. The professor had told his wife that he was presenting a paper to a conference on Hittite studies in London. And there was such a conference. I'd organized it myself.

"Why do you take the bloody tube?" asked Mr. Alice. "It can't be to save money."

"I would have thought the fact I've been standing on that corner waiting for you for the last twenty minutes demonstrates exactly why I didn't drive," I told him. He likes it that I don't just roll over and wag my tail. I'm a dog with spirit. "The average daytime speed of a vehicle through the streets of Central London has not changed in four hundred years. It's still under ten miles an hour. If the tubes are running, I'll take the tube, thanks."

"You don't drive in London?" asked the professor in the loud suit. Heavens protect us from the dress sense of American academics. Let's call him Macleod.

"I'll drive at night, when the roads are empty," I told him. "After midnight. I like driving at night."

Mr. Alice wound down the window and lit a small cigar. I could not help noticing that his hands were trembling. With anticipation, I guessed.

And we drove through Earls Court, past a hundred tall red-brick houses that claimed to be hotels, a hundred tattier buildings that housed guest houses and bed-and-breakfasts, down good streets and bad. Sometimes Earls Court reminds me of one of those old women you meet from time to time who's painfully proper and prissy and prim until she's got a few drinks into her, when she starts dancing on the tables and telling everybody within earshot about her days as a pretty young thing sucking cock for money in Australia or Kenya or somewhere.

Actually, that makes it sound like I like the place and, frankly, I don't. It's too transient. Things come and go and people come and go too damn fast. I'm not a romantic man, but give me South of the River, or the East End, any day. The East End is a proper place: it's where things begin, good and bad. It's the cunt and the arsehole of London; they're always close together. Whereas Earls Court is—I don't know what. The body analogy breaks down completely when you get out to there. I think that's because London is mad. Multiple personality problems. All these little towns and villages that grew and crashed into each other to make one big city but never forget their old borders.

So the chauffeur pulls up in a road like any other, in front of a high, terraced house that might have been a hotel at one time. A couple of the windows were boarded over. "That's the house," said the chauffeur.

"Right," said Mr. Alice.

The chauffeur walked around the car and opened the door for Mr. Alice. Professor Macleod and I got out on our own. I looked up and down the pavement. Nothing to worry about.

I knocked on the door, and we waited. I nodded and smiled at the spyhole in the door. Mr. Alice's cheeks were flushed, and he held his hands folded in front of his crotch, to avoid embarrassing himself. Horny old bugger.

Well, I've been there too. We all have. Only Mr. Alice, he can afford to indulge himself.

The way I look at it, some people need love, and some people don't. I think Mr. Alice is really a bit of a *don't,* all things considered. I'm a *don't* as well. You learn to recognize the type.

And Mr. Alice is, first and foremost, a connoisseur.

There was a bang from the door, as a bolt was drawn back, and the door was opened by an old woman of what they used to describe as "repulsive aspect." She was dressed in a baggy black one-piece robe. Her face was wrinkled and pouched. I'll tell you what she looked like. Did you ever see a picture of one of those cinnamon buns they said looked like Mother Teresa? She looked like that, like a cinnamon roll, with two brown raisin eyes peering out of her cinnamon roll face.

She said something to me in a language I did not recognize, and Professor Macleod replied haltingly. She stared at the three of us suspiciously, then she made a face and beckoned us in. She slammed the door behind us. I closed first one eye, then the other, encouraging them to adjust to the gloom inside the house.

The building smelled like a damp spice rack. I didn't like anything about the whole business; there's something about foreigners, when they're that foreign, that makes my skin crawl. As the old bat who'd let us in, who I had begun to think of as the Mother Superior, led us up flight after flight of stairs, I could see more of the black-robed women, peering at us out of doorways and down the corridor. The stair-carpet was frayed and the soles of my shoes made sticking noises as they pulled up from it; the plaster hung in crumbling chunks from the walls. It was a warren, and it drove me nuts. Mr. Alice shouldn't have to come to places like that, places where he couldn't be protected properly.

More and more shadowy crones peered at us in silence as we climbed our way through the house. The old witch with the cinnamon bun face talked to Professor Macleod as we went, a few words here, a few words there; and he in return panted and puffed at her, from the effort of climbing the stairs, and answered her as best he could.

"She wants to know if you brought the diamonds," he gasped.

"Tell her we'll talk about that once we've seen the merchandise," said Mr. Alice. He wasn't panting, and if there was the faintest tremble in his voice, it was from anticipation.

Mr. Alice has fucked, to my personal knowledge, half a brat-pack of the leading male movie stars of the last two decades, and more male models than you could shake your kit at; he's had the prettiest boys on five continents; none of them knew precisely who they were being fucked by, and all of them were very well paid for their trouble.

At the top of the house, up a final flight of uncarpeted wooden stairs, was the door to the attic, and flanking each side of the door, like twin tree trunks, was a huge woman in a black gown. Each of them looked like she could have held her own against a sumo wrestler. Each of them held, I kid you not, a scimitar: they were guarding the Treasure of the Shahinai. And they stank like old horses. Even in the gloom, I could see that their robes were patched and stained.

The Mother Superior strode up to them, a squirrel facing up to a couple of pit bulls, and I looked at their impassive faces and wondered where they originally came from. They could have been Samoan or Mongolian, could have been pulled from a freak farm in Turkey or India or Iran.

On a word from the old woman they stood aside from the door, and I pushed it open. It wasn't locked. I looked inside, in case of trouble, walked in, looked around, and gave the all-clear. So I was the first male in this generation to gaze upon the Treasure of the Shahinai.

He was kneeling beside a camp bed, his head bowed.

Legendary is a good word to use for the Shahinai. It means I'd never heard of them and didn't know anyone who had, and once I started looking for them even the people who had heard of them didn't believe in them.

"After all, my good friend," my pet Russian academic said, handing over his report, "you're talking about a race of people the sole evidence for the existence of which is half a dozen lines in Herodotus, a poem in the *Thousand and One Nights,* and a speech in the *Manuscrit Trouvé à Saragosse.* Not what we call reliable sources."

But rumors had reached Mr. Alice and he got interested. And what Mr. Alice wants, I make damned sure that Mr. Alice gets. Right now, looking at the Treasure of the Shahinai, Mr. Alice looked so happy I thought his face would break in two.

The boy stood up. There was a chamber pot half sticking out from beneath the bed, with a cupful of vivid yellow piss in the bottom of it. His robe was white cotton, thin and very clean. He wore blue silk slippers.

It was so hot in that room. Two gas fires were burning, one on each side of the attic, with a low hissing sound. The boy didn't seem to feel the heat. Professor Macleod began to sweat profusely.

According to legend, the boy in the white robe—he was seventeen at a guess, no more than eighteen—was the most beautiful man in the world. I could easily believe it.

Mr. Alice walked over to the boy, and he inspected him like a farmer checking out a calf at the market: peering into his mouth, tasting the boy, and looking at the lad's eyes and his ears; taking his hands and examining his fingers and fingernails; and then, matter-of-factly, lifting up his white robe and inspecting his uncircumcised cock before turning him round and checking out the state of his arse.

And through it all the boy's eyes and teeth shone white and joyous in his face.

Finally Mr. Alice pulled the boy toward him and kissed him, slowly and gently, on the lips. He pulled back, ran his tongue around his mouth, nodded. Turned to Macleod. "Tell her we'll take him," said Mr. Alice.

Professor Macleod said something to the Mother Superior, and her face broke into wrinkles of cinnamon happiness. Then she put out her hands.

"She wants to be paid now," said Macleod.

I put my hands, slowly, into the inside pockets of my mac and pulled out first one, then two black velvet pouches. I handed them both to her. Each bag contained fifty flawless D or E grade diamonds, perfectly cut, each in excess of five carats. Most of them picked up cheaply from Russia in the mid-nineties. One hundred diamonds: forty million dollars. The old woman tipped a few into her palm and prodded at them with her finger. Then she put the diamonds back into the bag, and she nodded.

The bags vanished into her robes, and she went to the top of the stairs and as loud as she could, she shouted something in her strange language.

From all through the house below us there came a wailing, like from a horde of banshees. The wailing continued as we walked downstairs through that gloomy labyrinth, with the young man in the white robe in the lead. It honestly made the hairs on the back of my neck prickle, that wailing, and the stink of wet-rot and spices made me gag. I fucking hate foreigners.

The women wrapped him up in a couple of blankets before they would let him out of the house, worried that he'd catch some kind of a chill despite the blazing July sunshine. We bundled him into the car.

I got a ride with them as far as the tube, and I went on from there.

I spent the next day, which was Wednesday, dealing with a mess in Moscow. Too many fucking cowboys. I was praying I could sort things out without having to personally go out there: the food gives me constipation.

As I get older, I like to travel less and less, and I was never keen on it in the first place. But I can still be hands-on whenever I need to be. I remember when Mr. Alice said that he was afraid that Maxwell was going to have to be removed from the playing field. I told him I was doing it myself, and I didn't want to hear another word about it. Maxwell had always been a loose cannon. Little fish with a big mouth and a rotten attitude.

Most satisfying splash I've ever heard.

By Wednesday night I was tense as a couple of wigwams, so I called a bloke I know, and they brought Jenny over to my flat in the Barbican. That put me in a good mood. She's a good girl, Jenny. Nothing sluttish about her at all. Minds her P's and Q's.

I was very gentle with her, that night, and afterward I slipped her a twenty-pound note.

"But you don't need to," she said. "It's all taken care of."

"Buy yourself something mad," I told her. "It's mad money." And I ruffled her hair, and she smiled like a schoolgirl.

Thursday I got a call from Mr. Alice's secretary to say that everything was satisfactory and I should pay off Professor Macleod.

We were putting him up in the Savoy. Now, most people would have taken the tube to Charing Cross, or to Embankment, and walked up the Strand to the Savoy. Not me. I took the tube to Waterloo station and walked north over Waterloo Bridge. It's a couple of minutes longer, but you can't beat the view.

When I was a kid, one of the kids in the dorm told me that if you held your breath all the way to the middle of a bridge over the Thames and you made a wish there, the wish would always come true. I've never had anything to wish for, so I do it as a breathing exercise.

I stopped at the call box at the bottom of Waterloo Bridge. (BUSTY SCHOOLGIRLS NEED DISCIPLINE. TIE ME UP TIE ME DOWN. NEW BLONDE IN TOWN.) I phoned Macleod's room at the Savoy. Told him to come and meet me on the bridge.

His suit was, if anything, a louder check than the one he'd worn on Tuesday. He gave me a buff envelope filled with word-processed pages: a sort of homemade Shahinai-English phrase book. *"Are you hungry?" "You must bathe now." "Open your mouth."* Anything Mr. Alice might need to communicate.

I put the envelope in the pocket of my mac.

"Fancy a spot of sightseeing?" I asked, and Professor Macleod said it was always good to see a city with a native.

"This work is a philological oddity and a linguistic delight," said Macleod as we walked along the Embankment. "The Shahinai speak a language that has points in common with both the Aramaic and the Finno-Ugric family of languages. It's the language that Christ might have spoken if he'd written the epistle to the primitive Estonians. Very few loanwords, for that matter. I have a theory that they must have been forced to make quite a few abrupt departures in their time. Do you have my payment on you?"

I nodded. Took out my old calf-skin wallet from my jacket pocket and pulled out a slip of brightly colored card. "Here you go."

We were coming up to Blackfriars Bridge. "It's real?"

"Sure. New York State Lottery. You bought it on a whim, in the airport, on your way to England. The numbers'll be picked on Saturday night. Should be a pretty good week, too. It's over twenty million dollars already."

He put the lottery ticket in his own wallet, black and shiny and bulging with plastic, and he put the wallet into the inside pocket of his suit. His hands kept straying to it, brushing it, absently making sure it was still there. He'd have been the perfect mark for any dip who wanted to know where he kept his valuables.

"This calls for a drink," he said. I agreed that it did, but, as I pointed out to him, a day like today, with the sun shining and a fresh breeze coming in from the sea, was too good to waste in a pub. So we went into an off-license. I bought him a bottle of Stoli, a carton of orange juice and a plastic cup, and I got myself a couple of cans of Guinness.

"It's the men, you see," said the Professor. We were sitting on a wooden bench looking at the South Bank across the Thames. "Apparently there aren't many of them. One or two in a generation. The Treasure of the Shahinai. The women are the guardians of the men. They nurture them and keep them safe.

"Alexander the Great is said to have bought a lover from the Shahinai. So did Tiberius, and at least two Popes. Catherine the Great was rumored to have had one, but I think it's just a rumor."

I told him I thought it was like something in a storybook. "I mean, think about it. A race of people whose only asset is the beauty of their men. So every century they sell one of their men for enough money to keep the tribe going for another hundred years." I took a swig of the Guinness. "Do you think that was all of the tribe, the women in that house?"

"I rather doubt it."

He poured another slug of vodka into the plastic cup, splashed some orange juice into it, raised his glass to me. "Mr. Alice," he said. "He must be very rich."

"He does all right."

"I'm straight," said Macleod, drunker than he thought he was, his forehead prickling with sweat, "but I'd fuck that boy like a shot. He was the most beautiful thing I've ever seen."

"He was all right, I suppose."

"You wouldn't fuck him?"

"Not my cup of tea," I told him.

A black cab went down the road behind us; its orange For Hire light was turned off, although there was nobody sitting in the back.

"So what is your cup of tea, then?" asked Professor Macleod.

"Little girls," I told him.

He swallowed. "How little?"

"Nine. Ten. Eleven or twelve, maybe. Once they've got real tits and pubes I can't get it up anymore. Just doesn't do it for me."

He looked at me as if I'd told him I liked to fuck dead dogs, and he didn't say anything for a bit. He drank his Stoli. "You know," he said, "back where I come from, that sort of thing would be illegal."

"Well, they aren't too keen on it over here."

"I think maybe I ought to be getting back to the hotel," he said.

A black cab came around the corner, its lights on this time. I waved it down and helped Professor Macleod into the back. It was one of our Particular Cabs. The kind you get into and you don't get out of.

"The Savoy, please," I told the cabbie.

"Righto, governor," he said, and took Professor Macleod away.

Mr. Alice took good care of the Shahinai boy. Whenever I went over for meetings or briefings the boy would be sitting at Mr. Alice's feet, and Mr. Alice would be twining and stroking and fiddling with his black-black hair. They doted on each other, you could tell. It was soppy and, I have to admit, even for a coldhearted bastard like myself, it was touching.

Sometimes, at night, I'd have dreams about the Shahinai women—these ghastly, batlike, hag-things, fluttering and roosting through this huge rotting old house, which was, at the same time, both Human History and St. Andrew's Asylum. Some of them were carrying men between them as they flapped and flew. The men shone like the sun, and their faces were too beautiful to look upon.

I hated those dreams. One of them, and the next day was a write-off, and you can take that to the fucking bank.

The most beautiful man in the world, the Treasure of the Shahinai, lasted for eight months. Then he caught the flu.

His temperature went up to 106 degrees, and his lungs filled with water and he was drowning on dry land. Mr. Alice brought in some of the best doctors in the world, but the lad just flickered and went out like an old lightbulb, and that was that.

I suppose they just aren't very strong. Bred for something else, after all, not strength.

Mr. Alice took it really hard. He was inconsolable—wept like a baby all the way through the funeral, tears running down his face, like a mother who had just lost her only son. It was pissing with rain, so if you weren't standing next to him, you'd not have known. I ruined a perfectly good pair of shoes in that graveyard, and it put me in a rotten mood.

I sat around in the Barbican flat, practiced knife throwing, cooked a spaghetti bolognaise, watched some football on the telly.

That night I had Alison. It wasn't pleasant.

The next day I took a few good men and we went down to the house in Earls Court to see if any of the Shahinai were still about. There had to be more Shahinai young men somewhere. It stood to reason.

But the plaster on the rotting walls had been covered up with stolen rock posters, and the place smelled of dope, not spice.

The warren of rooms was filled with Australians and New Zealanders. Squatters, at a guess. We surprised a dozen of them in the kitchen sucking narcotic smoke from the mouth of a broken R. White's Lemonade bottle.

We searched the house from cellar to attic, looking for some trace of the Shahinai women, something that they had left behind, some kind of clue, anything that would make Mr. Alice happy.

We found nothing at all.

And all I took away from the house in Earls Court was the memory of the breast of a girl, stoned and oblivious, sleeping naked in an upper room. There were no curtains on the window.

I stood in the doorway, and I looked at her for too long, and it painted itself on my mind: a full, black-nippled breast, which curved disturbingly in the sodium-yellow light of the street.

T. E. D. Klein

GROWING THINGS

Though he might deny it, T. E. D. Klein is something of a legendary—
and enigmatic—figure. His legendary status was established in a rush
in the 1980s; he was the first editor of the slick newsstand magazine
The Twilight Zone *even while he was distinguishing himself with*
such stunning stories as "Children of the Kingdom" and "Petey." In
1984 came his eagerly awaited novel The Ceremonies, *which was*
virtuosic in its execution and firmly established Klein in the top
pantheon of horror writers. The novel was followed in 1985 by Dark
Gods, *which collected the two stories already mentioned with two other*
long pieces.

Since that amazing torrent of work, T. E. D. Klein has been
quieter, but not quiet. The following story is both a treat and a pleasure
to present.

"**H**ey, honey, listen to this one. It's downright scary."

The magazine, drawn from near the middle of the pile, was yellowed, musty-smelling. Herb licked his lips with a fat tongue and squinted at the page with the corner turned down. " 'Dear Mr. Fixit: Early this spring a peculiar roundish bulge appeared under the linoleum in my bathroom, and now with the warm weather it's beginning to get larger, as if something is sprouting under there. My husband, who is not well, almost tripped over it yesterday. What is it, some sort of fungus? How can I get rid of it without having to rip up the linoleum? As we cannot afford expensive new flooring, we are relying on you.' Signed, 'Anxious.' "

"I shouldn't wonder she was anxious," said Iris from her cloud of lemon oil and beeswax. She'd been giving the old end table a vigorous polishing and was slightly out of breath. "Who wants to share their bathroom with a bunch of toadstools?"

"Don't worry, Fixit's got it under control. 'Dear Anxious: Sounds as if you have a pocket of moisture trapped between the floorboards and the linoleum. Often a damp basement is the culprit. Simply drill a hole up from the basement to release the moisture buildup, then seal the area with flash patch or creosote.' " Herb rubbed his chin. "Sounds simple enough to me."

"Not in *this* house."

"What do you mean?"

"We don't have a basement, remember? You'd have to get down on your belly and slither beneath the house, with all that muck down there."

"Hah, you're right! Certainly wouldn't want to do that!" Herb's stomach shook as he laughed. "Thank God the damned bathroom's new."

In fact, the bathroom, clean and professionally tiled, was one of the things that had sold them on the house. Herb liked long showers, and Iris—who, unlike Herb's first wife, had never had to make time for children—was given to leisurely soaks in the tub.

The rest of the place was in, at best, an indifferent state of repair. The rain gutters sagged, the windows needed caulking, and, if the house were to serve as anything more than a summer retreat from the city, the ancient coal-burning furnace in an alcove behind the kitchen would have to be replaced. Eventually, too, they'd have to add more rooms; at present the house was just a bungalow, a single floor of living space crowned by a not-too-well-insulated attic littered with rolls of cotton wadding, damaged furniture, and other bric-a-brac abandoned by the former owners. Who these owners were was uncertain; clearly the place hadn't been lived in for years, and—though the real estate lady had denied it—it had probably been on the market for most of that time.

The two of them, of course, had hoped for something better; they were, in their way, a pair of midlife romantics. But Herb's alimony payments and an unexpected drubbing from the IRS this April had forced them to be practical. Besides, they had three acres' worth of woods, and stars they could never have seen from the city, and bullfrogs chanting feverishly in the marsh behind the house. They had an old woodshed, a swaybacked garage that had once been a barn, and a sunken area near the forest's edge, overgrown with mushrooms and moss, that the real estate lady assured them had been a garden. They had each other. Did the house itself need work? As Herb had said airily when a skeptical friend asked if he knew anything about home repair, "Well, I know how to write a check."

Secretly he nourished the ambition of doing the work himself. Though he had barely picked up a hammer since he'd knocked together bookends for his parents in a high school shop class, he felt certain that a few carefully selected repair manuals and a short course of *This Old House* would see him through. If fate had steered him and Iris toward that creature of jest, the "handyman special," well, so be it. He would simply learn to be a handyman.

And fate, for once, had seemed to agree; for, among the artifacts left by the previous owners was a bookshelf stacked high with old magazines.

Actually, not all that old—from the late 1970s, in fact—but the humidity had aged them, so that they had taken on the fragile, jaundiced look of magazines from decades earlier. Iris had wanted to throw them away—"Those moldy old things," she'd said, curling her lip, "they smell of mildew. We'll fill up the shelves with books from local yard sales"—but Herb refused to hear of it. "They're perfect for a country house," he had said. "I mean, just look at this. *Home Handyman. Practical Gardener. Growing Things Organically. Modern Health.* Perfect rainy day reading."

Luckily for Herb, there were lots of rainy days in this part of the world, because after three months of homeowning it had become clear that reading do-it-yourself columns such as "Mr. Fixit"—a regular feature in *Home Handyman* magazine—was a good deal more fun than actually fixing anything. He'd enjoyed shopping for tools and had turned a corner of the garage into a rudimentary workshop; but now that the tools gleamed from their hooks on the wall and the necessary work space had been cleared, his enthusiasm had waned.

In fact, a certain lassitude had settled upon them both. Maybe it was the dampness. This was, by all accounts, one of the wettest summers on record; each week the local pennysaver sagged in their hands as they pulled it from the mailbox, and a book of stamps that Iris bought had long since stuck together. Dollars had grown limp in Herb's wallet. Today, with the summer sky once more threatening storms, he lay aside the *Handyman* and spent the afternoon with his nose buried in a back issue of *Country Kitchen,* while Iris, unable to transform an end table from the attic into something that passed for an antique, put away her beeswax and retreated to the bedroom for a nap.

It was growing dark by the time she awoke. Clouds covered the sky, but the rain had not come. Despite the afternoon's inactivity, they were both too tired to cook; instead they had dinner by candlelight at a roadside inn, along a desolate stretch of highway several miles beyond the town. They toasted one another's health and wished that they were just a few years younger.

The house felt chilly when they returned; the air seemed thick with moisture. They'd already had to buy themselves wool mattress pads to keep their sheets from growing clammy. Tonight, to take the dampness off, Herb built a fire, carefully examining the logs he carried inside for spiders and insects that could drop off and infest the house. He remembered a line he'd seen in *Practical Gardener,* something about being constantly on watch for "the blight on the peach and the worm in the rosebud."

This evening, though, it was *Home Handyman* that drew him back. He'd started weeks before with the older issues at the bottom of the pile and had steadily been working his way up. While on the couch Iris yawned over a contemporary romance, he engrossed himself in articles on wood-stove safety, building a patio, and—something he was glad he'd never have to worry about—pumping out a flooded basement.

The issue he'd just pulled out, from the top half of the pile, was less yellowed than the ones before. "Here's a letter," he announced, "from a man who's had trouble removing a tree stump next to his house. Mr. Fixit says he'd better get rid of it fast, or it'll attract termites." Herb shook his head. "Christ, you can't let down your guard for a second out here. And here's one from a man who built a chimney but didn't seal it properly." He chuckled. "The damn fool! Filled his attic with smoke." He eyed their fireplace speculatively, but it looked solid and substantial, the flames merry. He turned back to the magazine. The next page had the corner folded down. "Some guy asks about oil stains on a concrete floor. Mr. Fixit recommends a mixture of cream of tartar and something called 'oxalic acid.' How the hell are you supposed to find . . . Hey, listen to this, here's another one from that same woman who wrote in before. 'Dear Mr. Fixit: The advice you gave me previously, on getting rid of bulges under the linoleum in my bathroom by drilling up from the basement, was of little use, as we have no basement, and due to an incapacity my husband and I are unable to make our way beneath the house. The bulges—' "

Iris looked up from her book. "Before it was just *one* bulge."

"Well, hon," he said, thinking of her in the tub, "you know how it is with bulges." He made sure he saw her smile before turning back to the column. " 'The bulges have grown larger, and there's a definite odor coming from them. What should we do?' Signed, 'Still Anxious.' "

"That poor woman!" said Iris. She stretched and settled back into the cushions. "You don't suppose it could be radon, do you?"

"No, he says they may have something called 'wood bloat.' " Herb shuddered, savoring the phrase. " 'Forget about preserving the linoleum,' he says. 'Drill two holes deep into the center of the bulges and carefully pour in a solution of equal parts baking soda, mineral spirits, and vanilla extract. If that doesn't do the trick, I'd advise you to seek professional help.' "

"She should have done that in the first place," said Iris. "I'd love to know how she made out."

"Me, too," said Herb. "Let's see if the story's continued."

He flipped through the next few months of *Home Handyman*. There were leaky stovepipes, backed-up drains, and decaying roofs, but no mention of the bulges. From the couch came a soft bump as Iris lay back and let the book drop to the rug. Her eyes closed; her mouth went slack. Watching her stomach rise and fall in the firelight, he felt suddenly and peculiarly alone.

From outside came the whisper of rain—normally a peaceful sound, but tonight a troubling one; he could picture the land around the house, and beneath it, becoming a place of marsh and stagnant water, where God knows what might grow. The important thing, he knew, was to keep the bottom of the house raised above the ground, or else dampness would rot the timbers. Surely the crawl space under his feet was ample protection from the wetness; still, he wished that the house had a basement.

Softly, so as not to wake his wife, he tiptoed into the bathroom—still smelling pleasantly of paint and varnish—and stared pensively at the floor. For a moment, alarmed, he thought he noticed a hairline crack between two of the new tiles, where the floor was slightly uneven between the toilet and the shower stall; but the light was bad in here, and the crack had probably been there all along.

By the time he returned to the front room, the fire was beginning to go out. He'd have liked to add more wood, but he didn't want to risk waking Iris. Seating himself back on the rug with a pile of magazines beside him, he continued his search through the remaining issues of *Home Handyman,* right up till the point, more than three years in the past, when the issues stopped. He found no further updates from "Anxious"; he wasn't sure whether he was disappointed or relieved. The latter, he supposed; things must have come out okay.

The issues of *Handyman* were replaced by a pile, only slightly less yellowed and slightly less substantial, of *Modern Health,* with, predictably, its own advice column, this one conducted by a "Dr. Carewell." Shingles on roofs were succeeded by shingles on faces and legs; the cracked plaster and rotting baseboards gave way to hay fever and thinning hair.

"I have an enormous bunion on my right foot," one letter began, with a trace of pride. "I have a hernia that was left untreated," said another. Readers complained of plantar warts, aching backs, and coughs that wouldn't quit. It was like owning a home, Herb thought; you had to be constantly vigilant. Sooner or later, something always gave way and the rot seeped in. "Dear Dr. Carewell," one letter began, where the page corner had been turned down, "My husband and I are both increasingly incapacitated by a rash that has left large rose-red blotches all over our bodies. Could it be some sort of fungus? There is no pain or itching, but odd little bumps have begun to appear in the center." It was signed "Bedridden."

All this talk of breakdown and disease was depressing, and the mention of bed had made him tired. The fire had almost gone out. Glancing at the doctor's reply—it was cheerily reassuring, something about plenty of exercise and good organic vegetables—he got slowly to his feet. From another room came the creak of wood as the old house settled in for the night.

Iris snored softly on the couch. She looked so peaceful that he hated to wake her, but he knew she'd fall asleep again soon; the two of them always slept well, out here in the country. "Come on, hon," he whispered. "Bedtime." The sound of the rain no longer troubled him as he bent toward her, brushed back her hair, and tenderly planted a kiss on her cheek, rosy in the dying light.

F. Paul Wilson

◈

GOOD FRIDAY

F. Paul Wilson was paid more for his story in this book than for his first two novels with Doubleday in the 1970s. I know because he told me so, and also because I was at Doubleday at the time, and might even, though I thankfully don't remember, have ordered up the paltry checks for him.

How things have changed! Doubleday no longer cranks out two cheap hardcover science fiction novels a month, presold to schools and libraries (ah, cheap in price and production though they were, almost everyone involved loved them, and the line produced such classics in the horror field alone as the Shadows series, the Whispers anthologies, and the World Fantasy Award books), and F. Paul Wilson now writes highly acclaimed medical thrillers such as Deep as the Marrow, *as well as continuing to work in his first loves, the science fiction and horror fields (*Legacies, *a new Repairman Jack novel, appeared in 1997, fourteen years after the first one,* The Tomb*).*

For this book, he has produced something I very much wanted—a traditional vampire story.

"The Holy Father says there are no such things as vampires," Sister Bernadette Gileen said.

Sister Carole Hanarty glanced up from the pile of chemistry tests on her lap—tests she might never be able to return to her sophomore students—and watched Bernadette as she drove through town, working the shift on the old Datsun like a long-haul trucker. Her dear friend and fellow Sister of Mercy was thin, almost painfully so, with large blue eyes and short red hair showing around the white band of her wimple. As she peered through the windshield, the light of the setting sun ruddied the clear, smooth skin of her round face.

"If His Holiness said it, then we must believe it," Sister Carole said. "But we haven't heard anything from him in so long. I hope . . . ."

Bernadette turned toward her, eyes wide with alarm.

"Oh, you wouldn't be thinking anything's happened to His Holiness now, would you, Carole?" she said, the lilt of her native Ireland elbowing its way into her voice. "They wouldn't dare!"

Carole was momentarily at a loss as to what to say, so she gazed out the side window at the budding trees sliding past. The sidewalks of this little Jersey Shore town were empty, and hardly any other cars on the road. She and Bernadette had had to try three grocery stores before finding one with anything to sell. Between the hoarders and delayed or canceled shipments, food was getting scarce.

Everybody sensed it. How did that saying go? By pricking in my thumbs, something wicked this way comes . . .

Or something like that.

She rubbed her cold hands together and thought about Bernadette, younger than she by five years—only twenty-six—with such a good mind, such a clear thinker in so many ways. But her faith was almost childlike.

She'd come to the convent at St. Anthony's two years ago, and the two of them had established instant rapport. They shared so much. Not just a common Irish heritage, but a certain isolation as well. Carole's parents had died years ago, and Bernadette's were back on the Old Sod. So they became sisters in a sense that went beyond their sisterhood in the order. Carole was the big sister, Bernadette the little one. They prayed together, laughed together, walked together. They took over the convent kitchen and did all the food shopping together. Carole could only hope that she had enriched Bernadette's life half as much as the younger woman had enriched hers.

Bernadette was such an innocent. She seemed to assume that since the Pope was infallible when he spoke on matters of faith or morals he somehow must be invincible too.

Carole hadn't told Bernadette, but she'd decided not to believe the Pope on the matter of the undead. After all, their existence was not a matter of faith or morals. Either they existed or they didn't. And all the news out of Eastern Europe last fall had left little doubt that vampires were real.

And that they were on the march.

Somehow they had got themselves organized. Not only did they exist, but more of them had been hiding in Eastern Europe than even the most superstitious peasant could have imagined. And when the communist bloc crumbled, when all the former client states and Russia were in disarray, grabbing for land, slaughtering in the name of nation and race and religion, the vampires took advantage of the power vacuum and struck.

They struck high, they struck low, and before the rest of the world could react, they controlled all Eastern Europe.

If they had merely killed, they might have been containable. But because each kill was a conversion, their numbers increased in a geometric progression. Sister Carole understood geometric progressions better than most. Hadn't she spent years demonstrating them to her chemistry class by dropping a seed crystal into a beaker of supersaturated solution? That one crystal became two, which became four, which became eight, which became sixteen, and so on. You could watch the lattices forming, slowly at first, then bridging through the solution with increasing speed until the liquid contents of the beaker became a solid mass of crystals.

That was how it had gone in Eastern Europe, then spreading into Russia and into Western Europe.

The vampires became unstoppable.

All of Europe had been silent for months. Officially, at least. But a couple of the students at St. Anthony's High who had shortwave radios had told Carole of faint transmissions filtering through the transatlantic night recounting ghastly horrors all across Europe under vampire rule.

But the Pope had declared there were no vampires. He'd said it, but shortly thereafter he and the Vatican had fallen silent along with the rest of Europe.

Washington had played down the immediate threat, saying the Atlantic Ocean formed a natural barrier against the undead. Europe was quarantined. America was safe.

Then came reports, disputed at first, and still officially denied, of vampires in New York City. Most of the New York TV and radio stations had stopped transmitting last week. And now . . .

"You can't really believe vampires are coming into New Jersey, can you?" Bernadette said. "I mean, that is, if there were such things."

"It is hard to believe, isn't it?" Carole said, hiding a smile. "Especially since no one comes to Jersey unless they have to."

"Oh, don't you be having on with me now. This is serious."

Bernadette was right. It was serious. "Well, it fits the pattern my students have heard from Europe."

"But dear God, 'tis Holy Week! 'Tis Good Friday, it is! How could they dare?"

"It's the perfect time, if you think about it. There will be no mass said until the first Easter Mass on Sunday morning. What other time of the year is daily mass suspended?"

Bernadette shook her head. "None."

"Exactly." Carole looked down at her cold hands and felt the chill crawl all the way up her arms.

The car suddenly lurched to a halt and she heard Bernadette cry out, "Dear Jesus! They're already here!"

Half a dozen black-clad forms clustered on the corner ahead, staring at them.

"Got to get out of here!" Bernadette said, and hit the gas.

The old car coughed and died.

"Oh, no!" Bernadette wailed, frantically pumping the gas pedal and turning the key as the dark forms glided toward them. "No!"

"Easy, dear," Carole said, laying a gentle hand on her arm. "It's all right. They're just kids."

Perhaps "kids" was not entirely correct. Two males and four females who looked to be in their late teens and early twenties, but carried any number of adult lifetimes behind their heavily made-up eyes. Grinning, leering, they gathered around the car, four on Bernadette's side and two on Carole's. Sallow faces made paler by a layer of white powder, kohl-crusted eyelids, and black lipstick. Black fingernails, rings in their ears and eyebrows and nostrils, chrome studs piercing cheeks and lips. Their hair ranged the color spectrum, from dead white through burgundy to crankcase black. Bare hairless chests on the boys under their leather jackets, almost-bare chests on the girls in their black push-up bras and bustiers. Boots of shiny leather or vinyl, fishnet stockings, layer upon layer of lace, and everything black, black, black.

"Hey, look!" one of the boys said. A spiked leather collar girded his throat, acne lumps bulged under his whiteface. "Nuns!"

"Penguins!" someone else said.

Apparently this was deemed hilarious. The six of them screamed with laughter.

We're *not* penguins, Carole thought. She hadn't worn a full habit in years. Only the headpiece.

"Shit, are *they* gonna be in for a surprise tomorrow morning!" said a buxom girl wearing a silk top hat.

Another roar of laughter by all except one. A tall slim girl with three large black tears tattooed down one cheek, and blond roots peeking from under her black-dyed hair, hung back, looking uncomfortable. Carole stared at her. Something familiar there . . .

She rolled down her window. "Mary Margaret? Mary Margaret Flanagan, is that you?"

More laughter. " 'Mary Margaret'?" someone cried. "That's Wicky!"

The girl stepped forward and looked Carole in the eye. "Yes, sister. That used to be my name. But I'm not Mary Margaret anymore."

"I can see that."

She remembered Mary Margaret. A sweet girl, extremely bright, but so quiet. A voracious reader who never seemed to fit in with the rest of the kids. Her grades plummeted as a junior. She never returned for her senior year. When Carole had called her parents, she was told that Mary Margaret had left home. She'd been unable to learn anything more.

"You've changed a bit since I last saw you. What is it—three years now?"

"You talk about *change?*" said the top-hatted girl, sticking her face in the window. "Wait'll tonight. Then you'll *really* see her change!" She brayed a laugh that revealed a chromed stud in her tongue.

"Butt out, Carmilla!" Mary Margaret said.

Carmilla ignored her. "They're coming tonight, you know. The Lords of the Night will be arriving after sunset, and that'll spell the death of your world and the birth of ours. We will present ourselves to them, we will bare our throats and let them drain us, and then we'll join them. Then we will rule the night with them!"

It sounded like a canned speech, one she must have delivered time and again to her black-clad troupe.

Carole looked past Carmilla to Mary Margaret. "Is that what you believe? Is that what you really want?"

The girl shrugged her high thin shoulders. "Beats anything else I got going."

Finally the old Datsun shuddered to life. Carole heard Bernadette working the shift. She touched her arm and said, "Wait. Just one more moment, please."

She was about to speak to Mary Margaret when Carmilla jabbed her finger at Carole's face, shouting.

"Then you bitches and the candy-ass god you whore for will be fucking extinct!"

With a surprising show of strength, Mary Margaret yanked Carmilla away from the window.

"Better go, Sister Carole," Mary Margaret said.

The Datsun started to move.

"What the fuck's with you, Wicky?" Carole heard Carmilla scream as the car eased away from the dark cluster. "Getting religion or somethin'? Should we start callin' you 'Sister Mary Margaret' now?"

"She was one of the few people who was ever straight with me," Mary Margaret said. "So fuck off, Carmilla."

The car had traveled too far to hear more.

"What awful creatures they were!" Bernadette said, staring out the window in Carole's room. She hadn't been able to stop talking about the incident on the street. "Almost my age, they were, and such horrible language!"

Her convent room was little more than a ten-by-ten-foot plaster box with cracks in the walls and the latest coat of paint beginning to flake off the ancient embossed tin ceiling. She had one window, a crucifix, a dresser and mirror, a worktable and chair, a bed, and a nightstand as furnishings. Not much, but she gladly called it home. She took her vow of poverty seriously.

"Perhaps we should pray for them."

"They need more than prayer, I'd think. Believe me you, they're heading for a bad end." Bernadette removed the oversized rosary she wore looped around her neck, gathering the beads and its attached crucifix in her hand. "Maybe we could offer them some crosses for protection?"

Carole couldn't resist a smile. "That's a sweet thought, Bern, but I don't think they're looking for protection."

"Sure, and lookit after what I'm saying," Bernadette said, her own smile rueful. "No, of course they wouldn't."

"But we'll pray for them," Carole said.

Bernadette dropped into a chair, stayed there for no more than a heartbeat, then was up again, moving about, pacing the confines of Carole's room. She couldn't seem to sit still. She wandered out into the hall and came back almost immediately, rubbing her hands together as if washing them. ·

"It's so quiet," she said. "So empty."

"I certainly hope so," Carole said. "We're the only two who are supposed to be here."

The little convent was half empty even when all its residents were present. And now, with St. Anthony's School closed for the coming week, the rest of the nuns had gone home to spend Easter Week with brothers and sisters and parents. Even those who might have stayed around the convent in past years had heard the rumors that the undead might be moving this way, so they'd scattered south and west. Carole's only living relative was a brother who lived in California, and he hadn't invited her; even if he had, she couldn't afford to fly there and back to Jersey just for Easter. Bernadette hadn't heard from her family in Ireland for months.

So that left just the two of them to hold the fort, as it were.

Carole wasn't afraid. She knew they'd be safe here at St. Anthony's. The convent was part of a complex consisting of the church itself, the rectory, the grammar school and high school buildings, and the sturdy old, two-story rooming house that was now the convent. She and Bernadette had taken second-floor rooms, leaving the first floor to the older nuns.

Not *really* afraid, although she wished there were more people left in the complex than just Bernadette, herself, and Father Palmeri.

"I don't understand Father Palmeri," Bernadette said. "Locking up the church and keeping his parishioners from making the stations of the cross on Good Friday. Who's ever heard of such a thing, I ask you? I just don't understand it."

Carole thought she understood. She suspected that Father Alberto Palmeri was afraid. Sometime this morning he'd locked up the rectory, barred the door to St. Anthony's, and hidden himself in the church basement.

God forgive her, but to Sister Carole's mind, Father Palmeri was a coward.

"Oh, I do wish he'd open the church, just for a little while," Bernadette said. "I need to be in there, Carole. I *need* it."

Carole knew how Bern felt. Who had said religion was an opiate of the people? Marx? Whoever it was, he hadn't been completely wrong. For Carole, sitting in the cool, peaceful quiet beneath St. Anthony's gothic arches, praying, meditating, and feeling the presence of the Lord were like a daily dose of an addictive drug. A dose she and Bern had been denied today. Bern's withdrawal pangs seemed worse than Carole's.

The younger nun paused as she passed the window, then pointed down to the street.

"And now who in God's name would they be?"

Carole rose and stepped to the window. Passing on the street below was a cavalcade of shiny new cars—Mercedes Benzes, BMWs, Jaguars, Lincolns, Cadillacs—all with New York plates, all cruising from the direction of the parkway.

The sight of them in the dusk tightened a knot in Carole's stomach. The lupine faces she spied through the windows looked brutish, and the way they drove their gleaming luxury cars down the center line . . . as if they owned the road.

A Cadillac convertible with its top down passed below, carrying four scruffy men. The driver wore a cowboy hat, the two in the back sat atop the rear seat, drinking beer. When Carole saw one of them glance up and look their way, she tugged on Bern's sleeve.

"Stand back! Don't let them see you!"

"Why not? Who are they?"

"I'm not sure, but I've heard of bands of men who do the vampires' dirty work during the daytime, who've traded their souls for the promise of immortality later on, and for . . . other things now."

"Sure and you're joking, Carole!"

Carole shook her head. "I wish I were."

"Oh, dear God, and now the sun's down." She turned frightened blue eyes toward Carole. "Do you think maybe we should . . . ?"

"Lock up? Most certainly. I know what His Holiness said about there not being any such thing as vampires, but maybe he's changed his mind since then and just can't get word to us."

"Sure and you're probably right. You close these and I'll check down the hall." She hurried out, her voice trailing behind her. "Oh, I do wish Father Palmeri hadn't locked the church. I'd dearly love to say a few prayers there."

Sister Carole glanced out the window again. The fancy new cars were gone, but rumbling in their wake was a convoy of trucks—big, eighteen-wheel semis, lumbering down the center line. What were they for? What did they carry? What were they delivering to town?

Suddenly a dog began to bark, and then another, and more and more until it seemed as if every dog in town was giving voice.

To fight the unease rising within her like a flood tide, Sister Carole concentrated on the simple manual tasks of closing and locking her window and drawing the curtains.

But the dread remained, a sick, cold certainty that the world was falling into darkness, that the creeping hem of shadow had reached her corner of the globe, and that without some miracle, without some direct intervention by a wrathful God, the coming night hours would wreak an irrevocable change on her life.

She began to pray for that miracle.

*   *   *

The two remaining sisters decided to keep the convent of St. Anthony's dark tonight.

And they decided to spend the night together in Carole's room. They dragged in Bernadette's mattress, locked the door, and double-draped the window with the bedspread. They lit the room with a single candle and prayed together.

Yet the music of the night filtered through the walls and the doors and the drapes, the muted moan of sirens singing antiphon to their hymns, the muffled pops of gunfire punctuating their psalms, reaching a crescendo shortly after midnight, then tapering off to . . . silence.

Carole could see that Bernadette was having an especially rough time of it. She cringed with every siren wail, jumped at every shot. She shared Bern's terror, but she buried it, hid it deep within for her friend's sake. After all, Carole was older, and she knew she was made of sterner stuff. Bernadette was an innocent, too sensitive even for yesterday's world, the world before the vampires. How would she survive in the world as it would be after tonight? She'd need help. Carole would provide as much as she could.

But for all the imagined horrors conjured by the night noises, the silence was worse. No human wails of pain and horror had penetrated their sanctum, but imagined cries of human suffering echoed through their minds in the ensuing stillness.

"Dear God, what's happening out there?" Bernadette said after they'd finished reading aloud the Twenty-third Psalm.

She huddled on her mattress, a blanket thrown over her shoulders. The candle's flame reflected in her frightened eyes and cast her shadow, high, hunched, and wavering, on the wall behind her.

Carole sat cross-legged on her bed. She leaned back against the wall and fought to keep her eyes open. Exhaustion was a weight on her shoulders, a cloud over her brain, but she knew sleep was out of the question. Not now, not tonight, not until the sun was up. And maybe not even then.

"Easy, Bern—" Carole began, then stopped.

From below, on the first floor of the convent, a faint thumping noise.

"What's that?" Bernadette said, voice hushed, eyes wide.

"I don't know."

Carole grabbed her robe and stepped out into the hall for a better listen.

"Don't you be leaving me alone, now!" Bernadette said, running after her with the blanket still wrapped around her shoulders.

"Hush," Carole said. "Listen. It's the front door. Someone's knocking. I'm going down to see."

She hurried down the wide, oak-railed stairway to the front foyer. The knocking was louder here, but still sounded weak. Carole put her eye to the peephole, peered through the sidelights, but saw no one.

But the knocking, weaker still, continued.

"Wh-who's there?" she said, her words cracking with fear.

"Sister Carole," came a faint voice through the door. "It's me . . . Mary Margaret. I'm hurt."

Instinctively, Carole reached for the handle, but Bernadette grabbed her arm.

"Wait! It could be a trick!"

She's right, Carole thought. Then she glanced down and saw blood leaking across the threshold from the other side.

She gasped and pointed at the crimson puddle. "That's no trick."

She unlocked the door and pulled it open. Mary Margaret huddled on the welcome mat in a pool of blood.

"Dear sweet Jesus!" Carole cried. "Help me, Bern!"

"What if she's a vampire?" Bernadette said, standing frozen. "They can't cross the threshold unless you ask them in."

"Stop that silliness! She's hurt!"

Bernadette's good heart won out over her fear. She threw off the blanket, revealing a faded-blue, ankle-length flannel nightgown that swirled just above the floppy slippers she wore. Together they dragged Mary Margaret inside. Bernadette closed and relocked the door immediately.

"Call 911!" Carole told her.

Bernadette hurried down the hall to the phone.

Mary Margaret lay moaning on the foyer tiles, clutching her bleeding abdomen. Carole saw a piece of metal, coated with rust and blood, protruding from the area of her navel. From the fecal smell of the gore Carole guessed that her intestines had been pierced.

"Oh, you poor child!" Carole knelt beside her and cradled her head in her lap. She arranged Bernadette's blanket over Mary Margaret's trembling body. "Who did this to you?"

"Accident," Mary Margaret gasped. Real tears had run her black eye makeup over her tattooed tears. "I was running . . . fell."

"Running from what?"

"From *them*. God . . . terrible. We searched for them, Carmilla's Lords of the Night. Just after sundown we found one. Looked just like we always knew he would . . . you know, tall and regal and graceful and seductive and cool. Standing by one of those big trailers that came through town. My friends approached him but I sorta stayed back. Wasn't too sure I was really into having my blood sucked. But Carmilla goes right up to him, pulling off her top and baring her throat, offering herself to him."

Mary Margaret coughed and groaned as a spasm of pain shook her.

"Don't talk," Carole said. "Save your strength."

"No," she said in a weaker voice when it eased. "You got to know. This Lord guy just smiles at Carmilla, then he signals his helpers who pull open the back doors of the trailer." Mary Margaret sobbed. "Horrible! Truck's filled with these . . . *things!* Look human but they're dirty and naked and act like beasts. They like *pour* out the truck and right off a bunch of them jump Carmilla. They start biting and ripping at her throat. I see her go down and hear her screaming and I start backing up. My other friends try to run but they're pulled down too. And then I see one of the things hold up Carmilla's head and hear the Lord guy say, 'That's right, children. Take their heads. Always take their heads. There are enough of us now.' And that's when I turned and ran. I was running through a vacant lot when I fell on . . . this."

Bernadette rushed back into the foyer. Her face was drawn with fear. "Nine-one-one doesn't answer! I can't raise anyone!"

"They're all over town," Mary Margaret said after another spasm of coughing. Carole could barely hear her. She touched her throat— so cold. "They set fires and attack the cops and firemen when they arrive. Their human helpers break into houses and drive the people outside, where they're attacked. And after the things drain the blood, they rip the heads off."

"Dear God, why?" Bernadette said, crouching beside Carole.

"My guess . . . don't want any more vampires. Maybe only so much blood to go around and—"

She moaned with another spasm, then lay still. Carole patted her cheeks and called her name, but Mary Margaret Flanagan's dull, staring eyes told it all.

"Is she . . . ?" Bernadette said.

Carole nodded as tears filled her eyes. You poor misguided child, she thought, closing Mary Margaret's eyelids.

"She's died in sin," Bernadette said. "She needs anointing immediately! I'll get Father."

"No, Bern," Carole said. "Father Palmeri won't come."

"Of course he will. He's a priest and this poor lost soul needs him."

"Trust me. He won't leave that church basement for anything."

"But he must!" she said, almost childishly, her voice rising. "He's a priest."

"Just be calm, Bernadette, and we'll pray for her ourselves."

"We can't do what a priest can do," she said, springing to her feet. "It's not the same."

"Where are you going?" Carole said.

"To . . . to get a robe. It's cold."

My poor, dear, frightened Bernadette, Carole thought as she watched her scurry up the steps. I know exactly how you feel.

"And bring your prayer book back with you," she called after her.

Carole pulled the blanket over Mary Margaret's face and gently lowered her head to the floor. She waited for Bernadette to return . . . and waited. What was taking her so long? She called her name but got no answer.

Uneasy, Carole returned to the second floor. The hallway was empty and dark except for a pale shaft of moonlight slanting through the window at its far end. Carole hurried to Bern's room. The door was closed. She knocked.

"Bern? Bern, are you in there?"

Silence.

Carole opened the door and peered inside. More moonlight, more emptiness.

Where could—?

Down on the first floor, almost directly under Carole's feet, the convent's back door slammed. How could that be? Carole had locked it herself—dead-bolted it at sunset.

Unless Bernadette had gone down the back stairs and . . .

She darted to the window and stared down at the grassy area between the convent and the church. The high, bright moon had made a black-and-white photo of the world outside, bleaching the lawn below with its stark glow, etching deep ebony wells around the shrubs and foundation plantings. It glared from St. Anthony's slate roof, stretching a long, crocketted wedge of night behind its gothic spire.

And scurrying across the lawn toward the church was a slim figure wrapped in a long raincoat, the moon picking out the white band of her wimple, its black veil a fluttering shadow along her neck and upper back—Bernadette was too old-country to approach the church with her head uncovered.

"Oh, Bern," Carole whispered, pressing her face against the glass. "Bern, don't."

She watched as Bernadette ran up to St. Anthony's side entrance and began clanking the heavy brass knocker against the thick oak door. Her high, clear voice filtered faintly through the window glass.

"Father! Father Palmeri! Please open up! There's a dead girl in the convent who needs anointing! Won't you please come over?"

She kept banging, kept calling, but the door never opened. Carole thought she saw Father Palmeri's pale face float into view to Bern's right through the glass of one of the church's few unstained windows. It hovered there for a few seconds or so, then disappeared.

But the door remained closed.

That didn't seem to faze Bern. She only increased the force of her blows with the knocker, and raised her voice even higher until it echoed off the stone walls and reverberated through the night.

Carole's heart went out to her. She shared Bern's need, if not her desperation.

Why doesn't Father Palmeri at least let her in? she thought. The poor thing's making enough racket to wake the dead.

Sudden terror tightened along the back of Carole's neck.

. . . *wake the dead* . . .

Bern was too loud. She thought only of attracting the attention of Father Palmeri, but what if she attracted . . . others?

Even as the thought crawled across her mind, Carole saw a dark, rangy figure creep onto the lawn from the street side, slinking from shadow to shadow, closing in on her unsuspecting friend.

"Oh, my God!" she cried, and fumbled with the window lock. She twisted it open and yanked up the sash.

Carole screamed into the night. "Bernadette! Behind you! There's someone coming! Get back here now, Bernadette! *Now!*"

Bernadette turned and looked up toward Carole, then stared around her. The approaching figure had dissolved into the shadows at the sound of the shouted warnings. But Bernadette must have sensed something in Carole's voice, for she started back toward the convent.

She didn't get far—ten paces, maybe—before the shadowy form caught up to her.

"No!" Carole screamed as she saw it leap upon her friend.

She stood frozen at the window, her fingers clawing the molding on each side as Bernadette's high wail of terror and pain cut the night.

For the span of an endless, helpless, paralyzed heartbeat, Carole watched the form drag her down to the silver lawn, tear open her raincoat, and fall upon her, watched her arms and legs flail wildly, frantically in the moonlight, and all the while her screams, oh, dear God in Heaven, her screams for help were slim, white-hot nails driven into Carole's ears.

And then, out of the corner of her eye, Carole saw the pale face appear again at the window of St. Anthony's, watch for a moment, then once more fade into the inner darkness.

With a low moan of horror, fear, and desperation, Carole pushed herself away from the window and stumbled toward the hall. *Someone* had to help. On the way, she snatched the foot-long wooden crucifix from Bernadette's wall and clutched it against her chest with both hands. As she picked up speed, graduating from a lurch to a walk to a loping run, she began to scream—not a wail of fear, but a long, seamless ululation of rage.

Something was killing her friend.

The rage was good. It canceled the fear and the horror and the loathing that had paralyzed her. It allowed her to move, to keep moving. She embraced the rage.

Carole hurtled down the stairs and burst onto the moonlit lawn—

And stopped.

She was disoriented for an instant. She didn't see Bern. Where was she? Where was her attacker?

And then she saw a patch of writhing shadow on the grass ahead of her near one of the shrubs.

Bernadette?

Clutching the crucifix, Carole ran for the spot, and as she neared she realized it was indeed Bernadette, sprawled facedown, but not alone. Another shadow sat astride her, hissing like a reptile, gnashing its teeth, its fingers curved into talons that tugged at Bernadette's head as if trying to tear it off.

Carole reacted without thinking. Screaming, she launched herself at the creature, ramming the big crucifix against its exposed back. Light flashed and sizzled and thick black smoke shot upward in oily swirls from where cross met flesh. The thing arched its back and howled, writhing beneath the cruciform brand, thrashing wildly as it tried to wriggle out from under the fiery weight.

But Carole stayed with it, following its slithering crawl on her knees, pressing the flashing cross deeper and deeper into its steaming, boiling flesh, down to the spine, into the vertebrae. Its cries became almost piteous as it weakened, and Carole gagged on the thick black smoke that fumed around her, but her rage would not allow her to slack off. She kept up the pressure, pushed the wooden crucifix deeper and deeper into the creature's back until it penetrated the chest cavity and seared into its heart. Suddenly the thing gagged and shuddered and then was still.

The flashes faded. The final wisps of smoke trailed away on the breeze.

Carole abruptly released the shaft of the crucifix as if it had shocked her, and ran back to Bernadette. She dropped to her knees beside the still form and turned her over onto her back.

"Oh, no!" she screamed when she saw Bernadette's torn throat, her wide, glazed, sightless eyes, and the blood, so much blood smeared all over the front of her.

Oh no. Oh, dear God, please no! This can't be! This can't be real!

A sob burst from her. "No, Bern! Nooooo!"

Somewhere nearby, a dog howled in answer.

Or was it a dog?

Carole realized she was defenseless now. She had to get back to the convent. She leaped to her feet and looked around. Nothing moving. A yard or two away she saw the dead thing with her crucifix still buried in its back.

She hurried over to retrieve it, but recoiled from touching the creature. She could see now that it was a man—a naked man, or something that very much resembled one. But not quite. Some indefinable quality was missing.

Was it one of *them?*

This must be one of the undead Mary Margaret had warned about. But could this . . . this *thing* . . . be a vampire? It had acted like little more than a rabid dog in human form.

Whatever it was, it had mauled and murdered Bernadette. Rage bloomed again within Carole like a virulent, rampant virus, spreading through her bloodstream, invading her nervous system, threatening to take her over completely. She fought the urge to batter the corpse.

Bile rose in her throat; she choked it down and stared at the inert form prone before her. This once had been a man, someone with a family, perhaps. Surely he hadn't asked to become this vicious night thing.

"Whoever you were," Carole whispered, "you're free now. Free to return to God."

She gripped the shaft of the crucifix to remove it but found it fixed in the seared flesh like a steel rod set in concrete.

Something howled again. Closer.

She had to get back inside, but she couldn't leave Bern out here.

Swiftly, she returned to Bernadette's side, worked her hands through the grass under her back and knees, and lifted her into her arms. So light! Dear Lord, she weighed almost nothing.

Carole carried Bernadette back to the convent as fast as her rubbery legs would allow. Once inside, she bolted the door, then staggered up to the second floor with Bernadette in her arms.

She returned Sister Bernadette Gileen to her own room. Carole didn't have the energy to drag the mattress back across the hall, so she stretched her supine on the box spring of her bed. She straightened Bern's thin legs, crossed her hands over her blood-splattered chest, arranged her torn clothing as best she could, and covered her from head to toe with a bedspread.

And then, looking down at that still form under the quilt she had helped Bernadette make, Carole sagged to her knees and began to cry. She tried to say a requiem prayer but her grief-racked mind had lost the words. So she sobbed aloud and asked God, Why? How could He let this happen to a dear, sweet innocent who had wished only to spend her life serving Him? *Why?*

But no answer came.

When Carole finally controlled her tears, she forced herself to her feet, closed Bernadette's door, and stumbled into the hall. She saw the light from the front foyer and knew she shouldn't leave it on. She hurried down and stepped over the still form of Mary Margaret under the blood-soaked blanket. Two violent deaths here tonight in a house devoted to God. How many more outside these doors?

She turned off the light but didn't have the strength to carry Mary Margaret upstairs. She left her there and raced through the dark back to her own room.

Carole didn't know what time the power went out.

She had no idea how long she'd been kneeling beside her bed, alternately sobbing and praying, when she glanced at the digital alarm clock on her night table and saw that its face had gone dark and blank.

Not that a power failure mattered. She'd been spending the night by candlelight anyway. There was barely an inch of candle left, but that gave her no clue as to the hour. Who knew how fast a candle burned?

She was tempted to lift the bedspread draped over the window and peek outside, but was afraid of what she might see.

How long until dawn? she wondered, rubbing her eyes. This night seemed endless. If only—

Beyond her locked door, a faint squeak came from somewhere along the hall. It could have been anything—the wind in the attic, the old building settling, but it had been long, drawn out, and high-pitched. Almost like . . .

A door opening.

Carole froze, still on her knees, hands still folded in prayer, her elbows resting on the bed, and listened for it again. But the sound was not repeated. Instead, something else . . . a rhythmic shuffle . . . in the hall . . . approaching her door . . .

Footsteps.

With her heart punching frantically against the inner wall of her chest, Carole leaped to her feet and stepped close to the door, listening with her ear almost touching the wood. Yes. Footsteps. Slow. And soft, like bare feet scuffing the floor. Coming this way. Closer. They were right outside the door. Carole felt a sudden chill, as if a wave of icy air had penetrated the wood, but the footsteps didn't pause. They passed her door, moving on.

And then they stopped.

Carole had her ear pressed against the wood now. She could hear her pulse pounding through her head as she strained for the next sound. And then it came, more shuffling outside in the hall, almost confused at first, and then the footsteps began again.

Coming back.

This time they stopped directly outside Carole's door. The cold was there again, a damp, penetrating chill that reached for her bones. Carole backed away from it.

And then the doorknob turned. Slowly. The door creaked with the weight of a body leaning against it from the other side, but Carole's bolt held.

Then a voice. Hoarse. A single whispered word, barely audible, but a shout could not have startled her more.

"Carole?"

Carole didn't reply—*couldn't* reply.

"Carole, it's me. Bern. Let me in."

Against her will, a low moan escaped Carole. No, no, no, this couldn't be Bernadette. Bernadette was dead. Carole had left her cooling body lying in her room across the hall. This was some horrible joke. . . .

Or was it? Maybe Bernadette had become one of *them,* one of the very things that had killed her.

But the voice on the other side of the door was not that of some ravenous beast. It was . . .

"Please let me in, Carole. I'm frightened out here alone."

Maybe Bern *is* alive, Carole thought, her mind racing, ranging for an answer. I'm no doctor. I could have been wrong about her being dead. Maybe she survived. . . .

She stood trembling, torn between the desperate, aching need to see her friend alive and the wary terror of being tricked by whatever creature Bernadette might have become.

"Carole?"

Carole wished for a peephole in the door, or at the very least a chain lock, but she had neither, and she had to do something. She couldn't stand here like this and listen to that plaintive voice any longer without going mad. She had to *know.* Without giving herself any more time to think, she snapped back the bolt and pulled the door open, ready to face whatever awaited her in the hall.

She gasped. "Bernadette!"

Her friend stood just beyond the threshold, swaying, stark naked.

Not completely naked. She still wore her wimple, although it was askew on her head, and a strip of cloth had been layered around her neck to dress her throat wound. In the wan, flickering candlelight that leaked from Carole's room, she saw that the blood that had splattered her was gone. Carole had never seen Bernadette unclothed before. She'd never realized how thin she was. Her ribs rippled beneath the skin of her chest, disappeared only beneath the scant padding of her small breasts with their erect nipples; the bones of her hips and pelvis bulged around her flat belly. Her normally fair skin was almost blue-white. The only other colors were the dark pools of her eyes and the orange splotches of hair on her head and her pubes.

"Carole," she said weakly. "Why did you leave me?"

The sight of Bernadette standing before her, alive, speaking, had drained most of Carole's strength; the added weight of guilt from her words nearly drove her to her knees. She sagged against the door frame.

"Bern . . ." Carole's voice failed her. She swallowed and tried again. "I—I thought you were dead. And . . . what happened to your clothes?"

Bernadette raised her hand to her throat. "I tore up my nightgown for a bandage. Can I come in?"

Carole straightened and opened the door farther. "Oh, Lord, yes. Come in. Sit down. I'll get you a blanket."

Bernadette shuffled into the room, head down, eyes fixed on the floor. She moved like someone on drugs. But then, after losing so much blood, it was a wonder she could walk at all.

"Don't want a blanket," Bern said. "Too hot. Aren't you hot?"

She backed herself stiffly onto Carole's bed, then lifted her ankles and sat cross-legged, facing her. Mentally, Carole explained the casual, blatant way she exposed herself by the fact that Bernadette was still recovering from a horrific trauma, but that made it no less discomfiting.

Carole glanced at the crucifix on the wall over her bed, above and behind Bernadette. For a moment, as Bernadette had seated herself beneath it, she thought she had seen it glow. It must have been reflected candlelight. She turned away and retrieved a spare blanket from the closet. She unfolded it and wrapped it around Bernadette's shoulders and over her spread knees, covering her.

"I'm thirsty, Carole. Could you get me some water?"

Her voice was strange. Lower pitched and hoarse, yes, but that should be expected after the throat wound she'd suffered. No, something else had changed in her voice, but Carole could not pin it down.

"Of course. You'll need fluids. Lots of fluids."

The bathroom was only two doors down. She took her water pitcher, lit a second candle, and left Bernadette on the bed, looking like an Indian draped in a serape.

When she returned with the full pitcher, she was startled to find the bed empty. She spied Bernadette immediately, by the window. She hadn't opened it, but she'd pulled off the bedspread drape and raised the shade. She stood there, staring out at the night. And she was naked again.

Carole looked around for the blanket and found it . . . hanging on the wall over her bed . . .

Covering the crucifix.

Part of Carole screamed at her to run, to flee down the hall and not look back. But another part of her insisted she stay. This was her friend. Something terrible had happened to Bernadette and she needed Carole now, probably more than she'd needed anyone in her entire life. And if someone was going to help her, it was Carole. *Only* Carole.

She placed the pitcher on the nightstand.

"Bernadette," she said, her mouth as dry as the timbers in these old walls, "the blanket . . ."

"I was hot," Bernadette said without turning.

"I brought you the water. I'll pour—"

"I'll drink it later. Come and watch the night."

"I don't want to see the night. It frightens me."

Bernadette turned, a faint smile on her lips. "But the darkness is so beautiful."

She stepped closer and stretched her arms toward Carole, laying a hand on each shoulder and gently massaging the terror-tightened muscles there. A sweet lethargy began to seep through Carole. Her eyelids began to drift closed . . . so tired . . . so long since she'd had any sleep . . .

No!

She forced her eyes open and gripped Bernadette's hands, pulling them from her shoulders. She pressed the palms together and clasped them between her own.

"Let's pray, Bern. With me: Hail Mary, full of grace . . ."

"No!"

". . . the Lord is with thee. Blessed art thou . . ."

Her friend's face twisted in rage. "I said NO, damn you!"

Carole struggled to keep a grip on Bernadette's hands but she was too strong.

". . . amongst women . . ."

And suddenly Bernadette's struggles ceased. Her face relaxed, her eyes cleared, even her voice changed, still hoarse, but higher in pitch, lighter in tone as she took up the words of the prayer.

"And Blessed is the fruit of thy womb . . ." Bernadette struggled with the next word, unable to say it. Instead she gripped Carole's hands with painful intensity and loosed a torrent of her own words. "Carole, get out! Get out, oh, please, for the love of God, get out now! There's not much of me left in here, and soon I'll be like the ones that killed me and I'll be after killing you! So run, Carole! Hide! Lock yourself in the chapel downstairs but get away from me *now!*"

Carole knew now what had been missing from Bernadette's voice—her brogue. But now it was back. This was the real Bernadette speaking. She was back! Her friend, her sister, was back! Carole bit back a sob.

"Oh, Bern, I can help! I can—"

Bernadette pushed her toward the door. "*No one* can help me, Carole!" She ripped the makeshift bandage from her neck, exposing the deep, jagged wound and the ragged ends of the torn blood vessels within it. "It's too late for me, but not for you. They're a bad lot and I'll be one of them again soon, so get out while you—"

Suddenly Bernadette stiffened and her features shifted. Carole knew immediately that the brief respite her friend had stolen from the horror that gripped her was over. Something else was back in control.

Carole turned and ran.

But the Bernadette-thing was astonishingly swift. Carole had barely reached the threshold when a steel-fingered hand gripped her upper arm and yanked her back, nearly dislocating her shoulder. She cried out in pain and terror as she was spun about and flung across the room. Her hip struck hard against the rickety old spindle chair by her desk, knocking it over as she landed in a heap beside it.

Carole groaned with the pain. As she shook her head to clear it, she saw Bernadette approaching her, her movements stiff, more assured now, her teeth bared—so many teeth, and so much longer than the old Bernadette's—her fingers curved, reaching for Carole's throat. With each passing second there was less and less of Bernadette about her.

Carole tried to back away, her frantic hands and feet slipping on the floor as she pressed her spine against the wall. She had nowhere to go. She pulled the fallen chair atop her and held it as a shield against the Bernadette-thing. The face that had once belonged to her dearest friend grimaced with contempt as she swung her hand at the chair. It scythed through the spindles, splintering them like matchsticks, sending the carved headpiece flying. A second blow cracked the seat in two. A third and fourth sent the remnants of the chair hurtling to opposite sides of the room.

Carole was helpless now. All she could do was pray.

"Our Father, who art—"

"Too late for that to help you now, *Carole!*" she hissed, spitting her name.

". . . hallowed be Thy Name . . ." Carole said, quaking in terror as undead fingers closed on her throat.

And then the Bernadette-thing froze, listening. Carole heard it too. An insistent tapping. On the window. The creature turned to look, and Carole followed her gaze.

A face was peering through the window.

Carole blinked but it didn't go away. This was the second floor! How—?

And then a second face appeared, this one upside down, looking in from the top of the window. And then a third, and a fourth, each more bestial than the last. And as each appeared it began to tap its fingers and knuckles on the window glass.

"*No!*" the Bernadette-thing screamed at them. "You can't come in! She's mine! No one touches her but *me!*"

She turned back to Carole and smiled, showing those teeth that had never fit in Bernadette's mouth. "They can't cross a threshold unless invited in by one who lives there. *I* live here—or at least I did. And I'm not sharing you, Carole."

She turned again and raked a claw-like hand at the window. "Go A-*way!* She's MINE!"

Carole glanced to the left. The bed was only a few feet away. And above it—the blanket-shrouded crucifix. If she could reach it . . .

She didn't hesitate. With the mad tapping tattoo from the window echoing around her, Carole gathered her feet beneath her and sprang for the bed. She scrambled across the sheets, one hand outstretched, reaching for the blanket—

A manacle of icy flesh closed around her ankle and roughly dragged her back.

"Oh, no, bitch," said the hoarse, unaccented voice of the Bernadette-thing. "Don't even *think* about it!"

It grabbed two fistfuls of flannel at the back of Carole's nightgown and hurled her across the room as if she weighed no more than a pillow. The wind whooshed out of Carole as she slammed against the far wall. She heard ribs crack. She fell among the splintered ruins of the chair, pain lancing through her right flank. The room wavered and blurred. But through the roaring in her ears she still heard that insistent tapping on the window.

As her vision cleared she saw the Bernadette-thing's naked form gesturing again to the creatures at the window, now a mass of salivating mouths and tapping fingers.

"Watch!" she hissed. "Watch me!"

With that, she loosed a long, howling scream and lunged at Carole, arms curved before her, body arcing into a flying leap. The scream, the tapping, the faces at the window, the dear friend who now wanted only to slaughter her—it all was suddenly too much for Carole. She wanted to roll away but couldn't get her body to move. Her hand found the broken seat of the chair by her hip. Instinctively she pulled it closer. She closed her eyes as she raised it between herself and the horror hurtling toward her through the air.

The impact drove the wood of the seat against Carole's chest; she groaned as new stabs of pain shot through her ribs. But the Bernadette-thing's triumphant feeding cry cut off abruptly and devolved into a coughing gurgle.

Suddenly the weight was released from Carole's chest, and the chair seat with it.

And the tapping at the window stopped.

Carole opened her eyes to see the naked Bernadette-thing standing above her, straddling her, holding the chair seat before her, choking and gagging as she struggled with it.

At first Carole didn't understand. She drew her legs back and inched away along the wall. And then she saw what had happened.

Three splintered spindles had remained fixed in that half of the broken seat, and those spindles were now firmly and deeply embedded in the center of the Bernadette-thing's chest. She wrenched wildly at the chair seat, trying to dislodge the oak daggers but succeeded only in breaking them off at skin level. She dropped the remnant of the seat and swayed like a tree in a storm, her mouth working spasmodically as her hands fluttered ineffectually over the bloodless wounds between her ribs and the slim wooden stakes deep out of reach within them.

Abruptly she dropped to her knees with a dull thud. Then, only inches from Carole, she slumped into a splay-legged squat. The agony faded from her face and she closed her eyes. She fell forward against Carole.

Carole threw her arms around her friend and gathered her close.

"Oh, Bern, oh, Bern, oh, Bern," she moaned. "I'm so sorry. If only I'd got there sooner!"

Bernadette's eyes fluttered open and the darkness was gone. Only her own spring-sky blue remained, clear, grateful. Her lips began to curve upward but made it only halfway to a smile, then she was gone.

Carole hugged the limp cold body closer and moaned in boundless grief and anguish to the unfeeling walls. She saw the leering faces begging to crawl away from the window and she shouted at them though her tears.

"Go! That's it! Run away and hide! Soon it'll be light and then *I'll* come looking for *you!* For *all* of you! And woe to any of you that I find!"

She cried over Bernadette's body a long time. And then she

wrapped it in a sheet and held and rocked her dead friend in her arms until sunrise.

With the dawn she left the old Sister Carole Hanarty behind. The gentle soul, happy to spend her days and nights in the service of the Lord, praying, fasting, teaching chemistry to reluctant adolescents, and holding to her vows of poverty, chastity, and obedience, was gone.

The new Sister Carole had been tempered in the forge of the night and recast into someone relentlessly vengeful and fearless to the point of recklessness. And perhaps, she admitted with no shame or regret, more than a little mad.

She departed the convent and began her hunt.

Chet Williamson

EXCERPTS FROM THE
RECORDS OF THE NEW ZODIAC
AND THE DIARIES
OF HENRY WATSON FAIRFAX

Chet Williamson is a funny guy, and here he's produced a story that's both funny and horrifying at the same time. He has worked in both humor and horror (fields which are oddly compatible); in another book I edited years ago, I was able to reprint a piece he had originally written for The New Yorker *titled "Ghandi at the Bat."*

Horror readers know Williamson mainly by novels such as Ash Wednesday *and* Dreamthorp, *as well as by such short stories as "Yore Skin's Jes's Soft 'N Purty . . . He Said," which originally appeared in the landmark anthology* Razored Saddles *and which is one of the most singularly brilliant and disgusting tales ever published in the field—and not funny at all.*

(Note: The Zodiac was a New York City dining club established in 1868 and consisted of twelve gentlemen active in New York society. At least two volumes of the collected minutes of the meetings were privately published.)

September 18th, 20——:

Before I retired last night, I read a column which suggested that many of the outrages perpetrated by both children and adults might be due to the lack of civility in society. I cannot help but agree.

The final decades of the previous century witnessed a dreadful decline in civility, and this new century promises to be no more refined. We are on every side beset by adversarial imagery. The media poses everything in terms of battles, wars, and combat, and I find myself falling into this modern-day vernacular.

I recall (with chagrin) speaking before the board of our computer company just yesterday, and telling them that we should not rest until we have thoroughly crushed Tom Chambers's company, which is all that stands between us and a virtual legal monopoly on network servers. I described our position, quite accurately, as "outnumbered and outgunned," but suggested that sheer courage and resourcefulness could yet win the war, though I would also be willing to shift some cash from other Fairfax corporations into the fray. I went on to demonize Chambers as the head of an evil empire who would be content with nothing less than total domination of the world's computers.

Although that representation is certainly true, I am ashamed of my martial hyperbole, and my forebears would be ashamed of me as well. For a hundred and fifty years the Fairfaxes have conducted their many enterprises with restraint and even temper, and I feel the ghostly censure of my father, my grandfather, and my great-grandfather for betraying that tradition.

Therefore, in order to assuage my guilt, I plan to institute—or rather, reinstate—a tradition which, I believe, has long been neglected and which will, I trust, add a touch of civility and goodwill to the practices of at least a dozen businessmen, myself and my most powerful competitors among them. . . .

CONSTITUTION

Article I. This Club shall be known as the New Zodiac, modelled after the original Zodiac dining club founded in 1868.

Article II. It shall be made up of twelve members, or *Signs,* who shall be addressed by the zodiacal sign assigned to them by lot.

Article III. The New Zodiac shall meet for dinner on the final Saturday evening of every month, the place to be selected by that month's host, or *caterer,* who shall make all arrangements for the dinner, the cost of which shall be equally shared by the Signs. The cost of the wines and spirits shall be borne by the caterer.

CHARTER MEMBERS

Aquarius ....Mr. Frank Reynolds
Pisces ....Mr. Todd Arnold
Aries ....Mr. Jeff Condelli
Taurus ....Mr. Richard Rank
Gemini ....Mr. Thomas Chambers
Cancer ....Mr. Edward Devore
Leo ....Mr. John Thornton
Virgo ....Mr. Clark Taylor
Libra ....Mr. Bruce Levine
Scorpio ....Mr. Cary Black
Sagittarius ....Mr. David Walsh
Capricorn ....Mr. Henry Fairfax

November 25th:

I fear that I may have made a mistake in selecting the charter members of the New Zodiac. Only Ed Devore and John Thornton come, like myself, from old money, while the rest are all nouveau. The strength of the original Zodiac may have come from the fact that the Signs were all members of New York society in a time when society meant something. Through its history, the Zodiac boasted both J. P. Morgans, Senior and Junior, the Rev. Henry Van Dyke, Joseph H. Choate and John William Davis, both Ambassadors to the Court of St. James, Senator Nelson W. Aldrich, and other wealthy and powerful, and, above all, dignified, men who knew the importance of civility. In my effort to make the club more democratic, I simply selected the wealthiest and most powerful men, hoping to bring civility to those who most needed it, including myself.

But the first meeting was not as I had anticipated, even though I tried to recreate as best I could the original menu served at the very first dinner of the original Zodiac on February 29th, 1868. . . .

Minutes of the First Meeting of the New Zodiac

THE HOUGHTON CLUB, NEW YORK   NOVEMBER 24TH, 20——
Present at table: All Signs. Capricorn, caterer.

MENU:

Oysters	*Selle de mouton*
Potage à la Bagration	*Haricots vert*
Bouchées à la Reine	*Salade—laitue—fromage*
Terrapin à la Maryland	*Poudin glacé*
Suprême de volaille	*Gâteaux*
Asperges	*Fruits*
Roman punch	*Café*

WINES:
Krug 1982
Lafitte 1969
Chambertin 1947
Old brandy vintage 1895

It was moved by Brother Gemini to make Brother Capricorn, the member who initiated this series of dinners, the Secretary of the New Zodiac. A unanimous voice vote followed, after which Bro. Gemini observed that perhaps the extra work would keep Bro. Capricorn so busy that he would find no time "to f———over my business." Much pleasant laughter followed, and Bro. Capricorn accepted his new post.

Dinner seemed to be received well, although Bro. Aries had to be reminded that fruit was not to be thrown at his fellow Signs. "We are, after all," said Bro. Capricorn, "the New Zodiac and not the Drones' Club."

"What the hell's the Drones' Club?" Bro. Aries asked, and when informed stated that he had never heard of P. G. Wodehouse. "F———this Woodhead, whoever he is," he said, and tossed a strawberry, which hit Bro. Capricorn in the left eye, to the merriment of the company.

When the party was asked who would volunteer to cater the following month's dinner, Bro. Gemini offered to do so, upon receiving assurances in the form of each Sign's solemn word that whatever went on at the dinners would remain confidential. Bro. Gemini then made a vow of his own, that he would serve the Signs a feast at the next dinner "like no billionaire has ever tasted before, but which we all f———ing well deserve. It'll make what we had tonight seem like sh—t in comparison—as far as scarcity goes, anyway."

Bro. Gemini then inquired of Bro. Capricorn if he might borrow the two volumes of the original *Records of the Zodiac,* which he wished to consult for further menu ideas, and Bro. Capricorn happily agreed.

The evening was concluded by the relating of several humorous stories by Bros. Taurus, Libra, and Cancer concerning African-Americans, and some ribald anecdotes told by Bros. Virgo and Sagittarius about women who have worked under them.

Adjourned.

Capricorn, *Secretary*

. . . Most of them seemed to be Philistines, but I confess that I was not surprised to find Ed Devore joining in with the ethnic jokes. He's long had a prejudice against blacks, all the more so since his company was barred from doing any more business in South Africa, after nearly a century of high profits there. And though John Thornton didn't make a fool of himself as most of the others did, he seemed ready to join in at the slightest provocation, and I expect him to be equally frivolous at the next dinner.

At least they all seemed to be civil to each other, which is a start. And Condelli didn't throw any more food after my reprimand, except of course for the face-saving strawberry to show that my billions held no greater sway than his. Perhaps they will calm down in time. And perhaps Chambers's attention to the dinner he's catering will help to take his eye off his business long enough for us to make further inroads into his market share. I wonder, though, just what it is that he's planning to serve. . . .

Second Meeting

THE MEDIA MANSE, PORTLAND, OREGON DECEMBER 29TH, 20——
Present at table: All Signs. Gemini, caterer.

MENU:

Sea Tag oysters	*Soufflé aux épinards*
Potage crème d'orge régence	*Pommes Mont d'Or*
Timbale de crab	*Medaillon de foie gras*
Cubicle Steak à la Pompadour	*Salade Arlesienne*
Champion de Virginie, sauce	*Asperges, sauce Hollandaise*
champagne	*Omelette Norwegienne*

Wines:
Convent sherry 1894
Moët-Chandon 1969
Château Latour 1957
Musigny 1954
Hôtel de Paris
Blue Pipe Madeira
Holmes Rainwater Madeira 1879
Cognac Napoleon 1890

The sumptuous meal was a near-complete recreation, Brother Gemini so informed us, of a dinner put together in 1925 by J. P. Morgan Jr., the differences being the years of the vintages and the meat utilized in two of the entrées, of which he would say more later.

In further emulation of J. P. Morgan's magnanimity, Bro. Gemini presented the Signs with a linen tablecloth woven in Venice upon which were embossed all the signs of the zodiac, similar to the one Morgan had given to the original Zodiac.

As superb as was the meal (and its setting—Bro. Gemini's newly completed mansion that overlooks the Pacific), even more extraordinary were the wines and spirits. It was not until everyone had made their way through every vintage and was well fortified with the extraordinary Cognac that Bro. Gemini revealed to us the secret ingredient of the Cubicle Steak à la Pompadour and the Champion de Virginie, sauce champagne. Morgan Jr. had originally served Cotelettes de pigeouaux à la Pompadour and Jambon de Virginie, and all the Signs were curious as to with what meats Bro. Gemini had improved the recipes.

He informed us in a matter true to his personal style, transforming the dining room into a multimedia presentation area with a few spoken words. Screens dropped into place in response to the voice recognition technology, the room darkened, and Bro. Gemini then told us that although he would bear the cost of the wines and spirits, which amounted to well over a quarter million dollars (a bargain, he claimed, considering the short time in which his staff had to gather them), the shared cost of the dinner itself amounted to eight hundred and fifty thousand dollars each.

At the gasp from the Signs, Bro. Gemini inquired of Bro. Capricorn the cost of the previous dinner, which he had solely borne, and was told the amount was seventeen thousand dollars, not including the wines. Bro. Gemini admitted that there was quite a difference between seventeen thousand dollars and over ten million, but that his fellow Signs would understand when they realized just what it was of which they had partaken.

The presentation began then, a combination of video and still photography that showed in detail the process of harvesting the meat, with sections entitled "On the Hoof," "Making the Purchase," "The Butchering Process," and finally "In the Kitchen." Much of the material was more graphic than several of the Signs cared to see, your secretary included, and Bro. Cancer and Bro. Libra wasted both the meal and the wines by disgorging the entire contents of their stomachs into thoughtfully provided plastic-lined silk bags.

Still, no one left their seats, and at the end of the presentation, Bro. Gemini gave an eloquent defense and rationale for his menu selections, by the end of which nearly all the Signs were in agreement with him, and checks for each Sign's share were promised.

Bro. Aries was named the caterer of the next dinner, and assured his brother Signs that he would continue in the tradition established by Bro. Gemini.

Adjourned.

Capricorn, *Secretary*

   . . . Cubicle steak. Ed Devore and John Thornton, my old friends, actually laughed at that ghastly pun. Perhaps New England inbreeding has softened their brains so that they can find such a thing funny. Although Devore vomited at first, along with Levine, I think it was because of the graphic elements of the presentation rather than the knowledge of what they had ingested. They probably would have gotten sick at the sight of a steer being butchered, let alone a human being.

   Cubicle Steak and Champion de Virginie, Chambers's dreadful wordplay. Champion for Jambon, and it happens that Kevin Dupree, a purchasing agent in Chambers's company, was indeed the Virginia state spelling bee champion when he was in middle school, as his projected résumé told us.

   And what awful detail Chambers went into to carry out his parallels to the raising and purchasing of stock. We saw footage of Dupree "on the hoof," both at his job and with his family; we saw the chilling purchase, Chambers himself offering the man ten million dollars for his family if he would vanish forever; then Dupree's slow breaking down as the realization dawned that he was Chambers's body and soul, and that if he refused he and his family would be ruined, both financially and in other ways that only a man with a vast fortune might accomplish.

The butchering itself was numbing, nearly as deadening to me as it must have been to poor Dupree; then seeing the meat cooked and prepared for serving, and most coldhearted of all, seeing us eating it in footage that had been shot by hidden cameras only an hour before and then assembled by Chambers's flunkies.

By the end, some Signs looked sick, some merely uncomfortable, and some were smiling as though they were boys who had been caught stealing candy. But when Chambers began to speak, their faces changed. Though the man can be as coarse as a line worker, he can be as eloquently silver-tongued as the devil when required. He talked about the twelve of us as the true leaders of the country, the new lords of the world, and how our employees, from the humblest we never see to the executives who work closely with us, are all commodities, material to be bought and sold and used as needed. "Our intelligence and foresight and energy have given us the power," he said, "to enrich them or impoverish them . . . or devour them, if we will it."

And God help me, I could not tell the others that he was wrong. He had already proven himself right. He has seduced them, my friends along with my competitors. I could see their minds churning, thinking of how they might top Chambers's feast. Condelli is next month's caterer, and he seemed thrilled beyond measure at the prospect.

My desire to spread civility has set something quite the opposite into motion, and I do not see how I can stop it. Honor compels me to remain silent, but also to end what I have unwillingly begun. I would do so immediately, but if that is not possible, I have nearly a year until it is once again my turn to serve as caterer, and many things can happen in a year. . . .

Third Meeting

THE HAVENS, BALTIMORE, MARYLAND   JANUARY 26TH, 20——
Present at table: All Signs. Aries, caterer.

MENU:

Minestrone   *Small eggplant*
Roast leg of Philip Lamb,
mint sauce . . .

January 27th:

> . . . *Lamb was Condelli's Director of European Operations. At first I thought it possible that he simply might have contributed his leg and survived, since the cost was far less than for Chambers's dinner, but my investigations show that Philip Lamb has disappeared.*
>
> *Such an act boldly throws down the gauntlet for the other Signs. Lamb had been quite important to the success of Condelli's overseas ventures. It was as though Condelli was saying that anyone can lose an anonymous office drone, but he was willing to make a real* sacrifice. . . .

Fourth Meeting

DOUBLE R RANCH, DALLAS, TEXAS   FEBRUARY 23RD, 20——
Present at table: All Signs. Taurus, caterer.

MENU:

Shysters Rockefeller	Hot wings
Double R Chili with beaners	Texas fries
Bar-B-Q Veep . . .	

February 24th:

> . . . *bad enough that Rank would discard his two top drilling men from his Mexican offshore rigs, but to further weaken himself by barbecuing his distribution Vice-President for that terrible beef/veep pun was utterly foolish. But far worse was his disposal of his entire legal team as a mere appetizer. Of course, he'll put together another, but still it seems insane. . . .*

Fifth Meeting

THE DEVORE HOUSE, BOSTON, MA   MARCH 30TH, 20—
Present at table: All Signs. Cancer, caterer.

MENU:

Caviar	Dinde sauvage rôtie Parie aux
Potage velouté Chantilly	marrons
Roast breast of Mindy,	Gelée d'Airelles
sauce Nautun . . .	

March 31st:

> . . . *a return to fine dining after Rank's reprehensible Texas barbecue. But Devore has taken the whole thing to a new plateau—or an even lower depth. Perhaps he felt the only way to top Rank was to make more than just a business sacrifice. I have no doubt that he loved Mindy. She had been his mistress for seven years. Psychologically, a loss like that can be far more devastating to a man and his business than the loss of personnel alone can be, and I could see that Devore was feeling the loss deeply. It will be interesting to see the progress of his holdings over the next few months. Rank's growth has certainly been curtailed in the wake of his dinner. Perhaps after Chambers is dealt with, I might try a silent run at Double-R Industries. . . .*

Seventh Meeting

CEO de lait, rôti . . .

Ninth Meeting

Directeurs à la crème . . .

Eleventh Meeting

Pére à la organe . . .

Twelfth Meeting

THE TAYLOR HOUSE, MIAMI, FLORIDA   NOVEMBER 30TH, 20——
Present at table: All Signs. Virgo, caterer.

MENU:

Huitres	*Salade Nicoise*
Potage botsch polonais	*Asperges en branches,*
Vol-au-vent of very young virgin	*sauce mousseline*
sweetbread	*Bombe Alhambra*
Baron d'agneau Beauharnais	*Petis pois au beurre*
Pommes noisettes	

Wines:
Krug 1978
Château Latour 1946—Magnum
Clos de Vougeot 1948
Madeira, rainwater 1886
Napoleon brandy 1873

Most of the Signs seemed in somber mood this evening, in spite of Brother Virgo's splendid repast. Though Bro. Virgo himself seemed a bit glum, possibly over the business misfortunes that have adversely affected nearly all of the Signs, and possibly over the provenance of the sweetbreads, spirits seemed to lift as more and more spirits were consumed.

Several of the Signs joshed Bro. Gemini concerning the successful hostile takeover of his company by Bro. Capricorn, who protested that in spite of the technical terminology he felt no hostility toward Bro. Gemini at all, and hoped that Bro. Gemini reciprocated his goodwill. Bro. Capricorn concluded by telling Bro. Gemini that despite the tides of fortune there would always be a place for him at this table.

A full year now having passed since the first meeting of the New Zodiac, it falls to Bro. Capricorn once again to perform the function of caterer at next month's dinner, which, he informed his brother Signs, he expected them all to attend.

Adjourned.

Capricorn, *Secretary*

December 1st:
   . . . *his own daughter. They've become monsters, but at a woeful cost. No matter how tough and ruthless you may be, you cannot remain unmoved when serving up your own flesh and blood.*
   And your business *cannot remain unmoved when your guilt interferes with your attention to it, and you leave gaping holes in your corporate charts by butchering those who made it what it is.*
   Nor can that business remain unshaken when your surviving employees are individually informed of what has happened, by messages that remain on screen just long enough to read and then vanish forever from Fairfax Technologies' now universally used network servers.

December 9th:
   The Signs are all, save one, ruined, victims of their own hunger and the things that hunger brought. With my inside knowledge of their trou-

bles, it has been easy to buy them out and swallow them up in their weakened condition. The last one fell just this morning.

The companies of the Signs of the New Zodiac have been devoured.

Minutes of the Thirteenth and Final Meeting of the New Zodiac

THE FAIRFAX CLUB, NEW YORK   DECEMBER 28th, 20——
Present at table: All Signs. Capricorn, caterer.
Absent from their seats: Aquarius, Pisces, Aries, Taurus, Gemini, Cancer, Leo, Virgo, Libra, Scorpio, Sagittarius.

MENU:

Hors d'oeuvres a' la Aquarius   Pisces jardiniere
Potage queue de Aries   Taurus rôtis
Gemini pâté   Cancer à la crème
Leo d'agneau—mint sauce   Roast suckling Virgo
Libra Parmentiére   Scorpio à la casserole
Sagittarius de lait farci
au marrons

WINES:
Pol Roger extra dry 1956
Château Latour 1947
Tichner Madeira 1868
Café Anglais 1854

Discussion following the dinner was succinct. Brother Capricorn observed that sometimes there is no remedy for incivility in society but removal of the incivil elements. No one spoke in opposition to this remark.

After a brief period of silence, it was moved by Brother Capricorn that the New Zodiac be dissolved due to lack of members. The motion carried, 1–0.

Bro. Capricorn, having dined alone, offered to bear the entire cost of the dinner, and there were no objections.

The other Signs rested most comfortably, and most civilly.
Adjourned.

Capricorn, *Secretary*

Eric Van Lustbader

AN EXALTATION OF
TERMAGANTS

When Eric Van Lustbader's first best-selling novel, The Ninja, *was published in 1980, he presented a copy to me with the inscription "Forget those short stories already, and write a novel!" At the time I was privileged to work on his Sunset Warrior novels at Doubleday (see the introduction to F. Paul Wilson's story for comments about these cheaply produced Doubleday novels—then go out and buy the Sunset Warrior books, which are wonderful), and though I took his advice a few years later, I didn't abandon short fiction, and neither did he, to our good fortune.*

The Ninja proved to be only the first in a string of best-sellers for Lustbader (the most recent, Angel Eyes*)—but here, for you and me, he has written the following novelette, a tough and tender story with beautiful fantasy elements.*

I consider it the renewal of an old friendship.

Let me introduce you to the great love of my life. My grand affair with Ms. M lasted almost fifteen years. She wasn't pretty, and God knows she wasn't often fair, but she did lead me into some mighty special places—places I sure as hell never would have set foot in if it hadn't been for her. I bless her for that; but I also curse her. Every night I find new ways to curse her, and all the while I'm missing her so bad my stomach hurts like it's got a nest of nasty little demons inside it. And maybe it does. After what happened a couple of weeks ago it wouldn't surprise me, not even a smidgen.

Mescal's her name, yessir; and fucking up my head's her game. She did that every night while I tongue-kissed the smooth taste of her. Oh, yeah, you got it now. I've had a great galloping love affair with mescal for a long, long time. And she was one helluva jealous mistress, let me tell you. But no more. Not ever again. And here's why.

I used to make love shamelessly to my mistress all over Manhattan, but the place I liked best was called Helicon, so named no doubt because its owner, Mike, was Greek. See, Mount Helicon was the home of the Muses, or so the ancient Greeks believed, anyway. The bar was holed up a block away from the Holland Tunnel, on the ground floor of a cast-iron building you could see had been handsome as sin maybe seventy-five years ago. Inside was a long, narrow space with slowly turning fans dripping from a pressed-tin ceiling dating back to the turn of the century. The old millennium, not the one just passed. The tin was pressed into a nice pattern, which reminded me of some old Mexican tiles I had seen when I was living in Oaxaca. When I'd first met Ms. M. So long ago I can't remember the date. Hell, they don't make tiles like that anymore. Not since the craftsmen all got jobs making high-profile sneakers and nylon running suits, and assembling Personal Digital Assistants.

In any event, Helicon had lots to recommend it: sawdust on the floor, and the smell of old beer and even older grease hanging like well-won medals on a gaunt warrior. Not to mention the bar itself, which seemed to go on forever, scarred with the wounds of long-forgotten brawls and newly broken hearts. Best of all, the light was just dim enough so that when you looked at yourself in the panels of cloudy mirror behind the bar's polished mahogany surface you could just about convince yourself that you were someone else—someone you had once dreamed of becoming, maybe.

The particular day I'm thinking of I was sitting in a booth, making love to Ms. M, when the bar phone rang. Mike picked it up, spoke a moment, then held out the receiver.

"It's for you," he said to me.

I grabbed my mistress and brought her to a stool. Scooping up the receiver, I growled, "Yeah, what?"

"Jesus, Willie, it's ten-thirty in the morning. Are you drinking already?"

"Who the hell wants to know?" I took an extra-large hit of the mescal.

"It's worse than I imagined," the disapproving voice said. "It's Herman, your brother."

"Ah, that explains it," I said, cutting the sonuvabitch off. "You have no imagination."

"If you sobered up, you could get a real job."

"And, goddammit, my name isn't Willie!" My cheeks flushed red, I hung up.

"Wrong number," I told Mike as I slid the phone back down the bar. He just gave me a wry grin. He knew what was up. Mike and I had a relationship—the kind you can only have with a really top-flight bartender.

Back in my booth, I pushed aside the empty glass from my second drink and sipped some more mescal while I brooded about my empty office and the last contract I had signed. It had been six months and I hadn't put a word down on my notepad, let alone on my word processor. Idly, I considered calling Ray Michaels, my accountant, who made sure my life didn't go straight to hell in a handcart while I struggled through my affair with Ms. M. I thought maybe I ought to have him contact my publisher and tell her to forget it, give back the advance she'd sent me. Then I remembered I'd already blown it on that little month-long jaunt back to my old haunting grounds in Mexico. Just as well; I'd never reneged on a contract before and I had no intention of starting now. But what was I going to write about? I hadn't a clue.

I glanced up at the carved wooden ship's figurehead Mike had hung from the ceiling. She was half human, half bird, and because of that I had dubbed her Melpomene, the Muse of Tragedy. It was said that from the fertile union of Melpomene and the river god, Achelous, the marvelously sad and desperate Sirens had been born to endlessly sing the tormenting tune that lured unsuspecting sailors to their doom against the craggy shores upon which the Sirens were marooned. Sometime in my youth Melpomene had become my personal muse because I could in no other way put into perspective the tragedy that had befallen my family.

I looked up as the phone rang again. Mike gave me the eye while he listened to the voice at the other end of the line.

"If it's my damn brother again tell him to kiss my white writer's ass."

"It's Ray," Mike said, holding out the receiver.

I groaned as I took the phone. My accountant never called me unless he had a good reason. "Hey," I said.

"Bill, I just got off the phone with your brother." He sounded concerned. "He says you're in a mood."

"Does he, now? Let me see. It's ten-forty of a Monday morning, I'm on my third mescal, and I don't have a fucking thought in my head. So I'd say, yes, I'm in a mood."

Ray sighed. "He needs to talk to you."

"The rat bastard ran off with my wife, not to mention the proceeds of my pension plan, while he was what could be laughingly
called my business manager. He doesn't need to talk to me."

"Listen," Ray said patiently, "you sued him and got all the money
back. You could have put him in jail if you'd pressed charges."

"Don't think it doesn't eat at me."

"Then why didn't you?"

"It would have broken Donnatella's heart, that's why," I said.
"God knows why but my ex-wife loves the jerk."

"It's a new millennium," he said. "Bygones."

"Bull*shit*." I have to admit my teeth were clenched. "No fucking
way, bygones."

"Okay, be like that."

I heard some suspicious noises in the background and said, "What,
are you on the golf course?"

"Sixth tee," he affirmed. "You should come out with me and try
it sometime."

"And have to make conversation with the deadhead bankers you
play with? I'd rather be tortured by my termagant."

"Your what?"

"Termagant. Know what a harpy is?"

"Sure. A woman who never shuts up."

"A rose by any other name." I laughed. "Except this one stinks
to high heaven."

"Didn't you used to call Donnatella a termagant?"

"That would be an affirmative, good buddy." I looked up at the
wooden Melpomene. "And right now, my own personal muse has
become one. Ironic, isn't it?"

"Who was it said we all get what we deserve?"

"I believe it was you. Just now."

Ray sighed. "I assume you're blocked."

"Like a bowel full of bricks."

"There's still time to join me for the back nine. Get some gentle
sport in instead of all that death-wish extreme stuff you go in for,"
he said. "The sun's out, you know. The birds are chirping."

"Some of those birds are on the endangered species list. Just make
sure you don't clobber one with your driver."

"I'm not good with the driver," Ray said. "Off the sixth I use a
three wood."

"That's the difference between you and me, Ray. I'd use the driver and get to the green in two. Risk, old boy. Take the risk."

"I'm an accountant, remember? That word is not in my vocabulary." I could hear him say something to one of his deadheads and I wondered whether this conversation had lost him his turn. He didn't like to lose at golf. "Listen, this time your brother really did have something important to tell you."

"That would be a physical impossibility, like putting your head up your ass. Although in Herman's case . . ."

"Bill, can the crap. Lilly's dying."

"Um hum." I took another hit of mescal.

"Don't—I mean, don't for Christ's sake fall apart or anything."

"No chance of that, old boy."

"So I see. Well, I guess I shouldn't be surprised. You haven't seen her in, what . . . ?"

"Thirty years," I said.

"She's your sister."

"She was a retard," I corrected him. I found I was already talking about her in the past tense. "Couldn't move without spazzing all over the place, couldn't speak a single word. Couldn't hold a thought in her head, I shouldn't think."

"That's just plain cold, Bill."

I was getting fed up. "Listen, Ray, it wasn't you who had to live through the nightmare of childhood with Lilly, with her vomiting in your face, mewling all night like a cat with worms, trying to pull your hair out by the roots every time you came near her. It wasn't you who got into fights three or four times a week because your schoolmates were so fucking cruel. It wasn't you who had to live with parents who were so filled with dread, so utterly desperate they became helpless as children, taken advantage of time and again by con artists posing as doctors, healers, fortune-tellers. It wasn't you who had madness staring you in the face for fourteen years. Christ, the thought of it all makes my skin crawl."

He was silent for a time. "She's on the point of death now, Bill. Herman has made it clear he feels he has no obligation in the matter of arrangements. So what d'you want to do?"

"I want to forget she ever existed, that's what I want to do."

Ray sighed again. "When she dies I'll have her cremated, then."

"By all fucking means," I told him. "Scatter her spaz ashes to the four winds." I waited a moment. "And Ray?"

"Yes, Bill."

"Don't even think about telling me I have to be there when they do it."

That conversation set the tone. I was sour and pissed off when I got off the phone, and if I hadn't been, what happened next might have happened differently. But I was and it didn't.

What happened next was that the Tazzman breezed in. Not that I knew his name then; I'd never set eyes on him before.

"Hey, yo, whiteys, git yo hands in da air an do like I tell yo." The Tazzman was a tall, cadaverous black man with a sunken chest, wild hair like Jimi Hendrix and a face like Ike Turner, only he was very, very young. The studied meanness of his features seemed no more than a millimeter thick, as if stamped upon him by circumstance rather than by any aspect of his own nature. Mike and I decided to pay attention since he had a scary-looking machine pistol leveled at us.

He advanced into the bar, watching both of us with quick, nervous movements. "Yo," he said, addressing Mike, "I wancha money."

"Tell me something, kid, you ever do this before?" I said as Mike was about to reply. "I mean, it's eleven o'clock of a Monday morning. Nobody's in the place but me and Mike here. What kinda money you think he has in the till?" I could see from the disapproving glance Mike gave me that he was not a happy camper. Too bad. Someone had to take control of this situation, otherwise we'd both be fucked.

"Smart guy," the Tazzman snarled. "Yo gonna git yo smart white ass stuck all over dis here wall yo doan watchit." His wary, scared eyes took us both in. "Gimme what's inna till an whut you got on you."

I fanned open my wallet. The two fives made me feel briefly ashamed.

"Shee-*it!*" the Tazzman opined as he lifted the bills so expertly I hardly knew they were gone. "Ain't you even got a watch?"

"Time means nothing to me," I said, showing him my naked wrists. "Speaking of which, you don't look like you've eaten anything for a bunch."

The Tazzman chewed on his lip and glowered at me as he sized up the situation. He was as jumpy as a bear scenting humans, which should have warned me. But as I said, those phone calls put me in one pissy mood and I was ready to take up arms against the next person who crossed my path. Stupid, right? The ancient Greeks had a better word for it: *hubris.*

"Mike, make this guy a burger, would you?" Since the Tazzman couldn't make heads or tails out of this, I decided to press on. "What's your name?"

"Huh?" He seemed stupefied. I guess I couldn't blame him much. I doubt this robbery was going the way he had envisioned.

"You got a name, don't you?" I got up from my booth. "My name's Bill, and like I said before this here's Mike. What do your friends call you?"

"You makin' fun a me? I'll whup yo white ass, dass fo sho."

"I'm not making fun of you."

He squinted suspiciously at me. "Ain't got no friends." He pursed his lips, looking from me to Mike and back again. "I be da Tazzman on accounta my hair." He lifted one hand to touch it; it didn't seem to give an inch. "Kids say it make me look like a *Tazz*manian Devil, sumpin lak dat." That's how Tasmanian came out in his odd accent. He gestured at Mike with the machine pistol. "He really gone make me a bugga?"

"Sure," I said, giving Mike the high sign.

As Mike unwrapped a patty and slapped it on the griddle, I took a step toward the Tazzman. His nostrils flared as he smelled the frying beef and I took another step toward him. He didn't like that.

"Hey, muthafucka," he said, beginning to swing that damn weapon in my direction.

Mike yelled: "Bill, for Chrissake!"

And I threw Ms. M into the Tazzman's face. I don't know whether you know it or not but she gets into your eyes and she's one mean momma.

"Muth*afucka!*" the Tazzman said, with a thorough lack of originality.

He squeezed the trigger just as I slammed my left arm against the barrel of the machine pistol. A sound blast seemed to open a hole in my head, boring straight through to my brain. I trod hard on the Tazzman's instep, and he howled like a banshee. But I had underestimated the beanpole, just as I had misjudged the entire situation.

He got off a second squeeze. A hail of bullets stitched a lethal line across the mirrors. Mike tried to duck but he got in the way and was blasted back into the triple tier of liquor bottles behind him. Liquor and blood combined in one god-awful spew.

"Ah, hell," I said. As the machine pistol swung toward me, I kicked over a table, ducked behind it, then screamed as the high-velocity bullets shredded the solid oak tabletop as if it were paperboard.

I lurched drunkenly into the shadows at the rear of the bar, but the Tazzman was in full bore and he followed me. The machine pistol quit erupting long enough for him to slam home another magazine. How many did he have? I wondered as I ran.

I bypassed the doors to the rest rooms knowing that there was nowhere to run, nowhere to hide. The bullets were chattering into the old plaster as I hit the rear door. It wouldn't open! I fumbled with the deadbolt, then frantically pulled it open as constellations of lathe and wood flew past my head and struck me on the shoulder.

I hurtled into the stinking back alley where Mike dumped his garbage and his hamburger meat when it started to turn into a laboratory experiment.

And silence . . .

Silence?

Where was the unholy racket of the Tazzman's machine pistol? you might ask. But that was the least of it, because I wasn't in any stinking back alley. Turning around in a complete circle I could see that, well, let me put it this way, if I'd had a tiny terrier at my side I would no doubt have blurted out: "We're not in Kansas anymore, Toto."

I finally returned to the direction from which I'd come, but there was no filthy facade, no door back into Helicon; there was only air and space and light—glorious, luminous light. I was in a high-ceilinged room, looking out a tall window at a curiously familiar structure with a rounded dome that looked almost Middle Eastern. Lower down, a large city fanned away in the blue-and-gold dusk. But it had been morning just moments ago, and this place was definitely not Manhattan. The plethora of chimneys and mansard roofs made me think immediately of Europe.

Around me, the pale stucco walls were hung with paintings. These huge Impressionist canvasses were dense with color, vibrant with protean movement. They swirled about me like eddies in a stream.

"Do you like them?"

The voice was melodious, rich as Devonshire cream.

I turned around to see a woman with a long face whose determination made handsome features that were at best plain. She had a stern countenance eerily like the cursed headmistress of the Adirondack prep school I'd escaped to at the age of fourteen (even that had been better than my intolerable home life), then had promptly escaped *from*. Salt-and-pepper hair fell lankly to her slight shoulders and in one hand she held a cluster of paintbrushes, so I assumed she was the artist. She was dressed in an orange shirt and rust-colored trousers over which she wore a long red apron, stiff with dried paint. Even so, I could see a white pentagram stitched to its front. You might think this a curious getup, and you'd be right. But by far the most curious thing about her was her eyes. I swear they were the color of unpolished bronze, and they had no pupils.

"Lady, I don't know who you are but I'd be much obliged if you'd tell me where the hell I am. Also, do you have a drink—preferably something high in alcohol content."

"I was speaking of the paintings. Even though they are unfinished I'd be interested to know whether you find them effective." She spoke with the intensity possible only when one is consumed by a passion. Had she even heard what I'd said? No matter; her passion impelled me to give the paintings a more focused look. So far as I could tell they were all of the same subject: a series of landscapes deliberately interconnected by composition and style, caught at different times of the day and season. I was certain I didn't know what I was looking at and yet, curiously, that very certainty filled me with an inexpressible sadness, just as if I had been pierced through the heart.

"Sure, sure. They're beautiful," I told her. But I was still distracted, and in desperate need of a stiff drink. "Listen, I don't think you get it. One minute I was in a New York bar running from a madman with a machine pistol and the next I'm here. I'm asking you again, where *is* here?"

"Regard the paintings," she said in the slightly stilted locution of the European. Her arm rose and fell like the swell of the ocean. "They will tell you."

"Lady, for the love of—"

"Please," she said. "My name is Vav. And yours is William, yes?"

"Did you say Viv, like Vivian?" I wasn't sure I'd heard her right.

"No. *Vav.*" She enunciated it clearly. "It is a very old name—ancient, one might say. It is the Hebrew word for 'nail.' " She smiled, and her face broke open like a ripe melon spilling out its fragrant and delicious juice. "I am the nail that joins the beams overhead. I am the one who provides shelter to lost travelers."

Looking at that face I had to laugh; I had no other choice. I imagined she could make even a condemned criminal feel good about his final moments of life. "Well, that seems to be me, all right," I admitted. I took a quick glance out the window. "That wouldn't—Whoa! I mean, it couldn't possibly be Sacré-Coeur. Hell, that's in Paris."

"Yes, it is," she said.

"But that's impossible!" I closed my eyes, shook my head and opened them again. There was Sacré-Coeur. It hadn't dissolved in a sudden puff of smoke. "I must have lost my mind."

"Or most likely gained it." She chuckled. "Come now, do not be alarmed." She led me away from the window. "Have another look at the paintings, yes? I am creating them just for you."

"You mean you knew I was coming?" Why did that make me feel so good?

"That hardly seems possible, does it?" She laughed until I joined her, and we shared a joke the origin of which was beyond my ken. She took my arm as if we were old friends. "But come, tell me if anything here seems familiar," she urged as we moved slowly around the high-ceilinged room.

My brow furrowed in concentration. "Funny, I'd been thinking just that, but . . ." I shook my head. "Maybe when you've completed them."

"Obviously you need more time," she interrupted. She did this a lot, as if she was oddly pressed for time.

"All things considered, I think I'd prefer to get back home," I said.

"Didn't I hear mention of a madman with a machine pistol?" She stripped off her apron. "Why in the world would you want to go back there?"

I considered a moment, thinking of poor dead Mike and the Tazzman, Ray on my back about Lilly, and that sonuvabitch brother of mine, not to mention a writer's block as frightening as the death zone atop Mount Everest. Then I considered the unusual woman beside me, being in Paris on a perfect drizzly velvet night, and I felt a certain lightness of being I hadn't felt in I don't know how long. "To be honest, I can't think of a reason."

She squeezed my arm. "Good, then you'll come with me to the opening of the new exhibition."

I licked my lips. "First, I need a drink."

She went to an antique sideboard, poured a liquid into a squat glass of cut-crystal, and brought it back to me. I put the glass to my lips. My nostrils flared at the scent of mescal, and I threw my head back, downing it in one long swallow.

"That's always helped before, hasn't it," she said as I put the empty glass aside.

Normally, I'd be pissed as hell at that kind of comment, but Vav had a way of speaking that held no judgment. It was as if she were simply holding up for me to examine a facet of my life. It was entirely up to me what I thought of it.

"It certainly has its place," I said as we walked across the apartment's living room. I got a brief impression of deep-cream-colored walls, a long Deco-style sofa, a couple of Art Nouveau lamps, all of which seemed to have been put there with a minimum of thought. Then there was the antique Oriental carpet on which was curled a black cat with a single white spot in the center of its forehead. The cat awoke as we passed, its luminous citrine eyes following us as Vav led me out the front door.

At the bottom of a well-worn stone staircase, we found ourselves in a high, musty vestibule typical of Parisian apartment buildings. It smelled of stone softened by the dampness of the ages. A light came on as we entered, then winked out as we departed.

Mist borne like a flock of birds on the evening wind fluttered in gossamer veils past the iron streetlights. We began to walk east, into the night.

"The gallery is only a few blocks away," Vav said.

"Listen, I can see for myself I'm in Paris, but how the hell did I get here?"

We came to a curb and crossed the street on a fairly steep upgrade. "Which explanation would satisfy you?" she said. "The scientific, the metaphysical or the paranormal?"

"Which one is the truth?"

"Oh, I imagine they're all equally true . . . or false. It all depends on your particular point of view."

I shook my head in frustration. "But that's just it, you see. I don't *have* a point of view. To do so I would have to understand what is happening, and I don't."

She nodded, thinking through every word I said. "Perhaps it's only because you aren't ready yet to hear what I'm saying. In the same way you aren't ready to see the paintings."

As we turned left, then left again, past the Art Nouveau entrance to the Anvers Métro station, I curiously found my mind wandering backward in time. I saw with astonishing clarity my mother's face. She had been a handsome woman, powerful in many ways, weak and frightened in others. In her dealings with other people, for instance, she was rock solid and extremely forceful. Once I'd seen her wrangle the price of a Rolex watch down a hundred dollars by telling the shop owner she had nine sons (instead of the two she really did have), all of whom would one day require graduation presents just like this watch she'd picked out for me. I remember having to keep my eyes cast down lest I giggle into the shop owner's greedy face. Outside, the Rolex encircling my right wrist, my mother and I had laughed until we cried. That moment still reverberated inside me, though she was long gone.

On the other hand, my mother was riddled with fear and superstition, especially when it came to her children. Her own father, whom she had adored, had died when she was only fourteen. She once told me that when I was born she was consumed with all the terrible things that could happen to me: disease, accidents, being gulled by the evil people she imagined on all sides. She did not want me taken prematurely from her as her father had been. She dreamed of him, of seeing him asleep in his chair at night, in shirt and vest, carpet slippers on his feet, his gold pocket watch lying open in the palm of his hand, as if he needed its weight to ensure he'd wake up in time for work. She would pad softly across the living room and climb into his lap, curling like a dog, closing her eyes and dreaming of him.

My mother did not, as might have been expected, relax after I and my brother, Herman, were born. This, she would later tell me, was because she knew she was fated to have Lily. Lily confirmed my mother's worst fears, her essentially bleak view of the world. Of course she blamed herself for Lily's deformities. Of course she had a nervous breakdown. And of course this made everything worse, for us and for her. You could say with a fair degree of certainty that hers was a self-fulfilling prophesy. She was terrified of life and so she gave birth to a life that terrified her. Was it any wonder then that Lily horrified us? We learned, Herman and I, like all animals, by example.

It's not that I blame my mother. She could no more help herself than a robin could help but fly. That's what robins do: fly. And to be perfectly truthful Lily was an unholy terror. Not that she could help herself, either. But the truth is the truth, no matter how painful. There was simply no point in going near her, let alone trying to make contact. For a time, I tried to pity her, but though I could pity my mother I couldn't pity Lily. There simply wasn't enough of her. Then, I tried to pretend she didn't exist, but that didn't work, either. Nothing worked when it came to Lily—no diagnosis, no therapy, no form of rationalizing, nothing. Eventually, even her *Exorcist*-like twitching and drooling became banal, part of the scenery that's seen but no longer registers. She was a sad fact of life, like my dad's pathetic easy chair that was so smelly and decrepit we all wanted to throw it out.

A swelling burst of sound pulled me out of my odd reverie. Up ahead, I saw a crowd spilling out of a large arched, iron-clad doorway. I felt certain this must be the entrance to the gallery where the exhibition hung.

I wanted to go on, but instead I stopped dead in my tracks. My gaze had been drawn, possibly by an unexpected movement, to a shape crouched atop the ornate cornice at the corner of the building nearest us. It projected out over the sidewalk, a dark and sinister countenance that made my blood run cold. It was merely a gargoyle, I realized after this initial jolt, but it was unlike any I'd ever seen before. I squinted into the drizzly gloom. It appeared as if the thing was half man, half reptile. It had an eerie oblate head with a face that was wider than it was high. Oversized eyes flanked an inhumanly large mouth and a horrific ophidian snout.

"What has caught your attention?" Vav asked.

"The gargoyle above us."

"Ah." She nodded. "You know, don't you, that gargoyles were originally added to buildings to remind man of the dark side of his nature."

"Jesus, if this one represents someone's dark side I certainly never want to meet him. The thing is downright hideous." And yet I couldn't stop myself from staring up at it. Possibly this was because I had a personal horror of reptiles that dated back to when I was a child of seven. I'd been lost in the Mexican coastal swamps and had had a truly terrifying encounter with a crocodile intent on having me for lunch. I got the willies just recalling it.

"The crowd is big, isn't it?" Vav said without even turning her head to look.

"And getting bigger every moment, I'm happy to say." In truth, I was delighted to get my mind off the horror squatting above us. "You're obviously quite popular."

"Ah no, now you are confusing the messenger with the message," she said. "It's nothing to do with *me*. They have all come to see the *paintings*."

"But the paintings *are* you."

"Once you are there, you will see." She led me into the mouth of a dank alley along the near side of the stone building. Instantly, the city was obliterated by darkness.

"Shouldn't we be going into the gallery?" I asked.

"We must hurry," Vav said. "From what you have told me there is very little time."

"But I've told you nothing—"

I broke off. There was something about this alley, something oddly, eerily familiar, but I shook off the sensation as nonsense. Besides, I was too busy being the paranoid New Yorker, figuring the odds of us getting mugged. I felt a thoroughly unpleasant creeping along my spine the farther we went. It built to such a pitch that I was literally forced to glance back over my shoulder. I let out an ugly expletive as my worst fears were realized: a misshapen form was slouching behind us.

"What is it?" Vav had halted at my cry and now she turned.

"There's someone coming after us," I said. "Can't you see him?"

"I'm afraid I can't see anything," she said. "I thought you'd guessed. I'm quite blind."

"Oh, hell."

"No, no, it's all part of my gift," she said, misunderstanding me.

Out of the wok and into the inferno, I thought as I grabbed her by the arm and dragged her backward down the alley.

"Hurry," she said. "Hurry now, William."

The figure was gaining on us at an alarming rate. All of a sudden I knew what it felt like to have my blood run cold, because I found myself staring face-to-face—if you could call it that—with the hideous gargoyle. It was so hideous I could barely glance at it. Now I knew what had drawn my eye up to it in the first place: I had seen it stir. The problem was I hadn't been able to believe it. Now I had no choice. It was alive and it was after us.

"It's the gargoyle," I managed to get out. "Vav, if you have any idea what the hell is going on, now would be the time to tell me." Right about then it occurred to me that the Tazzman had shot me and this was really . . . Hell?

"Vav, tell me I'm not dead."

"It's worse than I had been led to believe," she said more to herself than to me. What mystery were her blind bronze eyes seeing? "Trust me, William, you're not dead."

No sooner had Vav said this than a gargoyle leapt at us with such frightening speed that it was all I could do to duck out of its way. A misshapen taloned hand swung across my vision and struck Vav with such force that she flew out of my grip and bounced like a ball against the stones of the alley. Then, to my surprise, the beast drew back as if sensing something I could neither see nor hear. Foolishly, I turned my back on the horror while I knelt beside her.

"William, are you there?"

"You know I am." There was blood all over, hot and sticky. "I've got to call an ambulance."

"Too late. You must get to the exhibition," she whispered. "It's absolutely vital."

"Vav, please tell me why." But she was gone, and I could feel the beast almost upon me, so I let her go and ran. But I had left it too late. One of its paws tripped me and I went sprawling face first onto the cobblestones. I tried to get up, but I seemed paralyzed. I had only strength enough to turn over. I saw it looming over me, its awful snout contorted in what seemed to be a ghastly grin.

I threw a hand across my face and at once I was seized by a violent bout of vertigo. The very cobblestones beneath me seemed to melt as I plunged into a dark and formless pit. I think I screamed. Then I must have lost consciousness, because the next thing I saw when I opened my eyes was a cool, leafy glade. Birds chirped and sang in the oak branches in counterpoint to the soft lazy drone of insects. I could smell clover and the tangy scents of loosestrife and mock orange. Looking up at the sky, I could see it was that time of the day when, having riven out the sunlight, the lovely cobalt of evening has spread like inscrutable words upon a page.

I heard a horse whinny and, turning my head, discovered close by a magnificent chestnut hunter-jumper cropping the grass. He was fitted out in English riding habit.

The quick beat of a horse's hooves caused me to look up into the face of a woman. She was quite striking, with emerald eyes and lustrous dark-blond hair that fell thick as the forest around us to the edge of her jawline. *Radiant,* that was the word one might use in defining her; radiant in the way few people ever are or could hope to be. Seated confidently astride a black mare with a white blaze in the center of its forehead, she was dressed in expensive but practical hunting togs of a deep blue, save for her silk shirt, which was milky-white.

"Are you quite all right?" she inquired in a delightful, clipped English accent.

"Should I be?" I asked. I wiped my eyes, which to my complete horror were leaking tears. I wanted to stop weeping but I could not. Already I missed Vav; I wanted her back. I realized that in her company for the first time in many years I had felt safe.

"From a distance it seemed as if you took a nasty fall, but now I'm here I do believe the forest bed of oak leaves bore the brunt of it."

I hadn't the faintest idea what she was talking about. But as I got up I discovered that I was brushing leaves and detritus from a pair of jodhpurs and high black hunting boots. And not a trace of Vav's blood which was seconds ago splattered all over me. I wept again, so copiously that I was obliged to turn away from her out of embarrassment.

"I guess I'm okay," I replied when I'd managed to pull myself together. I put a hand to my head. "Except for a bit of a headache."

"Hardly surprising, actually." She handed me an etched silver hip flask. "Here. You look like you could use this."

I unscrewed the cap, smelled the familiar aroma of mescal. I felt the familiar lure, but somehow something had changed inside me and I was put in mind of a fish rising to the baited hook. I hesitated a moment more before handing back the flask. "Some other time, perhaps."

She nodded. "Why don't I wait and ride the rest of the way with you."

I looked around. "Are we on some kind of steeplechase?"

"Yes, of course." She laughed, a sound like a thousand tinkling silver bells. "We're on a hunt, William."

Taking up the chestnut's reins, I slid my foot into the left stirrup. "And we would be . . . where?" I swung up into the saddle.

"Leicestershire. The East Midlands of England. The Charnwood Forest, to be precise."

"The heart of hunt country," I said. "The Cottesmore is run here, if memory serves."

"The great yearly foxhunt. Yes, indeed. But now without growing controversy." Her eyes crinkled in the most appealing manner. "Come on now." She dug the heels of her boots into the mare's flanks and the horse leapt forward. "I don't fancy missing all the fun, d'you?"

I urged the chestnut after her and at once he broke into a full gallop. To give you a fair idea of how this woman affected me, I confess that even while I was desperately trying to remember everything I'd been taught about riding, I was studying her features with ruthless concentration. Her rosy, cream-colored skin made her seem as if she was born for the hunt—or at the very least for the misty English countryside. She had a canny intelligence about her, an insouciant air that drew me in a way I could not fathom. If at that very moment someone had warned me about her—had accused her of being a murderess, to take the extreme—I would have laughed in his face and, putting heels to my steed's sweaty flanks, left him in the dust. Happy to be in her heady company. I had only just met her and already I felt as if I'd known her all my life. Some connection, intimate as an umbilical, bound us. She was like an unexpected present under the Christmas tree. *Are you really for me?* I wanted to ask while rubbing my eyes in disbelief.

"Hey, you know my name but I don't know yours," I called.

"Surely you know me, William." She lifted a hand and I saw with a start the webbing between her fingers. "I am Gimel, the weaver of realities, the font of ideas, the headwater of inspiration. I am like my namesake, the camel, filled to the brim with resources, a self-sufficient ship even in the most hostile climates."

At this moment, we emerged into a wide grassy field dotted with dandelion and foxglove. The specters of solid oaks marched ahead of us on either side, and in the gathering gloom I could just make out an oft-tramped path. As we began to follow it, I soberly reminded myself that all this frothing off at the mind was nothing more than an odd kind of fantasy left over, perhaps, from the tens of thousands of hormonal fever dreams I'd had during my appropriately bad adolescence. By bad I mean spoiled, like that blackish, moldy thing you find in your refrigerator after having been away for several months.

"I take it, then, we're on a foxhunt of our own," I said as I pulled abreast of her. I was so close I could breathe in her lovely scent.

"Oh, no. I would never be after anything so beautiful as a fox." When she shook her head her hair moved in the most provocative way. "We're after the beast."

"What beast?"

"You know perfectly well, William, so don't play me." She gave me a sharp look. I saw a flinty edge inside the gorgeous emeralds of her eyes and my heart turned over. Doctor, the oxygen! Stat! "The beast of beasts," she went on, oblivious to the arrow protruding from my heart. "There is only one so hideous, so needing of being hunted."

"Look, I admit to being more than slightly confused. I mean, just moments ago I was lying in a back alley of Paris with my friend's blood—"

"So you think of Vav as a friend? Curious. You only knew her a very short while."

"I'm a good judge of character," I replied somewhat angrily. "If you aren't also a friend of hers, you'd better declare it now."

She laughed. "My goodness, how quickly you jump to her defense." Close to me now, she leaned over and kissed me on the cheek and I heard those birds chirping in my head, the ones you see in the cartoons flying around Sylvester's head when Tweety has hit him a good one with a hammer. "Vav and I were like sisters. Closer, even, if you can imagine. Like two pieces of the same pie."

"I miss her."

"I'm hardly surprised," she said. "You were on your way to an exhibition of paintings. It's important you get there." She nodded as if to herself. "Absolutely vital, one might say."

"You mean you know how to get me back to Paris?"

"That wouldn't be wise, now would it? Besides, there's no need." She was posting a bit so I could keep pace. Her back was straight, her shoulders squared. She had about her that almost flagrant tomboy look I find irresistible. I imagined her striding through the forest like Diana, the mythical huntress, thighs flexing, muscles cording as she notched an arrow onto her bowstring, pulling it taut as her prey came into range. "The exhibition just went up in the Manor House. We'll get there as soon as we can. But first, we must see the hunt to its inevitable conclusion."

"If it's inevitable, why bother with it?" I said. "Why not just head straight for the Manor?"

Her brow furrowed. "One might as well ask why not exhale without inhaling first. It simply cannot be done. Laws of the universe, you know."

"These are the same laws that allow me to move from New York to Paris to the Charnwood Forest in the blink of an eye? Or to allow an exhibition of paintings in Paris to be here now?"

"Just so." She was oblivious to my irony. In fact, she appeared relieved. "I'm so pleased you and I are on the same page."

I groaned. A page of what strange book? I wondered.

"Don't worry," she called. "I'll get you where you need to go. Trust me, William."

I felt a tiny chill play against my spine, for that was just what Vav had said. At that moment, I made a decision. Spurring my horse on, I leaned over toward her. So far as I could determine, playing by the rules, odd though they might be, had done me no good at all. All change! I grabbed her reins and drew her off the trodden path.

"What are you doing?" she said, alarmed.

"To the Manor, wherever that is," I said. "Let the others handle the beast."

"What others?" We were side by side now, our thighs touching. "William, we're the only ones on this hunt."

"So much the better," I said. "No one will miss us when we don't go on."

"You don't understand."

I leaned in until I was close enough to smell her hair. "Now we're getting somewhere."

She licked her lips. At the fall of night her eyes were like cabochon jewels. For an instant I found myself wondering idly, crazily, if she was as blind as Vav.

"We must run the beast to ground," she said. "Otherwise, it will never let us get to the Manor House."

"Why?"

"William—" There was something in her face now, some hint of a wound so fresh, so deep it was still bleeding. "Vav ignored the beast at her own peril. Look what happened to her. I won't make the same mistake."

She looked so vulnerable. I put my hand on the side of her neck. "What mistake?"

She was trembling a little. "The paintings and the beast are intertwined. You can't see one without encountering the other. She thought she could take you directly to the paintings, that she could somehow circumvent the beast. But she was wrong."

"You keep talking about a beast, but what exactly do you mean? To my knowledge there *are* no beasts in Leicestershire, or for that matter anywhere in England. Large predators are extinct here, as they are in most of Europe."

Her eyes searched mine. "Vav didn't explain?"

"If she had I wouldn't be asking you, would I?" I said softly.

"It's an exercise in futility. You won't believe me, I promise you."

I kissed her cheek. "You mean you won't even give me the chance?"

This seemed to give her pause. I could sense that she was coming to a decision she would rather not make. "It's best if we keep moving while we talk."

I nodded and let go of her reins, following closely as she veered at an acute angle across the cool blue grassland into the inky shadows of the forest.

"The beast is a creature born of chaos," she said at last. "It hardly thinks as you or I know it; you can't reason with it or come to a compromise, but its reactions to stimuli are appallingly quick. It is pure evil."

"It attacked Vav before I could even take a breath."

"Poor Vav. She didn't have a chance," Gimel said in an odd tone of voice, as if she were speaking to herself. Then her gaze met mine across the short distance between us. "As I said, I won't make the same mistake."

I wanted to ask her what she meant, but all at once, inside the forest, everything changed. I don't mean the oak trees, or the coolness of the evening, the rich earthy smells or the very strong sense of being in this place. I don't quite know how to say this, but it was as if from the moment I had run out the back of Helicon I had been balancing on a taut wire. Now that wire had broken, and I was falling. Not literally, you understand. But figuratively I felt as if I were falling from one reality—or rather my *perception* of reality—into another. A bubble had burst and I suddenly found myself beneath the skin of the universe. I was inside looking out at the surface—the bright, shiny, all-too-familiar shell—of every mundane thing we take for granted. Now everything looked different to me. And with that feeling came a ripple of recognition, like the déjà vu of a vivid dream, of the unfinished paintings I'd seen in Vav's atelier. For just the briefest instant I glimpsed beneath their conventional Impressionist surface to what they were *about. It's nothing to do with me,* Vav had said in speaking about the exhibition. I hadn't understood her then. How could the exhibition *not* be about her? I had wondered in Paris. She was the artist. And yet now I was beginning to understand what she had meant. The paintings were what was important. Who had painted them was in a very real sense of no import.

"Wait!" I called out to Gimel. "Hold on a second!"

She whirled her horse around. "What is it?"

I was already dismounted. "There's something about this place . . . something familiar."

She jumped off her horse, and as it turned I saw attached to one side of the saddle an old-fashioned longbow—not one of those space-age-material composite bows hunters use nowadays—and a quiver of arrows. She came toward me with a pronounced limp, as if one leg were shorter than the other. Then I saw that her left leg was narrower and smaller than her right, withered like a dried stalk of wheat.

"Perhaps you have been to this part of the Charnwood Forest before."

I shook my head. "I've never been outside of London. But even if I had, that isn't what I mean." I was walking around the small glade. "What I'm feeling . . . It isn't as simple as that." She regarded me calmly, albeit with a certain degree of curiosity. "Do you think it's possible to know a place—I mean know it inside and out—without ever having set foot in it?"

"If one looks at only the physical world, no, of course not." She strode across the glade in her peculiar lopsided gait to stand in front of me. "But the universe is so much more than that, isn't it?" In the tone of her voice I could sense that she was asking something else entirely.

Curious how these moments of transition came upon me. Once again, I found my consciousness cast back in time. The image of Donnatella, slightly drunk, stood before me. I had met her in Mexico, where she had come with her husband and sister for a vacation. While her unconscionable husband was romancing her sister, Donnatella and I sat in quiet, leafy Oaxacan squares and drank mescal. This had the effect of keeping the stifling heat at bay and also of arousing us to seizures of unbridled passion. Thinking now about those erotically charged moments in her hotel room or in mine I could for the first time see where it all went wrong. They were fierce, those sexual encounters, yes, but—and it hurts so much to admit this—they were also essentially joyless. It hurt because it showed me how little we really had, what small people we were together. It occurred to me that with Herman, Donnatella was a better person—and that hurt as well. To say all of this hit me with the impact of an express train was something of an understatement. Up until that moment I was absolutely certain we had loved one another, even after she and Herman ran off together. But now I knew better. Our love, like a billboard with a half-naked model, had been nothing more than wishful thinking. The sad truth is that Donnatella and I coupled for all the wrong reasons, and we married for them as well. Twelve hours after her divorce came through, wham, it was done: we were married. It was a seductive but poisonous start we made for ourselves, sitting sprawl-legged, drunk on mescal and each other, groping moist flesh beneath the plank table, under the somnolent, watchful gaze of the Mexican waiters. To this day I hear the soulful strum of a Mexican guitar and my eyes glaze over. But I suppose the truth is that all the while Donnatella was pleasuring me she was thinking of her husband and her sister, and of revenge.

No, we never loved one another. Our personal flame wasn't even passion so much as rage—a rage at everything around us. And this rage—this demonic passion—made us safe. For a time. And then it vanished. You couldn't even say our relationship was over, because it had never really begun. I curiously never stopped liking her. With Lily she was a saint, going to see her almost every week when I never would. She and I had the most god-awful fights about that. She'd often say it was a mortal sin, my ignoring my sister, and who knows, perhaps she was right. Then again, being Roman Catholic, Donnatella was consumed with all the conflicting quirks and superstitions that go along with the religion. I often wondered how she rationalized two divorces. Once, when I asked her, she told me with a curious kind of contempt that her uncle knew the Pope and had managed to secure for her some form of dispensation. To this day, I have no idea whether or not that was true. Anyway, I'm not sure it matters. She was certainly kinder to my sister than she was to her own sister, but how can I fault her for that? I can't. I won't. She's a unique person and in the end I'm glad we met, even if I got to know her too well and too late. But when you come to the quick of it—when you strip away everything that doesn't matter—she was never mine, and the deepest pain comes from the years of self-delusion that she once was.

The enormity of these revelations made me sick to my stomach. It was as if the world had turned to ash, as if memory like some terrible swift scythe had mown down a shining field of illusion. *My* illusion. Now all at once Donnatella, the languorous, leafy Mexican square, the sweaty furtive couplings, the plangent guitar music outside the cracked hotel window wavered and grew insubstantial like a djinn vanishing into his lamp.

I was back in the Charnwood Forest in the ethereal darkness of the glade. Gimel was still close beside me. I could smell her slightly spicy scent.

"What were you just thinking?" she asked. "I could feel your tension."

"I was recalling my life," I said truthfully. "And, sadly, it occurred to me that it hasn't been what I'd thought it was."

"What is?" Her eyes were shining in the dark. "Whatever we can immediately know must be of poor value, don't you think?"

"I don't know you." I gripped her more tightly. "Not at all."

"Am I precious, then?" Her eyes danced as she smiled wickedly at me. "Is that your meaning?"

A cool stillness seemed to banish the rest of the world to a dim and hazy daguerreotype. Did the breeze cease to stir the oak leaves; did the birds cease their evening songs, the insects their nocturnal Morse code? It seemed that way to me. In Mexico, Donnatella had once told me that when she was with me nothing else was real. "Existence, it is the tip of the flame," she had said in the endearing way she had of reparsing the English language in her own image. "When I am in your arms I am in the flame, can you understand this?"

With Gimel I felt I was inside the flame, as if all existence resided in the minuscule space between us. But, in the end, the outside world intruded like a clammy and inauspicious wind. In the instant that my memories had overtaken me I had missed something, perhaps something crucial.

I was at once filled with apprehension. The smile had frozen on her face. I could see the skin on her arms had broken out into goose bumps.

"What's happened?" I said.

Then I heard it, too. Something quite large was making its way through the forest. As we stood without moving a muscle, straining to interpret the sound, I could tell it was heading directly for us.

"It's the beast," she whispered. "It's found us."

"We'd better get back on our horses," I said.

"Do you think that's wise?" She put a hand on my mount's bridle. "Now that we're here do you still believe the best choice is to run?"

"What else is there to do?" I said. "Will your arrows stop it?"

"I have no idea."

"That uncertainty doesn't make for good odds."

"What have odds to do with it?" All at once she seemed saddened. "Do you think Vav considered the odds when she took you down the Parisian alley?"

"I couldn't say."

"Then you're right," she said, abruptly letting go of the bridle. She sounded as if at any moment she would break into tears. "We'd better try to flee before it's too late."

But it was already too late. As I put one boot into the stirrup, the underbrush parted and a dark and ungainly shape rushed us from the shadows. The black mare reared up, snorting, her nostrils flared, and Gimel nocked an arrow to her bowstring. She drew back the string and let fly. Maybe it was a trick of the last of the evening's cobalt light, but the arrow seemed to disappear an instant before it would have pierced the beast's chest. With a soft cry, she hurled herself directly into the beast's path.

"No!" I shouted as the thing swung an enormous paw at her. It was immensely powerful. Even from that distance I could hear her neck crack. She was lifted off her feet by the terrific force of the blow, spun around so that I saw all the light had gone out of her eyes. She fell to the forest floor, her head at an unnatural angle.

My stomach turned over and I tried to get to her. But I also felt compelled to get a better look at this beast than I had at the gargoyle.

And yet I could only take it in with brief, furtive flicks of my eyes. It had the same hideous face I'd glimpsed out of the corner of my eye in the Parisian alley, but this time its body was definitely more animal than human. Just as it had before, it hesitated, but this time I thought I heard something, a far-off crack as if a rifle shot. Wasting no time, I gathered Gimel to me and dragged her into the mass of oaks. I picked her up amid the dense tangle of underbrush; she was as light as an infant. It was as if there was no substance to her, as if all that she had been had vanished the moment the beast had broken her neck.

Still I could not bear to let her go. She had sacrificed herself, throwing herself between me and the beast. But there was no time to lose. Behind me, the beast was crashing through the forest toward me. I turned and ran, stumbling over villages of roots and vines, colonies of pale toadstools. Once, I went down on my knees, but I never let go of Gimel. I could not imagine leaving her there for the beast to find and perhaps maul over. That would have been an inhuman act.

I have already said that her body was quite light, nevertheless it was an impediment amid the forest's tenacious undergrowth. As a consequence, I was rapidly losing ground to the beast, whose hellacious panting was like the roar of an immense vehicle about to run me down.

Without warning I emerged from the forest and went skidding dangerously down the brown bank to a rather wide stream. Quickly, I looked to left and right. There was no help for it but to go forward into the water. It was cold as ice, and far deeper than it had appeared from shore. I was already up to my waist and I wasn't yet at the deepest part. Behind me, the beast burst from the forest. Its momentum took it to the very edge of the water, where it reared back, bellowing in rage. Possibly it was afraid of water. My spirits rose as I kept going. Halfway across the stream, the water had risen as high as my breastbone. Light as she was, it was still an effort to keep Gimel's body in the air.

I looked back over my shoulder and gave an involuntary cry of terror. The beast was metamorphosing into a gigantic reptile. Scales popped out along its back, and a thick, wickedly spiked tail emerged from between its hind legs. Slithering on its pale belly, it entered the water and, with appalling speed, shot toward me.

All at once, I was seven years old, back in the Mexican swamps. The hot sun fell like a yoke around my shoulders and the back of my neck. The insects swarmed, feasting on my bare flesh. I had become separated from my father by a stand of liana-draped trees. He had been dozing, his back against the bole of a tree, and I, bored and restless, had wandered away. Now I no longer knew my way back through the maze of emerald foliage and muddy water to where he was no doubt already looking for me. And to make matters worse, I had stumbled upon a crocodile lazing in the shallows. It was gray-white and huge, its prehistoric ridged back, armor plate and mammoth hinged jaws making it seem as if it was a lethal weapon on four squat legs.

Christ, it was quick! The beast took off after me as if it had been expelled from a rocket launcher. Its maw was already open and I could see the double rows of razor-sharp teeth. The thing actually looked as if it was grinning at me. I screamed as I stumbled. I saw the thing racing toward me. Then a shot rang out, the croc leapt up, thrashing. Another shot, and its heavily muscled body whipsawed around, almost burying me. When it fell back into the brackish water it was so close to me I was drenched. The last flip of its tail cut my forearm. Then my father and Adolfo, our Mexican guide, had gathered me up. Adolfo wanted to rush me back to the jeep that had brought us here, but my father shook his head and handed me his thick hard-wood walking stick. I took it and slammed it down onto the croc's flat armored cranium. I did this again and again, grunting with the effort and the rage inside me, while Adolfo murmured like a prayer: *"Es muy malo."* It's very bad. I ignored him and didn't stop until I had broken through the bone, until in my mind I had hurt the beast quite as much as he had frightened me.

Like a dream, all this replayed in my head within the space of an eye-blink. The sense of déjà vu ended here, however, because I knew there was no Adolfo combing the area for me, ready to kill this beast before it got to me.

The thrashing drove waves against me. So this was it. It was my fate to die here; the beast was going to get a second chance to do what in another reality it might have done to me when I was seven. I could feel it in the night. No! I could not let it happen. Saying a quick prayer, I dropped Gimel's body and whirled to face it. Its jaws hinged open and, curling my hand into a fist, I jammed my upper arm vertically into the cavernous maw. Teeth ripped through skin and flesh, making me scream, but I would not budge. I'd used my arm like a stick to keep its jaws opened wide, for I'd learned very young that if you jammed a stick into a croc's mouth it couldn't snap it shut.

So there we were, locked together, me bleeding, the beast thrashing, trying to get its powerful tail on me. Sheer terror fought my growing fatigue to a standstill, but the beast's tail was coming closer and closer, thwapping the water viciously. The force of its attack was driving me backward downriver, and now I could feel the current quickening, swirling around me, sucking at me like a leviathan's mouth. It grew in strength until, all of a sudden, my feet were swept out from under me. I was whirled away with such force that even the beast's reflexes weren't fast enough to catch my arm. I was underwater, fully in the grip of the roaring current. I struggled to regain my balance; when that failed, I tried simply to get my head above the surface. Pain blossomed as I hit an underwater rock. I bounced off, spinning. A flash of pain snaked up my side. I gasped for air and began to choke on water. I no longer knew which direction was up or down. Then I struck something. Not another rock; this was soft and cylindrical. It was a body—Gimel's body. I encircled it with my arms and held on, riding out the current as my head rose into sweet air before I was plunged under again. But with my second gulp of air, I could feel the current lessening, and at last I was able to strike out for shore.

I pulled Gimel's white corpse up onto the sludgy bank and I lay there next to her, more dead than alive it seemed to me, for I felt a curious kinship with her. She had saved me from the beast as Vav had done in Paris. Her withered left leg now seemed as natural and necessary a part of her as her heart-shaped face. I felt her arm like a lifeline across my chest and I closed my eyes, wondering whether I was at last safe.

A moment more and it didn't matter, as I was cast into unconsciousness.

I awoke with rain in my face. It was still dark. I could have been out for an hour or twenty-four hours, there was no way of knowing. Thunder rumbled and, as I rose onto one elbow, a flash of lightning illuminated an utterly unfamiliar landscape. I lay in a swale at the edge of a forest; the stream that had carried me here was gone. Clearly, I was no longer in the Charnwood Forest. By the look of the thick stands of pines and American sugar maples I wasn't even in England anymore. And Gimel had vanished along with the stream. I rolled over onto the spot she had occupied and wondered at the deep sense of loss inside me.

At length, I pressed the heels of my hands against my eyes. The arm I'd jammed into the beast's mouth was as good as new. No blood at all. Naturally. The air was decidedly colder, and I shivered inside my damp clothes. I knew I had to get to some kind of shelter quickly or face the threat of hypothermia. I wondered where my next guide was, for this had been the pattern in my previous two realities. Sensing no one about, I rose and, choosing a direction at random, set off in that direction. I decided it was just as well that the pattern had been broken, since my two previous guides had ended up dead.

Because my father was a furniture restorer and coppersmith, I was born and raised in Hadley, Massachusetts, where he enjoyed an excellent reputation. This terrain, identical to the densely wooded hillsides of my childhood, put me immediately in mind of the one and only time I had consented to go on a family outing with Lily. I was used to those woods; I was twelve at the time this outing took place, and already I'd been out hunting plenty of times with my father. He loved to hunt the way most men his age loved to play golf. He was not a violent man, at least not with his family. But, once, I had seen him take apart a bully twice his size who had cut us off in heavy traffic. I had stood beside our car, staring openmouthed as he pummeled this giant senseless. Possibly he had aggression issues which were dealt with in our hunting. On the other hand, hunting required guile, cunning and a good degree of patience, none of which can exist for long within an aggressive individual.

Still, he did not do well with Lily, and though both he and my mother strenuously denied it, so far as I could tell his leaving could not have originated from any other source. I can't speak for my brother, but I did not do well with his departure. Of course I blamed Lily; I couldn't blame him or my mother, could I? Lily was such a convenient target, like that croc whose skull I stove in after Adolfo had shot it to death; by then it couldn't harm me, but it had sure as hell scared the living piss out of me.

Possibly Lily did, as well.

In any event, in the first few months after my father left, my mother was desperate for the rest of the family, so far as it was possible, to do everything together. I imagine it was her way of reassuring us that our world hadn't fallen apart. Years later, it occurred to me that she must have been reassuring herself, as well. Toward that end, she engineered this outing. Because I was the eldest sibling, it was my responsibility to collapse and unfold Lily's wheelchair, as well as to push her around while she screamed, barked, howled and generally sent chills up and down my spine.

It was a beautiful spring day in late May. The birds were twittering busily and the insects were droning. For some reason, the air was filled with butterflies, as if they all had broken out of their golden chrysalises at the same time. You can imagine how beautiful they were, but something about them—perhaps their erratic, skittish flight—seemed to terrify Lily. She rose up out of her wheelchair, screaming and clutching the air with her spastic fingers. When I made the mistake of coming around to try to calm her, she clawed at me with such ferocity she actually drew blood.

That's when I hit her. It was just a smack on her cheek with my open hand, and it startled me just as much as it must have startled her. Her eyes rolled in her head, her face filled with blood, but she was eerily silent for long minutes. Then she erupted into tears. She wept and moaned, rocking and shaking as if with a high fever.

My mother hurried over and boxed me hard on the ear before shoving me away. Then she knelt beside Lily and began the long and repugnant ritual of calming her down. While she tenderly stroked her forearms and murmured to her, while Lily wept and pulled at her hair, hateful Herman looked at me with the full-blown contempt of an adult. Not that he did anything to help Lily—I don't believe she ever liked him, and he knew it. But now he could lord it over me. He could say that *he'd* never lifted a hand to his sister.

"Billy, how could you," my mother said sometime later.

"Mom, look what she did to me. She drew blood, for God's sake."

"She couldn't help herself. She'd never intentionally hurt you. You know how much Lily cares for you."

"Mom, I don't know anything of the sort," I said defensively. "And to be brutally honest, neither do you. Can you tell if a mushroom likes you? No, 'cause a mushroom can't think."

Then she did something she had never done before or after. She grabbed me by my shirtfront and shook me like a rag doll. "Now you're talking like your father, young man, and I won't have it. Do you understand me?" She was mad as hell. "This is your sister you're talking about. Lily is a human being just like you or Herman."

"*Nobody* is like Herman."

"Billy, I'm serious. What does it take to get through to you these days?" All at once she let me go and all the fire went out of her. She appeared defeated, not just by me, but by life. The lens through which the world appeared to her was so distorted by her own past that she could not help but define us by the same severely restricted limits she used for herself. She turned back to Lily, but a moment before she did I could see the look of bitter sorrow that passed like a shroud across her face.

The memory of that bright, bloody afternoon faded as I reached the edge of the pines. I found myself beside a packed-dirt road. It was no more than a country lane, really. I looked in both directions, could see nothing, and went to my left. Given a choice, I always go left. The wind had picked up and so had the rain. Without the protection of the forest I began to shiver. I picked up my pace and within twenty minutes I could see lights burning in a house across a dark field of bare, furrowed rows. I hurried across its open expanse, the bitter wind making my sopping clothes adhere to my skin. I passed an old, rusted tractor that had about it a forlorn air, as if its owner had abandoned it suddenly and without much thought.

The house was old, in the Victorian style, complete with ornamental gingerbread, a wide covered porch and those turreted rooms that look like a witch's conical hat. The place looked gloomy. The fact that it was painted a battleship gray didn't help, but truthfully I never much cared for the Victorian style—too ornate to no good purpose to suit me.

In any event, I climbed the wide plank stairs onto the porch and out of the rain. I shook myself off like a dog before I rang the bell. A chime sounded deep inside the house, setting up peculiar vibrations that set my teeth on edge. When no one answered on my second ring, I tried the door. It wasn't locked.

Inside, I found myself in a magisterial vestibule that was oval in shape. Its main feature was a spiral staircase that grandly rose to the second floor. There was a living room to the right and a study to the left.

"Hello?" I called. "Anybody home?"

There was no reply. Save for the stertorous ticking of a grandfather clock, lacquered black with an etched white porcelain oval affixed just above its face. Had it been a human being I would have figured it was ill.

The study was lit by a wood fire in a massive stone fireplace so encrusted with charcoal it looked as if it had been used for centuries. As you can imagine, the crack and spark of the aromatic logs, as well as the heat itself, were very welcome. I placed myself beside the hearth and relaxed into the delicious heat. Within moments, I could feel my clothes drying out. While they did, I looked around the study. It was paneled in tiger-oak bookshelves. A chair rail ran around the room, and the molding and cornices were of a design and manufacture long out of date. A circular Aubusson rug covered the floor and an ornate ormolu chandelier hung unlit like a great spider waiting to be awakened.

When I was sufficiently warmed and my clothes no longer stuck to me like wet papier-mâché I made my way through the ground floor rooms without finding a living soul. Curiously, the place seemed well-lived-in. For instance, I discovered a plate of orange cheddar cheese and salt biscuits on the kitchen table, and on the massive gas stove a teakettle blackened now because someone had left the flame on while all the water had evaporated. I turned off the burner and almost seared my palm lifting the kettle to a cool spot.

I cursed just as I heard someone scream. Snatching up a large carving knife, I rushed out into the vestibule just as the scream came again, foreshortened this time by an odd and frightening liquid gurgle. It was a female voice and it had come from the second floor. I took the stairs three at a time.

"Hello?" I called at the top of the stairs. "Are you all right?"

I heard only a tiny whimper in reply.

Racing down the hall to my left, I kicked open the door to each room I passed. I was met with only darkness and the peculiar smell of disuse. Then I saw light seeping from under the door at the end of the hallway. I ran to the door and without hesitation threw it open.

I found myself in a huge bedroom, possibly the master suite. An enormous canopy bed occupied the right half of the room, while an uncomfortable-looking divan-and-chairs set in the baroque Louis Quatorze style stood guard on the other half. Between them, a woman lay curled on her left side. I heard her whimper again and rushed to her, kneeling down beside her. She opened her eyes, saw the carving knife and recoiled.

I dropped it immediately. "Don't be alarmed," I said as gently as I could. "I mean you no harm." I put a hand on her shoulder. "On the contrary."

I could only see the right side of her face, which was heart-shaped and strong-featured. She had long dark hair that swirled about her like the currents of a very deep pool. She had on a pink shantung silk blouse and moss-green trousers of the same material. Her feet were bare and I saw tattooed on the instep of one a crescent moon and a circle.

"Are you all right?" I asked again.

"Bring a candle over," she said. When I had complied and had lighted it for her, she took another look at me. "William, it *is* you."

"Do I know you?"

"My name is Daleth," she said. "I am the door, the moist leaf that protects and provides."

"What happened here?"

She rose up and turned her full face to me. I recoiled with a small cry I could not help but utter. The entire left side of her face was a raw pulp, newly burned by naked flame.

"My God," I whispered. "We've got to get you to a hospital."

"You found your way here, William," she said as I helped her up. "I wanted to meet you, to guide you here, but—" She collapsed against me and her head lolled on my chest without leaving an imprint of blood.

I helped her to the divan and arranged her on it. Her breathing was heavy, as tortured as the ticking of the old clock downstairs.

"It has come," she said. "The beast is already here, you see. It has violated the rules, which means that you must have done the same."

I immediately thought of my willfully changing the course of the hunt in the Charnwood Forest over Gimel's warning.

"I suppose I have," I said. "But I had no idea of the consequences."

"No," she said. "But that's just it, isn't it?"

"What do you mean?"

"All life has consequence, William. All life has value."

"Not this beast. It's already killed two people, and now look what it's done to you."

She regarded me from out of pitch-black eyes. "The beast—it's still here. Somewhere. Waiting to come into the light."

I retrieved the carving knife and hefted it. "This time I'm ready."

"What will you do?" she asked. "Pierce its skull as you did with the crocodile?"

I started. "How did you know about that?"

"How did I know your name?"

I stood up, shaking. "Who are you? Who are any of you?"

"I told you. My name is Daleth."

"You're termagants," I cried, "sent to torture me!"

She drew herself up. "Are you so undeserving of torture?" I was too stunned to answer. Possibly she never meant me to answer, because almost immediately she went on. "If so, then why do you torture yourself?"

"What . . . what do you mean?" I said hoarsely.

"Oh, you know perfectly well what I mean, William, sitting day after day in that bar, hiding yourself away from the world, losing your soul in that bottomless pit inside yourself."

"Hey!" I shouted. Now I truly was terrified. I'd told no one about that bottomless pit, not Donnatella, not Mike the bartender, not Ray my accountant. *No one.* "What in the name of holy hell is going on here?"

That was when she cocked her head and her black eyes opened wide. "You hear it, don't you, William?" The sound she was referring to came again, echoing eerily in the bowels of the house. "The beast is on the move again. It is coming out of the shadows."

"Fuck the beast."

"Yes"—she nodded—"*fuck* the beast, indeed." She cocked her head. "On the other hand, you cannot ignore it. And you can no longer run away. This is your last chance. Here is where you make your stand."

I could hear it now, and somehow the sound of its movements sent fresh shock waves of terror running through me.

"Tell me what the others didn't," I said. "Tell me how to kill it."

She looked up at me with something akin to astonishment. "It cannot be killed. I thought you knew that much."

"Damn you!" I cried. "Damn all you to hell!"

"Too late for that."

I turned and ran from the room. I held the knife in front of me, but I was sweating so profusely the hilt felt loose and slippery in my grip.

"Oh, God," I moaned in despair, "what is going to happen to me?" There was nobody to protect me, nobody to save me. Vav was dead, so was Gimel, and this one, this Daleth, was of no use at all. She had already proved that she couldn't stand up to the beast. That left me and only me.

You can no longer run away, she had said. To hell with that. I flew down the staircase and hurtled to the front door. It wouldn't open no matter how hard I pulled and pushed. I ran into the living room, ripped aside the heavy drapes and tried to open the window. It wouldn't budge. I looked at the storm-swept night outside and found even that preferable to remaining here. In a fit of rage, I picked up a chair and threw it at the window. I gaped in astonishment as the chair bounced off the pane of glass. I beat at the glass with my fists to no avail. Daleth was right, I couldn't run away.

This is your last chance, she had said. Did that mean I had blown my first two chances in Paris and Leicestershire? Chances at what?

"Hey!" I yelled at no one and everything. How could I play the game when I didn't know the rules or the object? "Dammit, this isn't fair!"

"Of course it's not fair," Daleth said, coming into the room. She seemed to have regained a good measure of her strength. "Whatever is?"

"But you know what this is about!" I shouted.

"I know *everything*."

"Then, for the love of God, why won't you tell me?"

She came close to me and I turned my head so I wouldn't have to see the horribly maimed side of her face. "Won't you look at me, William?" she said softly. "Don't you find me beautiful?"

She *was* beautiful, at least most of her. But what the beast had done to her had altered her forever. "Don't make me answer that."

"But it's an important question. Vital, one might say." Why did each termagant keep repeating what the others had said? How was it even possible? She kept moving to try to bring her left side into my line of sight, and I kept turning with her. "Don't you think it deserves an answer?"

"Don't do this, I beg you."

"You must answer, William. In your heart you know you must."

She was right. "You were beautiful, once," I blurted out. "But not now."

She was circling me like a hyena scenting the death throes. "Now you have no interest in me."

"I didn't say that."

Nipping at me like a termagant knowing her job was almost done. "Now you won't protect me."

"Don't put words in my mouth!" I screamed.

She spread her arms wide. "Time to make your stand, William."

"How can I when I don't even know what I'm fighting for."

"Oh, you know." She leaned in as she whispered. "It's your soul, William. Your very soul."

"Then I was right. I *am* dead!"

"No. Death is easy. This isn't." Now she was right up against me and I didn't even bother to turn aside. I stared at both sides of her, the beautiful and the horribly disfigured. And now something began to take shape in my mind. Something terribly, intimately familiar. "You know this beast, William. You know it very, very well. As I said, this is where you make your stand."

"But you said it couldn't be defeated."

"No." She gave me a penetrating look. "I said it can't be killed."

"Wait a minute. What are you saying?" Something familiar here—emotions or possibly a certain dynamic, I didn't know for sure—had triggered a memory I had long suppressed. I had misled myself; a long time ago I *had* told one person about the bottomless pit inside myself because in the frenzy of detonating teenage hormones it had become unbearable to keep it to myself. "You . . . it . . ." And then I knew. I knew it all. She saw it on my face and she smiled. It was a beautiful smile, a magnificent smile, a smile for the ages. "You and Vav and Gimel, you're all one, aren't you?"

She nodded. "Just different aspects."

I just stood, staring, unable to make a move.

"Go on, then," she whispered. "Time for you to root out the beast."

"I don't want to leave you," I said.

"If that is what you want," she answered me, "then you won't."

"But I have to know. . . . Is it also what you want?"

"It's what I've always wanted." She smiled that beatific smile. "But then you already knew that, didn't you?"

"Yes." I could barely speak, my throat was so clogged with emotion. "I guess I always did." I held out my hand. "Come on. I'll protect you, but I won't leave you again. Not ever."

She gave me a sad look, but she took my hand and I squeezed it hard. Together, we went out of the living room. In the study, I tried the wall switch, but the chandelier remained dark.

"I'm afraid that's one of the drawbacks of this place," she said. "The electricity is unreliable."

I found a suitable length of wood on the cordwood pile next to the hearth and twisted some old newspaper around one end. I stuck it into the fire. When it was burning well we went up the stairs. I held it before us, lighting the way.

We went along the hallway. Once again, I opened the door to each dark room. This time, the makeshift torch illuminated the interiors. I suppose at this point I wasn't surprised to see Vav's paintings hung on the walls. At last, I'd reached the art exhibition. I went from room to room in wonderment.

Each one was as clear as ice; they pierced my heart with bittersweet poignancy. "These are scenes from my childhood," I said as I studied the paintings. "Here are the forests where I hunted with Dad; here's the field where Herman and I used to play Tag and You're It; here's the lane that led to our house; and here's where . . ." I turned to my companion. "Here's where I slapped you." I put a hand up to her cheek. "Lily, will you ever forgive me?"

"I'm here," my sister said. "I brought you here with the power of my mind. It's all the power I have, you see. All the energy that would have gone into talking and walking and running, playing tennis and making love and . . . all the things everyone takes for granted, has been channeled into my mind. It had nowhere else to go."

"But why did you wait so long to do this?"

"This reality I built for myself takes a tremendous amount of energy—to bring you into it required a superhuman burst. I knew I could only do it once, and not for very long. So I waited until near the end." She smiled and touched my cheek in return. "Mom was right, you know. She could see underneath it all. I cared about you like no one else."

"But I was so cruel to you."

She pointed to the far side of the last room of the exhibition. *"Regarde ça,"* she said in Vav's warm voice.

I let go of her long enough to cross the room. There was a brick fireplace, soot-blackened, above which ran a carved oak mantelpiece. On the mantelpiece was a small, battered black-and-white photo, faded now with time. I peered at it. It was me, as a young boy. The sun must have been in my eyes for I was squinting. There was an expression on my face I knew well and didn't much care for. At first, I thought this was what Lily wanted me to see, but then I heard something stir. I looked down but could see nothing. I thrust the sputtering torch farther in front of me and I saw a dark figure huddled against the blackened firebrick. *Good Christ,* I thought. *It's the beast!* Instinctively, I brandished the carving knife, but it appeared to no longer be a threat. The face, when it raised its head, did not seem at all hideous. In fact, it seemed as familiar as that alleyway in Paris down which Vav had led me, as familiar as the Charnwood Forest glade where I had stopped with Gimel. I glanced back up at the old photo of myself, then back down at the beast. There was no fear inside me now, no loathing. I reached out to touch it and its darkness ran up my arm, its essence turning to ink that sank into my skin. In a moment, it had vanished with a faint pop. Astonished, I turned back to Lily. "The beast was me, wasn't it?" I said, though in truth I needed no real confirmation from her. "At least it was a part of me."

"The part you had to face," she said. "I told you it couldn't be killed—not without killing yourself, anyway. But you found the means to defeat it." She came toward me. "Understanding and forgiveness,

Billy." She put a hand on my arm. "If you can face me, if you can
love me now then surely you can forgive yourself."

"But you terrified me."

She put a hand against my mouth and I found myself trembling.
"And yet you fed me when you had to, you held me and rocked me
even when I vomited all over you. Herman never went near me. He
loathed me, just like Dad did."

"But that afternoon—I hit you."

"Yes, and I loved you all the more for it."

"What? I don't understand."

"It's simple, Billy. I struck you and drew blood."

"But you couldn't help it. It was just you spazzing—" I broke
off, shame flooding me anew.

"It's all right, Billy." She caressed me. "Don't you see, you reacted
as if I were a normal person. You treated me like you would anyone
else who had struck you. Even Mom, who loved me so desperately,
couldn't have done what you did, because she pitied me so. You
never pitied me, so when you reacted you did so from your true
being. For that I was so grateful, Billy, I cannot begin to tell you."

"Oh, Lily—" Bitter tears of remorse and self-loathing slid down
my cheeks. "I never suspected what was underneath. That you had—"
I gestured at the paintings.

"But you did, Billy." She took me over to a painting of a forest
glade drenched in sunlight and in something intangible that, just like
this reality she had created, was so much more. "That afternoon when
I drew blood and you hit me back was our connection, our communication. Before then, I was plagued by bouts of despair and black
thoughts of suicide. You reaffirmed for me my right to exist, my own
humanity." She smiled. "Vav, Gimel, Daleth—they're all pieces of
my personality and they all love you unconditionally."

I was overcome with shame. "My God, I never imagined—"

"How could you?" she said gently. Now she seemed to be holding
me as, moments before, I had been holding her. "That was okay,
you see. Because I could see underneath *your* facade. I knew what
was there."

"But I never came to see you."

"And yet we never lost touch, did we? Because Donnatella would
tell me all about you."

"She'd talk to you about me?"

"You were *all* she talked about, Billy. And she was so good at it, it was like having you in the room with me." Her dark eyes looked into mine. "She never stopped coming, even after the divorce."

"I didn't know that."

"She's here now."

I looked around. "In this house?"

Her voice grew soft as a candle flame. "No, at my bedside. The moment has come. I'm dying, Billy."

"No!" I pulled her close to me, wrapping my arms around her. "I won't let it happen. I won't lose you now, after I've just found you."

Lily shook her head. "We all have our time, Billy. Mine has come and gone."

"Then we'll stay here, in this fantastic world you've conjured. I'll keep you safe here. Nothing can harm you."

"Oh, Billy." She shook her head as I took her back out into the hallway. But I recoiled as soon as I looked over the banister. There was nothing below us. The entire ground floor had vanished into an odd kind of pearly-gray mist.

"What the hell—?"

"It's going, Billy. I'm growing weak. I can't maintain this world any longer."

"Then, teach me how to rebuild it," I said. "I'm strong. I'll do whatever it takes." Already I could see the mist curling up the staircase. Everything it touched instantly melted into it. It reached the second floor and the entire right wing vanished. I took Lily's hand, and we raced down what was left of the hallway. "Quick! Tell me how to rebuild this!"

"It won't work, Billy. You can't cheat death."

"But I don't want you to die!" Behind us, the rooms with the wondrous paintings of our childhood were one by one being devoured in the mist.

"And I don't want to leave you," Lily said as we reached the master suite, "but I must."

"There must be something you can do," I implored her.

Now it was she who led me inside. "Close the door and lock it," she said. When I did what she had asked, I saw that she was very pale. She collapsed into my arms, and I carried her to the huge canopied bed. As I laid her gently on it, she looked up at me and said, "All my life I've wanted to sleep one night in a bed like this." She glanced up at the canopy and I could see her artist's eyes taking in every nuance of color, form and texture. "It's heavenly, isn't it?" she whispered.

"Yes," I said. "That's just what it is. Heavenly." Beads of sweat stood out on her forehead and upper lip. "Lily—"

She turned her eyes on me. "Yes?"

"I love you."

"I know, Billy. I know."

I put my head on her stomach and we held each other for a long time. Then, very weakly, she said my name. I could feel the vibrations go through my entire body.

"Don't wish for Donnatella to love you any more than she does," Lily whispered. "Don't regret what you had with her."

"But it's over."

"Yes." She sighed. "It's over. But look to what lies ahead."

"I don't know what lies ahead."

"Yes," she whispered in a voice that had become all but insubstantial, "but that's the point, isn't it?"

I wept then, for her and for me—but also for us, for what we had had so briefly that was now gone. Gone without my being with her at the end. How I envied Donnatella! How I appreciated her anew for the good and loyal friend she had been to Lily!

When I opened my eyes I saw that I was in the alley behind Helicon. In my hand was a lotus flower of the purest white. As I touched its delicate petals, I knew this was what Lily had left me as proof that our time together had been no bizarre hallucination brought on by temporary madness or the mescal.

I suddenly thought of Mike. I jerked open the back door and rushed inside, ready to call 911.

"Hey, buddy," Mike said from his accustomed place behind the bar, "that was a helluva piss you took."

Stupefied, I merely blinked at him. "What?" Where were the smashed bottles and mirror, the bullet holes and the blood? Mike's blood.

"But, god*damn*— You're okay—" I was trying not to stammer.

"Except for a shitload of bills I have to pay, of course I am," Mike said. "Why wouldn't I be?"

"Because you were dead, that's why!" I looked around wildly. "Where's the crazy black guy with the machine pistol?"

"The only crazy guy I see is you. You're the only one's been in here this morning." Mike gave me the fish-eye. "You know, you've already had two mescals. Maybe that's enough till you get some break-fast in you. I'll fry you up some eggs."

I peered into my favorite booth, looking for the empty glass I'd left there, but there was nothing on the table save liquor rings, remind-ers of binges past. "But I've already had three drinks."

"Yeah?" Mike shoveled grease to the back of the griddle with a blackened spatula. He cracked open a couple of eggs and they started to sizzle. "Then you started drinking at home, my son, 'cause you've only had two here."

"Wait a minute." I was turning the lotus flower around and around, thinking about Lily and what the power of her mind had been able to achieve. "What time is it?"

Mike, still with a puzzled look on his face, glanced at his watch. "Ten twenty-eight."

"It's Monday morning, right?"

Poor Mike looked as if he didn't know whether to tend the eggs or call the boys at Bellevue. "Yeah, right. Why?"

"I don't know," I told him. But possibly I did. The call from Herman had come at ten-thirty. It seemed as if I was back at the moment before it all began. Could this have been the final extraordi-nary act Lily had performed with her mind, to give us both a chance to be together one last time before she died? "But I've got a funny feeling the phone is going to ring."

"Yeah, right," he guffawed. "And my name's Rudolph W. Giuliani."

The phone rang, and Mike started. "Jesus Christ," he said, staring at me.

"Maybe I ought to answer it." I reached for the phone and heard Herman's voice. Yep, that's exactly what she had done. I looked at Mike and winked. "It's for me."

Tim Powers

ITINERARY

I consider Tim Powers a new friend, since I made his acquaintance only through my pursuit of his work for this book. We hit it off immediately, and his editor at Avon only hates me a little bit for taking him away from his current novel project to write the following story. This is an event, since Powers writes an average of one short story per decade.

For those of you with your heads so firmly stuck in the sand of the horror/suspense field that you're not aware of his work, since winning science fiction's Phillip K. Dick Memorial Award for his novel The Anubis Gates *(which describes seventeenth-century England in minute detail), Powers has been considered one of the most important voices in the sf and fantasy fields; his work (other novels:* Earthquake Weather, Last Call, Expiration Date*) exhibits his own brand of "magic realism," combining elements of sf, fantasy, horror, the occult, psychiatry, surrealism, comedy, history, and just about anything else he feels like throwing into the brew—with magical results.*

As you're about to see, we're lucky to have him.

The day before the Santa Ana place blew up, the telephone rang at about noon. I had just walked the three blocks back from Togo's with a tuna-fish sandwich, and when I was still out in the yard I heard the phone ringing through the open window; I ran up the porch steps, trying to fumble my keys out of my pocket without dropping the Togo's bag, and I was panting when I snatched up the receiver in the living room. "Hello?"

I thought I could hear a hissing at the other end, but no voice. It was October, with the hot Santa Ana winds shaking the dry pods off the carob trees, and the receiver was already slick with my sweat. I used to sweat a lot in those days, what with the beer and the stress and all. "Hello?" I said again, impatiently. "Am I talking to a short circuit?" Sometimes my number used to get automatic phone calls from an old abandoned oil tank in San Pedro, and I thought I had rushed in just to get another of those.

It was a whisper that finally answered me, very hoarse; but I could tell it was a man: "Gunther! Jesus, boy—this is—Doug Olney, from Neff High School! You remember me, don't you?"

"Doug? Olney?" I wondered if he had had throat cancer. It had been nearly twenty years since I'd spoken to him. "Sure I remember! Where are you? Are you in town—"

"No time to talk. I don't want to—change any of your plans." He seemed to be upset. "Listen, a woman's gonna call your number in a minute; she's gonna ask for me. You don't know her. Say I just left a minute ago, okay?"

"Who is she—" I began, but he had already hung up.

As soon as I lowered the receiver into the cradle, the phone rang again. I took a deep breath and then picked it up again. "Hello?"

It was a woman, sure enough, and she said, "Is Doug Olney there?" I remember thinking that she sounded like my sister, who's married, in a common-law and probably unconsummated sense, to an Iranian who lives at De Gaulle Airport in France; though I hadn't heard from my sister since Carter was president.

I took a deep breath. "He just left," I said helplessly.

"I bet." A shivering sigh came over the line. "But I can't do any more." Again I was holding a dead phone.

We grew up in a big old Victorian house on Lafayette Avenue in Buffalo. The third floor had no interior partitions or walls, since it was originally designed to be a ballroom; by the time we were living there the days of balls were long gone, and that whole floor was jammed to capacity with antique furniture, wall to wall, floor to twelve-foot ceiling, back to front. My sister and I were little kids then, and we could crawl all through that vast lightless volume, up one canted couch and across the underside of an inverted table, squeezing past rolled carpets and worming between Regency chair legs. Of course there was no light at all unless we crowded into a space near one of the dust-filmed windows; and climbing back down to the floor, and then tracing the molding and the direction of the floor planks to the door, was a challenge. When we were finally able to stand up straight again out in the hall, we'd be covered with sour dust and not eager to explore in there again soon.

The nightmare I always had as a child was of having crept and wriggled to the very center of that room all by myself in the middle of the night, pausing roughly halfway between the floor and ceiling in pitch darkness on some sloped cabinet or sleigh bed—and then hearing a cautious scuffle from some remote cubic yard out there, in that three-dimensional maze of Cabriole legs and cartouches that you had to touch to learn the shapes of. And in the dream I knew it was some lonely boy who had hidden away up there with all the furniture years and years ago, and that he wanted to play, to show me whatever old shoe buckles or pocket watches or fountain pens he had found in drawers and coat pockets. I always pictured him skeletal and pale, though of course he'd be careful never to get near enough to the windows to be seen, and I knew he'd speak in a whisper.

I always woke up from that dream while it was still dark outside my window, and so tense that I'd simply lie without moving a muscle until I could see the morning light through my eyelids.

I was in the yard of the Santa Ana house early the next morning, sipping at a can of Coors beer and blinking tears out of my eyes as I tried to focus on the tomato vines through the sun glare on the white garden wall, when I heard a pattering like rain among the leaves. I sat down abruptly in the damp grass to push the low leaves aside.

It was bits of glass falling out of the sky. I touched one shard, and it was as hot as a serving plate. A cracking and thumping started up behind me then, and I fell over backward trying to stand up in a hurry. Red clay roof tiles were shattering violently on the grass and tearing the jasmine branches. The air was sharp with the acid smell of burned, broken stone, and then a hard punch of scorchingly hot air lifted me off my feet and rolled me over the top of the picnic table. I was lying facedown and breathless in the grass when the bass-note boom deafened me and stretched my hair out straight, so that it stood up from my scalp for days; I still have trouble combing it down flat, not that I try frequently.

The yard looked like a battlefield. All the rosebushes were broken off flush with the ground, and the ceramic duck that we'd had forever was broken into a hundred pieces. I was dimly glad that the duck had been able to tour California once in his otherwise uneventful life.

The eastern end of the house, where the kitchen had been, was broken wide open, with tar paper strips standing up along the roof edge like my hair, and beams and plaster chunks lay scattered out across the grass. Everything inside the kitchen was gone, the table and the refrigerator and the pictures on the wall. Propane is heavier than air, and it had filled the kitchen from the floor upward, until it had reached the pilot light on the stove.

The explosion had cracked my ribs and burned my eyebrows off and scorched my throat, and I think I got sick from radon or asbestos that had been in the walls. I took a day-long ride on a bus out here to San Bernardino to recuperate at my uncle's place, the same rambling old ranch-style house where we lived happily for a year right after we moved from New York, before my mother found the Santa Ana house and began making payments on it.

The ceramic duck might have been the first thing my mother bought for the house. He generally just sat in the yard, but shortly after my sister and I turned seven he was stolen. We didn't get very excited about that, but we were awestruck when the duck mysteriously showed up on the lawn again, six months later—because propped up against him in the dewy grass was a photo album full of pictures of the ceramic duck in various locations around the state: the duck in front of the flower bank at the entrance to Disneyland, the duck on a cable car seat in San Francisco, the duck sitting between the palm prints of Clark Gable; along with a couple of more mundane shots, like one of the duck just leaning against an avocado tree in somebody's yard out behind a weather-beaten old house. I think all the stories you hear about world-traveling lawn gnomes these days started with the humbler travels of our duck, back in '59. Or vice versa, I suppose.

My uncle's place hasn't changed at all since my sister and I explored every hollow and gully of the weedy acre and climbed the sycamores along the back fence so many years ago—our carved initials are still visible on the trunk of one of them, I discover, still only a yard above the dirt, though my sister isn't interested in seeing them now. There's a surprising lot of our toys, too, old wooden Lincoln Logs and Nike missile launchers; I've gathered them from among the weeds and put them near the back of the garage where my uncle supposedly keeps his beer, but she doesn't want to see them either.

Always in San Bernardino you see women on the noonday sidewalks wearing shorts and halter tops, and from behind they look young and shapely with their long brown legs and blond hair; but when the car you're in has driven past them, and you hike around in the passenger seat to look back, their faces are weary, and shockingly old. And at night along Base Line, under the occasional clusters of sodium-vapor lights, you can see that the bar parking lots are jammed with cars, but you can generally also see four or five horses tied up to a post outside the bar door. My uncle says this is a semidesert climate, right below the Cajon Pass and Barstow in the high desert, and so we get a lot of patches of mirage.

I'll let my sister drive me as far as the Stater Brothers market on Highland, though that doesn't cheer her up, probably because I mostly shoplift the fruits and cheese and crackers that are all I can keep down anymore. She flew back from France after I hurt myself, and when she can borrow an old car from a friend she drives out to visit me. She keeps trying to trick me into coming back to live in Santa Ana again, or anywhere besides my uncle's house—she wants to drive me to a hospital, actually—but I don't dare. I've told her not to tell anyone where I am, and I've taken a false name, not that anyone asks me.

Her family, I have to admit, has given her a lot of grief. Her husband was born in a part of Iran that was under British jurisdiction, and when he tried to go back there after going to school in England the Iranians said he was an enemy of the Shah; they took his passport and gave him some papers that permitted him to leave but never come back, and he got as far as Charles de Gaulle Airport, but France wouldn't let him in without a passport and Customs wouldn't let him get on another plane. He's lived on the Boutique Level of Terminal One now for decades, sleeping on a plastic couch and watching TV, and Lufthansa flight attendants give him travel kits so that he can shave and brush his teeth. My sister met him there during a layover on a European tour my mother bought for her right after high school, and now she's got a job and an apartment in Roissy so she can be near him. I keep telling her she's going to lose her job, staying away like this, but she says she has no choice, because nobody else can get through to me the way she still can. I'm *backward,* she says.

My uncle makes himself scarce when she drives up the dirt track out front in one beat old borrowed car or another; so does everybody. When I hobbled off the bus at his warped chain-link front gate, all scorched and blinking and hoarse and dizzy from the radon, he was waiting for me out in the front yard with his usual straw hat pulled down over his gray hair; all you really see is the bushy mustache. The house is empty now, just echoing rooms with one old black Bakelite telephone on the kitchen floor and a lot of wires sticking out of the walls where there used to be lights, but he told me I could sleep in my old room, and I've carried in some newspapers to make a nest in the corner there. I'm thinking about moving the nest into the closet.

"Don't bother anybody you might see here," my uncle told me on that first day. "Just leave 'em alone. They probably live here."

And I have seen a very old man in the kitchen, always crying quietly over the sink and wearing one of those senior citizen jumpsuits that zip up from the ankle to the neck; I've just nodded to him and discreetly shuffled past across the dusty linoleum. What could we have to say to each other that the other wouldn't already know? And a couple of times I've seen two kids out at the far end of the backyard. Let them play, I figure. My uncle is generally walking around in circles behind the garage trying to find his beer. There's a patch of mirage out there—if you step into the weeds by the edge of the driveway, walking away from the house, you find with no shift at all that you've just stepped *onto* the driveway, *facing* the house.

"It's been that way forever," he told me one day when he was taking a break from it, sitting on the hood of his wrecked old truck. "But one night a few winters ago I stepped out there and *wasn't* facing the house; and I was standing on one of your mom's long-ago rosebushes. The flowers were open, like they thought it was day, and the leaves were warm. Time doesn't pass, in mirages, everybody knows that—so I hopped right in the truck and bought two cases of Budweiser out of the cooler at Top Cat, and stashed 'em there right by the rosebush. The next morning it was the two-for-one-step mirage again, but whenever it slacks off, I know where there's a lot of cold beer."

I nodded a number of times, and so did he, and it was right after this conversation with him that I started keeping all our old toys back there.

Yesterday my sister came rocking up the dirt driveway in a shiny green Edsel, and when she braked it in a cloud of dust and clanked the door open I could see that she'd been crying at some point on the drive up. It's a long drive, and it takes a lot out of her.

My voice is gone because of the explosion having scorched my throat, so I stepped closer to her to be heard. "Come in the house and have . . . some water," I rasped—awkwardly, because she'd doing all this for my sake. We don't have any glasses, but she could drink it out of the faucet. "Or crackers," I added.

"I can't stand to see the inside of the house," she said crossly.

"We had good times in this house, *when we were all living* in it." She squinted out past the dogwood tree at the infinity of brown hillocks that is the backyard. "Let's talk out there."

"You're testy," I noted as I followed her up the dirt driveway, past the house. She was wearing a blue sundress that clung to her sweaty back.

"Why do you suppose that is, Gunther?"

I glanced around quickly, but there wasn't even a bird in the empty blue sky. "Doug," I reminded her huskily, trying to project my frail voice. The name had been suggested by the phone call I'd got on the day before the explosion, and certainly Doug Olney himself would never hear about the deception, wherever he might be. "Always, you promised."

We were walking out past the end of the driveway among the burr-weeds now, and I saw her shoulders shrug wearily. "Why do you suppose that is—Mr. Olney?" she called back to me.

I lengthened my stride to step up beside her. The soles of my feet must be tough, because the burrs never stick in my skin. "I bet it's expensive to rent a classic Edsel," I hazarded.

"Yes, it is." Her voice was flat and harsh. "Especially in the summer, with all the Mexican weddings. It's a '57, but it must have a new engine or something in it—I could hardly see the signs on the old Route 66 today. Just Foothill Boulevard all the way. I may not be able to come out here again, get through to you, not even your own *twin,* who *lived* here, *with* you! Not even in a car from those days. And Hakim needs me too." She turned to face me and stamped her foot. "He could figure some way to get out of that airport if he really wanted to! And look at you! Damn it—Doug—how long do you think a comatose body can *live,* even in a hospital like Western Medical, with its soul off hiding *incognito* somewhere?"

"Well, *soul* . . ."

"This is certainly unsanctified ground. Is it a crossroads? Have you got *rue* growing out here with the weeds?" She was crying again. "*Propane leak*. Why were you found out in the yard, out by the duck? You changed your mind, didn't you? You were trying to walk away from it. Good! Keep *on* walking away from it; don't stop here in the . . . in the terminal, the nowhere in-between. Walk right now to that silly old car back there, and let me drive you to Western Medical while I still can, while you can still make the trip. You can *wake up*."

I smiled at her and shook my head. I know now that I was never scared of the boy in the dark ballroom. I was tense with fear of each fresh unknown dawn, which the boy had found a way to hide from, but which always did come to me mercilessly shining right through my closed eyelids. I opened my mouth to croak some reassurance to her, but she was looking past me with an empty expression.

"Jesus," she said then, reverently, in a voice almost as hoarse as mine, "this is where that other picture was taken. The photo of the duck by the avocado tree. In the photo album, remember?" She pointed back toward the house. "There's no tree here now, but the angle of the house, the windows—look, it's the very same view, we just didn't recognize it then because we remembered this house freshly painted, not all faded and peeled like it is now, and like it was in the picture, and because in the picture there was a big distracting avocado tree in the foreground!"

I stood beside her and squinted through watering eyes against the sun glare. She might have been right—if you imagined a tree to the right, with the poor duck leaning against the trunk, this view was at least very like the one in that old photo album.

"The person with the camera was standing right here," she said softly.

Or *will be* standing, I thought.

"Could you drive me to Stater Brothers?" I said.

Several times I've gone out and looked since she drove away, and I'm still not sure she was right. The trouble is, I don't remember the photograph all that clearly. It might have been this house. All I can do is wait.

I don't imagine that I'll be going to Stater Brothers again soon, if ever. The trip was upsetting, with so many curdles and fractures of mirage in the harsh daylight that you'd think San Bernardino was populated by nothing but walking skeletons and one-hoss shays. I did get an avocado, along with my crackers and processed cheese-food slices, and my sister left off a box of our dad's old clothes because I've been wearing the scorched pants and shirt still, and she said it broke her heart to see me walking around all killed. I haven't looked in the box, but it stands to reason that there's one of those jumpsuits in it.

I know now that she's going back, at last, to poor stalled Hakim at the airport in Roissy. I called her from the phone in the kitchen here.

"I'm on my way to the hospital," I told her. "You can go back to France."

"You're—Gunth—I mean, *Doug,* where are you calling from?"

"I'm back in Santa Ana. I just want to change my clothes, try to comb my hair, before I get on a bus to the hospital."

"Santa Ana? What's the number there, I'll call you right back."

That panicked me. Helplessly I gave her the only phone number I could think of, my old Santa Ana number. "But I didn't mean to take up any more of your time," I babbled, "I just wanted to—"

"That's our old number," she said. "How can you be at our old number?"

"It—stayed with the house." If I could still sweat, I'd have been sweating. "These people who live here now don't mind me hanging around." The lie was getting ahead of me. "They like me; they made me a sandwich."

"I bet. Stay by the phone."

She hung up, and I knew it was a race then to see which of us would be able to dial the old number most rapidly. She must have been hampered by a rotary-dial phone too, because I got ringing out of the earpiece; and after it had rung four times I concluded that the number must be back in service again, because I would have got the recording by then if it had not been. My lips were silently mouthing *Please, please,* and I was aching with anxious hope that whoever answered the line would agree to go along with what I'd tell them to say.

Then the phone at the other end was lifted, and the voice said, breathlessly, "Hello?"

Of course I recognized him, and the breath clogged in my numb throat.

"Hello?" came the voice again. "Am I talking to a short circuit?"

Yes, I thought.

That oil tank in San Pedro hadn't been in use for years, but it had once been equipped with an automatic-dial switch to call the company's main office when its fuel was depleted; a stray power surge had apparently turned it on again, and the emergency number it called was by that time ours. Probably the oil tank hadn't had any fuel in it at all anymore, and only occasionally noticed. Certainly there had been nothing we could do about it.

"Gunther!" It hurt my teeth to say the name. "Jesus, boy—this is—Doug Olney, from Neff High School! You remember me, don't you?"

"Doug?" said the half-drunk, middle-aged man at the other end of the line, befuddledly wondering if I had throat cancer. "Olney? Sure I remember! Where are you? Are you in town—"

"No time to talk," I said, trying not to choke. What if Doug Olney, the real one, *had* been in town, in Santa Ana? Would this unhappy loser have suggested that the two of them get together for lunch? "I don't want to—" Stop you, I thought; save you, for damn sure. "—change any of your plans." My eyes were watering, even in the dim kitchen. "Listen, a woman's gonna call your number in a minute; she's gonna ask for me. You don't know her," I assured him; I didn't want him to be at all thinking he might. "Say I just left a minute ago, okay?"

"Who is she—"

I just hung up. You'll find out, I thought.

My uncle's beer appeared in the yard today, two cases of it, still cold from the cooler at Top Cat. The roses are still fresh, and I looked at the clip-cuts on some stems and tried to comprehend that my mother had cut the flowers only a few hours earlier, by the rosebush's time; the smears in the white dust on the rose hips were probably from her fingers. Sitting in the dirt driveway in the noonday sun, my uncle and I got all weepy and sentimental, and drank can after can of the Budweiser in toasts to missing loved ones, though probably nobody was in the house, and the two children were by then long gone from the backyard.

I've planted the golf-ball-sized seeds from the avocado, right where the tree was in the picture—if it was in fact a picture of this house. Eventually it will be a tree, and maybe one day the duck will be there, leaning on the trunk, on his way back from Disneyland and Grauman's Chinese Theater to the house where my sister and I are still seven years old. I plan to tag along, if he'll have me.

Nancy A. Collins

◈

CATFISH GAL BLUES

Nancy A. Collins made quite a name for herself with her Sonja Blue vampire books; she won a 1990 Bram Stoker Award (why don't they call them Brammies instead of Stokers?) for Sunglasses After Dark, *which was followed by* In the Blood *and* Paint It Black—*the three of them have been issued together as* The Sonja Blue Collection.*

Which isn't to say she's restricted herself to vampires. She's done comic book work (Swamp Thing), comic book novelizations (a novelization of the Fantastic Four), edited anthologies such as Forbidden Acts *(with Edward E. Kramer and Martin H. Greenberg), and even penned westerns* (Walking Wolf: A Weird Western).*

Here she gives us none of the above—but rather a folk tale, kind of a country legend that turns out for its protagonist to be . . . well, read on.

Flyjar is the kind of Southern town where time doesn't mean much. Maybe that's because there's little in the way of change between the seasons—the difference between winter and summer a mere fifteen degrees on average. And when you're as poor as most folks in Flyjar, there's not a whole lot of difference between one decade and another—or century, for that matter.

The two constants in Flyjar are poverty and the river. The town clings to the Mississippi like a child to its mama's skirt, and its fortunes—for good or ill—have been tied to the Big Muddy tighter than apron strings. At one time it had served as fueling stop for the riverboats that once traveled up and down the Father of All Waters. But those days were long gone, and all that remained of "the good old days" were some deteriorating wooden piers along the riverbanks.

Since most of the wharves extended several hundred feet into the river, there were plenty of crappies, channel cat and garfish free for the taking, provided you had the know-how and patience to catch them, as Sammy Herkimer, one of Flyjar's better fishermen, was quick to tell anyone who'd listen.

There were several docks to choose from, but Sammy's favorite was the one at Steamboat Bend. It was a mile or so from town and, because of that, was not in the best of shape. Since that meant keeping an eye on where you walked, not many of the locals used it, which suited Sammy just fine. Then one day, while he was sitting on the dock, sipping iced tea from a thermos, he was surprised to find himself joined by, of all people, Hop Armstrong.

Hop was the closest thing Flyjar had to a fancyman, since the good Lord had seen fit to bless him with good looks but had skimped in the ambition department. When it came to playing guitar and getting women to pay his way, Hop was second to none. But when it came to physical labor . . . well, that was another story.

"Lord A'mighty, Hop!" Sammy proclaimed, unable to hide his surprise. "What you doin' here? Someone set fire to your house?"

"You could say that." Hop grunted. "My woman said I had to bring home supper."

"That a fact?" Sammy said, raising an eyebrow.

Hop's most recent sugar mama was Lucinda Solomon, the proprietress of the local beauty parlor. Lucinda was good-looking and well-to-do, at least by Flyjar's standards. She was also notoriously strong-willed, and rumor had it that in living off Lucinda, Hop had finally met up with something approximating hard work.

Sammy glanced at the younger man's gear, noting with some amusement that while Hop had remembered to bring along his guitar, he hadn't bothered to pack a net. He returned his gaze to the river, shaking his head. After a long stretch of silence between the two, the older man spoke up abruptly.

"You know why they call this stretch of the river Steamboat Bend, Hop?"

"I figgered on account of it bein' a bend in the river and there was steamboats that used to come down it," he replied with a shrug.

"That's part of it, but it ain't the whole reason. A long time ago there was this big ole paddleboat that used to cruise up and down the river called *Delta Blossom*. She was a real fancy pleasure boat, with marble mantelpieces and crystal chandeliers and gold door handles. When folks heard *Delta Blossom* was coming, they ran from the houses and fields to watch her pass. Anyways, one day, without any warning,

Delta Blossom went down with all hands right about there," Sammy said, gesturing towards the middle of the river.

"Why did she sink?" Hop asked, a tinge of interest seeping into his voice.

"No one's rightly sure. Some said the boilers blew out th' side of the boat. Some said there was a fire belowdecks. Maybe it got its hull punched open by a submerged tree. Who can really know, after all this time? But my old granny used to swear up and down that *Delta Blossom* was scuttled by catfish gals."

Hop scowled at the older man. "You funnin' with me, ain't you, Sammy."

"No, sir, I ain't!" he said solemnly, shaking his head for emphasis. "Before there was any white or black folk, or even Indians living in these parts, there was catfish gals here. They live in the river, down where it's muddy and deep. They got the upper parts of women and from the waist down are big ole channel cats. They keep their distance from humans and, for the most part, are peaceful enough. Some folks said the catfish gals sank the *Delta Blossom* on account of one of them gettin' caught in the paddlewheel and crushed."

Hop turned to fix the older man with a curious stare. "You ever *seen* one of them catfish gals, Sammy?"

"No, I ain't. But I ain't gone lookin' for them, neither. But my granny said they was why no one hardly ever finds folks who are fool enough to go swimmin' in the river. They take the drowned bodies and stick 'em deep in the mud, until they get all blote up. That way their flesh is easier to eat . . ."

Hop grimaced. "Hush up about that! It's bad enough my woman's got me out here without you goin' on about catfish eatin' daid folks!"

"Sorry. I didn't realize you was sensitive on the subject." After another stretch of silence, Sammy nodded towards the guitar. "So— if you're here to fish, why the git-box?"

"Man can do more than one thing at a time, can't he?"

"I reckon so—but I don't recommend it. You'll scare off the fish."

"Mebbe I'll just charm me a catfish gal instead." Hop grinned.

"If anyone could, I reckon it'd be you." Sammy sighed as he reeled in his line. "Well, I caught me enough for one day. I better get on home so's I can clean this mess of crappies in time for supper. Good luck on charming them catfish gals, Hop. Y'all take care."

"Y'all too, Sammy," Hop replied absently, his gaze fixed on the river.

★   ★   ★

Hop had to admit that being out in the sunshine on a day like today wasn't all that bad. It wasn't too hot and there was a nice breeze coming off the water . . . plus, there was the added advantage of being out of his woman's line of sight.

Lucinda was far from an easy woman to please, and an even harder one to live with when riled. And she was most always riled. Hop knew the signs well enough by now to realize that his days of leisure at the feisty Miz Solomon's expense were drawing to their close, but he didn't like to jump ship unless he had a new girlfriend lined up. Unfortunately, for a man of his tastes and inclinations, Flyjar didn't have much in the way of available lady folk for him to choose from— so it looked like he was going to have to make do with Lucinda for a while longer. At least Steamboat Bend was remote enough that the chances of Lucinda's actually finding how hard he was—or wasn't— working at making sure there would be supper on the table come sundown were in his favor.

Hop pulled a forked stick from his tackle box and wedged it between the loose planks of the dock. After baiting the hook, he cast the line into the murky waters and propped the reel against the stick. Keeping one eye on the bobber, Hop leaned against the nearby wooden pylon and picked up his guitar.

There was not a time in his memory when music didn't come easy to him. Ever since he was knee-high, he'd been able to make a guitar do whatever it was he wanted of it. It was pretty much the same with women, too. Playing guitar came as natural to him as breathing and eating—and felt a lot more pleasant than chopping cotton or driving a tractor.

Hop scanned the deceptively calm surface of the river. It was so wide the current's strength was difficult to gauge with the naked eye. The only way to figure out just how powerful the river truly was was by the size of the driftwood and the speed at which it went past. There were days when full-grown oak trees raced one another to the Gulf of Mexico. Today was relatively placid, with only a few deadfalls the size of railroad ties headed downriver.

Hop found his mind turning once again to the story Sammy had told him. Not about the catfish gals—that was pure hokum if ever he heard it. What piqued his imagination was the *Delta Blossom*. Hop wondered what it must have been like back in those days, when the steamboats cruised the river, bringing glamour and wealth to pissant little towns like Flyjar.

To think that one of the grandest of the old paddlewheelers had come to its end a stone's throw from where he was sitting, taking all its splendor to the Mississippi's silty floor. All Hop had ever seen gracing the river were flat-bottomed barges and the occasional freighter or small leisure craft. These were hardly the kinds of boats that sparked the imagination and quickened the heart. Folks didn't flock to the levees just to watch a barge pass by.

Hop wondered if there was still anything left of the old *Delta Blossom* at the bottom of Steamboat Bend. There was no way to know. What secrets the river held it did not give up readily. Still, it didn't keep him from idly hoping to spot the sunken pleasure ship's outline.

In his mind's eye, he could see the long-lost floating pleasure palace, white as new cotton with towering double smokestack puffing away like a rich man's cigars as she made her way along the Mississippi. He could picture the Southern belles in hoop skirts lining the ship's second-story promenade, silk fans fluttering like caged birds, while riverboat gamblers in pristine linen suits and wide-brimmed hats tossed silver dollars and gold pieces onto the felt of the gaming tables. Hop saw himself dressed like Clark Gable in *Gone With the Wind,* tipping his hat to the young ladies of fashion gathered in the *Delta Blossom*'s grand salon for the evening's entertainment. What a swath he could have cut back then!

As his well-dressed phantom-self began to dance underneath the swaying crystal chandeliers with a young woman who looked a great deal like Vivien Leigh, Hop's nimble fingers were quick to provide the music. Granted, "Goodnight Irene" wasn't around at the time, but it was his daydream, after all, wasn't it?

As he played, a sudden movement in the middle of the river caught Hop's eye. From where he was sitting, it looked as if a swimmer had surfaced in the middle of the bend, near where Sammy said the *Delta Blossom* had gone down, then just as quickly submerged. But that was impossible.

Swimming in the Mississippi was only slightly less hazardous to your health than brushing your teeth with lit dynamite. Every so often some fool would get drunk enough to try to swim the river—and disappear without a trace ten feet from shore. If the family was lucky, the body would turn up a few days later, fifty miles downstream, snagged in the branches of a tree on the floodplain, looking more like a drowned pig than a human being. But what Hop saw hadn't looked anything like a floater popping to the surface. For one thing, it stayed in one place and didn't follow the current. Hop shaded his eyes against the sun, trying to get a better look, but there was nothing there. His attention was brought back closer to shore as the bobber on his line registered a strike. Hop dropped his guitar and snatched up the fishing rod, reeling in a ten-pound catfish.

It looked like Lucinda wasn't going to have anything to scold him about tonight, that much was for certain.

But as he headed back home, his fishing pole draped over one shoulder and his guitar slung over the other, Hop couldn't shake the feeling that he was being watched—and by something besides the catfish hanging from his belt.

That night as he was lying in bed, Lucinda snoring beside him, Hop got to thinking.

Maybe what Sammy Herkimer said about catfish gals wasn't all hogwash after all. He remembered reading in one of them yellow-backed magazines down at the barbershop about some kind of fish everyone thought was extinct being found in some foreign country a few years back. Besides, who was he to decide there weren't no such things as catfish gals, when he didn't know a soul who'd been to the bottom of the Mississippi and lived to tell the tale?

The very next day Hop went fishing without Lucinda telling him to.

He decided to try his luck again at Steamboat Bend. When he arrived at the dock, he was relieved to find he was alone. Hop set himself up on the dock just as he had the day before, but after a half hour of sitting and waiting for something to happen, he put down the fishing rod and picked up his guitar to pass the time.

Halfway into "Moanin' at Midnight," Hop heard what sounded like a fish slap the water near the pier. When he glanced up to see what had caused the noise, what he saw caused him to nearly drop his ax into the water below.

There was a human head bobbing in the water a hundred feet away from the dock. At the sound of his astonished gasp, the head ducked back down beneath the muddy surface without leaving so much as a ripple to mark its passing. Just as suddenly, there was a strike on Hop's line so powerful it nearly yanked his fishing pole into the river.

*   *   *

Although Lucinda was extremely pleased with the fifteen-pound catfish he brought home that evening, Hop didn't say anything about what he'd seen on the river. Something told him that whatever it was that was out at Steamboat Bend was best kept to himself.

The next day Hop didn't even bother casting his line into the river. He knew what was drawing the thing in the river to the dock, and it sure as hell wasn't the shiners he was using for bait.

He made his way to the very end of the landing, careful to avoid the loose and missing planks, and sat so his legs dangled over the edge. After a moment of deliberation, he decided "They Call Me Muddy Waters" would be an appropriate choice.

Just like before, the thing surfaced halfway through the song. Hop's heart was racing so fast it was hard to breathe, but he forced himself to keep playing. He didn't want to scare it off, so he kept playing, switching to "Pony Blues" once he'd finished with his first song.

While he played, Hop kept his head down, ignoring his audience as best he could. As he launched into "Circle Round the Moon" he risked glancing in the thing's direction, only to discover it was almost directly underneath his dangling feet, staring at him with big, dark eyes that seemed to be all pupil.

Hop was surprised at how human the catfish gal looked. From what Sammy had said, he'd pictured a fish in a fright wig, but that wasn't the case. Hell, he'd seen worse-looking women in church.

Her upper lip was extremely wide, with the familiar whiskers growing out of them, and she had slits instead of a nose, but outside of that she wasn't *too* ugly. Her hair was a real mess, though, with everything from twigs to what looked like live minnows caught in the tangled locks. He couldn't see much of what she looked like below the waterline, although he did glimpse vertical slits opening and closing down the sides of her neck.

Hop couldn't help but smile to himself when he saw how the catfish gal looked at him. Half fish or not, he knew what that look meant on a woman's face. He had her hooked but good and now was as good a time as any to reel her in.

Hop looked the catfish gal right in the eye and smiled. "Hello, lit'l fishie. You come to hear me play?"

The catfish gal's dreamy look was replaced by one of surprise. She

glanced around, as if confused by her surroundings, then shot backwards like a dolphin walking on its tail.

"Please! Don't go!" he shouted, stretching out one hand to stay
her retreat.

To his surprise, the catfish gal came to a sudden halt, regarding
him curiously, bobbing up and down in the Mississippi as easily as a
young girl treading water in a swimming pool.

"You ain't got nothin' to be scared of, lit'l fishie," Hop said,
smiling reassuringly. "I ain't gonna hurt you none. Do you want me
to play some more for you?" he asked, holding up his guitar.

The catfish gal nodded and lifted a dripping arm and pointed at
the guitar with a webbed forefinger. Hop smiled and obliged her by
picking up where he had left off on "Goin' Down Slow."

By the time the sun was starting to go down, Hop's hands were
cramping and his fingertips bloody. He'd played a little bit of almost
everything—blues, bluegrass, honky-tonk, camp songs, even a couple
of nursery songs—trying to figure out what the catfish gal liked and
didn't like: turned out she was partial to the blues—which made sense,
seeing how the blues was born on the banks of the Mississippi.

When he finally put aside his guitar, the catfish gal disappeared
beneath the river's muddy surface. A few seconds later a large catfish
came flying out of the water as if shot from a sling and landed on
the dock beside him. Hop picked up the floundering fish and shook
his head.

"I appreciate the thought," he said loudly. "But this ain't what
I'm lookin' for." After he tossed the fish back into the water, Hop
reached into his pocket and pulled out a silver dollar, which he held
up between his thumb and forefinger, so that it caught the sun's fading
rays. "If you want me to keep playing, you got to feed th' kitty. And
this here is what the kitty eats."

The catfish gal popped back to the surface, stared at the gleaming
coin for a long second, then submerged again. Hop shifted about
uneasily as first one minute, then another, elapsed without any sign of
the catfish gal. Maybe he pushed his luck a little too far too early. . . .

Something heavy and wet struck his chest, then dropped to the
deck with a metallic sound. Hop picked up the flat, circular piece of
slime-encrusted metal at his feet with trembling fingers. He scraped
the surface with his thumbnail and was rewarded not by the gleam of
silver—but the mellow shine of gold.

He gave out a whoop, then looked around to see if anyone might
have witnessed his good fortune, but he was alone on the landing, at

least as far as human company was concerned. Talk about falling in a honey pot!

And all for the price of a song.

As summer wore on, Hop Armstrong became a regular visitor to Steamboat Bend, showing up early and staying till late, and always leaving with heavy, if somewhat damp, pockets. On those occasions Sammy Herkimer was fishing off the dock, Hop was forced to wait the old angler out, but for the most part he didn't have to worry about being found out.

At first Lucinda had been suspicious of his newfound interest in fishing, but since he never came back smelling of perfume or wearing another woman's shade of lipstick on his collar, she eventually accepted his pastime as genuine. Of course, Lucinda had no way of knowing about the Folgers can full of old gold and silver coins he had stashed out in the garage, or about the bag of gold doorknobs hidden in the woodpile behind the house. Hop didn't see any need to tell her about his newfound wealth because that would lead to her asking him where he got it from, and where would he be then?

If he told Lucinda about the catfish gal, every man, woman and child in Flyjar would be lined up on the dock playing everything from a banjo to a Jew's harp trying to muscle in on his gig. The way Hop saw it, there was no call for him to ruin a good thing before he had to.

Once there weren't any more goodies coming his way from Lit'l Fishie, as he called her, he planned to take his Folgers can full of antique coins and gunnysack of doorknobs and head off to the big city—say, Jackson or Greenville. Hell, he might even go as far as New Orleans—maybe even Biloxi! He didn't really care where he ended up, just as long as it was someplace where the women were prettier and younger than those in Flyjar and you could buy beer on Sundays. Judging from how Lit'l Fishie was behaving during his more recent serenades, something told him it wouldn't be long before things dried up on her end, so to speak.

She kept swinging back and forth between acting skittish—disappearing every time a bullfrog croaked—and making kiss-kiss noises with that saddlebag mouth of hers. Hop might not know much, but he sure as hell knew women, and Lit'l Fishie was showing all the signs of a sugar mama running short on cash.

As he set out for Steamboat Bend that day, Hop decided it was going to be his last serenade for the catfish gal—and his final day as a citizen of Flyjar. Now that he'd found his fortune, it was time for him to strike out into the world and collect his fame.

Hop scanned the sky, frowning at the approaching clouds. It had rained off and on since sunrise, and there were puddles all along the rutted cow path that was the only road that led to the derelict landing at Steamboat Bend. As much as he disliked tramping through the mud, going out on foul-weather days meant he didn't have to worry about anyone snooping around.

Tightening his grip on his guitar strap, Hop hurried down the levee embankment and onto the deserted dock's wooden surface. He sat down on the end of the pier, as he always did, dangling his legs over the open water, and began to play "See My Grave Is Kept Clean."

Normally Lit'l Fishie broke surface about fifty yards away the moment he started to play, then moved in until she was staring up at him like a snake-tranced bird. Hop knew that look all too well. He saw it all the time in the eyes of the women whenever he played at the juke joints. He knew that if he said the word, Lit'l Fishie would roll in cornmeal and gladly throw herself in a red-hot frying pan.

He finished with the Blind Lemon and started into Leadbelly, but the catfish gal had yet to put in an appearance. Hop frowned. Maybe she couldn't hear him. He didn't really know where she lived, exactly, but he was under the impression she didn't stray that far from the Bend. He changed from Leadbelly to Son House, on the offhand chance that she didn't care for "Cotton Fields." When Lit'l Fishie still didn't show herself, Hop's frown deepened even further. It was time to pull out the stops. He began to play one of her favorites: "Up Jumped the Devil."

There was a bubbling sound directly below where he was sitting. Hop smiled knowingly at the shape lurking just below the murky water lapping against the pylon. Robert Johnson worked like a charm on women—whether they were two-legged or had gills.

"Why you so shy all of a sudden, darlin'?" he called out. "Why don't you show me that sweet face of yours?"

The bubbles at the end of the pier grew more intense, as if the water was boiling. Hop scowled and leaned forward, staring down between his dangling feet at the muddy water below.

"Lit'l Fishie—is that you?"

There was less than a heartbeat between the moment the thing with bumpy skin and gaping mouth filled with jagged teeth leapt from the water and when its powerful jaws snapped closed on Hop's legs. He was only able to scream just the once—a high, almost womanly shriek—before he was yanked, guitar and all, into the river.

The last thing Hop saw, before the silty waters of the Mississippi closed over him, was the catfish gal watching him drown, a sorrowful expression in her bruised eyes.

When Hop Armstrong went out fishing and never came back, most folks in Flyjar were of the opinion he'd found himself a new girlfriend and left Lucinda for greener pastures. A smaller group thought the handsome ne'er-do-well had gotten drunk and fallen through the dilapidated dock into the river below. In any case, no one really gave a good god damn, and after a couple of weeks there were other things to talk about down at the barbershop.

About three months after Hop disappeared, Sammy Herkimer snagged his line on something underneath the pier at Steamboat Bend. At first he thought he was just caught on some waterlogged reeds. But when he reeled his line back in, he found Hop's git-box hanging off the other end.

The guitar that had charmed so many ladies out of their drawers and their life's savings was now dripping slime, its neck splintered and body badly chewed up. Sammy shook his head as he freed the mangled instrument. He really wasn't surprised by what he'd found. In a way, he blamed himself for what happened to poor Hop. After all, when he'd told him about the catfish gals, he'd forgot to mention they weren't the *only* critters that made Steamboat Bend their home.

One thing about them gator boys: they sure are jealous.

Ramsey Campbell

◈

THE ENTERTAINMENT

Ramsey Campbell has done it all in the horror field—and he's refused to leave it. There from the beginning of the boom in the late 1970s, where brilliant stories like "McIntosh Willie" very quickly established him as a distinctive voice, he has continued to publish brilliantly in the genre to this day. His best tales are identifiable almost immediately as Campbellian; though his style owes something to Robert Aikman with its dreamlike, vaguely roiling quality, Campbell's images are unlike any others in imaginative fiction.

Campbell won the Stoker Award in 1994 for his collection Alone with the Horrors, *and his latest work can be found in a nonsupernatural novel (something of a departure),* The Last Voice They Hear, *as well as in the following typically creepy tale, written just for you and me.*

By the time Shone found himself back in Westingsea he was able to distinguish only snatches of the road as the wipers strove to fend off the downpour. The promenade where he'd seen pensioners wheeled out for an early dose of sunshine, and backpackers piling into coaches that would take them inland to the Lakes, was waving isolated trees that looked too young to be out by themselves at a gray sea baring hundreds of edges of foam. Through a mixture of static and the hiss on the windscreen a local radio station advised drivers to stay off the roads, and he felt he was being offered a chance. Once he had a room he could phone Ruth. At the end of the promenade he swung the Cavalier around an old stone soldier drenched almost black and coasted alongside the seafront hotels.

There wasn't a welcome in sight. A sign in front of the largest and whitest hotel said NO, apparently having lost the patience to light up its second word. He turned along the first of the narrow streets of boardinghouses, in an unidentifiable one of which he'd stayed with his parents most of fifty years ago, but the placards in the windows were just as uninviting. Some of the streets he remembered having been composed of small hotels had fewer buildings now, all of them care homes for the elderly. He had to lower his window to read the signs across the roads, and before he'd finished his right side was soaked. He needed a room for the night—he hadn't the energy to drive back to London. Half an hour would take him to the motorway, near which he was bound to find a hotel. But he had only reached the edge of town, and was braking at a junction, when he saw hands adjusting a notice in the window of a broad three-story house.

He squinted in the mirror to confirm he wasn't in anyone's way, then inched his window down. The notice had either fallen or been removed, but the parking area at the end of the short drive was unoccupied, and above the high thick streaming wall a signboard that frantic bushes were doing their best to obscure appeared to say most of HOTEL. He veered between the gateposts and came close to touching the right breast of the house.

He couldn't distinguish much through the bay window. At least one layer of net curtains was keeping the room to itself. Beyond heavy purple curtains trapping moisture against the glass, a light was suddenly extinguished. He grabbed his overnight bag from the rear seat and dashed for the open porch.

The rain kept him company as he poked the round brass bellpush next to the tall front door. There was no longer a button, only a socket harboring a large bedraggled spider that recoiled almost as violently as his finger did. He hadn't laid hold of the rusty knocker above the neutral grimace of the letter-slot when a woman called a warning or a salutation as she hauled the door open. "Here's someone now."

She was in her seventies but wore a dress that failed to cover her mottled toadstools of knees. She stooped as though the weight of her loose throat was bringing her face, which was almost as white as her hair, to meet his. "Are you the entertainment?" she said.

Behind her a hall more than twice his height and darkly papered with a pattern of embossed vines not unlike arteries led to a central staircase that vanished under the next floor up. Beside her a long-legged table was strewn with crumbled brochures for local attractions; above it a pay telephone with no number in the middle of its dial clung to the wall. Shone was trying to decide if this was indeed a hotel when the question caught up with him. "Am I . . ."

"Don't worry, there's a room waiting." She scowled past him and shook her head like a wet dog. "And there'd be dinner and a breakfast for anyone who settles them down."

He assumed this referred to the argument that had started or re-commenced in the room where the light he'd seen switched off had been relit. Having lost count of the number of arguments he'd dealt with in the Hackney kindergarten where he worked, he didn't see why this should be any different. "I'll have a stab," he said, and marched into the room.

Despite its size, it was full of just two women—of the breaths of one at least as wide as her bright pink dress, who was struggling to lever herself up from an armchair with a knuckly stick and collapsing red-faced, and of the antics of her companion, a lanky woman in the flapping jacket of a dark blue suit and the skirt of a grayer outfit, who'd bustled away from the light switch to flutter the pages of a television listings magazine before scurrying fast as the cartoon squirrel on the television to twitch the cord of the velvet curtains, an activity Shone took to have dislodged whatever notice had been in the win-dow. Both women were at least as old as the person who'd admitted him, but he didn't let that daunt him. "What seems to be the prob-lem?" he said, and immediately had to say "I can't hear you if you both talk at once."

"The light's in my eyes," the woman in the chair complained, though of the six bulbs in the chandelier one was dead, another miss-ing. "Unity keeps putting it on when she knows I'm watching."

"Amelia's had her cartoons on all afternoon," Unity said, darting at the television, then drumming her knuckles on top of an armchair instead. "I want to see what's happening in the world."

"Shall we let Unity watch the news now, Amelia? If it isn't some-thing you like watching you won't mind if the light's on."

Amelia glowered before delving into her cleavage for an object that she flung at him. Just in time to field it he identified it as the remote control. Unity ran to snatch it from him, and as a newsreader appeared with a war behind him Shone withdrew. He was lingering over closing the door while he attempted to judge whether the moun-tainous landscapes on the walls were vague with mist or dust when a man at his back murmured, "Come out, quick, and shut it."

He was a little too thin for his suit that was gray as his sparse hair. Though his pinkish eyes looked harassed, and he kept shrugging his shoulders as though to displace a shiver, he succeeded in producing enough of a grateful smile to part his teeth. "By gum, Daph said you'd sort them out, and you have. You can stay," he said.

Among the questions Shone was trying to resolve was why the man seemed familiar, but a gust of rain so fierce it strayed under the front door made the offer irresistible. "Overnight, you mean." He thought it best to check.

"That's the least," the manager presumably only began, and twisted round to find the stooped woman. "Daph will show you up, Mr. . . ."

"Shone."

"Who is he?" Daph said as if preparing to announce him.

"Tom Shone," Shone told her.

"Mr. Thomson?"

"Tom Shone. First name Tom."

"Mr. Tom Thomson."

He might have suspected a joke if it hadn't been for her earnestness, and so he appealed to the manager. "Do you need my signature?"

"Later, don't you fret," the manager assured him, receding along the hall.

"And as for payment . . . "

"Just room and board. That's always the arrangement."

"You mean you want me to . . ."

"Enjoy yourself," the manager called, and disappeared beyond the stairs into somewhere that smelled of an imminent dinner.

Shone felt his overnight bag leave his shoulder. Daph had relieved him of the burden and was striding upstairs, turning in a crouch to see that he followed. "He's forever off somewhere, Mr. Snell," she said, and repeated, "Mr. Snell."

Shone wondered if he was being invited to reply with a joke until she added, "Don't worry, we know what it's like to forget your name."

She was saying he, not she, had been confused about it. If she hadn't cantered out of sight his response would have been as sharp as the rebukes he gave his pupils when they were too childish. Above the middle floor the staircase bent towards the front of the house, and he saw how unexpectedly far the place went back. Perhaps nobody was staying in that section, since the corridor was dark and smelled old. He grabbed the banister to speed himself up, only to discover it wasn't much less sticky than a sucked lollipop. By the time he arrived at the top of the house he was furious to find himself panting.

Daph had halted at the far end of a passage lit, if that was the word, by infrequent bulbs in glass flowers sprouting from the walls.

Around them shadows fattened the veins of the paper. "This'll be you," Daph said, and pushed open a door.

Beside a small window under a yellowing lightbulb the ceiling angled almost to the carpet, brown as mud. A narrow bed stood in the angle, opposite a wardrobe and dressing table and a sink beneath a dingy mirror. At least there was a phone on a shelf by the sink. Daph passed him his bag as he ventured into the room. "You'll be fetched when it's time," she told him.

"Time? Time . . ."

"For dinner and all the fun, silly," she said with a laugh so shrill his ears wanted to flinch.

She was halfway to the stairs when he thought to call after her. "Aren't I supposed to have a key?"

"Mr. Snell will have it. Mr. Snell," she reminded him, and was gone.

He had to phone Ruth as soon as he was dry and changed. There must be a bathroom somewhere near. He hooked his bag over his shoulder with a finger and stepped into the twilight of the corridor. He'd advanced only a few paces when Daph's head poked over the edge of the floor. "You're never leaving us."

He felt absurdly guilty. "Just after the bathroom."

"It's where you're going," she said, firmly enough to be commanding rather than advising him, and vanished down the hole that was the stairs.

She couldn't have meant the room next to his. When he succeeded in coaxing the sticky plastic knob to turn, using the tips of a finger and thumb, he found a room much like his, except that the window was in the angled roof. Seated on the bed in the dimness on its way to dark was a figure in a toddler's blue overall—a teddy bear with large black ragged eyes or perhaps none. The bed in the adjacent room was strewn with photographs so blurred that he could distinguish only the grin every one of them bore. Someone had been knitting in the next room, but had apparently lost concentration, since one arm of the mauve sweater was at least twice the size of the other. A knitting needle pinned each arm to the bed. Now Shone was at the stairs, beyond which the rear of the house was as dark as that section of the floor below. Surely Daph would have told him if he was on the wrong side of the corridor, and the area past the stairs wasn't as abandoned as it looked: he could hear a high-pitched muttering from the dark, a voice gabbling a plea almost too fast for words, praying with such urgency the speaker seemed to have no time to pause for

breath. Shone hurried past the banisters that enclosed three sides of
the top of the stairs and pushed open the door immediately beyond
them. There was the bath, and inside the plastic curtains that someone
had left closed would be a shower. He elbowed the door wide, and
the shower curtains shifted to acknowledge him.

Not only they had. As he tugged the frayed cord to kindle the
bare bulb, he heard a muffled giggle from the region of the bath. He
threw his bag onto the hook on the door and yanked the shower
curtains apart. A naked woman so scrawny he could see not just her
ribs but the shape of bones inside her buttocks was crouching on all
fours in the bath. She peered wide-eyed over one splayed knobbly
hand at him, then dropped the hand to reveal a nose half the width
of her face and a gleeful mouth devoid of teeth as she sprang past
him. She was out of the room before he could avoid seeing her
shrunken disused breasts and pendulous gray-bearded stomach. He
heard her run into a room at the dark end of the corridor, calling out
"For it now" or perhaps "You're it now." He didn't know if the
words were intended for him. He was too busy noticing that the door
was boltless.

He wedged his shoes against the corner below the hinges and
piled his sodden clothes on top, then padded across the sticky linoleum
to the bath. It was cold as stone, and sank at least half an inch with
a loud creak as he stepped into it under the blind brass eye of the
shower. When he twisted the reluctant squeaky taps it felt at first as
though the rain had got in, but swiftly grew so hot he backed into
the clammy plastic. He had to press himself against the cold tiled wall
to reach the taps, and had just reduced the temperature to bearable
when he heard the doorknob rattle. "Taken," he shouted. "Someone's
in here."

"My turn."

The voice was so close the speaker's mouth must be pressed against
the door. When the rattling increased in vigor Shone yelled, "I won't
be long. Ten minutes."

"My turn."

It wasn't the same voice. Either the speaker had deepened his
pitch in an attempt to daunt Shone or there was more than one person
at the door. Shone reached for the sliver of soap in the dish protruding
from the tiles, but contented himself with pivoting beneath the shower
once he saw the soap was coated with gray hair. "Wait out there,"
he shouted. "I've nearly finished. No, don't wait. Come back in
five minutes."

The rattling ceased, and at least one body dealt the door a large soft thump. Shone wrenched the curtains open in time to see his clothes spill across the linoleum. "Stop that," he roared, and heard someone retreat—either a spectacularly crippled person or two people bumping into the walls as they carried on a struggle down the corridor. A door slammed, then slammed again, unless there were two. By then he was out of the bath and grabbing the solitary bath towel from the shaky rack. A spider with legs like long gray hairs and a wobbling body as big as Shone's thumbnail scuttled out of the towel and hid under the bath.

He hadn't brought a towel with him. He would have been able to borrow one of Ruth's. He held the towel at arm's length by two corners and shook it over the bath. When nothing else emerged, he rubbed his hair and the rest of him as swiftly as he could. He unzipped his case and donned the clothes he would have sported for dining with Ruth. He hadn't brought a change of shoes, and when he tried on those he'd worn, they squelched. He gathered up his soaked clothes and heaped them with the shoes on his bag, and padded quickly to his room.

As he kneed the door open he heard sounds beyond it: a gasp, another, and then voices spilling into the dark. Before he crossed the room, having dumped his soggy clothes and bag in the wardrobe that, like the rest of the furniture, was secured to a wall and the floor, he heard the voices stream into the house. They must belong to a coach party—brakes and doors had been the sources of the gasps. On the basis of his experiences so far, the influx of residents lacked appeal for him and made him all the more anxious to speak to Ruth. Propping his shoes against the ribs of the tepid radiator, he sat on the underfed pillow and lifted the sticky receiver.

As soon as he obtained a tone he began to dial. He was more than halfway through Ruth's eleven digits when Snell's voice interrupted. "Who do you want?"

"Long distance."

"You can't get out from the rooms, I'm afraid. There's a phone down here in the hall. Everything else as you want it, Mr. Thomson? Only I've got people coming in."

Shone heard some of them outside his room. They were silent except for an unsteady shuffling and the hushed sounds of a number of doors. He could only assume they had been told not to disturb him. "There were people playing games up here," he said.

"They'll be getting ready for tonight. They do work themselves up, some of them. Everything else satisfactory?"

"There's nobody hiding in my room, if that's what you mean."

"Nobody but you."

That struck Shone as well past enough, and he was about to make his feelings clear while asking for his key when the manager said, "We'll see you down shortly, then." The line died at once, leaving Shone to attempt an incredulous grin at the events so far. He intended to share it with his reflection above the sink, but hadn't realized until now that the mirror was covered with cracks or a cobweb. The lines appeared to pinch his face thin, to discolor his flesh and add wrinkles. When he leaned closer to persuade himself that was merely an illusion, he saw movement in the sink. An object he'd taken to be a long gray hair was snatched into the plughole, and he glimpsed the body it belonged to squeezing itself out of sight down the pipe. He had to remind himself to transfer his wallet and loose coins and keys from his wet clothes to his current pockets before he hastened out of the room.

The carpet in the passage was damp with footprints, more of which he would have avoided if he hadn't been distracted by sounds in the rooms. Where he'd seen the teddy bear someone was murmuring "Up you come to Mummy. Gummy gum." Next door a voice was crooning "There you all are," presumably to the photographs, and Shone was glad to hear no words from the site of the lopsided knitting, only a clicking so rapid it sounded mechanical. Rather than attempt to interpret any of the muffled noises from the rooms off the darker section of the corridor, he padded downstairs so fast he almost missed his footing twice.

Nothing was moving in the hall except rain under the front door. Several conversations were ignoring one another in the television lounge. He picked up the receiver and thrust coins into the box, and his finger faltered over the zero on the dial. Perhaps because he was distracted by the sudden hush, he couldn't remember Ruth's number.

He dragged the hole of the zero around the dial as far as it would go in case that brought him the rest of the number, and as the hole whirred back to its starting point, it did. Ten more turns of the dial won him a ringing padded with static, and he felt as if the entire house was waiting for Ruth to answer. It took six pairs of rings—longer than she needed to cross her flat—to make her say "Ruth Lawson."

"It's me, Ruth." When there was silence he tried reviving their joke. "Old Ruthless."

"What now, Tom?"

He'd let himself hope for at least a dutiful laugh, but its absence threw him less than the reaction from within the television lounge: a titter, then several. "I just wanted you to know—"

"You're mumbling again. I can't hear you."

He was only seeking to be inaudible to anyone but her. "I say, I wanted you to know I really did get the day wrong," he said louder. "I really thought I was supposed to be coming up today."

"Since when has your memory been that bad?"

"Since, I don't know, today, it seems like. No, fair enough, you'll be thinking of your birthday. I know I forgot that too."

A wave of mirth escaped past the ajar door across the hall. Surely however many residents were in there must be laughing at the television with the sound turned down, he told himself as Ruth retorted "If you can forget that you'll forget anything."

"I'm sorry."

"I'm sorrier."

"I'm sorriest," he risked saying, and immediately wished he hadn't completed their routine, not only since it no longer earned him the least response from her but because of the roars of laughter from the television lounge. "Look, I just wanted to be sure you knew I wasn't trying to catch you out, that's all."

"Tom."

All at once her voice was sympathetic, the way it might have sounded at an aged relative's bedside. "Ruth," he said, and almost as stupidly, "What?"

"You might as well have been."

"I might . . . you mean I might . . ."

"I mean you nearly did."

"Oh." After a pause as hollow as he felt he repeated the syllable, this time not with disappointment but with all the surprise he could summon up. He might have uttered yet another version of the sound, despite or even because of the latest outburst of amusement across the hall, if Ruth hadn't spoken. "I'm talking to him now."

"Talking to who?"

Before the words had finished leaving him Shone understood that she hadn't been speaking to him but about him, because he could hear a man's voice in her flat. Its tone was a good deal more than friendly to her, and it was significantly younger than his. "Good luck to you both," he said, less ironically and more maturely than he would have preferred, and snagged the hook with the receiver.

A single coin trickled down the chute and hit the carpet with a plop. Amidst hilarity in the television lounge several women were crying "To who, to who" like a flock of owls. "He's good, isn't he," someone else remarked, and Shone was trying to decide where to take his confusion bordering on panic when a bell began to toll as it advanced out of the dark part of the house.

It was a small but resonant gong wielded by the manager. Shone heard an eager rumble of footsteps in the television lounge, and more of the same overhead. As he hesitated, Daph dodged around the manager towards him. "Let's get you sat down before they start their fuss," she said.

"I'll just fetch my shoes from my room."

"You don't want to bump into the old lot up there. They'll be wet, won't they?"

"Who?" Shone demanded, then regained enough sense of himself to answer his own question with a weak laugh. "My shoes, you mean. They're the only ones I've brought with me."

"I'll find you something once you're in your place," she said, opening the door opposite the television lounge, and stooped lower to hurry him. As soon as he trailed after her she bustled the length of the dining room and patted a small isolated table until he accepted its solitary straight chair. This faced the room and was boxed in by three long tables, each place at which was set like his with a plastic fork and spoon. Beyond the table opposite him velvet curtains shifted impotently as the windows trembled with rain. Signed photographs covered much of the walls—portraits of comedians he couldn't say he recognized, looking jolly or amusingly lugubrious. "We've had them all," Daph said. "They kept us going. It's having fun keeps the old lot alive." Some of this might have been addressed not just to him, because she was on her way out of the room. He barely had time to observe that the plates on the Welsh dresser to his left were painted on the wood, presumably to obviate breakage, before the residents crowded in.

A disagreement over the order of entry ceased at the sight of him. Some of the diners were scarcely able to locate their places for gazing at him rather more intently than he cared to reciprocate. Several of them were so inflated that he was unable to determine their gender except by their clothes, and not even thus in the case of the most generously trousered of them, whose face appeared to be sinking into a nest of flesh. Contrast was provided by a man so emaciated his handless wristwatch kept sliding down to his knuckles. Unity and

Amelia sat facing Shone, and then, to his dismay, the last of the eighteen seats was occupied by the woman he'd found in the bath, presently covered from neck to ankles in a black sweater and slacks. When she regarded him with an expression of never having seen him before and delight at doing so now he tried to feel some relief, but he was mostly experiencing how all the diners seemed to be awaiting some action from him. Their attention had started to paralyze him when Daph and Mr. Snell reappeared through a door Shone hadn't noticed beside the Welsh dresser.

The manager set about serving the left-hand table with bowls of soup while Daph hurried over, brandishing an especially capacious pair of the white cloth slippers Shone saw all the residents were wearing. "We've only these," she said, dropping them at his feet. "They're dry, that's the main thing. See how they feel."

Shone could almost have inserted both feet into either of them. "I'll feel a bit of a clown, to tell you the truth."

"Never mind, you won't be going anywhere."

Shone poked his feet into the slippers and lifted them to discover whether the footwear had any chance of staying on. At once all the residents burst out laughing. Some of them stamped as a form of applause, and even Snell produced a fleeting grateful smile as he and Daph retreated to the kitchen. Shone let his feet drop, which was apparently worth another round of merriment. It faded as Daph and Snell came out with more soup, a bowl of which the manager brought Shone, lowering it over the guest's shoulder before spreading his fingers on either side of him. "Here's Tommy Thomson for you," he announced, and leaned down to murmur in Shone's ear. "That'll be all right, won't it? Sounds better."

At that moment Shone's name was among his lesser concerns. Instead he gestured at the plastic cutlery. "Do you think I could—"

Before he had time to ask for metal utensils with a knife among them, Snell moved away as though the applause and the coos of joy his announcement had drawn were propelling him. "Just be yourself," he mouthed at Shone.

The spoon was the size Shone would have used to stir tea if the doctor hadn't recently forbidden him sugar. As he picked it up there was instant silence. He lowered it into the thin broth, where he failed to find anything solid, and raised it to his lips. The brownish liquid tasted of some unidentifiable meat with a rusty undertaste. He was too old to be finicky about food that had been served to everyone. He swallowed, and when his body raised to protest he set about spooning the broth into himself as fast as he could without spilling it, to finish the task.

He'd barely signaled his intentions when the residents began to cheer and stamp. Some of them imitated his style with the broth while others demonstrated how much more theatrically they could drink theirs; those closest to the hall emitted so much noise that he could have thought part of the slurping came from outside the room. When he frowned in that direction, the residents chortled as though he'd made another of the jokes he couldn't avoid making.

He dropped the spoon in the bowl at last, only to have Daph return it to the table with a briskness not far short of a rebuke. While she and Snell were in the kitchen everyone else gazed at Shone, who felt compelled to raise his eyebrows and hold out his hands. One of the expanded people nudged another, and both of them wobbled gleefully, and then all the residents were overcome by laughter that continued during the arrival of the main course, as if this was a joke they were eager for him to see. His plate proved to bear three heaps of mush, white and pale green and a glistening brown. "What is it?" he dared to ask Daph.

"What we always have," she said as if to a child or to someone who'd reverted to that state. "It's what we need to keep us going."

The heaps were of potatoes and vegetables and some kind of mince with an increased flavor of the broth. He did his utmost to eat naturally, despite the round of applause this brought him. Once his innards began to feel heavy he lined up the utensils on his by no means clear plate, attracting Daph to stoop vigorously at him. "I've finished," he said.

"Not yet."

When she stuck out her hands he thought she was going to return the fork and spoon to either side of his plate. Instead she removed it and began to clear the next table. While he'd been concentrating on hiding his reaction to his food the residents had gobbled theirs, he saw. The plates were borne off to the kitchen, leaving an expectant silence broken only by a restless shuffling. Wherever he glanced, he could see nobody's feet moving, and he told himself the sounds had been Daph's as she emerged from the kitchen with a large cake iced white as a memorial. "Daph's done it again," the hugest resident piped.

Shone took that to refer to the portrait in icing of a clown on top of the cake. He couldn't share the general enthusiasm for it; the clown looked undernourished and blotchily red-faced, and not at all certain what shape his wide twisted gaping lips should form. Snell brought in a pile of plates on which Daph placed slices of cake, having cut it in half and removed the clown's head from his shoulders in the process, but the distribution of slices caused some debate. "Give Tommy Thomson my eye," a man with bleary bloodshot eyeballs said.

"He can have my nose," offered the woman he'd seen in the bath.

"I'm giving him the hat," Daph said, which met with hoots of approval. The piece of cake she gave him followed the outline almost precisely of the clown's sagging pointed cap. At least it would bring dinner to an end, he thought, and nothing much could be wrong with a cake. He didn't expect it to taste faintly of the flavor of the rest of the meal. Perhaps that was why, provoking a tumult of jollity, he began to cough and then choke on a crumb. Far too eventually Daph brought him a glass of water in which he thought he detected the same taste. "Thanks," he gasped anyway, and as his coughs and the applause subsided, managed to say, "Thanks. All over now. If you'll excuse me, I think I'll take myself off to bed."

The noise the residents had made so far was nothing to the uproar with which they greeted this. "We haven't had the entertainment yet," Unity protested, jumping to her feet and looking more than ready to dart the length of the room. "Got to sing for your supper, Tommy Thomson."

"We don't want any songs and we don't want any speeches," Amelia declared. "We always have the show."

"The show," all the diners began to chant, and clapped and stamped in time with it, led by the thumping of Amelia's stick. "The show. The show."

The manager leaned across Shone's table. His eyes were pinker than ever, and blinking several times a second. "Better put it on for them or you'll get no rest," he muttered. "You won't need to be anything special."

Perhaps it was the way Snell was leaning down to him that let Shone see why he seemed familiar. Could he really have run the hotel where Shone had stayed with his parents nearly fifty years ago? How old would he have to be? Shone had no chance to wonder while the question was "What are you asking me to do?"

"Nothing much. Nothing someone of your age can't cope with. Come on and I'll show you before they start wanting to play their games."

It wasn't clear how much of a threat this was meant to be. Just now Shone was mostly grateful to be ushered away from the stamping and the chant. Retreating upstairs had ceased to tempt him, and fleeing to his car made no sense when he could hardly shuffle across the carpet for trying to keep his feet in the slippers. Instead he shambled after the manager to the doorway of the television lounge. "Go in there," Snell urged, and gave him a wincing smile. "Just stand in it. Here they come."

The room had been more than rearranged. The number of seats had been increased to eighteen by the addition of several folding chairs. All the seats faced the television, in front of which a small portable theater not unlike the site of a Punch and Judy show had been erected. Above the deserted ledge of a stage rose a tall pointed roof that reminded Shone of the clown's hat. Whatever words had been inscribed across the base of the gable were as faded as the many colors of the frontage. He'd managed to decipher only ENTER HERE when he found himself hobbling towards the theater, driven by the chanting that had emerged into the hall.

The rear of the theater was a heavy velvet curtain, black where it wasn't greenish. A slit had been cut in it up to a height of about four feet. As he ducked underneath, the moldy velvet clung to the nape of his neck. A smell of damp and staleness enclosed him when he straightened up. His elbows knocked against the sides of the box, disturbing the two figures that lay on a shelf under the stage, their empty bodies sprawling, their faces nestling together upside down as though they had dragged themselves close for companionship. He turned the faces upwards and saw that the figures, whose fixed grins and eyes were almost too wide for amusement, were supposed to be a man and a woman, although only a few tufts of gray hair clung to each dusty skull. He was nerving himself to insert his hands in the gloves of the bodies when the residents stamped chanting into the room.

Unity ran to a chair and then, restless with excitement, to another. Amelia dumped herself in the middle of a sofa and inched groaning to one end. Several of the jumbo residents lowered themselves onto folding chairs that looked immediately endangered. At least the seating of the audience put an end to the chant, but everyone's gaze fastened on Shone until he seemed to feel it clinging to the nerves of his face. Beyond the residents, Snell mouthed, "Just slip them on."

Shone pulled the open ends of the puppets towards him and poked them gingerly wider, dreading the emergence of some denizen from inside one or both. They appeared to be uninhabited, however, and so he thrust his hands in, trying to think which of his kindergarten stories he might adapt for the occasion. The brownish material fitted itself easily over his hands, almost as snug as the skin it resembled, and before he was ready each thumb was a puppet's arm, the little fingers too, and three fingers were shakily raising each head as if the performers were being roused from sleep. The spectators were already cheering, a response that seemed to entice the tufted skulls above the stage. Their entrance was welcomed by a clamor in which requests gradually became audible. "Let's see them knock each other about like the young lot do these days."

"Football with the baby."

"Make them go like animals."

"Smash their heads together."

They must be thinking of Punch and Judy, Shone told himself—and then a wish succeeded in quelling the rest. "Let's have Old Ruthless."

"Old Ruthless" was the chant as the stamping renewed itself—as his hands sprang onto the stage to wag the puppets at each other. All at once everything he'd been through that day seemed to have concentrated itself in his hands, and perhaps that was the only way he could be rid of it. He nodded the man that was his right hand at the balding female and uttered a petulant croak. "What do you mean, it's not my day?"

He shook the woman and gave her a squeaky voice. "What day do you think it is?"

"It's Wednesday, isn't it? Thursday, rather. Hang on, it's Friday, of course. Saturday, I mean."

"It's Sunday. Can't you hear the bells?"

"I thought they were for us to be married. Hey, what are you hiding there? I didn't know you had a baby yet."

"That's no baby, that's my boyfriend."

Shone twisted the figures to face the audience. The puppets might have been waiting for guffaws or even groans at the echo of an old joke; certainly he was. The residents were staring at him with, at best, bemusement. Since he'd begun the performance the only noise had been the sidling of the puppets along the stage and the voices that caught harshly in his throat. The manager and Daph were gazing at him over the heads of the residents; both of them seemed to have forgotten how to blink or grin. Shone turned the puppets away from the spectators as he would have liked to turn himself. "What's up with us?" he squeaked, wagging the woman's head. "We aren't going down very well."

"Never mind, I still love you. Give us a kiss," he croaked, and made the other puppet totter a couple of steps before it fell on its face. The loud crack of the fall took him off guard, as did the way the impact trapped his fingers in the puppet's head. The figure's ungainly attempts to stand up weren't nearly as simulated as he would have preferred. "It's these clown's shoes. You can't expect anyone to walk in them," he grumbled. "Never mind looking as if I'm an embarrassment."

"You're nothing else, are you? You'll be forgetting your own name next."

"Don't be daft," he croaked, no longer understanding why he continued to perform, unless to fend off the silence that was dragging words and antics out of him. "We both know what my name is."

"Not after that crack you fetched your head. You won't be able to keep anything in there now."

"Well, that's where you couldn't be wronger. My name . . ." He meant the puppet's, not his own; that was why he was finding it hard to produce. "It's, you know, you know perfectly well. You know it as well as I do."

"See, it's gone."

"Tell me or I'll thump you till you can't stand up," Shone snarled in a rage that was no longer solely the puppet's, and brought the helplessly grinning heads together with a sound like the snapping of bone. The audience began to cheer at last, but he was scarcely aware of them. The collision had split the faces open, releasing the top joints of his fingers only to trap them in the splintered gaps. The clammy bodies of the puppets clung to him as his hands wrenched at each other. Abruptly something gave, and the female head flew off as the body tore open. His right elbow hit the wall of the theater, and the structure lurched at him. As he tried to steady it, the head of the puppet rolled under his feet. He tumbled backwards into the moldy curtains. The theater reeled with him, and the room tipped up.

He was lying on his back, and his breath was somewhere else. In trying to prevent the front of the theater from striking him he'd punched himself on the temple with the cracked male head. Through the proscenium he saw the ceiling high above him and heard the appreciation of the audience. More time passed than he thought necessary before several of them approached.

Either the theater was heavier than he'd realized or his fall had weakened him. Even once he succeeded in peeling Old Ruthless off his hand he was unable to lift the theater off himself as the puppet lay like a deflated baby on his chest. At last Amelia lowered herself towards him, and he was terrified that she intended to sit on him. Instead she thrust a hand that looked boiled almost into his face to grab the proscenium and haul the theater off him. As someone else bore it away she seized his lapels and, despite the creaking of her stick, yanked him upright while several hands helped raise him from behind. "Are you fit?" she wheezed.

"I'll be fine," Shone said before he knew. All the chairs had been pushed back against the windows, he saw. "We'll show you one of our games now," Unity said behind him.

"You deserve it after all that," said Amelia, gathering the fragments of the puppets to hug them to her breasts.

"I think I'd like—"

"That's right, you will. We'll show you how we play. Who's got the hood?"

"Me," Unity cried. "Someone do it up for me."

Shone turned to see her flourishing a black cap. As she raised it over her head, he found he was again robbed of breath. When she tugged it down he realized that it was designed to cover the player's eyes, more like a magician's prop than an element of any game. The man with the handless watch dangling from his wrist pulled the cords of the hood tight behind her head and tied them in a bow, then twirled her round several times, each of which drew from her a squeal only just of pleasure. She wobbled around once more as, having released her, he tiptoed to join the other residents against the walls of the room.

She had her back to Shone, who had stayed by the chairs, beyond which the noise of rain had ceased. She darted away from him, her slippered feet patting the carpet, then lurched sideways towards nobody in particular and cocked her head. She was well out of the way of Shone's route to the door, where Daph and the manager looked poised to sneak out. He only had to avoid the blinded woman and he would be straight up to his room, either to barricade himself in or to retrieve his belongings and head for the car. He edged one foot forward into the toe of the slipper, and Unity swung towards him. "Caught you. I know who that is, Mr. Tommy Thomson."

"No you don't," Shone protested in a rage at everything that had led to the moment, but Unity swooped at him. She closed her bony hands around his cheeks and held on tight far longer than seemed reasonable before undoing the bow of the hood with her right hand while gripping and stroking his chin with the other. "Now it's your turn to go in the dark."

"I think I've had enough for one day, if you'll excuse—"

This brought a commotion of protests not far short of outrage. "You aren't done yet, a young thing like you." "She's older than you and she didn't make a fuss." "You've been caught, you have to play." "If you don't it won't be fair." The manager had retreated into the doorway and was pushing air at Shone with his outstretched hands as Daph mouthed, "It's supposed to be the old lot's time." Her words and the rising chant of "Be fair" infected Shone with guilt, aggravated when Unity uncovered her reproachful eyes and held out the hood. He'd disappointed Ruth; he didn't need to let these old folk down too. "Fair enough, I'll play," he said. "Just don't twist me too hard."

He hadn't finished speaking when Unity planted the hood on his scalp and drew the material over his brows. It felt like the clammy bodies of the puppets. Before he had a chance to shudder it was dragging his eyelids down, and he could see nothing but darkness. The hood molded itself to his cheekbones as rapid fingers tied the cords behind his head. "Not too—" he gasped at whoever started twirling him across the room.

He felt as if he'd been caught by a vortex of cheering and hooting, but it included murmurs too. "He played with me in the bath." "He wouldn't let us in there." "He made me miss my cartoons." "That's right, and he tried to take the control off us." He was being whirled so fast he no longer knew where he was. "Enough," he cried, and was answered by an instant hush. Several hands shoved him staggering forward, and a door closed stealthily behind him.

At first he thought the room had grown colder and damper. Then, as his giddiness steadied, he understood that he was in a different room, farther towards the rear of the house. He felt the patchy lack of carpet through his slippers, though that seemed insufficient reason for the faint scraping of feet he could hear surrounding him to sound so harsh. He thought he heard a whisper or the rattling of some object within a hollow container level with his head. Suddenly, in a panic that flared like white blindness inside the hood, he knew Daph's last remark hadn't been addressed to him, nor had it referred to anyone he'd seen so far. His hands flew to untie the hood—not to see where he was and with whom, but which way to run.

He was so terrified to find the cord immovably knotted that it took him seconds to locate the loose ends of the bow. A tug at them released it. He was forcing his fingertips under the edge of the hood when he heard light dry footsteps scuttle towards him, and an article that he tried to think of as a hand groped at his face. He staggered backwards, blindly fending off whatever was there. His fingers encountered ribs barer than they ought to be, and poked between them to meet the twitching contents of the bony cage. The whole of him convulsed as he snatched off the hood and flung it away.

The room was either too dark or not quite dark enough. It was at least the size of the one he'd left, and contained half a dozen sagging armchairs that glistened with moisture, and more than twice as many figures. Some were sprawled like loose bundles of sticks topped with grimacing masks on the chairs, but nonetheless doing their feeble best to clap their tattered hands. Even those that were swaying around him appeared to have left portions of themselves elsewhere. All of them were attached to strings or threads that glimmered in the murk and led his reluctant gaze to the darkest corner of the room. A restless mass crouched in it—a body with too many limbs, or a huddle of bodies that had grown inextricably entangled by the process of withering. Some of its movement, though not all, was of shapes that swarmed many-legged out of the midst of it, constructing parts of it or bearing away fragments or extending more threads to the other figures in the room. It took an effort that shriveled his mind before he was able to distinguish anything else: a thin gap between curtains, a barred window beyond—to his left, the outline of a door to the hall. As the figure nearest to him bowed so close he saw the very little it had in the way of eyes peering through the hair it had stretched coquettishly over its face, Shone bolted for the hall.

The door veered aside as his dizziness swept it away. His slippers snagged a patch of carpet and almost threw him on his face. The doorknob refused to turn in his sweaty grasp, even when he gripped it with both hands. Then it yielded, and as the floor at his back resounded with a mass of uneven yet purposeful shuffling, the door juddered open. He hauled himself around it and fled awkwardly, slippers flapping, out of the dark part of the hall.

Every room was shut. Other than the scratching of nails or of the ends of fingers at the door behind him, there was silence. He dashed along the hall, striving to keep the slippers on, not knowing why, knowing only that he had to reach the front door. He seized the latch and flung the door wide and slammed it as he floundered out of the house.

The rain had ceased except for a dripping of foliage. The gravel glittered like the bottom of a stream. The coach he'd heard arriving—

an old private coach spattered with mud—was parked across the rear of his car, so close it practically touched the bumper. He could never maneuver out of that trap. He almost knocked on the window of the television lounge, but instead limped over the gravel and into the street, towards the quiet hotels. He had no idea where he was going except away from the house. He'd hobbled just a few paces, his slippers growing more sodden and his feet sorer at each step, when headlamps sped out of the town.

They belonged to a police car. It halted beside him, its hazard lights twitching, and a uniformed policeman was out of the passenger seat before Shone could speak. The man's slightly chubby concerned face was a wholesome pink beneath a street lamp. "Can you help me?" Shone pleaded. "I—"

"Don't get yourself in a state, old man. We saw where you came from."

"They boxed me in. My car, I mean, look. If you can just tell them to let me out—"

The driver moved to Shone's other side. He might have been trying to outdo his colleague's caring look. "Calm down now. We'll see to everything for you. What have you done to your head?"

"Banged it. Hit it with, you wouldn't believe me, it doesn't matter. I'll be fine. If I can just fetch my stuff—"

"What have you lost? Won't it be in the house?"

"That's right, at the top. My shoes are."

"Feet hurting, are they? No wonder with you wandering around like that on a night like this. Here, get his other arm." The driver had taken Shone's right elbow in a firm grip, and now he and his partner easily lifted Shone and bore him towards the house. "What's your name, sir?" the driver enquired.

"Not Thomson, whatever anyone says. Not Tommy Thomson or Tom either. Or rather, it's Tom all right, but Tom Shone. That doesn't sound like Thomson, does it? Shone as in shine. I used to know someone who said I still shone for her, you still shine for me, she'd say. Been to see her today as a matter of fact." He was aware of talking too much as the policemen kept nodding at him and the house with its two lit windows—the television lounge's and his—reared over him. "Anyway, the point is the name's Shone," he said. "Ess aitch, not haitch as some youngsters won't be told it isn't, oh en ee. Shone."

"We've got you." The driver reached for the empty bellpush, then pounded on the front door. It swung inwards almost at once, revealing the manager. "Is this gentleman a guest of yours, Mr. Snell?" the driver's colleague said.

"Mr. Thomson. We thought we'd lost you," Snell declared, and pushed the door wide. All the people from the television lounge were lining the hall like spectators at a parade. "Tommy Thomson," they chanted.

"That's not me," Shone protested, pedaling helplessly in the air until his slippers flew into the hall. "I told you—"

"You did, sir," the driver murmured, and his partner said even lower, "Where do you want us to take you?"

"To the top, just to—"

"We know," the driver said conspiratorially. The next moment Shone was sailing to the stairs and up them, with the briefest pause as the policemen retrieved a slipper each. The chant from the hall faded, giving way to a silence that seemed most breathlessly expectant in the darkest sections of the house. He had the police with him, Shone reassured himself. "I can walk now," he said, only to be borne faster to the termination of the stairs. "Where the door's open?" the driver suggested. "Where the light is?"

"That's me. Not me really, anything but, I mean—"

They swung him through the doorway by his elbows and deposited him on the carpet. "It couldn't be anybody else's room," the driver said, dropping the slippers in front of Shone. "See, you're already here."

Shone looked where the policemen were gazing with such sympathy it felt like a weight that was pressing him into the room. A photograph of himself and Ruth, arms around each other's shoulders with a distant mountain behind, had been removed from his drenched suit and propped on the shelf in place of the telephone. "I just brought that," he protested, "you can see how wet it was," and limped across the room to don his shoes. He hadn't reached them when he saw himself in the mirror.

He stood swaying a little, unable to retreat from the sight. He heard the policemen murmur together and withdraw, and their descent of the stairs, and eventually the dual slam of car doors and the departure of the vehicle. His reflection still hadn't allowed him to move. It was no use his telling himself that some of the tangle of wrinkles might be cobwebs, not when his hair was no longer graying but white. "All right, I see it," he yelled—he had no idea at whom. "I'm old. I'm old."

"Soon," said a whisper like an escape of gas in the corridor, along which darkness was approaching as the lamps failed one by one. "You'll be plenty of fun yet," the remains of another voice said somewhere in his room. Before he could bring himself to look for its source, an item at the end of most of an arm fumbled around the door and switched out the light. The dark felt as though his vision was abandoning him, but he knew it was the start of another game. Soon he would know if it was worse than hide-and-seek—worse than the first sticky unseen touch of the web of the house on his face.

Edward Lee

ICU

Edward Lee appeared like a gift on my doorstep. I don't mean literally; I mean only that his story "ICU" is one of the few in this book that I didn't specifically commission but which knocked my socks off when I had it in my hands. The story has the finger-snapping, graphic-image intensity of a Quentin Tarrantino script, with, I think, a little more juice in the veins and conscience in the cabeza.

Lee has published steadily in the field since the early 1980s; his work includes older books like Incubi *and* Succubi, *as well as more recent efforts such as* Sacrifice *(as Richard Kinion). A limited edition short story collection,* The Ushers and Other Stories, *was published in 1998.*

It chased him; it was *huge*. But what was it? He sensed its immensity gaining on him, pursuing him through unlit warrens, around cornerways of smothered flesh, and down alleys of ichor and blood . . .

Holy Mother of God.

When Paone fully woke, his mind felt wiped out. Dull pain and confinement crushed him, or was it paralysis? Warped images, voices, smears of light and color all massed in his head. Francis "Frankie" Paone shuddered in the terror of the nameless thing that chased him through the rabbets and fissures of his own subconscious mind.

Yes, he was awake now, but the chase led on:

Storming figures. Concussion. Blood squirting onto dirty white walls.

And like a slow-dissolve, Paone finally realized what it was that chased him. Not hitters. Not cops or feds.

It was *memory* that chased him.

But the memory of *what*?

The thoughts surged. *Where am I? What the hell happened to me?*

This latter query, at least, shone clear. Something *had* happened. Something devastating . . .

The room was a blur. Paone squinted through grit teeth; without his glasses he couldn't see three feet past his face.

But he could see enough to know.

Padded leather belts girded his chest, hips, and ankles, restraining him to a bed which seemed hard as slate. He couldn't move. To his right stood several metal poles topped by blurred blobs. A long line descended . . . to his arm. *IV bags,* he realized. The line came to an end at the inside of his right elbow. And all about him swarmed unmistakable scents: antiseptics, salves, isopropyl alcohol.

I'm in a fucking hospital, he acknowledged.

Someone must've dropped a dime on him. But . . . He simply couldn't remember. The memories hovered in fragments, still chasing his spirit without mercy. Gunshots. Blood. Muzzleflash.

His myopia offered even less mercy. Beyond the bed he could detect only a vague white perimeter, shadows, and depthless bulk. A drone reached his ears, like a distant air conditioner, and there was a slow, aggravating beep: the drip-monitor for his IV. Overhead, something swayed. *Hanging flowerpot?* he ventured. No, it reminded him more of one of those retractable arms you'd find in a doctor's office, like an X-ray nozzle. And the fuzzed ranks of shapes along the walls could only be cabinets, *pharmaceutical* cabinets.

Yeah, I'm in a hospital, all right, he realized. An ICU ward. It had to be. And he was buckled down good. Not just his ankles, but his knees too, and his shoulders. More straps immobilized his right arm to the IV board, where white tape secured the needle sunk into the crook of his elbow.

Then Paone looked at his left arm. That's all it was—an arm. There was no hand at the end of it. And when he raised his right leg . . .

Just a stump several inches below the knee.

Nightmare, he wished. But the chasing memories seemed too real for a dream, and so did the pain. There was *plenty* of pain. It hurt to breathe, to swallow, even to blink. Pain oozed through his bowels like warm acid.

Somebody fucked me up royal, he conceded. The jail ward, no doubt. *And there's probably a cop standing right outside the door.* He knew where he was now, but it terrified him not knowing exactly what had brought him here.

The memories raged, chasing, chasing . . .

Heavy slumps. Shouts. A booming, distorted voice . . . like a megaphone.

Jesus. He wanted to remember, yet again, he didn't. The memories *stalked* him: pistol shots, full-auto rifle fire, the feel of his own piece jumping in his hand.

"Hey!" he shouted. "How about some help in here!"

A click resounded to the left; a door opened and closed. Soft footsteps approached, then suddenly a bright, unfocused figure blurred toward him.

"How long have you been awake?" came a toneless female voice.

"Couple of minutes," Paone said. Pain throbbed in his throat. "Could you come closer? I can barely see you."

The figure obliged. Its features sharpened.

It wasn't a cop at all, it was a nurse. Tall, brunet, with fluid-blue eyes and a face of hard, eloquent lines. Her white blouse and skirt blurred like bright light. White nylons shone over sleek, coltish legs.

"Do you know where my glasses are?" Paone asked. "I'm near-sighted as hell."

"Your glasses fell off at the crime scene," she flatly replied.

Crime scene, came the bumbling thought.

"We've sent someone to recover them," she added. "It shouldn't be too long." Her vacant eyes appraised him. She leaned over to take his vitals. "How do you feel?"

"Terrible. My gut hurts like a son of a bitch, and my hand . . ." Paone, squinting, raised the bandaged left stump. "Shit," he muttered. He didn't even want to ask.

Now the nurse turned to finick with the IV monitor; Paone continued to struggle against the freight of chasing memory. More images churned in some mental recess. Fragments of wood and ceiling tile raining on his shoulders. The mad cacophony of what could only be machine gun fire. A head exploding to pulp.

Blank-faced, then, the nurse returned her gaze. "What do you remember, Mr. Paone?"

"I—" was all he said. He stared up. Paone never carried real ID on a run, and whatever he drove was either hot or chopped, with phony plates. The question ground out of his throat. "How do you know my name?"

"We know all about you," she said, unfolding a slip of paper. "The police showed us this teletype from Washington. Francis K. 'Frankie' Paone. You have seven aliases. You're thirty-seven years old, never been married, and you have no known place of legal residence.

In 1985 you were convicted of interstate flight to avoid prosecution, interstate transportation of obscene material depicting minors, and multiple violations of Section 18 of the United States Code. Two years ago you were released from Alderton Federal Penitentiary after serving sixty-two months of concurrent eleven- and five-year jail terms. You are a known associate of the Vinchetti crime family. You're a child pornographer, Mr. Paone."

Christ, a fuckin' burn, Paone realized. *Somebody set me up.* By now it wasn't hard to figure: lying in some ICU ward strapped to a bed, shot up like a hinged duck in a shooting gallery, one hand gone, one leg gone, and now this stolid bitch reading him his own rap sheet off an FBI fax. He sure as shit hadn't gotten busted taking down some candy store.

"You don't know what you're talking about," he said.

Her eyes blazed down. Her face could've been carved from stone. *Yeah.* Paone thought, *I'll bet she's got a couple kids herself flunking out of school and smoking pot. Bet her car just broke down and her insurance just went up and her hubby's late for dinner every night because he's too busy balling his secretary and snorting rails of coke off her tits, and all of a sudden it's my fault that the world's a shithouse full of perverts and pedophiles. It's my fault that a lot of people out there pay righteous cash for kiddie flicks, right, baby? Go ahead, blame me. Why not? Oh, hey, and how about the drug problem? And the recession and the Middle East and the ozone layer? That's all my fault too, right?*

Her voice sounded like she had gravel in her throat when again she asked: "What do you remember?"

The query haunted him. The bits of memory blurred along with the room in his myopic eyes—bullets popping into flesh, the megaphone grating, spent cartridges spewing out of wafts of smoke—and chased him further, stalking him as relentlessly as a wild cat running down a fawn, while Paone fled on, desperate to know yet never daring to look back. . . .

"Shit, nothing," he finally said. "I can't remember anything accept bits and pieces."

The nurse seemed to talk more to herself than to him. "A transient-global amnesic effect, retrograde and generally nonaphasic, induced by acute traumatic shock. Don't worry, it's a short-term symptom and quite commonplace." The big blue eyes bore back into him. "So I think I'll refresh your memory. Several hours ago, you murdered two state police officers and a federal agent."

Paone's jaw dropped.

At once the chase ended, the wild cat of memory finally falling down on its prey—Paone's mind. He remembered it all, the pieces falling into place as quickly as pavement to a ledge-jumper.

The master run. Rodz. The loops.

And all the blood.

Another day, another ten K, Paone thought, mounting the three flights of stairs to Rodz's apartment. He wore jersey gloves—no way he was rockhead enough to leave his prints anywhere near Rodz's crib. He knocked six times on the door, whistling "Love Me Tender" by the King.

"Who is it?" came the craggy voice.

"Santa Claus," Paone said. "You really should think about getting a chimney."

Rodz let him in, then quickly relocked the door. "Anyone tailing you?"

"No, just a busload of DJ agents and a camera crew from *60 Minutes*."

Rodz glowered.

Fuck you if you can't take a joke, Paone thought. He didn't much like Rodz—Newark slime, a whack. Nathan Rodz looked like an anorectic Tiny Tim after a bad facelift: long, frizzy black hair on the head of a pudgy medical cadaver, speedlines down his cheeks. Rodz was what parlance dubbed a "snatch-cam"—a subcontractor, so to speak. He abducted the kids, or got them on loan from freelance movers, then shot the tapes himself. "The Circuit" was what the Justice Department called the business: underground pornography. It was a 1.5-billion-dollar-per-year industry that almost no one knew about, a far cry from the *Debbie Does Dallas* bunk you rented down at Metro Video. Paone muled all kinds of underground: rape loops, "wet" S&M, animal flicks, scat, snuff, and (their biggest number) "kp" and "prepubes." Paone picked up the masters from guys like Rodz, then muled them to Vinchetti's mobile "dupe" lab. Vinchetti's network controlled almost all of the underground porn in the East; Paone was the middleman, part of the family. It all worked through mail drops and coded distro points. Vinchetti paid two grand for a twenty-minute master if the resolution was good; from there each master was duped hundreds of times and sold to clients with a taste for the perverse. "Logboys," the guys who did the actual rodwork, were hired freelance on the side; that way, nobody could spin on Vinchetti himself. Paone had seen some shit in his time—part of his job was to sample each master for quality: biker chicks on PCP blowing horses and dogs, addicts excreting on each other and often consuming the produce of their bowels. "Nek" flicks. "Bag" flicks. Logboys getting down on pregnant girls, retarded girls, amputees and deformees. And snuff. It amazed Paone, in spite of its grotesquery: people *paid* to see this stuff. They *got off* on it. *What a fucked-up world,* he thought a million times over, but, hey, supply and demand—that was the American Way, wasn't it? If Vinchetti didn't supply the clients, someone else would, and as long as the money was there . . .

I'll take my cut, Paone stonily thought.

The biggest orders were always for kp. According to federal stats, 10,000 kids disappeared each year and were never seen again; most of them wound up in the Circuit. The younger the kids, the more the tapes cost. Once kids got old (fourteen or fifteen) they were deemed as "beat," and they were either sold overseas or put out on the street to turn tricks for Vinchetti's pross net. One thing feeding the other. Yeah, it was a fucked-up world, all right, but that wasn't Paone's problem.

The competition was squat. Only one other East Coast family ran underground porn, the Bontes, and they had a beef with Vinchetti going way back. Both families fought for pieces of the hard market, but the Bontes only owned a trickle of the action, and Paone could've laughed at the reason. Dario Bonte, the don, thought it was unethical to victimize children. *Ain't that a laugh,* Paone had thought. *The son of a bitch'll string women out on junk and put them in scat films till they starve to death, but he won't do any kiddie.* What a chump. Most of the money was in kp anyway. No wonder Bonte was losing his ass. And every now and then some foreign outfit would try to move on Vinchetti's turf with kp from Europe.

But they never lasted very long.

All in all, Paone's job was simple: he bought the masters, muled them to the lab and kept the snatch-cams in line—guys like this muck-for-brains short-eyed scumbag Rodz.

"I got five for ya," said Rodz, "the usual." Rodz's voice was more annoying than nails across slate, a nasally, wet rasp. "But I been thinking, you know?"

"Oh, you think?" Paone asked. He'd never seen such a pit for an apartment. Little living room full of put-it-together-yourself furniture, smudged walls, tacky green-and-brown carpet tile; an odiferous kitchen. *Buckingham Fucking Palace this ain't.*

"Like two K a pop is getting pretty skimpy these days," Rodz went on. "Come on, man, for a fucking master that Vinchetti's crew'll dupe hundreds of times? That's serious green for him. But what about me? Every time I make a master for your man, I'm sticking my neck out a mile."

"That's because you were *born* with a mile-long neck, Ichabod."

"I think two-point-five at least is fair. I mean, I heard that the Bonte family's paying three."

"The Bontes don't do kiddie porn, grapehead," Paone informed him. "And anybody in the biz knows that."

"Yeah, but they do snuff and nek and all the other hard stuff. I'm the one busting my ass making the masters. I should be able to go to the highest bidder."

Paone stared him down. "Watch that, Rodz. No jive. You master for Vinchetti and Vinchetti only. Period. You want some advice? Don't even *think* about peddling your shit to some other family. The last guy who pulled a stunt like that, you know what happened to him? Jersey cops found him hanging upside-down in some apartment laundry room. Blowtorched. And they cut off his cock and Express Mailed it to his grandmother in San Bernardino."

Rodz's face did a twitch. "Yeah, well, like I was saying, two K a pop sounds pretty square."

I thought so, Paone regarded.

"So where's that green?"

Paone headed toward the back bedroom, where Rodz did his thing. "You don't touch doggie-doo till I see the fruits of your labor."

He sat down on a couch that had no doubt served as a prop in dozens of Rodz's viddies. High-end cameras and lights sat on tripods, not the kind of gear they sold down at Radio Shack. The masters had to be shot on large-format inch-and-a-quarter high-speed tape so the dupes retained good contrast. The five boxed tapes sat before a thirty-five-inch Sony Trinitron and a studio double-player by Thompson Electronics. "Good kids this time, too," Rodz complimented himself. "All level." Sometimes a kid would freak on camera, or space out; lots of them were screwed up from the get-go: Fetal Cocaine babies, Fetal Alcohol Syndrome, Battered Child Syndrome. There were times when Paone actually felt sad about the way things worked.

Now came the sadder part: Paone had to sit back and watch each master; lighting, resolution, and clarity all had to be good. He plugged in the first tape. . . .

Jesus, he thought. Pale movement flickered on the screen. They were always the same in a way. What bothered Paone most were the faces—the forlorn, tiny faces on the kids, the *look* while Rodz's stunt cocks got busy. *What do they think?* Paone wondered. *What goes on in their heads?* Every so often the kid would look into the camera and offer a stare that defied description. . . .

"At least let me UV the cash while you're watching," Rodz said.

"Yeah, yeah." Paone threw him the stuffed envelope. His face felt molded of clay as he watched on. Rodz always fronted his flicks with cutesy titles, like *Vaseline Alley, The Young and the Hairless, Stomper Room.* Meanwhile, Rodz himself donned nylon gloves and took out the band of century notes. Ten grand didn't look like much. He scanned each bill front and back with a Sirchie ultraviolet lamp. Technicians from Treasury worked liaison with DJ and the Bureau all the time. Their favorite game was to turn someone out and dust buy-money with invisible uranyl phosphate dyes. Dead solid perfect in court.

"Clean enough for ya?" Paone asked. "I mean, a clean guy like yourself?"

"Yeah, looks good." Rodz's face looked lit up as he inspected the bills. "Unsequenced numbers too. That's great."

Paone winced when he glanced back to the screen. In the last tape, here was Rodz himself, with his hair pulled back and a phony beard, doing the rodwork himself. Paone frowned.

"Sweet, huh?" Rodz grinned at himself on the screen. "Always wanted to be in pictures."

"You should get an Oscar. Best Supporting Pervert."

"It's some fringe bennie. And look who's talking about pervert. I just make the tapes. It's your people who distribute them."

Rodz had a point. *I'm just a player in the big game,* Paone reminded himself. When the money's good you do what you gotta do.

"I'm outa here," Paone said when the last master flicked off. He packed up the tapes and followed Rodz out to the living room. "I wish I could say it's been a pleasure."

Rodz chuckled. "You should be nicer to me. One day I might let you be in one of my flicks. You'd never be the same."

"Yeah? And you'll never be the same when I twist your head off and shove it up your ass."

By the apartment door, Rodz held the speedlined grin. "See you next time. . . . I'd offer to shake hands except I wouldn't want to get any slime on you."

"Thanks for the thought." Paone polished his glasses with a hand-kerchief, reached for the door, and—

Ka-CRACK!

"Holy shit!" Rodz yelled.

—the door blew out of its frame. Not kicked open, *knocked down,* and it was no wonder when Paone, in a moment of static shock, noted the size of the TSD cop stepping back with the steelhead door-ram. An even bigger cop three-pointed into the room with a cocked revolver.

"Freeze! Police!"

Paone moved faster than he'd ever moved in his life, got an arm around Rodz, and began to jerk back. Rodz gasped, pissing his pants, as Paone used him as a human shield. Two shots rang out, both of which socked into Rodz's upper sternum.

"Give it up, Paone!" the cop advised. "There's no way out!"

Bullshit, Paone thought. Rodz twitched, gargling blood down his front, then suddenly turned to dead weight. But the move gave Paone time to duck behind the kitchen counter and shuck his SIG 220 chock-full of 9mm hardball. *Move fast!* he directed himself, then sprang up, squeezed off two rounds, and popped back down. Both slugs slammed into the cop's throat. All Paone heard was the slump.

Shadows stiffened in the doorway. A megaphone boomed: "Francis Frankie Paone, you're surrounded by Justice Department agents and the state police. Throw down your weapon and surrender. Throw down your weapon and surrender, throw down your—" and on and on.

Paone shucked his backup piece—an ice-cold Colt snub—and tossed it over the counter. Another state cop and a guy in a suit blundered in. *Dumb fucks,* Paone thought. He sprang up again, squeezed off two sets of doubletaps. The cop twirled, taking both bullets in the chin. And the suit, a DJ agent, took his pair between the eyes. In the frantic glimpse, Paone had time to see the guy's head explode. A goulash of brains slapped the wall.

No way I'm going down. Paone felt surprisingly calm. *Back room. Window. Three-story drop into the bushes.* It was his only chance. . . .

But a chance he'd never get.

Before he could move out, the room began to . . . vibrate. Three state SWAT men in Kevlar charged almost balletically into the room, and after that the world turned to chaos. Bullets swept toward Paone in waves. M-16s on full-auto spewed hot brass and rattled away like lawn mowers, rip-stitching holes along the walls, tearing the kitchen apart. "I give up!" Paone shouted, but the volley of gunfire only increased. He curled up into a ball as everything around him began to disintegrate into flying bits. Clip after clip, the bullets came, bursting cabinets, chewing up the counter and the floor, and when there was little left of the kitchen, there wasn't much left of Paone. His left hand hung by a single sinew, his right leg looked gnawed off. Hot slivers of steel cooked in his guts.

Then: silence.

His stomach burned like swallowed napalm. His consciousness began to drift away with wafts of cordite. He sidled over; blood dotted his glasses. EMTs carried off the dead police as a man in blue utilities poked forward with a smoking rifle barrel. Radio squawk eddied fog-like in the hot air, and next Paone was being stretchered out over what seemed a lake of blood.

Dreamy moments later, red and white lights beat in his eyes. The doors of the ambulance slammed shut.

"Great God Almighty," he whispered.

"I told you you'd remember," the nurse said.

"How bad am I shot?"

"Not bad enough to kill you. IV antibiotics held off the peritoneal infection, and the EMTs got tourniquets on your arm and leg before you lost too much blood." Her eyes narrowed. "Lucky for you there's no death penalty in this state."

That's right, Paone slowly thought. And the fed statutes only allowed capital punishment if an agent was killed during a narcotics offense. They'd send him up for life with no parole, sure, but that beat fertilizing the cemetery. The fed slams were easier than a lot of the state cuts; plus, Paone was a cop-killer, and cop-killers got instant status in stir. No bulls would be trying to bust his cherry. *Things could be worse,* he recognized now. He remembered what he'd told that punk Rodz about taking things for granted; Paone stuck to his guns. He was busted, shot up like Swiss cheese, and had left a hand and a leg on Rodz's kitchen floor, but at least he was alive.

Yeah, he thought. *Hope springs eternal.*

"What are you smiling about?" the nurse asked.

"I don't know. Just happy to be alive, I guess . . . Yeah, that's it." It was true. Despite these rather irrefutable circumstances, Paone was indeed very happy.

"Happy to be alive?" The nurse looked coldly disgusted. "What about the men you murdered? They had wives, families. They had children. Those children are fatherless now. Those men are dead because of you."

Paone shrugged as best he could. "Life's a gamble. They lost and I won. They're the ones who wanted to play hardball, not me. If they hadn't fucked with me, their kids would still have daddies. I'm not gonna feel guilty for wasting a bunch of guys who tried to take me down."

It was ironic. The pain in his gut sharpened yet Paone couldn't help his exuberance. He wished he had his glasses so he could see the nurse better. Hell, he wished he had a cold beer too, and a smoke. He wished he wasn't in these damn hospital restraints. A little celebration of life seemed in order, like maybe he wouldn't mind putting the blocks on this ice-bitch nurse. Yeah, like maybe roll her over onto the bed and give that cold pussy of hers a good working over. *Bet that'd take some of the starch out of her sails.*

Paone, next, began to actually laugh. What a weird turn of the cards the world was. God worked in strange ways, all right. *At least He's got a sense of humor.* It was funny. *Those three cops bite the dust and I'm lying here all snug and cozy, gandering the Ice Bitch.* Paone's low and choppy laughter did not abate.

The nurse turned on the radio to drown out her patient's unseemly jubilation. Light news filled the air as she checked Paone's pulse and marked his IV bags. The newscaster droned the day's paramount events: A heat wave in Texas had killed a hundred people. Zero-fat butter to hit the market next week. The Surgeon General was imploring manufacturers to suspend production of silicon testicular implants, and a U.S. Embassy in Africa somewhere just got bombed. It made things even funnier: the world and all its silliness suddenly meant nothing to Paone. He was going to the slam. What difference did anything, good or bad, make to him now?

He squinted up when another figure came in. Through the room's blurred features, a face leaned over: a sixtyish guy, snow-white hair and a great bushy mustache. "Good evening, Mr. Paone," came the greeting. "My name's Dr. Willet. I wanted to stop by and see how you're doing. Is there anything I can get for you?"

"Since you asked, Doc, I wouldn't mind having my glasses back, and to tell you the truth I wouldn't mind having another nurse. This one here's about as friendly as a mad dog."

Willet only smiled in response. "You were shot up pretty bad but you needn't worry now about infection or blood loss. Those are always our chief concerns with multiple gunshot wounds. I'm happy to inform you that you're in surprisingly good shape considering what happened."

Jolly good, Paone thought.

"And I must say," Willet went on, "I've been anxious to meet you. You're the first child pornographer I've ever had the opportunity to speak with. In a bizarre sense, you're famous. The renegade outlaw."

"Well, I'd offer to give you an autograph," Paone joked, "but there's a problem. I'm left-handed."

"Good, good, that's the spirit. It's a man of character who can maintain a sense of levity after going through what you've—"

"Shhh!" the nurse hissed. She seemed jittery now, a pent-up blur. "This is it . . . I think this is it."

Paone made a face. From the radio, the newscaster droned on: ". . . in a year-long federal sting operation. One suspect, Nathan Rodz, was killed on-site in a frantic shootout with police. Two state police officers and one special agent from a Justice Department task force were also killed, according to authorities, by the second suspect, an alleged mob middleman by the name of Francis 'Frankie' Paone. Paone himself was under investigation for similar allegations, and thought to have direct ties with the Vinchetti crime family, which is said to control over fifty percent of all child pornography marketed in the U.S. Police spokesmen later announced that Paone, during the shootout, managed to escape the scene, and is currently the subject of a state-wide manhunt . . ."

Paone's thoughts seemed to slowly flatten. "What's this . . . Escaped?"

The nurse was smiling now. She opened a pair of black-framed glasses and put them on Paone's face. . . .

The blurred room, at last, came into focus.

What the fuck is this?

A tracked curtain surrounded him, as he would expect on an ICU ward, but then he noticed something else. It wasn't an X-ray nozzle that hung overhead; it was a retractable boom, complete with microphone. And one of the IV stands wasn't an IV stand at all; it was a stand for a directional halogen light.

"What the hell kind of hospital is this!" Paone demanded.

"Oh, it's not a hospital," Willet said. "It's a safe house."

"One of Don Dario Bonte's safe houses," the nurse was delighted to add.

Willet again. "And we're his private medical staff. Generally our duties are rather uninvolved. When one of the don's men gets shot or hurt, we take care of him, since the local hospital wouldn't be safe."

Bonte, Paone thought in slow dread. *Dario Bonte—Vinchetti's only rival . . .*

"And the police were all too happy to hand you over to our goodly employer," Willet continued. "Half of the state police are on Don Bonte's payroll . . . and this way, the suffering taxpayers are spared the cost of a trial."

Paone felt like he was about to throw up his heart.

The nurse's breasts shook when she giggled. "But we're not just going to kill you—"

"We've got some interesting games to play before we do that," Willet said. "See, our job was to make sure you survived until Junior could get here—"

A door clicked open, and then the nurse reeled back the curtain to reveal a typical basement. But that was not all Paone saw. Standing in the doorway before some steps was a frightfully muscular young man with short dark hair, chiseled features and—

Aw sweet Jesus holy shit—

—and a crotch so packed it looked like he had a couple of potatoes in his pants.

"Three guesses why they call him Junior," the nurse giggled on.

"And three more guesses as to what happens next," Willet said. Now he had shouldered a high-end Sony Betacam. "You see, Mr. Paone, *your* boss may own the market share for child pornography, but *our* boss owns a share of the rest. You know, the *really* demented stuff. And as a gut-shot amputee, you'll be able to provide us with a *very special* feature, don't you think?"

Paone vomited on himself when Junior began to lower his jeans. The nurse jammed a needle into Paone's arm, not enough sodium amytal to knock him out, but just enough to keep him from putting up much of a fight. Then the nurse took off his restraints and flipped him over.

"Don Bonte doesn't like child pornographers," she said.

The stitches across Paone's abdomen began to pop, and he could hear Junior's footsteps approach the bed.

"As they say," Willet enthused: "Lights, camera, action!"

P. D. Cacek

THE GRAVE

I admit, with some head-hanging, that I had to be pointed in P. D. Cacek's direction. One of the main reasons for the existence of my acknowledgments page at the front of this book is to pay thanks to certain people for "giving" me writers that would have slipped through the cracks in my brain (there are many such). For some reason Trish's work (she told me I could call her Trish), which has apparently caught fire recently (a novel, Night Prayers, *has been compared to Nancy Collins's Sonja Blue books, and there is also a story collection,* Leavings), *had escaped me. She is one of those writers whom Charles L. Grant would have lovingly tended in the garden of his Shadows series, and her clear head and careful, mood-evocative prose, immediately evident when I read "The Grave," were a breath of fresh air.*

If you don't agree, you're wrong.

It was as if someone had suddenly wrapped a thick layer of cotton around her. Things that had been ordinary and familiar became muted and removed.

If she hadn't been so frightened she might have even laughed at the feeling. Not that it was an entirely unpleasant sensation.

She could still hear the birds singing in the thick, autumn-bright canopy above her and identify each sweet trill and warble, caw, churr, chirp and whistle. She could smell the moss and moisture from the stream as it gurgled through the shallows not twenty feet behind her and she could feel the whispered urgency of the wind reminding her that she really should be heading home for supper. These things were familiar. These things had accompanied her for the last fifteen years as she walked the wooded path to and from her position as Bryner Elementary School's Head Librarian.

These things she heard and smelled and felt.

But she saw only the tiny grave.

The imaginary feel of cotton tightened around her.

For fifteen years she had walked that same path through the woods, had heard the same noises, felt the same seasonal changes, but until today she had never noticed it. Never saw it.

The grave.

It was a child's grave, she was sure of that even though she had no reason to be. Alone and abandoned and forgotten, the grave was tucked back into the shadows at the far end of a narrow gully; the tiny dirt mound in front of the weathered pink headstone

pink is for girls

all but eroded by the countless seasons

how many

of rain and snow and drought while she, and who knows how many others, passed by.

What kind of mother would bury her child, alone, in the woods? What kind of mother would do such a thing?

A bad mother, Elizabeth Hesse thought as she looked down at the little grave, a very *bad* mother.

"I would never have done that," she said out loud. "I would have been a good mother."

But even as she said the words she knew it wasn't true, because a good mother would have seen the grave before this.

And she hadn't.

Until today.

One of the things she was always telling the children who came into the library was, "Look. See the world. Don't just wander blindly through it. Notice everything."

Wonderful, hypocritical words. She had said them for fifteen years, every day for fifteen years . . . and still she hadn't noticed anything. Hadn't looked. Had wandered blindly back and forth in front of the grave for fifteen years of her own life and never seen it.

Until today.

A small sound began to whisper from Elizabeth's mouth, but she caught it with her fingers before it escaped. Her hand still smelled of the tuna sandwich she'd had for lunch; the fish oil stronger than the gardenia-scented liquid soap in the Teacher's Lounge.

Her father's company had sent a spray of gardenias to his funeral. Small and white, they had nevertheless filled the viewing room with their scent. Her mother had complained about that, saying it was overpowering.

There were no flowers on the small grave, just a thin blanket of autumn leaves.

It made Elizabeth shiver just looking at it. *A good mother would have tried to keep her baby warm. She would have done that if it had been her child. She would have been a good mother.* She wouldn't have buried it in the woods.

No.

Elizabeth closed her eyes and let her hand drop to the top button on her cardigan. It *wasn't* a real grave. What she had seen, and would see again when she opened her eyes, would be a rock that only *looked* like a headstone. She hadn't noticed it before because there was nothing *to* notice.

It's not a grave. It's not a grave. It's not—

Elizabeth kept repeating the words until she opened her eyes. And then the words and hope went away.

It was a grave . . . but perhaps only the grave of an animal.

Yes. That fit. It was the grave of some beloved pet that had died of old age or accident and been buried. Or a favorite dolly.

Elizabeth sighed. Of course, it had to be a joke or animal's grave. No mother in her right mind would bury a child so far away . . . from . . . *everything*. Alone. Abandoned.

Forgotten.

Good mothers just didn't do that sort of thing. Good mothers protected their children and made sure they were healthy and happy and . . .

But if the grave was only a childish fancy, then that meant some mother . . . some *bad* mother had let her child wander into the woods.

Alone!

Elizabeth turned and glanced quickly up and down the path.

The children *knew* they weren't supposed to play in the woods. It had been the subject of concern for years; probably even as far back as when she was a child. The woods were not safe, they never had been. Her own mother told her that repeatedly.

Only last November, the second day of the Thanksgiving holiday, Polly Winter, a fourth grader, had broken her ankle while playing a game of Hide-and-Seek with visiting cousins. Elizabeth had seen her just that morning from the library window and she was still limping, nearly a full year later, poor child. Poor, willful child.

Something rustled in the tall grass near the stand of red-leafed maple directly behind the

grave

gully and Elizabeth bit her lip. *The woods were not safe. The woods were secluded. The woods were lonely . . . so very lonely.*

Whatever was in the grave—doll or dog (*or child*)—it was alone and lonely, too.

A shiver followed Elizabeth as she stepped from smooth path to rock-rutted gully. Although she moved carefully and cautiously, the way her mother had taught her, her foot almost twisted out from under her and she saw herself sprawled unladylike in the dirt, skirt thrown back, legs spread wide.

Stop that!

Elizabeth kept her footing but stopped when another gust of wind rustled the maple leaves in front of her. *That was the sound she'd heard.* There was no one in the woods besides her. No children, no adults, no one to see her kneel in front of the tiny headstone.

It was pink granite flecked with black and silver; and it was cold against the palm of her hand, its edges smooth as butter, the chiseled inscription all but obliterated. With one finger, like a kindergartner connecting the dots with an oversized pencil, Elizabeth traced the letters carved into the stone one at a time.

This was no childish project or joke. No animal rested beneath the stone.

M. Y. P. R. E. C. I. O. U. S. O.

"My Precious One."

Elizabeth dropped her hand and sat back on her calves, felt the left knee of her nylons pop and send runners halfway up her thigh.

The grave was real . . . but she'd never noticed it before. But more importantly, none of the generations of schoolchildren she told to "Hush" and "Be quiet" had noticed it either.

And Heaven knows they noticed everything *else* worth whispering about during Free Reading Time: the broken water main that flooded out the toy shop, the broken-down car, the funny-looking cloud that had been all purple and orange, the new traffic lights, the old park benches, the way the sky looked before it snowed. They noticed everything but the grave. And they should have.

Because a grave, a real grave, was something much too wonderful and much too terrible not to talk about.

Rustling again. And not the wind. This time directly behind her. Louder. Closer. *Rustle. Rustle. Thump. Thump.*

Footsteps.

Elizabeth twisted toward the sound and leaned back against the small headstone. Protectively. The way a *good* mother . . . but not *this* child's mother would.

"Who's there?" she said in her *Librarian's* voice. "Is someone there?"

Rustle, thump . . . and what was that? A *giggle*? Sitting straighter, Elizabeth took a deep breath and began mentally going down her list of school troublemakers.

"Kenny Wisman, is that you?"

A brilliant boy with more energy than control, he was always looking for better and bigger pranks to justify his existence. Creating the small grave would be a minor accomplishment for a boy who had not-so-secretly christened her *Mz. Hesse-the-Pest*.

"Kenneth? If that's you, speak up now! I dislike being snuck up upon." Without thinking, without caring that she might be laughed at, Elizabeth reached back and hugged the headstone. "Show yourself this instant, young man, or else I'll be forced to call your mother and—"

A tufted blue jay screeched as it shot, arrowlike, from the underbrush in front of her and she screeched with it. When it called again, it was already a hundred yards away.

"Foolish," she said as she turned back to the grave and smiled. "I scared myself, wasn't that silly of me?"

Elizabeth brushed a fallen leaf off the stone. Perhaps no one, including herself, had noticed the grave until now because *now* was when *she* was supposed to find it. Perhaps it had been waiting all these years until she was ready to find it. To notice it. To care.

My Precious One.

"You're late."

Elizabeth carefully hung her shoulder bag on the coat rack and took a deep breath before answering.

"Yes, Mother. Sorry, Mother."

She had said the same thing (*yes Mother sorry Mother*) for as long as she could remember, with no variations or modifications, but tonight she noticed that the words stuck a little in her throat.

The same way she noticed how old and used up her mother looked when she walked into the dining room.

"My *God,* what have you done now? Just look at your clothes!"

Despite every effort not to, Elizabeth looked down and felt the same kind of chill that she had at the grave . . . a cold numbing that seeped through the layers of flesh and bone until it reached her lungs and made her gasp for air. She really was a mess. The hem of her skirt was stained with mud and a dead leaf clung to the ruined stocking just below her left knee. Although she didn't remember it happening, three buttons on her cardigan had torn away.

Elizabeth pulled the sweater closed to cover the mud-flecked blouse beneath. Funny, how she didn't notice when it happened . . . but, then again, she hadn't noticed so much before tonight. . . .

"What have you done?" her mother asked again, accusing, all but dropping the covered casserole dish on the table when she mirrored Elizabeth's action and reached up to clutch the front of her housedress.

"You've been raped, haven't you?" The words were cold and sharp and stinging, and left bruises where they hit. "I warned you about walking through those woods, Elizabeth, and now look what's happened. You're ruined. No man will ever look at you again."

Elizabeth fingered the broken thread from one of the missing buttons.

"No, Mother, I wasn't raped. I—tripped, that's all. That path was rather muddy." The chill moved from her lungs, giving Elizabeth a chance to catch her breath, and made itself comfortable in her untouched womb. "I'm fine."

"Oh." With a sigh, her mother dropped her hand and busied herself with the casserole. "Well, dinner is probably ruined thanks to your tardiness. I try to make sure everything is timed perfectly and you think nothing of wandering in whenever it pleases you."

"I didn't plan on being late, Mother."

"That's no excuse, Elizabeth. Now, go into the kitchen and wash your hands before the stew gets any colder than it already is." Sitting herself at the head of the table, her mother began ladling out the steaming chunks of meat and vegetables. "I'll not wait for you if you don't mind."

"No," Elizabeth said, nodding as she walked to the kitchen. "Of course not, Mother. I wouldn't expect you to."

Her mother grunted something in reply, but Elizabeth decided to not notice.

The water, though only lukewarm, stung the abrasions on Elizabeth's hands as she scrubbed them clean. For all of her life her mother had taught her that *pain* was the only thing you could truly believe. If whatever it was you did didn't hurt somehow, then it wasn't worth the effort.

Her mother had not been a good mother.

The chill in her womb rolled over lazily, like a kitten stretching in the sun, when Elizabeth turned off the taps and dried her hands. *Her mother didn't know* how *to be a good mother.*

Arms straight out in front, fingers pointing to the ceiling, Elizabeth turned her palms toward her and then back. And sighed.

Her poor hands were clean, but the flesh was red and swollen from the vigorous washing and two nails had snapped off at bizarre angles. She'd have to file and mend them before the Kindergarten's Story Hour in the morning.

The older children wouldn't notice, but the little ones . . . the *babies,* they saw everything. She had to be so careful around the babies.

My Precious One.

There was the clank and clatter of metal upon china from the dining room—her mother's subtle way of telling Elizabeth she was taking *much* too long at the assigned task.

But the clinking and clatter didn't stop when Elizabeth got back to the table.

"You didn't bring the dinner rolls, Elizabeth."

Elizabeth let her throbbing hands settle against the chill in her womb. *Her mother was not a good mother . . . but she'd show her, she'd show her.* "I didn't know I was supposed to, Mother."

Her mother's fork hit the side of the dinner plate and made it sing. "Well, isn't that just like you? I would have thought a grown woman, a supposedly *mature* woman would have taken it upon herself to notice if the dinner rolls were on the table or not and do something about it . . . without having her *Mommy* have to tell her. My God, Elizabeth, don't you notice anything?"

Not until today, Mother.

Elizabeth couldn't help but smile as she turned and walked back to the kitchen.

"And don't forget the butter," her mother whined. "You know I like butter on my rolls. And bring the jam. Strawberry. Not the marmalade like last night. Strawberry is for supper, marmalade is for breakfast. It's not that difficult a thing to remember, so I don't understand how you manage to forget so often."

Elizabeth picked up the jar with the bright red, plumb strawberries—*I forget because I don't like strawberry jam*—and dropped it into the sink.

"Oops."

"What was that?"

"I dropped the jam, Mother. I'm sorry." The jar of marmalade

felt cool against her palm as she carried it, the rolls and butter back
to the table. "I'll pick some more up tomorrow. And don't worry
about the kitchen, I'll clean it up after dinner. Would you like me to
butter you a roll, Mother?"

Her mother glared at her from across the table. "How could you
be so clumsy?"

Elizabeth ignored the question and spooned a large dollop of the
honey-gold marmalade onto a roll.

"Mother, have you ever heard of a grave out in the woods?"

"What?"

"A grave . . . a child's grave in the woods. Near the stream. Have
you ever heard mention of it?"

"Of course not," her mother said, ignoring the offered rolls and
butter as she returned her attention to the stew. "There are no graves
in the woods. Why would you ask such a thing, Elizabeth?"

"No reason," Elizabeth answered as she brought the marmalade-
laden roll toward her lips. "I heard a rumor."

"Rumors are just that," her mother growled. "I'm surprised you
paid it any notice."

The chill in Elizabeth's womb reached up and touched her heart.

"I am, too, Mother."

Her mother had stayed up past her usual ten o'clock bedtime just to
be difficult—puttering around the house in her robe and slippers and
refusing to go to bed when Elizabeth suggested it.

*A good mother would have gone to bed when she was supposed to. A
good mother would have* known *when to leave her child alone.*

"I'll know," Elizabeth said as she carefully unfolded the mud-
stained handkerchief that had been tucked away in the bottom of her
purse. "I'll be a good mother."

"Isn't that right? My Precious One."

The tiny skull, with its brittle fringe of dark brown hair and patina
of leathery flesh, fell onto its side when Elizabeth lifted it toward her
face. Presenting a cheek to be kissed.

So Elizabeth did. The way a good mother would.

The grave in the woods had been old, very old; its tiny occupant
all but gone to dust. Elizabeth had tried to be gentle, but the moment
her trembling hands touched the stained baby blanket (*pink, for girls*)
the body beneath crumbled.

She'd only managed to save the skull. Nothing else.

But that was enough.

"Poor little thing," Elizabeth whispered, and watched the baby hair tremble under her breath like summer wheat. "You've been alone for so long."

She kissed it again, to let it know it was loved. The feel of the dried skin against her lips wasn't that unpleasant, no more so than any other kiss she'd ever had to give; and away from the confines of the grave and stench of decay, her Precious One only smelled a bit musty . . . like a well-loved book.

But still it wasn't a *baby* smell. Babies weren't supposed to smell like books, they were supposed to smell sweet like candy, like flowers, like . . .

Elizabeth smiled as she stood up and hurried them both to her dressing table. Cupping her Precious One gently in one palm, she began to dig through the mounds of white panties and bras for the tiny indulgence she'd treated herself to. And hidden. Years ago.

The bottle of perfume was still sealed, still perfect; the price sticker still attached. Untouched, until now. Unloved. Until now.

Her mother didn't approve of perfume, but her *mother* wasn't going to be the one wearing it.

The scent of gardenias filled the room the moment Elizabeth lifted off the white cap. Unlike the day of her father's funeral, the fragrance made her happy. Humming softly, she held the bottle over her Precious One's forehead and let a crystal drop fall. It clung like dew to the sparse hair, but then a second drop, larger than the first and not expected, missed its target and fell onto the linen dresser scarf.

Leaving a mark. Leaving a stain.

Elizabeth gasped as the perfume bottle slipped from her fingers. It bled its clear, fragrant blood across the top of her dressing table and died.

The stench of gardenias was overpowering. Her mother would smell it. Her mother would find out.

And it was all her Precious One's fault.

"Bad baby!" Elizabeth hissed, and pinched the little chin between her thumb and forefinger; squeezed and saw the tiny right ear fall like a spent blossom.

How could she be a good mother to such a child?

"Now look what you've done. Can't you behave for just one moment?"

Elizabeth brushed the mummified skin off onto the floor and quickly mopped up the spilled perfume with the already soiled scarf.

The air was thick with the cloying scent and she almost gagged before she got the soaked linen into the laundry hamper.

It was only after she could catch her breath and breathe again that Elizabeth looked down at her baby. Another small flake of skin, perhaps the beginnings of an eyebrow, had fallen off.

"What am I going to do with you?"

Without waiting for an answer, Elizabeth took the tiny head in both hands and shook it. Something rattled inside the skull, but she knew she wasn't hurting her Precious One. She was only teaching it right from wrong, the way a *good* mother was supposed to.

"What kind of mother would I be if I didn't teach you?" she asked when she finally stopped, looking deep into the sunken, empty sockets. "Not a very good one, and I want to be a good mother. I have to be. Now, are you sorry you made such a mess? Yes, I'm sure you are."

Elizabeth leaned down to kiss the wrinkled forehead.

"Yes. All is forgiven. All right, time for bed. And no back talk . . . young lady."

Yes, she remembered. *Pink was for girls. Her Precious One was a girl.* How wonderful. She'd always wanted a daughter.

Her Precious One didn't utter so much as a whimper when Elizabeth, good mother that she was, carried her to the antique toy cabinet at the far end of the room to pick out a body.

There was really only one choice among the china dolls Elizabeth had collected since her own childhood—the cupid-faced infant in the long, imported lace christening gown.

It was supposed to be very expensive and very old, her mother had told her . . . but *her* mother had never been a *good* mother, not like Elizabeth was going to be, so it didn't matter what she'd said.

Elizabeth smashed the doll's head against the side of the cabinet and smiled at the pattern the china pieces made on the rug.

"Look," she said, holding her Precious One up to see, "like snow-flakes. All right, don't move and it won't hurt. Mother promises."

Her Precious One's withered neck slipped effortlessly onto the wooden dowel the doll's head had been molded around.

"Oh, my," Elizabeth said, tucking the lace collar in around the hardened flesh. Her Precious One's head wobbled a bit, but not much. "Oh, don't you look beautiful? Yes, you do . . . you look beautiful."

Elizabeth tickled and kissed and cooed and waltzed them both around the room that had been hers since birth. That would now be both of theirs.

Her mother's shout ended the dance. Like always.

"Elizabeth! It's almost midnight! Go to bed this instant . . . you have work in the morning."

Elizabeth stopped too quickly. Her Precious One's head tipped forward, chin against the embroidered yoke of the gown.

"Yes, Mother. Sorry, Mother," she shouted to her mother, then hissed to her child, "Sit up straight! A lady never slumps. I said sit up!"

Elizabeth shook her Precious One and watched the baby's head loll backwards. She was being obstinate. She was being a bad baby.

Her Precious One wasn't so precious after all. Maybe there had been a reason for the lonely grave in the woods. Maybe Elizabeth had been chosen to find it because she was the only one who could handle such a spoiled child.

Her Precious One had to be taught. A good mother had to teach her baby.

"I'm only doing this because I love you," Elizabeth said as she lay her Precious One over one arm and lifted her free hand into position.

"I'm going to be a *good* mother to you, but that means you have to be a *good* baby to me. It's only fair."

Elizabeth smiled. Her Precious One knew. Her Precious One understood. *She* was *a good mother.*

"Be brave," she whispered as she lifted her hand. "This will hurt me more than it will you."

When it didn't, Elizabeth consoled herself with the knowledge that there would be other occasions to prove she was a good mother.

Many occasions in the years to come.

Thomas Ligotti

THE SHADOW, THE DARKNESS

I'm convinced that without E-mail this book would have been vastly different—and taken twice as long to produce. The plain fact is, writers will respond to E-mail but not to telephone calls or written letters or, especially, home visits (there's a story behind that one). There's something at once impersonal and personal about E-mail; it's safe and at the same time intimate, providing instant access with a leisurely response (say, hours or at most a day) that seems, by snail-mail standards, lightning fast. I would compare it to the long-dead practice of multiple daily mail deliveries—remember how Sherlock Holmes was always getting and sending letters, all day long? Computers in general might be a pain in the arse, and the Internet might indeed prove to be evil, but without E-mail and the delete key on my word processor, I honestly don't know how I'd get anything done anymore.

Which brings me, in a fashion, to Thomas Ligotti, whom I was able to bother and remind and just plain keep in touch with because of E-mail. He was a pleasure to work with, won the Bram Stoker Award in 1997 for his story "The Red Tower," and is the author of the short story collection The Nightmare Factory, *which was itself nominated for a Stoker.*

Possibly because of E-mail, he has provided us with one of the stories in this book you won't be able to get out of your head.

It seemed that Grossvogel was charging us *entirely* too much money for what he was offering. Some of us, we were about a dozen in all, blamed ourselves and our own idiocy as soon as we arrived in that place which one neatly dressed old gentleman immediately dubbed the "nucleus of nowhere." This same gentleman, who a few days before had announced to several persons his abandonment of poetry writing due to the lack of what he considered proper appreciation of his innovative practice of the "Hermetic lyric," went on to say that such a place as the one in which we found ourselves was exactly what we should have expected, and probably what we idiots and failures deserved. We had no reason to expect anything more, he explained, than to end up in the dead town of Crampton, in a nowhere region of the country—of the world, in fact—during a dull season of the year that was pinched between such a lavish and brilliant autumn and what promised to be an equally lavish and brilliant wintertime. We were trapped, he said, completely stranded for all practical purposes, in a region of the country, and of the entire world, where all the manifestations of that bleak time of year, or rather its *absence* of manifestations, were so evident in the landscape around us, where everything was absolutely stripped to the bone, and where the pathetic emptiness of forms in their unadorned state was so brutally evident. When I pointed out that Grossvogel's brochure for this excursion, which he deemed a "physical-metaphysical excursion," did not strictly misrepresent our destination, I received only evil looks from several of the others at the table where we sat, as well as from the nearby tables of the small, almost miniature diner in which the whole group of us were now packed, filling it to capacity with the presence of exotic out-of-towners who, when they stopped bickering for a few moments, simply stared with a killing silence out the windows at the empty streets and broken-down buildings of the dead town of Crampton. The town was further maligned as a "drab abyss," the speaker of this phrase being a skeletal individual who always introduced himself as a "defrocked academic." This self-designation would usually provoke a query as to its meaning, after which he would, in so many words, elaborate on how his failure to skew his thinking to the standards of, as he termed it, the "intellectual marketplace," along with his failure to conceal his unconventional studies and methodologies, had resulted in his longtime inability to secure a position within a reputable academic institution, or within any sort of institution or place of business whatever. Thus, in his mind, his failure was more or less his ultimate distinction, and in this sense he was typical of those of us who were seated at the few tables and upon stools along the counter of that miniature diner, complaining that Grossvogel had charged us entirely too much money and to some degree misrepresented, in his brochure, the whole value and purpose of the excursion to the dead town of Crampton.

Taking my copy of Grossvogel's brochure from the back pocket of my trousers, I unfolded its few pages and laid them before the other three people who were seated at the same table as I. Then I removed my fragile reading glasses from the pocket of the old cardigan I was wearing beneath my even older jacket in order to scrutinize these pages once again, confirming the suspicions I had had about their meaning.

"If you're looking for the fine print—" said the man seated to my left, a "photographic portraitist" who often broke into a spate of coughing whenever he began to speak, as he did on this occasion.

"What I think my friend was going to say," said the man seated on my right, "was that we have been the victims of a subtle and intricate swindle. I say this on his behalf because this is the direction in which his mind works, am I right?"

"A *metaphysical swindle*," confirmed the man on my left, who had ceased coughing for the moment.

"Indeed, a metaphysical swindle," repeated the other man somewhat mockingly. "I would never have imagined myself being taken in by such a thing, given my experience and special field of knowledge. But this, of course, was such a subtle and intricate operation."

While I knew that the man on my right was the author of an unpublished philosophical treatise entitled *An Investigation into the Conspiracy Against the Human Race,* I was not sure what he meant by the mention of his "experience and special field of knowledge." Before I could inquire about this issue, I was brashly interrupted by the woman seated across the table from me.

"Mr. Reiner Grossvogel is a fraud, it's as simple as that," she said loud enough for everyone in the diner to hear. "I've been aware of his fraudulent character for some time, as you know. Even before his so-called metamorphic experience, or whatever he calls it—"

"Metamorphic recovery," I said by way of correction.

"Fine, his metamorphic recovery, whatever that's supposed to mean. Even before that time I could see that he was somebody who had all the makings of a fraud. He only required the proper conjunction of circumstances to bring this trait out in him. And then along came that supposedly near-fatal illness of his that he says led to that, I can barely say it, *metamorphic recovery*. After that he was able to realize all his unused talents for being the fraud he was always destined to be and always wanted to be. I joined in this farcical excursion, or whatever it is, only for the satisfaction of seeing everyone else find out what I always knew and always maintained about Reiner Grossvogel. You're all my witnesses," she finished, her wrinkled and heavily made-up eyes scanning our faces, and those of the others in the diner, for the affirmation she sought.

I knew this woman only by her professional name of Mrs. Angela.

Until recently she had operated what everyone among our circle re-ferred to as a "psychic coffeehouse." Among the goods and services offered by this establishment was a fine selection of excellent pastries that were made off the premises by Mrs. Angela herself, or so she claimed. Unfortunately, the business never seemed to prosper either on the strength of its psychic readings, which were performed by several persons in Mrs. Angela's employ, or on the strength of its excellent pastries and somewhat overpriced coffee. It was Mrs. Angela who first complained about the quality of both the service and the modest fare being offered to us in the Crampton diner. Not long after we arrived that afternoon and immediately packed ourselves into what seemed to be the town's only active place of business, Mrs. Angela called out to the young woman whose lonely task it was to cater to our group. "This coffee is incredibly bitter," she shouted at the girl, who was dressed in what appeared to be a brand-new white uniform. "And these doughnuts are stale, every one of them. What kind of place is this? I think this whole town and everything in it is a fraud."

When the girl came over to our table and stood before us I noticed that her uniform resembled that of a nurse more than it did an outfit worn by a waitress in a diner. Specifically it reminded me of the uniforms that I saw worn by the nurses at the hospital where Grossvogel was treated, and ultimately recovered, from what appeared at the time to be a very serious illness. While Mrs. Angela was berating the waitress over the quality of the coffee and doughnuts we had been served, which were included in the travel package that Grossvogel's brochure described as the "ultimate physical-metaphysical excursion," I was reviewing my memories of Grossvogel in that stark and conspicu-ously out-of-date hospital where he had been treated, however briefly, some two years preceding our visit to the dead town of Crampton. He had been admitted to this wretched facility through its emergency room, which was simply the rear entrance to what was not so much a hospital, properly speaking, but more a makeshift clinic set up in a decayed old building located in the same neighborhood where Grossvogel, and most of those who knew him, were forced to live due to our limited financial means. I myself was the one who took him, in a taxi, to this emergency room and provided the woman at the admittance desk with all the pertinent facts of his identification, since he was in no condition to do so himself. Later I explained to a nurse—whom I could not help looking upon merely as an emergency room attendant in a nurse's uniform, given that she seemed somehow lacking in medical expertise—that Grossvogel had collapsed at a local art gallery during a modest exhibit of his works. This was his first experience, I told the nurse, both as a publicly exhibited artist and as a victim of a sudden physical collapse. However, I did not mention that the art gallery to which I referred might have been more accurately depicted as an empty storefront that now and then was cleaned up and used for exhibitions or artistic performances of various types. Grossvogel had been complaining throughout the evening of abdominal pains, I informed the nurse, and then repeated to an emergency room physician, who also struck me as another medical attendant rather than as a legitimate doctor of medicine. The reason these abdominal pains increased throughout that evening, I speculated to both the nurse and the doctor, was perhaps due to Grossvogel's increasing sense of anxiety at seeing his works exhibited for the first time, since he had always been notoriously insecure about his talents as an artist and, in my opinion, had good reason to be. On the other hand there might possibly have been a serious organic condition involved, I allowed when speaking with the nurse and later with the doctor. In any case, Grossvogel finally collapsed on the floor of the art gallery and was unable to do anything but groan somewhat pitifully and, to be candid, somewhat irritatingly since that time.

After listening to my account of Grossvogel's collapse, the doctor instructed the artist to lie down upon a stretcher that stood at the end of a badly lighted hallway, while both the doctor and the nurse walked off in the opposite direction. I stood close by Grossvogel during the time that he lay upon this stretcher in the shadows of that makeshift clinic. It was the middle of the night by then, and Grossvogel's moaning had abated somewhat, only to be replaced by what I understood at that time as a series of delirious utterances. In the course of this rhetorical delirium the artist mentioned several times something that he called the "pervasive shadow." I told him that it was merely the poor illumination of the hallway, my own words sounding somewhat delirious to me due to the fatigue brought on by the events of that night, both at the art gallery and in the emergency room of that tawdry hospital. But Grossvogel—in his delirium, I supposed—only gazed about the hallway, as if he could not see me standing there or hear the words I had just spoken to him. And yet he now placed his hands over his ears, as though to shut out some painful and deafening sound. Afterwards I just stood there listening to Grossvogel murmur at intervals, no longer responding to his delirious and increasingly more elaborate utterances about the "pervasive shadow that causes things to be what they would not be" (and later: "the all-moving darkness that makes things do what they would not do").

After an hour or so of listening to Grossvogel, I noticed that the doctor and nurse were now standing close together at the other end of that dark hallway. They seemed to be conferring with each other for the longest time and every so often one or both of them would look in the direction where I was standing close by the prostrate and murmuring Grossvogel. I wondered how long they were going to carry on with what seemed to me a medical charade, a clinical dumbshow, while the artist lay moaning and now more frequently murmuring on the subject of the shadow and the darkness. Perhaps I dozed off on my feet for a moment, because it seemed that from out of nowhere the nurse was suddenly at my side and the doctor was no longer anywhere in sight. The nurse's white uniform now appeared almost luminous in the dingy shadows of that hallway. "You can go home now," she said to me. "Your friend is going to be admitted to the hospital." She then pushed Grossvogel on his stretcher toward the doors of an elevator at the end of the hallway. As soon as she reached these elevator doors they opened quickly and silently, pouring the brightest light into that dim hallway. When the doors were fully opened I could see the doctor standing inside. He pulled Grossvogel's stretcher into the brilliantly illuminated elevator while the nurse pushed the stretcher from behind. As soon as they were all inside, the elevator doors closed quickly and silently, and the hallway in which I was still standing seemed even darker and more dense with shadows than it had before.

The following day I visited Grossvogel at the hospital. He had been placed in a small private room in a distant corner of the institution's uppermost floor. As I walked toward this room, looking for the identifying number I had been given at the information desk downstairs, it seemed that none of the other rooms on that floor was occupied. It was only when I found the number I sought that I looked inside and actually saw a bed that was occupied, conspicuously so, since Grossvogel was a rather large-bodied individual who took up the full length and breadth of an old and sagging mattress. He seemed quite giantlike lying on that undersized, institutional mattress in that small, windowless room. There was barely enough space for me to squeeze myself between the wall and the bedside of the artist, who seemed to be still in much the same delirious condition as he had been the night before. There was no sign of recognition on his part that I was present in the room, although we were so close that I was practically on top of him. Even after I spoke his name several times his teary gaze betrayed no notice of my presence. However, as I began to sidle away from his bedside I was startled when Grossvogel firmly grabbed my arm with his enormous left hand, which was the hand he used for painting and drawing the works of his which had been exhibited in the storefront art gallery the previous evening. "Grossvogel," I said expectantly, thinking that finally he was going to respond, if only to speak about the pervasive shadow (that causes things to be what they would not be) and the all-moving darkness (that causes things to do what they would not do). But a few seconds later his hand became limp and fell from my arm onto the very edge of the misshapen institutional mattress on which his body again lay still and unresponsive.

After some moments I made my way out of Grossvogel's private room and walked over to the nurse's station on the same floor of the hospital to inquire about the artist's medical condition. The sole nurse in attendance listened to my request and consulted a folder with the name "Reiner Grossvogel" typed in one of its upper corners. After studying me some time longer than she had studied the pages concerning the artist, and now hospital patient, she simply said, "Your friend is being observed very closely."

"Is that all you can tell me?" I asked.

"His tests haven't been returned. You might ask about them later."

"Later today?"

"Yes, later today," she said, taking Grossvogel's folder and walking away into another room. I heard the squeaking sound of a drawer in a filing cabinet being opened and then suddenly being slammed shut again. For some reason I stood there waiting for the nurse to emerge from the room where she had taken Grossvogel's medical folder. Finally I gave up and returned home.

When I called the hospital later that day I was told that Grossvogel had been released. "He's gone home?" I said, which was the only thing that occurred to me to say. "We have no way of knowing where he's gone," the woman who answered the phone replied just before hanging up on me. Nor did anyone else know where Grossvogel had gone, for he was not at his home, and no one among our circle had any knowledge of his whereabouts.

*　　*　　*

It was several weeks, perhaps more than a month after Grossvogel's release from the hospital, and subsequent disappearance, that several of us had gathered, purely by chance, at the storefront art gallery where the artist had collapsed during the opening night of his first exhibit. By this time even I had ceased to be concerned in any way with Grossvogel or the fact that he had without warning simply dropped out of sight. Certainly he was not the first to do so among our circle, all of whom were more or less unstable, sometimes dangerously volatile persons who might involve themselves in questionable activities for the sake of some artistic or intellectual vision, or simply out of pure desperation of spirit. I think that the only reason any of us mentioned Grossvogel's name as we drifted about the art gallery that afternoon was due to the fact that his works still remained on exhibit, and wherever we turned we were confronted by some painting or drawing or whatnot of his which, in a pamphlet issued to accompany the show, I myself had written were "manifestations of a singularly gifted artistic visionary," when, in fact, they were without exception quite run-of-the-mill specimens of the sort of artistic nonsense that, for reasons unknown to all concerned, will occasionally gain a measure of success or even a high degree of prominence for its creator. "What am I supposed to do with all this junk?" complained the woman who owned, or perhaps only rented, the storefront building that had been set up as an art gallery. I was about to say to her that I would take responsibility for removing Grossvogel's works from the gallery, and perhaps even store them somewhere for a time, when the skeletal person who always introduced himself as a defrocked academic interjected, suggesting to the agitated owner, or at least operator, of the art gallery that she should send them to the hospital where Grossvogel had "supposedly been treated" after his collapse. When I asked why he had used the word *supposedly,* he replied, "I've long believed that place to be a dubious institution, and I'm not the only one to hold this view." I then asked if there was any credible basis for this belief of his, but he only crossed his skeletal arms and looked at me as if I had just insulted him in some way. "Mrs. Angela," he said to a woman who was standing nearby, studying one of Grossvogel's paintings as if she were seriously considering it for purchase. At that time Mrs. Angela's psychic coffeehouse had yet to prove itself a failed venture, and possibly she was thinking that Grossvogel's works, although inferior from an artistic standpoint, might in some way complement the ambience of her place of business, where patrons could sit at tables and receive advice from hired psychic counselors while also feasting on an array of excellent pastries.

"You should listen to what he says about that hospital," Mrs. Angela said to me without taking her eyes off that painting of Grossvogel's. "I've had a strong feeling about that place for a long time. There is some aspect of it that is extremely devious."

"Dubious," corrected the defrocked academic.

"Yes," answered Mrs. Angela. "It's not by any means someplace I'd like to wake up and find myself."

"I wrote a poem about it," said the neatly dressed gentleman who all this time had been prowling about the floor of the gallery, no doubt waiting for the most propitious moment to approach the woman who owned or rented the storefront building and persuade her to sponsor what he was forever touting as an "evening of Hermetic readings," which of course would prominently feature his own works. "I once read that poem to you," he said to the gallery owner.

"Yes, you read it to me," she confirmed in a monotone.

"I wrote it after being treated in the emergency room of that place very late one night," explained the poet.

"What were you treated for?" I asked him.

"Oh, nothing serious, as it turned out. I went home a few hours later. I was never admitted as a patient, I'm glad to say. That place, and I quote from my poem on the subject, was the 'nucleus of the abysmal.' "

"That's fine to say that," I said. "But could we possibly speak in more explicit terms?"

However, before I could draw out a response from the self-styled writer of Hermetic lyrics, the door of the art gallery was suddenly pushed open with a conspicuous force that all of us inside instantly recognized. A moment later we saw standing before us the large-bodied figure of Reiner Grossvogel. Physically he appeared to be, for the most part, much the same person I recalled prior to his collapse on the floor of the art gallery not more than a few feet from where I was now standing, bearing none of the traits of that moaning, delirious creature whom I had taken in a taxi to the hospital for emergency treatment. Nevertheless, there did seem to be something different about him, a subtle but thorough change in the way he looked upon what lay before him: whereas the gaze of the artist had once been characteristically downcast or nervously averted, his eyes now seemed completely direct in their focus and filled with a calm purpose.

"I'm taking away all of this," he said, gesturing broadly but quite gently toward the artworks of his that filled the gallery, none of which had been sold either on the opening night of his show or during the subsequent period of his disappearance. "I would appreciate your assistance, if you will give it," he added as he began taking down paintings from along the walls.

The rest of us joined him in this endeavor without question or comment, and laden with artworks both large and small we followed him out of the gallery toward a battered pickup truck parked at the curb in front. Grossvogel casually hurled his works into the back of the rented, or possibly borrowed, truck (since the artist was never known to possess any kind of vehicle before that day), exhibiting no concern for the damage that might be incurred by what he had once considered the best examples of his artistic output to date. There was a moment's hesitation on the part of Mrs. Angela, who was perhaps still considering how one or more of these works would look in her place of business, but ultimately she too began carrying Grossvogel's works out of the gallery and hurling them into the back of the truck, where they piled up like refuse, until the gallery's walls and floor-space were entirely cleared and the place looked like any other empty storefront. Grossvogel then got into the truck while the rest of us stood in wondering silence outside the evacuated art gallery. Putting his head out the open window of the rented or borrowed truck, he called to the woman who ran the gallery. She walked over to the driver's side of the truck and exchanged a few words with the artist before he started the engine of the vehicle and drove off. Returning to where we had remained standing on the sidewalk, she announced to us that, within the next few weeks, there would be a second exhibit of Grossvogel's work at the gallery.

This, then, was the message that was passed among the circle of persons with whom I consorted: that Grossvogel, after physically collapsing from an undisclosed ailment or attack at the first, highly unsuccessful exhibit of his works, was now going to present a second exhibit after summarily cleaning out the art gallery of those rather worthless paintings and drawings and whatnot of his already displayed to the public and hauling them away in the back of a pickup truck. Of course, Grossvogel's new exhibit was promoted in an entirely professional manner by the woman who owned the art gallery and who stood to gain financially from the sale of what, in the phrase of the advertising copy associated with this event, was somewhat awkwardly called a "radical and revisionary phase in the career of the celebrated artistic visionary Reiner Grossvogel." Nevertheless, due to the circumstances surrounding both the artist's previous and upcoming exhibits, the whole thing almost immediately devolved into a fog of delirious and sometimes lurid gossip and speculation. This development was wholly in keeping with the nature of those who comprised that circle of dubious, not to mention devious artistic and intellectual persons of which I had unexpectedly become a central figure. After all, it was I who had taken Grossvogel to the hospital following his collapse at the first exhibit of his works, and it was the hospital—already a subject of strange repute, as I discovered—that loomed so prominently within the delirious fog of gossip and speculation surrounding Grossvogel's upcoming exhibit. There was even talk of some special procedures and medications to which the artist had been exposed during his brief confinement at this institution that would account for his unexplained disappearance and subsequent reemergence in order to perpetrate what many presumed would be a startling "artistic vision." No doubt it was this expectation, this desperate hope for something of stunning novelty and lavish brilliance—which in the minds of some overly imaginative persons promised to exceed the domain of mere aesthetics—that led to the acceptance among our circle of the unorthodox nature of Grossvogel's new exhibit, as well as accounted for the emotional letdown that followed for those of us in attendance that opening night.

And, in fact, what occurred at the gallery that night in no way resembled the sort of exhibit we were accustomed to attending: the floor of the gallery and the gallery's walls remained as bare as the day when Grossvogel appeared with a pickup truck to cart off all his works from his old art show, while the new one, we soon discovered after arriving, was to take place in the small back room of the storefront building. Furthermore, we were charged a rather large fee in order to enter this small back room, which was illuminated by only a few lightbulbs of extremely low wattage dangling here and there from the ceiling. One of the lightbulbs was hung in a corner of the room directly above a small table which had a torn section of a bedsheet draped over it to conceal something that was bulging beneath it. Radiating out from this corner, with its dim lightbulb and small table, were several loosely arranged rows of folding chairs. These uncomfortable chairs were eventually occupied by those of us, about a dozen in all, who were willing to pay the large fee for what seemed to be an event more in the style of a primitive stageshow than anything resembling an art exhibit. I could hear Mrs. Angela in one of the seats behind me saying over and over to those around her, "What the hell is this?" Finally she leaned forward and said to me, "What does Grossvogel think he's doing? I've heard that he's been medicated to the eyeballs ever since he came out of that hospital." Yet the artist appeared lucid enough when a few moments later he made his way through the loosely arranged rows of folding chairs and stood beside the small table with the torn bedsheet draped over it and the low-watt lightbulb dangling above. In the confines of the art gallery's back room the large-bodied Grossvogel seemed almost gigantic, just as he had when lying upon that institutional mattress in his private room at the hospital. Even his voice, which was usually quiet, even somewhat wispy, seemed to be enlarged when he began speaking to us.

"Thank you all for coming here tonight," he began. "This shouldn't take very long. I have only a few things to say to you and then something that I would like to show you. It's really no less than a miracle that I'm able to stand here and speak to you in this way. Not too long ago, as some of you may recall, I suffered a terrible attack in this very art gallery. I hope you won't mind if I tell you a few things about the nature of this attack and its consequences, things which I feel are essential to appreciating what I have to show you tonight.

"Well, then, let me start by saying that, on one level, the attack I suffered in this art gallery during the opening night of an exhibit of my works was in the nature of a simple gastrointestinal upheaval, even if it was a quite severe episode of its type. For some time this gastrointestinal upheaval, this disorder of my digestive system, had been making its progress within me. Over a period of many years this disorder had been progressively and insidiously developing, on one level, in the depths of my body and, on another level altogether, in the darkest aspect of my being. This period coincided with, and in fact was a direct consequence of, my intense desire with respect to the field of art—which is to say, my desire to *do* something, i.e., create artworks, and my desire to *be* something, i.e., an artist. I was attempting during this period I speak of—and for that matter throughout most of my life—to *make something with my mind,* specifically to create works of art by the only possible means I believed were available to me, which was by using my mind or using my imagination or *creative faculties,* by using, in brief, some force or function of what people would call a soul or a spirit or simply a personal self. But when I found myself collapsed upon the floor of this art gallery, and later at the hospital, experiencing the most acute abdominal agony, I was overwhelmed by the realization that I had no mind or imagination that I could use, that there was nothing I could call a soul or self—those things were all nonsense and dreams. I realized, in my severe gastrointestinal distress, that the only thing that had any existence at all was this larger-than-average physical body of mine. And I realized that there was nothing for this body to *do* except to function in physical pain and that there was nothing for it to *be* except what it was—not an artist or creator of any kind but solely a mass of flesh, a system of tissues and bones and so forth, suffering the agonies of a disorder of its digestive system, and that anything I did that did not directly stem from these facts, especially producing works of art, was profoundly and utterly *false and unreal*. At the same time I also became aware of the force that was behind my intense desire to do something and to be something, particularly my desire to create utterly false and unreal works of art. In other words, I became aware of what in reality was *activating* my body."

Before continuing with the introductory talk that comprised the first part of his art exhibit, or artistic stageshow, as I thought of it, Grossvogel paused and for a moment seemed to be surveying the faces of the small audience seated in the back room of the gallery. What he had expressed to us concerning his body and its digestive malfunctions was on the whole comprehensible enough, even if certain points he was articulating seemed at the time to be questionable and his overall discourse somewhat unengaging. Yet we put up with Grossvogel's words, I believe, because we had thought that they were leading us into another, possibly more engaging phase of his experience, which in some way we already sensed was not wholly alienated from our own, whether or not we identified with its peculiarly gastrointestinal nature. Therefore we remained silent, almost respectfully so, considering the unorthodox proceedings of that night, as Grossvogel continued with what he had to tell us before the moment came when he unveiled what he had brought to show us.

"It is all so very, very simple," the artist continued. "Our bodies are but one manifestation of the energy, the *activating force* that sets in motion all the objects, all the bodies of this world and enables them to exist as they do. This activating force is something like a shadow that is not on the outside of all the bodies of this world but is *inside* of everything and thoroughly pervades everything—an all-moving darkness that has no substance in itself but that moves all the objects of this world, including those objects which we call our bodies. While I was in the throes of my gastrointestinal episode at the hospital where

I was treated, I descended, so to speak, to that deep abyss of entity where I could feel how this shadow, this darkness, was activating my body. I could also hear its movement, not only within my body but in everything around me, because the sound that it made was not the sound of my body. It was in fact the sound of this shadow, this darkness, which was a powerful roaring—the sound of strange and bestial oceans moving upon and incessantly consuming black and endless shores. Likewise I was to detect the workings of this pervasive and all-moving force through the sense of smell and the sense of taste, as well as the sense of touch with which my body is equipped. Finally I opened my eyes, for throughout much of this agonizing ordeal of my digestive system my eyelids were clenched shut in pain. And when I opened my eyes I found that I could see how everything around me, including my own body, was activated from within by this pervasive shadow, this all-moving darkness. And nothing looked as I had always known it to look. Before that night I had never experienced the world purely by means of my organs of physical sensation, which are the direct point of contact with that deep abyss of entity that I am calling the shadow, the darkness.

"I should confess that prior to my physical collapse at this very art gallery I had undergone a psychic collapse—a collapse of something false and unreal, of something nonsensical and dreamlike, it goes without saying, although it was all very genuine and real to me at the time. This collapse of my mind and my self was the result of how poorly my works of art were being received by those attending the opening night of my first exhibit, of how profoundly unsuccessful they were as artistic creations, miserably unsuccessful even in the sphere of false and unreal artistic creations. This unsuccessful exhibit demonstrated to me how thoroughly I had failed in my efforts to be an artist. Everyone at the exhibit could see how unsuccessful my artworks proved to be, and I could see everyone in the very act of witnessing my unmitigated failure as an artist. This was the psychic crisis which precipitated my physical crisis and the eventual collapse of my body into spasms of gastrointestinal torment. Once my mind and my personal sense of self had broken down, all that was left in operation were my organs of physical sensation, by means of which I was able for the first time to experience directly that deep abyss of entity that is the shadow, the darkness which had activated my intense desire to be a success at *doing* something and at *being* something, and thereby also activated my body as it moved within this world, just as all bodies are likewise activated. And what I experienced through direct sensory channels—the spectacle of the shadow inside of everything, the all-moving darkness—was so appalling that I was sure I would cease to exist. In some way, because of the manner in which my senses were now functioning, especially my aural and visual senses, I did in fact cease to exist as I had existed before that night. Without the interference of my mind and my imagination, all that nonsensical dreaming about my soul and my self, I was forced to see all things under the aspect of the shadow inside them, the darkness which activated them. And it was wholly appalling, more so than my words could possibly tell you."

Nevertheless, Grossvogel went on to explain in detail, to those of us who paid the exorbitant price to see his stageshow exhibit, the appalling way in which he was now forced to see the world around him, including his own body in its gastrointestinal distress, and how convinced he was that this vision of things would soon be the cause of his death, despite the measures taken to save him during his hospital sojourn. It was Grossvogel's contention that his only hope of survival was for him to perish completely, in the sense that the person, or the mind or self that had once been Grossvogel, would actually cease to exist. This necessary condition for survival, he maintained, prompted his physical body to undergo a "metamorphic recovery." Within a matter of hours, Grossvogel told us, he no longer suffered from the symptoms of acute abdominal pains which had initiated his crisis, and furthermore he was now able to tolerate the way in which he was permanently forced to see things, as he put it, "under the aspect of the shadow inside them, the darkness which activated them." Since the person who had been Grossvogel had perished, as Grossvogel explained to us, the body of Grossvogel was able to continue as a *successful organism* untroubled by the imaginary torments that had once been inflicted upon him by his fabricated mind and his false and unreal self. As he articulated the matter in his own words, "I am no longer *occupied* with my self or my mind." What we in the audience now saw before us, he said, was Grossvogel's body speaking with Grossvogel's voice and using Grossvogel's neurological circuitry but without the "imaginary character" known as Grossvogel; all of his words and actions, he said, now emanated directly from that same force which activates every one of us if we could only realize it in the way he was compelled to in order to keep his body alive. The artist emphasized in his own terribly calm way that in no sense did he choose his unique course of recovery. No one would willingly choose such a thing, he contended. Everyone prefers to continue their existence as a mind and a self, no matter what pain it causes them, no matter how false and unreal they might be, than to face the quite obvious reality of being only a body set in motion by this mindless, soulless, and selfless force which he designed as the shadow, the darkness. Nonetheless, Grossvogel disclosed to us, this is exactly the reality that he needed to admit into his system if his body was to continue its existence and to succeed as an organism. "It was purely a matter of physical survival," he said. "Everybody should be able to understand that. Anyone would do the same." Moreover, the famous metamorphic recovery in which Grossvogel the person died and Grossvogel the body survived was so successful, he informed his stageshow audience, that he immediately embarked upon a strenuous period of travel, mostly by means of inexpensive buslines that took him great distances across and around the entire country, so that he could look at various people and places while exercising his new faculty of being able to see the shadow that pervaded them, the all-moving darkness that activated them, since he was no longer subject to the misconceptions about the world that are created by the mind or imagination—those obstructing mechanisms which were now removed from his system—nor did he mistakenly imagine anyone or anything to possess a soul or a self. And everywhere he went he witnessed the spectacle that had previously so appalled him to the point of becoming a life-threatening medical condition.

"I could now know the world directly through the senses of my body," Grossvogel continued. "And I saw with my body what I could never have seen with my mind or imagination during my career as a failed artist. Everywhere I travelled I saw how the pervasive shadow, the all-moving darkness, was *using our world*. Because this shadow, this darkness has nothing of its own, no way to exist except as an activating force or energy, whereas we have our bodies, we are *only* our bodies. Whether they are organic bodies or nonorganic bodies, human or nonhuman bodies, makes no difference—they are all simply bodies and nothing but bodies, with no component whatever of a mind or a soul or a self. Hence the shadow, the darkness *uses our world for what it needs to thrive upon.* It *has* nothing except its activating energy, while we *are* nothing except our bodies. This is why the shadow, the darkness causes things to be what they would not be and to do what they would not do. Because without the shadow inside them, the all-moving blackness activating them, they would be only what they are—heaps of matter lacking any impulse, any urge to flourish, to *succeed* in this world. This state of affairs should be called what it is—an absolute nightmare. That is exactly what I experienced in the hospital when I realized, due to my intense gastrointestinal suffering, that I had no mind or imagination, no soul or self—that these were nonsensical and dreamlike intermediaries fabricated to protect human beings from realizing what it is we really are: only a collection of bodies activated by the shadow, the darkness. Those among us who are successful organisms to any degree, including artists, are so only by virtue of the extent to which we function as bodies and by no means as minds or selves. This is exactly the manner in which I had failed so exceptionally, since I was so convinced of the existence of my mind and my imagination, my soul and my self. My only hope lay in my ability to make a metamorphic recovery, to *accept in every way* the nightmarish order of things so that I could continue to exist as a successful organism even without the protective nonsense of the mind and the imagination, the protective dream of having any kind of soul or self. Otherwise I would have been annihilated by a fatally traumatic insanity brought on by the shock of this shattering realization. Therefore the person who was Grossvogel had to perish in that hospital—and good riddance—so that the body of Grossvogel could be free of its gastrointestinal crisis and go on to travel in all directions by various means of transportation, primarily the inexpensive transportation provided by interstate buslines, witnessing the spectacle of the shadow, the darkness using our world of bodies for what it needs to thrive upon. And after witnessing this spectacle it was inevitable that I should portray it in some form, not as an *artist who has failed* because he is using some nonsense called the mind or the imagination, but as a *body that has succeeded* in perceiving how everything in the world actually functions. That is what I have come to show you, to exhibit to you this evening."

I, who had been lulled or agitated by Grossvogel's discourse as much as anyone in the audience, was for some reason surprised, and even apprehensive, when he suddenly ended his lecture or fantasy monologue or whatever I construed his words to be at the time. It seemed that he could have gone on speaking forever in the back room of that art gallery where low-watt lightbulbs hung down from the ceiling, one of them directly above the table that was covered with a torn section of a bedsheet. And now Grossvogel was lifting one corner of the torn bedsheet to show us, at last, what he had created, not by using his mind or imagination, which he claimed no longer existed in him any more than did his soul or self, but by using only his body's organs of physical sensation. When he finally uncovered the piece completely and it was fully displayed in the dull glow of the lightbulb which hung directly above it, none of us demonstrated either a positive or negative reaction to it at first, possibly because our minds were so numbed by all the verbal buildup that had led to this moment of unveiling.

It appeared to be a sculpture of some kind. However, I found it initially impossible to give this object any generic designation, either artistic or nonartistic. It might have been anything. The surface of the piece was uniformly of a shining darkness, having a glossy sheen beneath which was spread a swirling murk of shades that appeared to be in motion, an effect which seemed quite credibly the result of some swaying of the lightbulb dangling above. And it seemed that as I gazed at this object, I could hear a faint roaring sound in which there was definitely something both beastlike and oceanic, as Grossvogel had earlier suggested to us. There was more than a casual resemblance in its general outline to some kind of creature, perhaps a grossly distorted version of a scorpion or a crab, since it displayed more than a few clawlike extensions reaching out from a central, highly shapeless mass. But it also appeared to have elements poking upwards, peaks or horns that jutted at roughly vertical angles and ended sometimes in a sharp point and sometimes in a soft, headlike bulge. Because Grossvogel had spoken so much about bodies, it was natural to see such forms, in some deranged fashion, as the basis of the object or as being incorporated into it somehow—a chaotic world of bodies of every kind, of shapes activated by the shadow inside them, the darkness that caused them to be what they would not be and to do what they would not do. And among these bodylike shapes I distinctly recognized the large-bodied figure of the artist himself, although the significance that Grossvogel had *implanted* himself therein escaped me as I sat contemplating this modest exhibit.

Whatever Grossvogel's sculpture may have represented in its parts or as a whole, it did project a certain suggestion of that "absolute nightmare" which the artist, so to speak, had elucidated during his lecture or fantasy monologue earlier that evening. Yet this quality of the piece, even for an audience that had more than a slight appreciation for nightmarish subjects and contours, was not enough to offset the high price we had been required to pay for the privilege of hearing about Grossvogel's gastrointestinal ordeal and self-proclaimed metamorphic recovery. Soon after the artist unveiled his work to us, each of our bodies rose out of those uncomfortable folding chairs and excuses for departing the premises were being spoken on all sides. Before making my own exit I noticed that inconspicuously displayed next to

Grossvogel's sculpture was a small card upon which was printed the title of the piece. "Tsalal No. 1," it read. Later I learned something about the meaning of this term, which, in the way of words, both illuminated and concealed the nature of the thing that it named.

The matter of Grossvogel's sculpture—of which he subsequently put out a series of several hundred, each of them with the same title followed by a number that placed it in a sequence of artistic production—was discussed at length as we sat waiting in the diner situated on the main street of the dead town of Crampton. The gentleman seated to my left at one of the few tables in the diner reiterated his accusations against Grossvogel.

"First he subjected us to an artistic swindle," said this person who was prone to sudden and protracted coughing spells, "and now he has subjected us to a metaphysical swindle. It was unheard of, charging us such a price for that exhibition of his, and now charging us so outrageously once again for this 'physical-metaphysical excursion.' We've all been taken in by that—"

"That absolute fraud," said Mrs. Angela when the man on my left was unable to complete his statement because he had broken into another fit of coughing. "I don't think he's even going to show up," she continued. "He induces us to come to this hole-in-the-wall town. He says that this is the place where we need to collect for this excursion of his. But he doesn't show his face anywhere around here. Where did he find this place, on one of those bus tours he was always talking about?"

It seemed that we had only ourselves and our own idiocy to blame for the situation we were in. Even though no one openly admitted it, the truth was that those of us who were present that day when Grossvogel entered the art gallery, gently requesting us to assist him in throwing all of his works on exhibit into the back of a battered pickup truck, were very much impressed with him. None of us in our small circle of artists and intellectuals had ever done anything remotely like that or even dreamed of doing something so drastic and full of drama. From that day it became our unspoken conviction that Grossvogel was on to something, and our disgraceful secret that we desired to attach ourselves to him in order to profit in some way by this association. At the same time, of course, we also resented Grossvogel's daring behavior and were perfectly ready to welcome another failure on his part, perhaps even another collapse on the floor of the gallery where he and his artworks had already once failed (to everyone's thorough satisfaction). Such a confusion of motives was more than enough reason for us to pay the exorbitant fee that Grossvogel charged for his new exhibit, which we afterward dismissed in one way or another.

Following the show that night I stood on the sidewalk outside the art gallery, listening once again to Mrs. Angela's implications regarding the true source of Grossvogel's metamorphic recovery and artistic inspiration. "Mr. Reiner Grossvogel has been medicated to the eyeballs ever since he came out of that hospital," she said to me as if for the first time. "I know one of the girls who works at the drugstore that fills his prescriptions. She's a very good customer of mine," she added, her wrinkled and heavily made-up eyes flashing with self-satisfaction. Then she continued her scandalous revelations. "I think you might know the kind of medications prescribed for someone with Grossvogel's medical condition, which really isn't a medical condition at all but a psychophysical disorder that I or any of the people who work for me could have told him about a long time ago. Grossvogel's brain has been swimming in all kinds of tranquilizers and antidepressants for months now, and not only that. He's also been taking an antispasmodic compound for that condition of his that he's supposed to have recovered from by such miraculous means. I'm not surprised he doesn't think he has a mind or any kind of self, which is all just an act in any case. *Antispasmodic*." Mrs. Angela hissed at me as we stood on the sidewalk outside the art gallery following Grossvogel's exhibit. "Do you know what that means?" she asked me, and then quickly answered her own question. "It means belladonna, a poisonous hallucinogenic. It means phenobarbital, a barbiturate. The girl from the drugstore told me all about it. He's been overdosing himself on all of these drugs, do you understand? That's why he's been seeing things in that peculiar way he would have us believe. It's not some shadow or whatever he says that's *activating* his body. I would know about something like that, now wouldn't I? I have a special gift that provides me with insight into things like that."

But despite her purported gifts, along with her genuinely excellent pastries, Mrs. Angela's psychic coffeehouse did not thrive as a business and ultimately went under altogether. On the other hand, Grossvogel's sculptures, which he produced at a prolific pace, were an incredible success, both among local buyers of artistic products and among art merchants and collectors across the country, even reaching an international market to some extent. Reiner Grossvogel was also celebrated in feature articles that appeared in major art magazines and nonartistic publications alike, although he was usually portrayed, in the words of one critic, as a "one-man artistic and philosophical freakshow." Nevertheless, Grossvogel was by any measure now functioning as a highly successful organism. And it was due to this success, which had never been approached by anyone else within our small circle of artists and intellectuals, that those of us who had abandoned Grossvogel upon hearing him lecture on his metamorphic recovery from a severe gastrointestinal disorder and viewing the first in his prodigious Tsalal series of sculptures, now once again attached ourselves and our failed careers to him and his unarguably successful body without a mind or a self. Even Mrs. Angela eventually became conversant with the "realizations" that Grossvogel had first espoused in the back room of that storefront art gallery and now disseminated in what seemed an unending line of philosophical pamphlets, which became almost as sought after by collectors as his series of Tsalal sculptures. Thus, when Grossvogel issued a certain brochure among the small circle of artists and intellectuals which he had never abandoned even after he had achieved such amazing financial success and celebrity, a brochure announcing a "physical-metaphysical excursion" to the dead town of Crampton, we were more than willing once more to pay the exorbitant price he was asking.

This was the brochure to which I referred the others seated at the table with me in the Crampton diner: the photographic portraitist who was subject to coughing jags on my left, the author of the unpublished philosophical treatise *An Investigation into the Conspiracy Against the Human Race* on my right, and Mrs. Angela directly across from me. The man on my left was still reiterating, with prolonged interruptions of his coughing (which I will here delete), the charge that Grossvogel had perpetrated a "metaphysical swindle" with his high-priced "physical-metaphysical excursion."

"All of Grossvogel's talk about that business with the shadow and the blackness and the nightmare world he purportedly was seeing . . . and then where do we end up—in some godforsaken town that went out of business a long time ago, and in some part of the country where everything looks like an overexposed photograph. I have my camera with me ready to create portraits of faces that have looked upon Grossvogel's shadowy blackness, or whatever he was planning for us to do here. I've even thought of several very good titles and concepts for these photographic portraits which I imagine would have a good chance of being published together as a book, or at least a portfolio in a leading photography magazine. I thought that at the very least I might have taken back with me a series of photographic portraits of Grossvogel, with that huge face of his. I could have placed that with almost any of the better art magazines. But where is the celebrated Grossvogel? He said he would be here to meet us. He said we would find out everything about that shadow business, as I understood him. Furthermore, I have my head prepared for those absolute nightmares that Grossvogel prattled on about in his pamphlets and in that highly deceptive brochure of his."

"This brochure," I said during one of the man's more raucous intervals of hacking, "makes no explicit promises about any of those things you've imagined to be contained there. It specifically announces that this is to be an excursion, and I quote, 'to a *dead* town during a time of year when one season is failing and the next is just beginning its rise to success.' Grossvogel's brochure also says that this is a '*finished* town, a *failed* town, a false and unreal setting that is the product of unsuccessful organisms and therefore a town that is exemplary of that extreme state of failure that may so distress human organic systems, particularly the gastrointestinal system, to the point of weakening its delusional and totally fabricated defenses—e.g., the mind, the self—and thus precipitating a crisis of nightmare realization involving . . .' and I think we're all familiar with the shadow-and-darkness talk which follows. The point is, Grossvogel promises nothing in this brochure except an environment redolent of failure, a sort of hothouse for failed organisms. The rest of it is entirely born of your own imaginations . . . and my own, I might add."

"Well," said Mrs. Angela, pulling the brochure I had placed on the table toward her, "did I imagine reading that, and *I* quote, 'suitable dining accommodations will be provided'? Bitter coffee and stale doughnuts are not what I consider suitable. Grossvogel is now a rich man, as everybody knows, and this is the best he can do? Until the day I closed down my business for good, I served superlative coffee, not to mention superlative pastries, even if I now admit that I didn't make them myself. And my psychic readings, mine and those of all my people, were as breathtaking as they come. Meanwhile, the rich man and that waitress there are practically poisoning us with this bitter coffee and these incredibly stale, cut-rate doughnuts. What I could use at this moment is some of that antispasmodic medicine Grossvogel's been taking in such liberal doses for so long. And I'm sure he'll have plenty of it with him if he ever shows his face around here, which I doubt he will after making us sick with his suitable dining accommodations. If you will excuse me for a moment."

As Mrs. Angela made her way toward the other side of the diner, I noticed that there were already a few others lined up outside the single door labeled REST ROOM. I glanced around at those still seated at the few tables or upon the stools along the counter of the diner, and there seemed to be a number of persons who were holding their hands upon their stomachs, some of them tenderly massaging their abdominal region. I too was beginning to feel some intestinal discomfort which might have been attributed to the poor quality of the coffee and doughnuts we had been served by our waitress, who now appeared to be nowhere in sight. The man sitting on my left had also excused himself and made his way across the diner. Just as I was about to get up from the table and join him and the others who were lining up outside the rest room, the man seated on my right began telling me about his "researches" and his "speculations" which formed the basis for his unpublished philosophical treatise *An Investigation into the Conspiracy Against the Human Race,* and how these related to his "intense suspicions" concerning Grossvogel.

"I should have known better than to have entered into this . . . excursion," the man said. "But I felt I needed to know more about what was behind Grossvogel's story. I was intensely suspicious with respect to his assertions and claims about his metamorphic recovery and about so many other things. For instance, his assertion—his realization, as he calls it—that the mind and the imagination, the soul and the self, are all simply *nonsense and dreams.* And yet he contends that what he calls the shadow, the darkness—the Tsalal, as his artworks are entitled—is *not* nonsense and dreams, and that it uses our bodies, as he claims, *for what it needs to thrive upon.* Well, really, what is the basis for dismissing his mind and imagination and so forth, but embracing the reality of his Tsalal, which seems no less the product of some nonsensical dream?"

I found the man's suspicious interrogations to be a welcome distraction from the intestinal pressure now building up inside me. In response to his question I said that I could only reiterate Grossvogel's explanation that he was longer experiencing things, that is, no longer *seeing* things, with his supposedly illusory mind and self, but with his body, which as he further contended, was activated, and entirely *occupied,* by the shadow that is the Tsalal. "This isn't by any means the most preposterous revelation of its kind, at least in my experience," I said in defense of Grossvogel.

"Nor is it in mine," he said.

"Besides," I continued, "Grossvogel's curiously named sculptures, in my opinion, have a merit and interest apart from a strictly metaphysical context and foundation."

"Do you know the significance of this word—*Tsalal*—that he uses as the sole title for all his artworks?"

"No, I'm afraid I have no notion of its origin or meaning," I regretfully confessed. "But I suppose you will enlighten me."

"Enlightenment has nothing to do with this word, which is ancient Hebrew. It means 'to become darkened . . . to become enshadowed,' so to speak. This term has emerged not infrequently in the course of my researches for my treatise *An Investigation into the Conspiracy Against the Human Race*. It occurs, of course, in numerous passages throughout the Old Testament—that potboiler of apocalypses both major and minor."

"Maybe so," I said. "But I don't agree that Grossvogel's use of a term from Hebrew mythology necessarily calls into question the sincerity of his assertions, or even their validity, if you want to take it that far."

"Yes, well, I seem not to be making myself clear to you. What I'm referring to emerged quite early in my researches and preliminary speculations for my *Investigation*. Briefly, I would simply say that it's not my intention to cast doubt on Grossvogel's Tsalal. My *Investigation* would prove me to be quite explicit and unequivocal on this phenomenon, although I would never employ the rather showy and somewhat trivial approach that Grossvogel has taken, which to some extent could account for the fabulous success of his sculptures and pamphlets, on the one hand, and, on the other, the abysmal failure of my treatise, which will remain forever unpublished and unread. All that aside, my point is not that this Tsalal of Grossvogel's *isn't* in some way an actual phenomenon. I know only too well that the mind and the imagination, the soul and the self, are not only the nonsensical dreams that Grossvogel makes them out to be. They are in fact no more than a cover-up—as false and unreal as the artwork Grossvogel was producing before his medical ordeal and recovery. Grossvogel was able to penetrate this fact by some extremely rare circumstance which no doubt had something to do with his medical ordeal."

"His gastrointestinal disorder," I said, feeling more and more the symptoms of this malady in my own body.

"Exactly. It's the precise mechanics of this experience of his that interested me enough to invest in his excursion. This is what remains so obscure. There is nothing obvious, if I may say, about his Tsalal or its mechanism, yet Grossvogel is making what to my mind are some fascinating claims and distinctions with such overwhelming certitude. But he *is* certainly mistaken, or possibly is being devious on one point at least. I say this because I know that he has not been entirely forthcoming about the hospital where he was treated. In my researches for *An Investigation* I have looked into such places and how they operate. I know for a fact that the hospital where Grossvogel was treated is an extremely rotten institution, an absolutely rotten institution. Everything about it is a sham and a cover-up for the most gruesome goings-on, the true extent of which I'm not sure even those involved with such places realize. It's not a matter of any sort of depravity, so to speak, or of malign intent. There simply develops a sort of . . . collusion, a rotten alliance on the part of certain people and places. They are in league with . . . well, if only you could read my *Investigation* you would know the sort of nightmare that Grossvogel was faced with in that hospital, a place reeking of nightmares. Only in such a place could Grossvogel have confronted those nightmarish realizations he has discoursed upon in his countless pamphlets and portrayed in his series of Tsalal sculptures, which he says were not the product of his mind or imagination, or his soul or his self, but only the product of what he was seeing with his body and its organs of physical sensation—the shadow, the darkness. The mind and all that, the self and all that, are only a cover-up, only a fabrication, as Grossvogel says. They are that which cannot be seen with the body, which cannot be sensed by any organ of physical sensation. This is because they are actually nonexistent cover-ups, masks, disguises for the thing that is activating our bodies in the way Grossvogel explained—activating them and using them for what it needs to thrive upon. They are the work, the artworks in fact, *of the Tsalal itself*. Oh, it's impossible to simply tell you. I wish you could read my *Investigation*. It would have explained everything; it would have revealed everything. But how could you read what was never written in the first place."

"Never written?" I inquired. "Why was it never written?"

"Why?" he said, pausing for a moment and grimacing in pain. "The answer to that is exactly what Grossvogel has been preaching in both his pamphlets and in his public appearances. His entire doctrine, if it can even be called that, if there could ever be such a thing in any sense whatever, is based on the nonexistence, the imaginary nature, of everything we believe ourselves to be. Despite his efforts to express what has happened to him, he must know very well that there are no

words that are able to explain such a thing. Words are a total obfusca-
tion of the most basic fact of existence, the very conspiracy against
the human race that my treatise might have illuminated. Grossvogel
has experienced the essence of this conspiracy firsthand, or at least has
claimed to have experienced it. Words are simply a cover-up of this
conspiracy. They are the ultimate means for the cover-up, the ultimate
artwork of the shadow, the darkness—its ultimate artistic cover-up.
Because of the existence of words, we think that there exists a mind,
that some kind of soul or self exists. This is just another of the infinite
layers of the cover-up. But there is no mind that could have written
An Investigation into the Conspiracy Against the Human Race—no mind
that could write such a book and no mind that could read such a
book. There is no one at all who can say anything about this most
basic fact of existence, no one who can betray this reality. And there
is no one to whom it could ever be conveyed."

"That all seems impossible to comprehend," I objected.

"It just might be, if only there actually were anything to comprehend, or anyone to comprehend it. But there are no such
beings."

"If that's the case," I said, wincing with abdominal discomfort,
"then who is having this conversation?"

"Who indeed?" he answered in a distantly rhetorical tone. "Nevertheless, I would like to continue speaking. Even if this is only nonsense and dreams I feel the need to perpetuate it all. Especially at this
moment, when I feel this pain taking over my mind and my self.
Pretty soon none of this will make any difference. No," he said in a
dead voice. "It doesn't matter now."

I noticed that he had been staring out the front window of the
diner for some time, gazing at the town. Some of the others in the
diner were doing the same, dumbstruck at what they saw and ago-
nized, as I was, by the means by which they were seeing it. The
vacant scene of the town's empty streets and the desolate season that
had presided over the surrounding landscape, that place we had complained was absent of any manifestations of interest when we first
arrived there, was undergoing a visible metamorphosis to the eyes of
many of us, as though an eclipse were occurring. But what we were
now seeing was not a darkness descending from far skies but a shadow
which was arising from within the dead town around us, as if a torrent
of black blood had begun roaring through its pale body—roaring like
a distant ocean moving in a bestial surge toward its shores. I realized
that I had suddenly and unknowingly joined in the forefront of those

who were affected by the changes taking place, even though I literally had no *idea* what was happening, no knowledge that came to my mind, which had ceased to function in the way it once did, leaving my body in a dumb state of agony, its organs of sensations registering the gruesome spectacle of things around me: other bodies eclipsed by the shadow swirling inside their skins, some of them still speaking as though they were persons who possessed a mind and a self, imaginary entities still complaining in human words about the pain they were only beginning to realize, crying out above the increasing roar for remedies as they entered the "nucleus of the abysmal," and still seeing with their minds even up to the very moment when their minds abandoned them entirely, dissipating like a mirage, able to say only how everything appeared to their minds, how the shapes of the town outside the windows of the diner were turning all crooked and crabbed, reaching out toward them as if with claws and rising up like strange peaks and horns into the sky, which was no longer pale and gray but swirling with the pervasive shadow, the all-moving darkness that they could finally see so perfectly because now they were seeing with their bodies, only with their bodies pitched into a great roaring blackness of pain. And one voice called out—a voice that both moaned and coughed—that there was a face outside, a "face across the entire sky," it said. The sky and town were now both so dark that perhaps only someone preoccupied with the human face could have seen such a thing among that world of churning shadows outside the windows of the diner. Soon after that the words all but ceased, because bodies in true pain do not speak. The very last words I remember were those of a woman who screamed for someone to take her to a hospital. And this was a request which, in the strangest way, had been anticipated by the one who had induced us to make this "physical-metaphysical excursion" and whose body had already mastered what our bodies were only beginning to learn—the nightmare of a body that is being used and that knows what is using it, making things be what they would not be and do what they would not do. I sensed the presence of a young woman who had worn a uniform as white as gauze. She had returned. And there were others like her who moved among us, their forms being the darkest of all, and who knew how to minister to our pains in order to effect our metamorphic recovery. We did not need to be brought to their hospital, since the hospital and all its rottenness had been brought to us.

$\star$ $\quad$ $\star$ $\quad$ $\star$

And as much as I would like to say everything that happened to us in the town of Crampton (whose deadness and desolation seem an illusion of paradise after having its hidden life revealed to our eyes) . . . as much as I would like to say how it was that we were conveyed from that region of the country, that nucleus of nowhere, and returned to our distant homes . . . as much as I would like to say precisely what assistance and treatments we might have received that delivered us from that place and the pain we experienced there, I cannot say anything about it at all. Because when one is saved from such agony, the most difficult thing in the world is to question the means of salvation: the body does not know or care what takes away its pain and is incapable of questioning these things. For that is what we have become, or what we have all but become—bodies without the illusion of minds or imaginations, bodies without the distractions of souls or selves. None of us among our circle questioned this fact, although we have never spoken of it since our . . . recovery. Nor have we spoken of the absence of Grossvogel from our circle, which does not exist in the way it once did, that is to say, as an assemblage of artists and intellectuals. We became the recipients of what someone designated as the "legacy of Grossvogel," which was more than a metaphorical expression, since the artist had in fact bequeathed to each of us, on the condition of his "death or disappearance for a stipulated period of time," a share in the considerable earnings he had amassed from the sales of his works.

But this strictly monetary inheritance was only the beginning of the success that all of us from that abolished circle of artists and intellectuals began to experience, the seed from which we began to grow out of our existence as failed minds and selves into our new lives as highly successful organisms, each in our own field of endeavor. Of course we could not have failed, even if we tried, in attaining whatever end we pursued, since everything we have experienced and created was a phenomenon of the shadow, the darkness which reached outwards and reached upwards from inside us to claw and poke its way to the heights of a mountainous pile of human and nonhuman bodies. These are all we have and all we are; these are what is used and thrived upon. I can feel my own body being used and cultivated, the desires and impulses that are pulling it to succeed, that are *tugging* it toward every kind of success. There is no means by which I could ever oppose these desires and impulses, now that I exist solely as a body which seeks only its efficient perpetuation so that it may be thrived upon by what needs it. There is no possibility of my resisting what needs to thrive upon us, no possibility of betraying it in any way. The medications that I and the others now consume in such prodigious quantities serve only to further the process of our cultivation, this growing and pulling and using of our bodies. And even if this little account of mine—my own Tsalal, if you will (nevermind the pronouns)—even if this little chronicle seems to disclose secrets that might undermine the nightmarish order of things, it does nothing but support and promulgate that order. Nothing can resist or betray this nightmare because nothing exists that might *do* anything, that might *be* anything that could realize a success in that way. The very idea of such a thing is only nonsense and dreams.

There could never be anything written about the "conspiracy against the human race," because the phenomenon of a conspiracy requires a multiplicity of agents, a division of sides, one of which is undermining the other in some way and the other having an existence that is able to be undermined. But this is no such multiplicity or division, no undermining or resistance or betrayal on either side. What exists is only this *pulling,* this *tugging* upon all of the bodies of this world. But these bodies have a collective existence only in a taxonomic or perhaps a topographical sense and in no way constitute a collective entity, an agency that might be the object of a conspiracy. And a collective entity called the human race cannot exist where there is only a collection of nonentities, of bodies which are themselves only provisional and will be lost one by one, the whole collection of them always approaching nonsense, always dissolving into dreams. There can be no conspiracy in a void, or rather in a black abyss. There can only be this tugging of all these bodies toward that ultimate success which it seems my large-bodied friend realized when he was finally used to the fullest extent, his body used up, *entirely consumed* by what needed it to thrive.

"There is only one true and final success for the shadow that makes things what they would not be," Grossvogel proclaimed in the very last of his pamphlets. "There is only one true and final success for the all-moving blackness that makes things do what they would not do," he wrote. And these were the very last lines of that last pamphlet. Grossvogel could not explain himself or anything else beyond these unconcluded statements. He had run out of the words that (to quote someone who shall remain as nameless as only a member of the human race can be) are the ultimate artwork of the shadow, the darkness—its ultimate artistic cover-up. Just as he could not resist it as his body was pulled toward that ultimate success, he could not betray it with his words.

It was during the winter following the Crampton excursion that I began fully to see where these last words of Grossvogel were leading. Late one night I stood gazing from a window as the first snow of the season began to fall and become increasingly more prolific throughout each dark hour during which I observed its progress with my organs of physical sensation. By that time I could see what was inside the falling flakes of snow, just as I could see what was inside all other things, activating them with its force. And what I saw was a black snow tumbling with an incessant roar from a black sky. There was nothing recognizable in that sky—certainly no familiar visage spread out across the night and implanted into it. There was only this roaring blackness above and this roaring blackness below. There was only this consuming, proliferating, roaring blackness whose only true and final success was in the mere perpetuation of itself as successfully as it could in a world where nothing exists that could ever hope to be anything else except what it needs to thrive upon . . . until everything is entirely consumed and there is only one thing remaining in all existence and it is an infinite body of roaring blackness activating itself and thriving upon itself with eternal success in the deepest abyss of entity. Grossvogel could not resist or betray it, even if it was an absolute nightmare, the ultimate physical-metaphysical nightmare. He ceased to be a person so that he could remain a successful organism. "Anyone would do the same," he said.

And no matter what I say I cannot resist or betray it. No one could do so because there is no one here. There is only this body, this shadow, this darkness.

Rick Hautala

KNOCKING

Rick Hautala's novel Night Stone *was famous for its cover (which sported a hologram, a publishing first) as well as for its contents. Like Ramsey Campbell, he has refused to abandon the field, and has steadfastly kept to the path he laid out years ago with such subsequent horror and thriller novels as* Impulse, Dark Silence, *and* Cold Whisper.

For 999, Rick came up with a dandy piece, which actually features the millennium, something I wanted to avoid. But somehow in this story I didn't mind at all, since the millennium is just background—like the Dune-like worms in Star Wars, *which made my jaw drop, not because they were so neat but because Lucas had the nerve to just make them background.*

This story is not about the millennium at all. It's about something much more scary: the human mind.

The streets were on fire.

For the last six weeks, once the sun was down, Martin Gordon wouldn't leave his house.

He didn't dare.

He hadn't seen any news reports since the television stations had gone off the air last week. It had been even longer since he'd read a current newspaper or magazine. But he didn't need anyone to tell him that being out after dark was dangerous. From his second-floor bedroom window, he could see marauding bands of young people, their black silhouettes outlined like hot metal against the dancing flames of the burning city as they roved the streets.

The millennial celebrations had started in early December. At first they had been nothing more than sporadic nightly celebrations; but for the last few weeks, they had continued from dusk until dawn as throngs of people moved from city block to city block. What had started as a spontaneous celebration quickly turned into wanton destruction as people's frustrations and insecurities took over. It wasn't long before the burning and looting began.

Martin had quit his job on Monday of last week. He thought *quit* might be too strong a word. There was no superior left at the factory for him to give his notice to, so one morning he simply stopped showing up.

He didn't mind being out of work all that much. He'd never really liked his job in the first place, and now he had plenty of time to do the things he enjoyed doing, such as working on his model railroad. Of course, with no electricity, he couldn't run the trains. In the gathering darkness, he could only admire the work he'd done that day and hope that—eventually—once the electricity was restored, he could run them again.

For the last several days, however, he'd spent most of the daylight hours reinforcing the barricades around his house. He'd sacrificed nearly all of the heavy oak doors from inside the house to cover the downstairs windows. He picked up some heavy-duty screws at the hardware store and, after cutting the doors in half, screwed them securely into the window frames. Someone would have to be damned serious about breaking in to remove one of them.

Getting food was becoming an increasing problem. Martin had run out of ready cash a while ago. All of the city's banks had closed their doors by the second week of December, so his paltry savings were locked up where he couldn't get at them.

Ultimately it didn't matter because all of the grocery stores within walking distance of his house had been looted, anyway. Without electricity, all of the perishables had gone bad, but Martin had enough dried and canned food squirreled away to last him at least a month or so, maybe longer if he was careful. As it was, his meals were pretty uninspired—usually nothing more than cold baked beans or vegetables eaten straight from the can. All he could hope was that the situation would eventually calm down and the police would restore order so everything could start getting back to normal.

Whatever normal was in the year 2000.

Every day, as soon as the sun started to set, Martin would make sure the front and back doors were secure, then settle down for a cold meal from a can before going upstairs, where he could keep an eye on the front yard from his bedroom window. Then, usually sometime after midnight, he'd settle down to sleep.

He'd gotten so he could sleep through just about anything, unless a roving band of party-goers came too close to the house. When things started to get out of control, he would wake up and sit on his bed with his loaded shotgun cradled like a baby in his lap. The only light he used was a single candle, which he placed behind him so it would illuminate the bedroom doorway without blinding him if there was any trouble.

So far, though, there hadn't been any trouble, and for some reason, tonight was unusually quiet. The millennium rioting was still in full swing, but some distance away. When Martin looked out the upstairs window, he could see the fire-lit buildings in the distance and hear the sounds of music and riotous voices, laughing and calling out in wild abandon.

"Christ, some celebration," he muttered.

He was in the habit of talking out loud to himself, having lived alone for the last eight years, ever since his mother had died. He had never known his father, who, according to his mother, had left the family when Martin was only one year old. Like a lot of men in tough economic times, one day he'd gone to the store for cigarettes and never come back.

There was a sharp winter chill in the air, so after listening to the distant block party for a while, Martin decided it was safe to close the window and settle down to sleep. Because there was no heat in the house—even if there had been electricity to run the furnace, there hadn't been any oil deliveries in weeks—his mattress was heaped high with blankets and comforters. His breath made puffy white clouds as he lay down in the darkness and watched the dull orange flicker of flames against the city skyline.

He had just drifted off to sleep when he was suddenly startled awake.

For a panicky instant, Martin wasn't sure what had awakened him. The sounds of the celebrations were still far off in the distance. Concerned, he looked around the darkened bedroom, sure that he had heard . . . something. But what?

Could there be someone in the house?

He felt a tingling rush of apprehension.

It was possible, he supposed, but he didn't see how anyone could have gotten in without making enough noise to wake him up sooner.

Moving slowly so as to make as little sound as possible, Martin sat up and reached over the side of the bed to where his shotgun leaned against the wall. He felt better once it was in hand. Tossing the bedcovers aside, he swung his feet to the floor. A numbing chill ran up the back of his legs the instant his bare feet hit the icy floorboards.

Standing in a defensive crouch, he tried to stop his teeth from chattering as he waited for the sound to come again. Shivers teased like bony fingertips playing the xylophone up and down his spine. The hair at the nape of his neck prickled with anticipation until—very faintly—he heard the sound again.

It was the sound of someone knocking . . .

. . . knocking on the front door.

Martin's heart pulsed heavily in his chest as he thumbed the hammer back on the shotgun and took a few cautious steps forward. He was breathing rapidly, trailing his frosty breath like a tangled scarf over his shoulders.

Before he made it to the now-doorless doorway of his bedroom, the knocking came again, louder this time. It echoed through the cold, dark house, which resonated like the insides of a huge kettledrum.

Martin was shivering terribly when he stepped out into the hallway and paused to look over the railing. His eyes seemed to be taking too long to adjust to the darkness as he stared at the front door, positive that he could see it push inward with each heavy blow as the knocking sounded again.

Tightening his grip on the shotgun, he started down the stairs, his gaze focused on the narrow windows on either side of the door. He wanted to catch some indication of who was out there on the doorstep, but all he could see was the deep, black stain of the night, pressing against the glass like a stray cat, wanting to be let in.

Martin took a deep breath, preparing to call out a challenge or warning, but his voice failed him, caught like a fish hook in his throat.

He didn't like this.

Not one bit.

But in spite of his rising tension, he kept moving forward. Every step creaked beneath his weight, setting his teeth on edge until he made it down to the foyer.

The only light in the house came from the single candle burning upstairs in his bedroom. Hardly enough light to see by. The darkness within the house pressed close, squeezing against him like soft, crushed velvet. When he realized that he was holding his breath, he let it out in a long, slow whistle. His hands were shaking as he raised the shotgun and aimed it at the front door.

Even though he was expecting it and was convinced that he was ready for it, his heart skipped a beat when the knocking came again.

One . . . two . . . three times, the heavy blows pounded against the door.

And then they stopped.

The sudden silence hummed in Martin's ears as he stood in the foyer, too frightened to say or do anything.

His anticipation spiked as he waited for the sound to come again. He looked furtively from side to side as though expecting to see something creeping up behind him in the darkness even though he told himself that there was nothing there. His gaze returned to the door when the unseen person on the other side began knocking again, even harder.

Was it a friend? Martin wondered. Someone who'd stopped by to check if he was all right?

That didn't seem likely.

Martin didn't have any real friends. He pretty much kept to himself, having gotten used to being alone after so many years tending to his invalid mother before she died.

Thinking of his mother sent a tickling electric current racing up his back.

What if that's her out there? he wondered, unable to repress the deep shudder that shook his insides. He couldn't help but remember how during those last horrible years, when she was ill and bedridden, she would bang on the wall to get his attention, pulling him away from his time alone with his trains.

He tried not to think it, but the sounds were practically identical.

"No!" he told himself. "Mother is dead!"

He tried not to imagine what she would look like, her wizened form hunched on the crumbling cement stairs, wrapped against the cold in her yellowing burial shroud as she banged on the door to be let in. Her skin, gray with the rot of the grave, would be falling off in large, ragged chunks as each knock rang out like a hammer on an ancient Chinese gong.

But no!

That couldn't be her.

He had seen her coffin lowered into the ground.

She was dead!

Even if he hadn't smothered her with her pillow, like the detective who had come by several times had suggested, she was dead and buried! And even if he had done something like that, he would have done it only out of mercy, to end her long suffering following the paralyzing stroke.

He told himself that he shouldn't let his imagination get fired up like this. It wasn't healthy. There was definitely someone out there, make no mistake, but it wasn't—it couldn't be his mother!

But it was someone, and when whoever it was began hammering on the door again, Martin told himself that, if they didn't stop it and go away real soon, he was going to unload both barrels of his shotgun on them without warning.

He didn't care who it was.

Even if it was some little kid who'd lost a kitten and was going from door to door looking for it. Or some crazed drunk or drug addict, lost and, thinking he was home, pounding on the wrong door to be let in.

It didn't matter.

Hell, even if it did matter, Martin didn't care.

Anyone with any common sense was safe inside his own home as soon as it got dark. The only people out and about at this hour were dangerous people who deserved to die if they were going to bother decent people, like Martin, who wanted nothing but to be left alone.

He'd shoot if he had to.

He hadn't heard the news lately, but he was sure there must have been numerous deaths—murders and accidental deaths—since the celebrations began. One more death in a city this size wasn't even going to be noticed. Not when the police had so many other things to take care of.

Still, Martin didn't dare to call out, much less go to the door.

Instead, he walked to the wall opposite the front door and, leaning back against the closed closet door—one of the few remaining inside the house—slid slowly down into a sitting position on the floor with his shotgun poised and aimed at the front door.

The knocking continued unabated, the blows coming more rapidly now, the heavy thumping booming louder and louder. Martin was convinced that, before long, the door would be smashed to splinters. In spite of the cold night, thin trickles of sweat ran down his face. His eyes felt like they were bugging from their sockets as he watched . . . and waited . . . wishing that the knocking would stop and the person would go away and leave him alone.

But that didn't happen, and Martin couldn't stop wondering who it might be. He kept tossing possible scenarios over in his mind until he thought of something that made his pulse skip a beat. He felt suddenly light-headed with anxiety.

What if it was his father, come home after all these years?

Could that be possible?

Martin had lived his whole life in this house with his mother, so if, by some extraordinary circumstance, his father was still alive, he would naturally come back here first, if only to see if his family still lived here.

Martin's forefinger brushed lightly against the trigger of the shotgun. He grit his teeth so hard he could hear low grinding noises deep inside his head. His vision pulsed and swirled in front of him, creating a vortex of darkness spinning within deeper darkness.

The pounding on the door was so loud now that it seemed to be as much inside his head as outside. Blow after blow rained down against the wood, and each blow resonated inside Martin's skull until he was trembling like a man wracked with fever.

Go away! he thought but didn't dare say out loud.

Go away!

Leave me alone!

And still the knocking continued, keeping time with the painful beating of his heart, which thundered in his ears so hard it made his neck ache.

Please . . . For the love of God . . . Just go away!

But the knocking didn't let up. It grew louder and louder until—finally—Martin realized that he was going to have to go to the door and confront whomever it was.

His body was rigid and throbbing with pain as he rose slowly to his feet. He maintained such a tight grip on his shotgun that, for a moment or two, his fingers were paralyzed, unable to move.

Martin told himself to stay in control, that he had to deal with this now or it would only get worse. He would be in serious trouble if he opened the door and the person—whoever was out there—saw even a hint of fear or hesitation on his part.

His feet dragged heavily on the wooden floor, making loud rasping sounds, but not loud enough to drown out the incessant hammering on the door.

Martin licked his lips and took a shuddering breath that made his chest feel like it was constricted by thick iron bands. The sour pressure in his stomach grew painfully intense, and he had to concentrate to make his arms move as he raised the shotgun and pointed it at the door.

Go away! Now! Before you regret it, Martin wanted to call out, but horrible images of his dead mother and the father he had never known filled his mind.

Could it be both of them out there on the stoop?

He felt curiously weighed down as he moved toward the door. It was like being trapped in a dream. No matter how many steps he took, the front door seemed to withdraw from him, getting farther away rather than closer.

Martin shook his head and slapped himself on the cheek, trying to convince himself that he was awake. This was real. It was really happening.

And all the while, the heavy pounding on the door continued without letting up.

Watching like a dissociated observer, Martin raised his hand and reached out for the door lock. The other hand held the shotgun at chest level, his forefinger on the trigger and already starting to squeeze.

A prickling wave of pain rolled up his arm to his shoulder as he slowly withdrew the metal clasp of the chain lock and let it drop. It made a rough, grating noise as it swung back and forth like a pendulum against the door, bouncing every time the knocking from the other side vibrated the door.

Holding his breath so long it hurt, Martin grasped the dead bolt and turned it slowly to the right. Every nerve in his body was sizzling like overloaded wires as he waited for the lock to click open.

He was swept up in a flood of vertigo and was afraid that he would pass out before he could get the door open and confront whomever was out there on his doorstep. They must have heard him undo the lock, he thought, so they would have plenty of time to run away before he got the door open.

Martin jumped when the lock clicked, sounding as sharp as the snap of a whip. He reached quickly for the doorknob, gave it a savage twist, and pulled back to throw the door open.

But the doorknob slipped from his hand as if it were greased.

Momentarily confused, Martin stood back. He was breathing so heavily his throat made a dull roaring sound. Sweat tickled his ribs as it ran down the inside of his shirt. The sound of the knocking continued, so loud now it made his vision jump in time with it.

The gun felt suddenly heavy in his hand, and he placed it on the floor, leaning it against the wall within easy reach. He wiped his sweaty palms on his pants legs before taking hold of the doorknob again and giving it another violent turn.

He heard the cylinder mechanism click. This time when he pulled back, he kept his grip, but—still—the door wouldn't open.

Martin muttered a curse under his breath, but he could barely hear his own voice above the constant pounding on the door. He could feel the deep vibration in the palm of his hand, like a wasp sting, but he ignored it as he twisted the doorknob back and forth several times, all the while pulling back with all his strength.

Still, the door wouldn't open.

It wouldn't even budge.

This isn't possible, Martin thought, sure that whoever was out there still knocking was holding the door shut with the other hand so he couldn't open it.

Panting heavily, Martin moved to the left. Bending low, he peered out the side window. The night was dense and black except for the distant glow of fire on the horizon. As far as he could see, there was no one out there.

The doorstep was empty.

A sudden gust of wind blew a flurry of snow from the edge of the porch roof. The ice crystals glittered like diamond dust in the flickering orange glow before drifting down into the darkness. For just an instant, Martin imagined that the shower of snow had assumed a vague human form. He cleared his throat, preparing to call out, but his voice was locked up inside his chest.

The knocking continued without stopping.

Martin jumped and let out a startled yelp when he saw an alley cat leap from the trash cans to the top of the fence that bordered his property. But even if the sound had stopped, he knew that the cat couldn't have been the one doing it.

Shivering wildly, he moved back to the door. After making sure the dead bolt and chain lock were unlocked, he grasped the doorknob again with both hands. The muscles in his wrists and forearms knotted like twisted wire as shivering vibrations ran up his arms to his shoulders and neck.

A pathetic whimper escaped Martin as he ratcheted the doorknob quickly back and forth. The door couldn't have been shut tighter if it had been nailed shut. Bracing one foot against the doorjamb, he leaned back and pulled with all his strength, but the door still wouldn't budge.

Who's out there? Martin wanted to call out. *Why are you doing this?* But his throat felt flayed and raw.

His heart was thumping heavily in his ears as the knocking grew steadily louder, thundering through the dark house, keeping time with his hammering pulse.

Every muscle in Martin's body tensed as he leaned back as far as he could, struggling to open the door. He sucked in shallow gulps of air that felt like he was sipping fire. Finally, in a high, broken voice, he forced out a whisper.

"Mother?"

The instant those words left his mouth, the knocking ceased. Leaden silence merged with the darkness and filled the air.

The silence stretched.

Then, from every door still in the house, from the hall closet, the basement, the kitchen pantry, came knocking.

Martin screamed. Waves of rising panic swept through him. He raised his arm above his head and brought it down hard against the front door.

"Let me out!"

Tears stung his eyes as he brought his fist down repeatedly against the door, knocking so hard that it wasn't long before his hands were bruised and bloodied.

"Let . . . me . . . out!" he said between wrenching sobs. "Let . . . me . . . out!"

He collapsed forward, pressing his forehead against the cold, unyielding wood as he continued to pound with both fists. His body was wrung out, burning with exhaustion. Tears gushed from his eyes.

The only sound that filled the house now was the weakening blows he made against the door.

He didn't even hear himself ask as he continued to knock, "Who's . . . there . . . ?"

David Morrell

RIO GRANDE GOTHIC

Yes, David Morrell wrote First Blood *and created the famous character* John Rambo. *Yes, he's the best-selling author of such novels as* Brotherhood of the Rose *and* Double Image. *He's also a heck of a nice fellow, a gentleman in person, and probably pats dogs on the head when he passes them in the street. He also writes stories as good as his novels, such as the one you're about to read.*

The protagonist of "Rio Grande Gothic" is a classic Morrell hero, a man forced by circumstances to change roles from the hunter to the hunted. Like much of Morrell's best work, the pace is fast and the action nearly continuous.

And this time, it's also creepy as hell.

When Romero finally noticed the shoes on the road, he realized that he had actually been seeing them for several days. Driving into town along Old Pecos Trail, passing the adobe-walled Santa Fe Woman's Club on the left, approaching the pueblo-style Baptist church on the right, he reached the crest of the hill, saw the jogging shoes on the yellow median line, and steered his police car onto the dirt shoulder of the road.

Frowning, he got out and hitched his thumbs onto his heavy gun belt, oblivious to the roar of passing traffic, focusing on the jogging shoes. They were laced together, a Nike label on the back. One was on its side, showing how worn its tread was. But they hadn't been in the middle of the road yesterday, Romero thought. No, yesterday, it had been a pair of leather sandals. He remembered having been vaguely aware of them. And the day before yesterday? Had it been a pair of women's high heels? His recollection wasn't clear, but there had been *some* kind of shoes—of that he was certain. What the . . . ?

After waiting for a break in traffic, Romero crossed to the median and stared down at the jogging shoes as if straining to decipher a riddle. A pickup truck crested the hill too fast to see him and slow down, the wind it created ruffling his blue uniform. He barely paid attention, preoccupied by the shoes. But when a second truck sped over the hill, he realized that he had better get off the road. He withdrew his nightstick from his gun belt, thrust it under the tied laces, and lifted. Feeling the weight of the shoes dangling from the nightstick, he waited for a minivan to speed past, then returned to his police car, unlocked its trunk, and dropped the shoes into it. Probably that was what had happened to the other shoes, he decided. A sanitation truck or someone working for the city must have stopped and cleared what looked like garbage. This was the middle of May. The tourist season would soon be in full swing. It wasn't good to have visitors seeing junk on the road. I'll toss these shoes in the trash when I get back to the station, he decided.

The next pickup that rocketed over the hill was doing at least fifty. Romero scrambled into his cruiser, flicked on his siren, and stopped the truck just after it ran a red light at Cordova.

He was forty-two. He had been a Santa Fe policeman for fifteen years, but the thirty thousand dollars he earned each year wasn't enough for him to afford a house in Santa Fe's high-priced real estate market, so he lived in the neighboring town of Pecos, twenty miles northeast, where his parents and grandparents had lived before him. Indeed, he lived in the same house that his parents had owned before a drunk driver, speeding the wrong way on the Interstate, had hit their car head-on and killed them. The modest structure had once been in a quiet neighborhood, but six months earlier a supermarket had been built a block away, the resultant traffic noise and congestion blighting the area. Romero had married when he was twenty. His wife worked for an Allstate Insurance agent in Pecos. Their twenty-two-year-old son lived at home and wasn't employed. Each morning, Romero argued with him about looking for work. That was followed by a different argument in which Romero's wife complained that he was being too hard on the boy. Typically, he and his wife left the house not speaking to each other. Once trim and athletic, the star of his high school football team, Romero was puffy in his face and stomach from too much takeout food and too much time spent behind a steering wheel. This morning, he had noticed that his sideburns were turning gray.

*   *   *

By the time he finished with the speeding pickup truck, a house burglary he was sent to investigate, and a purse snatcher he managed to catch, Romero had forgotten about the shoes. A fight between two feuding neighbors who happened to cross paths with each other in a restaurant parking lot further distracted him. He completed his paperwork at the police station, attended an after-shift debriefing, and didn't need much convincing to go out for a beer with a fellow officer rather than muster the resolve to make the twenty-mile drive to the tensions of his home. He got in at ten, long after his wife and son had eaten. His son was out with friends. His wife was in bed. He ate leftover fajitas while watching a rerun of a situation comedy that hadn't been funny the first time.

The next morning, as he crested the hill by the Baptist church, he came to attention at the sight of a pair of loafers scattered along the median. After steering sharply onto the shoulder, he opened the door and held up his hands for traffic to stop while he went over, picked up the loafers, returned to the cruiser, and set them in the trunk beside the jogging shoes.

"Shoes?" his sergeant asked back at the station. "What are you talking about?"

"Over on Old Pecos Trail. Every morning, there's a pair of shoes," Romero said.

"They must have fallen off a garbage truck."

"Every morning? And only shoes, nothing else? Besides, the ones I found this morning were almost new."

"Maybe somebody was moving and they fell off the back of a pickup truck."

"Every morning?" Romero repeated. "These were Cole Hahns. Expensive loafers like that don't get thrown on top of a load of stuff in a pickup truck."

"What difference does it make? It's only shoes. Maybe somebody's kidding around."

"Sure," Romero said. "Somebody's kidding around."

"A practical joke," the sergeant said. "So people will wonder why the shoes are on the road. Hey, *you* wondered. The joke's working."

"Yeah," Romero said. "A practical joke."

*   *   *

The next morning, it was a battered pair of Timberland work boots. As Romero crested the hill by the Baptist church, he wasn't surprised to see them. In fact, the only thing he had been uncertain about was what type of footwear they would be.

If this is a practical joke, it's certainly working, he thought. Whoever's doing it is awfully persistent. Who . . .

The problem nagged at him all day. Between investigating a hit-and-run on St. Francis Drive and a break-in at an art gallery on Canyon Road, he returned to the crest of the hill on Old Pecos Trail several times, making sure that other shoes hadn't appeared. For all he knew, the joker was dumping the shoes during the daytime. If so, the plan Romero was thinking about would be worthless. But after the eighth time he returned and still didn't see more shoes, he told himself he had a chance.

The plan had the merit of simplicity. All it required was determination, and of that he had plenty. Besides, it would be a good reason to postpone going home. So after getting a Quarter Pounder and fries, a Coke and two large containers of coffee from McDonald's, he headed toward Old Pecos Trail as dusk thickened. He used his private car, a five-year-old, dark blue Jeep Cherokee—no sense in being conspicuous. He considered establishing his stakeout in the Baptist church's parking lot. That would give him a great view of Old Pecos Trail. But at night, with his car the only one in the lot, he'd be conspicuous. Across from the church, though, East Lupita Road intersected with Old Pecos Trail. It was a quiet residential area, and if he parked there, he couldn't be seen by anyone driving along Old Pecos. In contrast, he himself would have a good view of passing traffic.

It can work, he thought. There were streetlights on Old Pecos Trail but not on East Lupita. Sitting in darkness, munching on his Quarter Pounder and fries, using the caffeine in the Coke and the two coffees to keep himself alert, he concentrated on the illuminated crest of the hill. For a while, the headlights of passing cars were frequent and distracting. After each vehicle passed, he stared toward the area of the road that interested him, but no sooner did he focus on that spot than more headlights sped past, and he had to stare harder to see if anything had been dropped. He had his right hand ready to turn the ignition key and yank the gearshift into forward, his right foot primed to stomp the accelerator. To relax, he turned on the radio for fifteen-minute stretches, careful that he didn't weaken the battery.

Then traffic became sporadic, making it easy to watch the road. But after an eleven o'clock news report in which the main item was about a fire in a store at the De Vargas mall, he realized the flaw in his plan. All that caffeine. The tension of straining to watch the road.

He had to go to the bathroom.

But I went when I picked up the food.

That was then. Those were two large coffees you drank.

Hey, I had to keep awake.

He squirmed. He tensed his abdominal muscles. He would have relieved himself into one of the beverage containers, but he had crumbled all three of them when he stuffed them into the bag that the Quarter Pounder and fries came in. His bladder ached. Headlights passed. No shoes were dropped. He pressed his thighs together. More headlights. No shoes. He turned his ignition key, switched on his headlights, and hurried toward the nearest public rest room, which was on St. Michael's Drive at an all-night gas station because at eleven-thirty most restaurants and takeout places were closed.

When he got back, two cowboy boots were on the road.

"It's almost one in the morning. Why are you coming home so late?"

Romero told his wife about the shoes.

"Shoes? Are you crazy?"

"Haven't you ever been curious about something?"

"Yeah, right now I'm curious why you think I'm stupid enough to believe you're coming home so late because of some old shoes you found on the road. Have you got a girlfriend, is that it?"

"You don't look so good," his sergeant said.

Romero shrugged despondently.

"You been out all night, partying?" the sergeant joked.

"Don't I wish."

The sergeant became serious. "What is it? More trouble at home?"

Romero almost told him the whole story, but remembering the sergeant's indifference when he'd earlier been told about the shoes, Romero knew he wouldn't get much sympathy. Maybe the opposite. "Yeah, more trouble at home."

After all, what he'd done last night was, he had to admit, a little strange. Using his free time to sit in a car for three hours, waiting for . . . If a practical joker wanted to keep tossing shoes on the road, so what? Let the guy waste his time. Why waste my own time trying to catch him? There were too many real crimes to be investigated. What am I going to charge the guy with? Littering?

Throughout his shift, Romero made a determined effort not to go near Old Pecos Trail. A couple of times during a busy day of interviewing witnesses about an assault, a break-in, another purse snatching, and a near-fatal car accident on Paseo de Peralta, he was close enough to have swung past Old Pecos Trail on his way from one incident to another, but he deliberately chose an alternate route. Time to change patterns, he told himself. Time to concentrate on what's important.

At the end of his shift, his lack of sleep the previous night caught up to him. He left work exhausted. Hoping for a quiet evening at home, he followed congested traffic through the dust of the eternal construction project on Cerrillos Road, reached Interstate 25, and headed north. Sunset on the Sangre de Cristo Mountains tinted them the blood color for which the early Spanish colonists had named them. In a half hour, I'll have my feet up and be drinking a beer, he thought. He passed the exit to St. Francis Drive. A sign told him that the next exit, the one for Old Pecos Trail, was two miles ahead. He blocked it from his mind, continued to admire the sunset, imagined the beer he was going to drink, and turned on the radio. A weather report told him that the high for the day had been seventy-five, typical for mid-May, but that a cold front was coming in and that the night temperature could drop as much as forty degrees, with a threat of frost in low-lying areas. The announcer suggested covering any recently purchased tender plants. The average frost-free day was May 15, but . . .

Romero took the Old Pecos Trail exit.

Just for the hell of it, he thought. Just to have a look and settle my curiosity. What can it hurt? As he crested the hill, he was surprised to notice that his heart was beating a little faster. Do I really expect to find more shoes? he asked himself. Is it going to annoy me that they were here all day and I didn't come over to check? Pressure built in his chest as that section came into view. He breathed deeply . . .

And exhaled when he saw that there wasn't anything on the road. There, he told himself. It was worth the detour. I proved that I'd have wasted my time if I drove over here during my shift. I can go home now without being bugged that I didn't satisfy my curiosity.

But all the time he and his wife sat watching television while they ate Kentucky Fried Chicken (their son was out with friends), Romero felt restless. He couldn't stop thinking that whoever was dumping the shoes would do so again. The bastard will think he's outsmarted me. You? What are you talking about? He doesn't have the faintest idea who you are. Well, he'll think he's outsmarted whoever's picking up the shoes. The difference is the same.

The beer that Romero had been looking forward to tasted like water.

And of course the next morning, damn it, there was a pair of women's tan pumps five yards away from each other along the median. Scowling, Romero blocked morning traffic, picked up the pumps, and set them in the trunk with the others. Where the hell is this guy getting the shoes? he thought. These pumps are almost new. So are the loafers I picked up the other day. Who throws out perfectly good shoes, even for a practical joke?

When Romero was done for the day, he phoned his wife to tell her, "I have to work late. One of the guys on the evening shift got sick. I'm filling in." He caught up on some paperwork he needed to do. Then he went to a nearby Pizza Hut and got a medium pepperoni with mushrooms and black olives, to go. He also got a large Coke and two large coffees, but this time he'd learned his lesson and came prepared with an empty plastic gallon jug that he could urinate in. More, he brought a Walkman and earphones so he wouldn't have to use the car's radio and worry about wearing down the battery.

Confident that he hadn't forgotten anything, he drove to the stakeout. Santa Fe had its share of dirt roads, and East Lupita was one of them. Flanked by chamisa bushes and Russian olive trees, it had widely spaced adobe houses and got very little traffic. Parked near the corner, Romero saw the church across from him, its bell tower reminding him of a pueblo mission. Beyond were the piñon-dotted Sun Mountain and Atalaya Ridge, the sunset as vividly blood-colored as it had been the previous evening.

Traffic passed. Studying it, he put on his headphones and switched the Walkman from CD to radio. After finding a call-in show (was the environment truly as threatened as ecologists claimed?), he sipped his Coke, dug into his pizza, and settled back to watch traffic.

An hour after dark, he realized that he had indeed forgotten something. The previous day's weather report had warned about low night temperatures, possibly even a frost, and now Romero felt a chill creep up his legs. He was grateful for the warm coffee. He hugged his chest, wishing that he'd brought a jacket. His breath vapor clouded the windshield so that he often had to use a handkerchief to clear it. He rolled down his window, and that helped control his breath vapor, but it also allowed more cold to enter the vehicle, making him shiver. Moonlight reflected off lingering snow on top of the mountains, especially at the ski basin, and that made him feel even colder. He turned on the Jeep and used its heater to warm him. All the while, he concentrated on the dwindling traffic.

Eleven o'clock, and still no shoes. He kept reminding himself that it had been about this hour two nights earlier when he had been forced to leave to find a rest room. When he had returned twenty minutes later, he had found the cowboy boots. If whoever was doing this followed a pattern, there was a good chance that something would happen in the next half hour.

Stay patient, he thought.

But as had happened two nights earlier, the Coke and the coffees finally had their effect. Fortunately, he had that problem taken care of. He grabbed the empty gallon jug from the seat beside him, twisted its cap off, positioned the jug beneath the steering wheel, and started to urinate, only to squint from the headlights of a car that approached behind him, reflecting in his rearview mirror.

His bladder muscles tensed, interrupting the flow of urine. Jesus, he thought. Although he was certain that the driver wouldn't be able to see what he was doing, he felt self-conscious enough that he quickly capped the jug and set it on the passenger floor.

Come on, he told the approaching car. He needed to urinate as bad as ever and urged the car to pass him, to turn onto Old Pecos Trail and leave, so he could grab the jug again.

The headlights stopped behind him.

What in God's name? Romero thought.

Then rooflights began to flash, and Romero realized that what was behind him was a police car. Ignoring his urgent need to urinate, he rolled down his window and placed his hands on top of the steering wheel, where the approaching officer, not knowing who was in the car or what he was getting into, would be relieved to see them.

Footsteps crunched on the dirt road. A blinding flashlight scanned the inside of Romero's car, assessing the empty pizza box, lingering over the yellow liquid in the plastic jug. "Sir, may I see your license and registration, please?"

Romero recognized the voice. "It's okay, Tony. It's me."

"Who . . . Gabe?"

The flashlight beam hurt Romero's eyes.

"Gabe?"

"The one and only."

"What the hell are you doing out here? We had several complaints about somebody suspicious sitting in a car, like he was casing the houses in the neighborhood."

"It's only me."

"Were you here two nights ago?"

"Yes."

"We had complaints then, too, but when we got here, the car was gone. What are you doing?" the officer repeated.

Trying not to squirm from the pressure in his abdomen, Romero said, "I'm on a stakeout."

"Nobody told me about any stakeout. What's going on that—"

Realizing how long it would take to explain the odd-sounding truth, Romero said, "They've been having some attempted break-ins over at the church. I'm watching to see if whoever's been doing it comes back."

"Man, sitting out here all night—this is some piss-poor assignment they gave you."

"You have no idea."

"Well, I'll leave before I draw any more attention to you. Good hunting."

"Thanks."

"And next time, tell the shift commander to let the rest of us know what's going on so we don't screw things up."

"I'll make a point of it."

The officer got back in his cruiser, turned off the flashing lights, passed Romero's car, waved, and steered onto Old Pecos Trail. Instantly, Romero grabbed the plastic jug and urinated for what seemed a minute and a half. When he finished and leaned back, sighing, his sense of relaxation lasted only as long as it took him to study Old Pecos Trail again.

The next thing, he scrambled out of his car and ran cursing toward a pair of men's shoes—they turned out to be Rockports—lying laced together in the middle of the road.

*   *   *

"Did you tell Tony Ortega you'd been ordered to stake out the Baptist church?" his sergeant demanded.

Romero reluctantly nodded.

"What kind of bullshit is that? Nobody put you on any stakeout. Sitting in a car all night, acting suspicious. You'd better have a damned good reason for—"

Romero didn't have a choice. "The shoes."

"What?"

"The shoes I keep finding on Old Pecos Trail."

His eyes wide, the sergeant listened to Romero's explanation. "You don't put in enough hours? You want to donate a couple nights free overtime on some crazy—"

"Hey, I know it's a little unusual."

"A *little*?"

"Whoever's dumping those shoes is playing some kind of game."

"And you want to play it with him."

"What?"

"He leaves the shoes. You take them. He leaves more shoes. You take them. You're playing his game."

"No, it isn't like that."

"Well, what *is* it like? Listen to me. Quit hanging around that street. Somebody might shoot you for a prowler."

When Romero finished his shift, he found a dozen old shoes piled in front of his locker. Somebody laughed in the lunchroom.

"I'm Officer Romero, ma'am, and I guess I made you a little nervous last night and two nights earlier. I was in my car, watching the church across the street. We had a report that somebody might try to break in. It seems you thought *I'm* the one who might try breaking in. I just wanted to assure you the neighborhood's perfectly safe with me parked out there."

"I'm Officer Romero, sir, and I guess I made you a little nervous last night and two nights earlier."

This time, he had everything under control. No more large Cokes and coffees, although he did keep his plastic jug, just in case. He made sure to bring a jacket, although the frost danger had finally passed and the night temperature was warmer. He was trying to eat better, too, munching on a *burrito grande con pollo* from Felipe's, the best Mexican takeout in town. He settled back and listened to the radio call-in show on the Walkman. The program was still on the environmental theme: "Hey, man, I used to be able to swim in the rivers when I was a kid. I used to be able to eat the fish I caught in them. I'd be nuts to do that now."

It was just after dark. The headlights of a car went past. No shoes. No problem. Romero was ready to be patient. He was in a rhythm. Nothing would probably happen until it usually did—after eleven. The Walkman's earphones pinched his head. He took them off and readjusted them as headlights sped past, heading to the right, out of town. Simultaneously, a different pair of headlights rushed past, heading to the left, *into* town. Romero's window was down. Despite the sound of the engines, he heard a distinct *thunk,* then another. The vehicles were gone, and he gaped at two hiking boots on the road.

Holy . . .

Move! He twisted the ignition key and yanked the gearshift into drive. Breathless, he urged the car forward, its rear tires spewing stones and dirt, but as he reached Old Pecos Trail, he faced a hurried decision. Which driver had dropped the shoes? Which car? Right or left?

He didn't have any jurisdiction out of town. Left! His tires squealing on the pavement, he sped toward the receding taillights. The road dipped, then rose toward the stoplight at Cordova, which was red and which Romero hoped would stay that way, but as he sped closer to what he now saw was a pickup truck, the light changed to green, and the truck drove through the intersection.

Shit.

Romero had an emergency light on the passenger seat. Shaped like a dome, it was plugged into the cigarette lighter. He thrust it out the window and onto the roof, where its magnetic base held it in place. Turning it on, seeing the reflection of its flashing red light, he pressed harder on the accelerator. He sped through the intersection, rushed up behind the pickup truck, blared his horn, and nodded when the truck went slower, angling toward the side of the road.

Romero wasn't in uniform, but he did have his 9mm Beretta in a holster on his belt. He made sure that his badge was clipped onto the breast pocket of his denim jacket. He aimed his flashlight toward a load of rocks in the back of the truck, then carefully approached the driver. "License and registration, please."

"What seems to be the trouble, Officer?" The driver was Anglo, young, about twenty-three. Thin. With short sandy hair. Wearing a red-and-brown-checked work shirt. Even sitting, he was tall.

"You were going awfully fast coming over that hill by the church."

The young man glanced back, as if to remind himself that there'd been a hill.

"License and registration," Romero repeated.

"I'm sure I wasn't going more than the speed limit," the young man said. "It's forty there, isn't it?" He handed over his license and pulled the registration from a pouch on the sun visor above his head.

Romero read the name. "Luke Parsons."

"Yes, sir." The young man's voice was reedy, with a gentle politeness.

"P.O. Box 25, Dillon, New Mexico?" Romero asked.

"Yes, sir. That's about fifty miles north. Up past Espanola and Embudo and—"

"I know where Dillon is. What brings you down here?"

"Selling moss rocks at the roadside stand off the Interstate."

Romero nodded. The rocks in the back of the truck were valued locally for their use in landscaping, the lichenlike moss that speckled them turning pleasant muted colors after a rain. Hardscrabble vendors gathered them in the mountains and sold them, along with homemade birdhouses, self-planed roof-support beams, firewood, and vegetables in season, at a clearing off a country road that paralleled the Interstate.

"Awful far from Dillon to be selling moss rocks," Romero said.

"Have to go where the customers are. Really, what's this all a—"

"You're selling after dark?"

"I wait until dusk in case folks coming out of Harry's Road House or the steak house farther along decide to stop and buy something. Then I go over to Harry's and get something to eat. Love his barbecued vegetables."

This wasn't how Romero had expected the conversation to go. He had anticipated that the driver would look uneasy because he'd lost the game. But the young man's politeness was disarming.

"I want to talk to you about those shoes you threw out of the car. There's a heavy fine for—"

"Shoes?"

"You've been doing it for several days. I want to know why—"

"Officer, honestly, I haven't the faintest idea what you're talking about."

"The shoes I saw you throw onto the road."

"Believe me, whatever you saw happen, it wasn't me doing it. Why would I throw shoes on the road?"

The young man's blue eyes were direct, his candid look disarming. Damn it, Romero thought, I went after the wrong car.

Inwardly, he sighed.

He gave back the license and registration. "Sorry to bother you."

"No problem, Officer. I know you have to do your job."

"Going all the way back to Dillon tonight?"

"Yes, sir."

"As I said, it's a long way to travel to sell moss rocks."

"Well, we do what we have to do."

"That's for sure," Romero said. "Drive safely."

"I always do, Officer. Good night."

"Good night."

Romero drove back to the top of the hill, picked up the hiking shoes, and put them in the trunk of his car. It was about that time, a little before ten, that his son was killed.

He passed the crash site on the way home to Pecos. Seeing the flashing lights and the silhouettes of two ambulances and three police cars on the opposite section of the Interstate, grimacing at the twisted wrecks of two vehicles, he couldn't help thinking, Poor bastards. God help them. But God didn't, and by the time Romero got home, the medical examiner was showing the state police the wallet that he had taken from the mutilated body of what seemed to be a young Hispanic male.

Romero and his wife were arguing about his late hours when the phone rang.

"Answer it!" she yelled. "It's probably your damned girlfriend."

"I keep telling you I don't have a—" The phone rang again. "Yeah, hello."

"Gabe? This is Ray Becker with the state police. Sit down, would you?"

As Romero listened, he felt a cold ball grow inside him. He had never felt so numb, not even when he'd been told about the deaths of his parents.

His wife saw his stunned look. *"What is it?"*

Trembling, he managed to overcome his numbness enough to tell her. She screamed. She never stopped screaming until she collapsed.

★   ★   ★

Two weeks later, after the funeral, after Romero's wife went to visit her sister in Denver, after Romero tried going back to work (his sergeant advised against it, but Romero knew he'd go crazy just sitting around home), the dispatcher sent him on a call that forced him to drive up Old Pecos Trail by the Baptist church. Bitterly, he remembered how fixated he had been on this spot not long ago. Instead of screwing around wondering about those shoes, I should have stayed home and paid attention to my son, he thought. Maybe I could have prevented what happened.

There weren't any shoes on the road.

There weren't any shoes on the road the next day or the day after that.

Romero's wife never came back from Denver.

"You have to get out more," his sergeant told him.

It was three months later, the middle Saturday of August. As a part of the impending divorce settlement and as a way of trying to stifle memories, Romero had sold the house in Pecos. With his share of the proceeds, he had moved to Santa Fe and risked a down payment on a modest house in the El Dorado subdivision. It didn't make a difference. He still had the sense of carrying a weight on his back.

"I hope you're not talking about dating."

"I'm just saying you can't stay holed up in this house all the time. You have to get out and do something. Distract yourself. While I think of it, you ought to be eating better. Look at the crap in this fridge. Stale milk, a twelve-pack of beer, and some leftover Chicken McNuggets."

"Most of the time I'm not hungry."

"With a fridge like this, I don't doubt it."

"I don't like cooking for myself."

"It's too much effort to make a salad? I tell you what. Saturdays, Maria and I go to the Farmers' Market. Tomorrow morning, you come with us. The vegetables don't come any fresher. Maybe if you had some decent food in this fridge, you'd—"

"What's wrong with me the Farmers' Market isn't going to cure."

"Hey, I'm knocking myself out trying to be a friend. The least you can do is humor me."

★   ★   ★

The Farmers' Market was near the old train station, past the tracks, in an open area the city had recently purchased called the Rail Yard. Farmers drove their loaded pickups in and parked in spaces they'd been assigned. Some set up tables and put up awnings. Others just sold from the back of their trucks. There were taste samples of everything from pies to salsa. A bluegrass band played in a corner. Somebody dressed up as a clown wandered through the crowd.

"See, it's not so bad," the sergeant said.

Romero walked listlessly past stands of cider, herbal remedies, free-range chicken, and sunflower sprouts. In a detached way, he had to admit, "Yeah, not so bad." All the years he'd worked for the police department, he'd never been here—another example of how he'd let his life pass him by. But instead of motivating him to learn from his mistakes, his regret only made him more depressed.

"How about some of these little pies?" the sergeant's wife asked. "You can keep them in the freezer and heat one up when you feel like it. They're only one or two servings, so you won't have any leftovers."

"Sure," Romero said, not caring. "Why not?" His dejected gaze drifted over the crowd.

"What kind?"

"Excuse me?"

"What kind? Peach or butter pecan?"

"It doesn't matter. Choose some for me."

His gaze settled on a stand that offered religious icons made out of corn husks layered over carved wood: Madonnas, manger scenes, and crosses. The skillfully formed images were painted and covered with a protective layer of varnish. It was a traditional Hispanic folk art, but what caught Romero's attention wasn't the attractiveness of the images but rather that an Anglo instead of a Hispanic was selling them as if he'd made them.

"This apple pie looks good, too," the sergeant's wife said.

"Fine." Assessing the tall, thin, sandy-haired man selling the icons, Romero added, "I know that guy from somewhere."

"What?" the sergeant's wife asked.

"Nothing. I'll be back in a second to get the pies." Romero made his way through the crowd. The young man's fair hair was extremely short. His thin face emphasized his cheekbones, making him look as if he'd been fasting. He had an aesthetic quality similar to that on the faces of the icons he was selling. Not that he looked ill. The opposite. His tan skin glowed.

His voice, too, seemed familiar. As Romero approached, he heard the reedy gentle tone with which the young man explained to a customer the intricate care with which the icons were created.

Romero waited until the customer walked off with her purchase. "Yes, sir?"

"I know you from somewhere, but I just can't seem to place you."

"I wish I could help you, but I don't think we've met."

Romero noticed the small crystal that hung from a woven cord on the young man's neck. It had a hint of pale blue in it, as if borrowing some of the blue in the young man's eyes. "Maybe you're right. It's just that you seem so awfully—"

Movement to his right distracted him, a young man carrying a large basket of tomatoes from a pickup truck and setting it next to baskets of cucumbers, peppers, squash, carrots, and other vegetables on a stand next to this one.

But more than the movement distracted him. The young man was tall and thin, with short sandy hair and a lean aesthetic face. He had clear blue eyes that seemed to lend some of their color to the small crystal hanging from his neck. He wore faded jeans and a white T-shirt, the same as the young man to whom Romero had been talking. The white of the shirt emphasized his glowing tan.

"You *are* right," Romero told the first man. "We haven't met. Your brother's the one I met."

The newcomer looked puzzled.

"It's true, isn't it?" Romero asked. "The two of you are brothers? That's why I got confused. But I still can't remember where—"

"Luke Parsons." The newcomer extended his hand.

"Gabe Romero."

The young man's forearm was sinewy, his handshake firm.

Romero needed all of his discipline and training not to react, his mind reeling as he remembered. Luke Parsons? Christ, this was the man he had spoken to the night his son had been killed and his life had fallen apart. To distract himself from his memories, he had come to this market, only to find someone who reminded him of what he was desperately trying to forget.

"And this is my brother Mark."

"Hello."

"Say, are you feeling all right?"

"Why? What do you—"

"You turned pale all of a sudden."

"It's nothing. I just haven't been eating well lately."

"Then you ought to try this." Luke Parsons pointed toward a small bottle filled with brown liquid.

Romero narrowed his eyes. "What is it?"

"Home-grown echinacea. If you've got a virus, this'll take care of you. Boosts your immune system."

"Thanks but—"

"When you feel how dramatically it picks you up—"

"You make it sound like drugs."

"God's drug. Nothing false. If it doesn't improve your well-being, we'll give you a refund."

"There you are," Romero's sergeant said. "I've been looking all over for you." He noticed the bottle in Romero's hand. "What's *that*?"

"Something called home-grown . . ." The word eluded him.

"Echinacea," Luke Parsons said.

"Sure," the sergeant's wife said. "I use it when we get colds. Boosts the immune system. Works like a charm. Lord, these tomatoes look wonderful."

As she started buying, Luke told Romero, "When your appetite's off, it can mean your body needs to be detoxified. These cabbage, broccoli, and cauliflower are good for that. Completely organic. No chemicals of any kind ever went near them. And you might try *this*." He handed Romero a small bottle of white liquid.

"Milk thistle," the sergeant's wife said, glancing at the bottle while selecting green peppers. "Cleans out the liver."

"Where on earth did you learn about this stuff?" the sergeant asked.

"Rosa down the street got interested in herbal remedies," she answered as the three of them crossed the train tracks carrying sacks of vegetables. "Hey, this is Santa Fe, the world's capital of alternate medicines and New Age religions. If you can't beat 'em, join 'em."

"Yeah, those crystals around their necks. They're New Agers for sure," Romero said. "Did you notice their belts were made of hemp? No leather. Nothing from animals."

"No fried chicken and take-out burgers for those guys." The sergeant gave Romero a pointed look. "They're as healthy as can be."

"All right, okay, I get it."

"Just make sure you eat your greens."

★   ★   ★

The odd part was that he actually did start feeling better. Physically, at least. His emotions were still as bleak as midnight, but as one of the self-help books he'd read had said, "One way to heal yourself is from the body to the soul." The echinacea (ten drops in a glass of water, the typed directions said) tasted bitter. The milk thistle tasted worse. The salads didn't fill him up. He still craved a pepperoni pizza. But he had to admit, the vegetables at the Farmers' Market were as good as any he'd come across. No surprise. The only vegetables he'd eaten before came from a supermarket, where they'd sat for God knew how long, and that didn't count all the time they'd been in a truck on the way to the store. They'd probably been picked before they were ready so they wouldn't ripen until they reached the supermarket, and then there was the issue of how many pesticides and herbicides they'd been doused with. He remembered a radio call-in show that had talked about poisons in food. The program had dealt with similar problems in the environment and—

Romero shivered.

That program had been the one he'd listened to in his car the night he'd been waiting for the shoes to drop and his son had been killed.

Screw it. If I'm going to feel this bad, I'm going to eat what I want.

It took him only fifteen minutes to drive in from El Dorado and get a big take-out order of ribs, fries, cole slaw, and plenty of barbecue sauce. He never ate in restaurants anymore. Too many people knew him. He couldn't muster the energy for small talk. Another fifteen minutes and he was back at home, watching a lawyer show, drinking beer, gnawing on ribs.

He was sick before the ten o'clock news.

"I swear, I'm keeping to my diet. Hey, don't look at me like that. I admit I had a couple of relapses, but I learned my lesson. I've never eaten more wholesome food in my life."

"Fifteen pounds. That health club I joined really sweats the weight off."

★   ★   ★

"Hi, Mark."

The tall, thin, sandy-haired young man behind the vegetables looked puzzled at him.

"What's wrong?" Romero asked. "I've been coming to this market every Saturday for the past six weeks. You don't recognize me by now?"

"You've confused me with my brother." The man had blue eyes, a hint of their color in the crystal around his neck. Jeans, a white T-shirt, a glowing tan, and the thin-faced, high-cheekboned aesthetic look of a saint.

"Well, I know you're not Luke. I'm sure I'd recognize *him*."

"My name is John." His tone was formal.

"Pleased to meet you. I'm Gabe Romero. Nobody told me there were *three* brothers."

"Actually—"

"Wait a minute. Let me guess. If there's a Mark, Luke, and John, there's got to be a Matthew, right? I bet there are *four* of you."

John's lips parted slightly, as if he wasn't accustomed to smiling. "Very good."

"No big deal. It's my business to deduce things," Romero joked.

"Oh? And what business is—" John straightened, his blue eyes as cold as a star, watching Luke come through the crowd. "You were told not to leave the stand."

"I'm sorry. I had to go to the bathroom."

"You should have gone before we started out."

"I did. But I can't help it if—"

"That's right. You can't help me if you're not here. We're almost out of squash. Bring another basket."

"I'm really sorry. It won't happen again."

Luke glanced self-consciously at Romero, then back at his brother, and went to get the squash.

"Are you planning to buy something?" John asked.

You don't exactly win friends and influence people, do you? Romero thought. "Yeah, I'll take a couple of those squash. I guess with the early frost that's predicted, these'll be the last of the tomatoes and peppers, huh?"

John simply looked at him.

"I'd better stock up," Romero said.

★　　★　　★

He had hoped that the passage of time would ease his numbness, but each season only reminded him. Christmas, New Year's, then Easter, and too soon after that, the middle of May. Oddly, he had never associated his son's death with the scene of the accident on the Interstate. Always the emotional connection was with that section of road by the Baptist church at the top of the hill on Old Pecos Trail. He readily admitted that it was masochism that made him drive by there so often as the anniversary of the death approached. He was so preoccupied that for a moment he was convinced that he had willed himself into reliving the sequence, that he was hallucinating as he crested the hill and for the first time in almost a year saw a pair of shoes on the road.

Rust-colored, ankle-high hiking boots. They so surprised him that he slowed down and stared. The close look made him notice something so alarming that he slammed on his brakes, barely registering the squeal of tires behind him as the car that followed almost hit the cruiser. Trembling, he got out, crouched, stared even more closely at the hiking boots, and rushed toward his two-way radio.

The shoes had feet in them.

As an approaching police car wailed and officers motioned for traffic to go past on the shoulder of the road, Romero stood with his sergeant, the police chief, and the medical examiner, watching the lab crew do its work. His cruiser remained where he had stopped it next to the shoes. A waist-high screen had been put up.

"I'll know more when we get the evidence to the lab," the medical examiner said, "but judging from the straight clean lines, I'm assuming that something like a power saw was used to sever the feet from the legs."

Romero bit his lower lip.

"Anything else you can tell us right away?" the police chief asked.

"There isn't any blood on the pavement, which means that the blood on the shoes and the stumps of the feet was dry before they were dropped here. The discoloration of the tissue suggests that at least twenty-four hours passed between the crime and the disposal."

"Anybody notice anything else?"

"The size of the shoes," Romero said.

They looked at him.

"Mine are tens. These look to be sevens or eights. My guess is, the victim was female."

The same police officers who had left the pile of old shoes in front of Romero's locker now praised his instincts. Although he had long since discarded the various shoes that he had collected in the trunk of the police car and of his private vehicle, no one blamed him. After all, so much time had gone by, who could have predicted that the shoes would be important? Still, he remembered what kind they had been, just as he remembered that he had started noticing them almost exactly a year ago, around the fifteenth of May.

But there was no guarantee that the person who had dropped the shoes a year ago was the person who had left the severed feet. All the investigating team could do was deal with the little evidence they had. As Romero suspected, the medical examiner eventually determined that the victim had indeed been a woman. Was the person responsible a tourist, someone who came back to Santa Fe each May? If so, would that person have committed similar crimes somewhere else? Inquiries to the FBI revealed that over the years numerous murders by amputation had been committed throughout the United States, but none matched the profile that the team was dealing with. What about missing persons reports? Those in New Mexico were eliminated, but as the search spread, it became clear that so many thousands of people disappeared in the United States each month that the investigation team would need more staff than it could ever hope to have.

Meanwhile, Romero was part of the team staking out that area of Old Pecos Trail. Each night, he used a night-vision telescope to watch from the roof of the Baptist church. After all, if the killer stayed to his pattern, other shoes would be dropped, and perhaps—God help us, Romero thought—they too would contain severed feet. If he saw anything suspicious, all he needed to do was focus on the car's license plate and then use his two-way radio to alert police cars hidden along Old Pecos Trail. But night after night, there was nothing to report.

A week later, a current model red Saturn with New Hampshire plates was found abandoned in an arroyo southeast of Albuquerque. The car was registered to a thirty-year-old woman named Susan Crowell, who had set out with her fiancé on a cross-country car tour three weeks earlier. Neither she nor her fiancé had contacted their friends and relatives in the past eight days.

★   ★   ★

May became June, then July. The Fourth of July pancake breakfast in the historic plaza was its usual success. Three weeks later, Spanish Market occupied the same space, local Hispanic artisans displaying their paintings, icons, and woodwork. Tourist attendance was down, the sensationalist publicity about the severed feet having discouraged some visitors from coming. But a month after that, the similar but larger Indian Market occurred, and memories were evidently short, for now the usual thirty thousand tourists thronged the plaza to admire Native American jewelry and pottery.

Romero was on duty for all of these events, making sure that everything proceeded in an orderly fashion. Still, no matter the tasks assigned to him, his mind was always back on Old Pecos Trail. Some nights, he couldn't stay away. He drove over to East Lupita, watched the passing headlights on Old Pecos Trail, and brooded. He didn't expect anything to happen, not as fall approached, but being there made him feel on top of things, helped focus his thoughts, and in an odd way gave him a sense of being close to his son. Sometimes, the presence of the church across the street made him pray.

One night, a familiar pickup truck filled with moss rocks drove by. Romero remembered it from the night his son had been killed and from so many summer Saturdays when he'd watched baskets of vegetables being carried from it to a stand at the Farmers' Market. He had never stopped associating it with the shoes. Granted, at the time he'd been certain that he'd stopped the wrong vehicle. He didn't have a reason to take the huge step of suspecting that Luke Parsons had anything to do with the murders of Susan Crowell and her fiancé. Nonetheless, he had told the investigation team about that night previous year, and they had checked Luke out as thoroughly as possible. He and his three brothers lived with their father on a farm in the Rio Grande gorge north of Dillon. They were hard workers, kept to themselves, and stayed out of trouble.

Seeing the truck pass, Romero didn't have a reason to make it stop, but that didn't mean he couldn't follow it. He pulled onto Old Pecos Drive and kept the truck's taillights in view as it headed into town. It turned right at the state capitol building and proceeded along Paseo de Peralta until on the other side of town it steered into an Allsup's gas station.

Romero chose a pump near the pickup truck, got out of his Jeep, and pretended to be surprised by the man next to him.

"Luke, it's Gabe Romero. How are you?"

Then he *was* surprised, realizing his mistake. This wasn't Luke.

"*John?* I didn't recognize you."

The tall, thin, sandy-haired, somber-eyed young man assessed him. He lowered his eyes to the holstered pistol on Romero's hip. Romero had never worn it to the Farmers' Market. "I didn't realize you were a police officer."

"Does it matter?"

"Only that it's reassuring to know my vegetables are safe when you're around." John's stern features took the humor out of the joke.

"Or your moss rocks." Romero pointed toward the back of the truck. "Been selling them over on that country road by the Interstate? That's usually Luke's job."

"Well, he has other things to do."

"Yeah, now that I think of it, I haven't seen him at the market lately."

"Excuse me. It's been a long day. It's a long drive back."

"You bet. I didn't mean to keep you."

Luke wasn't at the Farmer's Market the next Saturday or the final one the week after that.

Late October. There'd been a killing frost the night before, and in the morning there was snow in the mountains. Since the Farmers' Market was closed for the year and Romero had his Saturday free, he thought, Why don't I take a little drive?

The sunlight was cold, crisp, and clear as Romero headed north along Highway 285. He crested the hill near the modernistic Sante Fe Opera House and descended from the juniper-and-piñon-dotted slopes of town into a multicolored desert, its draws and mesas stretching dramatically away toward white-capped mountains on each side. No wonder Hollywood made so many westerns here, he thought. He passed the Camel Rock Indian casino and the Cities of Gold Indian casino, reaching what had once been another eternal construction project, the huge interchange that led west to Los Alamos.

But instead of heading toward the atomic city, he continued north, passing through Espanola, and now the landscape changed again, the hills on each side coming closer, the narrow highway passing between the ridges of the Rio Grande gorge. WATCH OUT FOR FALLING ROCK, a sign said. Yeah, I intend to watch out, he thought. On his left, partially screened by leafless trees, was the legendary Rio Grande, narrow, taking its time in the fall, gliding around curves, bubbling over boulders. On the far side of the river was Embudo Station, an old stagecoach stop the historic buildings of which had been converted into a microbrewery and a restaurant.

He passed it, heading farther north, and now the gorge began to widen. Farms and vineyards appeared on both sides of the road, where silt from melting during the Ice Age had made the soil rich. He stopped in Dillon, took care that his handgun was concealed by his zipped-up windbreaker, and asked at the general store if anybody knew where he could find the Parsons farm.

Fifteen minutes later, he had the directions he wanted. But instead of going directly to the farm, he drove to a scenic view outside town and waited for a state police car to pull up beside him. During the morning's drive, he had used his cellular phone to contact the state police barracks farther north in Taos. After explaining who he was, he had persuaded the dispatcher to send a cruiser down to meet him.

"I don't anticipate trouble," Romero told the burly trooper as they stood outside their cars and watched the Rio Grande flow through a chasm beneath them. "But you never know."

"So what do you want me to do?"

"Just park at the side of the highway. Make sure I come back out of the farm."

"Your department didn't send you up here?"

"Self-initiative. I've got a hunch."

The trooper looked doubtful. "How long are you going to be in there?"

"Considering how unfriendly they are, not long. Fifteen minutes. I just want to get a sense of the place."

"If I get a call about an emergency down the road . . ."

"You'll have to go. But I'd appreciate it if you came back and made sure I left the property. On my way to Santa Fe, I'll stop at the general store in Dillon and leave word that I'm okay."

The state trooper still looked doubtful.

"I've been working on this case a long time," Romero said. "Please, I'd really appreciate the help."

The dirt road was just after a sign that read, TAOS, 20 MILES. It was on the left of the highway and led down a slope toward fertile bottomland. To the north and west, ridges bordered the valley. Well-maintained rail fences enclosed rich, black soil. The Parsonses were certainly hard workers, he had to admit. With cold weather about to arrive, the fields had been cleared, everything ready for spring.

The road headed west toward a barn and outbuildings, all of them neat-looking, their white appearing freshly painted. A simple wood frame house, also white, had a pitched metal roof that gleamed in the autumn sun. Beyond the house was the river, about thirty feet wide, with a raised footbridge leading across to leafless aspen trees and scrub brush trailing up a slope.

As he drove closer, Romero saw movement at the barn, someone getting off a ladder, putting down a paint can. Someone else appeared at the barn's open doors. A third person came out of the house. They were waiting in front of the house as Romero pulled up and stopped.

This was the first time he'd seen three of the brothers together, their tall, lean, sandy-haired, blue-eyed similarities even more striking. They wore the same denim coveralls with the same blue wool shirts underneath.

But Romero was well enough acquainted with them that he could tell one from another. The brother on the left, about nineteen, must be the one he had never met.

"I assume you're Matthew." Romero got out of the car and walked toward them, extending his hand.

No one made a move to shake hands with him.

"I don't see Luke," Romero said.

"He has things to do," John said.

Their features were pinched.

"Why did you come here?" Mark asked.

"I was driving up to Taos. While I was in the neighborhood, I thought I'd drop by and see if you had any vegetables for sale."

"You're not welcome."

"What kind of attitude is that? For somebody who's been as good a customer as I have, I thought you might be pleased to see me."

"Leave."

"But don't you want my business?"

"Matthew, go in the house and bring me the phone. I'm going to call the state police."

The young man nodded and turned toward the house.

"That's fine," Romero said. "I'll be on my way."

★   ★   ★

The trooper was at the highway when Romero drove out.

"Thanks for the backup."

"You'd better not thank me. I just got a call about you. Whatever you did in there, you really pissed them off. The dispatcher says, if you come back they want you arrested for trespassing."

". . . the city's attorney," the police chief said.

The man's handshake was unenthusiastic.

"And this is Mr. Daly, the attorney for Mr. Parsons," the chief said.

An even colder handshake.

"Mr. Parsons you've definitely met," the chief said.

Romero nodded to John.

"I'll get right to the point," Daly said. "You've been harassing my client, and we want it stopped."

"Harassing? Wait a minute. I haven't been harassing—"

"Detaining the family vehicle without just cause. Intimidating my client and his brothers at their various places of business. Following my client. Confronting him in public places. Invading his property and refusing to leave when asked to. You crowd him just about everywhere he goes, and we want it stopped or we'll sue both you and the city. Juries don't like rogue cops."

"Rogue cop? What are you talking about?"

"I didn't come here to debate this." Daly stood, motioning for John to do the same. "My client's completely in the right. This isn't a police state. You, your department, and the city have been warned. Any more incidents, and I'll call a press conference to let every potential juror know why we're filing the lawsuit."

With a final searing gaze, Daly left the room. John followed almost immediately but not before he gave Romero a victimized look that made Romero's face turn warm with anger.

The office became silent.

The city attorney cleared his throat. "I don't suppose I have to tell you to stay away from him."

"But I haven't done anything wrong."

"Did you follow him? Did you go to his home? Did you ask the state police in Taos for backup when you entered the property?"

Romero looked away.

"You were out of your jurisdiction, acting completely on your own."

"These brothers have something to do with—"

"They were investigated and cleared."

"I can't explain. It's a feeling that keeps nagging at me."

"Well, *I* have a feeling," the attorney said. "If you don't stop exceeding your authority, you're going to be out of a job, not to mention in court trying to explain to a jury why you harassed a group of brothers who look like advertisements for hard work and family values. Matthew, Mark, Luke, and John, for God sake. If it wouldn't look like an admission of guilt, I'd recommend your dismissal right now."

Romero got the worst assignments. If a snowstorm took out power at an intersection and traffic needed to be directed by hand, he was at the top of the list to do it. Anything that involved the outdoors and bad weather, he was the man. Obviously, the police chief was inviting him to quit.

But Romero had a secret defense. The heat that had flooded his face when John gave him that victimized look hadn't gone away. It had stayed and spread, possessing his body. Directing traffic in a foot of snow, with a raging storm and a wind chill near zero? No problem. Anger made him as warm as could be.

John Parsons had arrogantly assumed he'd won. Romero was going to pay him back. May 15. That was about the time the shoes had appeared two years ago, and the severed feet last year. The chief was planning some surveillance on that section of Old Pecos Trail, but nobody believed that if the killer planned to act again, he'd be stupid enough to be that predictable. For certain, Romero wasn't going to be predictable. He wasn't going to play John's game and risk his job by hanging around Old Pecos Trail so that John could drive by and claim that the harassment had started again. No, Old Pecos Trail didn't interest him anymore. On May 15, he was going to be somewhere else.

Outside Dillon. In the Rio Grande gorge.

He planned it for quite a while. First, he had to explain his absence. A vacation. He hadn't taken one last year. San Francisco. He'd never been there. It was supposed to be especially beautiful in the spring. The chief looked pleased, as if he hoped Romero would look for a job there.

Second, his quarry knew the kind of car he drove. He traded his five-year-old green Jeep for a three-year-old blue Ford Explorer.

Third, he needed equipment. The night-vision telescope he'd used to watch Old Pecos Trail from the top of the church had made darkness so vivid that he bought a similar model from a military surplus store. He went to a camera store and bought a powerful zoom lens for the 35mm camera he had at home. Food and water for several days. Outdoor clothing. Something to carry everything in. Hiking shoes sturdy enough to support all the weight.

His vacation started on May 13. When he'd last driven to Dillon, autumn had made the Rio Grande calm, but now the spring snowmelt widened and deepened it, cresting it into a rage. Green trees and shrubs bordered the foaming water as white-water rafters shot through roiling channels and jounced over hidden rocks. As he drove past the entrance to the Parsons farm, he worried that one of the brothers might drive out and notice him, but then he reminded himself that they didn't know this car. He stared to his left at the rich black land, the white buildings in the distance, and the glinting metal roof of the house. At the far edge of the farm, the river raged high enough that it almost snagged the raised footbridge.

He put a couple of miles between him and the farm before he stopped. On his left, a rest area underneath cottonwoods looked to be the perfect place. A few other cars were there, all of them empty. White-water rafters, he assumed. At the end of the day, someone would drive them back to get their vehicles. In all the coming and going, his car would be just one of many that were parked there. To guard against someone's wondering why the car was there all night and worrying that he had drowned, he left a note on his dashboard that read, "Hiking and camping along the river. Back in a couple of days."

He opened the rear hatch, put on the heavy backpack, secured its straps, locked the car, and walked down a rocky slope, disappearing among bushes. He had spent several evenings at home, practicing with the fully loaded knapsack, but his brick floors hadn't prepared him for the uneven terrain that he now labored over—rocks, holes, and fallen branches, each jarring step seeming to add weight to his backpack. More, he had practiced in the cool of evening, but now, in the heat of the day, with the temperature predicted to reach a high of eighty, he sweated profusely, his wet clothes clinging to him.

His pack weighed sixty pounds. Without it, he was sure he could have reached the river in ten minutes. Under the circumstances, he took twenty. Not bad, he thought, hearing the roar of the current. Emerging from the scrub brush, he was startled by how fast and high the water was, how humblingly powerful. It was so swift that it created a breeze, for which he was grateful as he set down his backpack and flexed his stiff shoulders. He drank from his canteen. The water had been cool when he had left the house but was now tepid, with a vague metallic taste.

Get to work, he told himself.

Without the backpack, the return walk to the car was swift. In a hurry, he unlocked the Explorer, removed another sack, relocked the car, and carried his second burden down the slope into the bushes, reaching the river five minutes sooner than he had earlier. The sack contained a small rubber raft, which after he used a pressurized cannister to inflate it had plenty of room for himself and his backpack. Making sure that the latter was securely attached, he studied the heaving water, took a deep breath, exhaled, and pushed it into the river.

Icy water splashed across him. If not for his daily workouts on exercise machines, he never would have had the strength to paddle so hard and fast, constantly switching sides, keeping the raft from spinning. But the river carried him downstream faster than he had anticipated. He was in the middle, but no matter how hard he fought, he didn't seem to be getting closer to the other side. He didn't know what scared him worse, being overturned or not reaching the opposite bank before the current carried him to the farm. Jesus, if they see me . . . He worked his arms to their maximum. Squinting to see through spray, he saw that the river curved to the left. The current on the far side wasn't as strong. Paddling in a frenzy, he felt the raft shoot close to the bank. Ten feet. Five. He braced himself. The moment the raft jolted against the shore, he scrambled over the front rim, landed on the muddy bank, almost fell into the water, righted himself, and dragged the raft onto the shore.

His backpack sat in water in the raft. Hurriedly, he freed the straps that secured it, then dragged it onto dry land. Water trickled out the bottom. He could only hope that the waterproof bags into which he had sealed his food, clothes, and equipment had done their job. Had anyone seen him? He scanned the ridge behind him and the shore across from him—they seemed deserted. He overturned the raft, dumped the water out of it, tugged the raft behind bushes, and concealed it. He set several large rocks in it to keep it from blowing away, then returned to the shore and satisfied himself that the raft couldn't be seen. But he couldn't linger. He hoisted his pack onto his shoulders, ignored the strain on his muscles, and started inland.

Three hours later, after following a trail that led along the back of the ridge that bordered the river, he finished the long, slow, difficult hike to the top. The scrub brush was sparse, the rocks unsteady under his waffle-soled boots. Fifteen yards from the summit, he lowered his backpack and flexed his arms and shoulders to ease their cramps. Sweat dripped from his face. He drank from his canteen, the water even more tepid, then sank to the rocks and crept upward. Cautiously, he peered over the top. Below were the white barn and outbuildings. Sunlight gleamed off the white house's pitched metal roof. Portions of the land were green from early crops, one of which Romero recognized even from a distance: lettuce. No one was in view. He found a hollow, eased into it, and dragged his backpack after him. Two rocks on the rim concealed the silhouette of his head when he peered down between them. River, field, farmhouse, barn, more fields. A perfect vantage point.

Still, no one was in view. Some of them are probably in Santa Fe, he thought. As long as nothing's happening, this is a good time to get settled. He removed his night-vision telescope, his camera, and his zoom lens from the backpack. The waterproof bags had worked— the equipment was dry. So were his food and his sleeping bag. The only items that had gotten wet were a spare shirt and pair of jeans that, ironically, he had brought with him in case he needed a dry change of clothes. He spread them out in the sun, took another look at the farm—no activity—and ravenously reached for his food. Cheddar cheese, wheat crackers, sliced carrots, and a dessert of dehydrated apricots made his mouth water as he chewed them.

Five o'clock. One of the brothers crossed from the house to the barn. Hard to tell at a distance, but through the camera's zoom lens, Romero thought he recognized Mark.

Six-thirty. Small down there, the pickup truck arrived. It got bigger as Romero adjusted the zoom lens and recognized John getting out. Mark came out of the barn. Matthew came out of the house. John look displeased about something. Mark said something. Matthew stayed silent. They entered the house.

Romero's heart beat faster with the satisfaction that he was watching his quarry and they didn't know it. But his exhilaration faded as dusk thickened, lights came on in the house, and nothing else happened. Without the sun, the air cooled rapidly. As frost came out of his mouth, he put on gloves and a jacket.

Maybe I'm wasting my time, he thought.

Like hell. It's not the fifteenth yet.

The temperature continued dropping. His legs cold despite the jeans he wore, he squirmed into the welcome warmth of his sleeping bag and chewed more cheese and crackers as he switched from the zoom lens to the night-vision telescope. The scope brightened the darkness, turning everything green. The lights in the windows were radiant. One of the brothers left the house, but the scope's definition was a little grainy, and Romero couldn't tell who it was. The person went into the barn and returned to the house ten minutes later.

One by one, the lights went off. The house was soon in darkness.

Looks like the show's over for a while, Romero thought. It gave him an opportunity to get out of his sleeping bag, work his way down the slope, and relieve himself behind a bush. When he returned, the house seemed as quiet as when he had gone away.

Again, he reminded himself, today's not important. Tomorrow might not be, either. But the *next* day's the fifteenth.

He checked that his handgun and his cellular phone were within easy reach (all the comforts of home), settled deeper into the sleeping bag, and refocused the night-vision scope on the farm below. Nothing.

The cold made his eyes feel heavy.

A door slammed.

Jerking his head up, Romero blinked to adjust his eyes to the bright morning light. He squirmed from his sleeping bag and used the camera's zoom lens to peer down at the farm. John, Mark, and Matthew had come out of the house. They marched toward the nearest field, the one that had lettuce in it. The green shoots glistened from the reflection of sunlight off melted frost. John looked as displeased as on the previous evening, speaking irritably to his brothers. Mark said something in return. Matthew said nothing.

Romero frowned. This was one too many times that he hadn't seen Luke. What had happened to him? Adjusting the zoom lens, he watched the group go into the barn. Another question nagged at him. The police report had said that the brothers worked for their father, that this was their father's land. But when Romero had come to the farm the previous fall, he hadn't seen the father.

Or yesterday.

Or this morning.

Where the hell was he? Was the father somehow responsible for the shoes and . . .

Were the father and Luke not on the farm because they were somewhere else, doing . . .

The more questions he had, the more his mind spun.

He tensed, seeing a glint of something reflect off melted frost on grass beside the barn door. Frowning harder, he saw the glint dart back and forth, as if alive. Oh, my Jesus, he thought, suddenly realizing what it was, pulling his camera away from the rim. He was on the western ridge, staring east. The sun above the opposite ridge had reflected off his zoom lens. If the light had reflected while the brothers were outside . . .

The cold air felt even colder. Leaving the camera and its zoom lens well below the rim, he warily eased his head up and studied the barn. Five minutes later, the three brothers emerged and began to do chores. Watching, Romero opened a plastic bag of Cheerios, Wheat Chex, raisins, and nuts that he'd mixed together, munching the trail mix, washing it down with water. From the drop in temperature the previous night, the water in his canteen was again cold. But the canteen was almost empty. He had brought two others, and they would last him for a while. Eventually, though, he was going to have to return to the river and use a filtration pump to refill the canteens. Iodine tablets would kill the bacteria.

By mid-afternoon, the brothers were all in one field, Matthew on a tractor, tilling the soil, while John and Mark picked up large rocks that the winter had forced to the surface, carrying them to the back of the pickup truck.

I'm wasting my time, he thought. They're just farmers, for God sake.

Then why did John try to get me fired?

He clenched his teeth. With the sun behind his back, it was safe to use the camera's zoom lens. He scanned the farm, staring furiously at the brothers. The evening was a replay of the previous one. By ten, the house was in darkness.

Just one more day, Romero thought. Tomorrow's the fifteenth. Tomorrow's what I came for.

Pain jolted him into consciousness. A walloping burst of agony made his mind spin. A third cracking impact sent a flash of red behind his eyes. Stunned, he fought to overcome the shock of the attack and thrashed to get out of his sleeping bag. A blow across his shoulders knocked him sideways. Silhouetted against the starry sky, three figures surrounded him, their heavy breath frosty as they raised their clubs to strike him again. He grabbed his pistol and tried to free it from the sleeping bag, but a blow knocked it out of his numbed hand an instant before a club across his forehead made his ears ring and his eyes roll up.

He awoke slowly, his senses in chaos. Throbbing in his head. Blood on his face. The smell of it. Coppery. The nostril-irritating smell of stale straw under his left cheek. Shadows. Sunlight through cracks in a wall. The barn. Spinning. His stomach heaved.

The sour smell of vomit.

"Matthew, bring John," Mark said.

Rumbling footsteps ran out of the barn.

Romero passed out.

The next time he awoke, he was slumped in a corner, his back against a wall, his knees up, his head sagging, blood dripping onto his chest.

"We found your car," John said. "I see you changed models."

The echoing voice seemed to come from a distance, but when Romero looked blearily up, John was directly before him.

John read the note Romero had left on the dashboard. " 'Hiking and camping along the river. Back in a couple of days.' "

Romero noticed that his pistol was tucked under John's belt.

"What are we going to do?" Mark asked. "The police will come looking for him."

"So what?" John said. "We're in the right. We caught a man with a pistol who trespassed on our property at night. We defended ourselves and subdued him." John crumbled the note. "But the police won't come looking for him. They don't know he's here."

"You can't be sure," Mark said.

Matthew stood silently by the closed barn door.

"Of course, I can be sure," John said. "If this was a police operation, he wouldn't have needed this note. He wouldn't have been worried that someone would wonder about the abandoned car. In fact, he wouldn't have needed his car at all. The police would have driven him to the drop-off point. He's on his own."

Matthew fidgeted, continuing to watch.

"Isn't that right, Officer Romero?" John asked.

Fighting to control the spinning in his mind, Romero managed to get his voice to work. "How did you know I was up there?"

No one answered.

"It was the reflection from the camera lens, right?" Romero sounded as if his throat had been stuffed with gravel.

"Like the Holy Spirit on Pentecost," John said.

Romero's tongue was so thick he could barely speak. "I need water."

"I don't like this," Mark said. "Let him go."

John turned toward Matthew. "You heard him. He needs water."

Matthew hesitated, then opened the barn door and ran toward the house.

John returned his attention to Romero. "Why wouldn't you stop? Why did you have to be so persistent?"

"Where's Luke?"

"See, that's what I mean. You're so damnably persistent."

"We don't need to take this any further," Mark warned. "Put him in his car. Let him go. No harm's been done."

"Hasn't there?"

"You just said we were in the right to attack a stranger with a gun. After it was too late, we found out who he is. A judge would throw out an assault charge."

"He'd come back."

"Not necessarily."

"I guarantee it. Wouldn't you, Officer Romero? You'd come back."

Romero wiped blood from his face and didn't respond.

"Of course, you would," John said. "It's in your nature. And one day you'd see something you shouldn't. It may be you already have."

"Don't say anything more." Mark warned.

"You want to know what this is about?" John asked Romero.

Romero wiped more blood from his face.

"I think you should get what you want," John said.

"No," Mark said. "This can't go on anymore. I'm still not convinced he's here by himself. If the police are involved . . . It's too risky. It has to stop."

Footsteps rushed toward the barn. Only Romero looked as Matthew hurried inside, carrying a jug of water.

"Give it to him," John said.

Matthew warily approached, like someone apprehensive about a wild animal. He set the jug at Romero's feet and darted back.

"Thank you," Romero said.

Matthew didn't answer.

"Why don't you ever speak?" Romero asked.

Matthew didn't say anything.

Romero's skin prickled. "You can't."

Matthew looked away.

"Of course. Last fall when I was here, John told you to bring him the phone so he could call the state police. At the time, I didn't think anything of it." Romero waited for the swirling in his mind to stop. "I figured he was sending the weakest one of the group, so if I made trouble he and Mark could take care of it." Romero's lungs felt empty. He took several deep breaths. "But all the time I've been watching the house, you haven't said a word."

Matthew kept looking away.

"You're mute. That's why John told you to bring the phone. Because you couldn't call the state police yourself."

"Stop taunting my brother and drink the water," John said.

"I'm not taunting him. I just—"

"Drink it."

Romero fumbled for the jug, raised it to his lips, and swallowed, not caring about the sour taste from having been sick, wanting only to clear the mucus from his mouth and the gravel in his throat.

John pulled a clean handkerchief from his windbreaker pocket and threw it to him. "Pour water on it. Wipe the blood from your face. We're not animals. There's no need to be without dignity."

Baffled by the courtesy, Romero did what he was told. The more they treated him like a human being, the more chance he had of getting away from here. He tried desperately to think of a way to talk himself out of this. "You're wrong about the police not being involved."

"Oh?" John raised his eyebrows, waiting for Romero to continue.

"This isn't official, sure. But I do have backup. I told my sergeant what I planned to do. The deal is, if I don't use my cell phone to call him every six hours, he'll know something's wrong. He and a couple of friends on the force will come here looking for me."

"My, my. Is that a fact."

"Yes."

"Then why don't you call him and tell him you're all right?"

"Because I'm *not* all right. Look, I have no idea what's going on here, and all of a sudden, believe me, it's the last thing I want to find out. I just want to get out of here."

The barn became terribly silent.

"I made a mistake." Romero struggled to his feet. "I won't make it again. I'll leave. This is the last time you'll see me." Off balance, he stepped out of the corner.

John studied him.

"As far as I'm concerned, this is the end of it." Romero took another step toward the door.

"I don't believe you."

Romero stepped past him.

"You're lying about the cell phone and about your sergeant," John said.

Romero kept walking. "If I don't call him soon—"

John blocked his way.

"—he'll come looking for me."

"And here he'll find you."

"Being held against my will."

"So we'll be charged with kidnapping?" John spread his hands. "Fine. We'll tell the jury we were only trying to scare you to keep you from continuing to stalk us. I'm willing to take the chance that they won't convict us."

"What are you talking about?" Mark said.

"Let's see if his friends really come to the rescue."

Oh, shit, Romero thought. He took a further step toward the door.

John pulled out Romero's pistol.

"No!" Mark said.

"Matthew, help Mark with the trapdoor."

"This has to stop!" Mark said. *"Wasn't what happened to Matthew and Luke enough?"*

Like a tightly wound spring that was suddenly released, John whirled and struck Mark with such force that he knocked him to the floor. "Since when do you run this family?"

Wiping blood from his mouth, Mark glared up at him. "I don't. *You* do."

"That's right. I'm the oldest. That's always been the rule. If you'd have been meant to run this family, you'd have been the firstborn."

Mark kept glaring.

"Do you want to turn against the rule?" John asked.

Mark lowered his eyes. "No."

"Then help Matthew with the trapdoor."

Romero's stomach fluttered. All the while John aimed the pistol at him, he watched Mark and Matthew go to the far left corner, where it took both of them to shift a barrel of grain out of the way. They lifted a trapdoor, and Romero couldn't help bleakly thinking that someone pushing from below wouldn't have a chance of moving it when the barrel was in place.

"Get down there," John said.

Romero felt dizzier. Fighting to repress the sensation, he knew that he had to do something before he felt any weaker.

If John wanted me dead, he'd have killed me by now.

Romero bolted for the outside door.

"Mark!"

Something whacked against Romero's legs, tripping him, slamming his face hard onto the floor.

Mark had thrown a club.

The three brothers grabbed him. Dazed, the most powerless he'd ever felt, he thrashed, unable to pull away from their hands, as they dragged him across the dusty floor and shoved him through the trapdoor. If he hadn't grasped the ladder, he'd have fallen.

"You don't want to be without water." John handed the jug down to him.

A chill breeze drifted from below. Terrified, Romero watched the trapdoor being closed over him and heard the scrape of the barrel being shifted back into place.

God help me, he thought.

But he wasn't in darkness. Peering down, he saw a faint light and warily descended the ladder, moving awkwardly because of the jug he held. At the bottom, he found a short tunnel and proceeded along it. An earthy musty smell made his nostrils contract. The light became brighter as he neared its source in a small plywood-walled room that he saw had a wooden chair and table. The floor was made from plywood, also. The light came from a bare bulb attached to one of the sturdy beams in the ceiling. Stepping all the way in, he saw a cot on the left. A clean pillow and blanket were on it. To the right, a toilet seat was attached to a wooden box positioned above a deep hole in the ground. I'm going to lose my mind, he thought.

The breeze, weak now that the trapdoor was closed, came from a vent in an upper part of the farthest wall. Romero guessed that the duct would be long and that there would be baffles at the end so that, if Romero screamed for help, no one who happened to come onto the property would be able to hear him. The vent provided enough air that Romero wasn't worried about suffocating. There were plenty of other things to worry about, but at least not that.

The plywood of the floor and walls was discolored with age. Nonetheless, the pillow and the blanket had been stocked recently— when Romero raised them to his nose, there was a fresh laundry smell beneath the loamy odor that it had started absorbing.

The brothers couldn't have known I'd be here. They were expecting someone else.

Who?

Romero smelled something else. He told himself that it was only his imagination, but he couldn't help sensing that the walls were redolent with the sweaty stench of fear, as if many others had been imprisoned here.

His own fear made his mouth so dry that he took several deep swallows of water. Setting the jug on the table, he stared apprehensively at a door across from him. It was just a simple old wooden door, vertical planks held in place by horizontal boards nailed to the top, middle, and bottom, but it filled him with apprehension. He knew that he had to open it, that he had to learn if it gave him a way to escape, but he had a terrible premonition that something unspeakable waited on the other side. He told his legs to move. They refused. He told his right arm to reach for the doorknob. It, too, refused.

The spinning sensation in his mind was now aggravated by the short quick breaths he was taking. I'm hyperventilating, he realized, and struggled to return his breath rate to normal. Despite the coolness of the chamber, his face dripped sweat. In contrast, his mouth was drier than ever. He gulped more water.

Open the door.

His body reluctantly obeyed, his shaky legs taking him across the chamber, his trembling hand reaching for the doorknob. He pulled.

Nothing happened, and for a moment he thought that the door was locked, but when he pulled harder, the door creaked slowly open, the loamy odor from inside reaching his nostrils before his eyes adjusted to the shadows in there.

For a terrible instant, he thought he was staring at bodies. He almost stumbled back, inwardly screaming, until a remnant of his sanity insisted that he stare harder, that what he was looking at were bulging burlap sacks.

And baskets.

And shelves of . . .

Vegetables.

Potatoes, beets, turnips, onions.

Jesus, this was the root cellar under the barn. Repelled by the musty odor, he searched for another door. He tapped the walls, hoping for a hollow sound that would tell him there was an open space, perhaps another room or even the outside, beyond it.

He found nothing to give him hope.

"Officer Romero?" The faint voice came from the direction of the trapdoor.

Romero stepped out of the root cellar and closed the door.

"Officer Romero?" The voice sounded like John's.

Romero left the chamber and stopped halfway along the corridor, not wanting to show himself. A beam of pale light came down through the open trapdoor. "What?"

"I've brought you something to eat."

A basket sat at the bottom of the ladder. Presumably John had lowered it by a rope and then pulled the rope back up before calling to Romero.

"I'm not hungry."

"If I were you, I'd eat. After all, you have no way of telling when I might bring you another meal."

Romero's empty stomach cramped.

"Also, you'll find a book in the basket, something for you to pass the time. D. H. Lawrence. Seems appropriate since he lived on a ranch a little to the north of us outside Taos. In fact, he's buried there."

"I don't give a shit. What do you intend to do with me?" Romero was startled by how shaky his voice sounded.

John didn't answer.

"If you let me go right now, I'll forget this happened. None of this has gone so far that it can't be undone."

The trapdoor was closed. The pale beam of light disappeared.

Above, there were scraping sounds as the barrel was put back into place.

Romero wanted to scream.

He picked up the basket and examined its contents. Bread, cheese, sliced carrots, two apples . . . and a book. It was a tattered blue hardback without a cover. The title on its spine read, *D. H. Lawrence: Selected Stories.* There was a bookmark at a story called "The Woman Who Rode Away." The pages in that section of the book had been so repeatedly turned that the upper corners were almost worn through.

The blows to Romero's head made him feel as if a spike had been driven into it. Breathing more rapidly, dizzier than ever, he went back to the chamber. He put the basket on the table, then sat on the cot and felt so weak that he wanted to lie down, but he told himself that he had to look at the story. One thing you could say for certain about John, he wasn't whimsical. The story was important.

Romero opened the book. For a harrowing moment, his vision doubled. He strained to focus his eyes, and as quickly as the problem had occurred, it went away, his vision again clear. But he knew what was happening. I've got a concussion.

I need to get to a hospital.

Damn it, concentrate.

"The Woman Who Rode Away."

The story was set in Mexico. It was about a woman married to a wealthy industrialist who owned bountiful silver mines in the Sierra Madre. She had a healthy son and daughter. Her husband adored her. She had every comfort she could imagine. But she couldn't stop feeling smothered, as if she was another of her husband's possessions, as if he and her children owned her. Each day, she spent more and more time staring longingly at the mountains. What's up there? she wondered. Surely it must be something wonderful. The secret villages. One day, she went out horseback riding and never came back.

Romero stopped reading. The shock of his injuries had drained him. He had trouble holding his throbbing head up. At the same time, his empty stomach cramped again. I have to keep up my strength, he thought. Forcing himself to stand, he went over to the basket of food, chewed on a carrot, and took a bite out of a freshly baked, thickly crusted chunk of bread. He swallowed more water and went back to the cot.

The break hadn't done any good. As exhausted as ever, he reopened the book.

The woman rode into the mountains. She had brought enough

food for several days, and as she rode higher, she let her horse choose whatever trails it wanted. Higher and higher. Past pines and aspens and cottonwoods until, as the vegetation thinned and the altitude made her light-headed, Indians greeted her on the trail and asked where she was going. To the secret villages, she told them. To see their houses and to learn about their gods. The Indians escorted her into a lush valley that had trees, a river, and groups of low flat gleaming houses. There, the villagers welcomed her and promised to teach her.

Romero saw double again. Frightened, he struggled to control his vision. The concussion's getting worse, he thought. Fear made him weaker. He wanted to lie down, but he knew that, if he fell asleep, he might never wake up. Shout for help, he thought in a panic.

To whom? Nobody can hear me. Not even the brothers.

Rousing himself, he went over to the table, bit off another chunk of bread, ate a piece of apple, and sat down to finish the story. It was supposed to tell him something, he was sure, but so far he hadn't discovered what it was.

The woman had the sense of being in a dream. The villagers treated her well, bringing her flowers and clothes, food and drinks made of honey. She spent her days in a pleasant languor. She had never slept so long and deeply. Each evening, the pounding of drums was hypnotic. The seasons turned. Fall became winter. Snow fell. The sun was angry, the villagers said on the shortest day of the year. The moon must be given to the sun. They carried the woman to an altar, took off her clothes, and plunged a knife into her chest.

The shocking last page made Romero jerk his head up. The woman's death was all the more unnerving because she knew it was coming and she surrendered to it, didn't try to fight it, almost welcomed it. She seemed apart from herself, in a daze.

Romero shivered. As his eyelids drooped again, he thought about the honey drinks that the villagers had kept bringing her.

They must have been drugged.

Oh, shit, he thought. It took all of his willpower to raise his sagging head and peer toward the basket and the jug on the table.

The food and water are drugged.

A tingle of fear swept through him, the only sensation he could still feel. His head was so numb that it had stopped aching. His hands and feet didn't seem to be a part of him. I'm going to pass out, he thought sickly.

He started to lie back.

No.

Can't.

Don't.

Get your lazy ass off this cot. If you fall asleep, you'll die.

Mind spinning, he wavered to his feet. Stumbled toward the table. Banged against it. Almost knocked it over. Straightened. Lurched toward the toilet seat. Bent over it. Stuck his finger down his throat. Vomited the food and water he'd consumed.

He wavered into the corridor, staggered to the ladder, gripped it, turned, staggered back, reached the door to the root cellar, turned, and stumbled back to the ladder.

He did it again.

You have to keep walking.

And again.

You've got to stay on your feet.

His knees buckled. He forced them to straighten.

His vision turned gray. He stumbled onward, using his arms to guide him.

It was the hardest thing he had ever done. It took more discipline and determination than he knew he possessed. I won't give up, he kept saying. It became a mantra. I won't give up.

Time became a blur, delirium a constant. Somewhere in his long ordeal, his vision cleared, his legs became stronger. He allowed himself to hope, when his headache returned, the drug was wearing off. Instead of wavering, he walked.

And kept walking, pumping himself up. I have to be ready, he thought. As his mind became more alert, it nonetheless was seized by confusion. Why had John wanted him to read the story? Wasn't it the same as a warning not to eat the food and drink the water?

Or maybe it was an explanation of what was happening. A choice that was offered. Spare yourself the agony of panic. Eat from the bounty of the earth and surrender as the woman had done.

Like hell.

Romero dumped most of the water down the toilet seat. It helped to dissipate his vomit down there so that it wouldn't be obvious what he had done. He left a small piece of bread and a few carrot sticks. He bit into the apples and spit out the pieces, leaving cores. He took everything else into the root cellar and hid it in the darkest corner behind baskets of potatoes.

He checked his watch. It had been eleven in the morning when they had forced him down here. It was now almost midnight. Hearing the faint scrape of the barrel being moved, he lay down on the cot, closed his eyes, dangled an arm onto the floor, and tried to control his frantic breathing enough to look unconscious.

"Be careful. He might be bluffing."

"Most of the food's gone."

"Stay out of my line of fire."

Hands grabbed him, lifting. A dead weight, he felt himself being carried along the corridor. He murmured as if he didn't want to be wakened. After securing a harness around him, one brother went up the ladder and pulled on a rope while the other brothers lifted him. In the barn, as they took off the harness, he moved his head and murmured again.

"Let's see if he can stand," John said.

Romero allowed his eyelids to flicker.

"He's coming around," Mark said.

"Then he can help us."

They carried him into the open. He moved his head from side to side, as if aroused by the cold night air. They put him in the back of the pickup truck. Two brothers stayed with him while the other drove. The night was so cold that he allowed himself to shiver.

"Yeah, definitely coming around," John said.

The truck stopped. He was lifted out and carried into a field. Allowing his eyelids to open a little farther, Romero was amazed at how bright the moon was. He saw that the field was the same one that he had seen the brothers tilling and removing stones from the day before.

They set him on his feet.

He pretended to waver.

Heart pounding, he knew that he had to do something soon. Until now, he had felt helpless against the three of them. The barn had been too constricting a place in which to try to fight. He needed somewhere in the open, somewhere that allowed him to run. This field was going to have to be it. Because he knew without a doubt that this was where they intended to kill him.

"Put him on his knees," John said.

"It's still not too late to stop this," Mark said.

"Have you lost your faith?"

"I . . ."

"Answer me. Have you lost your faith?"

". . . No."

"Then put him on his knees."

Romero allowed himself to be lowered. His heart was beating so frantically that he feared it would burst against his ribs. A sharp stone hurt his knees. He couldn't allow himself to react.

They leaned him forward on his hands. Like an animal. His neck was exposed.

"Prove your faith, Mark."

Something scraped, a knife being pulled from a scabbard.

It glinted in the moonlight.

"Take it," John said.

"But—"

"Prove your faith."

A long tense pause.

"Yes," John said. "Lord, accept this sacrifice in thanks for the glory of your earth and the bounty that comes from it. The blood of—"

Feeling another sharp rock, this one beneath his palm, Romero gripped it, spun, and hurled it as strongly as he could at the head of the figure nearest him. The rock made a terrible crunching noise, the figure groaning and dropping, as Romero charged to his feet and yanked the knife from Mark's hands. He drove it into Mark's stomach and stormed toward the remaining brother, whom he recognized as John because of the pistol in his hand. But before Romero could strike him with the knife, John stumbled back, aiming, and Romero had no choice except to hurl the knife. It hit John, but whether it injured him, Romero couldn't tell. At least it made John stumble back farther, his aim wide, the gunshot plowing into the earth, and by then Romero was racing past the pickup truck, into the lane, toward the house.

John fired again. The bullet struck the pickup truck.

Running faster, propelled by fear, Romero saw the lights of the house ahead and veered to the left so he wouldn't be a silhouette. A third shot, a bullet buzzing past him, shattered a window in the house. He stretched his legs to the maximum. His chest heaved. As the house got larger before him, he heard the roar of the pickup truck behind him. I have to get off the lane. He veered farther to the left, scrambled over a rail fence, and raced across a field of chard, his panicked footsteps mashing the tender shoots.

Headlights gleamed behind him. The truck stopped. A fourth shot broke the silence of the valley. John obviously assumed that in this isolated area there was a good chance a neighbor wouldn't hear. Or care. Trouble with coyotes.

A fifth shot stung Romero's left shoulder. Breathing rapidly and hoarsely, he zigzagged. At the same time, he bent forward, running as fast as he could while staying low. He came to another fence, squirmed between its rails, and rushed into a further field, crushing further crops—radishes, he dimly thought.

The truck roared closer along the lane.

Another roar matched it, the roiling power of the Rio Grande as Romero raced nearer. The lights of the house were to his right now. He passed them, reaching the darkness at the back of the farm. The river thundered more loudly.

Almost there. If I can—

Headlights glaring, the truck raced to intercept him.

Another fence. Romero lunged between its rails so forcefully that he banged his injured shoulder, but he didn't care—moonlight showed him the path to the raised footbridge. He rushed along it, hearing the truck behind him. The churning river reflected the headlights, its fierce whitecaps beckoning. With a shout of triumph, he reached the footbridge. His frantic footsteps rumbled across it. Spray from the river slicked the boards. His feet slipped. The bridge swayed. Water splashed over it. He lost his balance, nearly tumbled into the river, but righted himself. A gunshot whistled past where he had been running before he fell. Abruptly, he was off the bridge, diving behind bushes, scurrying through the darkness on his right. John fired twice toward where Romero had entered the bushes as Romero dove to the ground farther to the right. Desperate not to make noise, he fought to slow his frenzied breathing.

His throat was raw. His chest ached. He touched his left shoulder and felt cold liquid mixed with warm: water and blood. He shivered. Couldn't stop shivering. The headlights of the truck showed John walking onto the footbridge. The pistol was in his right hand. Something else was in his left. It suddenly blazed. A powerful flashlight. It scanned the bushes. Romero pressed himself lower to the ground.

John proceeded across the bridge. "I've been counting the same as you have!" he shouted to be heard above the force of the current. "Eight shots! I checked the magazine before I got out of the truck. Seven more rounds, plus one in the firing chamber!"

Any moment the flashlight's glare would reach where Romero was hiding. He grabbed a rock, thanked God that it was his left shoulder that had been injured, and used his right arm to hurl the rock. It bounced off the bridge. As Romero scurried farther upriver, John swung the flashlight toward where he had been and fired.

This time, Romero didn't stop. Rocks against a pistol weren't going to work. He might get lucky, but he doubted it. John knew which direction he was in, and whenever Romero risked showing himself to throw another rock, John had a good chance of capturing him in the blaze of the flashlight and shooting him.

Keep going upriver, he told himself. Keep making John follow. Without aiming, he threw a rock in a high arc toward John but didn't trick him into firing without a target. Fine, Romero thought, scrambling through the murky bushes. Just as long as he keeps following.

The raft, he kept thinking. They found my campsite. They found my car.

But did they find the raft?

In the darkness, it was hard to get his bearings. There had been a curve in the river, he remembered. Yes. And the ridge on this side angled down toward the water. He scurried fiercely, deliberately making so much noise that John was bound to hear and follow. He'll think I'm panicking, Romero thought. To add to the illusion, he threw another high arcing rock toward where John was stalking him.

A branch lanced his face. He didn't pay any attention. He just rushed onward, realized that the bank was curving, saw the shadow of the ridge angling down to the shore, and searched furiously through the bushes, tripping over the raft, nearly banging his head on one of the rocks that he had put in it to prevent a wind from blowing it away.

John's flashlight glinted behind him, probing the bushes.

Hurry!

Breathless, Romero took off his jacket, stuffed it with large rocks, set it on the rocks that were already in the raft, and dragged the raft toward the river. Downstream, John heard him and redirected the flashlight, but not before Romero ducked back into the bushes, watching the current suck the raft downstream. In the moonlight and the glint of the flashlight, the bulging jacket looked as if Romero were hunkered down in the raft, hoping not to be shot as the raft sped past.

John swung toward the river and fired. He fired again, the muzzle flash bright, the gunshots barely audible in the roar of the current, which also muted the noises that Romero made as he charged from the bushes and slammed against John, throwing his injured arm around John's throat while he used his other hand to grab John's gun arm.

The force of hitting John propelled them into the water. Instantly, the current gripped them, its violence as shocking as the cold. John's face was sucked under. Clinging to him, straining to keep him under, Romero also struggled with the river, its power thrusting him through the darkness. The current heaved him up, then dropped him. The cold was so fierce that already his body was becoming numb. Even so, he kept squeezing John's throat and struggling to get the pistol away from him. A huge tree limb scraped past. The current upended him. John broke the surface. Romero went under. John's hands pressed him down. Frenzied, Romero kicked. He thought he heard a scream as John let go of him and he broke to the surface. Five feet away, John fought to stay above the water and aim the pistol. Romero dove under. Hearing the shot, he used the force of the current to add to his effort as he thrust himself farther under water and erupted from the surface to John's right, grabbing John's gun arm, twisting it.

You son of a bitch, Romero thought,. If I'm going to die, you're going with me. He dragged John under. They slammed against a boulder, the pain making Romero cry out under water. Gasping, he broke to the surface. Saw John ahead of him, aiming. Saw the head-lights of the truck illuminating the footbridge. Saw the huge tree limb caught in the narrow space between the river and the bridge. Before John could fire, he slammed into the branch. John collided with it a moment later. Trapped in its arms, squeezed by the current, Romero reached for the pistol as John aimed it point-blank. Then John's face twisted into surprised agony as a boulder crashed down on him from the bridge and split his skull open.

Romero was barely aware of Matthew above him on the foot-bridge. He was too paralyzed with horror, watching blood stream down John's face. An instant later, a log hurtled along the river, struck John, and drove him harder against the tree branch. In the glare of the headlights, Romero thought he saw wood protruding from John's chest as he, the branch, and the log broke free of the bridge and swirled away in the current. Thrust along with him, Romero stretched his arms up, trying to claw at the bridge. He failed. Speeding under it, reaching the other side, he tensed in apprehension of the boulder that he would bang against and be knocked unconscious by when something snagged him. Hands. Matthew was on his stomach on the bridge, stretching as far down as he could, clutching Romero's shirt. Romero struggled to help him, trying not to look at Matthew's crushed forehead and right eye from where Romero had hit him with the rock. Gripping Matthew's arms, pulling himself up, Romero felt debris crash past his legs, and then he and Matthew were flat on the footbridge, breathing hoarsely, trying to stop trembling.

"I hate him," Matthew said.

For a moment, Romero was certain that his ears were playing tricks on him, that the gunshots and the roar of the water were making him hear sounds that weren't there.

"I hate him," Matthew repeated.

"My God, you can talk."

For the first time in twelve years, he later found out.

"I hate him," Matthew said. "Hatehimhatehimhatehimhatehim."

Relieving the pressure of silence that had built up for almost two thirds of his life, Matthew gibbered while they went to check Mark and found him dead, while they went to the house and Romero phoned the state police, while they put on warm clothes and Romero did what he could for Matthew's injury and they waited for the police to arrive, while the sun rose and the investigators swarmed throughout the farm. Matthew's hysterical litany became ever more speedy and shrill until a physician finally had to sedate him and he was taken away in an ambulance.

The state trooper whom Romero had asked for backup was part of the team. When Romero's police chief and sergeant heard what had happened, they drove up from Santa Fe. By then the excavations had started, and the bodies were showing up. What was left of them, anyway, after their blood had been drained into the fields and they'd been cut into pieces.

"Good God, how many?" the state trooper exclaimed as more and more body parts, most in extreme stages of decay, were found under the fields.

"As long as Matthew can remember, it's been happening," Romero said. "His mother died giving him birth. She's under one of the fields. The father died from a heart attack three years ago. They never told anybody. They just buried him out there someplace. Every year on the last average frost date, May fifteenth, they've sacrificed someone. Most of the time it was a homeless person, no one to be missed. But last year it was Susan Crowell and her fiancé. They had the bad luck of getting a flat tire right outside the farm. They walked down here and asked to use a phone. When John saw the out-of-state license plate . . ."

"But why?" the police chief asked in dismay as more body parts were discovered.

"To give life to the earth. That's what the D. H. Lawrence story was about. The fertility of the earth and the passage of the seasons. I guess that's as close as John was able to come to explaining to his victims why they had to die."

"What about the shoes?" the police chief asked. "I don't understand about the shoes."

"Luke dropped them."

"The fourth brother?"

"That's right. He's out there somewhere. He committed suicide."

The police chief looked sick.

"Throughout the spring, until the vegetables were ready for sale, Luke drove back and forth from the farm to Santa Fe to sell moss rocks. Each day, he drove along Old Pecos Trail. Twice a day, he passed the Baptist church. He was as psychologically tortured as Matthew, but John never suspected how close he was to cracking. That church became Luke's attempt for absolution. One day, he saw old shoes on the road next to the church."

"You mean he didn't drop the first ones?"

"No, they were somebody's idea of a prank. But they gave him an idea. He saw them as a sign from God. Two years ago, he started dropping the shoes of the victims. They'd always been a problem. Clothes will decay readily enough. But shoes take a lot longer. John told him to throw them in the trash somewhere in Santa Fe. Luke couldn't bring himself to do that any more than he could bring himself to go into the church and pray for his soul. But he could drop the shoes outside the church in the hopes that he'd be forgiven and that the family's victims would be granted salvation."

"And the next year, he dropped shoes with feet in them," the sergeant said.

"John had no idea that he'd taken them. When he heard what had happened, he kept him a prisoner here. One morning, Luke broke out, went into one of the fields, knelt down, and slit his throat from ear to ear."

The group became silent. In the background, amid a pile of upturned rich black soil, someone shouted that they'd found more body parts.

★   ★   ★

Romero was given paid sick leave. He saw a psychiatrist once a week for four years. On those occasions when people announced that they were vegetarians, he answered, "Yeah, I used to be one, but now I'm a carnivore." Of course, he couldn't subsist on meat alone. The human body required the vitamins and minerals that vegetables provided, and although Romero tried vitamin pills as a substitution, he found that he couldn't do without the bulk that vegetables provided. So he grudgingly ate them, but never without thinking of those delicious, incredibly large, shiny, healthy-looking tomatoes, cucumbers, peppers, squash, cabbage, beans, peas, carrots, and chard that the Parsons brothers had sold. Remembering what had fertilized them, he chewed and chewed, but the vegetables always stuck in his throat.

Peter Schneider

DES SAUCISSES, SANS DOUTE

If you don't have a sense of humor, I strongly suggest you skip this next piece. As I said in the introduction to Chet Williamson's story earlier in this volume, horror and humor are strangely and strongly attracted to one another—and you may never find a better example of it than what follows. "Des Saucisses, Sans Doute" is a telling, hilarious, and possibly sick (in the tradition of The National Lampoon*) parody, and manages, in a faux introductory headnote and the very short "story" which follows it by the imaginary author Pamela Jergens, to effectively skewer everything we hold sacred and serious in this field.*

Peter Schneider's writing résumé is not as long as it should be, but his publishing one is longer than your leg. He's been a marketing executive at some of the major publishing houses in New York City, as well as the founder of Hill House Books, which produced a stellar edition of Peter Straub's Ghost Story, *which is still considered one of the finest private editions of its time.*

As I warned, if you don't know how to laugh don't read this piece— but if you do, prepare to laugh out loud. The fancy and ominous-sounding French title, by the way, translates as "The Hot Dogs, Without Doubt."

Pamela Jergens

DES SAUCISSES, SANS DOUTE

Pamela Jergens is one of our new breed of writers of le horreur, *as I like to call it. She's had a number of stories published in* Dead 'Uns, Le Journale de Mort, *and* Cry Like a Baby . . . A Dead Baby. *She's also the author of the "Fiendish Funsters," a horror-based young adult series published by Blood Press. Pamela proclaims, "I truly have two lives—my normal, average American life as a professional businesswoman . . . and my other life, where I live out on the word processor the dark fantasies that come to me, almost unbidden. There is a strict dichotomy between my two lives—one does not encroach on the other. If they did, I would lose touch* *with who I am . . . and what I want to be." In her other, normal, average American life Pamela conducts a high-powered career as a magazine editor (for such journals as* Cry Like a Baby . . . A Dead Baby, Dead 'Uns, *and* Le Journale de Mort). *She also serves as the publisher and CEO of Blood Press. "I disdain the recent works of the so-called splatterpunks," says Pamela. "My work is instead the* matériel *of the night . . . of the dark places that live within us, expressed through only the subtlest of metaphors and signals . . . where the true horror may be within ourselves, not in the ravings of werewolves or vampires. I feel my work is in the tradition of Nathaniel Hawthorne or Max Shulman—the "quiet" horror of* Rapaccini's Daughter *or* Dobie Gillis—*the horror, indeed, of ourselves." And here you can just imagine the authoress tapping herself on the temple. So now, for those of you in a contemplative and inner-examining mood, is* "Des Saucisses, Sans Doute."*

I brandished the severed left tit of the blond chick in one hand. It had not been a clean cut—Momma never got me braces when I was growing up.

She lay, cowering and crying, in the corner of the room, the front of her fabulous bod smeared with blood and offal.

"Hey, baby," I crowed as I picked up her D-cup bra. "Let's play David and Goliath." I plopped the moist handful of tissue into the left cup and swirled the entire contraption around my head, until finally it let go of its grisly burden, which flew, arrow-like, across the room, only to land on the far wall with a hideous *groooop*, leaving a trail not unlike a snail, only bloodier, as it made its way down the plasterboard of the wall. The pale brown nipple detached itself and fell to the hardwood floor with a faint *plumph*.

She cried harder and harder, and buried her face in her hands.

I thought back to a few hours before, when I had met Donnalie in the pub down the street from my apartment. She was not beautiful in the classic sense. Her hideous cleft palate, her wandering left eye, and her nose, eaten away by tertiary syphilis . . . all flaws in and of themselves, yet together they made her look noble, like a mare roaming the hills of Loch Lomond, wind blowing her mane in a tangle of uproarious curls. After a few minutes of conversation, we left for the warmth . . . and promised brandies . . . of my inexpensive apartment over the Jibblesworth store. And now, I found myself in a situation that defied even the farthest reaches of a maniac's mind. It had started with a kiss . . . and ended with a kitchen knife.

Suddenly my tongue shot out of my mouth, enlarging at a rapid rate and splitting into a tempered steel fork. I strode over to Donnalie,

my protruding tongue now six feet in length and hard as granite.
"Lookth at this," I lisped, as my abnormally prehensile tongue stabbed
down onto her legs. Over and over the forked tongue fell, until finally
her legs gave way at the knees. I keened in delight as I grabbed the
severed limbs. Reaching around and grabbing two extension cords
from the wall, I feverishly lashed the limbs to my own legs, making
sure that the feet extended a good six inches beyond my own. Clam-
bering to my "feet," I stumbled across the room, roaring with laughter. "Look, Donnalie, I don't need elevator shoes . . . I got elevator
feets!" (My height—only 5'3" at maturity—had always been an issue
in my psyche.) Mercifully, however, Donnalie had fainted dead away.

The alarm blared, sending piercing shards of noise into my shattered
sleep. I clutched the pillow closer to my head, trying to drown out
the tintinnabulations crescendoing in my screeching brain. Finally, I
gave up the fight and swung out of bed, cradling my pained head in
my hands. Suddenly the memories of the night before crashed blind-
ingly into my consciousness. "My God!" I thought. "Did I do that?"
My cat, Mr. Menick, leapt to the floor as I realized I had spoken my
thoughts instead of just thinking them. I jumped to my feet and raced
into the kitchen, where the events of the previous evening seemed to
have occurred. Sighing with relief, I slumped against the refrigerator.
No, there was no blood, no breasts, staining the lovely white walls of
my modern *prepatoire de manger*. Everything was as it should be.

I crept over to the stove and poured into a large mug the dregs
of the coffee I had prepared the morning before. I stared out the
window, at the robin redbreasts bob, bob, bobbin' outside at the
birdfeeder, as I pulled a Thomas's English muffin out of the box, split
it open with my stainless steel forked tongue, and watched the surface
of my coffee as a taupe nipple bobbed insouciantly to the surface.

The End?

Ed Gorman

ANGIE

Ed Gorman, like Joe Lansdale and a few others in this book, has worn many hats—which is an apt description, since he's been a Western writer, and the image of Ed in a cowboy hat just isn't something I can hold in my head. He's also been a book editor (as one example, he edited, with Martin H. Greenberg, one of the most successful and lauded horror anthologies of the 1980s, Stalkers*), magazine editor (*Mystery Scene*), columnist (*Cemetery Dance magazine*), mystery writer (*A Cry of Shadows *and the more recent thrillers* Black River Falls *and* Cold Blue Midnight*), and, of course, horror writer (short stories under his own name, novels under the name of Daniel Ransom). The fact that he's managed to distinguish himself in all these capacities is remarkable, and ample proof of his energy and versatility.*

For 999, Gorman has produced a cold-eyed and sneaky little study of human nature; if Guy de Maupassant were still around, he might have penned this story.

Roy said, "He heard us last night."

Angie said, "Heard what?"

"Heard us talking about Gina."

"No, he didn't. He was asleep."

"That's what I thought. But I went back to the can one time and I saw his door was open and I looked in there and he was sittin' up in bed, wide awake. Listenin'."

"He probably'd just woken up."

"He heard us talkin'."

"How do you know?"

"I asked him," Roy said.

"Yeah? And what did he say?"

"He said he didn't."

"See, I told ya."

"Well, he was lyin'."

"How do you know?" she said.

"He's my son, ain't he? That's how I know. I could tell by his face."

"So what if he did hear?"

Roy looked at her, astonished. "So what if he did? He'll go to the cops."

"The cops? Roy, you're crazy. He's nine years old and he's your *son*."

"That little bastard don't give two turds about me, Angie. He was strictly a mama's boy. And now that he knows—"

He didn't need to say it. Angie had been waitressing at a truck stop when she'd met Roy. He was living in a trailer with his son, Jason, and his wife, Gina. He went for Angie immediately. On her nights off, he'd take her to Cedar Rapids, where they'd go to a couple of dance clubs. They always had a great time except when Roy got real drunk and started trouble with black guys who were dating white girls. Roy had some friends who were always talking about blowing up places with blacks and Jews and fags in them. Roy always gave them a certain percentage of his robbery money. That's what Roy did. He robbed banks, usually small-town ones that were located on the edge of town. Roy was a pro. He figured everything out carefully in advance. He knew the exit routes and where the bank kept the video surveillance cameras, and he checked out the teller windows in advance to see which clerk looked most vulnerable. He'd served six years in Fort Madison for sticking up a gas station when he was nineteen. He was thirty-six now and vowed never to be caught again. What she liked about him was that he had a goal in life. There was this one bank in Des Moines where he said he could get half a million on a payroll Friday. They'd go to Vegas and then they'd go see this whites-only compound up in the Utah mountains. That was the only part that Angie didn't like. She didn't understand politics and Roy and his buddies always carrying on about Jews and queers and colored people bored her. She had a way of looking awake when she was really *not* awake. She did that practically every time Roy and his buddies started talking about some militia deal they had heard about and intended to join.

The wife got wind of the courtship between Roy and Angie, though, and raised hell. She wouldn't give him a divorce, and she threatened to tell the cops about all his robberies all over the Midwest. So one rainy night he killed her. Shoved a knife into her right breast, which silenced her, and then cut her throat. He loaded her into a body bag and packed a hundred pounds of hand weights in there with her and then drove his two-year-old Ford out to the river that very moonglow night and threw her in just below the dam. The only trouble Roy had was his son, Jason. The kid just kept wailin' and carryin' on about where's my mom, where's my mom? He hadn't wanted the kid in the first place, had beat the shit out of her, but she still wouldn't get an abortion. Even back then he'd had the dream of this big Des Moines bank on payroll Friday, and who wanted a kid along when you had all the cash with you? But Gina had her way and Roy was stuck with the little prick. And now Jason had overheard him talkin' about killin' his mother. Roy knew that somehow, some way, the little prick would turn him in.

Roy said, "Don't worry, I'll handle it."

She watched him carefully. "Sometimes you scare the shit out of me, Roy. You really do. He's your own flesh and blood."

"I didn't want him. *Gina* wanted him."

"And you killed Gina."

"For *you*," he said. "I killed her for *you*." Then, "Shit, honey, here we go again. Arguin'. This ain't what I want and it ain't what you want, either. You c'mere now." Then, "A kid like that, he's a ball and chain."

He liked it when she sat in his lap. He liked to feel her up to the point that his erection got so big and bulgy it was downright painful. She'd wriggle on it and make him even crazier. Then, as now, they'd go in on their big mussed sleepwarm bed and do the trick.

Afterward, today, he said, "I better get into town. I want to be there at noontime. See what the place is like around then."

He was scoping out a bank. He was planning to rob it day after tomorrow. Their cash supply was way way down. The trailer park manager was on Roy's ass for back rent.

Roy said, "Don't say nothin' to him when he gets home from school."

"All right."

"You just let me handle everything."

"All right."

"It'll be better for us," Roy said, trying to make her feel better. "Haulin' that kid everywhere we go, that isn't the kind of life we want. We want to be free, babe. That's just the kind of people we are. Free."

Roy had killed people before and it had never bothered her. But never a kid before, that she knew of. And his *own* kid to boot.

He kissed her breasts a final time and then said, "I'll figure out what to do about Jason and then you'n me'll go dancin' tonight. Okay?"

"Okay, Roy."

Roy was gonna kill him for sure.

One day, when Angie was thirteen, her grandmother said, "That body of hers is gonna get her in trouble someday." The irony being that Grandmother herself had had a body just like it—killer breasts and hips that made young men weep in public—when she'd been young. And so had Angie's mother, the person Grandmother was talking to.

The thing being that the worst trouble Grandmother had ever gotten in was getting knocked up by a soldier home on leave from WW II, a pregnancy that had brought Angie's mother, Suzie, into the world. The worst Suzie had ever gotten into, in turn, was getting knocked up by a Vietnam soldier home on leave, a pregnancy that had brought *Angie* into the world.

Angie, however, got into a lot more trouble than just spreading her sweet young thighs. She saw a TV show one night where this beautiful girl was referred to as a "kept woman," a woman who lounged about an expensive apartment all day, looking just great, while this older man paid her rent, gave her endless numbers of gifts, and practically groveled every time the kept woman was even faintly displeased. An Iowa girl with a wondrous body like Angie's, was it any wonder she'd want to be a kept woman, too?

When she was fifteen, she ran away from home in the company of a thirty-two-year-old woman from Omaha who took her to a hotel in Des Moines. Angie slept with ten men in three years and made just over a thousand dollars. One of the men had been black, and that gave her some pause. She could just hear her dad if he ever found out about her (A) screwing men for money or (B) screwing a *black man* for money.

She went back home. Her dad, who worked as an appliance service repair man for Al's American Appliances, didn't have the money for a private shrink so they sent her to the county Human Services Department, where she saw this counselor for free. She spent two hours filling out the Minnesota Multiphasic Personality Test, which just about bored her ass off. He kept peeking in the room and asking her if she was about done. That's what he *pretended* to do, anyway. What he was really doing was staring at her breasts. He'd fallen in love with them the moment they walked in the door. She ended up screwing him on the side. He had a wife who worked at Wal-Mart in Cedar Rapids and two little girls, one of whom was lame in some way and whom he got all sad about sometimes. He was thirty-eight and bald and felt guilty about screwing her and cheating on his wife and all but he said that her tits just made him dizzy when he touched them, just dizzy. He kept her in rap CDs. She loved rap. The way the gangsters in the rap videos took care of their girlfriends. That's what she wanted. She wanted to meet some guy who'd give her a life of ease. A kept woman. No work. No hassle. No sweat. Just sit around some fancy apartment and read comic books and watch MTV and porno movies. She loved porno movies. The thing was, she didn't like sex very much, except for masturbating, but if sex was the price she had to pay for a life of ease, so be it.

She dropped the counselor as soon as she managed to get through high school. She got a job in Cedar Rapids as a clerk in a Target store. She lasted three weeks. She took her paycheck and bought a very sexy dress and then she started hanging out in the lawyer bars downtown. Her first couple of months, things went pretty good. She hadn't found a guy who'd make her an official kept woman, but she'd found several guys who'd give her a little money now and then, enough money for a nice little apartment and a six-year-old Oldsmobile.

But things did not go well after a time. She caught the clap and profoundly displeased a couple of the men who gave her money. Then she ran into two men who were long of tongue but short of wallet, a car salesman who drove them around in sleek new Caddies, and a supper club owner who wore her like a pinkie ring. They were full of promises but had no real money. The Caddie man had two wives and two alimonies; and the supper club man owed the IRS boys so much in back taxes, he could barely afford a pack of gum. He'd had a supper club over in Rock Island several years back, and he'd been charged with tax evasion, later dropped to a simple (if overwhelming) tax debt.

Then, the worst thing of all happened. On the night of her twenty-sixth birthday, Angie got busted for prostitution. She was in a downtown bar sitting with a couple of hookers she knew getting birthday party drunk, when one of the lawyers suggested they all go out to his houseboat. Well, they did, and the cops followed them.

Angie insisted that she accepted gifts but never cash for sex per se but it was a distinction apparently too subtle for the minds of the gendarmes. They hated these two particular lawyers and were gleeful about arresting them. Cedar Rapids had a new police station and Angie was impressed with it. She saw a couple of cute young cops, too, and thought she wouldn't mind dating a cop. It was probably fun. She was booked and fingerprinted and charged. It all, like much of Angie's life, had a dream-like quality. She was just walking through it—as if her life was a TV show and she was simply watching it—the reality of her trouble not hitting her until the next day when her name appeared in the paper. The Cedar Rapids paper was read by everybody in her hometown. Angie called home and tried to explain. Her mother was in tears, her father enraged. They told her not, definitely *not,* to attend the family reunion two weekends hence.

Now it was two years later and Angie was living with Roy, who robbed banks and killed people when he thought it was necessary. She saw plainly now that he was never going to have the kind of money it took to make her a kept woman. Hell, he'd even hinted a few times that she should get another waitress job to help out with the rent and the food. Plus, there were the people he'd killed, three that she knew of for sure. The only one that really bothered her was his wife. Killing his wife was a real personal thing, and it scared Angie. Killing his own son scared her even more.

She spent the afternoon getting depressed about her bikinis. School would be out in a week. Swimming pools would be opening up. Time to flaunt her body. But this year there was too much of her body to flaunt. She'd put on twenty pounds. Ripples of cellulite could be seen on the back of her thighs. She wished now Roy hadn't talked her into getting his name tattooed on both her boobs.

At three-thirty, Jason came home. He was a skinny, sandy-haired kid with a lot of freckles and eyeglasses so thick they made you feel sorry for him. Kids like Jason always got picked on by other kids.

Something was wrong. He usually went to the refrigerator and got himself some milk and a piece of the pie Angie always kept on hand for both of them. Roy had a whiskey tooth, not a sweet tooth. Then Jason usually sat at the dining room table and watched *Batman.* But not today. He just muttered a greeting and went back to his little room and closed the door. Something really was wrong and she figured she knew what it was. She slipped a robe on over her bikini—

you shouldn't be around him, your tits hangin' out that way, Roy said whenever she wore a bikini around the trailer—and went back to his room and knocked gently. She could never figure out what he thought of her. He was almost always polite but never more than that.

"I'm asleep," he said.

She giggled. "If you were asleep, you couldn't say 'I'm asleep.' "

"I just don't feel like talkin', Angie."

She decided to risk it. "You heard us talkin' last night, didn't you, Jason?"

There was a long silence. "No."

"About your mom."

"No."

"About what happened to her."

There was another long silence. "He killed her. I heard him say so."

So Roy was right. The kid *had* heard.

She opened the door and went in. He lay on the bed. He still had his sneakers on. A Spawn comic book lay across his chest. Sunlight angled in through the dirty window on the west wall and picked out the blond highlights in his hair.

She went over and sat down next to him. The springs made a noise. She tried not to think about her weight, or how her bikinis fit her. She was definitely going on a diet. She was going to be a kept woman, and one thing a kept woman had to do was keep her body good.

She said, "I just wanted you to know that I didn't have nothin' to do with it, what he did, I mean."

"Yeah," he said. "I know."

"And I also wanted you to know that your daddy isn't a bad man."

"Yes, he is."

"Sometimes he is. But not all the time."

"He broke your rib, didn't he?"

"He didn't mean to hit me that hard. He was just drunk was all. If he'd been sober, he wouldn't have hit me that hard."

"They say in school that a man shouldn't hit a woman at all."

"Well," she said, "you know what your daddy says about schools. That they're run by Jews and queers and colored people."

He stared at her. "I'm gonna turn him in."

She got scared. "Oh, honey, don't you *ever* say that to your daddy." She knew that Roy was looking for an excuse, any excuse, to kill Jason. "Promise me you won't. He'd get so mad he'd—"

She didn't need to finish her sentence. She sensed that the kid knew what she was talking about.

She said, "Is that a good comic book?"

"Not as good as Batman."

"Then how come you don't get Batman?"

"I already read it for this month."

"Oh."

She leaned forward and kissed him on the forehead. She'd never done that before. He was a nice kid. "You remember what I said now. You never say anything in front of your daddy about turnin' him in. You hear me?"

"Yeah, I guess so."

"You take a nap now."

She stood up.

Her mother had once said, "You give a man plenty of starch and a good piece of meat, he'll never complain about you *or* your cookin'." Angie had told this to Roy once and he'd grinned at her and pawed one of her breasts and said, "All depends on what kind of meat you're talkin' about." At the time, Angie had found his remark hilarious.

There was nothing to smile about as she made the Kraft cheese and macaroni while the pork chops sizzled in the oven. He was going to kill his own son. She couldn't get over it. His own son.

Forty-five minutes later, the three of them ate dinner. As always, Jason said grace to himself the way his mom had taught him. While he did this, Roy made a face and rolled his eyes. Little sissy sonofabitch, he'd drunkenly said to Jason one night, sayin' grace like that.

Roy said, "Guess what I found today?"

Angie said, "What?"

"I was talkin' to the boy."

"Oh," Angie said, irritated with his tone of voice. "Pardon me for living."

She got up from the table and carried her dishes to the sink.

"Guess what I found today?" Roy said to Jason.

"What?"

"A real great spot for fishin'."

"Oh."

"For you and me. I always wanted to teach you how to fish."

"I thought you *hated* to fish," Jason said.

"Not anymore. I love fishin', don't I, babe?"

"Yeah," Angie said from the sink, where she was cleaning off her plate. "He loves fishin'."

Angie knew immediately that Roy had figured out how to kill the kid. He hated fishing, and even more he hated do anything with the kid.

After supper, Jason went into his room. Most kids would be out playing in the warm spring night. Not Jason. He had a little twelve-inch TV in there and he had a lot of X-Files novels, too. He was well set up.

While she was doing the dishes, and Roy was sitting at the table nursing a Hamms from the bottle and watching some skin on the Playboy Channel, she said, "You're gonna do it."

"Yes, I am."

"He's your own flesh and blood."

He came over and pressed against her. He had a hard-on. Seems he always had a hard-on. She didn't have no complaints in that department. He groped her and kissed her neck and said, "We're free kind of people, Angie. Free. And with the kid along, we'll never be free. Especially with what he knows about us. One phone call from him and we'll be in the slammer."

"But he's your own son."

Jason's door opened. He went to the john. Roy said, "You let me take care of it."

Twenty minutes later, Roy and Jason, they left. She couldn't think of any way to stop them without coming right out and warning Jason about what was going on.

She paced. She paced and gunned whiskey from a Smurfs glass. She was so agitated her heart felt like thunder in her chest and every few minutes her right arm jerked grotesquely.

And then she remembered the gun. She didn't even know what kind of gun it was. One of her lawyer friends had given it to her once when one of her old boyfriends was hassling her. She'd shot it a few times. She knew how to use it. She kept it in the bureau underneath the crotchless panties Roy had bought her, his joke always being that he'd personally eaten the crotch out of them.

She got the gun and she went after them. Her only thought was the river. About half a mile on the other side of some hardwoods was a cliff and below it fast water that ran to a dam near Cedar Rapids. One time they'd been walking and Roy said it was a perfect place to throw a body. His cellmate, a lifer Roy had a lot of respect for, had said that while bodies did occasionally wash up right away, there was a better chance they'd give you a five-, six-day head start from the law.

The dying day was indigo in the sky, indigo and salmon pink and mauve spreading like a stain beneath a few northeasterly thunderheads and a biting wind that tasted of rain. Rainstorms always scared her. When she was little, she'd always hidden in the closet, her two older sisters laughing at her, scaredy-pants, scaredy-pants. But she didn't care. She'd hidden anyway.

The way she found them, they were sitting on a picnic table near the cliff, father and son, just talking. Darkness was slowly making them grainy, and soon would make them invisible.

Roy said, "What the hell you doing here?"

"She can be here if she wants to," Jason said.

She smiled. The kid liked her and that made her feel good.

"I guess I need to go to the bathroom," Jason said.

He walked over to the hardwoods and disappeared.

"I was afraid you already did something to him," Angie said.

He looked at her. Shrugged. "It's harder than I thought it would be."

"He's your own flesh and blood."

"Yeah, yeah, I guess that's it. I started to do it a couple times but I couldn't go through with it. I mean, it's not like shootin' a stranger or anything."

"Let's go back."

He shook his head. "Oh, no. You go back alone."

"But if you can't do it, why you want to stay out here?"

"I didn't say I *can't* do it. I just said it's harder than I thought it was. It's just gonna take me a little time is all. Now, you get that sweet ass of yours back home and wait for me. We'll be pullin' out tonight."

"Pullin' out?"

They could see Jason coming back toward them.

"Yeah," Roy said in a whispering voice, "school'll be askin' questions, him not around anymore. Better off pullin' out tonight."

Jason walked up. "Dad tell you there's twenty-pound fish in that river?"

"Yeah," she said, "that's what he said."

"Angie's got to get back home. She's makin' us a surprise."

"A surprise?" Jason said, excited. "What kinda surprise?"

"Well, if she tells ya, it won't be much of a surprise, will it?"

Jason grinned. "No, I guess not."

"You head home, babe," Roy said. "We'll be up'n a while."

She wanted to argue but you didn't argue with Roy. You didn't argue and win, anyway. And you got bruises and bumps and breaks for *not* winning.

"Guess I better go," she said.

"I can't wait to see the surprise," Jason said.

She went back but she didn't go home. She stood inside the hardwoods, inside the shadows, inside the night, and watched them.

He couldn't do it. That's what she was hoping. That when it came right down to it, he just couldn't do it. She said a couple of prayers.

But he did it. Pulled the gun out, grabbed Jason by the shoulder and started dragging him across the grassy space between picnic table and cliff.

All this was instinct: her running, her screaming. Roy looked real pissed when he saw her. He got distracted from the kid and the kid tried wrestling himself away, swinging his arms wild, trying to kick, trying to bite.

Roy didn't have any warning about her gun. She got up close to him and jerked it out of the back pocket of her Levi's and killed him point-blank. Three bullets in the side of the head.

He went over on his side and shit his pants before he hit the ground. The smell was awful.

The weird thing was how the kid reacted. You'd think he'd be grateful that she'd killed the sonofabitch. But he knelt next to Roy and wailed and rocked back and forth and held a dead cold white hand in his hand and then wailed some more. Maybe, she thought, maybe it was because his mom was dead, too. Maybe losin' both your folks, maybe it was too much to handle, even if your own flesh-and-blood dad *had* tried to kill you.

She dragged Roy over and pushed him off the cliff into the river. The stars were on the water tonight and the choppy waves glistened.

She dragged the boy away. He fought at first, biting, kicking, wrestling, and all. She let him have a good hard slap, though, and that settled him down. He kept cryin' but he did what she told him.

"How you doin'?"

"All right."

"You hungry?"

"Sort of, I guess."

"You'll like Colorado. Wait till you see the mountains."

"You didn't have to kill him."

"He was gonna kill *you*."

He didn't say anything for a long time. They were nearing the Nebraska border. The land was getting flatter. Cows, crying with prairie sorrow, tossed in their earthen beds, while nightbirds collected chorus-like in the trees, making the leafy branches thrum with their song. It was nice with the windows rolled down and all the summery Midwest roaring in your ears.

Sixty-three miles before they hit the border, just after ten o'clock, they found the Empire Motel, one of those 1950s jobs with the office in the middle and eight stucco-sided rooms fanned out on either side.

Angie rented a room and bought a bunch of candy and potato chips from the vending machine. She rented a sci-fi video from the manager for Jason.

She got him into the shower and then into bed and played the movie for him. He didn't last long. He was asleep in no time. She turned out the lights and got into bed herself. She was tired. Or thought she was, anyway. But she couldn't sleep. She lay there and thought about Roy and about when she was a little girl and about being a kept woman. It had to happen for her someday. It just had to. Then she remembered what she'd looked like in those bikinis. God, she really had to go on a diet.

She lay like this for an hour. Then she heard car doors opening and male laughter. She decided to go peek out the window. Two nice-looking, nicely dressed guys were carrying a suitcase apiece into a room two doors away. They were driving this just-huge new Lincoln. Sight of them made her agitated. She wanted a drink and to hear some music. Maybe dance a little. And laugh. She needed a good laugh.

Fifteen minutes later, she was fixed up pretty good, white tank top and red short-shorts, the ones where her cheeks were exposed to erotic perfection, her hair all done up nice, and enough perfume so that she smelled really good.

The kid wouldn't miss her. He'd be fine. He'd be sleeping and the door would be locked and he'd be just fine.

*   *   *

Their names were Jim Durbin and Mike Brady. They were from Cedar Rapids and they owned a couple of computer stores and they were going to open a big new one in Denver. Ordinarily, Jim would fly but Mike was scared to fly. And ordinarily, they would stay in a nicer motel than this but they couldn't find anything else on the road. Her excuse for knocking on their door this late was the front office didn't have a cigarette machine and she was out and she heard them still up and she wondered if either of them had a few cigarettes they'd loan her. Jim said he didn't smoke but Mike did. Jim said he'd been trying for years to get Mike to quit. How do you like that? Jim said. Guy doesn't mind risking lung cancer every day of his life but he won't get on an airplane?

They had a nice bottle of I. W. Harper and invited her in. It was obvious Mike was interested in her. Jim was married. Mike was just going through a divorce he called "painful." He said his wife ended up running off with this doctor she was on this charity committee with. Jim said Mike needed a good woman to rebuild Mike's self-esteem. That was a word Angie heard a lot. She liked the daytime talk shows and they talked a lot about self-esteem. There was a transvestite prostitute on just last week, as a matter of fact, and Angie felt sorry for the poor thing. He/she said that's all he/she was looking for, self-esteem.

Angie got sort of drunk and spent her time talking to Mike while Jim took a shower and got ready for bed. Angie could tell he was taking a real long time to give Mike and her a chance to be alone. And then they were making out and his hands were all over her and then she was down on her knees next to his bed and doing him and he was gasping and groaning and bucking and just going crazy and it made her feel powerful and wonderful to make a man this happy, especially a broken-hearted one.

When Jim came back, wearing a red terry-cloth robe and rubbing his crew cut with a white towel, Angie and Mike were sitting in chairs and having another drink.

"So, what's going on?" Jim said.

"Well," Mike said, and he looked like a teenager, excited and nervous at the same time, "I was going to ask Angie if she'd like to come to Denver with me. Spend a couple of weeks while we get the grand opening all set up and everything."

Jim said, still rubbing his crew cut with the white towel, "This is a guy who does everything first-class, Angie, let me tell you. You should see his condo. The view of the city. Unbelievable."

"You like Jet Skiing?" Mike said.

"Sure," Angie said, though she wasn't exactly sure what it was.

"Well, I've got *two* Jet Skis and they're a ball. Believe me, we could have a lot of fun. You could stay at my condo and do what you like during the day—shop or whatever—and then at night, we'll get together again."

Jim said, "God, Angie, you're a miracle worker. This sounds like my old buddy Mike Brady. I haven't heard him sound this happy in three or four years."

Mike grinned. "Maybe I'm in love."

And he leaned over and slid his arm around Angie's neck and gave her a big whiskey kiss on the mouth.

All she could think of was how strange it was. Maybe she'd met the man who was going to make her into a kept woman. And this one wasn't married, either. He could marry her somewhere down the line.

She said, "Wait till I tell Jason."

Mike gave her a funny look. "Jason? Who's Jason?"

Jim came over, too. "Yeah, who's Jason?"

"Oh, sort of my stepson, I guess you'd say."

"You're traveling with a kid?" Mike said.

"Yeah."

Mike didn't have to say anything. It was all in his face. He'd been outlining an orgy of activities and she went and ruined it all with reality. A kid. A fucking kid.

"Oh," Mike said, finally.

"He's a real nice kid," Angie said. "Real quiet and everything."

"I'm sure he's a nice kid, Angie," Jim said. "But I don't think that's what Mike had in mind. Nothing against kids, you understand. I've got two of my own and Mike's got three."

"I love kids," Mike said, as if somebody had accused him otherwise.

"He wouldn't be any trouble," Angie said. "He really wouldn't."

Mike and Jim looked at each other and Jim said, looking at Angie now, "You know what we should do? Why don't we take your phone number, you know where you're staying in Omaha and every-thing, and then Mike can give you a call when he gets settled into his condo?"

Mike didn't have nerve enough to say good-bye so Jim was doing it for him.

A ball and chain, she remembered Roy said about Jason. Mike wasn't going to call. Jim was just saying that. And she'd be somewhere in Omaha, maybe with a waitress job or something. And pretty soon school would roll around and she'd have to worry about school clothes and getting him enrolled in a new school and everything. While somebody else would be living with Mike in his Denver condo, and Jet Skiing, whatever that was, and using Mike's American Express to buy new clothes and stuff.

She said, "You know if there's a river around here somewhere?"

"A river?" Jim said.

"Yes," she said. "A river."

Next morning at seven A.M. she knocked on the door. A sleepy pajamaed Jim opened it. "Hey," he said. "How's it goin'?" He sounded a little leery of seeing her. He'd obviously hoped they'd put the Denver matter to rest last night.

"Guess what?" she said.

"What?"

"I said I was sort of Jason's stepmother? Well, actually, I'm his aunt. My sister lives about ten miles from here and has troubles with depression. She wanted me to take him for a while but she stopped by the room here real early this morning and picked him up. Said she was feeling a lot better."

Mike could be seen over Jim's shoulder now. He said, excited, "So you don't have the kid anymore?"

"Free, white and twenty-one," she said.

"You're going to Denver!" he said.

Jim said, "I'm going to get some breakfast down the road. I'll be back in an hour or so."

He got dressed quick and left.

They did it their first time right in Mike's mussed bed. Only once or twice did she think of the kid, and how she'd smothered him in the room. She hadn't had any trouble finding the river. She had to give it to Roy. The ball-and-chain business. She had liked the kid but he really was a ball and chain.

A few hours later, they left for Denver. That night, they had spare ribs for supper at a roadside place. They drank a lot of wine, or vino, as Jim kept calling it, and Mike as a joke licked some of the rib sauce off her fingers. She was scared about later, when she went to sleep. Maybe she'd have nightmares about the kid. But she snuggled up to Mike real good and after they made love, they lay in the darkness sharing his cigarette and talking about Denver and she ended up not having any dreams at all.

Al Sarrantonio

THE ROPY THING

Joe R. Lansdale, Hisownself here. Writing about Al Sarrantonio. He was too modest to do it, so someone had to do it, and I've read just about everything he's written and have known him for years and love his short fiction.

When I was learning to write, one of the writers I was most impressed with and wanted to emulate was Al Sarrantonio. Here was a guy who had a unique point of view. He was always his own man, but he reminded me a bit of the best of Bradbury, had that same poetic echo. He reminded me a bit of an unsung short story writer, Kit Reed. Had that same sort of inexplicable subtext that spoke to your most inner self but wasn't something you could define in words.

That's what Al's done here. He's written another of his beautiful little fables via horror fiction. It has that special thing that makes a good story more than a story. It has echo beyond the words.

—J.R.L. (Hisownself)

The ropy thing got most of the neighborhood while Suzie and Jerry were watching Saturday morning cartoons on TV. Then the cable went out and Jerry's dad put on the radio but then that went out too. By then Suzie and Jerry were watching the ropy thing from the big picture window in Jerry's living room. The ropy thing was very fast, and sometimes they saw only its tip stretched high and straight, or formed into a loop, or snaking over a house or between trees or moving over cars. It hesitated, then shot into the moving van in front of Suzie's house across the street, pulling a fat uniformed mover out, coiling around him head to toe like a mummy and then yanking him down into the ground. It pulled Suzie's mom into the ground too, catching her as she tried to run back into the house from where she had been directing the movers from the curb.

"We're getting out!" Jerry's dad shouted, giving Jerry a strange look, and the ropy thing got him in the front yard between the garage and the car. Behind him was Jerry's mom, with an armful of pillows, and the ropy thing got her too. It got Jerry's sister, Jane, as she was sneaking away from the house to be with her boyfriend, Brad, down the block. Suzie and Jerry watched the ropy thing jump out of the bushes in front of Brad's house like a coiled black spring, getting Jane right in front of Brad, just as she reached to hold his hand. Brad turned to run but it got him too, shooting up out of the lawn and over the sidewalk, thin and fast. It whipped around Brad and squeezed him into two pieces, top and bottom, then pulled both halves down.

Suzie and Jerry ran up to the attic, and the ropy thing snaked up around the house but didn't climb that high and then went away. From the small octagonal attic window they watched it wrap around the Myers' house and pull the Myers' baby from the second-story window. Then it curled like a cat around the Myers' house's foundation, circling three times around and twitching, and stayed there.

"This is just like—" Jerry said, turning to Suzie, fear in his voice.

"I know," Suzie said, hushing him.

When they looked back at the Myers' house all the windows were broken and the porch posts had been ripped away, and the ropy thing was gone. They spied it down the block to the right, waving lazily in the air before whipping down; then they saw it up the block to the left, moving between two houses into the street to catch a running boy who looked like Billy Carson.

The day rose, a summer morning with nothing but heat.

The afternoon was hotter, an oven in the attic.

The ropy thing continued its work.

They discovered that the ropy thing could climb as high as it wanted when they retrieved Jerry's dad's binoculars and found the ropy thing wrapped like a boa constrictor around the steeple of the Methodist church in the middle of town, blocks away. It pulled something small, kicking and too far away to hear, out of the belfry and then slid down and away.

"I'm telling you it's—" Jerry said again.

Peering through the binoculars, Suzie again hushed him, but not before he finished: "—just like my father's trick."

★   ★   ★

They spent that night in the attic with the window cracked open for air. The ropy thing was outside, moving under the light of the moon. Twice it came close, once breaking the big picture window on the ground floor, then shooting up just in front of the attic window, tickling the opening with its tip, making Jerry, who was watching, gasp, but then flying away.

They found a box of crackers and ate them. The ropy thing's passings in front of the moon made vague, dark-gray shadows on the attic's ceiling and walls.

"Do you think it's happening everywhere?" Jerry asked.

"What do *you* think?" Suzie replied, and then Jerry remembered Dad's battery shortwave radio that pulled in stations from all over the world. It was in the back of the attic near the box of flashlights.

He got it and turned it on, and up and down the dial there was nothing but hissing.

"Everywhere . . ." Jerry whispered.

"Looks that way," Suzie answered.

"It can't be . . ." Jerry said.

Suzie ate another cracker.

Suddenly, Jerry dropped the radio and began to cry. "But it was just a trick my father played on me! It wasn't real!"

"It seemed real at the time, didn't it?" Suzie asked.

Jerry continued to sob. "He was *always* playing tricks on me! After I swallowed a cherry pit he hid a bunch of leaves in his hand and made believe he pulled them from my ear—he told me the cherry pit had grown inside and that I was now filled with a cherry tree! Another time he swore that a spaceship was about to land in the backyard, then he made me watch out the big picture window while he snuck into the back and threw a toy rocket over the roof so that it came down in front of me!" He looked earnest and confused. "He was always doing things like that!"

"You believed the tricks while they were happening, didn't you?" Suzie asked.

"Yes! But—"

"Maybe if you believe something hard enough, it happens for real."

Jerry was frantic. "But it was just a trick! You were with me, you saw what he did! He buried a piece of rope in the backyard, then brought us out and pulled the rope partway out of the ground, and said it was part of a giant monster, the Ropy Thing, which filled up the entire Earth until it was just below the surface—and that anytime it wanted it would throw out its ropy tentacles and grab everybody, and pull them down and suck them into its pulsating jelly body—"

He looked at Suzie with a kind of pleading on his face. "It wasn't *real!*"

"You believed."

"It was just a trick!"

"But you believed it was real," Suzie said quietly. She was staring at the floor. "Maybe because my mother was moving, taking me away from you, you believed so hard that you made it real." She looked up at him. "Maybe that's why it hasn't gotten us— because you did it."

She went to him and held him, stroking his hair with her long, thin fingers.

"Maybe you did it because you love me," she said.

Jerry looked up at her, his eyes still wet with tears. "I *do* love you," he said.

They ate all the food in the house after a week, and then moved to the Myers' house and ate all their food, and then to the Janzens' next door to the Myers'. They ate their way, uninvited guests, down one block and up the next. They ran from house to house at twilight or dawn. The ropy thing never came near them, busy now with catching all the neighborhood's dogs and cats.

Even when they did see the ropy thing, it stayed away, poking into a house on the next block, straining up straight, nearly touching the clouds, black and almost oily in the sun, like an antenna. It disappeared for days at a time, and once they saw a second ropy thing, through the telescope in the house they were living in, so far away from their own now that they didn't even know their hosts' names. They were near the edge of town, and the next town over had its own ropy thing curling up into the afternoon, rising up like a shoot here and there, pausing for a moment before bending midriff to point at the ropy thing in their own neighborhood. Their own ropy thing bent and pointed back at it.

Suzie looked at Jerry, who wanted to cry.

"Everywhere," she said.

★   ★   ★

As the summer wore on the squirrels disappeared, and then the birds and crickets and gnats and mosquitoes. Jerry and Suzie moved from house to house, town to town, and sometimes when they were out they saw the ropy thing pulling dragonflies into the ground, swatting flies dead and yanking them away. Everywhere it was the same: the ropy thing had rid every town, every house, every place, of people and animals and insects. Even the bees in the late summer were gone, as if the ropy thing had saved them for last, and now pulled them into its jelly body along with every-thing else alive. In one town they found a small zoo, and paused to look with wonder at the empty cages, the clean gorilla pit, the lapping water empty of seals.

There was plenty to eat, and water to drink, and soda in cans, and finally when they were done with the towns surrounding their town they rode a train, climbing into its engine and getting the diesel to fire and studying the controls and making it move. The engine made a sound like caught thunder. Even Jerry laughed then, putting his head out of the cab to feel the wind like a living thing on his face. Suzie fired the horn, which bellowed like a bullfrog. They passed a city, and then another, until the train ran out of fuel and left them in another town much like their own.

They moved on to another town after that, and then another after that, and always the ropy thing was there, following them, a sentinel in the distance, rising above the highest buildings, its end twitching.

Summer rolled toward autumn. Now, even when he looked at Suzie, Jerry never smiled anymore. His eyes became hollow, and his hands trembled, and he barely ate.

Autumn arrived, and still they moved on. In one nameless town, in one empty basement of an empty house, Jerry walked trembling to the workbench and took down from its pegboard a pair of pliers. He handed them to Suzie and said, "Make me stop believing."

"What do you mean?"

"Get the ropy thing out of my head."

Suzie laughed, went to the workbench herself and retrieved a flashlight, which she shined into Jerry's ears.

"Nothing in there but wax," she said.

"I don't want to believe anymore," Jerry said listlessly, sounding like a ghost.

"It's too late," Suzie said.

Jerry lay down on the floor and curled up into a ball.

"Then I want to die," he whispered.

Winter snapped at the heels of autumn. The air was apple cold, but there were no more apples. The ropy thing spent the fall yanking trees and bushes and late roses and grass into the ground.

It was scouring the planet clean of weeds and fish and amoebas and germs.

Jerry stopped eating, and Suzie had to help him walk.

Idly, Jerry wondered what the ropy thing would do after it had killed the Earth.

Suzie and Jerry stood between towns gazing at a field of dirt. In the distance the ropy thing waved and worked, making corn stalks disappear in neat rows. Behind Jerry and Suzie, angled off the highway into a dusty ditch, was the car that Suzie had driven, telephone books propping her up so that she could see over the wheel, until it ran out of gas. The sky was a thin dusty blue-gray, painted with sickly clouds, empty of birds.

A few pale snowflakes fell.

"I want it to end," Jerry whispered hoarsely.

He had not had so much as a drink of water in days. His clothes were rags, his eyes sunken with grief. When he looked at the sky now his eyeballs ached, as if blinded by light.

"I . . . want it to stop," he croaked.

He sat deliberately down in the dust, looking like an old man in a child's body. He looked up at Suzie, blinked weakly.

When he spoke, it was a soft question: "It wasn't me, it was you who did it."

Suzie said nothing, and then she said, "I believed. I believed because I had to. You were the only one who ever loved me. They were going to take me away from you."

There was more silence. In the distance, the ropy thing finished with the cornfield, stood at attention, waiting. Around its base a cloud of weak dust settled.

Quietly, Jerry said, "I don't love you anymore."

For a moment, Suzie's eyes looked sad—but then they turned to something much harder than steel.

"Then there's nothing left," she said.

Jerry sighed, squinting at the sky with his weak eyes.

The ropy thing embraced him, almost tenderly.

And as it pulled him down into its pulsating jelly body, he saw a million ropy things, thin and black, reaching up like angry fingers to the Sun and other stars beyond.

Gene Wolfe

THE TREE IS MY HAT

This is a true story: I once heard a fellow editor say he would quit his job and become Gene Wolfe's unpaid valet just so Wolfe could continue, without distraction, to write the kind of stories he writes.

Man, oh man, how's that for a testimonial?

I get the feeling that editor isn't alone.

Since he burst onto the science fiction scene in the 1970s with stories like "The Fifth Head of Cerberus," Gene Wolfe has been one of the treasures of that field, as well as the related fields of fantasy and horror to which he sometimes lends his talents. His longer work is best represented by his Severian the Torturer books, which at this time number four; they have been omnibused in The Book of the New Sun. *His writing is literary, perfumed with allusion, special, and unlike any other writer's.*

For us he has produced a special piece with an odd title that will make all the sense in the world once you've read the story.

---

30 Jan. I saw a strange stranger on the beach this morning. I had been swimming in the little bay between here and the village; that may have had something to do with it, although I did not feel tired. Dived down and thought I saw a shark coming around the big staghorn coral. Got out fast. The whole swim cannot have been more than ten minutes. Ran out of the water and started walking.

There it is. I have begun this journal at last. (Thought I never would.) So let us return to all the things I ought to have put in and did not. I bought this the day after I came back from Africa.

No, the day I got out of the hospital—I remember now. I was wandering around, wondering when I would have another attack, and went into a little shop on Forty-second Street. There was a nice-looking woman in there, one of those good-looking black women, and I thought it might be nice to talk to her, so I had to buy something. I said, "I just got back from Africa."

She: "Really. How was it?" Me: "Hot."

Anyway, I came out with this notebook and told myself I had not wasted my money because I would keep a journal, writing down my attacks, what I had been doing and eating, as instructed; but all I could think of was how she looked when she turned to go to the back of the shop. Her legs and how she held her head. Her hips.

After that I planned to write down everything I remember from Africa, and what we said if Mary returned my calls. Then it was going to be about this assignment.

31 Jan. Setting up my new Mac. Who would think this place would have phones? But there are wires to Kololahi, and a dish. I can chat with people all over the world, for which the agency pays. (Talk about soft!) Nothing like this in Africa. Just the radio, and good luck with that.

I was full of enthusiasm. "A remote Pacific island chain." Wait . . .

P.D.: "Baden, we're going to send you to the Takanga Group."

No doubt I looked blank.

"It's a remote Pacific island chain." She cleared her throat and seemed to have swallowed a bone. "It's not going to be like Africa, Bad. You'll be on your own out there."

Me: "I thought you were going to fire me."

P.D.: "No, no! We wouldn't do that."

"Permanent sick leave."

"No, no, no! But, Bad." She leaned across her desk and for a minute I was afraid she was going to squeeze my hand. "This will be rough. I'm not going to try to fool you."

Hah!

Cut to the chase. This is nothing. This is a bungalow with rotten boards in the floors that has been here since before the British pulled out, a mile from the village and less than half that from the beach, close enough that the Pacific-smell is in all the rooms. The people are fat and happy, and my guess is not more than half are dumb. (Try and match that around Chicago.) Once or twice a year one gets yaws or some such, and Rev. Robbins gives him arsenic. *Which cures it.* Pooey!

There are fish in the ocean, plenty of them. Wild fruit in the jungle, and they know which you can eat. They plant yams and breadfruit, and if they need money or just want something, they dive for pearls and trade them when Jack's boat comes. Or do a big holiday boat trip to Kololahi.

There are coconuts too, which I forgot. They know how to open them. Or perhaps I am just not strong enough yet. (I look in the mirror, and ugh.) I used to weigh two hundred pounds.

"You skinny," the king says. "Ha, ha, ha!" He is really a good guy, I think. He has a primitive sense of humor, but there are worse things. He can take a jungle chopper (we said upanga but they say heletay) and open a coconut like a pack of gum. I have coconuts and a heletay but I might as well try to open them with a spoon.

1 Feb. Nothing to report except a couple of wonderful swims. I did not swim at all for the first couple of weeks. There are sharks. I know they are really out there because I have seen them once or twice. According to what I was told, there are saltwater crocs, too, up to fourteen feet long. I have never seen any of those and am skeptical, although I know they have them in Queensland. Every so often you hear about somebody who was killed by a shark, but that does not stop the people from swimming all the time, and I do not see why it should stop me. Good luck so far.

2 Feb. Saturday. I was supposed to write about the dwarf I saw on the beach that time, but I never got the nerve. Sometimes I used to see things in the hospital. Afraid it may be coming back. I decided to take a walk on the beach. All right, did I get sunstroke?

Pooey.

He was just a little man, shorter even than Mary's father. He was too small for any adult in the village. He was certainly not a child, and was too pale to have been one of the islanders at all.

He cannot have been here long; he was whiter than I am.

Rev. Robbins will know—ask tomorrow.

3 Feb. Hot and getting hotter. Jan. is the hottest month here, according to Rob Robbins. Well, I got here the first week in Jan. and it has never been this hot.

Got up early while it was still cool. Went down the beach to the village. (Stopped to have a look at the rocks where the dwarf disappeared.) Waited around for the service to begin but could not talk to Rob, he was rehearsing the choir—"Nearer My God to Thee."

Half the village came, and the service went on for almost two hours. When it was over I was able to get Rob alone. I said if he would drive us into Kololahi I would buy our Sunday dinner. (He has a jeep.) He was nice, but no—too far and the bad roads. I told him I had personal troubles I wanted his advice on, and he said, "Why don't we go to your place, Baden, and have a talk? I'd invite you for lemonade, but they'd be after me every minute."

So we walked back. It was hotter than hell, and this time I tried not to look. I got cold Cokes out of my rusty little fridge, and we sat on the porch (Rob calls it the veranda) and fanned ourselves. He knew I felt bad about not being able to do anything for these people, and urged patience. My chance would come.

I said, "I've given up on that, Reverend."

(That was when he told me to call him Rob. His first name is Mervyn.) "Never give up, Baden. Never." He looked so serious I almost laughed.

"All right, I'll keep my eyes open, and maybe someday the Agency will send me someplace where I'm needed."

"Back to Uganda?"

I explained that the A.O.A.A. almost never sends anyone to the same area twice. "That wasn't really what I wanted to talk to you about. It's my personal life. Well, really two things, but that's one of them. I'd like to get back together with my ex-wife. You're going to advise me to forget it, because I'm here and she's in Chicago; but I can send E-mail, and I'd like to put the bitterness behind us."

"Were there children? Sorry, Baden. I didn't intend it to hurt."

I explained how Mary had wanted them and I had not, and he gave me some advice. I have not E-mailed yet, but I will tonight after I write it out here.

"You're afraid that you were hallucinating. Did you feel feverish?" He got out his thermometer and took my temperature, which was nearly normal. "Let's look at it logically, Baden. This island is a hundred miles long and about thirty miles at the widest point. There are eight villages I know of. The population of Kololahi is over twelve hundred."

I said I understood all that.

"Twice a week, the plane from Cairns brings new tourists."

"Who almost never go five miles from Kololahi."

"Almost never, Baden. Not never. You say it wasn't one of the villagers. All right, I accept that. Was it me?"

"Of course not."

"Then it was someone from outside the village, someone from another village, from Kololahi, or a tourist. Why shake your head?"

I told him.

"I doubt there's a leprosarium nearer than the Marshalls. Anyway, I don't know of one closer. Unless you saw something else, some other sign of the disease, I doubt that this little man you saw had leprosy. It's a lot more likely that you saw a tourist with pasty white skin greased with sun blocker. As for his disappearing, the explanation seems pretty obvious. He dived off the rocks into the bay."

"There wasn't anybody there. I looked."

"There wasn't anybody there you saw, you mean. He would have been up to his neck in water, and the sun was glaring on the water, wasn't it?"

"I suppose so."

"It must have been. The weather's been clear." Rob drained his Coke and pushed it away. "As for his not leaving footprints, stop playing Sherlock Holmes. That's harsh, I realize, but I say it for your own good. Footprints in soft sand are shapeless indentations at best."

"I could see mine."

"You knew where to look. Did you try to backtrack yourself? I thought not. May I ask a few questions? When you saw him, did you think he was real?"

"Yes, absolutely. Would you like another one? Or something to eat?"

"No, thanks. When was the last time you had an attack?"

"A bad one? About six weeks."

"How about a not-bad one?"

"Last night, but it didn't amount to much. Two hours of chills, and it went away."

"That must have been a relief. No, I see it wasn't. Baden, the next time you have an attack, severe or not, I want you to come and see me. Understand?"

I promised.

"This is Bad. I still love you. That's all I have to say, but I want to say it. I was wrong, and I know it. I hope you've forgiven me." And sign off.

4 Feb. Saw him again last night, and he has pointed teeth. I was shaking under the netting, and he looked through the window and smiled. Told Rob, and said I read somewhere that cannibals used to file their teeth. I know these people were cannibals three or four generations back, and I asked if they had done it. He thinks not but will ask the king.

"I have been very ill, Mary, but I feel better now. It is evening here, and I am going to bed. I love you. Good night. I love you." Sign off.

5 Feb. Two men with spears came to take me to the king. I asked if I was under arrest, and they laughed. No ha, ha, ha from His Majesty this time, though. He was in the big house, but he came out and we went some distance among hardwoods the size of office buildings smothered in flowering vines, stopping in a circle of stones: the king, the men with spears, and an old man with a drum. The men with spears built a fire, and the drum made soft sounds like waves while the king made a speech or recited a poem, mocked all the while by invisible birds with eerie voices.

When the king was finished, he hung this piece of carved bone around my neck. While we were walking back to the village, he put his arm around me, which surprised me more than anything. He is bigger than a tackle in the NFL, and must weigh four hundred pounds. It felt like I was carrying a calf.

Horrible, *horrible* dreams! Swimming in boiled blood. Too scared to sleep anymore. Logged on and tried to find something on dreams and what they mean. Stumbled onto a witch in L.A.—her home page, then the lady herself. (I'll get you and your little dog too!) Actually, she seemed nice.

Got out the carved bone thing the king gave me. Old, and probably ought to be in a museum, but I suppose I had better wear it as long as I stay here, at least when I go out. Suppose I were to offend him? He might sit on me! Seems to be a fish with pictures scratched into both sides. More fish, man in a hat, etc. Cord through the eye. Wish I had a magnifying glass.

6 Feb. Still haven't gone back to bed, but my watch says Wednesday. Wrote a long E-mail, typing it in as it came to me. Told her where

I am and what I'm doing, and begged her to respond. After that I went outside and swam naked in the moonlit sea. Tomorrow I want to look for the place where the king hung this fish charm on me. Back to bed.

Morning, and beautiful. Why has it taken me so long to see what a beautiful place this is? (Maybe my heart just got back from Africa.) Palms swaying forever in the trade winds, and people like heroic bronze statues. How small, how stunted and pale we have to look to them!

Took a real swim to get the screaming out of my ears. Will I laugh in a year when I see that I said my midnight swim made me understand these people better? Maybe I will. But it did. They have been swimming in the moon like that for hundreds of years.

E-mail! God bless E-mail and whoever invented it! Just checked mine and found I had a message. Tried to guess who it might be. I wanted Mary, and was about certain it would be from the witch, from Annys. Read the name and it was "Julius R. Christmas." Pops! Mary's Pops! Got up and ran around the room, so excited I could not read it. Now I have printed it out, and I am going to copy it here.

"She went to Uganda looking for you, Bad. Coming back tomorrow, Kennedy, AA 47 from Heathrow. I'll tell her where you are. Watch out for those hula-hula girls."

SHE WENT TO UGANDA LOOKING FOR ME

7 Feb. More dreams—little man with pointed teeth smiling through the window. I doubt that I should write it all down, but I knew (in the dream) that he hurt people, and he kept telling me he would not hurt me. Maybe the first time was a dream too. More screams.

Anyway, I talked to Rob again yesterday afternoon, although I had not planned on it. By the time I got back here I was too sick to do anything except lie on the bed. The worst since I left the hospital, I think.

Went looking for the place the king took me to. Did not want to start from the village, kids might have followed me, so I tried to circle and come at it from the other side. Found two old buildings, small and no roofs, and a bone that looked human. More about that later. Did not see any marks, but did not look for them either. It was black on one end like it had been in a fire, though.

Kept going about three hours and wore myself out. Tripped on a chunk of stone and stopped to wipe off the sweat, and Blam! I was there! Found the ashes and where the king and I stood. Looked around wishing I had my camera, and there was Rob, sitting up on four stones that were still together and looking down at me. I said, "Hey, why didn't you say something?"

And he said, "I wanted to see what you would do." So he had been spying on me; I did not say it, but that was what it was.

I told him about going there with the king, and how he gave me a charm. I said I was sorry I had not worn it, but anytime he wanted a Coke I would show it to him.

"It doesn't matter. He knows you're sick, and I imagine he gave you something to heal you. It might even work, because God hears all sorts of prayers. That's not what they teach in the seminary, or even what it says in the Bible. But I've been out in the missions long enough to know. When somebody with good intentions talks to the God who created him, he's heard. Pretty often the answer is yes. Why did you come back here?"

"I wanted to see it again, that's all. At first I thought it was just a circle of rocks, then when I thought about it, it seemed like it must have been more."

Rob kept quiet; so I explained that I had been thinking of Stonehenge. Stonehenge was a circle of big rocks, but the idea had been to look at the positions of certain stars and where the sun rose. But this could not be the same kind of thing, because of the trees. Stonehenge is out in the open on Salisbury Plain. I asked if it was some kind of a temple.

"It was a palace once, Baden." Rob cleared his throat. "If I tell you something about it in confidence, can you keep it to yourself?"

I promised.

"These are good people now. I want to make that clear. They seem a little childlike to us, as all primitives do. If we were primitives ourselves—and we were, Bad, not so long ago—they wouldn't. Can you imagine how they'd seem to us if they didn't seem a little childlike?"

I said, "I was thinking about that this morning before I left the bungalow."

Rob nodded. "Now I understand why you wanted to come back

here. The Polynesians are scattered all over the South Pacific. Did you know that? Captain Cook, a British naval officer, was the first to explore the Pacific with any thoroughness, and he was absolutely astounded to find that after he'd sailed for weeks his interpreter could still talk to the natives. We know, for example, that Polynesians came down from Hawaii in sufficient numbers to conquer New Zealand. The historians hadn't admitted it the last time I looked, but it's a fact, recorded by the Maori themselves in their own history. The distance is about four thousand miles."

"Impressive."

"But you wonder what I'm getting at. I don't blame you. They're supposed to have come from Malaya originally. I won't go into all the reasons for thinking that they didn't, beyond saying that if it were the case they should be in New Guinea and Australia, and they're not."

I asked where they had come from, and for a minute or two he just rubbed his chin; then he said, "I'm not going to tell you that either. You wouldn't believe me, so why waste breath on it? Think of a distant land, a mountainous country with buildings and monuments to rival Ancient Egypt's, and gods worse than any demon Cotton Mather could have imagined. The time . . ." He shrugged. "After Moses but before Christ."

"Babylon?"

He shook his head. "They developed a ruling class, and in time those rulers, their priests and warriors, became something like another race, bigger and stronger than the peasants they treated like slaves. They drenched the altars of their gods with blood, the blood of enemies when they could capture enough, and the blood of peasants when they couldn't. Their peasants rebelled and drove them from the mountains to the sea, and into the sea."

I think he was waiting for me to say something; but I kept quiet, thinking over what he had said and wondering if it were true.

"They sailed away in terror of the thing they had awakened in the hearts of the nation that had been their own. I doubt very much if there were more than a few thousand, and there may well have been fewer than a thousand. They learned seamanship, and learned it well. They had to. In the Ancient World they were the only people to rival the Phoenicians, and they surpassed even the Phoenicians."

I asked whether he believed all that, and he said, "It doesn't matter whether I believe it, because it's true."

He pointed to one of the stones. "I called them primitives, and they are. But they weren't always as primitive as they are now. This was a palace, and there are ruins like this all over Polynesia, great buildings of coral rock falling to pieces. A palace and thus a sacred place, because the king was holy, the gods' representative. That was why he brought you here."

Rob was going to leave, but I told him about the buildings I found earlier and he wanted to see them. "There is a temple, too, Baden, although I've never been able to find it. When it was built, it must have been evil beyond our imagining. . . ." He grinned then, surprising hell out of me. "You must get teased about your name."

"Ever since elementary school. It doesn't bother me." But the truth is it does, sometimes.

More later.

Well, I have met the little man I saw on the beach, and to tell the truth (what's the sense of one of these if you are not going to tell the truth?) I like him. I am going to write about all that in a minute.

Rob and I looked for the buildings I had seen when I was looking for the palace but could not find them. Described them, but Rob did not think they were the temple he has been looking for since he came. "They know where it is. Certainly the older people do. Once in a while I catch little oblique references to it. Not jokes. They joke about the place you found, but not about that."

I asked what the place I had found had been.

"A Japanese camp. The Japanese were here during World War Two."

I had not known that.

"There were no battles. They built those buildings you found, presumably, and they dug caves in the hills from which to fight. I've found some of those myself. But the Americans and Australians simply bypassed this island, as they did many other islands. The Japanese soldiers remained here, stranded. There must have been about a company, originally."

"What happened to them?"

"Some surrendered. Some came out of the jungle to surrender and were killed. A few held out, twenty or twenty-five, from what I've heard. They left their caves and went back to the camp they had built when they thought Japan would win and control the entire

Pacific. That was what you found, I believe, and that's why I'd like to see it."

I said I could not understand how we could have missed it, and he said, "Look at this jungle, Baden. One of those buildings could be within ten feet of us."

After that we went on for another mile or two and came out on the beach. I did not know where we were, but Rob did. "This is where we separate. The village is that way, and your bungalow the other way, beyond the bay."

I had been thinking about the Japs, and asked if they were all dead, and he said they were. "They were older every year and fewer every year, and a time came when the rifles and machine guns that had kept the villages in terror no longer worked. And after that, a time when the people realized they didn't. They went to the Japanese camp one night with their spears and war clubs. They killed the remaining Japanese and ate them, and sometimes they make sly little jokes about it when they want to get my goat."

I was feeling pretty rocky and knew I was in for a bad time, so I came back here. I was sick the rest of the afternoon and all night, chills, fever, headache, the works. I remember watching the little vase on the bureau get up and walk to the other side, and sit back down, and seeing an American in a baseball cap float in. He took off his cap and combed his hair in front of the mirror, and floated back out. It was a Cardinals cap.

Now about Hanga, the little man I see on the beach.

After I wrote all that about the palace, I wanted to ask Rob a couple of questions and tell him Mary was coming. All right, no one has actually said she was, and so far I have heard nothing from her directly, only the one E-mail from Pops. But she went to Africa, so why not here? I thanked Pops and told him where I am again. He knows how much I want to see her. If she comes, I am going to ask Rob to re-marry us, if she will.

Started down the beach, and I saw him; but after half a minute or so he seemed to melt into the haze. I told myself I was still seeing things, and I was still sick; and I reminded myself that I promised to go by Rob's mission next time I felt bad. But when I got to the end of the bay, there he was, perfectly real, sitting in the shade of one of the young palms. I wanted to talk to him, so I said, "Okay if I sit down, too? This sun's frying my brains."

He smiled (the pointed teeth are real) and said, "The tree is my hat."

I thought he just meant the shade, but after I sat he showed me, biting off a palm frond and peeling a strip from it, then showing me how to peel them and weave them into a rough sort of straw hat, with a high crown and a wide brim.

We talked a little, although he does not speak English as well as some of the others. He does not live in the village, and the people who do, do not like him although he likes them. They are afraid of him, he says, and give him things because they are. They prefer he stay away. "No village, no boat."

I said it must be lonely, but he only stared out to sea. I doubt that he knows the word.

He wanted to know about the charm the king gave me. I described it and asked if it brings good luck. He shook his head. "No *malhoi*." Picking up a single palm fiber, "This *malhoi*." Not knowing what *malhoi* meant, I was in no position to argue.

That is pretty much all, except that I told him to visit when he wants company; and he told me I must eat fish to restore my health. (I have no idea who told him I am ill sometimes, but I never tried to keep it a secret.) Also that I would never have to fear an attack (I think that must have been what he meant) while he was with me.

His skin is rough and hard, much lighter in color than the skin of my forearm, but I have no idea whether that is a symptom or a birth defect. When I got up to leave, he stood too, and came no higher than my chest. Poor little man.

One more thing. I had not intended to put it down, but after what Rob said maybe I should. When I had walked some distance toward the village, I turned back to wave to Hanga, and he was gone. I walked back, thinking that the shade of the palm had fooled me; he was not there. I went to the bay, thinking he was in the water as Rob suggested. It is a beautiful little cove, but Hanga was not there, either. I am beginning to feel sympathy for the old mariners. These islands vanished when they approached.

At any rate, Rob says that *malhoi* means "strong." Since a palm fiber is not as strong as a cotton thread, there must be something wrong somewhere. (More likely, something I do not understand.) Maybe the word has more than one meaning.

Hanga means "shark," Rob says, but he does not know my friend Hanga. Nearly all the men are named for fish.

*   *   *

More E-mail, this time the witch. "There is danger hanging over you. I feel it and know some higher power guided you to me. Be careful. Stay away from places of worship, my tarot shows trouble for you there. Tell me about the fetish you mentioned."

I doubt that I should, and that I will E-mail her again.

9 Feb. I guess I wore myself out on writing Thursday. I see I wrote nothing yesterday. To tell the truth, there was nothing to write about except my swim in Hanga's bay. And I cannot write about that in a way that makes sense. Beautiful beyond description. That is all I can say. To tell the truth, I am afraid to go back. Afraid I will be disappointed. No spot on earth, even under the sea, can be as lovely as I remember it. Colored coral, and the little sea-animals that look like flowers, and schools of blue and red and orange fish like live jewels.

Today when I went to see Rob (all right, Annys warned me; but I think she is full of it) I said he probably likes to think God made this beautiful world so we could admire it; but if He had, He would have given us gills.

"Do I also think that He made the stars for us, Baden? All those flaming suns hundreds and thousands of light-years away? Did God create whole galaxies so that once or twice in our lives we might chance to look up and glimpse them?"

When he said that I had to wonder about people like me, who work for the Federal Government. Would we be driven out someday, like the people Rob talked about? A lot of us do not care any more about ordinary people than they did. I know P.D. does not.

A woman who had cut her hand came in about then. Rob talked to her in her own language while he treated her, and she talked a good deal more, chattering away. When she left I asked whether he had really understood everything she said. He said, "I did and I didn't. I knew all the words she used, if that's what you mean. How long have you been here now, Baden?"

I told him and he said, "About five weeks? That's perfect. I've been here about five years. I don't speak as well as they do. Sometimes I have to stop to think of the right word, and sometimes I can't think of it at all. But I understand when I hear them. It's not an elaborate language. Are you troubled by ghosts?"

I suppose I gawked.

"That was one of the things she said. The king has sent for a woman from another village to rid you of them, a sort of witch-doctress, I imagine. Her name is Langitokoua."

I said the only ghost bothering me was my dead marriage's, and I hoped to resuscitate it with his help.

He tried to look through me and may have succeeded; he has that kind of eyes. "You still don't know when Mary's coming?"

I shook my head.

"She'll want to rest a few days after her trip to Africa. I hope you're allowing for that."

"And she'll have to fly from Chicago to Los Angeles, from Los Angeles to Melbourne, and from there to Cairns, after which she'll have to wait for the next plane to Kololahi. Believe me, Rob, I've taken all that into consideration."

"Good. Has it occurred to you that your little friend Hanga might be a ghost? I mean, has it occurred to you since you spoke to him?"

Right then, I had that "what am I doing here" feeling I used to get in the bush. There I sat in that bright, flimsy little room with the medicine smell, and a jar of cotton balls at my elbow, and the noise of the surf coming in the window, about a thousand miles from any-place that matters; and I could not remember the decisions I had made and the plans that had worked or not worked to get me there.

"Let me tell you a story, Baden. You don't have to believe it. The first year I was here, I had to go to town to see about some building supplies we were buying. As things fell out, there was a day there when I had nothing to do, and I decided to drive up to North Point. People had told me it was the most scenic part of the island, and I convinced myself I ought to see it. Have you ever been there?"

I had not even heard of it.

"The road only goes as far as the closest village. After that there's a footpath that takes two hours or so. It really is beautiful, rocks standing above the waves, and dramatic cliffs overlooking the ocean. I stayed there long enough to get the lovely, lonely feel of the place and make some sketches. Then I hiked back to the village where I'd left the jeep and started to drive back to Kololahi. It was almost dark.

"I hadn't gone far when I saw a man from our village walking along the road. Back then I didn't know everybody, but I knew him. I stopped, and we chatted for a minute. He said he was on his way to see his parents, and I thought they must live in the place I had just left. I told him to get into the jeep, and drove back, and let him out.

He thanked me over and over, and when I got out to look at one of the tires I was worried about, he hugged me and kissed my eyes. I've never forgotten that."

I said something stupid about how warmhearted the people here are.

"You're right, of course. But, Baden, when I got back, I learned that North Point is a haunted place. It's where the souls of the dead go to make their farewell to the land of the living. The man I'd picked up had been killed by a shark the day I left, four days before I gave him a ride."

I did not know what to say, and at last I blurted out, "They lied to you. They had to be lying."

"No doubt—or I'm lying to you. At any rate, I'd like you to bring your friend Hanga here to see me if you can."

I promised I would try to bring Rob to see Hanga, since Hanga will not go into the village.

Swimming in the little bay again. I never thought of myself as a strong swimmer, never even had much chance to swim, but have been swimming like a dolphin, diving underwater and swimming with my eyes open for what has got to be two or two and a half minutes if not longer. Incredible! My God, wait till I show Mary!

You can buy scuba gear in Kololahi. I'll rent Rob's jeep or pay one of the men to take me in his canoe.

11 Feb. I let this slide again, and need to catch up. Yesterday was very odd. So was Saturday.

After I went to bed (still full of Rob's ghost story and the new world underwater) and *crash*! Jumped up scared as hell, and my bureau had fallen on its face. Dry rot in the legs, apparently. A couple of drawers broke, and stuff scattered all over.

I propped it back up and started cleaning up the mess, and found a book I never saw before, *The Light Garden of the Angel King,* about traveling through Afghanistan. In front is somebody's name and a date, and "American Overseas Assistance Agency." None of it registered right then.

But there it was, spelled out for me. And here is where he was, Larry Scribble. He was an Agency man, had bought the book three years ago (when he was posted to Afghanistan, most likely) and brought it with him when he was sent here. I only use the top three drawers, and it had been in one of the others and got overlooked when somebody (who?) cleared out his things.

Why was he gone when I got here? He should have been here to brief me, and stayed for a week or so. No one has so much as mentioned his name, and there must be a reason for that.

Intended to go to services at the mission and bring the book, but was sick again. Hundred and nine. Took medicine and went to bed, too weak to move, and had this very strange dream. Somehow I knew somebody was in the house. (I suppose steps, although I cannot remember any.) Sat up, and there was Hanga smiling by my bed. "I knock. You not come."

I said, "I'm sorry. I've been sick." I felt fine. Got up and offered to get him a Coke or something to eat, but he wanted to see the charm. I said sure, and got it off the bureau.

He looked at it, grunting and tracing the little drawings on its sides with his forefinger. "No tie? You take loose?" He pointed to the knot.

I said there was no reason to, that it would go over my head without untying the cord.

"Want friend?" He pointed to himself, and it was pathetic. "Hanga friend? Bad friend?"

"Yes," I said. "Absolutely."

"Untie."

I said I would cut the cord if he wanted me to.

"Untie, please. Blood friend." (He took my arm then, repeating, "Blood friend!")

I said all right and began to pick at the knot, which was complex; and at that moment, I swear, I heard someone else in the bungalow, some third person who pounded on the walls. I believe I would have gone to see who it was then, but Hanga was still holding my arm. He has big hands on those short arms, with a lot of strength in them.

In a minute or two I got the cord loose and asked if he wanted it, and he said eagerly that he did. I gave it to him, and there was one of those changes you get in dreams. He straightened up, and was at least as tall as I am. Holding my arm, he cut it quickly and neatly with his teeth and licked the blood, and seemed to grow again. It was as if some sort of defilement had been wiped away. He looked intelligent and almost handsome.

Then he cut the skin of his own arm just like mine. He offered it to me, and I licked his blood like he had licked mine. For some reason I expected it to taste horrible, but it did not; it was as if I had gotten seawater in my mouth while I was swimming.

"We are blood friends now, Bad," Hanga told me. "I shall not harm you, and you must not harm me."

That was the end of the dream. The next thing I remember is lying in bed and smelling something sweet, while something tickled my ear. I thought the mosquito netting had come loose, and looked to see, and there was a woman with a flower in her hair lying beside me. I rolled over; and she, seeing that I was awake, embraced and kissed me.

She is Langitokoua, the woman Rob told me the king had sent for, but I call her Langi. She says she does not know how old she is, and is fibbing. Her size (she is about six feet tall, and must weigh a good two-fifty) makes her look older than she is, I feel sure. Twenty-five, maybe. Or seventeen. I asked her about ghosts, and she said very matter-of-factly that there is one in the house but he means no harm.

Pooey.

After that, naturally I asked her why the king wanted her to stay with me; and she solemnly explained that it is not good for a man to live by himself, that a man should have someone to cook and sweep, and take care of him when he is ill. That was my chance, and I went for it. I explained that I am expecting a woman from America soon, that American women are jealous, and that I would have to tell the American woman Langi was there to nurse me. Langi agreed without any fuss.

What else?

Hanga's visit was a dream, and I know it; but it seems I was sleepwalking. (Perhaps I wandered around the bungalow delirious.) The charm was where I left it on the dresser, but the cord was gone. I found it under my bed and tried to put it back through the fish's eye, but it will not go.

E-mail from Annys: "The hounds of hell are loosed. For heaven's sake be careful. Benign influences rising, so have hope." Crazy if you ask me.

E-mail from Pops: "How are you? We haven't heard from you. Have you found a place for Mary and the kids? She is on her way."

$\star$ $\star$ $\star$

What kids? Why the old puritan!

Sent a long E-mail back saying I had been very ill but was better, and there were several places where Mary could stay, including this bungalow, and I would leave the final choice to her. In fairness to Pops, he has no idea where or how I live, and may have imagined a rented room in Kololahi with a monkish cot. I should send another E-mail asking about her flight from Cairns; I doubt he knows, but it may be worth a try.

Almost midnight, and Langi is asleep. We sat on the beach to watch the sunset, drank rum-and-Coke and rum-and-coconut-milk when the Coke ran out, looked at the stars, talked, and made love. Talked some more, drank some more, and made love again.

There. I had to put that down. Now I have to figure out where I can hide this so Mary never sees it. I will not destroy it and I will not lie. (Nothing is worse than lying to yourself. *Nothing.* I ought to know.)

Something else in the was-it-a-dream category, but I do not think it was. I was lying on my back in the sand, looking up at the stars with Langi beside me asleep; and I saw a UFO. It was somewhere between me and the stars, sleek, dark, and torpedo-shaped, but with a big fin on the back, like a rocket ship in an old comic. Circled over us two or three times, and was gone. Haunting, though.

It made me think. Those stars are like the islands here, only a million billion times bigger. Nobody really knows how many islands there are, and there are probably a few to this day that nobody has ever been on. At night they look up at the stars and the stars look down on them, and they tell each other, "They're coming!"

Langi's name means "sky sister" so I am not the only one who ever thought like that.

Found the temple!!! Even now I cannot believe it. Rob has been looking for it for five years, and I found it in six weeks. God, but I would love to tell him!

Which I cannot do. I gave Langi my word, so it is out of the question.

We went swimming in the little bay. I dove down, showing her corals and things that she has probably been seeing since she was old enough to walk, and she showed the temple to me. The roof is gone if it ever had one, and the walls are covered with coral and the sea-creatures that look like flowers; you can hardly see it unless somebody shows you. But once you do it is all there, the long straight walls, the main entrance, the little rooms at the sides, everything. It is as if you were looking at the ruins of a cathedral, but they were decked in flowers and bunting for a fiesta. (I know that is not clear, but it is what it was like, the nearest I can come.) They built it on land, and the water rose; but it is still there. It looks hidden, not abandoned. Too old to see, and too big.

I will never forget this: How one minute it was just rocks and coral, and the next it was walls and altar, with a fifty-foot branched coral like a big tree growing right out of it. Then an enormous gray-white shark with eyes like a man's came out of the shadow of the coral tree to look at us, worse than a lion or a leopard. My god, was I ever scared!

When we were both back up on the rocks, Langi explained that the shark had not meant to harm us, that we would both be dead if it had. (I cannot argue with that.) Then we picked flowers, and she made wreaths out of them and threw them in the water and sang a song. Afterward she said it was all right for me to know, because we are us; but I must never tell other *mulis*. I promised faithfully that I would not.

She has gone to the village to buy groceries. I asked her whether they worshiped Rob's God in the temple underwater. (I had to say it like that for her to understand.) She laughed and said no, they worshiped the shark god so the sharks would not eat them. I have been thinking about that.

It seems to me that they must have brought other gods from the mountains where they lived, a couple of thousand years ago, and they settled here and built that temple to their old gods. Later, probably hundreds of years later, the sea came up and swallowed it. Those old gods went away, but they left the sharks to guard their house. Someday the water will go down again. The ice will grow thick and strong on Antarctica once more, the Pacific will recede, and those murderous old mountain gods will return. That is how it seems to me, and if it is true I am glad I will not be around to see it.

I do not believe in Rob's God, so logically I should not believe in them either. But I do. It is a new millennium, but we are still playing by the old rules. They are going to come to teach us the new ones, or that is what I am afraid of.

Valentine's Day. Mary passed away. That is how Mom would have said it, and I have to say it like that, too. Print it. I cannot make these fingers print the other yet.

Can anybody read this?

Langi and I had presented her with a wreath of orchids, and she was wearing them. It was so fast, so crazy.

So much blood, and Mary and kids screaming.

I had better backtrack or give this up altogether.

There was a boar hunt. I did not go, remembering how sick I had been after tramping through the jungle with Rob, but Langi and I went to the pig roast afterward. Boar hunting is the men's favorite pastime; she says it is the only thing that the men like better than dancing. They do not have dogs and do not use bows and arrows. It is all a matter of tracking, and the boars are killed with spears when they find them, which must be really dangerous. I got to talk to the king about this hunt, and he told me how they get the boar they want to a place where it cannot run away anymore. It turns then and defies them, and may charge; but if it does not, four or five men all throw their spears at once. It was the king's spear, he said, that pierced the heart of this boar.

Anyway it was a grand feast with pineapples and native beer, and my rum, and lots of pork. It was nearly morning by the time we got back here, where Mary was asleep with Mark and Adam.

Which was a very good thing, since it gave us a chance to swim and otherwise freshen up. By the time they woke up, Langi had prepared a fruit tray for breakfast and woven the orchids, and I had picked them for her and made coffee. Little boys, in my experience, are generally cranky in the morning (could it be because we do not allow them coffee?) but Adam and Mark were sufficiently over-whelmed by the presence of a brown lady giant and a live skeleton that conversation was possible. They are fraternal twins, and I think they really are mine; certainly they look very much like I did at their age. The wind had begun to rise, but we thought nothing of it.

"Were you surprised to see me?" Mary was older than I remembered, and had the beginnings of a double chin.

"Delighted. But Pops told me you'd gone to Uganda, and you were on your way here."

"To the end of the earth." (She smiled, and my heart leaped.) "I never realized the end would be as pretty as this."

I told her that in another generation the beach would be lined with condos.

"Then let's be glad that we're in this one." She turned to the boys. "You have to take in everything as long as we're here. You'll never get another chance like this."

I said, "Which will be a long time, I hope."

"You mean that you and . . .?"

"Langitokoua." I shook my head. (Here it was, and all my lies had melted away.) "Was I ever honest with you, Mary?"

"Certainly. Often."

"I wasn't, and you know it. So do I. I've got no right to expect you to believe me now. But I'm going to tell you, and myself, God's own truth. It's in remission now. Langi and I were able to go to a banquet last night, and eat, and talk to people, and enjoy ourselves. But when it's bad, it's horrible. I'm too sick to do anything but shake and sweat and moan, and I see things that aren't there. I—"

Mary interrupted me, trying to be kind. "You don't look as sick as I expected."

"I know how I look. My mirror tells me every morning while I shave. I look like death in a microwave oven, and that's not very far from the truth. It's liable to kill me this year. If it doesn't, I'll probably get attacks on and off for the rest of my life, which is apt to be short."

There was a silence that Langi filled by asking whether the boys wanted some coconut milk. They said they did, and she got my hele-tay and showed them how to open a green coconut with one chop. Mary and I stopped talking to watch her, and that's when I heard the surf. It was the first time that the sound of waves hitting the beach had ever reached as far inland as my bungalow.

Mary said, "I rented a Range Rover at the airport." It was the tone she used when she had to bring up something she really did not want to bring up.

"I know. I saw it."

"It's fifty dollars a day, Bad, plus mileage. I won't be able to keep it long."

I said, "I understand."

"We tried to phone. I had hoped you would be well enough to come for us, or send someone."

I said I would have had to borrow Rob's jeep if I had gotten her call.

"I wouldn't have known where you were, but we met a native, a very handsome man who says he knows you. He came along to show us the way." (At that point, the boys' expressions told me something was seriously wrong.) "He wouldn't take any money for it. Was I wrong to offer to pay him? He didn't seem angry."

"No," I said, and would have given anything to get the boys alone. But would it have been different if I had? When I read this, when I really get to where I can face it, the thing I will miss on was how fast it was—how fast the whole thing went. It cannot have been an hour between the time Mary woke up and the time Langi ran to the village to get Rob.

Mark lying there whiter than the sand. So thin and white, and looking just like me.

"He thought you were down on the beach, and wanted us to look for you there, but we were too tired," Mary said.

That is all for now, and in fact it is too much. I can barely read this left-handed printing, and my stump aches from holding down the book. I am going to go to bed, where I will cry, I know, and Langi will cuddle me like a kid.

Again tomorrow.

17 Feb. Hospital sent its plane for Mark, but no room for us. Doctor a lot more interested in my disease than my stump. "Dr. Robbins" did a fine job there, he said. We will catch the Cairns plane Monday.

I should catch up. But first: I am going to steal Rob's jeep tomorrow. He will not lend it, does not think I can drive. It will be slow, but I know I can.

19 Feb. Parked on the tarmac, something wrong with one engine. Have I got up nerve enough to write about it now? We will see.

Mary was telling us about her guide, how good-looking, and all he told her about the islands, lots I had not known myself. As if she were surprised she had not seen him sooner, she pointed and said, "Here he is now."

There was nobody there. Or rather, there was nobody Langi and I or the boys could see. I talked to Adam (to my son Adam, I have to get used to that) when it was over, while Rob was working on

Mark and Mary. I had a bunch of surgical gauze and had to hold it as tight as I could. There was no strength left in my hand.

Adam said Mary had stopped and the door opened, and she made him get in back with Mark. *The door opened by itself.* That is the part he remembers most clearly, and the part of his story I will always remember, too. After that Mary seemed to be talking all the time to somebody he and his brother could not see or hear.

She screamed, and there, for just an instant, was the shark. He was as big as a boat, and the wind was like a current in the ocean, blowing us down to the water. I really do not see how I can ever explain this.

No takeoff yet, so I have to try. It is easy to say what was not happening. What is hard is saying what was, because there are no words. The shark was not swimming in air. I know that is what it will sound like, but it (he) was not. We were not under the water, either. We could breathe and walk and run just as he could swim, although not nearly so fast, and even fight the current a little.

The worst thing of all was he came and went and came and went, so that it seemed almost that we were running or fighting him by flashes of lightning, and sometimes he was Hanga, taller than the king and smiling at me while he herded us.

No. The most worst thing was really that he was herding everybody but me. He drove them toward the beach the way a dog drives sheep, Mary, Langi, Adam, and Mark, and he would have let me escape. (I wonder sometimes why I did not. This was a new me, a me I doubt I will ever see again.)

His jaws were real, and sometimes I could hear them snap when I could not see him. I shouted, calling him by name, and I believe I shouted that he was breaking our agreement, that to hurt my wives and my sons was to hurt me. To give the devil his due, I do not think he understood. The old gods are very wise, as the king told me today; still, there are limits to their understanding.

I ran for the knife, the heletay Langi opened coconuts with. I thought of the boar, and by God I charged them. I must have been terrified. I do not remember, only slashing at something and someone huge that was and was not there, and in an instant was back again. The sting of the wind-blown sand, and then up to my arms in foaming water, and cutting and stabbing, and the hammerhead with my knife and my hand in its mouth.

We got them all out, Langi and I did. But Mark has lost his leg, and jaws three feet across had closed on Mary. That was Hanga himself, I feel sure.

Here is what I think. I think he could only make one of us see him at a time, and that was why he flashed in and out. He is real. (God knows he is real!) Not really physical the way a stone is, but physical in other ways that I do not understand. Physical like and unlike light and radiation. He showed himself to each of us, each time for less than a second.

Mary wanted children, so she stopped the pill and did not tell me. That was what she told me when I drove Rob's jeep out to North Point. I was afraid. Not so much afraid of Hanga (though there was that, too) but afraid she would not be there. Then somebody said "Banzai!" It was exactly as if he were sitting next to me in the jeep, except that there was nobody there. I said "Banzai" back, and I never heard him again; but after that I knew I would find her, and I waited for her at the edge of the cliff.

She came back to me when the sun touched the pacific, and the darker the night and the brighter the stars, the more real she was. Most of the time it was as if she were really in my arms. When the stars got dim and the first light showed in the east, she whispered, "I have to go," and walked over the edge, walking north with the sun to her right and getting dimmer and dimmer.

I got dressed again and drove back and it was finished. That was the last thing Mary ever said to me, spoken a couple of days after she died.

She was not going to get back together with me at all; then she heard how sick I was in Uganda, and she thought the disease might have changed me. (It has. What does it matter about people at the "end of the earth" if you cannot be good to your own people, most of all to your own family?)

Taking off.

We are airborne at last. Oh, Mary! Mary starlight!

*   *   *

Langi and I will take Adam to his grandfather's, then come back and stay with Mark (Brisbane or Melbourne) until he is well enough to come home.

The stewardess is serving lunch, and for the first time since it happened, I think I may be able to eat more than a mouthful. One stewardess, twenty or thirty people, which is all this plane will hold. News of the shark attack is driving tourists off the island.

As you see, I can print better with my left hand. I should be able to write eventually. The back of my right hand itches, even though it is gone. I wish I could scratch it.

Here comes the food.

An engine has quit. Pilot says no danger.

He is out there, swimming beside the plane. I watched him for a minute or more until he disappeared into a thunderhead. "The tree is my hat." Oh, God.

Oh my God!

My blood brother.

What can I do?

Edward Bryant

STYX AND BONES

Edward Bryant is another writer who wears many hats (though, as far as I know, no cowboy hat—though he does live in Denver and was raised in Wyoming). For a long time he has been a respected reviewer for Locus *magazine, where his specialty is this field, and he has occasionally—but not often enough—turned out short stories with a technical facility that is to be envied. He is another in the long list of writers who migrated from science fiction to horror, but has never left his roots behind and has managed to make both fields his comfortable home. His early, highly regarded science fiction work such as* Cinnabar, *a series of linked stories about a future California on a dying Earth, eventually gave way to equally well regarded work in the horror genre, the latest example of which is the following, a bone-chilling (yes, that's a pun, but also a literal description) example of the classic love-revenge tale.*

He dreamed he woke up dead.

Dead. Crushed. Every nerve pulled excruciatingly away from each muscle and each shattered bone. Awake and dead.

That was the confusion. The contradiction didn't occur to him until later. Much later. Now was only the pain.

Christ, he thought. *What's wrong?* It hurt so very much, and the least of the agony was a wasp drilling through his inner ear. He tried to reach to block the sound, but that motion only cranked the pain to a level that nauseated him. He couldn't raise his arms anyway.

Not a wasp. *No . . .* The noise was the telephone on the bedside table. He grabbed for it instinctively—*tried* to grab, could not. *What was wrong with his arms?* He bucked against the mattress, the tan print comforter sliding away from his lower body. Legs slipped off the mattress, feet slapping against the carpet and the slick mess of spilled magazines.

He smelled something heavy and terrible.

The sheet stuck to him as his body, levered upright, lurched against the bed table. His left arm swung around loosely, hand smacking the phone. It felt like incandescent steel wire flaring up molten inside his shoulder. He screamed.

The telephone tumbled to the floor as the handset swung around the base of the banker's lamp. The receiver jiggled up and down as if the coiled cord were the hemp rope dangling someone newly executed.

If he could have gotten his breath he might have cried. He heard the modulated wasp buzzing coming from the telephone earpiece. The tone was familiar and angry. He knew who it was. It didn't matter.

He needed help and so he sank to his knees attempting to align his face with the receiver.

"—the fuck are you doing, jerkweed?" the tinny voice was saying. "Too early for you? I told you last night I was coming over today to pick up my stuff."

His voice caught on a sob. "I need help," he gasped out. *"Please."*

Silence. Then the tenor of her voice changed. Curiosity and alarm replaced the fury with the suddenness of a carousel projector clicking ahead to the next slide. "Danny? What's wrong?"

"I don't know," he said. "I can't move."

"You're paralyzed?"

"No, no. My arms. *They* don't work. And it hurts," he said. "It hurts like a son of a bitch."

"Is this a goddamn trick?" she said. "Are you telling me the truth?"

"Yes," he said, voice catching on a sob he couldn't help. "Louisa, I swear to God something's really, really wrong."

"I'm on my way," she said.

"You got your key?" Danny said. "I can't unlock the door."

"I've got the key," Louisa answered. "I was gonna sharpen it like a razor and cut your balls off." Her voice sounded perfectly controlled. "I'm leaving now, baby. Hang on."

Danny heard the click as she set down her phone. He listened as the computerized phone company warning came, then the ear-rasping alert tone, finally silence on the line. Even if he used his teeth, there was no way he could hang up his phone.

He tried to sit up straight on the edge of the bed, wishing he were anywhere else, *anyone* else.

What's happened to me? he thought. Was he whining? Of course he was whining. It hurt too damned much to be brave.

In the twenty minutes it took for Louisa to drive over, he managed to stagger downstairs to the kitchen. It was a cold, cold January morning and something had obviously happened to the heat. A few wisps of warmth emanated from the register just inside the kitchen. He stood there quietly, aching, attempting to soak up what furnace air he could.

He heard the front door open and close.

"Danny?" she called.

"In the kitchen."

He listened to the steps approach. He wanted to shut his eyes. Louisa poked her head through the kitchen doorway and surveyed him, eyes wide, head to feet. "Danny, sweetie, you are a mess." Her voice sounded sincere but amazed. She wrinkled her nose.

He knew how he appeared, standing naked save for his soiled briefs, back against the register, hands dangling in front of him with the thumbs locked together, liquid excrement drying in thin rivulets down his legs to the floor. Louisa shook her head. She involuntarily reached out toward him. As soon as her fingertips touched his arm, he cried out. She jerked back. "It hurts that much?" He nodded, jaws clenched. "You called a doctor?" He shook his head. "No," she said, "I guess you really couldn't." Louisa looked up at him from her five-feet-even vantage, chocolate eyes serious beneath the pixie-cut raven bangs. "First thing, maybe get you cleaned up a little?"

He nodded. "It's gotta help. Then call Dr. King."

"Call Dr. King now," she said. "Bath'll wait."

"Phone's upstairs," he said. "I couldn't hang it up."

"I'll take care of everything," Louisa said soothingly. "Don't you worry."

She followed him up the stairs. The cats were nowhere to be seen. He didn't blame them.

In the bedroom she unwound the receiver cord from around the lamp, then stood contemplating the bed. "We gotta get that cleaned up quick. Doctor'll wait. No one'll be able to live in this house with that stink."

"My briefs and the sheets," he said. "Just seal 'em in a plastic garbage bag and set them out in the trash. The comforter's expensive—maybe you can throw it over the picnic table in the backyard and let it dry. Then put it in another bag and I'll have it dry-cleaned."

She nodded and gingerly rolled the down comforter into a loose cylinder. "Bags in the kitchen?"

"In the broom closet."

In a few minutes Louisa was back with black mylar bags into which she matter-of-factly stuffed the soiled sheets. "Those too." She pointed at his briefs.

"They aren't much," he protested. "But it's cold up here."

"They're gross," she said evenly. "After you're clean you can wear a nice warm robe."

He tried to put his thumbs beneath the waistband. He couldn't. "What about Dr. King?"

She grabbed the waistband and skinned the briefs down his legs. "I changed my mind again. The doc can wait. You need some attention first."

There were two bathrooms in the house, both on the second floor. Only one had a tub and shower. Danny stepped into the tub and braced himself as she twisted the water knob. Nothing happened. "No pressure," she said. "No water at all."

"I should have let the faucets drip last night," he said. "I'll bet the pipes are frozen."

"Downstairs too?"

He started to shrug. Stopped. "It may be okay down there."

"I'll check. You stay here." In a minute she yelled from the foot of the stairs, "Water's running down here. I'll be up in a second." Actually it took quite a few seconds, but she started her own solo bucket brigade of saucepans full of steaming tap water.

He yelled as the first half gallon of what felt like scalding water cascaded down his back.

"Don't be a baby," she said. "You're just cold. I've checked the temperature. It'll be all right." Louisa poured another panful, then wet a washrag and began to scrub him down. After the first few shocks, he had to admit the water felt good. With his hands locked thumb to thumb in front of him, he stared down at the brown eddy swirling in the drain. He felt more water, more scrubbing. Eventually the draining water ran clear.

"Okay, step out of there." She toweled him down, attempting to be gentle when the cotton plush dragged across his shoulders. When he was reasonably dry, Louisa draped the blue terry cloth robe around his shoulders and belted it at the waist. "Now lie down. We'll call the doctor."

The soiled sheets were no longer on the bed, but the mattress was still wet and stained. It looked as though Louisa had given it a good scrubbing. She spread a bath towel across the area, then fluffed out a cheap quilt from the linen rack. "Okay, lie down." She efficiently flipped open an old wool blanket and drew it up to his waist. "Comfy?"

"I guess," he said. "Comfy as I'm gonna get." He knew he didn't really feel comfortable. But then who knew when his life was going to improve? Lie down while he could. He did so, gingerly flopping back against the mound of pillows Louisa had stacked.

Only after he'd painfully settled himself, he groaned.

"What's the matter?" said Louisa.

"I gotta pee."

"I'll help you up," she said.

"I'm not sure I can make it. My back and shoulders feel like they're going to come apart if I move."

"Hmm," said Louisa. "You got a chamber pot?"

"No."

"Hold on," she said, turning and exiting the bedroom.

"Where are you going?"

Her voice floated back from the stairwell. "The kitchen."

Danny concentrated on using the muscles on the nether side of his bladder. Suddenly he couldn't think of anything in the world he wanted more than to relieve himself.

Louisa returned with an empty plastic two-liter diet Coke bottle and a pair of shears. His eyes widened. "What're the scissors for?"

She clicked them mischievously. "In case I have to whittle you down so you'll fit the neck of this bottle."

"Ha ha," he said. "How about just trimming the neck?"

"Don't think you'll fit?"

"Even today," he said, "it looks like too tight a squeeze."

With a single scissors jab, she punched a hole at the base of the bottle neck, then snipped a generous hole. "Big enough?"

"As long as I don't sneeze. Looks sharp." He spread his legs a little farther apart as she placed the bottle between his thighs. Louisa deftly inserted his flaccid penis into the hole. It occurred to him that the last time she'd touched him there, she hadn't been nearly so clinical. But today he felt absolutely no excitement.

Just relief.

When he was done, she took the bottle away to the bathroom, then brought it back emptied and rinsed.

"So far, so good," she said.

"Will you call Dr. King?" Danny said. He knew the GP's office number by heart. Louisa held the receiver to his ear and he heard the clinic's receptionist answer. The woman tried to put him on hold; he argued eloquently. In less than a minute, the doctor was on the line.

Danny explained what had happened after his waking this morning from a sound sleep. Dr. King asked whether anyone was with him. "My friend Louisa." He glanced at her. "I think she'll drive me." She nodded vigorously. "Okay," he said. "One o'clock it is." She hung up the phone.

"Want some food?" she said.

He shook his head. "Coffee'd be good." The phone rang. "Weezie," he said. "Would you get that?"

She picked up the receiver. "Danny Royal's home," she said perkily. Then her expression darkened. "I don't think this is a good time for you to talk to him." Danny formed the word *who* with his lips. She shook her head. "He's not feeling very well right now." Pause. "No, call back another time. Or maybe not at all." Set the phone back in its cradle.

"Should I ask?" Danny said.

"Your *good friend* Iffie," Louisa said. Ice rimed her words. "She said she dreamed you were in trouble."

Danny stared back at her. "Hey, Ifetayo really is my friend. You know that. And she's Yoruba, by way of a family sidetrack to Port au Prince. She dreams, it's worth listening to."

"Let's get something straight," said Louisa angrily. "Friday night, I walked in and found *your friend* in your bed. With you, asshole."

"You should have called ahead," said Danny.

"Lame," she replied. "I think you were playing us off against each other for God knows how long."

"Ifetayo was really uncomfortable with this," he said placatingly. "Like I told you, she bowed out of the whole thing. I think she was pretty angry."

"Just like me?" Louisa's voice dripped venom briefly. "I meant it when I told you I was going to come by today to pick up my stuff—the cards, the sweaters, everything I ever gave you, every bit of myself."

His voice stayed calm. "So why didn't you?"

"Don't be an idiot. When I called you, and when I came over

and saw you . . . You're a mess, Danny. You're in trouble. I think you're really sick. I want to take care of you." She set one cool hand gently on his forehead. "I love you. God knows why, but I do." Her voice ran down like a clock spring unwinding and she stopped.

"Did she say anything else?" Danny said. "Ifetayo?"

"You jerk," said Louisa. He felt her fingers tighten on his head, the nails beginning to dig into the skin. She took a deep breath. "She said you'd regret everything that's happened."

"A threat?" he said.

She shrugged. "How do I know? She's not my kind of people."

They stared at each other until Danny finally lowered his eyes. "I don't know how many times I can say it, Weezie. I'm sorry. I'm really sorry."

"You can say it lots," she answered. "Maybe eventually I'll believe it." After a time she said, "Danny, you really are a double-dyed prick bastard."

He tried to lighten things. He said, "Sticks and stones will break my bones, sweetie. Words won't hurt me."

"You ever hear about the river?" she said. "I'm guessing you have."

He looked bewildered. "What river?"

"The river Styx, dummy. Like the group. You know it was the river of hate? *Burning* hate? It circled hell nine times. That's a *lot* of anger, Danny."

He shook his head. "You've been reading up on all this?"

"I read more than you give me credit for, baby. I'm not just a stupid little costume girl." Then the anger left her voice again. She bent down and kissed him gently on the lips. "I'll make some coffee now." Louisa turned toward the door, then said over her shoulder, "I really will take care of you. You know that, don't you?"

She didn't wait for an answer.

Alone now, he lay there on the bed and tried to figure out what had happened. No, he thought, Louisa was by no means a stupid costume girl. True, he had never been knocked out by her intellect, but he'd realized a long time before that she was hardly unintelligent. It's just that he'd been doing his own thinking with definitely the wrong head when he'd met Louisa on the Papa Legba shoot. He'd been directing the musical video script he'd written for the distasteful speed metal group; she'd been paid by their manager some incredible pittance to keep their mutant Caribbean neo-Goth costumes stitched together. Also she was taking care of the quintet's hair and makeup.

Danny thought she was cute. And she responded. At the time, he didn't think it was wise to tell her about his on-again, off-again affair with Ifetayo. On that day, at that moment, it was off again, but he'd known the climate could change at any time. And it had.

So for the next two months he had tried with increasing desperation to balance the two women in his life, until the horrific Friday night when Louisa's unexpected visit had caught Danny in a highly compromising situation with Ifetayo. It had been like mixing oil and gasoline—and Danny's very presence, it seemed, was the match.

Screaming, crying, threatening, and the silence that was always more heartbreaking. The two women had left his house at different times, in different directions, and he'd guessed it unlikely that he would see either one again.

Until Sunday morning. Today.

Louisa entered the bedroom with a tray. She smiled. "Cream and sugar, sweetie, just like you always want it."

Did she know that about him? he thought. Well, obviously she did. "Thank you," he said.

She extended the cup of scalding coffee toward him—he held his breath—and she didn't spill a drop.

Dr. King was a brusque blond woman in her fifties who acknowledged Louisa's presence with a handshake and then proceeded to poke and prod Danny's body, hmm-ing and ah-ing when he winced at her fingers probing his arms and shoulders.

"We'll do a blood workup," she finally said. "But I suspect the verdict will be myositis."

"So what *is* that?" said Danny.

"Essentially a severe inflammation of the muscle tissue," she said, brow furrowing. "Sometimes virally triggered. It can be painful. You should recover."

"*Should* recover?" he said, realizing his voice was rising a little. "I've only got another week."

The doctor looked at him, expression puzzled. "You're not going to *die* from this, Daniel."

"No," he said. "What I mean is, my Guild health insurance expires in another week."

"Can't you renew it?"

"Not without a work contract," he said. "I had some hopes for a job, but I'm not gonna be able to work with my arms like this."

Louisa cleared her throat. Both Danny and Dr. King swiveled their heads to stare at her. "I can take dictation," she said. "I can help out."

"On the medical side of this," said Dr. King to Danny, "I could hospitalize you." She grimaced. "For a week. I don't think the myositis will be gone by then."

"I can take care of you at home," said Louisa. "You saw what I accomplished just this morning. I can keep you fed and clean, and medicated, if it comes to that."

Silence pooled in the examination room. Finally Dr. King shrugged. "I've got no problem with home care."

Danny opened his mouth to speak.

"Great!" said Louisa forcefully. "It's settled."

That afternoon, Danny and Louisa worked out some coping mechanisms. Much as he hated the indignity, she brushed his teeth, being exquisitely careful not to lacerate his gums. Then she worked out a system to skootch behind the pillows on the bed, and, lacing her fingers together into a double fist, to push against the small of his back so that he could more easily sit upright and get to his feet. At Danny's suggestion, she brought the cordless phone up from the office. He told her to fasten it securely to an eighteen-inch length of wooden lath with masking tape. He learned to dial it at arm's length, then to hold it to his head using the lath extension. As for the two-liter bottle with the widened hole, *nothing* improved on that.

When Danny got tired, Louisa left him to go shop for groceries. He slipped into an exhausted sleep. And dreamed.

Outlined by the moonlight shining through the east window, Ifetayo stood at the foot of his bed. His eyes flickered open and he admired the woman's supple musculature. There had been a time when he'd verbally compared her to a great jungle cat. That was just after he had hired her to work on a contract basis for him as an Internet researcher. She had laughed and asked him if he thought the image was at all racist. He wasn't sure, so kept that image to himself from then on.

"Hi, gorgeous," he said, mouth dry. "I'd get up—"

"—but you can't," she finished. "I know that very well." She brushed her long dark hair back from the one eye it had covered. "I wanted to see you before . . ." She hesitated.

"Before what?" Danny didn't like the sound of that.

"Before whatever may happen happens," Ifetayo finished.

"Don't give me any alt.philosophy," Danny said. "What's happening to me?"

Her generous lips curved in a smile half hidden by the darkness. "I don't like you much, lover."

Danny discovered he could barely force words from his own lips. "You mean you hate me?"

She seemed to ignore the question. "You'll get a gift," she said. Ifetayo sighed, sounding more sad than angry. Then she showed her teeth when she spoke. "You deserve anything you get."

"Iffie—" he said, unaccountably panicked.

The look was hard to read. "When you lie down with bitches—" she started to say.

And vanished. The moonlight evaporated. The bedroom flooded with austere late-afternoon sun. Danny blinked and drew in a ragged breath.

Louisa stood in the doorway. "Miss me?" she said.

Danny was never able to remember what he had for supper that night. He did recall that Louisa had fed him like a child, one bite at a time via fork or spoon. Going to sleep was akin to passing out.

In the morning, the phone rang and Louisa answered. It was Dr. King. Louisa handed the lath-handled portable over to Danny.

"I've got some test results back," said the doctor. "As I suspected, your CPK is elevated, which supports the myositis scenario. But I'm wondering if perhaps the inflammation is secondary."

"What do you mean?"

"I happened to run into my favorite bone man this morning. He reminded me that secondary myositis can be the immune system's natural reaction to bone fragments in the tissue after a fracture."

"I'm not sure I understand."

"Can your friend—uh, Louisa?—bring you in this afternoon? I'm scheduling you for an MRI."

"What are you looking for?" said Danny.

Dr. King's reply was terse. "Fractures."

"He'll be there," said Louisa on the other phone.

*   *   *

The bone specialist at the hospital came across as a bit dubious about the need for the MRI scan. He asked Danny if the patient were *sure* he had simply awakened in pain. There was no trauma? he asked.

"I didn't even fall out of bed," Danny answered.

Maybe, the bone man suggested with a smile, one of Danny's old flames had sneaked in during the night with a ballpeen hammer and got in a few good licks before making her escape.

Danny was not amused.

He glanced at Louisa, who silently formed an interrogative word with her lips.

Ifetayo?

Danny shook his head. Iffie was quite angry with him, feeling he had betrayed her. But she wasn't malevolent. Was she? He didn't think so. He wished he could be more sure.

The MRI experience was painless but exhausting. The orderlies slid him off the gurney onto a ramp that in turn slipped into a claustrophobic tube that reminded Danny of a *Star Trek* prop. They gave him headphones and a choice of audio channels. He chose '80s pop.

Once he was crammed inside the tube, the music switched on and it was hard-core country. Then the magnetic scan sequences started and a sound like bones being ground in the teeth of a T-rex drowned out Jimmie Rodgers and Ernest Tubb.

Nearly an hour later, Danny was more than ready when the operators wheeled his ramp out of the bright white tube.

"The radiologist will look at all this," said the bone man. "We'll call you."

When they arrived back at Danny's house, they found a small parcel wrapped in brown butcher paper, tied with red yarn, waiting on the doorstep. There was no tag.

Inside, Louisa opened it for him. They both stared at the tiny black stone effigy. It gleamed with oil, exuding a sharp fragrance that opened Danny's sinuses instantly.

"The hell?" he said. He hesitated. "Voodoo?"

"Ifetayo," said Louisa flatly. She did not elaborate. "You want me to toss it?"

He shook his head. "Destroying it could be a trap. Just put it in a safe place."

"I won't let her do anything to you," Louisa said. "I love you." She kissed him, gently trailing the fingers of her right hand down the side of his face to the level of his mouth. She touched his lips. "You're tired. You ought to go back to bed."

"I'm ready," he said.

Ifetayo again appeared to him in his dream, though it was an experience akin to watching a blurry TV channel under siege from lightning strikes and rising static. Standing at the foot of his bed, she wore a multicolored long tribal dress. Danny realized he had never seen her clad in anything but conventional Western clothing.

". . . my name . . ." he heard her say, ". . . meaning." She looked frustrated, then appeared to attempt to repeat herself. ". . . Yoruba. It means 'love brings happiness.' " Some sort of cosmic interference blurred the sound. Ifetayo looked distressed. ". . . can mean so many things . . ." Her hand wove sinuously in the air between them. Danny glimpsed what might have been a cocoon of some sort, gleaming with an inner light.

Then Iffie blinked out of existence as if another hand had thrown a power switch.

Danny recalled no more of his dreams that night.

First thing in the morning, the radiologist called. Yes, Danny's bones did betray breaks. His right shoulder owned up to two long fractures just below the ball joint; his left shoulder, at least one. The bone doctor came on the line and expressed some wonderment.

"It's possible—" he said, and then interrupted himself. "You're sure there was no trauma you can recall?" There wasn't. "It's possible," he continued, "that you suffered convulsions in your sleep. Muscles can do that, you know. It's uncommon, but they can fracture some major bones."

Danny considered that, thought about his own body betraying him in so hideous a way. "But why?" he said.

"Hard to say at this point. A sharp drop in blood glucose level, perhaps. Maybe a reaction triggered by sleep apnea. There could be a neurological basis." He was silent for a few moments. "I'll talk with Dr. King. We may start some series of diagnostics."

Danny kept his own silence for a while before breaking it. "But soon," he said. "The tests should be as soon as possible." He didn't have the energy to explain himself.

The bone man agreed and rang off.

Louisa noted his evident distress and gently seated herself on the mattress beside him. "Don't worry, sweetie. No matter what happens with the doctors, I'll take care of you. I'll see that nothing else happens."

"Gonna shoot Ifetayo if it turns out she's put the juju on me?" he said, half serious.

"Yes," she answered, sounding completely serious. "She can't hurt you."

"Relax," he said, trying to affect some healthy bravado. "It isn't your job to be my bodyguard."

"But I love you," said Louisa. "I love you so very much." She hesitated. "Don't you love me too?"

It was his turn to hesitate. "I like you a lot," he said. "I'm really grateful for everything you're doing."

"But you don't love me?"

He heard an edge in her voice. "I probably will," he said. "Give me some time."

She did not sound placated. "Don't wait too long, Danny." She got up and walked across the hall to the smaller bathroom. The door closed behind her. Danny thought he could hear her crying. But when she finally came back out, her face was dry and she was smiling.

"We're going out to eat," she said. "To celebrate."

"Celebrate what?" he said. "I'm not exactly in a good space for going out."

"Celebrating our love," Louisa said. "And don't you worry about a thing." With that, she put clean socks and running shoes on his feet. Dressed in boxer shorts, he allowed her carefully to maneuver his arms through the sleeves of his long trench coat.

"Anybody checks, they'll think I'm a pervert on the way to a schoolyard," he said.

"Trust me." She led him down to the car and drove him to a very dark restaurant where they could sit in relative seclusion to the side of the dining room. With her help, he ordered soups and puddings and coffee. The dishes lined up like little soldiers, each with a thick straw extending up toward his mouth.

He didn't expect to like the experience. Getting out cheered him, he discovered.

The glow started to dissipate once they returned home. The caller ID indicated that Ifetayo had called. "Don't phone her back," Louisa said.

"This is my house," Danny said. My rules, he *almost* said. When he gingerly dialed Iffie's number, he got a "this number is not presently in service," intercept. "I should drive over," he said. "It might be important."

"No," Louisa said. "You can't do that."

"Will you drive me over?"

"No."

He heard the anger in her voice, and backed off. "Maybe tomorrow."

"No," she said. "Never."

They talked little more before he decided to go to sleep.

Ifetayo did not come to him in his dreams.

Danny awoke hearing—and feeling—the bones of his toes snapping. The little toes twitched, convulsed, broke like twigs being trampled underfoot. Then the next in line, as the pain grew, right up to and including the big toes. Both of them.

Crack!

He screamed at the dream.

It was not a dream.

The small bones in the arch of his right foot began to vibrate, then to bend under internal pressure. He remembered tugging the wishbone at childhood Thanksgivings and Christmases. The pain was intense. But it was multiplied by the ripping, crunching *sounds,* noises of destruction that arrowed right to his gut. He doubled up on the bed and tried to reach his feet, to massage them the way he used to soothe charley horses. It did no good—he couldn't make his arms work.

All those tiny bones destroyed themselves as he cried out.

Then Louisa was there with warm towels to wipe his sweaty face and to lay wet wraps across the savage pain in his feet. "There now," she said. "It will be okay. We'll manage the pain."

"Why?" he said, mind blurry with the tortured electricity from his feet and shoulders. "Why why why why . . ." He stopped when he was out of breath. It didn't take long.

"She won't hurt you again," Louisa said.

The meaning came through to him finally. "Who? Ifetayo?"

"Of course." Louisa continued mopping his forehead. "Now try to rest. Just breathe through the pain. You won't be able to walk for a while. But don't worry. I'll take care of everything. I love you."

A thought came to him. "Weezie, that *thing* Iffie left on the porch yesterday. The one you put in a safe place? I think you better destroy it."

"I already did, lover," she said reassuringly.

"Good." He shook his head. Words swam in his head and it was hard to articulate them in his throat. "I never believed in black magic."

"You don't have to," Louisa said. "It works anyway."

He began to sink away from consciousness, trying to elude the pain from which he'd begun to think there truly was no escaping. Louisa said something he couldn't quite make out. "What?"

"The river Styx is deep and wide," she said. "So much hate flows there." Then it was as though she'd switched channels. "The cats are out of hiding. I fed them. They like me."

"What do you . . ." He didn't find out *what* she meant. Blessed unconsciousness arrived first.

When he awoke again, Danny could barely move at all. Louisa sat beside the bed with a cup of hot coffee brewed and ready. She carefully helped him sip it.

"I'm afraid your legs aren't doing so well," she said.

"They hurt like my shoulders," he whimpered.

"You'll be staying at home for a while," she said sympathetically. "I'll make sure you're all right."

"We don't have to drive over to see Ifetayo," Danny said.

"Damn straight," she replied. "Wouldn't do much good anyway."

"What do you mean?"

She didn't answer. "That woman hated you," Louisa said. "The effigy I destroyed? The one she left? That was to make you impotent. I guess she figured it was poetic justice." Louisa sighed. "But she had no *right.*"

Danny tried to raise his head to look at her. His fingers crawled along the top of the blanket like crippled spiders.

She glanced down. "Careful," she said. "Any more mischief and things could happen to all ten of those, even the thumbs." Then she grinned sunnily. "But I told you, I can take dictation. You'll do fine."

"What the hell are you talking about?" he mumbled. His vision suddenly irised in on something new crowning the bureau behind her. It was his picture in an antique metal frame. Something else leaned against the frame. It looked like a Ken doll wrapped tightly in mono-filament—so much stranded bondage it could have been cocooned for the winter. Those tight bonds looked as though they were pulling the doll's limbs out of true, contorting them into unnatural positions. The arms, legs, hands, there the bonds stretched the thickest and tightest.

The meaning started percolating through his bleary, pain-shot mind. Weezie *loved* him.

As though reading his mind, she said, "Danny, I'll love you forever. I couldn't let *her* injure you. There was no way. I'll take care of you always. Count on it."

This was a delirium he knew he would not wake from.

It was hard now to hold on to anything secure. But he knew something beyond all else as he stared up at her serene smile.

Love will always triumph over hate.

Always.

Steven Spruill

HEMOPHAGE

I find it fitting and highly pleasing that Steve Spruill and F. Paul Wilson have provided this book's two vampire stories, because, when I met them, a long time ago in a publishing galaxy far, far away, they were the best of friends (they still are, and not too long ago collaborated on a novel, Nightkill), *each turning out wonderful books for the Doubleday Science Fiction line I've already mentioned ad nauseum (see headnotes for Wilson and Lustbader).*

Since those days of tiny advances, Spruill has done just fine for himself; he is the author of thirteen novels, the last five of which have been Literary Guild selections. A trilogy based on the fascinating characters you are about to meet was completed in 1998; it consists of Rulers of Darkness, Daughter of Darkness, *and* Lords of Light.

"Hemophage" is set between the last two novels. In Spruill's own words (which I happen to agree with): "It gives us a glimpse of the powerful and complex creatures who just might be the reality behind the vampire myth."

The first whiff of blood, as the elevator doors parted, was rather like rose stems steeping in a vase, and then the carnal undertones hit, making Merrick's throat crawl. The cage settled a prodding inch, but he held fast, staring out at umber carpeting, gray wallpaper chased with silver. In the box of light from the elevator, dust motes swirled, telling him of people hurrying back and forth. No one visible from in here, though. He could press "Close," tell the uniform in the lobby he'd left something in the car, and get back home to Katie where he belonged. But the corpse had already become part of him, atoms from her veins soaking with each breath into his own capillaries.

Merrick let go and stepped into the hall, his palms prickling where the handrail had dug in. Behind him, the light narrowed and vanished with a thump, leaving the pallid flush of twenty-five-watt sconces, too far apart. *They do like it dark. One of them could slip through here with no fear of being seen, even if a tenant suddenly stepped out. . . .*

Merrick's jaw clenched. Damn the lieutenant, wouldn't take no, just a quick look, please. He couldn't know what he was asking.

Another uniform waited at the open door near the end of the hall. Glare from a flashbulb backlit him as he held up a hand. "This is a crime scene. If you'll just turn around—"

"I'm Merrick Chapman."

The cop straightened and blushed. "Yes, sir—sorry. I thought you'd be older."

You thought right, son.

A tiny entrance foyer gave way to a narrow hall on the left and a compact living room straight ahead, the parquet sketched with Persian carpets. A recliner in the corner drew his eye and he knew at once it had been a favored place. Plant stands spilled lacy fronds on either side and a pole lamp behind cast perfect light for reading. A romance novel lay open on the floor, spine up, bright plumage spread. Two evidence technicians on their knees worked around the chair with gloved hands.

"Lieutenant!"

Des, behind him. Turning, Merrick was startled at how much weight the man had gained, the glints of white in the ebony hair. Still a sharp dresser, but none of the Masai motifs he'd once favored in his braces and ties. Just a black silk blazer, now, white shirt and charcoal pants, a uniform of responsibility.

"Lieutenant, yourself."

"You're looking good, Merrick. Damn, rub in some Grecian Formula and you retired yesterday. 'Course, then we'd have to account for me." He cast a rueful look at his belly. "Thanks for coming. I owe you. Hell, I owed you before."

"You don't owe me anything, Des."

"Right. It was some other Merrick who twisted arms to get me his old job."

"Still think it was a favor?"

"Sure as hell beats sitting stakeout and bumping chairbacks in the squad room. And I can still get out of my nice office when I want." He glanced over his shoulder, down the narrow hall, nothing remotely like want in his face. "Stepansky catch you on the way in?"

"The guy at the door? What'd you tell him, anyway?"

"Just your name. Good kid, bucking for detective, hangs around our guys at the watering holes, listening to the war stories. You still hold the record for closing homicides, you know."

Merrick felt an uneasy surprise. People at the department were still talking about him? But what did it matter? He didn't have that much to hide anymore.

Des held out a pair of latex gloves. As Merrick pulled them on, images flashed through his mind of skin marbled with lividity, staring eyes, other blood, dark and fragrant, no two scents ever quite the same. For a second, he thought again of fleeing, far too late.

"She's in the bathroom," Des said.

Merrick followed down the narrow hall, glimpsing a tiny bedroom to one side, bed neatly made under a country quilt. The bathroom was big enough, pink and green tiles from a fifties remodeling. She lay in the tub, eyes closed, lips parted, as if she'd dozed off. Her plain face would have been prettier in life. The blood in the water half obscured her body. Merrick looked and there it was, beside the tub near her shoulder—a chef's knife with a long, sharply honed blade now gleaming with blood. Des fished out an alabaster forearm. The slash was deep, running down the wrist, not across. Bending closer, Merrick examined the wound, dizzied by the intoxicating smell. His throat locked and then he was able to swallow. He dipped a hand into the water.

Stone cold.

Nerves tightened along his spine, but he said, "What makes this murder?"

"Don't you think the water should be darker? I've seen four or five bathtub suicides and you usually can't make out the body, unless an arm stayed out to bleed on the floor. And the wrist—no priors. How'd she know to make that cut? She's not a shrink. She sold vacations in a travel agency."

"Note?"

Des shook his head.

Merrick looked at him. "You testing me, Des?"

The lieutenant grinned, and for a second the years dropped away.

"I'm sure you noticed," Merrick said, "that the blood on the knife is still drying, which means this isn't even an hour old. So why is the water cold?"

"Exactly. No one would get into a cold tub to slit their wrists. Whoever did this didn't count on her landlady letting herself in to return a curling iron."

Shutting his eyes, Merrick envisioned a tall figure that looked like a man slipping down the dim hallway toward this apartment. Or maybe climbing up the brick outside to a cocked window. He saw the woman sitting in her chair reading, looking up, maybe, as she felt a change in the air. But she wouldn't see her killer because he would be reaching out mentally, finding the capillaries in her retinas and pinching off the blood flow to create a blind spot that her mind would then paper over with the familiar, safe contours of her apartment. Next he would dilate her jugulars, dumping the blood from her brain, catching her as she fell. He would barely feel her weight as he carried her to the bathroom in arms that could lift a truck, hands that could smash through a wall. She'd had no chance, none at all, because vampires weren't real. Actually, this woman probably *had* seen her killer, but only in the deepest phosphors of her brain, where no expectations exist to fill in the blind spots. Novelists had dragged forth images of the blood eaters, distorted by their fevered imaginations, and Hollywood had thrown these distortions up on the screen, and ironically, being revealed in the false light of myth had only made the secret of the ages more secure. Yes, we know about vampires, and the thing we know best is that they are fiction.

Okay, no cross or wooden stake would have saved this woman, but an alarm linked to a camera might have. How long had the hemophage who'd been here tonight passed among humans, taking what it needed—two hundred years, a thousand? Had it roamed, in the dead of night, the trampled fields of Hastings and Waterloo, drinking the blood of the dying? How many bodies had it left in the woods, where the teeth of other animals would erase its own? Now you could nail a killer from a hair or a trace of his blood—provided he was human. But if it was an auto accident, a house fire, a missing person, a suicide, you didn't even look.

"What I want to know now," Des said, "is where's the rest of the blood? It sure as hell isn't on the floor. And it's not inside her, either, she's white as Wonder Bread. Do you think he could be back—our vampire killer?"

Our vampire killer.

"I assumed he was dead," Des mused. "In fact, I had this theory that you killed him."

Merrick gave him a sharp look.

He held up his hands. "Hey, I'm not accusing. But you spent night and day hunting the vicious bastard, and then you stopped and he stopped."

Merrick saw the vault in the ground out in the Virginia woods, the rows of cots in the commons for those too weakened by lack of blood to move anymore. He saw Abezi-Thibod, Balberith, Procel, lying there in the indigo half-light, white hair fanned on the pillows. The faces of dead pharaohs, until you saw an eye glitter with hatred. Others screamed and pounded behind the iron doors around the commons, where he'd put the fresh captures, and where, at last, he had put Zane.

Nausea spiked up his throat. He should never have come here. The nightmare was over, must stay over.

"Oh, you went through the motions," Des said, "for a few months after the last killing. But you'd never have retired if you'd thought he was still out there. Or so I hoped."

"You think I would catch him and, instead of bringing him in, just kill him?"

"Your secret would have been safe with me."

Merrick felt a weight in his chest. *Judge, jury, executioner.*

Des looked uncomfortable. "Look, I'm sorry. I shouldn't have said that. I've never known anyone with more integrity. I knew all along it was probably just wishful thinking. I did keep screening VICAP for years after his killings stopped, to see if they'd start up somewhere else. They didn't. And this sure isn't the same MO. The killer thirteen years ago was flaunting it. This . . ." Des looked at the corpse in the tub and swallowed. "This is sly, Merrick. Whoever did this never meant to be discovered—we only caught it by dumb luck. But the missing blood means I've got to consider our boy from thirteen years ago. How many crazy sons of bitches are tipped enough to think they're vampires?" Des shook his head. "Where's the rest of her blood? And don't tell me he drank it."

Merrick put a hand on Des's arm. "Don't let this get to you. It might be nothing. Maybe she was a real slow clotter and that's why the knife's still wet. Maybe this happened three hours ago, time enough for the water to go cold."

"You think maybe?" Hope and doubt struggled on Des's face. "What the hell, maybe." He blew out a breath. "I'll see what labs has to say. I'll keep you posted."

"Don't."

"Yeah. I guess you had enough of crazy sons of bitches to last you a lifetime."

Merrick said nothing.

"Sorry for laying this on you."

"Don't worry about it."

"Say hello to Katie for me," Des said.

"You bet." Merrick's mood lightened a shade. Katie, his life now. At this hour, they should be drinking coffee in the den, talking about her day at the hospital. Then they'd head upstairs. . . .

But he could not go home yet, not until he was sure.

Merrick pulled to a stop, cut off his headlights and waited while the dust drifted past. Leaning across to the passenger seat, he scanned Zane's place. The livestock-style gate clung with a tentacle of rusty chain to its post, blocking the driveway. No car, no lights on in the farmhouse, but that meant nothing.

Merrick's stomach knotted with tension. Pulling to the tilting shoulder, he shut off the engine, got out. The midnight air, heavy and still, was ideal for listening, cold enough to conduct the barest sound. Tuning out the soft tick of the cooling engine block, he detected a rustle in the field by the house and homed on it, eyes prickling as the weeds lightened in a red-tinged semblance of daylight. A raccoon reared up to peer back at him, then hurried away.

He turned back to the house. With the darkness that had cloaked it bleached away, its shabbiness was depressingly apparent. Paint which would be a pale yellow in daylight curled from the porch posts. Masking tape meandered across the front window, patching a crack in the glass with naked indifference. In a few more weeks, the two big maples that flanked the front porch would leaf out to hide some of the flaws, but now the place looked desolate.

"Come."

Zane's voice, muffled. Merrick saw him then, a tall, gray shape floating into the rectangle of cracked window. Skirting the gate, he hiked up the grassy incline to the front porch, his chest tight with dread. Boards creaked under his feet, a final alarm system that could not be unplugged. Twanging screen door, and then the knob, cool, resisting. Merrick backed up a few steps. Zane gazed out at him, no expression on the smooth, dark face. He'd cropped his sable hair close as a panther's pelt. His eyes were chips of jade.

"I got a call tonight. A young woman dead in her bath. Her wrists were slit, a lot of blood missing. You?"

"I don't do that anymore. I take a little while they sleep. I want to kill them, but I don't. We are the lions and they are the zebras, but they all wake up the next morning. Because I'm just like you, now. You saw to that."

Merrick took the lash without flinching, the scars already laid down by his own hand. How could right feel so wrong? He had let the logic trap him: only he could stop Zane, ergo if he did not, the blood was on his hands, too.

So I buried my own son thirteen years ago to save a legion of strangers. Because they look like us. They blaze up and fade in the blink of an eye, yet wear our faces. And we theirs. Has Zane forgotten his own human mother?

Merrick's heart compressed. Five hundred years, her bones to dust, but he would never forget her. There she was in Zane, now, her dark beauty subtly reshaped into the face of a Bedouin sheik, forever young.

"You got what you came for," Zane said.

In his mind, Merrick heard the same voice screaming, *No don't leave me, please. . . .*

But I did leave him.

Merrick saw the cell in his mind, as he had forced himself to do each day: Zane, hunched over on his cot, pressed down by the endless, dark sameness, trapped there with no future, only his memories, all the hunts, the spraying blood. Had he seen them there in the dark— ghosts with torn throats and crimson chests, their lips mouthing silent rebukes?

Had he prayed? *Let me out and I'll never kill again.*

And then a faint tremor combs the soles of his feet. Pressing his palms to the floor, he holds his breath, waiting for another, fearing delusion. The earth heaves, its dull rumble drowned out by a deafening crack as the concrete tears open from ceiling to floor, showering him with grit. Heart pounding into his throat, he leaps to the wall and presses an eye to the fracture, blinking against the cascade of dirt, yelling in relief as he finds the jagged line of daylight, two inches, all he needs. . . .

Merrick felt the shine of deliverance bathe his own eyes. A miracle. Was that you, God? Or the devil? Whoever caused that earthquake, I thank you. Another chance, for both of us.

Jagged gears of longing twisted in his throat. He pictured Zane using the transfusion packs, taking just a little, leaving them their lives—or deaths?

Had the woman in the apartment tonight chosen for herself?

Maybe.

Suicide. A slow clotter, that was all.

Yes.

He put his palm against the glass.

Beyond it, the green gaze softened.

For a moment, Merrick could see his son again, and then Zane faded back into the red shadows of the empty room.

Michael Marshall Smith

THE BOOK OF
IRRATIONAL NUMBERS

Michael Marshall Smith has quickly established himself as both a horror writer and the author of future-thrillers such as One of Us *and* Spares. *The movie people are after him (watch out!), but hopefully they won't take him away from us, or from the production of his singularly weird and chilling fiction.*

Watch this guy: he may be one of those writers who gets real big, real fast.

If so, like I said, I hope it doesn't stop him from turning out work like "The Book of Irrational Numbers." You'll recognize the story type pretty quickly—but it's the execution, and the unique study of the protagonist's mind-set, that make this tale so effective.

A nice clean page. Page three. 3 x 3 = 9, hence 0. The beginning. When I start a new notebook I never use the first piece of paper, because you know it's going to get scuffed up. I always leave both sides of that one blank, and start writing on the second piece of paper, where it will be protected from dirt. It's usually hobbies that I use notebooks for. I feel like writing a different type of thing now. Don't really know how to go about it. Blah blah blah words words words. Letters must add up to something, but I'm not sure what. Writing something down makes it feel like yesterday's news. Almost nothing actually *is* yesterday's news, though. Most of it is still going on. Today was a reasonable day like most others. I was due to paint a house just on the other side of town and I got most of the prepping done in the morning but then it started to rain, so I had to leave it be.

$14^2 = 196$. $8.56^2 = 73.2736$.

Roanoke is a funny place to live. Not quite in the middle of nowhere, close by the Blue Ridge Mountains. Of Virginia. Never seen a lonesome pine around here: there's billions of them. I quite like it though. There's plenty of work. People always need things done to their houses. There's not much else to do, and you've got a hell of a job finding anywhere to eat or drink in the evening, especially on Sundays. The only place is Macados, a burger bar in the center of town. Lots of high schoolers, though that's okay. They're not so rich that they're obnoxious. Most of them are pretty good kids. Basically it's a town with a couple of malls, a small airport. In winter you can go driving up in the mountains, find secret places. I drove back from Richmond once along the Ridge and passed all these little homesteads. People looked up at me like they'd never seen a car before. The land that time forgot.

Virtually the most important thing I have ever discovered is the idea of digital roots. To find the digital root of a number, the aim is to reduce it to a single digit. You achieve this by adding up all its existing digits: 943521, for example, adds up to $9 + 4 + 3 + 5 + 2 + 1 = 24$. This, of course, still has two digits, so you add them together $2 + 4 = 6$. The digital root of 943521, therefore, is 6. What is interesting, however, is that to speed up this process you can simply cast out the 9s. If there's a 9 in the number, or any of the digits add up to 9, you can ignore them. In 943521, therefore, you ignore the 9, and also ignore the 4 and 5, which add up to 9. This leaves you with $3 + 2 + 1$, which gives you 6. The same answer.

I ended up here completely by chance. I don't know, can't chart the steps, which brought me this way. I don't know. I don't remember anything in particular, but then maybe it could have been something so small that I wouldn't have thought it was important enough. I can remember some books some conversations some dreams some things I saw. But nothing spectacular. No major blows to the head.

You look for what makes sense.

Susan the new girl who works in the bookstore is lovely. She's got a great smile and she always looks so cheerful and as if she knows something funny is going to happen sooner or later. And she's prime.

I guess it's a vacation job or something. She noticed my accent straightaway. I think she thinks it's cool. I hope so.

Gerry was on the phone again earlier this evening, hassling everyone about what we're doing for the Millennium. Max is getting all hot and bothered about it too. Who cares? Everybody thinks that the year 2000 is going to be the big one. It's not. We're already there. It's already started. Cast out the 9s, and see how it is so. Last year was 1998. $1 + 9 + 9 + 8 = 27$, and $2 + 7$ (or ignore the 9s and just add 1 and 8) $= 9$; cast it out. Zero, in other words. 1998 is ground zero or the end of things, a nothing year in modulo 9. 1999, on the other hand, has a digital root of 1. 1999 is year 1; 2000 roots down to 2. 2000 isn't the start of anything, it's after it has already begun. Millenniums don't mean anything to real people. Their lives revolve around much smaller circles. You strip things down. If you can't reduce a number down any further, then it means something. Otherwise it's just addition.

Got the Macillsons' house painted today. Did some work inside for them too, fixing up stuff. Think their neighbor might need some work done too. So it goes, luckily.

It's very much like something breaks. When it's done, you go through this hell. Like grief. At first the units are minutes, and then hours. Weeks, months. Cycles of guilt and grief and sometimes glee. Once you've been through it once, it's different. The first time you're culpable, there's no getting away from it. Afterwards it's different. All the structures, once so hard, become fluid forever, like a bag full of broken glass in treacle. When you push your hand in, it's sweet and sharp together.

People are nice to me, but that just makes me feel sad and guilty, because I know I'm not very nice. It's really painful. I have good friends, and I always have a laugh with the guys at the store where I buy my materials. Susan at the bookstore waves now when she sees me go by. I don't deserve it. I want to be nice. It's important to me. I was nice once, I think, and bits of me still are. I used to drive miles, for example, every weekend, to see someone. I had it in me then, the capacity for being good. I still do. Bits of me seem not to be touched by it all. But they're no help, either, and you have to wonder where the energy, the motivation and glee come from. Doesn't any of it come from that part of me, the part I like? It must do: or if not, why is it so powerless? It must be very weak to be unable to do anything, in which case it's obviously not so blameless after all. It's all very well being that little flinchy man, sitting up in a high tower of the castle, behind a locked door, wanting no part of it. Weak, afraid; rational at the heart of the irrational. Rationality is weak; it has no moment, contributes to no interesting sums. All it does is cringe.

The weather was colder again today. I don't feel hunted, exactly. It's as if someone is reaching out of the dark towards me, as if the opaque brown fog is beginning to bulge as someone pushes against it from the outside. Think this is going to be a cold winter.

Seventeen is the last year of being young. I remember when I was a kid, about fourteen, I guess, thinking how weird it would feel to be older. I could just about understand the ages of sixteen and seventeen. Eighteen seemed one of those ages like twenty-one where it's not so much an age as a legal marker. A boundary line. You don't think, Oh, it's going to be like so-and-such being eighteen, you just think about the things that aren't going to be illegal anymore. Nineteen, though. That seemed really old. Being nineteen was grown up and over the wall. Of course it doesn't seem that way now. But it did then. Now I realize that 19 is 1 and 9, and $1 + 9 = 10$ and $1 + 0 = 1$. The first year of being old. $1 + 8$ is 9, a ground zero year.

You have to watch everything very carefully.

I think about people waiting for birthday cards, Christmas cards. A phone call which isn't going to come. Mothers, mainly. I wish I could say it made a big difference, but it doesn't.

Squaring numbers is very easy. You just take the number and multiply it by itself. Anybody can do that. It's an easy road to travel, like time in the usual direction.

Roads. I remember that time, back in England, when I drove up to Cambridge from London on the M11 motorway. If there's any bad weather anywhere in the world, it'll be on the M11. I'm telling you. It feels as if the road has been built to make the worst of it. There are high stretches, where strong winds seem to grab hold of the car and drag it towards other lanes; average stretches, where rain seems to sheet into the windscreen almost parallel to the ground; and then there are the dips. Especially just outside Cambridge there are long low patches, where fog collects and sits in a clump like porridge in a bowl. I used to have a girlfriend who lived there. For a year, in fact over a year, I used to drive up the M11 every weekend. I saw it in spring, summer, autumn, winter—and regardless, the weather there was worse than anywhere else. One night in October I drove down the slipway onto the motorway and found myself completely enveloped in fog. For the next ten miles visibility wasn't even as far as the end of the hood of the car. I couldn't see a damned thing. I couldn't see my own headlights, never mind anyone else's. I drove slower and slower and slower. I knew that after the next junction the road gradually got a little higher, pulled itself out of the trough all around the town. I kept waiting for the junction. Nothing passed me, and I saw no other cars, no headlights on the other side of the carriageway, no taillights on my own. After a long time I passed the first exit. Usually the fog lifted then. On that night it stayed exactly the same. Just as thick, just as deadening, just as much like driving slowly through the middle of a monstrous snowdrift that reached up to the sky. There was no sound, except for the hum of the engine. I'd turned the radio off, to avoid distraction. I couldn't see a thing outside the car, except for slow swirls within the mist. I'd been going for about thirty-five or forty minutes when I started to feel uneasy, and after another ten I was beginning to get really nervous. I knew the M11 like the back of my hand, and a message was starting to persistently knock on the back of my mind, where the autopilot sits and keeps an eye on things. Isn't it about time, it was saying, that we passed another exit? In normal conditions, I would pass the first exit about ten minutes into the journey, and the second at the half hour mark. This night was far from normal, and I was driving much slower than usual. But it was now at least fifty minutes since I'd passed the first exit. I couldn't have gone by the second without noticing: the massive exit signs by the side of the road were just about the only thing which I had been able to see at the beginning of the journey. So where was the second? I drove for another ten minutes. Still no cars on my side of the road, and no headlights on the other. I drove on for five further minutes, picking the speed up slightly. I was just a little . . . concerned. Ten minutes later a shape finally loomed out of the fog, and I breathed a sigh of relief. The journey was halfway over, and I'd seen the second exit. As I lit a cigarette, finally able to spare some concentration from the road, I thought for a moment. How long would it have taken for me to have started panicking? How long would I have had to wait before too long became *far* too long, before I'd started to feel in my heart of hearts that something had gone wrong, that the exit had disappeared and I was crawling along an endless fog-buried road into nothingness, the real world left behind?

Someone is after me now. Definitely. I know they are. It's an odd position to be in. Everyone else will always side with the hunter. Which I'm not. Some people in my position call themselves that, but it's pure vaingloriousness. I assume he's a policeman. He doesn't know who I am yet, but he's there. I'm not even sure how I know this. I'm not sure how I know a lot of things. Maybe I'm noticing little signs without really realizing what they are. I don't really know what to do about him. I'm not going to give myself up, or give myself away if I can help it, but—maybe he could even be my friend. He must understand some of it, which would help. I *don't* understand. That's part of it. I don't understand why I can't just be nice. You read books and a lot of people are just 1, 2, 3 . . . "these are the reasons why." An easy addition. I'm not, as far as I can remember. I don't have the excuse. I've got a fair number of friends, and they come round or I go see them and we hang out, but it's like the whole thing's in two dimensions. It's like a painted glass window—one stone, and it's going to fall apart. I'm just not nice, and it makes me sad, because some people are nice to me and I want to be nice, but can't. Not anymore. Once is enough, too much. It taints your life.

I was in the bookstore again today, bought some books and had a cup of coffee. I had a chat with Susan again too. The place wasn't very busy. I told her a couple of digital root tricks. Like . . . take any number (say, 4201); add the digits ($4 + 2 + 0 + 1 = 7$); take the sum away from the original number ($4201 - 7 = 4194$)—and the result will always have a digital root of 9. Or . . . take any number (say, 94213); scramble the digits in any order you like (32941, for instance); and subtract the smaller number from the bigger ($94213 - 32941 = 61272$). Guess what—digital root of 9 again. Those 9s, they get around. She thought the tricks were pretty cool. We got talking about symmetrical numbers, and how they don't come along in years very often. 1991; 2002; 2112; 2222. When I got home I realized something. If you look at the digital roots, the sequence goes $1 + (9 + 9) + 1 = 2$; in the same way $2002 = 4$; $2112 = 6$; $2222 = 8$. The *even* numbers. Then 2332 gives you 1, 2442 gives you 3, 2552 gives you

5, and 2662 gives you 7. The *odd* numbers. Which is kind of interesting. Maybe.

Gerry spends a hundred bucks a month on porn. There's a place in Greensboro. We got really drunk a couple months ago and he told me about it. Nothing weird, just people having sex. It obviously bothers him, but he can't stop doing it. He tries, he buys, he purges. Funny what accountants get up to.

Fall in Roanoke is driving foggy roads.

My twenties didn't make any sense to me. Or my early thirties. I used to be able to understand ages. Up until you're twenty, they make sense. Each year from the early teens onwards is such a huge step, until you're twenty, when they start getting smaller and smaller again. The teens. So many things become possible. Each year is like a quantum leap. After that—you just keep getting a little older and smaller. You have birthdays, and sometimes people remember them and sometimes they don't. When you were sixteen, and one of your friends had a birthday and became seventeen, you sure as hell knew about it. It meant your friend had gone to another planet. They stood taller than you. They were older. There's no difference between being twenty-seven and twenty-eight. Or forty-three and forty-four. You've been around the ring too many times. Forty-four is who-gives-a-shit, whatever modulo you're on.

It's like falling in love.

The Greeks knew a lot about math, but they didn't know about zero. Seriously. They had no 0, which meant they didn't understand how numbers relate to people and what they do. The difference between 0 and 1 is the biggest difference in the world, far greater than that between 2 and 3; because they're just additional counts, whereas 0 is never having done it at all. They knew very little about the irrational, and nothing about the quiet that lies beyond even that. They liked perfection, the Greeks. Perfect numbers, for example, which are the sum of the numbers that you can divide them by: $6 = 1 + 2 + 3$; $28 = 1 + 2 + 4 + 7 + 14$. They are also, as it happens, the sum of consecutive whole numbers: $6 = 1 + 2 + 3$; $28 = 1 + 2 + 3 + 4 + 5 + 6 + 7$. Kind of neat. But perfect numbers are very, very rare: irrationality is far more common. They say Pythagoras just pretended irrational numbers didn't exist. Just couldn't handle the idea. Shows how you can be a really bright guy and still know shit.

There's one under the kitchen floor. It's not even a very big kitchen. But there's one under there, about a foot under, lying face up. It's covered in concrete, and there's good quality slate laid on top. But sometimes when I see one of my friends standing in there I think, Jesus, that's really bad. Last time it happened was when Max and Julie were round, and Max was fixing us drinks in the kitchen. It's like the floor goes transparent for a moment, and I can see her lying there, below people's feet. Not literally, of course. I don't get visions. If anything, I'm too rational. Other times, for longish stretches, I just forget, and then the remembering is very bad. It's like, Jesus, what have I done? What can I do about it? And the answer is always— nothing. It's too late now to go back. It's always been too late. On the one hand it's disgusting, and pathetic and sick. But in everyday life images will pop into my mind, pictures, memories of things I've done. I push them away, but the pictures and memories feel warm and comforting and glorious, like the robes of a king in exile. After a while they come more often, and the sense of glee will start to strengthen, and that's when I know it's going to happen again. The dance begins, a dance where I'm my own partner, but I can't work out who's leading. It's a wonderful dance while it lasts.

Slim, slender, small. The little ones are like the digital root of breasts. You don't need great big lumps of flesh to prove you're a woman. It's in the face, in the nature. Stripped down to the essential.

Imagining is okay.

I would have to be very careful. Because of this guy. I wonder what he's like. I wonder what's going to happen. Whether he's righteously angry or just doing his job. And I wonder why I'm so convinced he's there, whether there's some structure that I'm sensing but just can't see. Maybe I need new sums.

So locked up that even when drunk you never get near it.

17 is prime. If you think about it, if someone's seventeen they're not yet an adult but they're no longer a child. Not least because it has no factors. 16 is two 8s or four 4s, come to that. I'm not getting involved

with multiples of children. The prime numbers between 10 and 20 are 13, 17, and 19. 19 is too old. 13 is a child. 17 is indivisible by anything except 1 and 17, which is right, because there's one seventeen-year-old there. One real person. It is disgusting. I know that. But it's also the only thing which has any reality or point. If I could only lose the guilt, and remain the same person, I could be happy. But I can't, because I want to be nice.

I had a dream once where I had a number, and squared it, and the result was 2. When I woke up I wanted to write the number down, but I'd forgotten it.

Forever the pull between what I want and the need to be nice. So many people live their lives like that. I don't know any perfect numbers in real life. Max is married, but he wants to sleep with other women. Not because he doesn't love Julie. He does. You only have to look at them to see how much they care about each other. But he just wants to sleep with other women. He told me this once, very stoned, but I knew anyway. You only have to watch his eyes. Hunger and guilt. His argument is that monogamy is artificial. He says that in the animal kingdom very few species mate for life, that it makes biological and evolutionary sense for the male to spread his genes as widely as possible: increase the chance of fertilization, and introduce as much variation into the gene pool as possible. Which may be true. But I suspect he just wants to bite some different nipples for a change. Meanwhile he has, I suspect, absolutely no idea that Julie throws up about one meal in three. He's just not very observant, I guess.

I was talking with Susan again today, showing her some more number tricks. She likes the way they dance. She's sharing a house with two other girls, but her friends have gone home for the vacation. It's funny the way she talks to me. Careful, polite—because I'm older. But friendly too. She's just finding her way.

I want to be whole, but you can only be whole if you tell, and I can't possibly tell. So who is that person that people know, and if they like you, what does it mean? Most things you can confess. You can absolve yourself by mentioning it, however lightly, by saying "Oh God, you'll never guess what I did, silly me." Not this. You can't absolve this. I have good friends. But not that good. No friends are that good. My secret keeps me apart from everyone. At least if you're an alcoholic you can try to admit it in front of yourself, God and one other person. Everyone says "Hey, that's a bad thing," but then they want to help you. I can only admit it to the first two: and believe me, it's the third that makes the difference. It must be, otherwise there's no way out of this, except death. That's why some people want to be caught: not to be stopped, not for the publicity, but just so you can get it out. Admitting it to God makes no difference. So far as I can tell, he doesn't care.

Today was Sunday, and it was snowing. I spent all day indoors tinkering with stuff. There was a guy working on the fence of the house opposite. He didn't look familiar. Paranoia is dangerous, because it can make you behave oddly. You have to behave properly. You have to be rational in the heart of irrationality.

It's not like half of these little idiots matter. For a year, they're prime. Then just machines pushing machines with baby machines in them. Not prime, not even perfect. Just blobs.

Irrational numbers are those which cannot be accurately expressed as a fraction, whose decimal places ramble randomly on. Like the square root of 2, which starts 1.41421356237 . . . and then goes on and on and on. Pi is also an irrational number: very fucking irrational, in fact—pi is a number that's off its face on drugs. People have spent their lives calculating it to millions and millions of places, and still there's no pattern, and no precise value. Pi is the ratio of a circle's circumference to its radius. You work out the circumference of a circle through the equation $c = \pi r$, where r is the radius—the distance from the exact center of the circle to the ring. Of course if you have the circumference, you can work out the radius by reversing the process and dividing by pi. But whichever way you do it, pi is still involved. And pi is irrational. The length of the radius can be as precise as you like—5.00 centimeters, 12 inches, 100 meters exactly—but the circumference is still going to have a never-ending series of numbers on the right-hand side of the decimal point, because of pi. You can use an approximation like 3.14 or 3.141592653589793, but you're never going to know the exact value, because there isn't one. There is uncertainty and darkness at the heart of something as simple as a circle.

★   ★   ★

I am the radius. I am rational when the circle of the world is not. Of course it works the other way too: when the circumference is rational, the radius is not. Perhaps I am that radius instead.

I haven't been to the bookstore for a week.

I could make it easier. I could move to Nevada or somewhere. Seventy towns in an area the size of a European country. But I won't. That would be giving in. I don't want to live in Nevada, for fuck's sake. It's pretty enough but there's nothing else happening there. Going there would be allowing it to become all of my life. There's nothing to do except go to Las Vegas, and those numbers ain't never going to be on your side. The occasional transgression I can talk myself round from. But if I lived in Nevada, every morning when I woke up I would know there was only one reason for my being there. It would become my whole life, instead of just part of it. Why else would you live in Nevada? Plus I imagine that people there are pretty good at fixing up their own houses.

Maybe I can just keep hanging on.

Him and me, and poor little pi in the middle—waiting to make one of us irrational. Maybe they've stopped looking, or maybe they were never looking in the first place. Sometimes it's very difficult for me to tell what are rational fears and what are not. It's such a cliff to step out over—"I did *what?*" Like having your heart in an elevator when someone cuts the cord holding it up. Then you reach out and steady yourself, and pull yourself back. You walk away from the shaft. But you know it's there. Waking in the middle of the night, cold panic. Nothing happens. Eventually you get back to sleep.

But Christ, the times when I don't have to do it. It's wonderful. I feel so strong. When I can recall what's happened, the things that have been done, and feel okay about them. When it just seems uninteresting and strange, and I can think to myself, I'm never doing that again. Not in the way I feel immediately afterwards, when I just feel sick about the whole thing and my balls ache and I'm flooded and sit in the living room scrubbed clean: but in a calm, dispassionate way. No, I think, I'm not going to do that again. I know I've done it, but that was then. This is now, and I don't need it anymore. It was bad, but it's gone. I did it, but I don't anymore. It's finished. It's over. It hasn't been yet, though. It's never been over yet.

Julie and Max looked happy tonight.

More than half my mind is always somewhere else. Even my friends seem like someone else's, because only part of me is ever really with them. The rest of me is out on the trail, walking by myself. I remember another time driving on the M11 one summer afternoon, I realized that all of the cars coming the other way had their lights on and their wipers going. I thought this was strange until I noticed that it actually was raining on the other side of the road. It was dry on the northbound side, wet on the southbound.

I didn't mean to go in, but I had a coffee at the shop opposite and saw her in the window, serving a customer. So I finished up and went into the bookstore.

17 is prime and a perfect age. 1 plus 7 is 8, and thus the digital root of the perfect age is 8. I'm thirty-five now, in 1999, the year of 1, of starting. The digital root of 35 is 8 too—and I have this sense of someone closing in. This can hardly be a coincidence. Perhaps I'll always be in danger when my age collapses to the same age as the girls', when they have the same digital root. It makes sense—it makes us too closely linked. When I was twenty-six I wasn't doing this, so I was safe. Forty-four will be dangerous. Fifty-three. Sixty-two. But I can't believe I'll still be doing this then. I jog, but I can't see me being fit enough at sixty-two. It's no walk in the park, this kind of thing. And will it make any sense to be doing this when my hair is gray and every part of me is scrawning out apart from a little pale paunch? Surely something will have burnt out by then. Interestingly, if you follow Wilson's test for primes, taking $(p - 1)^!$ to be congruent with $-1 \bmod p$, we find that the primeness of 17 leaves us with 16 as the value (in base 10) of -1 modulo 17. Half of 16 is 8. Again, rather convenient. All the 8s, 2^3, of course. I still can't work out whether that means I should take eight a year. It seems far too much. I'm happier with low primes, like 3, 5 or 7. Even 7 seems weak and greedy. 5 is better. It's worked for me so far. I don't like 2 as a prime, even though it passes Wilson. It just doesn't feel right. The heart of 2 is irrational. The heart of a seventeen-year-old makes sense. To them. To me.

★   ★   ★

I don't really remember the first time. You'd think you would. I remember little flashes of it, little sparks of darkness, but I can't really remember the whole thing. I remember where she's buried. I remember that all too well. Sometimes when I'm lying in bed and I feel okay, I slowly start to feel something reaching out for me. I realize that there's a bit of my brain which will always be standing in a patch of forest a little way from Epping, watching over a grave, standing guard over a woman maybe no one else even misses that much. She was short on family. She wasn't 17 of course, but she was 29. She was still prime, albeit a higher prime. But the actual doing of it, not really. I tend to remember the more recent ones most. You do, don't you. Because it's more recent. But even they are just a few still images, like I was really drunk. I wasn't. But it's like that. It's not like the normal things you do. I guess that's kind of funny, in a way. It's really not like the normal things you do.

Susan was kind of glum today. She'd had an argument with her landlord or the guy who owns the house they let or whoever he is. Leaking roof, which is no fun when it's this wet and this cold and going to get wetter and colder. I told her that I know something about such things. You should have seen her smile.

I tried to work out once, from first principles, how you find the square root of a number. Without a calculator. It did my head in. From school I distantly remembered that you think of a number close to it, whose square you know, and adjust it up and down by trial and error, until you're pretty close. But that's not very precise. It's not very attractive. It's such a simple thing, squaring something. Such an easy step. You take a number and multiply it by itself. Anyone can work that out. But finding the square root, reversing the process? There must be a way back, I thought. Once you've walked down a road, there must be some way home. I found out in the end. You use the Newton-Raphson equation for successive approximations:

$$x_{i+1} = (x_i + tx_i)/2$$

It bites its tail. You feed a number into the equation, then feed the result back in, and feed that result back in—and keep working it, and keep working it. Until you stop. Except that with many numbers, even a simple number like 2, you never do. You never stop. The result is irrational, and goes on forever. I can put as many primes through the loop as I like, and the decimals will never stop. I can never find the number that I squared to make 2. It's not there anymore. There's no way back. It's tainted.

My age always reduces to 8, when the year root is 1. The root of 17 is 8. 8 plus 1 is 9, which casts itself out. The sum of me is always on the other side of the barrier, cast out. Nothing can be done about it. Always driving in the rain, with no turning in sight.

Tomorrow evening, at eight o'clock, I'm going to an address just outside of town. To fix a roof as a favor.

That's all.

Joe R. Lansdale

MAD DOG SUMMER

*The highest compliment one writer can pay to another is to admit he
wishes he'd written something by the other scribbler. Joe Lansdale has
written two things I fervently wish I'd written. One of them is the piece
you're about to read. If you look up the phrase "Southern Gothic" in the
future you're likely to find "Mad Dog Summer" reproduced in its entirety
as the definition. I do not say this lightly.*

*Anyone who hasn't been in a cave for the last fifteen years knows
that Lansdale has excelled in the horror, western, suspense, and comic
book fields; much of his work exhibits "crossover" features which blur
(annihilate might be a better word) the distinctions between genres.
This is a very good thing—not because it's a gimmick but because
there are no reasons for those distinctions to be there, except to limit
less masterful writers.*

*The other piece of Joe's I wish I'd written? "The Night They Missed
the Horror Show."*

News, as opposed to rumor, didn't travel the way it does now. Not
back then. Not by radio or newspaper it didn't. Not in East Texas.
Things were different. What happened in another county was often
left to that county.

World news was just that, something that was of importance to
us all. We didn't have to know about terrible things that didn't affect
us in Bilgewater, Oregon, or even across the state in El Paso, or up
northern state way in godforsaken Amarillo.

All it takes now for us to know all the gory details about some
murder is for it to be horrible, or it to be a slow news week, and it's
everywhere, even if it's some grocery clerk's murder in Maine that
hasn't a thing to do with us.

Back in the thirties a killing might occur several counties over
and you'd never know about it unless you were related, because as I

said, news traveled slower then, and law enforcement tried to take care of their own.

On the other hand, there were times it might have been better had news traveled faster, or traveled at all. If we had known certain things, perhaps some of the terrible experiences my family and I went through could have been avoided.

What's done is done though, and even now in my eighties, as I lie here in the old folks' home, my room full of the smell of my own decaying body, awaiting a meal of whatever, mashed and diced and tasteless, a tube in my shank, the television tuned to some talk show peopled by idiots, I've got the memories of then, nearly eighty years ago, and they are as fresh as the moment.

It all happened in the years of nineteen thirty-one and -two.

I suppose there were some back then had money, but we weren't among them. The Depression was on, and if we had been one of those with money, there really wasn't that much to buy, outside of hogs, chickens, vegetables and the staples, and since we raised the first three, with us it was the staples.

Daddy farmed a little, had a barbershop he ran most days except Sunday and Monday, and was a community constable.

We lived back in the deep woods near the Sabine River in a three-room white house he had built before we were born. We had a leak in the roof, no electricity, a smoky wood stove, a rickety barn, and an outhouse prone to snakes.

We used kerosene lamps, hauled water from the well, and did a lot of hunting and fishing to add to the larder. We had about four acres cut out of the woods, and owned another twenty-five acres of hard timber and pine. We farmed the cleared four acres of sandy land with a mule named Sally Redback. We had a car, but Daddy used it primarily for his constable business and Sunday church. The rest of the time we walked, or me and my sister rode Sally Redback.

The woods we owned, and the hundreds of acres of it that surrounded our land, was full of game, chiggers and ticks. Back then in East Texas, all the big woods hadn't been timbered out and they didn't all belong to somebody. There were still mighty trees and lots of them, lost places in the forest and along the riverbanks that no one had touched but animals.

Wild hogs, squirrels, rabbits, coons, possums, some armadillo, and all manner of birds and plenty of snakes were out there. Sometimes you could see those darn water moccasins swimming in a school down the river, their evil heads bobbing up like knobs on logs. And woe unto the fella fell in amongst them, and bless the heart of the fool who believed if he swam down under them he'd be safe because a moccasin couldn't bite under water. They not only could, but would.

Deer roamed the woods too. Maybe fewer than now, as people grow them like crops these days and harvest them on a three-day drunk during season from a deer stand with a high-powered rifle. Deer they've corn fed and trained to be like pets so they can get a cheap free shot and feel like they've done some serious hunting. It costs them more to shoot the deer, ride its corpse around and mount its head, than it would cost to go to the store and buy an equal amount of beefsteak. Then they like to smear their faces with the blood after the kill and take photos, like this makes them some kind of warrior.

But I've quit talking, and done gone to preaching. I was saying how we lived. And I was saying about all the game. Then too, there was the Goat Man. Half goat, half man, he liked to hang around what was called the swinging bridge. I had never seen him, but sometimes at night, out possum hunting, I thought maybe I heard him, howling and whimpering down there near the cable bridge that hung bold over the river, swinging with the wind in the moonlight, the beams playing on the metal cables like fairies on ropes.

He was supposed to steal livestock and children, and though I didn't know of any children that had been eaten, some farmers claimed the Goat Man had taken their livestock, and there were some kids I knew claimed they had cousins taken off by the Goat Man, never to be seen again.

It was said he didn't go as far as the main road because Baptist preachers traveled regular there on foot and by car, making the preaching rounds, and therefore making the road holy. It was said he didn't get out of the woods that made up the Sabine bottoms. High land was something he couldn't tolerate. He needed the damp, thick leaf mush beneath his feet, which were hooves.

Dad said there wasn't any Goat Man. That it was a wive's tale heard throughout the South. He said what I heard out there was water and animal sounds, but I tell you, those sounds made your skin crawl, and they did remind you of a hurt goat. Mr. Cecil Chambers, who worked with my daddy at the barbershop, said it was probably a panther. They showed up now and then in the deep woods, and they could scream like a woman, he said.

Me and my sister Tom—well, Thomasina, but we all called her Tom 'cause it was easier to remember and because she was a tomboy—roamed those woods from daylight to dark. We had a dog named Toby that was part hound, part terrier, and part what we called fiest.

Toby was a hunting sonofagun. But the summer of nineteen thirty-one, while rearing up against a tree so he could bark at a squirrel he'd tracked, the oak he was under lost a rotten limb and it fell on him, striking his back so hard he couldn't move his back legs or tail. I carried him home in my arms. Him whimpering, me and Tom crying.

Daddy was out in the field plowing with Sally, working the plow around a stump that was still in the field. Now and then he chopped at its base with an ax and had set fire to it, but it was stubborn and remained.

Daddy stopped his plowing when he saw us, took the looped lines off his shoulders and dropped them, left Sally Redback standing in the field hitched up to the plow. He walked part of the way across the field to meet us, and we carried Toby out to him and put him on the soft plowed ground and Daddy looked him over. Daddy moved Toby's paws around, tried to straighten Toby's back, but Toby would whine hard when he did that.

After a while, as if considering all possibilities, he told me and Tom to get the gun and take poor Toby out in the woods and put him out of his misery.

"It ain't what I want you to do," Daddy said. "But it's the thing has to be done."

"Yes sir," I said.

These days that might sound rough, but back then we didn't have many vets, and no money to take a dog to one if we wanted to. And all a vet would have done was do what we were gonna do.

Another thing different was you learned about things like dying when you were quite young. It couldn't be helped. You raised and killed chickens and hogs, hunted and fished, so you were constantly up against it. That being the case, I think we respected life more than some do now, and useless suffering was not to be tolerated.

And in the case of something like Toby, you were often expected to do the deed yourself, not pass on the responsibility. It was unspoken, but it was pretty well understood that Toby was our dog, and therefore, our responsibility. Things like that were considered part of the learning process.

We cried a while, then got a wheelbarrow and put Toby in it. I already had my twenty-two for squirrels, but for this I went in the house and swapped it for the single-shot sixteen-gauge shotgun, so there wouldn't be any suffering. The thought of shooting Toby in the back of the head like that, blasting his skull all over creation, was not something I looked forward to.

Our responsibility or not, I was thirteen and Tom was only nine. I told her she could stay at the house, but she wouldn't. She said she'd come on with me. She knew I needed someone to help me be strong.

Tom got the shovel to bury Toby, put it over her shoulder, and we wheeled old Toby along, him whining and such, but after a bit he quit making noise. He just lay there in the wheelbarrow while we pushed him down the trail, his back slightly twisted, his head raised, sniffing the air.

In short time he started sniffing deeper, and we could tell he had a squirrel's scent. Toby always had a way of turning to look at you when he had a squirrel, then he'd point his head in the direction he wanted to go and take off running and yapping in that deep voice of his. Daddy said that was his way of letting us know the direction of the scent before he got out of sight. Well, he had his head turned like that, and I knew what it was I was supposed to do, but I decided to prolong it by giving Toby his head.

We pushed in the direction he wanted to go, and pretty soon we were racing over a narrow trail littered with pine needles, and Toby was barking like crazy. Eventually we run the wheelbarrow up against a hickory tree.

Up there in the high branches two big fat squirrels played around as if taunting us. I shot both of them and tossed them into the wheelbarrow with Toby, and darned if he didn't signal and start barking again.

It was rough pushing that wheelbarrow over all that bumpy wood debris and leaf and needle-littered ground, but we did it, forgetting all about what we were supposed to do for Toby.

By the time Toby quit hitting on squirrel scent, it was near nightfall and we were down deep in the woods with six squirrels—a bumper crop—and we were tuckered out.

There Toby was, a dadburn cripple, and I'd never seen him work the trees better. It was like Toby knew what was coming and was trying to prolong things by treeing squirrels.

We sat down under a big old sweetgum and left Toby in the wheelbarrow with the squirrels. The sun was falling through the trees like a big fat plum coming to pieces. Shadows were rising up like dark men all around us. We didn't have a hunting lamp. There was just the moon and it wasn't up good yet.

"Harry," Tom said. "What about Toby?"

I had been considering on that.

"He don't seem to be in pain none," I said. "And he treed six dadburn squirrels."

"Yeah," Tom said, "but his back's still broke."

"Reckon so," I said.

"Maybe we could hide him down here, come every day, feed and water him."

"I don't think so. He'd be at the mercy anything came along. Darn chiggers and ticks would eat him alive." I'd thought of that because I could feel bites all over me and knew tonight I'd be spending some time with a lamp, some tweezers and such myself, getting them off all kinds of places, bathing myself later in kerosene, then rinsing. During the summer me and Tom ended up doing that darn near every evening.

"It's gettin' dark," Tom said.

"I know."

"I don't think Toby's in all that much pain now."

"He does seem better," I said. "But that don't mean his back ain't broke."

"Daddy wanted us to shoot him to put him out of his misery. He don't look so miserable to me. It ain't right to shoot him he ain't miserable, is it?"

I looked at Toby. There was mostly just a lump to see, lying there in the wheelbarrow covered by the dark. While I was looking he raised his head and his tail beat on the wooden bottom of the wheelbarrow a couple of times.

"Don't reckon I can do it," I said. "I think we ought to take him back to Daddy, show how he's improved. He may have a broke back, but he ain't in pain like he was. He can move his head and even his tail now, so his whole body ain't dead. He don't need killin'."

"Daddy may not see it that way, though."

"Reckon not, but I can't just shoot him without trying to give him a chance. Heck, he treed six dadburn squirrels. Mama'll be glad to see them squirrels. We'll just take him back."

We got up to go. It was then that it settled on us. We were lost. We had been so busy chasing those squirrels, following Toby's lead, we had gotten down deep in the woods and we didn't recognize anything. We weren't scared, of course, least not right away. We roamed these woods all the time, but it had grown dark, and this immediate place wasn't familiar.

The moon was up some more, and I used that for my bearings. "We need to go that way," I said. "Eventually that'll lead back to the house or the road."

We set out, pushing the wheelbarrow, stumbling over roots and ruts and fallen limbs, banging up against trees with the wheelbarrow and ourselves. Near us we could hear wildlife moving around, and I thought about what Mr. Chambers had said about panthers, and I thought about wild hogs and wondered if we might come up on one rootin' for acorns, and I remembered that Mr. Chambers had also said this was a bad year for the hydrophobia, and lots of animals were coming down with it, and the thought of all that made me nervous enough to feel around in my pocket for shotgun shells. I had three left.

As we went along, there was more movement around us, and after a while I began to think whatever it was was keeping stride with us. When we slowed, it slowed. We sped up, it sped up. And not the way an animal will do, or even the way a coach whip snake will sometimes follow and run you. This was something bigger than a snake. It was stalking us, like a panther. Or a man.

Toby was growling as we went along, his head lifted, the hair on the back of his neck raised.

I looked over at Tom, and the moon was just able to split through the trees and show me her face and how scared she was. I knew she had come to the same conclusion I had.

I wanted to say something, shout out at whatever it was in the bushes, but I was afraid that might be like some kind of bugle call that set it off, causing it to come down on us.

I had broken open the shotgun earlier for safety sake, laid it in the wheelbarrow and was pushing it, Toby, the shovel, and the squirrels along. Now I stopped, got the shotgun out, made sure a shell was in it, snapped it shut and put my thumb on the hammer.

Toby had really started to make noise, had gone from growling to barking.

I looked at Tom, and she took hold of the wheelbarrow and started pushing. I could tell she was having trouble with it, working it over the soft ground, but I didn't have any choice but to hold on to the gun, and we couldn't leave Toby behind, not after what he'd been through.

Whatever was in those bushes paced us for a while, then went silent. We picked up speed, and didn't hear it anymore. And we didn't feel its presence no more neither. Earlier it was like we was walking along with the devil beside us.

I finally got brave enough to break open the shotgun and lay it in the wheelbarrow and take over the pushing again.

"What was that?" Tom asked.

"I don't know," I said.

"It sounded big."

"Yeah."

"The Goat Man?"

"Daddy says there ain't any Goat Man."

"Yeah, but he's sometimes wrong, ain't he?"

"Hardly ever," I said.

We went along some more, and found a narrow place in the river, and crossed, struggling with the wheelbarrow. We shouldn't have crossed, but there was a spot, and someone or something following us had spooked me, and I had just wanted to put some space between us and it.

We walked along a longer time, and eventually came up against a wad of brambles that twisted in amongst the trees and scrubs and vines and made a wall of thorns. It was a wall of wild rosebushes. Some of the vines on them were thick as well ropes, the thorns like nails, and the flowers smelled strong and sweet in the night wind, almost sweet as sorghum syrup cooking.

The bramble patch ran some distance in either direction, and encased us on all sides. We had wandered into a maze of thorns too wide and thick to go around, and too high and sharp to climb over, and besides they had wound together with low hanging limbs, and it was like a ceiling above. I thought of Brer Rabbit and the briar patch, but unlike Brer Rabbit, I had not been born and raised in a briar patch, and unlike Brer Rabbit, it wasn't what I wanted.

I dug in my pocket and got a match I had left over from when me and Tom tried to smoke some corn silk cigarettes and grapevines, and I struck the match with my thumb and waved it around, saw there was a wide space in the brambles, and it didn't take a lot of know-how to see the path had been cut in them. I bent down and poked the match forward, and I could see the brambles were a kind of tunnel, about six feet high and six feet wide. I couldn't tell how far it went, but it was a goodly distance.

I shook the match out before it burned my hand, said to Tom, "We can go back, or we can take this tunnel."

Tom looked to our left, saw the brambles were thick and solid, and in front of us was a wall of them too. "I don't want to go back because of that thing, whatever it is. And I don't want to go down that tunnel neither. We'd be like rats in a pipe. Maybe whatever it is knew it'd get us boxed in like this, and it's just waitin' at the other end of that bramble trap for us, like that thing Daddy read to us about. The thing that was part man, part cow."

"Part bull, part man," I said. "The Minotaur."

"Yeah. A minutetar. It could be waitin' on us, Harry."

I had, of course, thought about that. "I think we ought to take the tunnel. It can't come from any side on us that way. It has to come from front or rear."

"Can't there be other tunnels in there?"

I hadn't thought of that. There could be openings cut like this anywhere.

"I got the gun," I said. "If you can push the wheelbarrow, Toby can sort of watch for us, let us know something's coming. Anything jumps out at us, I'll cut it in two."

"I don't like any of them choices."

I picked up the gun and made it ready. Tom took hold of the wheelbarrow handles. I went on in and Tom came after me.

The smell of roses was thick and overwhelming. It made me sick. The thorns sometimes stuck out on vines you couldn't see in the dark. They snagged my old shirt and cut my arms and face. I could hear Tom back there behind me, cussing softly under her breath as she got scratched. I was glad for the fact that Toby was silent. It gave me some kind of relief.

The bramble tunnel went on for a good ways, then I heard a rushing sound, and the bramble tunnel widened and we came out on the bank of the roaring Sabine. There were splits in the trees above, and the moonlight come through strong and fell over everything and looked yellow and thick like milk that had turned sour. Whatever had been pacing us seemed to be good and gone.

I studied the moon a moment, then thought about the river. I said, "We've gone some out of the way. But I can see how we ought to go. We can follow the river a ways, which ain't the right direction, but I think it's not far from here to the swinging bridge. We cross that, we can hit the main road, walk to the house."

"The swinging bridge?"

"Yeah," I said.

"Think Momma and Daddy are worried," Tom asked.

"Yeah," I said. "Reckon they are. I hope they'll be glad to see these squirrels as I think they'll be."

"What about Toby?"

"We just got to wait and see."

The bank sloped down, and near the water there was a little trail ran along the edge of the river.

"Reckon we got to carry Toby down, then bring the wheelbarrow. You can push it forward, and I'll get in front and boost it down."

I carefully picked up Toby, who whimpered softly, and Tom, getting ahead of herself, pushed the wheelbarrow. It, the squirrels, shotgun and shovel went over the edge, tipped over near the creek.

"Damn it, Tom," I said.

"I'm sorry," she said. "It got away from me. I'm gonna tell Mama you cussed."

"You do and I'll whup the tar out of you. 'Sides, I heard you cussin' plenty."

I gave Toby to Tom to hold till I could go down a ways, get a footing and have him passed to me.

I slid down the bank, came up against a huge oak growing near the water. The brambles had grown down the bank and were wrapped around the tree. I went around it, put my hand out to steady myself, and jerked it back quick. What I had touched hadn't been tree trunk, or even a thorn, but something soft.

When I looked I saw a gray mess hung up in brambles, and the moonlight was shining across the water and falling on a face, or what had been a face, but was more like a jack-o'-lantern now, swollen and round with dark sockets for eyes. There was a wad of hair on the head like a chunk of dark lamb's wool, and the body was swollen up and twisted and without clothes. A woman.

I had seen a couple of cards with naked women on them that Jake Sterning had shown me. He was always coming up with stuff like that 'cause his daddy was a traveling salesman and sold not only Garrett Snuff but what was called novelties on the side.

But this wasn't like that. Those pictures had stirred me in a way I didn't understand but found somehow sweet and satisfying. This was stirring me in a way I understood immediately. Horror. Fear.

Her breasts were split like rotted melons cracked in the sun. The brambles were tightly wrapped around her swollen flesh and her skin was gray as cigar ash. Her feet weren't touching the ground. She was held against the tree by the brambles. In the moonlight she looked like a fat witch bound to a massive post by barbed wire, ready to be burned.

"Jesus," I said.

"You're cussin' again," Tom said.

I climbed up the bank a bit, took Toby from Tom, laid him on the soft ground by the riverbank, stared some more at the body. Tom slid down, saw what I saw.

"Is it the Goat Man?" she asked.

"No," I said. "It's a dead woman."

"She ain't got no clothes on."

"No, she ain't. Don't look at her, Tom."

"I can't help it."

"We got to get home, tell Daddy."

"Light a match, Harry. Let's get a good look."

I considered on that, finally dug in my pocket. "I just got one left."

"Use it."

I struck the match with my thumb and held it out. The match wavered as my hand shook. I got up as close as I could stand to get. It was even more horrible by match light.

"I think it's a colored woman," I said.

The match went out. I righted the wheelbarrow, shook mud out of the end of the shotgun, put it and the squirrels and Toby back in the wheelbarrow. I couldn't find the shovel, figured it had slid on down into the river and was gone. That was going to cost me.

"We got to get on," I said.

Tom was standing on the bank, staring at the body. She couldn't take her eyes off of it.

"Come on!"

Tom tore herself away. We went along the bank, me pushing that wheelbarrow for all I was worth, it bogging in the soft dirt until I couldn't push it anymore. I bound the squirrels' legs together with some string Tom had, and tied them around my waist.

"You carry the shotgun, Tom, and I'll carry Toby."

Tom took the gun, I picked Toby up, and we started toward the swinging bridge, which was where the Goat Man was supposed to live.

Me and my friends normally stayed away from the swinging bridge, all except Jake. Jake wasn't scared of anything. Then again, Jake wasn't

smart enough to be scared of much. Story on him and his old man
was you cut off their head they wouldn't be any dumber.

Jake said all the stories you heard about the swinging bridge were
made up by our parents to keep us off of it 'cause it was dangerous.
And maybe that was true.

The bridge was some cables strung across the Sabine from high
spots on the banks. Some long board slats were fastened to the cables
by rusty metal clamps and rotting ropes. I didn't know who had built
it, and maybe it had been a pretty good bridge once, but now a lot
of the slats were missing and others were rotten and cracked and the
cables were fastened to the high bank on either side by rusty metal
bars buried deep in the ground. In places, where the water had washed
the bank, you could see part of the bars showing through the dirt.
Enough time and water, the whole bridge would fall into the river.

When the wind blew, the bridge swung, and in a high wind it
was something. I had crossed it only once before, during the day, the
wind dead calm, and that had been scary enough. Every time you
stepped, it moved, threatened to dump you. The boards creaked and
ached as if in pain. Sometimes little bits of rotten wood came loose
and fell into the river below. I might add that below was a deep spot
and the water ran fast there, crashed up against some rocks, fell over
a little falls, and into wide, deep water.

Now, here we were at night, looking down the length of the
bridge, thinking about the Goat Man, the body we'd found, Toby,
and it being late, and our parents worried.

"We gotta cross, Harry?" Tom asked.

"Yeah," I said. "Reckon so. I'm gonna lead, and you watch where
I step. The boards hold me, they're liable to hold you."

The bridge creaked above the roar of the river, swaying ever so
slightly on its cables, like a snake sliding through tall grass.

It had been bad enough trying to cross when I could put both
hands on the cables, but carrying Toby, and it being night, and Tom
with me, and her trying to carry the shotgun . . . Well, it didn't
look promising.

The other choice was to go back the way we had come, or to
try another path on down where the river went shallow, cross over
there, walk back to the road and our house. But the river didn't
shallow until some miles away, and the woods were rough, and it was
dark, and Toby was heavy, and there was something out there that
had been tracking us. I didn't see any other way but the bridge.

I took a deep breath, got a good hold on Toby, stepped out on the first slat.

When I did the bridge swung hard to the left, then back even more violently. I had Toby in my arms, so the only thing I could do was bend my legs and try to ride the swing. It took a long time for the bridge to quit swinging, and I took the next step even more gingerly. It didn't swing as much this time. I had gotten a kind of rhythm to my stepping.

I called back to Tom, "You got to step in the middle of them slats. That way it don't swing so much."

"I'm scared, Harry."

"It's all right," I said. "We'll do fine."

I stepped on a slat, and it cracked and I pulled my foot back. Part of the board had broken loose and was falling into the river below. It hit with a splash, was caught up in the water, flickered in the moonlight, and was whipped away. It churned under the brown water, went over the little falls and was gone.

I stood there feeling as if the bottom of my belly had fell out. I hugged Toby tight and took a wide step over the missing slat toward the next one. I made it, but the bridge shook and I heard Tom scream. I turned and looked over my shoulder as she dropped the shotgun and grabbed at the cable. The shotgun fell longways and hung between the two lower cables. The bridge swung violently, threw me against one of the cables, then to the other side, and I thought I was a goner for sure.

When the bridge slowed, I lowered to one knee on the slat, pivoted and looked at Tom. "Easy," I said.

"I'm too scared to let go," Tom said.

"You got to, and you got to get the gun."

It was a long time before Tom finally bent over and picked up the gun. After a bit of heavy breathing, we started on again. That was when we heard the noise down below and saw the thing in the shadows.

It was moving along the bank on the opposite side, down near the water, under the bridge. You couldn't see it good, because it was outside of the moonlight, in the shadows. Its head was huge and there was something like horns on it and the rest of it was dark as a coal bin. It leaned a little forward, as if trying to get a good look at us, and I could see the whites of its eyes and chalky teeth shining in the moonlight.

"Jesus, Harry," Tom said. "It's the Goat Man. What do we do?"

I thought about going back. That way we'd be across the river from it, but then again, we'd have all the woods to travel through, and for miles. And if it crossed over somewhere, we'd have it tracking us again, because now I felt certain that's what had been following us in the brambles.

If we went on across, we'd be above it, on the higher bank, and it wouldn't be that far to the road. It was said the Goat Man didn't ever go as far as the road. That was his quitting' place. He was trapped here in the woods and along the banks of the Sabine, and the route them preachers took kept him away from the road.

"We got to go on," I said. I took one more look at those white eyes and teeth, and started pushing on across. The bridge swung, but I had more motivation now, and I was moving pretty good, and so was Tom.

When we were near to the other side, I looked down, but I couldn't see the Goat Man no more. I didn't know if it was the angle, or if it had gone on. I kept thinking when I got to the other side it would have climbed up and would be waiting.

But when we got to the other side, there was only the trail that split the deep woods standing out in the moonlight. Nothing on it.

We started down the trail. Toby was heavy and I was trying not to jar him too much, but I was so frightened, I wasn't doing that good of a job. He whimpered some.

After we'd gone on a good distance, the trail turned into shadow where the limbs from trees reached out and hid it from the moonlight and seemed to hold the ground in a kind of dark hug.

"I reckon if it's gonna jump us," I said, "that'd be the place."

"Then let's don't go there."

"You want to go back across the bridge?"

"I don't think so."

"Then we got to go on. We don't know he's even followed."

"Did you see those horns on his head?"

"I seen somethin'. I think what we oughta do, least till we get through that bend in the trail there, is swap. You carry Toby and let me carry the shotgun."

"I like the shotgun."

"Yeah, but I can shoot it without it knocking me down. And I got the shells."

Tom considered this. "Okay," she said.

She put the shotgun on the ground and I gave her Toby. I picked up the gun and we started around the dark curve in the trail.

I had been down this trail many times in the daylight. Out to the swinging bridge, but except for that one other time, I had never crossed the bridge until now. I had been in the woods at night before, but not this deep, and usually with Daddy.

When we were deep in the shadow of the trail nothing leaped out on us or bit us, but as we neared the moonlit part of the trail we heard movement in the woods. The same sort of movement we had heard back in the brambles. Calculated. Moving right along with us.

We finally reached the moonlit part of the trail and felt better. But there really wasn't any reason for it. It was just a way of feeling. Moonlight didn't change anything. I looked back over my shoulder, into the darkness we had just left, and in the middle of the trail, covered in shadow, I could see it. Standing there. Watching.

I didn't say anything to Tom about it. Instead I said, "You take the shotgun now, and I'll take Toby. Then I want you to run with everything you got to where the road is."

Tom, not being any dummy, and my eyes probably giving me away, turned and looked back in the shadows. She saw it too. It crossed into the woods. She turned and gave me Toby and took the shotgun and took off like a bolt of lightning. I ran after her, bouncing poor Toby, the squirrels slapping against my legs. Toby whined and whimpered and yelped. The trail widened, the moonlight grew brighter, and the red clay road came up and we hit it, looked back.

Nothing was pursuing us. We didn't hear anything moving in the woods.

"Is it okay now?" Tom asked.

"Reckon so. They say he can't come as far as the road."

"What if he can?"

"Well, he can't . . . I don't think."

"You think he killed that woman?"

"Figure he did."

"How'd she get to lookin' like that?"

"Somethin' dead swells up like that."

"How'd she get all cut? On his horns?"

"I don't know, Tom."

We went on down the road, and in time, after a number of rest stops, after helping Toby go to the bathroom by holding up his tail and legs, in the deepest part of the night, we reached home.

It wasn't entirely a happy homecoming. The sky had grown cloudy and the moon was no longer bright. You could hear the cicadas chirping and frogs bleating off somewhere in the bottoms. When we entered into the yard carrying Toby, Daddy spoke from the shadows, and an owl, startled, flew out of the oak and was temporarily outlined against the faintly brighter sky.

"I ought to whup y'all's butts," Daddy said.

"Yes sir," I said.

Daddy was sitting in a chair under an oak in the yard. It was sort of our gathering tree, where we sat and talked and shelled peas in the summer. He was smoking a pipe, a habit that would kill him later in life. I could see its glow as he puffed flames from a match into the tobacco. The smell from the pipe was woody and sour to me.

We went over and stood beneath the oak, near his chair.

"Your mother's been terrified," he said. "Harry, you know better than to stay out like that, and with your sister. You're supposed to take care of her."

"Yes sir."

"I see you still have Toby."

"Yes sir. I think he's doing better."

"You don't do better with a broken back."

"He treed six squirrels," I said. I took my pocketknife out and cut the string around my waist and presented him with the squirrels. He looked at them in the darkness, laid them beside his chair.

"You have an excuse," he said.

"Yes sir," I said.

"All right, then," he said. "Tom, you go on up to the house and get the tub and start filling it with water. It's warm enough you won't need to heat it. Not tonight. You bathe, then you get after them bugs on you with the kerosene and such, then hit the bed."

"Yes sir," she said. "But Daddy . . ."

"Go to the house, Tom," Daddy said.

Tom looked at me, laid the shotgun down on the ground and went on toward the house.

Daddy puffed his pipe. "You said you had an excuse."

"Yes sir. I got to runnin' squirrels, but there's something else. There's a body down by the river."

He leaned forward in his chair. "What?"

I told him everything that had happened. About being followed, the brambles, the body, the Goat Man. When I was finished, he said, "There isn't any Goat Man, Harry. But the person you saw, it's possible he was the killer. You being out like that, it could have been you or Tom."

"Yes sir."

"Suppose I'll have to take a look early morning. You think you can find her again?"

"Yes sir, but I don't want to."

"I know, but I'm gonna need your help. You go up to the house now, and when Tom gets through, you wash up and get the bugs off of you. I know you're covered. Hand me the shotgun and I'll take care of Toby."

I started to say something, but I didn't know what to say. Daddy got up, cradled Toby in his arms and I put the shotgun in his hand.

"Damn rotten thing to happen to a good dog," he said.

Daddy started walking off toward the little barn we had out back of the house by the field.

"Daddy," I said. "I couldn't do it. Not Toby."

"That's all right, son," he said, and went on out to the barn.

When I got up to the house, Tom was on the back porch in the tub and Mama was scrubbing her vigorously by the light of a lantern hanging on a porch beam. When I came up, Mama, who was on her knees, looked over her shoulder at me. Her blond hair was gathered up in a fat bun and a tendril of it had come loose and was hanging across her forehead and eye. She pushed it aside with a soapy hand. "You ought to know better than to stay out this late. And scaring Tom with stories about seeing a body."

"It ain't a story, Mama," I said.

I told her about it, making it brief.

When I finished, she was quiet for a long moment. "Where's your daddy?"

"He took Toby out to the barn. Toby's back is broken."

"I heard. I'm real sorry."

I listened for the blast of the shotgun, but after fifteen minutes it still hadn't come. Then I heard Daddy coming down from the barn, and pretty soon he stepped out of the shadows and into the lantern light, carrying the shotgun.

"I don't reckon he needs killin'," Daddy said. I felt my heart lighten, and I looked at Tom, who was peeking under Mama's arm as Mama scrubbed her head with lye soap. "He could move his back legs a little, lift his tail. You might be right, Harry. He might be better. Besides, I wasn't any better doin' what ought to be done than you, son. He takes a turn for the worse, stays the same, well . . . In the meantime, he's yours and Tom's responsibility. Feed and water him, and you'll need to manage him to do his business somehow."

"Yes sir," I said. "Thanks, Daddy."

Daddy sat down on the porch with the shotgun cradled in his lap. "You say the woman was colored?"

"Yes sir."

Daddy sighed. "That's gonna make it some difficult," he said.

Next morning I led Daddy out there by means of the road and the trail up to the swinging bridge. I didn't want to cross the bridge again. I pointed out from the bank the spot across and down the river where the body could be found.

"All right," Daddy said. "I'll manage from here. You go home. Better yet, get into town and open up the barbershop. Cecil will be wondering where I am."

I went home, out to the barn to check on Toby. He was crawling around on his belly, wiggling his back legs some. I left Tom with the duty to look after Toby being fed and all, then I got the barbershop key, saddled up Sally Redback, rode her the five miles into town.

Marvel Creek wasn't much of a town really, not that it's anything now, but back then it was pretty much two streets. Main and West. West had a row of houses, Main had the General Store, a courthouse, post office, the doctor's office, the barbershop my daddy owned, a couple other businesses, and sometimes a band of roving hogs that belonged to Old Man Crittendon.

The barbershop was a little one-room white building built under a couple of oaks. It was big enough for one real barber chair and a regular chair with a cushion on the seat and a cushion fastened to the back. Daddy cut hair out of the barber chair, and Cecil used the other.

During the summer the door was open, and there was just a screen door between you and the flies. The flies liked to gather on the screen and cluster like grapes. The wind was often hot.

Cecil was sitting on the steps reading the Tyler newspaper when I arrived. I tied Sally to one of the oaks, went over to unlock the door, and as I did, I gave Cecil a bit of a rundown, letting him know what Daddy was doing.

Cecil listened, shook his head, made a clucking noise with his tongue, then we were inside.

I loved the aroma of the shop. It smelled of alcohol, disinfectants, and hair oils. The bottles were in a row on a shelf behind the barber chair, and the liquid in them was in different colors, red and yellow and a blue liquid that smelled faintly of coconut.

There was a long bench along the wall near the door and a table with a stack of magazines with bright covers. Most of the magazines were detective stories. I read them whenever I got a chance, and sometimes Daddy brought the worn ones home.

When there weren't any customers, Cecil read them too, sitting on the bench with a hand-rolled cigarette in his mouth, looking like one of the characters out of the magazines. Hard-boiled, carefree, efficient.

Cecil was a big man, and from what I heard around town and indirectly from Daddy, ladies found him good-looking. He had a well-tended shock of reddish hair, bright eyes and a nice face with slightly hooded eyes. He had come to Marvel Creek about two months back, a barber looking for work. Daddy, realizing he might have competition, put him in the extra chair and gave him a percentage.

Daddy had since halfway regretted it. It wasn't that Cecil wasn't a good worker, nor was it Daddy didn't like him. It was the fact Cecil was too good. He could really cut hair, and pretty soon, more and more of Daddy's customers were waiting for Cecil to take their turn. More mothers came with their sons and waited while Cecil cut their boys' hair and chatted with them while he pinched their kids' cheeks and made them laugh. Cecil was like that. He could chum up to anyone in a big-city minute.

Though Daddy never admitted it, I could see it got his goat, made him a little jealous. There was also the fact that when Mama came down to the shop she always wilted under Cecil's gaze, turned red. She laughed when he said things that weren't that funny.

Cecil had cut my hair a few times, when Daddy was busy, and the truth was, it was an experience. Cecil loved to talk, and he told great stories about places he'd been. All over the United States, all over the world. He had fought in World War I, seen some of the dirtiest fighting. Beyond admitting that, he didn't say much about it. It seemed to pain him. He did once show me a French coin he wore around his neck on a little chain. It had been struck by a bullet and dented. The coin had been in his shirt pocket, and he credited it with saving his life.

But if he was fairly quiet on the war, on everything else he'd done he was a regular blabbermouth. He kidded me some about girls, and sometimes the kidding was a little too far to one side for Daddy, and he'd flash a look at Cecil, and I could see them in the mirror behind the bench, the one designed for the customer to look in while the barber snipped away. Cecil would take the look, wink at Daddy and change the subject. But Cecil always seemed to come back around to it, taking a real interest in any girlfriend I might have, even if I didn't really have any. Doing that, he made me feel as if I were growing up, taking part in the rituals and thoughts of men.

Tom liked him too, and sometimes she came down to the barbershop just to hang around him and hear him flatter and kid her. He loved to have her sit on his knee and tell her stories about all manner of things, and if Tom was interested in the stories I can't say, but she was certainly interested in Cecil, who was like a wild uncle to both her and me.

But what was most amazing about Cecil was the way he could cut hair. His scissors were like an extension of himself. They flashed and turned and snipped with little more than a flex of his wrist. When I was in his chair pruned hair haloed around me in the sunlight and my head became a piece of sculpture, transformed from a mass of unruly hair to a work of art. Cecil never missed a beat, never poked you with the scissor tips—which Daddy couldn't say—and when he was finished, when he had rubbed spiced oil into your scalp and parted and combed your hair, when he spun you around to look in the closer mirror behind the chairs, you weren't the same guy anymore. I felt I looked older, more manly, when he was finished. Maybe a little like those guys on the magazine covers myself.

When Daddy did the job, parted my hair, put on the oil, and let me out of the chair (he never spun me for a look like he did his adult customers), I was still just a kid. With a haircut.

Since on this day I'm talking about, Daddy was out, and haircuts for me were free, I asked Cecil if he would cut my hair, and he did, finishing with hand-whipped shaving cream and a razor around my ears to get those bits of hair too contrary for scissors. Cecil used his hands to work oil into my scalp, and he massaged the back of my neck with his thumb and fingers. It felt warm and tingly in the heat and made me sleepy.

No sooner had I climbed down from the chair than Old Man Nation drove up in his mule-drawn wagon and he and his two boys came in. Mr. Ethan Nation was a big man in overalls with tufts of hair in his ears and crawling out of his nose. His boys were big, redheaded, jug-eared versions of him. They all chewed tobacco, had brown teeth, and spat when they spoke. Most of their conversation was tied to or worked around cuss words not often spoken in that day and time. They never came in to get a haircut. They cut their own hair with a bowl and scissors. They liked to sit in the chairs and read what words they could out of the magazines and talk about how bad things were.

Cecil, though no friend of theirs, always managed to be polite, and, as Daddy often said, he was a man liked to talk, even if he was talking to the devil.

No sooner had Old Man Nation taken a seat than Cecil said, "Harry says there's been a murder." It was like it was a fact he was proud to spread around, but since I'd been quick to tell him and was about to burst with the news myself, I couldn't blame him none.

Once the word was out, there was nothing for me to do but tell it all. Well, almost all. For some reason I left the Goat Man out of it. I don't know exactly why, but I did.

When I was finished, Mr. Nation said, "Well, one less nigger wench ain't gonna hurt the world none. I was down in the bottoms, came across one of them burr-head women, I don't know, I might be inclined to do her in myself. They're the ones make the little ones. Drop babies like the rest of us drop turds. I might want her to help me out some first, though, you know what I mean. I mean, hell, they're niggers, but for about five minutes the important thing is they're all pink on the inside."

His boys smirked. Cecil said, "Watch your language," and moved his head in my direction.

"Sorry, son," Mr. Nation said. "Your pa's looking in on this, huh?"

"Yes sir," I said.

"Well, he's probably upset about it. He was always one to worry about the niggers. It's just another shine killin', boy, and he ought to leave it alone, let them niggers keep on killin' each other, then the rest of us won't have to worry with it."

At that moment, something changed for me. I had never really thought about my father's personal beliefs, but suddenly it occurred to me his were opposite those of Mr. Nation, and that Mr. Nation, though he liked our barbershop for wasting time, spouting his ideas and reading our magazines, didn't really like my daddy. The fact that he didn't, that Daddy had an opposite point of view to this man, made me proud.

In time, Mr. Johnson, a preacher, came in, and Mr. Nation, feeling the pressure, packed him and his two boys in their wagon and went on down the road to annoy someone else. Late in the day, Daddy came in, and when Cecil asked him about the murder, Daddy looked at me, and I knew then I should have kept my mouth shut.

Daddy told Cecil what I had told him, and little else, other than he thought the woman hadn't gotten caught up there by high water but had been bound there with those briars, like she was being showcased. Daddy figured the murderer had done it.

That night, back at the house, lying in bed, my ear against the wall, Tom asleep across the way, I listened. The walls were thin, and when it was good and quiet, and Mama and Daddy were talking, I could hear them.

"Doctor in town wouldn't even look at her," Daddy said.

"Because she was colored?"

"Yeah. I had to drive her over to Mission Creek's colored section to see a doctor there."

"She was in our car?"

"It didn't hurt anything. After Harry showed me where she was, I came back, drove over to Billy Gold's house. He and his brother went down there with me, helped me wrap her in a tarp, carry her out and put her in the car."

"What did the doctor say?"

"He reckoned she'd been raped. Her breasts had been split from top to bottom."

"Oh, my goodness."

"Yeah. And worse things were done. Doctor didn't know for sure, but when he got through looking her over, cutting on her, looking at her lungs, he thought maybe she'd been dumped in the river still alive, had drowned, been washed up and maybe a day or so later, someone, most likely the killer, had gone down there and found her, maybe by accident, maybe by design, and had bound her against that tree with the briars."

"Who would do such a thing?"

"I don't know. I haven't even an idea."

"Did the doctor know her?"

"No, but he brought in the colored preacher over there, Mr. Bail. He knew her. Name was Jelda May Sykes. He said she was a local prostitute. Now and then she came to the church to talk to him about getting out of the trade. He said she got salvation about once a month and lost it the rest of the time. She worked some of the black juke joints along the river. Picked up a little white trade now and then."

"So no one has any ideas who could have done it?"

"Nobody over there gives a damn, Marilyn. No one. The coloreds don't have any high feelings for her, and the white law enforcement let me know real quick I was out of my jurisdiction. Or as they put it, 'We take care of our own niggers.' Which, of course, means they don't take care of them at all."

"If it's out of your jurisdiction, you'll have to leave it alone."

"Taking her to Mission Creek was out of my jurisdiction, but where she was found isn't out of my jurisdiction. Law over there figures some hobo ridin' the rails got off over there, had his fun with her, dumped her in a river and caught the next train out. They're probably right. But if that's so, who bound her to the tree?"

"It could have been someone else, couldn't it?"

"I suppose, but it worries me mightily to think that there's that much cruelty out there in the world. And besides, I don't buy it. I think the same man killed her and displayed her. I did a little snoopin' while I was over in Mission Creek. I know a newspaperman over there, Cal Fields."

"He the older man with the younger wife? The hot patootie?"

"Yeah. He's a good guy. The wife ran off with a drummer, by the way. That doesn't bother Cal any. He's got a new girlfriend. But what he was tellin' me was interestin'. He said this is the third murder in the area in eighteen months. He didn't write about any of 'em in the paper, primarily because they're messy, but also because they've all been colored killings, and his audience don't care about colored killings. All the murders have been of prostitutes. One happened there in Mission Creek. Her body was found stuffed in a big ole drainpipe down near the river. Her legs had been broken and pulled up and tied to her head."

"Goodness."

"Cal said he'd just heard the rumor of the other. Cal gave me the name of the editor of the colored paper. I went over and talked to him, a fella named Max Greene. They did do a report on it. He gave me a back issue. The first one was killed January of last year, a little farther up than Mission Creek. They found her in the river too. Her private parts had been cut out and stuffed in her mouth."

"My God. But those murders are some months apart. It wouldn't be the same person, would it?"

"I hope so. Like I said, I don't want to think there's two or three just like this fella runnin' around. Way the bodies are mistreated, sort of displayed, something terribly vulgar done to them. I think it's the same man.

"Greene was of the opinion the murderer likes to finish 'em by drowning 'em. Even the one found in the drainpipe was in water. And the law over there is probably right about it being someone rides the rails. Every spot was near the tracks, close to some little jumping-off point with a juke joint and a working girl. But that don't mean he's a hobo or someone leaves the area much. He could just use the trains to go to the murder sites."

"The body Harry found. What happened to it? Who took it?"

"No one. Honey, I paid to have her buried in the colored cemetery over there. I know we don't have the money, but . . ."

"Shush. That's all right. You did good."

They grew quiet, and I rolled on my back and looked at the ceiling. When I closed my eyes I saw the woman's body, ruined and swollen, fixed to the tree by vines and thorns. And I saw the bright eyes and white teeth in the dark face of the horned Goat Man. I remembered looking over my shoulder and seeing the Goat Man standing in shadow in the middle of the wooded trail, watching me.

Eventually, in my dream I reached the road, and then I fell asleep.

After a while, things drifted back to normal for Tom and me. Time is like that. Especially when you're young. It can fix a lot of things, and what it doesn't fix, you forget, or at least push back and only bring out at certain times, which is what I did, now and then, late at night, just before sleep claimed me. Eventually it was all a distant memory.

Daddy looked around for the Goat Man a while, but except for some tracks along the bank, some signs of somebody scavenging around down there, he didn't find anyone. But I heard him telling Mama how he felt he was being watched, and that he figured there was someone out there knew the woods as well as any animal.

But making a living took the lead over any kind of investigation, and my daddy was no investigator anyway. He was just a small-town constable who mainly delivered legal summonses and picked up dead bodies with the justice of the peace. And if they were colored, he picked them up without the justice of the peace. So, in time the murder and the Goat Man moved into our past.

By that fall, Toby had actually begun to walk again. His back wasn't broken, but the limb had caused some kind of nerve damage. He never quite got back to normal, but he could get around with a bit of stiffness, and from time to time, for no reason we could see, his hips would go dead and he'd end up dragging his rear end. Most of the time, he was all right, and ran with a kind of limp, and not very fast. He was still the best squirrel dog in the county.

Late October, a week short of Halloween, when the air had turned cool and the nights were crisp and clear and the moon was like a pumpkin in the sky, Tom and me played late, chasing lightning bugs and each other. Daddy had gone off on a constable duty, and Mama was in the house sewing, and when we got good and played out, me and Tom sat out under the oak talking about this and that, and suddenly we stopped, and I had a kind of cold feeling. I don't know if a person really has a sixth sense. Maybe it's little things you notice unconsciously. Something seen out of the corner of the eye. Something heard at the back of a conversation. But I had that same feeling Daddy had spoken of, the feeling of being watched.

I stopped listening to Tom, who was chattering on about something or another, and slowly turned my head toward the woods, and there, between two trees, in the shadows, but clearly framed by the light, was a horned figure, watching us.

Tom, noticing I wasn't listening to her, said, "Hey."

"Tom," I said, "be quiet a moment and look where I'm lookin'."

"I don't see any—" Then she went quiet, and after a moment, whispered: "It's him . . . It's the Goat Man."

The shape abruptly turned, crunched a stick, rustled some leaves, and was gone. We didn't tell Daddy or Mama what we saw. I don't exactly know why, but we didn't. It was between me and Tom, and the next day we hardly mentioned it.

A week later, Janice Jane Willman was dead.

We heard about it Halloween night. There was a little party in town for the kids and whoever wanted to come. There were no invitations. Each year it was understood the party would take place and you could show up. The women brought covered dishes and the men brought a little bit of hooch to slip into their drinks.

The party was at Mrs. Canerton's. She was a widow, and kept books at her house as a kind of library. She let us borrow them from her, or we could come and sit in her house and read or even be read to, and she always had some cookies or lemonade, and she wasn't adverse to listening to our stories or problems. She was a sweet-faced lady with large breasts and a lot of men in town liked her and thought she was pretty.

Every year she had a little Halloween party for the kids. Apples. Pumpkin pie and such. Everyone who could afford a spare pillowcase made a ghost costume. A few of the older boys would slip off to West

Street to soap some windows, and that was about it for Halloween. But back then, it seemed pretty wonderful.

Daddy had taken us to the party. It was another fine cool night with lots of lightning bugs and crickets chirping, and me and Tom got to playing hide and go seek with the rest of the kids, and while the person who was it was counting, we went to hide. I crawled up under Mrs. Canerton's house, under the front porch. I hadn't no more than got up under there good, than Tom crawled up beside me.

"Hey," I whispered. "Go find your own place."

"I didn't know you was under here. It's too late for me to go anywhere."

"Then be quiet," I said.

While we were sitting there, we saw shoes and pants legs moving toward the porch steps. It was the men who had been standing out in the yard smoking. They were gathering on the porch to talk. I recognized a pair of boots as Daddy's, and after a bit of moving about on the porch above us, we heard the porch swing creak and some of the porch chairs scraping around, and then I heard Cecil speak.

"How long she been dead?"

"About a week I reckon," Daddy said.

"She anyone we know?"

"A prostitute," Daddy said. "Janice Jane Willman. She lives near all them juke joints outside of Mission Creek. She picked up the wrong man. Ended up in the river."

"She drown?" someone else asked.

"Reckon so. But she suffered some before that."

"You know who did it?" Cecil asked. "Any leads?"

"No. Not really."

"Niggers." I knew that voice. Old Man Nation. He showed up wherever there was food and possibly liquor, and he never brought a covered dish or liquor. "Niggers find a white woman down there in the bottoms, they'll get her."

"Yeah," I heard a voice say. "And what would a white woman be doin' wanderin' around down there?"

"Maybe he brought her there," Mr. Nation said. "A nigger'll take a white woman he gets a chance," Mr. Nation said. "Hell, wouldn't you if you was a nigger? Think about what you'd be gettin' at home. Some nigger. A white woman, that's prime business to 'em. Then, if you're a nigger and you've done it to her, you got to kill her so no one knows. Not that any self-respectin' white woman would want to live after somethin' like that."

"That's enough of that," Daddy said.

"You threatenin' me?" Mr. Nation said.

"I'm sayin' we don't need that kind of talk," Daddy said. "The murderer could have been white or black."

"It'll turn out to be a nigger," Mr. Nation said. "Mark my words."

"I heard you had a suspect," Cecil said.

"Not really," Daddy said.

"Some colored fella, I heard," Cecil said.

"I knew it," Nation said. "Some goddamn nigger."

"I picked a man up for questioning, that's all."

"Where is he?" Nation asked.

"You know," Daddy said, "I think I'm gonna have me a piece of that pie."

The porch creaked, the screen door opened, and we heard boot steps entering into the house.

"Nigger lover," Nation said.

"That's enough of that," Cecil said.

"You talkin' to me, fella?" Mr. Nation said.

"I am, and I said that's enough."

There was some scuttling, movement on the porch, and suddenly there was a smacking sound and Mr. Nation hit the ground in front of us. We could see him through the steps. His face turned in our direction, but I don't think he saw us. It was dark under the house, and he had his mind on other things. He got up quick like, leaving his hat on the ground, then we heard movement on the porch and Daddy's voice. "Ethan, don't come back on the porch. Go on home."

"Who do you think you are to tell me anything?" Mr. Nation said.

"Right now, I'm the constable, and you come up on this porch, you do one little thing that annoys me, I will arrest you."

"You and who else?"

"Just me."

"What about him? He hit me. You're on his side because he took up for you."

"I'm on his side because you're a loudmouth spoiling everyone else's good time. You been drinkin' too much. Go on home and sleep it off, Ethan. Let's don't let this get out of hand."

Mr. Nation's hand dropped down and picked up his hat. He said, "You're awfully high and mighty, aren't you?"

"There's just no use fighting over something silly," Daddy said.

"You watch yourself, nigger lover," Mr. Nation said.

"Don't come by the barbershop no more," Daddy said.

"Wouldn't think of it, nigger lover."

Then Mr. Nation turned and we saw him walking away.

Daddy said, "Cecil. You talk too much."

"Yeah, I know," Cecil said.

"Now, I was gonna get some pie," Daddy said. "I'm gonna go back inside and try it again. When I come back out, how's about we talk about somethin' altogether different?"

"Suits me," someone said, and I heard the screen door open again. For a moment I thought they were all inside, then I realized Daddy and Cecil were still on the porch, and Daddy was talking to Cecil.

"I shouldn't have spoken to you like that," Daddy said.

"It's all right. You're right. I talk too much."

"Let's forget it."

"Sure . . . Jacob, this suspect. You think he did it?"

"No. I don't."

"Is he safe?"

"For now. I may just let him go and never let it be known who he is. Bill Smoote is helping me out with him right now."

"Again, I'm sorry, Jacob."

"No problem. Let's get some of that pie."

On the way home in the car our bellies were full of apples, pie and lemonade. The windows were rolled down and the October wind was fresh and ripe with the smell of the woods. As we wound through those woods along the dirt road that led to our house, I began to feel sleepy.

Tom had already nodded off. I leaned against the side of the car and began to halfway doze. In time, I realized Mama and Daddy were talking.

"He had her purse?" Mama said.

"Yeah," Daddy said. "He had it, and he'd taken money from it."

"Could it be him?"

"He says he was fishing, saw the purse and her dress floating, snagged the purse with his fishing line. He saw there was money inside, and he took it. He said he figured a purse in the river wasn't something anyone was going to find, and there wasn't any name in it, and it was just five dollars going to waste. He said he didn't even consider that someone had been murdered. It could have happened that way. Personally, I believe him. I've known old Mose all my life. He taught me how to fish. He practically lives on that river in that boat of his. He wouldn't harm a fly. Besides, the man's seventy years old and not in the best of health. He's had a hell of a life. His wife ran off forty years ago and he's never gotten over it. His son disappeared when he was a youngster. Whoever raped this woman had to be pretty strong. She was young enough, and from the way her body looked, she put up a pretty good fight. Man did this had to be strong enough to . . . Well, she was cut up pretty bad. Same as the other women. Slashes along the breasts. Her hand hacked off at the wrist. We didn't find it."

"Oh dear."

"I'm sorry, honey. I didn't mean to upset you."

"How did you come by the purse?"

"I went by to see Mose. Like I always do when I'm down on the river. It was layin' on the table in his shack. I had to arrest him. I don't know I should have now. Maybe I should have just taken the purse and said I found it. I mean, I believe him. But I don't have evidence one way or the other."

"Hon, didn't Mose have some trouble before?"

"When his wife ran off some thought he'd killed her. She was fairly loose. That was the rumor. Nothing ever came of it."

"But he could have done it?"

"I suppose."

"And wasn't there something about his boy?"

"Telly was the boy's name. He was addleheaded. Mose claimed that's why his wife run off. She was embarrassed by that addleheaded boy. Kid disappeared four or five years later and Mose never talked about it. Some thought he killed him too. But that's just rumor. White folks talkin' about colored folks like they do. I believe his wife ran off. The boy wasn't much of a thinker, and he may have run off too. He liked to roam the woods and river. He might have drowned, fallen in some hole somewhere and never got out."

"But none of that makes it look good for Mose, does it?"

"No, it doesn't."

"What are you gonna do, Jacob?"

"I don't know. I was afraid to lock him up over at the courthouse. It isn't a real jail anyway, and word gets around a colored man was involved, there won't be any real thinking on the matter. I talked Bill Smoote into letting me keep Mose over at his bait house."

"Couldn't Mose just run away?"

"I suppose. But he's not in that good a health, hon. And he trusts me to investigate, clear him. That's what makes me nervous. I don't know how. I thought about talking to the Mission Creek police, as they have more experience, but they have a tendency to be a little emotional themselves. Rumor is, sheriff over there is in the Klan, or used to be. Frankly, I'm not sure what to do."

I began to drift off again. I thought of Mose. He was an old colored man who got around on shore with use of a cane. He had white blood in him. Red in his hair, and eyes as green as spring leaves. Mostly you saw him in his little rowboat fishing. He lived in a shack alongside the river not more than three miles from us. Living off the fish he caught, the squirrels he shot. Sometimes, when we had a good day hunting or fishing, Daddy would go by there and give Mose a squirrel or some fish. Mose was always glad to see us, or seemed to be. Up until a year ago, I used to go fishing with him. It was then Jake told me I ought not. That it wasn't right to be seen with a nigger all the time.

Thinking back on that, I felt sick to my stomach, confused. Mose had taught my daddy to fish, I had gone fishing with him, and suddenly I deserted him because of what Jake had said.

I thought of the Goat Man again. I recalled him standing below the swinging bridge, looking up through the shadows at me. I thought of him near our house, watching. The Goat Man had killed those women, I knew it. And Mose was gonna take the blame for what he had done.

It was there in the car, battered by the cool October wind, that I began to formulate a plan to find the Goat Man and free Mose. I thought on it for several days after, and I think maybe I had begun to come up with something that seemed like a good idea to me. It probably wasn't. Just some thirteen-year-old's idea of a plan. But it didn't really matter. Shortly thereafter, things turned for the worse.

It was a Monday, a couple days later, and Daddy was off from the barbershop that day. He had already gotten up and fed the livestock, and as daybreak was making through the trees, he come and got me up to help tote water from the well to the house. Mama was in the kitchen cooking grits, biscuits, and fatback for breakfast.

Me and Daddy had a bucket of water apiece and were carrying them back to the house, when I said, "Daddy. You ever figure out what you're gonna do with ole Mose?"

He paused a moment. "How'd you know about that?'

"I heard you and Mama talkin'."

He nodded, and we started walking again. "I can't leave him where he is for good. Someone will get onto it. I reckon I'm gonna have to take him to the courthouse or let him go. There's no real evidence against him, just some circumstantial stuff. But a colored man, a white woman, and a hint of suspicion . . . He'll never get a fair trial. I got to be sure myself he didn't do it."

"Ain't you?"

We were on the back porch now, and Daddy set his bucket down and set mine down too. "You know, I reckon I am. If no one ever knows who it was I arrested, he can go on about his business. I ain't got nothin' on him. Not really. Something else comes up, some real evidence against him, I know where he is."

"Mose couldn't have killed those women. He hardly gets around, Daddy."

I saw his face redden. "Yeah. You're right."

He picked up both buckets and carried them into the house. Mama had the food on the table, and Tom was sitting there with her eyes squinted, looking as if she were going to fall face forward in her grits any moment. Normally, there'd be school, but the schoolteacher had quit and they hadn't hired another yet, so we had nowhere to go that day, me and Tom.

I think that was part of the reason Daddy asked me to go with him after breakfast. That, and I figured he wanted some company. He told me he had decided to go down and let Mose loose.

We drove over to Bill Smoote's. Bill owned an icehouse down by the river. It was a big room really, with sawdust and ice packed in there, and people came and bought it by car or by boat on the river. He sold right smart of it. Up behind the icehouse was the little house where Bill lived with his wife and two daughters that looked as if they had fallen out of an ugly tree, hit every branch on the way down, then smacked the dirt solid. They was always smilin' at me and such, and it made me nervous.

Behind Mr. Smoote's house was his barn, really more of a big ole shed. That's where Daddy said Mose was kept. As we pulled up at Mr. Smoote's place alongside the river, we saw the yard was full of cars, wagons, horses, mules and people. It was early morning still, and the sunlight fell through the trees like Christmas decorations, and the river was red with the morning sun, and the people in the yard were painted with the same red light as the river.

At first I thought Mr. Smoote was just having him a big run of customers, but as we got up there, we saw there was a wad of people coming from the barn. The wad was Mr. Nation, his two boys, and some other man I'd seen around town before but didn't know. They had Mose between them. He wasn't exactly walking with them. He was being half dragged, and I heard Mr. Nation's loud voice say something about "damn nigger," then Daddy was out of the car and pushing through the crowd.

A heavyset woman in a print dress and square-looking shoes, her hair wadded on top of her head and pinned there, yelled, "To hell with you, Jacob, for hidin' this nigger out. After what he done."

It was then I realized we was in the middle of the crowd, and they were closing around us, except for a gap that opened so Mr. Nation and his bunch could drag Mose into the circle.

Mose looked ancient, withered and knotted like old cowhide soaked in brine. His head was bleeding, his eyes were swollen, his lips were split. He had already taken quite a beating.

When Mose saw Daddy, his green eyes lit up. "Mr. Jacob, don't let them do nothin'. I didn't do nothin' to nobody."

"It's all right, Mose," he said. Then he glared at Mr. Nation. "Nation, this ain't your business."

"It's all our business," Mr. Nation said. "When our womenfolk can't walk around without worrying about some nigger draggin' 'em off, then it's our business."

There was a voice of agreement from the crowd.

"I only picked him up 'cause he might know something could lead to the killer," Daddy said. "I was comin' out here to let him go. I realized he don't know a thing."

"Bill here says he had that woman's purse," Nation said.

Daddy turned to look at Mr. Smoote, who didn't acknowledge Daddy's look. He just said softly under his breath, "I didn't tell 'em he was here, Jacob. They knew. I just told 'em why you had him here. I tried to get them to listen, but they wouldn't."

Daddy just stared at Mr. Smoote for a long moment. Then he turned to Nation, said, "Let him go."

"In the old days, we took care of bad niggers prompt like," Mr. Nation said. "And we figured out somethin' real quick. A nigger hurt a white man or woman, you hung him, he didn't hurt anyone again. You got to take care of a nigger problem quick, or ever' nigger around here will be thinkin' he can rape and murder white women at will."

Daddy spoke calmly. "He deserves a fair trial. We're not here to punish anyone."

"Hell we ain't," someone said.

The crowd grew tighter around us. I turned to look for Mr. Smoote, but he was gone from sight.

Mr. Nation said, "You ain't so high and mighty now, are you, Jacob? You and your nigger-lovin' ways aren't gonna cut the mustard around here."

"Hand him over," Daddy said. "I'll take him. See he gets a fair trial."

"You said you were gonna turn him loose," Nation said.

"I thought about it. Yes."

"He ain't gonna be turned loose, except at the end of the rope."

"You're not gonna hang this man," Daddy said.

"That's funny," Nation said. "I thought that's exactly what we were gonna do."

"This ain't the wild west," Daddy said.

"No," Nation said. "This here is a riverbank with trees, and we got us a rope and a bad nigger."

One of Mr. Nation's boys had slipped off while Daddy and Mr. Nation were talking, and when he reappeared, he had a rope tied in a noose. He slipped it over Mose's head.

Daddy stepped forward then, grabbed the rope and jerked it off of Mose. The crowd let out a sound like an animal in pain, then they were all over Daddy, punching and kicking. I tried to fight them, but they hit me too, and the next thing I knew I was on the ground and legs were kicking at us and then I heard Mose scream for my daddy, and when I looked up they had the rope around his neck and were dragging him along the ground.

One man grabbed the end of the rope and threw it over a thick oak limb, and in unison the crowd grabbed the rope and began to pull, hoisting Mose up. Mose grabbed at the rope with his hands and his feet kicked.

Daddy pushed himself up, staggered forward, grabbed Mose's legs and ducked his head under Mose and lifted him. But Mr. Nation blindsided Daddy with a kick to the ribs, and Daddy went down and Mose dropped with a snapping sound, started to kick and spit foam. Daddy tried to get up, but men and women began to kick and beat him. I got up and ran for him. Someone clipped me in the back of the neck, and when I come to everyone was gone except me and Daddy, still unconscious, and Mose hung above us, his tongue long and black and thick as a sock stuffed with paper. His green eyes bulged out of his head like little green persimmons.

On hands and knees I threw up until I didn't think I had any more in me. Hands grabbed my sides, and I was figuring on more of a beating, but then I heard Mr. Smoote say, "Easy, boy. Easy."

He tried to help me up, but I couldn't stand. He left me sitting on the ground and went over and looked at Daddy. He turned him over and pulled an eyelid back.

I said, "Is he . . . ?"

"No. He's all right. He just took some good shots."

Daddy stirred. Mr. Smoote sat him up. Daddy lifted his eyes to Mose. He said, "For Christ sake, Bill, cut him down from there."

Mose was buried on our place, between the barn and the field. Daddy made him a wooden cross and carved MOSE on it, and swore when he got money he'd get him a stone.

After that, Daddy wasn't quite the same. He wanted to quit being a constable, but the little money the job brought in was needed, so he stayed at it, swearing anything like this came up again he was gonna quit.

Fall passed into winter, and there were no more murders. Those who had helped lynch Mose warmed themselves by their self-righteousness. A bad nigger had been laid low. No more women would die—especially white women.

Many of those there that day had been Daddy's customers, and we didn't see them anymore at the shop. As for the rest, Cecil cut most of the hair, and Daddy was doing so little of it, he finally gave Cecil a key and a bigger slice of the money and only came around now and then. He turned his attention to working around the farm, fishing and hunting.

When spring came, Daddy went to planting, just like always, but he didn't talk about the crops much, and I didn't hear him and Mama talking much, but sometimes late at night, through the wall, I could hear him cry. There's no way to explain how bad it hurts to hear your father cry.

They got a new schoolmaster come that spring, but it was decided school wouldn't pick up until the fall, after all the crops had been laid by. Cecil started teaching me how to cut hair, and I even got so I could handle a little trade at the shop, mostly kids my age that liked the idea of me doing it. I brought the money home to Mama, and when I gave it to her, she nearly always cried.

For the first time in my life, the Depression seemed like the Depression to me. Tom and I still hunted and fished together, but there was starting to be more of a gulf between our ages. I was about to turn fourteen and I felt as old as Mose had been.

That next spring came and went and was pleasant enough, but the summer set in with a vengeance, hot as hell's griddle, and the river receded some and the fish didn't seem to want to bite, and the squirrels and rabbits were wormy that time of year, so there wasn't much use in that. Most of the crops burned up, and if that wasn't bad enough, mid-July, there was a bad case of the hydrophobia broke out. Forest animals, domesticated dogs and cats were the victims. It was pretty awful. Got so people shot stray dogs on sight. We kept Toby close to the house, and in the cool, as it was believed by many that an animal could catch rabies not only by being bitten by a diseased animal but by air when it was hot.

Anyway, it got so folks were calling it a mad dog summer, and it turned out that in more ways than one they were right.

Clem Sumption lived some ten miles down the road from us, right where a little road forked off what served as a main highway then. You wouldn't think of it as a highway now, but it was the main road, and if you turned off of it, trying to cross through our neck of the woods on your way to Tyler, you had to pass his house, which was situated alongside the river.

Clem's outhouse was over near the river, and it was fixed up so what went out of him and his family went into the river. Lot of folks did that, though some like my daddy were appalled at the idea. It was that place and time's idea of plumbing. The waste dropped down a slanted hole onto the bank and when the water rose, the mess was carried away. When it didn't, flies lived there on mounds of dark mess, buried in it, glowing like jewels in rancid chocolate.

Clem ran a little roadside stand where he sold a bit of vegetables now and then, and on this hot day I'm talking about, he suddenly had the urge to take care of a mild stomach disorder, and left his son, Wilson, in charge of the stand.

After doing his business, Clem rolled a cigarette and went out beside the outhouse to look down on the fly-infested pile, maybe hoping the river had carried some of it away. But dry as it was, the pile was bigger and the water was lower, and something pale and dark lay facedown in the pile.

Clem, first spying it, thought it was a huge, bloated, belly-up catfish. One of those enormous bottom crawler types that were reputed by some to be able to swallow small dogs and babies.

But a catfish didn't have legs.

Clem said later, even when he saw the legs, it didn't register with him that it was a human being. It looked too swollen, too strange to be a person.

But as he eased carefully down the side of the hill, mindful not to step in what his family had been dropping along the bank all summer, he saw that it was indeed a woman's bloated body lying facedown in the moist blackness, and the flies were as delighted with the corpse as they were with the waste.

Clem saddled up a horse and arrived in our yard sometime after that. This wasn't like now, when medical examiners show up and cops measure this and measure that, take fingerprints and photos. My father and Clem pulled the body out of the pile and dipped it into the river for a rinse, and it was then that Daddy saw the face of Marla Canerton buried in a mass of swollen flesh, one cold dead eye open, as if she were winking.

The body arrived at our house wrapped in a tarp. Daddy and Clem hauled it out of the car and toted it up to the barn. As they walked by, me and Tom, out under the big tree, playing some game or another, could smell that terrible dead smell through the tarp, and with no wind blowing, it was dry and rude to the nostrils and made me sick.

When Daddy came out of the barn with Clem, he had an ax handle in his hand. He started walking briskly down to the car, and I could hear Clem arguing with him. "Don't do it, Jacob. It ain't worth it."

We ran over to the car as Mama came out of the house. Daddy calmly laid the ax handle in the front seat, and Clem stood shaking his head. Mama climbed into the car and started on Daddy. "Jacob, I know what you're thinkin'. You can't."

Daddy started up the car. Mama yelled out, "Children. Get in. I'm not leavin' you here."

We did just that, and roared off leaving Clem standing in the yard bewildered. Mama fussed and yelled and pleaded all the way over to Mr. Nation's house, but Daddy never said a word. When he pulled up in Nation's yard, Mr. Nation's wife was outside hoeing at a pathetic little garden, and Mr. Nation and his two boys were sitting in rickety chairs under a tree.

Daddy got out of the car with his ax handle and started walking toward Mr. Nation. Mama was hanging on his arm, but he pulled free. He walked right past Mrs. Nation, who paused and looked up in surprise.

Mr. Nation and his boys spotted Daddy coming, and Mr. Nation slowly rose from his chair. "What the hell you doin' with that ax handle?" he asked.

Daddy didn't answer, but the next moment what he was doing with that ax handle became clear. It whistled through the hot morning air like a flaming arrow and caught Mr. Nation alongside the head about where the jaw meets the ear, and the sound it made was, to put it mildly, akin to a rifle shot.

Mr. Nation went down like a windblown scarecrow, and Daddy stood over him swinging the ax handle, and Mr. Nation was yelling and putting up his arms in a pathetic way, and the two boys came at Daddy, and Daddy turned and swatted one of them down, and the other tackled him. Instinctively, I started kicking at that boy, and he came off Daddy and climbed me, but Daddy was up now, and the ax handle whistled, and that ole boy went out like a light and the other one, who was still conscious, started scuttling along the ground on all fours with a motion like a crippled centipede. He finally got upright and ran for the house.

Mr. Nation tried to get up several times, but every time he did that ax handle would cut the air, and down he'd go. Daddy whapped on Mr. Nation's sides and back and legs until he was worn out, had to back off and lean on the somewhat splintered handle.

Nation, battered, ribs surely broken, lip busted, spitting teeth, looked at Daddy, but he didn't try to get up. Daddy, when he got his wind back, said, "They found Marla Canerton down by the river. Dead. Cut the same way. You and your boys and that lynch mob didn't do nothin' but hang an innocent man."

"You're supposed to be the law?" Nation said.

"If'n I was any kind of law, I'd have had you arrested for what you did to Mose, but that wouldn't have done any good. No one around here would convict you, Nation. They're scared of you. But I ain't. I ain't. And if you ever cross my path again, I swear to God, I'll kill you."

Daddy tossed the ax handle aside, said "Come on," and we all started back to the car. As we passed Mrs. Nation, she looked up and leaned on her hoe. She had a black eye and a swollen lip and some old bruises on her cheek. She smiled at us.

We all went to Mrs. Canerton's funeral. Me and my family stood in the front row. Cecil was there. Just about everyone in town and around about, except the Nations and some of the people who had been in the lynch mob that killed Mose.

Within a week Daddy's customers at the barbershop returned, among them members of the lynch party, and the majority of them wanted him to cut their hair. He had to go back to work regularly. I don't know how he felt about that, cutting the hair of those who had beaten me and him that day, that had killed Mose, but he cut their hair and took their money. Maybe Daddy saw it as a kind of revenge. And maybe we just needed the money.

Mama took a job in town at the courthouse. With school out, that left me to take care of Tom, and though we were supposed to stay out of the woods that summer, especially knowing there was a murderer on the loose, we were kids and adventurous and bored.

One morning me and Tom and Toby went down to the river and walked along the bank, looking for a place to ford near the swinging bridge. Neither of us wanted to cross the bridge, and we used the excuse that Toby couldn't cross it, but that was just an excuse.

We wanted to look at the briar tunnel we had been lost in that night, but we didn't want to cross the bridge to get there. We walked a long ways and finally came to the shack where Mose had lived, and we just stood there looking at it. It had never been much, just a hovel made of wood and tin and tarpaper. Mose mostly set outside of it in an old chair under a willow tree that overlooked the river.

The door was wide open, and when we looked in there, we could see animals had been prowling about. A tin of flour had been knocked over and was littered with bugs. Other foodstuff was not recognizable. They were just glaze matted into the hard dirt floor. A few pathetic possessions were lying here and there. A wooden child's toy was on a shelf and next to it a very faded photograph of a dark black woman that might have been Mose's wife.

The place depressed me. Toby went inside and sniffed about and prowled in the flour till we called him out. We walked around the house and out near the chair, and it was then, looking back at the house, I noted there was something hanging on a nail on the outside wall. It was a chain, and from the chain hung a number of fish skele-tons, and one fresh fish.

We went over and looked at it. The fresh fish was very fresh, and in fact, it was still damp. Someone had hung it there recently, and the other stack of fish bones indicated that someone had been hanging fish there on a regular basis, and for some time, like an offering to Mose. An offering he could no longer take.

On another nail nearby, strings tied together, was a pair of old shoes that had most likely been fished from the river, and hung over them was a water-warped belt. On the ground, leaning against the side of the house below the nail with the shoes, was a tin plate and a bright blue river rock and a mason jar. All of it laid out like gifts.

I don't know why, but I took the dead fish down, all the old bones, and cast them into the river and put the chain back on the nail. I tossed the shoe and belt, the plate, rock and mason jar into the river. Not out of meanness, but so the gifts would seem to be taken.

Mose's old boat was still up by the house, laid up on rocks so it wouldn't rot on the ground. A paddle lay in its bottom. We decided to take it and float it upriver to where the briar tunnels were. We loaded Toby in the boat, pushed it into the water and set out. We floated the long distance back to the swinging bridge and went under it, looking for the Goat Man under there, waiting like Billy Goat Gruff.

In shadow, under the bridge, deep into the bank, was a dark indention, like a cave. I imagined that was where the Goat Man lived, waiting for prey.

We paddled gently to the riverbank where we had found the woman bound to the tree by the river. She was long gone, of course, and the vines that had held her were no longer there.

We pulled the boat onto the dirt and gravel bank and left it there as we went up the taller part of the bank, past the tree where the woman had been, and into the briars. The tunnel was the same, and it was clear in the daytime that the tunnel had, as we suspected, been cut into the briars. It was not as large or as long a tunnel as it had seemed that night, and it emptied out into a wider tunnel, and it too was shorter and smaller than we had thought. There were little bits of colored cloth hung on briars all about and there were pictures from Sears catalogs of women in underwear and there were a few of those playing cards like I had seen hung on briars. We hadn't seen all that at night, but I figured it had been there all along.

In the middle of the tunnel was a place where someone had built a fire, and above us the briars wrapped so thick and were so inter-twined with low-hanging branches, you could imagine much of this place would stay almost dry during a rainstorm.

Toby was sniffing and running about as best his poor old damaged back and legs would allow him.

"It's like some kind of nest," Tom said. "The Goat Man's nest."

A chill came over me then, and it occurred to me that if that was true, and if this was his den instead of the cave under the bridge, or one of his dens, he might come home at any time. I told Tom that, and we called up Toby and got out of there, tried to paddle the boat back upriver, but couldn't.

We finally got out and made to carry it along the bank, but it was too heavy. We gave up and left it by the river. We walked past the swinging bridge and for a long ways till we found a sandbar. We used that to cross, and went back home, finished the chores, cleaned ourselves and Toby up before Mama and Daddy came chugging home from work in our car.

Next morning, when Mama and Daddy left for town and work, me and Tom and Toby went at it again. I had a hunch about Mose's old shack, and I wanted to check it out. But my hunch was wrong. There was nothing new hung from the nails or leaned against the wall. But there was something curious. The boat we had left on the bank was back in its place atop the rocks with the paddle inside.

It was that night, lying in bed, that I heard Mama and Daddy talking. After Daddy had beaten Mr. Nation and his boys with the ax handle, his spirit had been restored. I heard him tell Mama: "There's this thing I been thinking, honey. What if the murderer wanted people to think it was Mose, so he made a big to-do about it to hide the fact he done it. Maybe he was gonna quit doin' it, but he couldn't. You know, like some of them diseases that come back on you when you think you're over it."

"You mean Mr. Nation, don't you?" Mama said.

"Well, it's a thought. And it come to me it might be one of them boys, Esau or Uriah. Uriah has had a few problems. There's lots of talk about him torturin' little animals and such, stomping the fish he caught on the bank, for no good reason other than he wanted to."

"That doesn't mean he killed those women."

"No. But he likes to hurt things and cut them up. And the other'n, Esau. He starts fires, and not like some kids will do, but regular like. He's been in trouble over it before. Folks like that worry me."

"That still don't mean they're murderers."

"No. But if Nation was capable of such a thing, it would be like him to blame it on a colored. Most people in these parts would be quick to accept that. I've heard a couple of lawmen say when you don't know who did it, go out and get you a nigger. It calms people down, and it's one less nigger."

"That's terrible."

"Of course it is. But there's some like that. If Nation didn't do it, and he knows one or both of them worthless boys did it, he might have been coverin' up for him."

"You really think that's possible, Jacob?"

"I think it's possible. I don't know it's likely, but I'm gonna keep my eye on 'em."

Daddy made sense about Mr. Nation and his boys. I had seen Mr. Nation a couple of times since the day Daddy gave him his beating, and when he saw me, he gave me a look that could have set fire to rocks, then went his way. Esau had even followed me down Main Street one day, scowling, but by the time I reached the barbershop, he had turned and gone between a couple of buildings and out of sight.

But all that aside, I still put my odds on the Goat Man. He had been near the site of the body me and Tom had found, and he had followed us out to the road, as if we were to be his next victims. And I figured only something that wasn't quite human would be capable of the kind of things that had happened in those bottoms with those women.

Poor Mrs. Canerton had always been so nice. All those books. The Halloween parties. The way she smiled.

As I drifted off to sleep I thought of telling Daddy about the Sears catalog pictures and the cloth and such in the briar tunnel, but being young like I was then, I was more worried about getting in trouble for being where I wasn't supposed to be, so I kept quiet. Actually, thinking back now, it wouldn't have mattered.

That summer, from time to time, me and Tom slipped off and went down to Mose's old cabin. Now and then there would be a fish on the nail, or some odd thing from the river, so my hunch had been right all along. Someone was bringing Mose gifts, perhaps unaware he was dead. Or maybe they had been left there for some other reason.

We dutifully took down what was there and returned it to the river, wondering if maybe it was the Goat Man leaving the goods. But when we looked around for sign of him, all we could find were prints from someone wearing large-sized shoes. No hoof prints.

As the summer moved on, it got hotter and hotter, and the air was like having a blanket wrapped twice around your head. Got so you hardly wanted to move mid-day, and for a time we quit slipping off down to the river and stayed close at home.

That Fourth of July, our little town decided to have a celebration. Me and Tom were excited because there was to be firecrackers and some Roman candles and all manner of fireworks, and, of course, plenty of home-cooked food.

Folks were pretty leery, thinking that the killer was probably still out there somewhere, and the general thinking had gone from him being some traveling fellow to being someone among us.

Fact was, no one had ever seen or heard of anything like this, except for Jack the Ripper, and we had thought that kind of murder was only done in some big city far away.

The town gathered late afternoon before dark. Main Street had been blocked off, which was no big deal as traffic was rare anyway, and tables with covered dishes and watermelons on them were set up in the street, and after a preacher said a few words, everyone got a plate and went around and helped themselves. I remember eating a little of everything that was there, zeroing in on mashed potatoes and gravy, mincemeat, apple, and pear pies. Tom ate pie and cake and nothing else except watermelon that Cecil helped her cut.

There was a circle of chairs between the tables and behind the chairs was a kind of makeshift stage, and there were a handful of folks with guitars and fiddles playing and singing now and then, and the men and womenfolk would gather in the middle and dance to the tunes. Mama and Daddy were dancing too, and Tom was sitting on Cecil's knee and he was clapping and keeping time to the music, bouncing her up and down.

I kept thinking Mr. Nation and his boys would show, as they were always ones to be about when there was free food or the possibility of a drink, but they didn't. I figured that was because of Daddy. Mr. Nation might have looked tough and had a big mouth, but that ax handle had tamed him.

As the night wore on, the music was stopped and the fireworks were set. The firecrackers popped and the candles and such exploded high above Main Street, burst into all kinds of colors, pinned themselves against the night, then went wide and thin and faded. I remember watching as one bright swathe did not fade right away, but dropped to earth like a falling star, and as my eyes followed it down, it dipped behind Cecil and Tom, and in the final light from its burst, I could see Tom's smiling face, and Cecil, his hands on her shoulders, his face slack and beaded with sweat, his knee still bouncing her gently, even though there was no music to keep time to, the two of them looking up, awaiting more bright explosions.

Worry about the murders, about there being a killer amongst us, had withered. In that moment, all seemed right with the world.

When we got home that night we were all excited, and we sat down for a while under the big oak outside and drank some apple cider. It was great fun, but I kept having that uncomfortable feeling of being watched. I scanned the woods, but didn't see anything. Tom didn't seem to have noticed, and neither had my parents. Not long after a possum presented itself at the edge of the woods, peeked out at our celebration and disappeared back into the darkness.

Daddy and Mama sang a few tunes as he picked his old guitar, then they told stories a while, and a couple of them were kind of spooky ones, then we all took turns going out to the outhouse, and finally to bed.

Tom and I talked some, then I helped her open the window by her bed, and the warm air blew in carrying the smell of rain brewing.

As I lay in bed that night, my ear to the wall, I heard Mama say: "The children will hear, honey. These walls are paper thin."

"Don't you want to?"

"Of course. Sure."

"The walls are always paper thin."

"You're not always like you are tonight. You know how you are when you're like this."

"How am I?"

Mama laughed. "Loud."

"Listen, honey. I really, you know, need to. And I want to be loud. What say we take the car down the road a piece. I know a spot."

"Jacob. What if someone came along?"

"I know a spot they won't come along. It'll be real private."

"Well, we don't have to do that. We can do it here. We'll just have to be quiet."

"I don't want to be quiet. And even if I did, it's a great night. I'm not sleepy."

"What about the children?"

"It's just down the road, hon. It'll be fun."

"All right . . . All right. Why not?"

I lay there wondering what in the world had gotten into my parents, and as I lay there I heard the car start up and glide away down the road.

Where could they be going?

And why?

It was really some years later before I realized what was going on. At the time it was a mystery. But back then I contemplated it for a time, then nodded off, the wind turning from warm to cool by the touch of oncoming rain.

Sometime later I was awakened by Toby barking, but it didn't last and I went back to sleep. After that, I heard a tapping sound. It was as if some bird were pecking corn from a hard surface. I gradually opened my eyes and turned in my bed and saw a figure at the open window. When the curtains blew I could see the shape standing there, looking in. It was a dark shape with horns on its head, and one hand was tapping on the windowsill with long fingernails. The Goat Man was making a kind of grunting sound.

I sat bolt upright in bed, my back to the wall.

"Go away!" I said.

But the shape remained and its gruntings changed to whimpers. The curtains blew in, back out, and the shape was gone. Then I noticed that Tom's bed, which was directly beneath the window, was empty.

I had helped open that window.

I eased over to her bed and peeked outside. Out by the woods I could see the Goat Man. He lifted his hand and summoned me.

I hesitated. I ran to Mama and Daddy's room, but they were gone. I dimly remembered before dropping off to sleep they had driven off in the car, for God knows what. I went back to our little room and assured myself I was not dreaming. Tom was gone, stolen by the Goat Man, most likely, and now the thing was summoning me to follow. A kind of taunt. A kind of game.

I looked out the window again, and the Goat Man was still there. I got the shotgun and some shells and pulled my pants on, tucked in my nightshirt, and slipped on my shoes. I went back to the window and looked out. The Goat Man was still in his spot by the woods. I slid out the window and went after him. As soon as he saw my gun, he ducked into the shadows.

As I ran, I called for Mama and Daddy and Tom. But no one answered. I tripped and went down. When I rose to my knees I saw that I had tripped over Toby. He lay still on the ground. I put the shotgun down and picked him up. His head rolled limp to one side. His neck was broken.

Oh God. Toby was dead. After all he had been through, he had been murdered. He had barked earlier, to warn me about the Goat Man, and now he was dead and Tom was missing, and Mama and Daddy had gone off somewhere in the car, and the Goat Man was no longer in sight.

I put Toby down easy, pushed back the tears, picked up the shotgun and ran blindly into the woods, down the narrow path the Goat Man had taken, fully expecting at any moment to fall over Tom's body, her neck broken like Toby's.

But that didn't happen.

There was just enough moon for me to see where I was going, but not enough to keep every shadow from looking like the Goat Man, coiled and ready to pounce. The wind was sighing through the trees and there were bits of rain with it, and the rain was cool.

I didn't know if I should go on or go back and try and find Mama and Daddy. I felt that no matter what I did, valuable time was being lost. There was no telling what the Goat Man was doing to poor Tom. He had probably tied her up and put her at the edge of the woods before coming back to taunt me at the window. Maybe he had wanted me too. I thought of what had been done to all those poor women, and I thought of Tom, and a kind of sickness came over me, and I ran faster, deciding it was best to continue on course, hoping I'd come up on the monster and would get a clear shot at him and be able to rescue Tom.

It was then that I saw a strange thing in the middle of the trail. A limb had been cut, and it was forced into the ground, and it was bent to the right at the top and whittled on to make it sharp. It was like a kind of arrow pointing the way.

The Goat Man was having his fun with me. I decided I had no choice other than to go where the arrow was pointing, a little trail even more narrow than the one I was on.

I went on down it, and in the middle of it was another limb, this one more hastily prepared, just broken off and stuck in the ground, bent over at the middle and pointing to the right again.

Where it pointed wasn't hardly even a trail, just a break here and there in the trees. I went that way, spiderwebs twisting into my hair, limbs slapping me across the face, and before I knew it my feet had gone out from under me and I was sliding over the edge of an embankment, and when I hit on the seat of my pants and looked out, I was at the road, the one the preachers traveled. The Goat Man had brought me to the road by a shortcut and had gone straight down it, because right in front of me, drawn in the dirt of the road, was an arrow. If he could cross the road or travel down it, that meant he could go anywhere he wanted. There wasn't any safe place from the Goat Man.

I ran down the road, and I wasn't even looking for sign anymore. I knew I was heading for the swinging bridge, and across from that the briar tunnels, where I figured the Goat Man had taken her. That would be his place, I reckoned. Those tunnels, and I knew then that the tunnels were where he had done his meanness to those women before casting them into the river. By placing that dead colored woman there, he had been taunting us all, showing us not only the place of the murder but the probable place of all the murders. A place where he could take his time and do what he wanted for as long as he wanted.

When I got to the swinging bridge, the wind was blowing hard and it was starting to rain harder. The bridge lashed back and forth, and I finally decided I'd be better off to go down to Mose's cabin and use his boat to cross the river.

I ran down the bank as fast as I could go, and when I got to the cabin my sides hurt from running. I threw the shotgun into the boat, pushed the boat off its blocks, let it slide down to the edge of the river. It got caught up in the sand there, and I couldn't move it. It had bogged down good in the soft sand. I pushed and pulled, but no dice. I started to cry. I should have crossed the swinging bridge.

I grabbed the shotgun out of the boat and started to run back toward the bridge, but as I went up the little hill toward the cabin, I saw something hanging from the nail there that gave me a start.

There was a chain over the nail, and hanging from the chain was a hand, and part of a wrist. I felt sick. Tom. Oh God. Tom.

I went up there slowly and bent forward and saw that the hand was too large to be Tom's, and it was mostly rotten with only a bit of flesh on it. In the shadows it had looked whole, but it was anything but. The chain was not tied to the hand, but the hand was in a half fist and the chain was draped through its fingers, and in the partial open palm I could see what it held was a coin. A French coin with a dent in it. Cecil's coin.

I knew I should hurry, but it was as if I had been hit with a stick. The killer had chopped off one of his victim's hands. I remembered that. I decided the woman had grabbed the killer, and the killer had chopped at her with something big and sharp, and her hand had come off.

This gave me as many questions as answers. How did Cecil's coin get in the hand, and how did it end up here? Who was leaving all these things here, and why? Was it the Goat Man?

Then there was a hand on my shoulder.

As I jerked my head around I brought up the shotgun, but another hand came out quickly and took the shotgun away from me, and I was looking straight into the face of the Goat Man.

The moon rolled out from behind a rain cloud, and its light fell into the Goat Man's eyes, and they shone, and I realized they were green. Green like ole Mose's eyes.

The Goat Man made a soft grunting sound and patted my shoulder. I saw then his horns were not horns at all but an old straw hat that had rotted, leaving a gap in the front, like something had taken a bite out of it, and it made him look like he had horns. It was just a straw hat. A dadburn straw hat. No horns. And those eyes. Ole Mose's eyes.

And in that instant I knew. The Goat Man wasn't any goat man at all. He was Mose's son, the one wasn't right in the head and was thought to be dead. He'd been living out here in the woods all this time, and Mose had been taking care of him, and the son in his turn had been trying to take care of Mose by bringing him gifts he had found in the river, and now that Mose was dead and gone, he was still doing it. He was just a big dumb boy in a man's body, wandering the woods wearing worn-out clothes and shoes with soles that flopped.

The Goat Man turned and pointed upriver. I knew then he hadn't killed anyone, hadn't taken Tom. He had come to warn me, to let me know Tom had been taken, and now he was pointing the way. I just knew it. I didn't know how he had come by the hand or Cecil's chain and coin, but I knew the Goat Man hadn't killed anybody. He had been watching our house, and he had seen what had happened, and now he was trying to help me.

I broke loose from him and ran back to the boat, tried to push it free again. The Goat Man followed me down and put the shotgun in the boat and grabbed it and pushed it out of the sand and into the river and helped me into it, waded and pushed me out until the current had me good. I watched as he waded back toward the shore and the cabin. I picked up the paddle and went to work, trying not to think too much about what was being done to Tom.

Dark clouds passed over the moon from time to time, and the raindrops became more frequent and the wind was high and slightly cool with the dampness. I paddled so hard my back and shoulders began to ache, but the current was with me, pulling me fast. I passed a whole school of water moccasins swimming in the dark, and I feared they might try to climb up into the boat, as they liked to do, thinking it was a floating log and wanting a rest.

I paddled quickly through them, spreading the school, and one did indeed try to climb up the side, but I brought the boat paddle down on him hard and he went back in the water, alive or dead I couldn't say.

As I paddled around a bend in the river, I saw where the wild briars grew, and in that moment I had a strange sinking feeling. Not only for fear of what I might find in the briar tunnels, but fear I might find nothing at all. Fear I was all wrong. Or that the Goat Man did indeed have Tom. Perhaps in Mose's cabin, and had been keeping her there, waiting until I was out of sight. But if that was true, why had he given my gun back? Then again, he wasn't bright. He was a creature of the woods, same as a coon or a possum. He didn't think like regular folks.

All of this went through my head and swirled around and confused itself with my own fears and the thought of actually cutting down on a man with a shotgun. I felt like I was in a dream, like the kind I'd had when I'd had the flu the year before and everything had swirled and Mama and Daddy's voices had seemed to echo and there were shadows all around me, trying to grab at me and pull me away into who knows where.

I paddled up to the bank and got out and pulled the boat up on shore best I could. I couldn't quite get it out of the water since I was so tuckered out from paddling. I just hoped it would hang there and hold.

I got the shotgun out and went up the hill quietly and found the mouth of the tunnel just beyond the tree, where me and Tom and Toby had come out that night.

It was dark inside the briars, and the moon had gone away behind a cloud and the wind rattled the briars and clicked them together and bits of rain sliced through the briars and mixed with the sweat in my hair, ran down my face and made me shiver. July the Fourth, and I was cold.

As I sneaked down the tunnel, an orange glow leaped and danced and I could hear a crackling sound. I trembled and eased forward and came to the end of the tunnel, and froze. I couldn't make myself turn into the other tunnel. It was as if my feet were nailed the ground.

I pulled back the hammer on the shotgun, slipped my face around the edge of the briars, and looked.

There was a fire going in the center of the tunnel, in the spot where Tom and I had seen the burn marks that day, and I could see Tom lying on the ground, her clothes off and strewn about, and a man was leaning over her, running his hands over her back and forth, making a sound like an animal eating after a long time without food. His hands flowed over her as if he was playing a piano. A huge machete was stuck up in the dirt near Tom's head, and Tom's face was turned toward me. Her eyes were wide and full of tears, and tied around her mouth was a thick bandanna, and her hands and feet were bound with rope, and as I looked the man rose and I saw that his pants were undone and he had hold of himself, and he was walking back and forth behind the fire, looking down at Tom, yelling, "I don't want to do this. You make me do this. It's your fault, you know? You're getting just right. Just right."

The voice was loud, but not like any voice I'd ever heard. There was all the darkness and wetness of the bottom of the river in that voice, as well as the mud down there, and anything that might collect in it.

I hadn't been able to get a good look at his face, but I could tell from the way he was built, the way the fire caught his hair, it was Mr. Nation's son, Uriah.

Then he turned slightly, and it wasn't Uriah at all. I had merely thought it was Uriah because he was built like Uriah, but it wasn't.

I stepped fully into the tunnel and said, "Cecil?"

The word just came out of my mouth, without me really planning to say it. Cecil turned now, and when he saw me his face was like it had been earlier, when Tom was being bounced on his knee and the fireworks had exploded behind him. He had the same slack-jawed look, his face was beaded in sweat.

He let go of his privates and just let them hang out for me to see, as if he were proud of them and that I should be too.

"Oh, boy," he said, his voice still husky and animal-like. "It's just gone all wrong. I didn't want to have to have Tom. I didn't. But she's been ripenin', boy, right in front of my eyes. Every time I saw her, I said, no, you don't shit where you eat, but she's ripenin', boy, and I thought I'd go to your place, peek in on her if I could, and then I seen her there, easy to take, and I knew tonight I had to have her. There wasn't nothing else for it."

"Why?"

"Oh, son. There is no why. I just have to. I have to do them all. I tell myself I won't, but I do. I do."

He eased toward me.

I lifted the shotgun.

"Now, boy," he said. "You don't want to shoot me."

"Yes, sir. I do."

"It ain't something I can help. Listen here. I'll let her go, and we'll just forget about this business. Time you get home, I'll be out of here. I got a little boat hid out, and I can take it downriver to where I can catch a train. I'm good at that. I can be gone before you know it."

"You're wiltin'," I said.

His pee-dink had gone limp.

Cecil looked down. "So I am."

He pushed himself inside his pants and buttoned up as he talked. "Look here. I wasn't gonna hurt her. Just feel her some. I was just gonna get my finger wet. I'll go on, and everything will be all right."

"You'll just go down the river and do it again," I said. "Way you come down the river to us and did it here. You ain't gonna stop, are you?"

"There's nothing to say about it, Harry. It just gets out of hand sometime."

"Where's your chain and coin, Cecil?"

He touched his throat. "It got lost."

"That woman got her hand chopped off, she grabbed it, didn't she?"

"I reckon she did."

"Move to the left there, Cecil."

He moved to the left, pointed at the machete. "She grabbed me, I chopped her with that, and her hand came off. Damndest thing. I got her down here and she got away from me and I chased her. And she grabbed me, fought back. I chopped her hand off and it went in the river. Can you imagine that . . . How did you know?"

"The Goat Man finds things in the river. He hangs them on Mose's shack.

"Goat Man?"

"You're the real Goat Man."

"You're not making any sense, boy."

"Move on around to the side there."

I wanted him away from the exit on that other side, the one me and Tom had stumbled into that night we found the body.

Cecil slipped to my left, and I went to the right. We were kind of circling each other. I got over close to Tom and I squatted down by her, still pointing the shotgun at Cecil.

"I could be gone for good," Cecil said. "All you got to do is let me go."

I reached out with one hand and got hold of the knot on the bandanna and pulled it loose. Tom said, "Shoot him! Shoot him! He stuck his fingers in me. Shoot him! He took me out of the window and stuck his fingers in me."

"Hush, Tom," I said. "Take it easy."

"Cut me loose. Give me the gun and I'll shoot him."

"All the time you were bringin' those women here to kill, weren't you?" I said.

"It's a perfect place. Already made by hobos. Once I decided on a woman, well, I can easily handle a woman. I always had my boat ready, and you can get almost anywhere you need to go by river. The tracks aren't far from here. Plenty of trains run. It's easy to get around. Now and then I borrowed a car. You know whose? Mrs. Canerton. One night she loaned it to me, and well, I asked her if she wanted to go for a drive with me while I ran an errand. And she liked me, boy, and I just couldn't contain myself. All I had to do was bring them here, and when I finished, I tossed out the trash."

"Daddy trusted you. You told where Mose was. You told Mr. Nation."

"It was just a nigger, boy. I had to try and hide my trail. You understand. It wasn't like the world lost an upstanding citizen."

"We thought you were our friend," I said.

"I am. I am. Sometimes friends make you mad, though, don't they? They do wrong things. But I don't mean to."

"We ain't talkin' about stealin' a piece of peppermint, here. You're worse than the critters out there with hydrophobia, 'cause you ain't as good as them. They can't help themselves."

"Neither can I."

The fire crackled, bled red colors across his face. Some of the rain leaked in through the thick wad of briars and vines and limbs overhead, hit the fire and it hissed. "You're like your daddy, ain't you? Self-righteous."

"Reckon so."

I had one hand holding the shotgun, resting it against me as I squatted down and worked the knots free on Tom's hands. I wasn't having any luck with that, so I got my pocketknife out of my pants and cut her hands loose, then her feet.

I stood up, raised the gun, and he flinched some, but I couldn't cut down on him. It just wasn't in me, not unless he tried to lay hands on us.

I didn't know what to do with him. I decided I had no choice but to let him go, tell Daddy and have them try and hunt him down. Tom was pulling on her clothes when I said, "You'll get yours eventually."

"Now you're talkin', boy."

"You stay over yonder, we're goin' out."

He held up his hands. "Now you're using some sense."

Tom said, "You can't shoot him, I can."

"Go on, Tom."

She didn't like it, but she turned down the tunnel and headed out. Cecil said, "Remember, boy. We had some good times."

"We ain't got nothin'. You ain't never done nothing with me but cut my hair, and you didn't know how to cut a boy's hair anyway." I turned and went out by the tunnel. "And I ought to blow one of your legs off for what you done to Toby."

We didn't use the opening in the tunnel that led to the woods because I wanted to go out the way I'd come and get back to the boat. We got on the river it would be hard for him to track us, if that was his notion.

When we got down to the river, the boat, which I hadn't pulled up good on the shore, had washed out in the river, and I could see it floating away with the current.

"Damn," I said.

"Was that Mose's boat?" Tom asked.

"We got to go by the bank, to the swinging bridge."

"It's a long ways," I heard Cecil say.

I spun around, and there he was up on the higher bank next to the tree where me and Tom had found the body. He was just a big shadow next to the tree, and I thought of the Devil come up from the ground, all dark and evil and full of bluff. "You got a long ways to go, children. A long ways."

I pointed the shotgun at him and he slipped behind the tree out of sight, said, "A long ways."

I knew then I should have killed him. Without the boat, he could follow alongside us easy, back up in the woods there, and we couldn't even see him.

Me and Tom started moving brisk like along the bank, and we could hear Cecil moving through the woods on the bank above us, and finally we didn't hear him anymore. It was the same as that night when we heard the sounds near and in the tunnel. I figured it had been him, maybe come down to see his handiwork at the tree there, liking it perhaps, wanting it to be seen by someone. Maybe we had come down right after he finished doing it. He had been stalking us, or Tom, maybe. He had wanted Tom all along.

We walked fast and Tom was cussing most of it, talking about what Cecil had done with his fingers, and the whole thing was making me sick.

"Just shut up, Tom. Shut up."

She started crying. I stopped and got down on one knee, let the shotgun lay against me as I reached out with both hands and took hold of her shoulders.

"I'm sorry, Tom, really. I'm scared too. We got to keep ourselves together, you hear me?"

"I hear you," she said.

"We got to stay the course here. I got a gun. He don't. He may have already given up."

"He ain't give up, and you know it."

"We got to keep moving."

Tom nodded, and we started out again, and pretty soon the long dark shadow of the swinging bridge was visible across the river, and the wind was high, and the bridge thrashed back and forth and creaked and groaned like hinges on rusty doors.

"We could go on down a ways, Tom, but I think we got to cross by the bridge here. It's quicker, and we can be home sooner."

"I'm scared, Harry."

"So am I."

"Can you do it?"

Tom sucked in her top lip and nodded. "I can."

We climbed up the bank where the bridge began and looked down on it. It swung back and forth. I looked down at the river.

White foam rose with the dark water and it rolled away and crashed over the little falls into the broader, deeper, slower part of the river. The rain came down on us and the wind was chilly, and all around the woods seemed quiet, yet full of something I couldn't put a name to. Now and again, in spite of the rain, the clouds would split and the moon would shine down on us, looking as if it were something greasy.

I decided to cross first, so if a board gave out Tom would know. When I stepped on the bridge, the wind the way it was, and now my weight, made it swing way up and I darn near tipped into the water. When I reached out to grab the cables, I let go of the shotgun. It went into the water without any sound I could hear and was instantly gone.

"You lost it, Harry," Tom yelled from the bank.

"Come on, just hang to the cables."

Tom stepped onto the bridge, and it swung hard and nearly tipped again.

"We got to walk light," I said, "and kind of together. When I take a step, you take one, but if a board goes, or I go, you'll see in time."

"If you fall, what do I do?"

"You got to go on across, Tom."

We started on across, and we seemed to have gotten the movement right, because we weren't tipping quite so bad, and pretty soon we were halfway done.

I turned and looked down the length of the bridge, past Tom. I didn't see anyone tryin' to follow.

It was slow going, but it wasn't long before we were six feet from the other side. I began to breathe a sigh of relief. Then I realized I still had a ways to go yet till we got to the wide trail, then the road, and now I knew there wasn't any road would stop Cecil or anyone else. It was just a road. If we got that far, we still had some distance yet, and Cecil would know where we were going, and Mama and Daddy might not even be home yet.

I thought if we got to the road I might try and fool him, go the other way, but it was a longer distance like that to someone's house, and if he figured what we were doin', we could be in worse trouble.

I decided there wasn't nothing for it but to head home and stay cautious. But while all this was on my mind, and we were about to reach the opposite bank, a shadow separated from the brush and dirt there and became Cecil.

He held the machete in his hand. He smiled and stuck it on the dirt, stayed on solid ground, but took hold of both sides of the cables that held up the swinging bridge. He said, "I beat you across, boy. Just waited. Now you and little Tom, you're gonna have to take a dip. I didn't want it this way, but that's how it is. You see that, don't you? All I wanted was Tom. You give her to me, to do as I want, then you can go. By the time you get home, me and her, we'll be on our way."

"You ain't got your dough done in the middle," I said.

Cecil clutched the cables hard and shook them. The bridge swung out from under me and I found my feet hanging out in midair. Only my arms wrapped around one of the cables was holding me. I could see Tom. She had fallen and was grabbing at one of the board steps, and I could see bits of rotten wood splintering. The board and Tom were gonna go.

Cecil shook the cables again, but I hung tight, and the board Tom clung to didn't give. I glanced toward Cecil and saw another shape coming out of the shadows. A huge one, with what looked like goat horns on its head.

Mose's boy, Telly.

Telly grabbed Cecil around the neck and jerked him back, and Cecil spun loose and hit him in the stomach, and they grappled around there for a moment, then Cecil got hold of the machete and slashed it across Telly's chest. Telly let out with a noise like a bull bellowing, leaped against Cecil, and the both of them went flying onto the bridge. When they hit, boards splintered, the bridge swung to the side and up and there was a snapping sound as one of the cables broke in two, whipped out and away from us and into the water. Cecil and Telly fell past us into the Sabine. Me and Tom clung for a moment to the remaining cable, then it snapped, and we fell into the fast rushing water after them.

I went down deep, and when I came up, I bumped into Tom. She screamed and I screamed and I grabbed her. The water churned us under again, and I fought to bring us up, all the while clinging to Tom's collar. When I broke the surface of the water I saw Cecil and Telly in a clench, riding the blast of the Sabine over the little falls, flowing out into deeper, calmer waters.

The next thing I knew, we were there too, through the falls, into the deeper, less rapid flowing water. I got a good grip on Tom and started trying to swim toward shore. It was hard in our wet clothes, tired like we were; and me trying to hang on to and pull Tom, who wasn't helping herself a bit, didn't make it any easier.

I finally swam to where my feet were touching sand and gravel, and I waded us on into shore, pulled Tom up next to me. She rolled over and puked.

I looked out at the water. The rain had ceased and the sky had cleared momentarily, and the moon, though weak, cast a glow on the Sabine like grease starting to shine on a hot skillet. I could see Cecil and Telly gripped together, a hand flying up now and then to strike, and I could see something else all around them, something that rose up in a dozen silvery knobs that gleamed in the moonlight, then extended quickly and struck at the pair, time after time.

Cecil and Telly had washed into that school of water moccasins, or another just like them, had stirred them up, and now it was like bull whips flying from the water, hitting the two of them time after time.

They washed around a bend in the river with the snakes and went out of sight.

I was finally able to stand up, and I realized I had lost a shoe. I got hold of Tom and started pulling her on up the bank. The ground around the bank was rough, and then there were stickers and briars, and my one bare foot took a beating. But we went on out of there, onto the road and finally to the house, where Daddy and Mama were standing in the yard yelling our names.

The next morning they found Cecil on a sandbar. He was bloated up and swollen from water and snakebites. His neck was broken, Daddy said. Telly had taken care of him before the snakebite.

Caught up in some roots next to the bank, his arms spread and through them and his feet wound in vines, was Telly. The machete wound had torn open his chest and side. Daddy said that silly hat was still on his head, and he discovered that it was somehow wound into Telly's hair. He said the parts that looked like horns had washed down and were covering his eyes, like huge eyelids.

I wondered what had gotten into Telly, the Goat Man. He had led me out there to save Tom, but he hadn't wanted any part of stopping Cecil. Maybe he was afraid. But when we were on the bridge, and Cecil was getting the best of us, he had come for him.

Had it been because he wanted to help us, or was he just there already and frightened? I'd never know. I thought of poor Telly living out there in the woods all that time, only his daddy knowing he was there, and maybe keeping it secret just so folks would leave him alone, not take advantage of him because he was addleheaded.

In the end, the whole thing was one horrible experience. I remember mostly just lying in bed for two days after, nursing all the wounds in my foot from stickers and such, trying to get my strength back, weak from thinking about what almost happened to Tom.

Mama stayed by our side for the next two days, leaving us only long enough to make soup. Daddy sat up with us at night. When I awoke, frightened, thinking I was still on the swinging bridge, he would be there, and he would smile and put out his hand and touch my head, and I would lie back and sleep again.

Over a period of years, picking up a word here and there, we would learn that there had been more murders like those in our area, all the way down from Arkansas and over into Oklahoma and some of North Texas. Back then no one pinned those on one murderer. The law just didn't think like that then. The true nature of serial killers was unknown. Had communication been better, had knowledge been better, perhaps some, or all, of what happened that time long ago might have been avoided.

And maybe not. It's all done now, those long-ago events of nineteen thirty-one and -two.

Now, I lie here, not much longer for the world, and with no desire to be here or to have my life stretched out for another moment, just lying here with this tube in my shank, waiting on mashed peas and corn and some awful thing that will pass for meat, all to be hand-fed to me, and I think of then and how I lay in bed in our little house next to the woods, and how when I awoke Daddy or Mama would be there, and how comforting it was.

So now I close my eyes with my memories of those two years, and that great and horrible mad dog summer, and I hope this time when I awake I will no longer be of this world, and Mama and Daddy, and even poor Tom, dead before her time in a car accident, will be waiting, and perhaps even Mose and the Goat Man and good old Toby.

Bentley Little

THE THEATER

In 1991 Bentley Little won the Bram Stoker Award for best first novel with The Revelation, *and it's been all uphill since. Subsequent books include* The Mailman, Dominion, The Ignored, *and* The Store, *the premise of which, that chain stores are insidious agents in modern life, would sound just plain silly if it (a) weren't so true and (b) wasn't rendered so utterly creepy by Little's approach.*

Creepy is a good way to describe Little's work; I detect the influences of Ramsey Campbell and the other Irrealists in his stories, a dreamlike quality underpinned with lurking dread.

"The Theater" was one of the very first stories I bought for this volume; you're about to see why.

It was ten to nine, almost closing time, and Putnam desperately had to take a leak. He pressed his legs together, gritting his teeth. There was no one in the bookstore. The last customer had left moments before, after spending two hours and no money, and no one else had come in since. He thought for a moment, then decided to close for the night. Or, rather, his bladder decided for him. Mr. Carr would have a fit if he knew, but Putnam was sure that the old man would rather have him lock up than leave the store open while he was indisposed.

Grabbing the ring of keys from the shelf beneath the register, he hurried around the counter to the front door. He fumbled for the right key, found it, and slipped it into the slot, turning until there was an audible click. He flipped the window sign over, from "Yes We're OPEN" to "Sorry We're CLOSED," then ran as quickly as he could to the bathroom at the back of the store.

He made it just in time.

It was with a welcome unhurried sense of relief that Putnam walked back out into the little utility alcove at the rear of the store. Glancing up as he finished buckling his belt, he found himself looking at the narrow wooden door directly across from the bathroom. He frowned. He'd been working at the bookstore for nearly a month now, since school had gotten out, and while he knew he had seen the door before, he had never really taken notice of it.

Something about that bothered him.

He reached out and attempted to turn the faded metal knob, but the door was locked. He rattled the knob and considered trying some of the other keys on the ring to see if one of them would open the door, but then thought he'd better ask Mr. Carr first. It was probably just a closet, but there might be a storage room for rare books or something back there, and he didn't want to get into any trouble.

Pocketing the keys, he walked back out to the front of the store.

He asked Mr. Carr about the door the next morning, while taking inventory. He'd expected the old man to simply tell him what was back there, to explain, in the same bored, slightly condescending voice in which he explained everything else, what was in the room. He was not prepared for the reaction he received.

Fear.

Terror.

It was like something out of a movie. Mr. Carr grew visibly pale, the color draining from his cheeks and lips, and his eyes widened comically. He reached out, grabbed Putnam's arm and squeezed, bony fingers digging painfully into muscle. "You didn't go up there, did you?"

"Up where? I just asked what was behind the door."

Mr. Carr licked his lips. "It's my fault. I should've told you before." He loosened his grip, his hand dropping, but his voice remained frightened. "There's a stairway behind the door. It leads up to a theater. These shops here"—he gestured toward the wall and, presumably, the boutique and dress store beyond—"used to be connected. Upstairs was a theater. The first opera theater in this part of the state, and the only one ever in this county. For a while, in the early 1900s, before the owners went bankrupt, they attracted top talent. Caruso performed here. A lot of big stars did. But there weren't enough people around here at that time to support such a theater, and they went out of business. The building was empty for a while, then someone else bought it and divided the bottom floor into these shops. The top floor and the theater were sealed off."

Putnam waited, expecting more, but the old man turned away, bending down to examine the stack of books at his feet. Putnam remained unmoving. He stared down at Mr. Carr's hands as the old man picked up a dusty leatherbound volume. The book wavered in the shop owner's trembling grasp. Why was Mr. Carr so frightened? He thought of asking, but as he gazed down at the shiny bald spot nestled in the middle of the old man's thin white hair, he decided against it.

He knelt down to help with the inventory.

On Sundays, Putnam worked alone. Mr. Carr always did his book buying on Sunday, hitting the swap meets, estate sales and thrift shops, leaving Putnam to manage the store by himself. Like most small businesses in the older downtown area, the bookstore closed at six on this day, and Putnam was usually home in time to catch *60 Minutes*.

But tonight he had other plans.

He locked up at five minutes after six, following the late departure of a college student who'd picked up used copies of several textbooks, and he flipped over the sign and shut off the lights at the front of the store before heading back to the rear alcove. He stood for a moment in front of the door, trying to see if he could discern any difference between it and the door to the bathroom, trying to see if he could pick up any negative vibrations, but there was nothing, only the slight secret childish rush of excitement that came from knowing he was about to do something forbidden.

He started trying keys.

The door opened on the fourth attempt, and Putnam turned the knob slowly, pushing in. Behind the door there was indeed a stairway, a narrow series of low wooden steps covered with a carpet of gray dust. The high walls were also wood, and from a pipe running lengthwise up the center of the sloping ceiling protruded two bare bulbs of ancient vintage. He stared into the dimness at the top of the stairs. This must have been a side entrance to the theater, he realized, the stairway used by stagehands and caterers. He began walking up. There were no handrails, which made him feel a little off balance, but he steadied himself by placing his hands on the walls. He took the steps two at a time.

He paused at the top. Here, stretching away from him, was a

hallway that apparently ran the length of the building and ended somewhere above the boutique or the dress shop or the jewelry store
beyond. The corridor was dark, illuminated only slightly at this end
by the light from the bookstore below and at the other end not at
all. Within the darkness were areas of deeper darkness, and he had
the distinct impression that there were doorways leading off from the
corridor into other rooms. It was too dark to see, though, to tell for
sure, and he hurried back downstairs, got the flashlight from under
the front counter and ran back up.

At the top of the stairs, he turned on the flashlight and shone it
down the corridor. There were doorways but no doors, and he walked
through the one closest to him. The yellow beam of his light played
over bare walls, a dusty radiator and a bricked window. At the far
end of the room's left wall was another doorway, and he strode across
the hardwood floor, his footsteps echoing in the silence, and shone
his light into the black opening. He saw a claw-footed bathtub, a
freestanding sink and an old toilet. He stared for a moment into the
bathroom, feeling vaguely uneasy, then quickly turned around and
walked back through the larger room into the corridor.

He walked down the hall and into the next doorway. And the
next. And the next.

This had been a theater? It looked more like a hotel. All of the
rooms leading off from the hallway were bedrooms and adjacent bathrooms with identical back-to-back floor plans, each a carbon copy of
the last. He continued his exploration, his disquiet increasing as he
made his way down the corridor. The first few rooms he'd entered
were empty, but in all of the others the furniture remained undis-
turbed: canopied beds, nightstands with kerosene lamps, dark wood
bureaus, high-backed chairs. Each room had a radiator and a sealed
window which, at one time, must have faced the street.

He stepped into the last room.

And saw, sitting in a dusty sheet-covered chair, a dead man.

He jumped, dropped the flashlight, almost screamed.

He was about to run away when he saw by the dissipated illumination of the downed flashlight that the figure in the chair was not a
man at all. Nor was it dead. It had never been alive. It was a dummy:
a pair of pants and a shirt stuffed with cloth, topped by a rag-covered
wigmaker's head.

He reached down and picked up the light, shining it first on the
figure, then, more slowly, around the room. This was not a bedroom.
It was longer and narrower, and the floor sloped visibly forward. Thick

dusty red curtains framed the brick window. There were no beds here, no nightstands, only four chairs, one of which, the one hosting the dummy, faced the door, the other three facing a wall.

No, not a wall.

A stage.

Putnam took a step into the room.

This was what was left of the original theater.

Now he felt afraid. He had been expecting something grand, a huge theater with an orchestra pit and a balcony, a gigantic auditorium with filigreed columns and plush velvet-backed chairs. He had not been expecting this grimy narrow room with its lone dummy audience and its pitifully primitive munchkin stage, and the strangeness of it all cast everything in a sinister light.

You didn't go up there, did you?

He pointed his flashlight toward the raised stage. Facing him from the platform was a tableau of small figures the size of dolls, horrid ugly things attired in garments of sackcloth and hair. He stepped closer, past the seated dummy, and focused the beam of his light on the figure nearest him. It was a nasty and horribly unnatural thing. The head, larger than the body, was made from a type of squash: a yam or pumpkin or something in between. The eyes were inset marbles, the nose whittled wood. Real teeth, human teeth, appeared to have been set in the upper and lower gums of the carved opening that was a mouth.

He felt suddenly chilled, but his flashlight moved on, to the others. The small figures each wore different expressions, different clothes, but they were all equally hideous and all seemed to be made from the same materials. They were all posed or positioned in aspects of movement, as though they had been frozen in mid-performance.

Without thinking, Putnam found himself stepping next to the stage. It was cold here, a frigid breeze blew in from somewhere, but the drop in temperature affected him only peripherally. He already felt frozen inside. He reached out and touched a tentative finger to the nearest doll. The figure was warm to his touch. And squishy.

He drew back, feeling repulsed and sickened, practically stumbling over his feet in his effort to get away from the stage. The finger with which he had touched the doll felt slightly slimy, and he held it out in front of him, as if to keep it from contaminating the rest of his body.

He made his way back toward the door, careful not to touch anything. He hated the dolls and he hated the theater. Hated them with a passion. It was a strangely irrational feeling, not one he would have expected, and not one that he stopped to analyze. He just wanted to get out of this place and get back to the bookstore. There was something wrong with what was up here, and that wrongness, which had at first frightened him, now filled him with an irrational loathing.

He hurried out of the theater and into the hallway, and by the time he reached the stairway at the far end he was running. He sprinted down the steps two at a time, and when he reached the bottom, he slammed the door behind him and with trembling fingers locked it. He wanted to wash his finger, but he did not want to stay in the bookstore any longer—not alone, not with that room upstairs—so instead of going into the bathroom he quickly turned off the rest of the lights in the store, and locked the door on his way out.

He stood for a moment in the street in front of the bookstore, sweating, breathing heavily, looking up at the long building. He had never noticed that the series of shops here were all housed within a single structure—their facades were all so different—and he never would have figured out on his own that the building contained a second story. Now that he knew, though, he could see the cleverly camouflaged sections of brick that blocked the upstairs windows. He started counting from the bookstore on, to determine which bricked window hid the theater, but gave it up instantly. He didn't want to know.

Shivering, he hurried around the side of the building to the parking lot where he had left his car.

At home, five minutes later, he went immediately into the bathroom to wash his finger. He scrubbed his skin with Dove, then with Ajax, but the slimy feeling would not go away. He opened the medicine cabinet, took out a box of Band-Aids and used several of them to wrap up his finger, and that felt a little better.

"Putnam!" his mom called from the kitchen. "Is that you? Are you home?"

"Yeah!" he called back. "I'm home!" His voice sounded different to himself, quiet, though he was yelling.

"Get ready for dinner, then!"

He stepped into the hallway. "What are we having?"

His mom peeked her head around the corner of the kitchen. "Chicken and fried zucchini."

Zucchini.

He blinked. In his mind, he saw his mother caressing the squash, putting a wig on top of it, carving out eyes, a nose, a mouth. He met her gaze across the hallway. His heart leaped in his chest. Was she looking at him strangely? Was that suspicion he saw behind her smile?

He looked away. This was insanity. This was crazy. Still, as his mom went back into the kitchen, he found that he was afraid to follow her, afraid he would see on the counter next to the sink one of those dolls from the theater.

He took a deep breath, trying to keep his hands from shaking. What was that theater? What were those dolls and why did their existence disturb him so? And why was it that the other figure, the dummy, did not have the same effect on him? Indeed, he found that when he thought of that seated form now, thought of those stuffed clothes in the chair, that wigmaker's head facing the door, he felt oddly comforted.

"Putnam! Get your sister! It's time to eat!"

"Okay, Mom!" His voice sounded better now, louder, more normal, and he walked out to the family room where Jenny was seated on the carpet in front of the television.

Next to her on the floor was one of the squash dolls, its vegetative face framed by frizzy black hair, its overlarge mouth fixed permanently in an unnatural smile.

Putnam's heart lurched in his chest. "What are you doing with that?" he demanded. He grabbed the doll from the floor and picked it up, squeezed it. He felt the warm slimy squishiness in his hands and instinctively dropped the figure again, stomping on it with both feet, crushing it.

Jenny stared up at him in shock, then burst into tears. "You killed her!" she cried.

He looked down at the broken form beneath his foot. It was a plastic baby girl with chubby cheeks and platinum blond hair. A mass-produced toy, nothing more.

Jenny was still crying. "Why did you kill my Dolly?"

He tried to swallow, tried to talk, but his mouth stayed open and no saliva or words would come. He hurried back down the hall and into the bathroom, barely making it to the toilet before he threw up.

He was sick the next day, really sick, not faking it, but when he called Mr. Carr to tell the old man that he wouldn't be in, there was silence on the other end of the line.

He cleared his throat. "I'll probably be in tomorrow, though," he said.

Mr. Carr's voice was quiet. "You went up there, didn't you? You saw the theater."

He thought of lying, thought of saying nothing, but he looked at the Band-Aids on his finger and he found himself whispering, "Yes."

Silence again. "They can't get down," Mr. Carr said finally. "They can never get down."

Putnam shook his head into the receiver, though the old man couldn't see it. "I can't—" he began.

"I told you not to go up there."

"I'll send you the keys. I . . . I can't go back."

"You will," Mr. Carr said sadly.

"No." Putnam felt tears welling in his eyes.

"Yes you will."

"No." He was crying now, the tears coursing down his cheeks. "No."

"Yes," Mr. Carr said softly.

Putnam hung up the phone, held the receiver, picked it up again. "Yes," he whispered to the dial tone.

The bookstore was the only place where he didn't think about the theater, about the dolls. At home, in the mall, on the streets, he could not get the images out of his head. He kept anticipating appearances by one of the figures or its brethren, appearances which never arrived. He kept expecting to see the small horrid shapes in cars, behind bushes, in bathrooms, on shelves.

But when he came to work each morning, it was as if a switch was shut off inside his head, denying the thoughts and images all access to his brain. The moment he walked through the doorway, he was able to function normally, was like his old self, able to think of the past, the present and the future without the specter of those . . . things . . . intruding.

He did not talk to Mr. Carr about what he'd seen, and the old man did not mention the episode.

The thought occurred to him that everything was preplanned, predestined, that things were supposed to work out this way and could not have worked out any other. In this scenario, he was meant to find a job at the bookstore, meant to discover the door, meant to sneak upstairs.

Meant to see the theater.

He forced himself to think of something else. That line of

thinking frightened him. To ascribe such power to the theater and its inhabitants, to admit that they had any meaning or resonance at all in the world beyond the stairs, meant that the ideas and beliefs he had held all of his life were nothing more than comforting and reassuring lies.

He told himself that it had all been coincidence. Bad luck.

He tried to believe it.

At home, his mom continued to be interested in politics and her career. His sister continued to be interested in playing and television.

He took to walking through the neighborhood and driving around the city alone. Both activities scared him, and he thought that perhaps that was why he forced himself to go through with them.

He was walking past the liquor store on the corner of Eighth and Center one evening when he was accosted by a hairy bearded man who grabbed his shoulders while looking wildly up and down the street. The man was wearing a dirty mismatched suit jacket and pants, and he smelled of sweat, vomit and old alcohol. His crooked teeth were colored in several gradations of yellow.

"Where's Bro?" the man demanded.

"Who's Bro?"

"My dog, man! Bro's my damn dog! You seen him?"

Putnam shook his head, backed up away from the man. "No," he said. "I don't think so. W-what's he look like?"

Something shifted, something in his perception, something in the man's face, something in the air itself. The man smiled, and the rotted teeth in his mouth looked suddenly

fake.

"He's about six inches high," the man said, and his voice was no longer high and hysterical but calm and low and reasonable. "He's orange and squishy and he used to be a yam."

Putnam fell back, caught himself against the liquor store door, and felt the scream rise in his throat.

"Huh?" the man asked, his voice wild again. "A big black sucker? Looks like a damn Doberman?"

"No!" Putnam screamed. "I've never seen your dog!"

He ran all the way home.

A week or so later, his mom added two new crops to her garden at the side of the house.

She planted pumpkins and summer squash.

*   *   *

Mr. Carr grew even colder, stiffer and more contemptuous than he had been before, the understanding he had momentarily exhibited on the phone that day gone and apparently forgotten. He seldom talked to Putnam now and when he did it was out of necessity and with a rarefied sort of disgusted disdain. The old man seemed to be deliberately attempting to anger him, and it seemed to Putnam as though Mr. Carr was trying to get him to quit.

He had the unsettling impression that the bookstore owner was, in some strange way, jealous of him.

But he could not quit, as much as he often wanted to. The bookstore was hell to him, and his insides knotted each day when he drove to work and looked up at the hidden second floor of the building, but the store offered the only sanctuary from the twisted tortured thoughts that festered in his brain. It was only within the boundaries of those walls that he was able to think of the dummy in the audience instead of the figures on the stage.

Mr. Carr or no Mr. Carr, he needed to work at the store.

On Sunday, Mr. Carr did not go book hunting. He stayed at the store, unpacking old boxes, shelving, leaving Putnam to run the register. It was at lunchtime that Putnam noticed that the old man was not around, not in any of the aisles, not in the oversized closet that served as a stockroom, not in the bathroom.

That meant there was only one place he could be.

Putnam considered leaving, taking off for lunch, going home or going to McDonald's. He considered staying at the register, waiting for Mr. Carr to return.

But instead he went upstairs.

He was not sure why he decided to return to the theater. There was no logical reason for it. He knew Mr. Carr was up there, so he would not be learning any new information by going up to the theater. He did not really want to go—the idea of seeing those things again made him feel nauseous.

But he went nonetheless.

He took the flashlight from under the counter. Mr. Carr had left the door in the alcove unlocked, and Putnam closed it behind him as he tiptoed up the steps. In the hallway, he walked quietly, careful not to make a sound, and he passed the rows of identical empty doorways until finally he reached the last one. He was nervous—his heart was pounding, and his palms were so sweaty he could barely hold on to the flashlight—but he took a deep breath, swallowed hard and shone the light into the theater.

Onto Mr. Carr.

The old man was seated in the chair farthest from the dummy, and he was naked. His shoes and shirt and pants lay in the dusty floor at his feet.

On his body, in various positions and poses, were the dolls.

Putnam stared. The old man had to know that the flashlight was shining on him, but he didn't seem to care. He touched one figure on his lap, then another on his shoulder, shivering as his fingers stroked the slimy cheeks, ran through the horrible coarse hair.

He was smiling.

Putnam still hated the theater, still hated the dolls, was still filled with an irrational anger and intense loathing. But he was also, somehow, envious of Mr. Carr. Some small part of him, he realized, wanted to be naked too, wanted to be sitting in one of the chairs for the audience, wanted to be close to the dolls.

He dropped the flashlight and ran back down the hallway to the stairs.

He ran downstairs and out of the store.

He did not go back, and when the next day his mom told him that Mr. Carr had phoned and had asked him to call him at the bookstore, Putnam told her that, to Mr. Carr, he was never home.

He returned to the bookstore himself, though, two days later. He pretended to be a customer, snuck in while Mr. Carr was busy at the counter, hid from the old man in the aisles, but when he left several hours later, walking on the far side of a departing couple, he saw the bookstore owner smiling at him, shaking his head. The smile was sad, and Putnam hurried out to his car feeling guilty and ashamed.

In the dream he was a farmer, and for miles in every direction, as far as the eye could see, spreading outward from the house, were fields upon fields of squash.

*   *   *

He killed Mr. Carr on a Sunday, after the last customers had left, after the store was closed. He clubbed the bookstore owner to death with an oversized zucchini, bringing down the huge heavy vegetable on the frail old man's head again and again and again and again until there was no face left, only a pulpy flattened featureless mess, until the zucchini was soft and shapeless.

Putnam stood over the old man's unmoving form, breathing heavily, his hands and clothes splattered with blood. He felt tired, felt good, but there was also a sense of incompletion, a sensation of unfulfillment, and he wandered up and down the aisles, still clutching the zucchini, unable to focus on the missing piece of the puzzle. Then his gaze landed upon an unopened box of books, on the X-Acto knife atop the cardboard, and everything clicked into place.

He began pulling books from the shelves, opening their covers and tearing out the pages until there was a small mountain of crumpled paper at his feet. He hurried back up the aisle and took off the old man's shoes and socks, pants and underwear, shirt and T-shirt.

He stuffed the clothes with paper, tied them together with packaging twine.

Using the X-Acto knife, he carved the zucchini into something resembling a human figure. He cut a swath of his own hair and pasted it to the squishy scalp with an adhesive of spit and the bookstore owner's blood.

Both of his projects were unfinished—half-assed, haphazard attempts at art—but they were the best he could manage at this time, under these circumstances, and he hoped that they were good enough. He grabbed the headless paper-stuffed dummy and the naked crude doll and brought them upstairs.

In the theater, he put Mr. Carr's stuffed clothes on the chair next to the other dummy and placed the doll on the stage. His hatred was back, but it was not as strong as it had been before, and underneath the loathing was longing. He took off his clothes, folding them neatly and laying them on the floor. He stood there for a moment, feeling the strange cold breeze caress his naked skin, then climbed onto the stage. He picked up the doll he had made, then its brethren. Lying flat on the dusty boards, he placed the small figures on top of his body, in theatrical positions, shivering slightly at the warm sliminess.

He positioned the final figure on his chest. Nothing happened for a moment. Then, suddenly, his hatred was gone, replaced by something like contentment, and in the silence of the theater he thought he heard an echo of singing.

He wanted to sit up, wanted to see if anything was happening, but he was enjoying it all too much, and he remained prone, still. The singing grew louder.

He closed his eyes, waiting.

And on his body, in the dark, the dolls began to move.

Thomas F. Monteleone

REHEARSALS

Tom Monteleone's breakout novel, The Blood of the Lamb, *deservedly won 1993's Stoker Award for best novel. He followed it up with* Night of Broken Souls *and* The Resurrectionist. *He's also known for his early science fiction work (he was another writer willing to make the jump from sf to horror, with successful results) and as the publisher of Borderlands Press, as well as the editor of the excellent Borderlands anthologies.*

"Rehearsals" is a Twilight Zone *story all the way; if Rod Serling were still around I think he would snap this one up in a second. In fact, it's so much of a* TZ *story that I've had a hard time since reading it believing that I didn't* see *it as one of the show's episodes. Quite an homage, I'd say—as well as a testament to Monteleone's ability.*

Dominic Kazan walked through the darkness, convinced he was not alone.

The idea cut through him like a razor as he fumbled for the light switch. Where was the damned thing? A sense of panic rose in him like a hot column of vomit in his throat, but he fought it down as his fingers tripped across the switch.

Abruptly, the lobby took shape in the dim light.

It, like the rest of the Barclay Theatre, was deserted. Crowds, actors, stagehands—everyone except for Dominic—had left hours ago. And he knew he should be alone. He was the janitor/night watchman for the Barclay, accustomed to, and actually comfortable with, the solitude. But for the last few nights, he could not escape the sensation there was something else lurking in the darkness of the big building.

Something that seemed to be waiting for him.

He enjoyed working alone; he had been alone most of his life. He did not mind working in almost total darkness; he had lived in a different kind of darkness most of his life.

But this feeling that he was not alone was beginning to bother him, actually frighten him. And he didn't want to have any bad feelings about the Barclay. It was his only true home, and he loved his job there. There was something special about being intimate with the magic of the theater—the props and costumes, the make-believe world of sets and flats. Sometimes he would come to work early, just to watch the hive-like activity of the stagehands and actors, feeling the magic-world come to life.

All his life, there seemed to be something stalking him. A mindless kind of thing, a thing of failure and despair. Somehow, it always caught up with him, and threw his life into chaos. He wondered if it was on his trail again.

Tonight. Trying to make him run away again.

And he was so tired, tired of running away . . .

. . . Away from the fragile dreams of his childhood, the traumas of adolescence, and the failures of manhood. His father used to tell him there were only two kinds of people in the world: Winners and Losers—and his son was definitely in the second group.

Thirty-two years old, and it looked like the old man had been right. His life already a worn-out patchquilt of pain and defeat. After pulling a stint in the army, he had drifted all over the country taking any unskilled job he could find.

Seasonal, mindless work in Lubbock oil fields, Biloxi docks, Birmingham factories. Ten years of nomad-living and nomad-losing.

When he had been much younger, he had tried to figure out why things never worked out for him. Physically, Dominic was almost handsome with his thick dark hair and bright blue eyes.

And mentally, he could always hold his own. He used to read lots of comics and books and never missed a Saturday afternoon double-feature. He even watched a play now and then, back when they used to run them on live television.

But after he left home and never looked back, things seemed to just get worse. After ten years, he started getting the idea that maybe he should go home and try to start over. The letter telling him that his father had died was now five years old, and he had not gone back then. He had not even contacted his mother about it, and that always bothered him.

Something gnawed at his memories and his guilt, and he had

finally quit his rigging job and started hitching east through the South—Louisiana, Mississippi, Alabama, Georgia.

One night, he was sitting in a roadhouse outside of Atlanta, drinking Bud on tap, watching a well-dressed guy next to him trying to drown himself in dry martinis. They had started talking, as lonely drinkers often will. The guy was obviously successful, middle-aged, and out-of-place in the roadside bar.

At one point, Dominic had mentioned that he was going home, back to the city of his birth. The stylish man laughed and slurred something about Thomas Wolfe. When Dominic questioned the response, the man said, "Don't you remember him? He's the guy who said 'You can't go home again,' and then he wrote a long, god-awful boring book to prove it."

Dominic never understood what the man was talking about until he reached his hometown. It was a large East Coast city, and it had changed drastically in his absence. Lots of remembered landmarks had vanished; the streets seemed cold, alien.

For several days, he gathered the courage to return to his old neighborhood, to face his mother after so many years.

When he was finally ready, arriving at the corner street, the correct address, he found his house was *gone*.

The entire street, which had once been a cramped, stifling heap of tenements, row houses, and basement shops, had been wiped out of existence. Urban renewal had invaded the neighborhood, grinding into dust all the bricks and mortar, all the memories.

In its place stood a monstrous building—a monolith of glass and steel and shaped concrete called the Barclay Theatre. At first he saw it as an intruder, a silent, hulking thing which had utterly destroyed his past, occupying the space where his little house had once stood. Perhaps Thomas Wolfe knew what he was talking about.

But after thinking about it, he thought it was ironic that it was, of all things, a theater that wiped out his memories.

Ironic indeed.

In the days that followed, he tried to locate his mother, but with no success. She had vanished, and a part of him was glad. It would have been difficult to face her as a man with no future, and now, not even a past. For no good reason, he decided to stay on in the city, taking day-labor jobs and a room at the YMCA.

As Dominic drifted into summer, he had made no friends, had not found a steady job, and had given up finding his mother. He read books from the library, went to matinee movies, and lived alone with his broken dreams. Occasionally he would walk back to his old neighborhood, as though hoping to see his house one final time. And on each visit, he would stand in the light-pool of a street lamp to stare at the elegant presence of the Barclay.

He seemed to feel an attraction to the place, old dreams stirring in a locked room of his mind. One day, when he saw an ad in the paper for a janitor/night watchman at the theater, he ran all the way to apply.

They hired him on a probational basis, but Dominic didn't mind the qualification. He made a point of being on time and very meticulous in his work. As the weeks passed, he felt a growing warmth in his heart for the Barclay; it became a haven of safety and security—a place where he could live with the old dreams.

When his diligence was rewarded with a permanent position and a raise in salary, he was very happy. He began coming early to watch current productions, and he learned the theater jargon of the stagehands, actors, and directors. The dreamscapes of the theater became real to him, and he absorbed the great tragedies, laughed at clever comedies.

But late at night, when the crowds had dispersed, was the time he loved the best. He would go into the main auditorium and listen to the lights cooling and crackling behind their gels, and think about that night's performance—comparing to past nights, to what he figured were the playwright's intentions. For the first time in his life, he was happy.

But then something changed. The feelings of not being alone started to grow out of the shadows, growing more intense . . .

. . . until tonight, and he felt that he could bear it no longer. There was a small voice in his mind telling him to run from the place and never return.

No, he thought calmly. No more running. Not ever again.

Above his head, the cantilevered balcony hung like a giant hammer ready to fall. He stepped into the main auditorium and listened to the darkness. The aisle swept down towards the stage where the grand drape and act curtain pulled back to reveal the set of the current play. Pushing a carpet sweeper slowly over the thick pile, Dominic noticed how truly dark the theater was. The exit light seemed dim and distant. Row upon row of seats surrounded him, like a herd of round-shouldered creatures huddled in deep shadows.

The entire theater seemed to be enclosing him like an immense vault, a dark hollow tomb. He knew there was something there with him. Acid boiled in his stomach, his throat caked with chalk.

Looking away from the empty seats back to the stage, he noticed that something had changed. Something was wrong.

The set for the currently running production was Nick's Place— a San Francisco saloon described in Saroyan's *The Time of Your Life*. But that set was gone. Somehow, it had been struck and changed overnight. An impossibility, Dominic knew, yet he stared into the darkness and could make out the configurations of a totally different set.

Walking closer, his eyes adjusting to the dim illumination of the Exit signs, Dominic picked up the details of the set—a shabby, gray-walled living room with a kitchenette to the right.

Dumpy green chairs with doilies on the arms, a couch with maroon and silver stripes, end tables with glass tops and a mahogany liquor cabinet with a tiny-screened Emerson television on top.

It was a spare, simple room.

A familiar room.

For an instant, Dominic recoiled at the thought. It couldn't *be*. It wasn't possible. But he recognized the room, down to its smallest details. As if the set designer had invaded a private memory, the set was a perfect replica of his parents' house. The house which had been located where the theater now stood. As Dominic stared in awe and disbelief, he could see that there was nothing dreamy and out-of-focus about the set. He stood before something with hard edges and substance, something real, and not distorted by the lens of memory.

Without thinking, he stepped closer and suddenly the stage lights heated up. The fixtures on the set cast off their grayish hues and burst into full color. An odd swelling sensation filled Dominic's chest, almost becoming a distinct pain. The pain of many years and many emotions. The thought occurred to him that someone might be playing a very cruel joke on him, and he turned to check the light booth up above and beyond the balcony. But it was dark and empty.

The sound of a door opening jarred him.

Turning back to the stage he saw a woman wearing a turquoise housedress and beige slippers enter the room from stage left.

She had a roundish face going towards plump and her eyes were flat and lackluster. There was an essential weariness about her.

Dominic felt tears growing in his eyes, a tightness in his throat, as he looked, stunned, at his *mother*.

"Mom! Mom, what're you doing here? Hey, Mom!"

But she did not hear him. Mechanically, his mother began setting a simple table with paper napkins, Melmac plates, and plain utensils. Dominic ran up to the edge of the stage and yelled at her but she ignored him. It became clear that she could neither see nor hear him— as though they were dimensions apart, as though he saw everything through a one-way mirror.

What the hell was going on?

Dominic grappled with the sheer insanity of it all, trying to make sense out of the hallucinated moment, when it continued.

The door at stage center flew open and his father entered the set.

At the sight of the man, something tightened around Dominic's heart like a fist, staggering him. His father was dead. And yet, there he was, standing in the doorway full of sweat and shine and dirt. There was a defiance in the old man's posture, in the way he slammed the door shut behind him. He wore greasy chino pants and a plaid flannel shirt. One hand carried a beat-up lunch pail with the word "Kazan" stenciled on the side; the other the evening paper.

Dropping the lunch bucket on the kitchen table, his father moved quickly to his favorite chair and unflapped the paper. If he had acknowledged the presence of his wife, Dominic had missed it. There was a somehow surreal quality to the scene—suggesting more than was actually taking place. He sensed this moment could have been taking place at any point in their lives over perhaps a twenty-year span.

Dominic fought off the emotional waves which crashed over him, trying to concentrate on the images on the stage. He was surprised to see how plain his mother actually was—not the pretty woman of his memories—and how much smaller and less imposing his father seemed. Again the convex glass of memory had worked its distorted magic.

The door at stage left abruptly opened and a small, frightfully thin boy of perhaps nine years entered the room. The boy had large ears, bright blue eyes, and Brylcreem-slicked dark hair. Dominic felt stunned as he recognized the boy as *himself.*

He had never realized how frail and odd he had looked as a child; he winced as he heard the young boy speak in a high-pitched voice.

                          BOY
        Hi, Daddy!

The boy advanced to his father's chair, carrying a sheaf of papers.

BOY (cont'd)
Look what me and Beezie are goin' to do . . . !

The greeting was met with silence. His father's face remained hidden behind the newspaper.

MOTHER
Joseph, the boy is talkin' to you.

FATHER
Eh! What does he want?

The paper dropped to the working man's lap, and the father stared at his son with a slack, almost hostile expression.

BOY
Daddy, look! Beezie and me are goin' to direct a play! And we're goin' to charge ten cents apiece for all the kids to come and see it.
(hands some papers to his father)
Here's some drawings I made. . . . See, this is Snow White's house, and—

FATHER
Play? Snow White . . . ? That's a fairy tale, ain't it?

BOY
Yeah, it's like the Walt Disney movie, and—

The father laughed roughly.

FATHER
A fairy tale is for a buncha fairies!
(he sweeps out his hand, scattering the drawings across the floor)
That's nothin' for a boy to be up to! Plays are for fairies . . . you want to be a fairy, boy?

BOY
But, Daddy, it's a good show, and—

FATHER
Listen, pick up this crap and get it outta here. And don't let me hear no more about it. You oughta be out playin' ball . . . not foolin' with this pansy crap!

Dominic stood in the aisle, his mind reeling from the impact of the scene. How he remembered that night! His father had so thoroughly crushed him that evening that he had given up the play with his friend. He had let a little piece of himself die that night.

A sudden anger surged through him as he forced his mind back to the rest of the memory, and he remembered what happened when he'd started picking up his drawings.

Up on the stage, his younger self was bending down, reaching out for the scattered papers.

Stepping closer to the stage, Dominic cried out, *"Watch it!* Don't let him get to them first . . . he's going to tear them up!"

The skinny, dark-haired boy paused, looked out into the darkness of the audience, as though listening. His mother and father had clearly heard nothing, and for a moment seemed to be arrested in time.

BOY

(looking down towards Dominic)
What did you say?

"Dad's going to tear up your drawings . . . if you let him," said Dominic. "So pick them up now, fast. Then tell him what you're thinking, what you're *feeling*."

BOY

Who are you?

Dominic swallowed hard, forced himself to speak in a clear, calm voice. "You know who I am. . . ."

BOY

(smiling)
Yeah, I guess I do. . . .

The boy turned back to the stage and quickly grabbed all his drawings as his father reached down a large hand and tried to snatch them away.

BOY

No! You leave them alone! You leave *me* alone!

FATHER

(a bit shocked by the boy's words)
What're ya gonna do? Grow up and be a fruitcake?
Whatsamatter with baseball? Too tough on ya?

The boy held the papers to his chest, paused to look out into the darkness at Dominic, then back to his father. The boy was breathing hard, obviously scared, but there was a new strength in the way he stood, staring at his father. He was almost sobbing, but he forced the words to come out clearly.

BOY
Yeah, I like baseball just fine. But I like this stuff, too. And . . . and, I don't care if you don't like it. 'Cause I do! And that's what's important!

The boy ran from the room, carrying his drawings. His father stared after him for a moment, then returned to his newspaper, trying to act unaffected by the small exchange. His mother stood by the table with a beaten, joyless expression on her face.

The stage lights dimmed quickly, fading everything into darkness. Dominic blinked his eyes as the figures of his parents became phantoms in the shadows, growing faint, insubstantial.

Another blink of his eyes and they were gone. Slowly the set began to metamorphose back into the barroom of Nick's Place.

Dominic's heart cried out silently, but it was too late. The vision, or whatever it had been, had vanished.

He took an aisle seat, let out a long breath. Rubbing his eyes, he felt the fine patina of sweat on his face. His heartbeats were loud and heavy. What the hell had been going on?

He had been awake, yet he felt as though he had just snapped out of a trance. He felt crazy, but he knew that he was not dreaming, not unless his whole life had been a nightmare.

It had seemed so real. How obvious the dynamics of his family seemed to him now. He wondered why he had never seen what things were really like when he was a kid. But then, maybe he did know back then. . . .

Children picked up things on a different level than adults.

They hadn't spent much time building up defense mechanisms and rationalizations for all the shitty things that happen in the world. Kids take everything straight, no chaser. It's later on we all start bull-shitting ourselves.

Dominic stood up and looked about the auditorium as an eerie sensation washed over him. It was as though he was the only person left in the whole world. He felt so totally alone. And he knew that it was time to get away from this place. Try to forget all the pain—isn't that what life is all about?—not wallow in it.

He walked back to the lobby, slipped through a side door, and then down a long corridor to his office. After turning out the lights, he locked up, headed for the employees' exit. Just as he reached the fire door, he heard footsteps in the shadows behind him. He whirled quickly and saw a small, hunched-over black man carrying a broom.

"Evenin', Mr. Kazan . . ." said the voice. "Oh, hi, Sam," said Dominic. "Take it easy now. Good night."

He pushed out the door to the parking lot, leaving the old janitor/ night watchman alone in the building.

The next day when Dominic Kazan awoke, he felt somehow *changed,* but there was nothing he could think of which would explain the feeling. He had no memory of the previous night's experience, other than a nagging question in his mind. It was a crazy idea he must have been dreaming about, but there was something he wanted to know.

That afternoon, before going down to the Barclay, Dominic stopped at the City Office Building to speak to some people in the records division of the Department of Urban Planning. They were as cooperative as bureaucrats can be, and after more than two hours of hassling around, Dominic chanced upon a few intriguing facts.

In the theater that evening after the performance, Dominic went about his duties. As stage manager, he had to make certain that all the props were back in place for the next show, that the set was restored to precurtain readiness; and that all the light and sound cues were in the proper order in the technician's booth. He went through his tasks slowly, waiting for the rest of the Barclay personnel to depart the large building. Entering the main auditorium, Dominic walked down the aisle and sat in the first row of the orchestra seats. A silence pervaded the place as he closed his eyes, letting his thoughts run free. His discovery at the Department of Urban Planning kept replaying in his mind—the proscenium stage of the Barclay occupied the very same space that was once filled by his parents' house in the middle of the old neighborhood block.

Dominic opened his eyes slowly, focusing on the stage. As though on cue, the lights heated up, gradually filling the set with hard illumination. But this time, he did feel fear as much as anticipation. He felt like he was about to embark upon a long-awaited trip.

Dominic looked up to see his familiar living room warming under the stage lights. . . .

The door opened and his father entered the room. He wore his usual work clothes, carried an evening paper and his lunch pail. Normally a quick-moving, broad-shouldered man who seemed to radiate force and raw power, Joseph Kazan appeared stooped and oddly defeated.

FATHER
Louisa! Louisa, where are you?

There was no immediate reply and he shrugged as he moved to his favorite chair. He began to open his folded newspaper, then threw it to the floor in disgust. A door opened at stage left and Dominic's mother appeared carrying a dish towel.

MOTHER
Joseph? What are you doing home so early?

Joseph looked at her with anger in his eyes, his lips curled back slightly. Suddenly the anger drained away from him. Looking away from his wife, he spoke with great effort.

FATHER
We got laid off again today . . . Got mad at my
foreman. I left after he told us all not to come in
tomorrow morning.

There was a pained expression in his mother's face.

MOTHER
Why do they always do this right before
Christmas? It's not fair.

FATHER
I'll have to find somethin' quick. We got bills to
keep up. Nobody's hirin' now, though . . . the
bastards!

His mother moved to his father's chair, put a hand on his shoulder.

MOTHER
Well, we've gotten by before . . . we'll do it again.

Joseph shook his head, slapped his leg absently.

FATHER
Some husband I been! A man's spozed to take care
of things! Take care of his family better'n this!

The door at stage center opened and an adolescent version of
Dominic entered the room. He was carrying a stack of books under
his arm, his parka under the other.

> BOY
>
> Hi, Mom . . . hey, Dad, what're you doing home
> early?

> FATHER
>
> (ignoring the question)
> Where you been?

> BOY
>
> We had a rehearsal after school. Just got finished.
> (to his mother)
> Can I have an apple or something, Mom?

> FATHER
>
> Rehearsal-what? Another one of them plays?

> BOY
>
> C'mon, Dad, you know I'm doing a play for the one-
> act contest at school. I wrote it myself, remember?

His father shook his head slowly, wiped his mouth with obvious
irritation, then looked at his mother.

> FATHER
>
> I'm worryin' about takin' care of this family, he's
> out writin' stuff for faggots!

His mother touched her husband's shoulder again.

> MOTHER
>
> Joseph, please don't take it out on him. . . .

> BOY
>
> Yeah, Dad. We've been through this stuff before,
> haven't we?

Dominic's father did not speak as he exploded from his chair and
backhanded the teenager across the face with one quick, furious motion. The force of the blow slammed the boy's head against the wall
and he staggered away, dazed and glassy-eyed.

FATHER
More! You want more! You smart-assed kid! You
don't speak to your father like that . . . not
never!

His mother moved to help her wounded son.

MOTHER
You didn't have to hit him like that.

FATHER
You stay away from him, goddammit! I oughta give
it to him twice as hard! He don't respect his father.
At his age he oughta be out workin' like a *man*. He
oughta be helpin' his family!

The teenaged boy looked at his father with terror in his eyes. He
appeared helpless, but he forced himself to speak.

BOY
What do you want from me? What have I ever done
to hurt you?

FATHER
(in mocking effeminate voice)
What have I ever done to hurt you!

His father grinned at his little joke, then raised his hand towards
the boy, just to watch him shy away.

FATHER (cont'd)
I'll tell you what you done . . . you ain't acted like
a man! And that hurts more'n anything. But that's
gonna stop. As of today you're gonna be a man.

BOY
What do you mean?

FATHER
You're goin' to work.

BOY
But I already have a job. . . .

> FATHER
>
> Ha! You call that paper route a job? I'm talkin'
> about a *real* job. Make some *real* money! It's about
> time you started helpin' your mother and me.

> BOY
>
> But what about school?

His father laughed, then stared at him defiantly.

> FATHER
>
> What about it? You're old enough to quit . . . so
> now you'll quit! I hadda leave school in the fifth
> grade! You think you're any better'n me?

> BOY
>
> But, Dad, I don't want to quit school. I can't quit
> *now*.

> FATHER
>
> Don't tell me what you "can't" or what you "want"
> 'cause that don't mean shit to me! I'm tellin' you
> what you gotta do 'cause I'm your father! That
> school's just fillin' your head with a bunch of crazy
> shit anyway. . . .

> BOY
>
> Dad, I can't believe this. . . .

> FATHER
>
> Shut up and listen to me or I'll bust you again!

Dominic had been watching the scene with a morbid fascination and a growing anger. Things seemed so much clearer now—how things worked in his family. He could not allow his younger self to succumb to the ravings of a beaten, humiliated man.

Without thinking further, he stood up and called out to the younger version of himself: "Hey! You tell him to keep his hands off you! And that if he tries anything again . . . you're going to stop him!"

As before, neither his father nor his mother seemed to have heard Dominic's voice. But the adolescent boy reacted immediately. He turned to the edge of the stage and peered into the darkness.

> BOY
> What did you say? Is it you again?

"Yes," said Dominic, his voice almost catching in his throat. "It's me . . . now tell him what I told you. Tell him what you're thinking. What you're *really* thinking."

Dominic watched the boy nod and turn back towards his father. There was a sensation of great tension in the air, like an electrical storm gathering on a humid day.

> BOY
> You can't hit me like that anymore.

The boy stood there, seeming to radiate a new strength.

> FATHER
> What?

> BOY
> You can't hit me—just because you feel like doing
> it. I haven't done anything wrong and I'm tired of
> you making me feel like I have.

> FATHER
> I'll bust you any goddamned time I—

> BOY
> No! No you won't! I won't let you!

His father smiled and shifted his weight from one foot to the other, his arms hanging loose as though ready for a fight.

> FATHER
> Well, what's this? A little *manliness* after all this
> time, huh? How about that?

> BOY
> I'm not quitting school. And you can't make me do
> it. There're things I want to do with my life that I
> can't do if I quit school.

His father looked at him silently, a confused expression on his face.

>   BOY (cont'd)
> There're things I want to do . . . things that you
> could *never* do.

>   FATHER
> What the hell's that spozed to mean?

>   BOY
> You have to understand something, Dad. I'm not
> going to be made responsible for anybody's life . . .
> except my own. Especially not yours. I can't live
> your life, but I *have* to live mine.

>   FATHER
> *(looking confused, off balance)*
> Listen, you little shit . . .

>   BOY
> No, Dad, I think it's time *you* listened. Maybe for
> the first time in your life.

The boy turned and walked to the door stage center, opening it.

>   BOY
> I'm going out for a while.

He exited the stage, leaving his father standing mute and stripped
of his power.

Dominic fell back in the theater seat as the stage quickly darkened
and the figures and props dissolved into the shadows.

In an instant the set was gone. He felt rigid and tense and there
was a soft roaring in his ears like the sound of a seashell. He felt as
though he had just awakened from a dream. But he knew it had been
no dream.

A memory?

Perhaps. But as he sat there in the darkness, he had the feeling he
had no memories. That the scene he had just witnessed was a solitary
moment, a free-floating, always existing piece of the timestream. A
moment out of time.

What is *happening* to me? The thought ate through him like a
furious acid, leaving him with a vague sense of panic. Standing up,
he knew that he must leave the place. Dominic walked up the aisle
to the lobby, refusing to look back at the dark stage.

The light in the lobby comforted him and he felt better immediately. Already, the fears and crazy thoughts were fading away. It's all right now. Better get on home. As he moved towards the exit, he heard a sound and stopped. A door slipping its latch.

"Mr. Kazan!" said a familiar voice. "What're you still doing here?"

Turning, Dominic saw Bob Yeager, the Barclay's stage manager, standing in the doorway of his office.

"Oh, hi, Bob. I was . . . I was just going over a few things. Just getting ready to leave."

Yeager rubbed his beard, grinned. "Just getting over those first-night jitters, huh? I can understand that, yes sir."

Dominic smiled uneasily. "Yeah, the first night's always the worst . . ."

"Hey, you did a great job, Mr. Kazan. Just fine."

"I did?"

Yeager nodded, smiled.

"I suppose I'll have to take your word for it," said Dominic. "Well, I guess I'd better be heading home. Good night."

When he arrived at his town house, he found that he couldn't sleep. He had the nagging sensation that something was wrong, that something in his life was out of whack, out of sync, but he couldn't pin it down. After making a cup of instant coffee, he wandered into his den, where a typewriter and a pile of manuscript pages awaited him on a large messy desk.

Sitting down, he decided to go back to that play he had been trying to write. Every actor thinks he can be a playwright, right? Some ideas started flowing as Dominic began to type, and it was very late before he went to bed.

The next evening's performance had gone better than opening night, but it was still rough. Dominic was playing the part of Alan in Wilson's *Lemon Sky,* and although the director was pleased with his characterization, Dominic was not. He had learned long ago that you cannot merely please your audience; you must also please yourself.

He remained in the dressing room, dawdling and taking his time, waiting for everyone else to leave. The rest of the cast planned to meet at their favorite bistro for drinks and food, and he had declined politely. There would be time for such things later. Tonight, Dominic felt compelled to go back into the theater itself, back into the empty darkness where careers were made or destroyed. He was not really certain why he felt the need to stay behind. But he had feelings, or rather, memories. Or perhaps they were dreams . . . or memories of dreams. Or . . .

He was not certain what they were, but he felt convinced that the answers lay in the dark shadows of the auditorium.

Finally, everyone had cleared out and he left the dressing room for the theater itself. As he entered through the lobby doors, he saw no one, not even Sam. There were no lights other than the green, glowing letters of the exit lights, and as he moved down the aisle, he had the sensation of entering an abandoned cathedral. The darkness seemed to crowd about him like a thick fog, and he began to feel strangely light-headed. As he drew himself deeper into the vast sea of empty seats, he could see the dim outlines of the set beyond the open act curtain—a modern suburban home in El Cajon, California.

Then slowly, the stage lights crackled as they gathered heat and bathed the stage in light and life. The shapes which took form and color were again the props of a tortured childhood.

The shabby living room, the kitchenette, worn carpets and dingy curtains.

The door at stage center opened and his mother entered, wearing a simple, tailored suit. Her hair was silvering and had been puffed by a beauty shop. She appeared elegant in a simply stated manner. He had never remembered his mother looking like that. She looked about the room as though expecting someone to be home.

MOTHER
Dominic, where are you? Dominic?

She appeared perplexed as she closed the door, calling his name again. Then turning towards the footlights, she looked beyond them to where he stood transfixed.

MOTHER (cont'd)
Oh, *there* you are. Dominic, come up here! Come to me. . . .

The recognition startled him, but he felt himself responding as though wrapped in the web of a dream. There was an unreality about the moment, a sensation which prompted him to question nothing, to merely react.

And he did.

Climbing up and onto the stage as the heat of the lights warmed him, he felt as though he was passing through a barrier.

It was that magic which every actor feels when the curtain rises and he steps forth, but it was also very different this time. . . .

> DOMINIC
> Where's Dad? He wasn't there, was he?

> MOTHER
> (*looking away*)
> No, Dominic . . . I'm sorry. I don't know where he
> is. He never came home from work.

She paused to straighten a doily on the arm of the sofa, then turned back to him.

> MOTHER (cont'd)
> But, Dominic, it was *wonderful!* So beautiful a play,
> I never seen! And *you* were wonderful! I am so
> proud of you, my son!

Dominic smiled and walked over to her and hugged her. It was the first time he could remember doing such a thing in a long, long time. Overt affection in his home had been a rarity, something shunned and almost feared.

> DOMINIC
> Thanks, Mom.

> MOTHER
> I always knew you were a good boy. I always knew
> you would make me proud someday.

> DOMINIC
> Did you?

He pulled away from her, looked at her intently.

> DOMINIC (cont'd)
> Then why didn't you ever tell me when I was a
> kid? Back when I really needed it.

His mother turned away, stared into the sink.

> MOTHER
>
> You wouldn't understand, Dominic. You don't know
> how many times I wanted to say something,
> but . . .

> DOMINIC
>
> But it was him, wasn't it? Christ, Mom, were you
> that much afraid of him that you could just stand
> by and watch him destroy your only son?

> MOTHER
>
> Don't talk like that, Dominic. I prayed for you,
> Dominic . . . I prayed into the night that you would
> be stronger than me, that you would stand up to
> him. I did what I *could*, Dominic. . . .

> DOMINIC
>
> I think I needed more than prayers, Mom . . . but
> that's okay. I understand. I'm sorry I jumped on
> you like that.

Then came the sound of a key fumbling in a lock. The click of
the doorknob sounded loud and ominous. The door swung open
slowly to reveal his father, obviously drunk, leaning against the threshold. Joseph Kazan shambled onto the set, seemingly unaware of anyone
else's presence. He collapsed in his usual chair and stared out into
empty space.

> DOMINIC
>
> Where have you been?

His father looked at him with a hardness, unaffected by the glaze
in his eyes.

> FATHER
>
> What the fuck you care?

> DOMINIC
>
> You're my father. I care. Sons are supposed to care
> about their fathers . . . or haven't you heard?

FATHER

(coughing)

Don't get wise with me! I can still get out of this chair and whomp you one!

DOMINIC

(smiling sadly)

Is that the only form of communication you know?—"Whomping" people?

FATHER

(laughing)

Ah, it's not even worth it! You and your fancy words . . . What do you know about bein' a man?

DOMINIC

Dad, I wanted you to be there tonight. You *knew* I wanted you there . . . didn't you?

His father looked at him and the hardness in his eyes seemed to soften a bit. Looking away, Joseph Kazan spoke in a low voice.

FATHER

Yeah . . . yeah, I knew.

DOMINIC

So why weren't you there? Did it really feel better to crawl into one of those sewers you call a bar and get filthy drunk? Did you think that getting juiced would make it all go away? What do—

FATHER

Shut up! Shut up before I whomp ya!

His father had put his hands over his ears, trying to shut out the offending words.

DOMINIC

No, I don't think so. I don't think you'll be "whomping" anybody. Ever again.

FATHER

That's brave words from a wimp like you.

DOMINIC
Don't talk to me about "brave." Why didn't you
come to the play tonight? *My* play! Your *son's* play!

FATHER
What're you talkin' about?

DOMINIC
What were you afraid of, Dad? That maybe some of
your buddies might see you? Might catch you going
to see a bunch of "faggots"?

FATHER
Hah! See, you even admit it yourself!

Dominic's mother moved in between the two men.

MOTHER
Oh God, look at you two! So much anger . . . so
much hate. Please, stop it . . . !

DOMINIC
Hate? No, Mom, that's not right. A lack of love,
maybe . . . but not really hate. There's a
difference.

FATHER
(*looking at his son*)
What the hell do you know?

DOMINIC
I think that's the heart of the problem around
here—not enough love in this house. There isn't
any love here. No warmth . . . no love.

FATHER
Shit, I'll tell y'about love! I worked for yer Mom for
thirty-five years. Worked hard! Did she ever have
to go out'n take a job like other guys' wives? Shit,
no!

His father was trembling as he spoke, his florid face puffy and
shining with sweat.

DOMINIC

There's more to love than that, Dad. Like the love between you and me . . . When I was a kid, did you ever just sit down and play with me? Did you ever tell me stories, or try to make me laugh? How about going fishing together, or flying a kite? Did we ever do anything like that?

FATHER

A man has to work!

DOMINIC

Did you really love your work _that_ much?

FATHER

What do y'mean?

DOMINIC

Did you love your work more than me?

FATHER
(confused, angry)
Don't talk no bullshit to me!

DOMINIC

It's not bullshit, Dad. Listen, when I was little—no brothers or sisters—I spent a lot of time alone. Sometimes I needed someone to guide me, to teach me.

FATHER

I never ran out and never came home at night . . . ask your mother! I was always there, every night!

DOMINIC
(smiling sadly)
Oh, yeah, you were there physically. But never emotionally, can't you see that? I can remember seeing other kids out doing things with their fathers, and I can remember really _hating_ them— because they had something I never did. That kind of stuff hurt me a lot more than your belt ever did.

His father did not respond, but looked down at his lap, where he had unconsciously knotted his hands together.

> MOTHER
> Dominic, leave him alone now. Let's all have some
> coffee, and we can—

> DOMINIC
> No, Mom. Let's finish it. Let's get it all out. It's
> been a long time coming.
> *(to his father)*
> Hey, Dad . . . do you know I have *no* memories of
> you ever encouraging me to do *anything*? Except all
> that macho shit.

> FATHER
> *What* kind of shit?

> DOMINIC
> Remember when I saved my paper route money
> and bought that cheap guitar?

> FATHER
> Yeah, so . . . ?

> DOMINIC
> But I guess you've forgotten how you screamed and
> yelled that you couldn't afford music lessons, and
> music was only for "fairies" anyhow?

> FATHER
> I ain't sure . . .

> DOMINIC
> Well, *I'm* sure. And when I told you I'd teach
> myself how to play it, you laughed, remember?

> FATHER
> Did I?

> DOMINIC
> Yes, and I don't have to strain to recall how that
> felt. It's carved right into my heart. The whole
> goddamned scene.

FATHER

So who ever heard of anybody teachin' themselves
to play music? It's crazy!

DOMINIC

Yeah, maybe . . . but I *did* teach myself, didn't I?
And I played in a band until that night I came
home late from a dance and you were waiting for
me behind the door—Remember that, Dad? The
night you smashed my guitar over the sink?

His father looked away from him. He seemed truly embarrassed
now.

DOMINIC (cont'd)

That's what my life's been like, Dad; me doing
interesting things *despite* what I got from you. Or
maybe I should say what I *didn't* get from you!

FATHER

That's horsehshit.

DOMINIC

(shaking his head)
I wish it was. I really do. But it's all true, Dad. All
true.

FATHER

Why don't you just shut up!

DOMINIC

Because I'm not finished yet. What's the matter,
am I threatening you? I think that's what the
problem has always been—you never liked the way
your wide-eyed kid had some natural curiosity
about the world, did you?

FATHER

(sounding tired now)
You're not making any sense.

DOMINIC

Well, try this one: you weren't only threatened by
your son, but just about *everybody*. Anybody you

thought was more intelligent than you, or more
educated, or had more money . . . you always had
something shitty to say about all of them, didn't
you?

FATHER

Now, it ain't like that!

DOMINIC

Wait! Let me finish. So then you wake up one
morning and you realize that your own weirdo kid
was not going to grow up to be a beer-drinking
macho man, you just gave up, didn't you?

FATHER

What do you mean?

DOMINIC

I mean that when you saw that your own kid was
turning out to be a hell of a lot different from
you—but very much like all those kinds of people
you feared and therefore despised—then you
stopped being a father to that strange son.

FATHER

I what?

DOMINIC

Didn't you know that all I wanted was a little
approval? A little love?

FATHER

You talk like you got it all figured out . . . what do
you think you are—a doctor or something?

DOMINIC

(grinning)
No. No "doctor" . . . just a son. And if I haven't
"figured it all out," at least I'm trying. You never
even tried!

His father stared at him and tried to speak, but no words would
come. His lower lip trembled slightly from the effort.

> DOMINIC
>
> Don't you understand why I'm telling you all this?
> Don't you understand what I've been trying to
> say?

His father shook his head quickly, uttered a single word.

> FATHER
>
> No. . . .

> DOMINIC
>
> I can't think of anything else to say. No other way
> to make you understand . . . except to just tell you,
> Dad. I don't know why, but after all the years, and
> after all the pain, I know that I still love you, that I
> have to love you.

He walked closer to his father and stared into his eyes, searching
for some glimmer of understanding.

> DOMINIC (cont'd)
>
> I love you, Dad.
> *(pause)*
> And I need to hear the same thing from you.

There was a long silence as father and son regarded each other.
Dominic could feel the presence of some great force gathering over
the stage. Then he saw the tears forming in his father's eyes.

> FATHER
>
> *(stepping forward)*
> Oh, Dominic. . . .

His father grabbed him up in his arms and pulled him close. For
an instant, Dominic resisted, but then relaxed, falling into the embrace
with his father.

> FATHER
>
> My son . . . what happened to us?
> *(pause)*
> I . . . *love* you!
> I *do* love you!

Dominic felt the barrel chest of his father close against his own and he was very conscious of how strange a sensation it was. Suddenly there was a great roaring in his ears and he was instantly terrified, disoriented. His father had relaxed his emotional embrace and Dominic pulled back and looked into the man's face.

He was only vaguely aware of the stage lights quickly fading to black, but in the last instant of illumination he saw that his father no longer stood before him. He now stared into the face of a stranger.

An actor.

The roaring sound had coalesced into something recognizable, and Dominic turned to look out into the brimming audience—a sea of people who were on their feet, clamoring, applauding wildly.

Then the curtain closed, sealing him off from them, from the torrent of appreciation.

He was only half aware of his two fellow actors—the ones who had portrayed his father and mother—as they moved to each side of him, joining their hands in his.

The lights came up as the curtain reopened. The audience renewed its furious applause, and suddenly he understood.

Feeling a flood of warmth and a special sense of gratitude, Dominic Kazan stepped forward to take his bow.

finale

Dennis L. McKiernan

DARKNESS

I knew Dennis McKiernan before he was a published writer. In fact, though it's not polite to brag, I can claim that I discovered him, a fact of which I'm very proud.

What I can't claim to have had any part in is his talent, which blossomed through the eighties and into the nineties, mostly in the fantasy field, where he has distinguished himself mightily. His heroic tales are in the tradition of J. R. R. Tolkien, but he has made the genre his own, with such books as Dragon Doom, The Iron Tower Trilogy *(consisting, oddly enough, of three volumes), and* The Silver Call Duology *(consisting of, you guessed it, two).*

For this book he has produced a singular tale; if Tom Monteleone's is a Twilight Zone *piece then this is a* Night Gallery *one—a Serling-like tale with a dash of color, though it concerns the opposites of light and dark.*

It makes a very nice "duology" with Monteleone's story.

It is always Dark.
Light only hides the Darkness.
—DANIEL KIAN MC KIERNAN

The taxi pulled in through the open, wrought iron gates and up a long, sweeping driveway with weeping willows looming in the chill darkness to either side. In the backseat, Harlow leaned forward to get a better look.

Wow . . . !

The moonlight glanced across the snow and highlighted white-laden topiary here and there as well as glimmered on the ice of a landscaped pond. A gazebo sat on the shore of the lakelet, snow on its octagonal roof. Ahead sat the house, the manse: white and two stories and elegant.

Twenty, twenty-five rooms, at least. Perhaps one for each year of my age.

As the cab pulled into a circular turnaround and stopped, Harlow could see a man standing at the front door and shielding his eyes from the headlights, a glitter of keys in his gloved hand.

Harlow got out. "Mr. Maxon?"

Tall and silver-haired, the man moved forward on the broad single step before the door and removed a glove and extended his open hand, his smile revealing angular teeth, and he said, "Mr. Winton, I presume." The two men shook hands, Maxon's grip cold.

The taxi driver hefted a cheap suitcase out from the trunk and set it to the wide stoop. "That'll be sixteen dollars."

"Just charge it to my account, Roddy," said Maxon.

The driver touched the bill of his cap and stepped back to his cab.

As the taxi pulled away, Maxon jingled the keys and softly said, "Well, let's get to it," and turned toward the door.

Picking up his imitation-leather luggage, Harlow followed, stepping through the doorway just as Maxon flipped a switch, and with a faint clicking throughout the house, light flooded the foyer and the rooms beyond, both upstairs and down. "Holy . . . !" Harlow set his suitcase down and squinted against the brightness and glanced at Maxon, the lawyer pale and pasty, almost cadaverous in this glare.

"Your great-uncle was a most peculiar man, Harlow, and you are the last in his line."

"Yeah, but all this light. His electric bill must have been enormous."

"He can afford it, or rather, could." Maxon closed the door and shed his overcoat. "And you can afford it as well, if you care to keep it this way. Personally, if it were mine to do, I'd get rid of the lights and turn this house back into a place of elegant comfort, which you can afford as well. In fact, there's not much you can't afford, within reason. There is but a single hindrance in your uncle's will, the stipulation being that the relative who inherits must live in this place or lose it all: fortune, house, everything."

Harlow grinned. "No trouble there. But, lord, all these lights. Can't we turn some off?"

Maxon shook his head. "I'm afraid not. They are either all on or all off."

Harlow cocked an eyebrow. "And this one switch, it controls them all?"

"Actually, every switch in the house does. As I understand it, each one feeds into a master control box, and the lights all go on and off together. Relay driven, I believe. There's a remote somewhere that will do the same, control the lights, that is."

"Like a TV remote?"

Maxon nodded. "Here, give me your parka and we'll take a tour."

Harlow peeled out of his coat and handed it to Maxon, the lawyer opening the door to a brightly lit foyer closet.

Harlow's eyes widened. "Even the closets?"

"Even those," replied Maxon, hanging both garments inside. He started to reach for the suitcase, but Harlow said, "No, no. Let me," and set it in the closet himself. Maxon grinned at the vigorous young man and said, "Now for the tour."

Every room, every chamber inside the house was illuminated by panels of light mounted on walls and ceilings. Each of the rooms was sparsely furnished, and of what furniture there was, much was made of molded glass or clear plastic or Lucite or some such, Harlow couldn't tell which. And wherever furniture of a different sort sat, floor panels cast light in the space below. Even the tall, king-sized four-poster had light panels underneath. "No place for monsters," said Harlow upon seeing this last. "Monsterless closets, too."

As they walked down to the first floor Harlow asked, "Is the whole house this way?"

Maxon nodded and led him to the kitchen, where luminous panels lit the interiors of cabinets, even though the shelves and doors were made of clear glass, as were the dishes within. Many utensils were transparent, sitting in their illumined drawers. And all appliances were lighted inside and out.

"My, my," said Harlow.

"Indeed," replied Maxon, and opened the door to the brightly lit garage. Inside sat a large gasoline-powered, motor-driven generator— a Honda—its exhaust feeding through a clear plastic pipe vented to the outside, the machine sitting silent but ready. Inside as well sat a BMW, a heavy-duty power cord running to it from the wall, its interior glowing with light.

"Even the car?"

Again Maxon nodded. "In the trunk are a number of batteries— on a charger—to power the light panels within."

Glove compartment, trunk, under the seats, inside the dash, under the hood: all were blazing.

Harlow frowned. "With all that light in the car, how did he see to drive at night?"

"He didn't," replied Maxon. "He didn't go out at night; but he wanted to be ready, just in case."

"In case of what?"

Maxon shrugged. "In case he had to, I suppose."

"Was he always this way? I mean, I didn't know anything about him—didn't even know I had a great-uncle until you contacted me."

"A good thing, that," said Maxon. "Else Massachusetts would have gotten it all—but for me running you down."

"Well, I'm glad you did. But again I ask: was he always this way?"

"No. When he was younger, much like your age, he traveled the world: Africa, India, Tibet, the Orient, the Outback, the Pampas, wherever: he saw them all. But rather suddenly, it seems, he stopped. Holed up in this house. Hired workers to make the changes to put light everywhere. A beacon in the dark, so to speak. The neighbors call this 'the lighthouse.'"

As they stepped back into the kitchen, Harlow sighed. "Lighthouse it is; there's not a shadow in this place. Was he afraid of the dark?"

"Perhaps," replied Maxon, now walking down the hall to the foyer. "As I said, he never went out at night."

Harlow looked about. "I wonder what he would have done in a blackout?"

As Maxon opened the closet and slipped into his overcoat he said, "Why, nothing. Should the power fail, the lights switch over to backup batteries; then the generator in the garage takes over."

"Oh." Harlow saw Maxon to the door. As the lawyer stepped outside and into the snowy November night, Harlow asked, "By the way, how did he die?"

"His heart gave out. The housekeeper, she found him in the recreation room; he'd been watching TV, it seems."

Harlow jerked a thumb over his shoulder. "In that glare?"

Maxon turned up a hand.

"Hmm," mused Harlow. "Regardless. Too bad I didn't know him. Perhaps I would have liked him."

"Perhaps you would have at that. He's buried out back in the family plot." Maxon looked at his watch. "Well, I'm due elsewhere. I'll drop in tomorrow night and we'll go over the assets and set up your bank and brokerage accounts, among other things."

"Uhh, can't we take care of it in the daylight, rather than in this glare?"

"I'm sorry, Harlow, I'm simply not available until tomorrow evening."

"Oh, I didn't know. Then tomorrow night it is. Any special time?"

"Shall we say eight?"

"Fine by me."

"Oh," said Maxon, fishing about under his coat, "these are yours." He handed the keys to Harlow. Then: "Well, I'm gone. Have a nice night."

"But wait, how will you get to wherever you're going?"

"It isn't far, and I need the exercise," replied Maxon.

Harlow watched as the lawyer trudged down the drive, and in spite of the moonlight, the man seemed to fade into the shadows. When he could see him no more, Harlow closed the door and stepped into well-lighted rooms.

Over the next three days, Harlow explored the house and property— fifty-four acres in all—discovering the family graveyard, finding the remains of an old cabin in a grove of trees to the north, briefly sitting in the snow-laden gazebo and surveying his new world. During it all he pondered his future. For the first time in his life, Harlow had money. Oh, not that he had been a vagrant before, but instead he had been a man with little to his name, not even relatives—no mother, no father, no foster parents—rather he had been raised, if you could call it that, in an orphanage. Yet now all that was changed: he *had* had kinfolk, kinfolk he never knew yet kinfolk nevertheless, kindred buried on these very grounds in a rather large family plot, many of the gravestones undated and without names. Regardless, thanks to one of these kindred, a heretofore unknown great-uncle, now he had money to spend. He was twenty-five and fairly rich and all he had to do was live in this splendid house . . . or it would be splendid as soon as he got rid of the glare, for he had decided that he would take up Maxon's suggestion and turn this house back into a place of elegant comfort. After that was done, he would then consider taking on a job, or perhaps a career, though Maxon had said he would never have to work again.

He hired a housekeeper and a cook, but they refused to stay in the place at night, saying that there was too much light. But Harlow suspected there was more to it than that, for often he saw the two

His heart pounding, sweat pouring, his moans turning to whines, Harlow managed to wrench himself fully awake, and gasping, he fumbled at the bedside lamp, finally finding the switch, snapping it on, and no one, nothing, no *thing,* stood at the foot of his bed.

Lord, I'm jumping at shadows.

Feeling drained, still it was a long time before Harlow fell back to sleep.

The next day Harlow got a dog, a rottweiler. Yet it seemed cowed by the unfamiliar surroundings, or so Harlow thought, and he literally had to drag it into the house. At the first chance it got it bolted out the door. Harlow never saw it again.

Son of a bitch.

Harlow had a monitored burglar alarm installed: all the doors and windows were armed, and in several of the downstairs rooms he had motion detectors positioned, tripped by heat plus movement. He accidentally triggered the alarm himself several times before learning all the codes and remembering when to disarm the system—the damn *whoop, whoop, whoop* of the electronic klaxon nearly causing him to jump out of his skin. But he was the only one, the only *thing,* to set off the alarm; nothing else tripped the siren and sent a call to the monitoring company, nor from them to the police.

One evening after a walk, Harlow returned to the house and opened the door to a closet—"Christ!" he shouted, and leaped back as something black in the darkness twisted up and away. His heart thudding, Harlow snapped on the closet light. Nothing was there but two jackets hanging on the coat rod. Harlow snapped off the light and swung the door to and fro, watching its shadow move. It didn't look the same.

Days went by, and still flickers of movement in the darkness caught Harlow's eye, while now and again someone or some *thing* stood in the black at the foot of his bed.

God, no wonder my granduncle had lights all over this pl— Oh my, but wait!

Harlow stepped to the phone and punched in a number.

"This is Harlow Winton. Ask him to give me a call. Yes: w-i-n-t-o-n. He has my number."

That night the phone rang. "Winton here. . . . Oh, Arthur, thanks for returning my— . . . Yes, yes, I'm fine. . . . What? . . . Right. . . . Tell me . . . my uncle, how did they find him? I mean, you said he was . . . Yes, that's right. Watching TV. How do you—? . . . I see. The remote was in his hand. The TV remote? Oh, my. . . . No, no.

No reason, just curious." Harlow sighed and looked about. "Thank you, Arthur. Yes, yes, thank you."

Harlow pushed the handset off button.

Damn! He grabbed the TV remote instead of the one for the lights.

Replacing the handset in the cradle, Harlow stepped away from the escritoire, noting for the first time just how dark were the shadows beneath.

After that return call from Maxon, things seemed to get worse. The feeling that something loomed behind him in the dark, or waited in the shadows in the next room, became overwhelming. And Harlow began reaching around door frames to flip on the lights before entering a darkened room, as well as reaching back around to flip off the lights behind. And now and again in the corner of his eye he thought he saw shadows following after, slithering down the hallways behind.

And at times he thought he heard slow breathing. But when he listened . . . nothing.

Oh God. Am I going mad or is something really here? And if something is here—if some thing is here—then I've got to get out. But wait. No. I can't leave. I'd lose everything. I have to live here, in this house, in this house where my uncle died in the dark . . . of fright, I think. Or maybe the thing killed him.

Days passed. Nights passed. And Harlow's dread worsened. And as his fear of darkness grew, so did his desire to be quit of this thing.

It's the thing I need to get rid of. But how? Bring back all those lights, all that glare? All that hideous transparent furniture? No sir. I got rid of those goddamned things, and I'll never bring them back. Besides, that was my uncle's solution, and you see what it got him: dead, that's what, killed by terror. Instead, I want this thing gone forever, not merely hiding from light.

An unremitting grinding knot settled deep in the pit of his stomach, and every day, every night, it seemed to grow worse and worse. His appetite waned and he lost weight; his hands trembled all the time.

And he began whispering to himself.

And he was weary, for although he had tried sleeping in the day, he simply couldn't; in the orphanage it had been taps at ten and reveille at six: it was ingrained in his life. But although he went to bed at night, he couldn't bring himself to turn out the light, and so he slept with it on—if it could be called sleeping—the closet door open, its light on as well.

And then one night as he got into bed, Harlow leapt the last yard or so to keep his feet from coming too close to the darkness beneath.

God, what am I doing? Am I a child?

But from that point on, he continued to leap to reach the bed, and upon wakening, he leapt out as well, even in the light of day.

And he acquired a stammer.

And at night, now and again, he was certain he heard what must be the *thing* moving through the house, in the halls and along the stairway; oh, not that he listened to the scrape of footsteps creeping through the dark, but rather he perceived a faint sibilant rustle, like dead leaves stirring in a chill wind.

And Harlow grew gaunt and wasted as the days and nights passed, while blackness shifted and slithered in shadow and a *thing* haunted the dark.

And still neither his housekeeper nor his cook would stay in the place at night, now saying that it was too dark. And they would leave before the sun went down and arrive again after it rose.

It was a blustery March night when the doorbell rang, and turning on the lights as he went, Harlow found Maxon standing at the door.

"Hob's nails, Harlow," said the silver-haired lawyer, "you look rather haggard, drained. Aren't you sleeping well?"

"Quick, quick, A-Arthur, come in. It's d-dark out there; come in."

"Oh, I wouldn't do that, Harlow. A bodyguard to protect you from *shadows*?"

Harlow giggled. Startled by the sound, he slapped his hand across his mouth. Then through his fingers he whispered, "P-pretty insane, hey?" It was uncertain as to whether Harlow was speaking to himself or to Arthur Maxon.

"Have you seen a doctor?"

"A-a shrink, don't you m-mean?"

"No. A family practitioner. You look twenty years older, my boy."

Again Harlow giggled.

"I'm worried about you, lad. You need to keep up your energy."

"I-I'm thinking of l-leaving this p-place. There's something here. Something dreadful."

"Oh, Harlow, don't say that. You'd lose a fortune. Besides, I've served this estate for many long years and will certainly see to its needs for many more long years to come. And so, my boy, I want you to stay and see to your health; it's in the best interests of all."

With Arthur urging Harlow to stick it out and to take care of himself, and Harlow clamping his hand over his own mouth to keep from giggling, the conversation dwindled to nought.

The evening ended with Harlow standing well back in the lighted foyer and watching while Arthur strode away from the house to fade into the darkness of night.

Weeks passed, while shadows shifted, and blackness breathed, and something stood in the darkness beyond. And during those same weeks, Harlow continued to decline, his vigor slipping away on tides of fear. And he was prone to fits of babbling, and spasms of giggling whispers. Even so, he held on to one rational thought, or so it seemed to him:

I want this thing, *whatever it is, not only gone but dead.*

Harlow began thinking of weapons—pistols, shotguns, rifles—something certain to kill, and then he remembered what Harry Callahan had said about a 44 magnum being the most powerful handgun in the world, able to blow heads clean off. *That's what I need: something to blow this thing's head clean off!*

But still Harlow had a major problem: how do you kill a thing that you can't see, a thing which flees from the light?

How can I get a good shot at it? I need to know where it is. I need to clearly see it, that's what. But how can I see something in the dar—?

Wait! That's it! Night-vision goggles! Or do they call them scopes? No matter, it's those things they use in the army to see in the dark. You wear them on your head, like that guy in Silence of the Lambs—*Buffalo Bill; yeah, Buffalo Bill—they multiply even the faintest of light and . . .*

His mind abuzz with possibilities, with plans, Harlow hardly slept at all. And he sat in bed, his blankets clutched to his chin, and giggled at the cleverness of his secret plan and now and then slapped his hand over his mouth to keep the secret from popping out . . . and watched as silent shadows slid up the stairs and along the walls in the hallway just outside the bedroom door, just at the limit of light.

The next day he bought a .44 magnum. A Dirty Harry gun. The dealer had said the fifty-caliber Desert Eagle was even more powerful, but Harlow insisted upon the Smith and Wesson .44, and he wanted it *now*. Upon seeing the haggard man's Beemer and the wad of money he offered, the proprietor temporarily closed shop and pulled the shades and turned on all the lights—as the hollow-eyed wretch had insisted, standing away from even the faintest of shadows. The dealer then said that *this one time* he would make an exception and sell the gun right away. No waiting period. No need for a license. And also just happened to have the night-vision goggles, too, for an appropriate price. Harlow turned down a laser sight, for even though the red beam was narrow, still it was light, and the *thing* might flee.

Hands shaking, Harlow drove home, careful to not speed or make a turn without signaling, obeying all traffic laws. He didn't want to get stopped now. *No, no.* They *might take the gun away.*

Impatiently he dithered about until the cook and the housekeeper were gone, and then, his heart thudding, he sat at the kitchen table and loaded the Smith and Wesson, sliding the 240-grain hollow-points into the waiting chambers.

It seems only fitting that I kill this thing *in the rec room. I mean, that's where it took advantage of a brownout and killed my uncle when the relays released and the lights went out. Killed him in the night in darkness, just as I'm going to kill it.*

Harlow picked up the night-vision goggles and slipped them on and adjusted them for fit, taking care not to accidentally flip on the amplifier switch.

It won't do to drive the goggles into overload here in the light of day. Better to wait till the depths of the night. Yes, the depths of the night. That's when I'll do it. When darkness fills every nook and cranny of the house. Turnabout, fair play, and all of that.

Harlow tittered, his voice tight with fear, but then he clamped his lips tight shut to keep the secret within.

It was nearly mid of night when—gun in hand, night goggles riding on his forehead—Harlow walked away from the kitchen, turning on lights ahead, turning them off behind.

Don't want lights on anywhere when I click that last switch and plunge everything into darkness.

His heart was hammering in dread.

But a loaded .44 magnum was gripped in his sweaty fist.

Finally he reached the recreation room.

Gasping for breath, he stepped about, turning off every light but one, as shadows crept inward and mustered all 'round.

Slick with sweat, his mouth dry, Harlow wiped his palms on his denims, then cocked the .44.

With a trembling hand he reached for the last lamp . . . and hesitated.

Come on, Harlow. It's you with the gun and the goggles. You can get this punk.

His lungs heaving, Harlow clicked off the last lamp.

Blackness pitched into the room.

Jesus Jesus, I can't— The thing—

Biting back a cry, Harlow jerked the goggles down over his eyes and slapped on the night-vision power. The light amplifier bloomed on, and Harlow could see—

God I can see!

—in a limited cone of vision, the greenish images ghostly. But he could see.

With the cocked .44 thrust out before him, Harlow jerked his head this way and that, looking for, seeking . . . what? He did not know. Whatever it was. The *thing*.

"C-come on, asshole!" he cried, his voice high, strained. "M-motherfucker!"

Left, right, he swept his tunnel vision.

And then he knew—

My God, it's behind me!

—and he jerked about to see—

Harlow reeled back, his bowels and bladder loosing, the gun falling from his hand to strike the floor, the thunderous explosion lost under terrified screams as he shrieked and shrieked and shrieked. . . .

When the taxi pulled away in the crisp October night, Gloria, twenty-two, picked up her cheap suitcase and followed the silver-haired man into the elegant manse. With a faint clicking throughout, light flooded the foyer and the rooms beyond, both upstairs and down. Maxon turned to the healthy young lady, a predatory grin on his cadaverous face, and he said, "Your great-uncle was a most peculiar man, Miss Willoughby, and you are the last in his line."

William Peter Blatty

ELSEWHERE

Is there anyone out there who hasn't heard of The Exorcist? *Though an Oscar sits on Bill Blatty's mantel for the screenplay to the movie version, it will always be the book that stands out in my mind: without benefit of a screen, William Peter Blatty flat out scared the crap out of me—and millions of others. In the process, he also, along with Ira Levin, cracked open the commercial fiction door to allow horror fiction in. This is the same door that Stephen King would kick in a few years later.*

What many readers may not know is that Blatty (who received the Stoker Award for Lifetime Achievement in 1998) had a distinguished career in the movies before The Exorcist, *producing screenplays for such films as* What Did You Do in the War, Daddy? *and* A Shot in the Dark.

After the success of The Exorcist, *he continued his film success, writing and eventually directing (*"Killer" Kane *and* The Exorcist III*); he also continued to produce fiction, which brings us to the stunning piece that follows.*

It is not only fitting but just that we end a book like this with a new short novel from William Peter Blatty. Elsewhere *is a slick, extremely well written, unsettling, and at times terrifying haunted house story; it also evidences the sly and sophisticated humor that is Blatty's hallmark. I was very lucky to obtain it for you—you're even luckier to read it.*

I was with a tribe on Mount Elgon, in East Africa. . . . During a palaver, I incautiously uttered the word *selelteni,* which means "ghosts." Suddenly a deathly silence fell on the assembly. The men glanced away, looked in all directions, and some of them made off.

CARL JUNG, *Psychology and the Occult*

Once I was afraid of dying. Now what I fear are the dead.

Why did I come to this place? Was it loneliness? Pride? The money? The creak of the floors, the color of the air, all things are a terror to me here. The house is bright, my companions amusing; why do I find myself thinking in whispers? Is it merely that the dark is coming on? I doubt it; I have touched the other side many times, it's my business. But this time it's different: something is wrong, something unfixable, like an ancient grief, like hell.

The rain has finally stopped, there's the sun, hate-red and breathing silent at the rim of the world. I ask why I'm frightened? Listen! Voices. Whispers. They're coming from the walls. Inside them.

Jesus save me from this night!

From the Diary of Anna Trawley, Tuesday, 8:22 P.M.

PART ONE

Chapter One

A pale pink telephone wedged at her chin, Joan Freeboard edgily stood at her desk while she rustled through message slips, frowning and impatient, as if searching for the one that would explain why she'd been born. A second line began to flash. She eyed it.

"Yeah, I know you already said you're coming," she scolded in a petulant, husky voice; in her accent one heard organ grinders strolling through the tenements, the flapping of a wash hung out to dry upon a roof. "So what? You need constant reminding, Terry," she hounded. "You remember what night and what time?"

She listened, pursed her lips, then tossed the slips to her desk. "I knew it. Write it down: Friday night at six o'clock. And remember, don't bring the freaking dogs!"

She punched into the flashing line.

"Yeah, Freeboard."

She wrinkled up her nose in distaste.

"Harry?"

Freeboard shifted her weight and fiddled with an earring, a southwestern dangle of stone and blue beads. Thirty-four, she wore short blond hair in bangs and had lost green eyes in a Kewpie doll face that masked a will with the grip of gravity. She lifted an incredulous eyebrow. "Co-list a contemporary in Greenwich, Harry? Are you out of your freaking *mind*? Ever since that cookbook lady bought a Tudor all the yuppies ever want there is something 'authentic,' meaning dark and depressing and falling all to shit. Look, you go and get the cookbook lady to build herself a house made out of glass, something round or triangular or shaped like a saucer and looks like it probably *landed* in Greenwich and then maybe after that we can talk, okay? So what else? Make it quick would you please? I'm in a hurry."

A middle-aged secretary quietly entered, despondent, her hair in a bun, just divorced. Freeboard handed her the copy for an ad, mouthing *"Times."* The secretary nodded and drooped away. Freeboard watched her with pity and then spoke into the phone. "No, Thursday's bad for me, Harry," she said grimly. "How about never? Is never good for you?" She crashed the pink telephone down on its cradle. "Dumb, boring, arrogant shithead!" she told it. "I've already screwed you! Why in shit would you think I'd want to screw you *again*?"

She snatched up her jacket and purse from a chair, told the secretary "Take a long lunch today, Millie," and strode out into the windowed Trump Tower arcade and then out to Fifth Avenue and its bustle, its squalls of stalled traffic in shadowed May. From the curbside she hailed a Yellow Cab and got into it.

"Where to?"

Freeboard hesitated, staring straight ahead. Something had found her. What was it? Some vague premonition. Of what? And what had she dreamed last night? she wondered.

"Where we goin'?"

"Somewhere else," Freeboard murmured.

"Somewhere else?"

She came back, and her dimpled chin jutted up slightly, as if with a child's defiance and grit. "Seven-seventy East River Drive," she commanded. The cab and her thoughts lurched forward into gridlock, into the patterned sleep of her life.

"This is it," she said assuredly half an hour later.

She was standing in a slowly ascending construction elevator with a couple from Hinsdale, Illinois, who were searching for a condo in Manhattan. Quiet, staring down at the elevator floor, they wore red hard hats over thoughtful expressions and hair that was white as the Arctic fox. Freeboard adjusted her own hard hat and finished, "You can't get newer than this."

The elfin elevator operator nodded. Stooped, middle-aged, looking older than his years, he wore a floppy and torn old gray wool sweater and was missing both his upper and lower front teeth. "Best views," he grunted gummily. "Yeah. Ya see everythin'—the Williamsboig Bridge, the whole river. Sly Stallone is gonna take a place here. I seen him yestiddy."

The building soared breathless above the East River. The couple wanted "new"; they had seen enough "old"—apartments for sale by their current occupants. "Why is it," the husband had grumbled, "that in all of these terribly expensive apartments, every room where a guest might go looks great, but you walk into any other room, like the kitchen, and the place looks like the embryo ward in *Alien*." Across from the Museum of Natural History, the master bedroom of a luxury apartment had only a single illumination, a naked bulb suspended by a wire coiling down from a crumbling and smoke-stained ceiling; in another a shower stall was situated in the middle of a bedroom wall: the occupant was using it to store women's shoes; and later, in the chic and stately Dakota, the walls of an apartment the couple had inspected were completely covered over by massive paintings of nude men and women looking earnest and absorbed while engaged in injecting themselves with drugs.

"Oh, well, they could be diabetics," the wife had noted kindly.

"You smell real good."

Freeboard turned a dead gaze to the elevator operator. He was eyeing her with grudging surmise. "Peach bubble bath," Freeboard told him inscrutably. The scent wafted up from her neck.

"Nice earrings," the operator nodded.

"Thanks."

"Hey, Eddie, come *on,* fer chrissakes! *Hold up!*"

An irritated workman was pounding on a door as the elevator creakily lurched up past him. The diminutive operator called down loudly, "You guys all smell like crap! You stink! I got real nice people with me here!"

The workman's voice rumbled up in a guttural threat:

"You're gonna pay for this, Eddie, you fuck!"

The couple from Hinsdale liked the apartment. Then something extraordinary occurred: standing at a window and breathing in plaster dust as she absently stared at a motor launch plowing white furrows in the murk of the river, Joan Freeboard, relentless pursuer of escrows, indomitable Realtor of the Year many times, whirled around to the couple and asked impulsively, "Are you sure you want to live in the city? It's mean and it's dirty and crowded and ugly."

What the hell am I saying? thought the Realtor, aghast.

She glanced at the launch again. Something about it. What? She wrinkled her brow. She didn't know. She turned back to the couple and struggled to recover:

"How about a contemporary in Greenwich?"

The strangeness pursued her. Later in the day, the deal done, papers signed, Freeboard found herself walking to Manhattan's last Automat, where she sat at a speckled-beige table with a heaping plate of steaming white rice and baked beans, stirred and mixed them together and ate them ravenously. For her drink she'd taken wedges of lemon that were meant for iced tea from an open bin, squeezed the juice into a glass filled with ice and cold water and now added sugar from a shaker on the table, just as she had done in her impoverished teens. The rice and beans filled her warmly now. Had they not she might have filled an empty bowl with hot water, added salt and gobs of catsup from the bottle on her table, then stirred it to smoothness: tomato soup. Why am I doing this? she wondered. She looked over at the banks of small-windowed compartments of food that would unlock when fed coins through a slot. She was searching for the hot apple pie with rum sauce. Once a March wind had blown a dollar to her chest and that was the day she'd been able to afford it. Where was it? Perhaps she had room for one bite.

"You come here often?"

Freeboard shifted her glance to the homeless bum now seated across from her like a curse. His greasy gray hair flowed down to his shoulders and he wore an old oversized army overcoat, a soiled denim shirt and khaki pants.

"Ya look like an actress. Ever done any actin'? I'm a castin' agent," the bum asserted. He smelled of stale wine and the air of packing crates and of doorways and steamy grates. A big toe poked up through a hole in his sneaker. The nail needed clipping.

"Also a producer," he added urbanely.

"Yeah, right, you remind me of David O'Selznick."

"Remind? Who the hell ya think you're talkin' to, kiddo? Show a little respect here, okay? Show some class. I see ya ain't got no money for food. I could help you."

"You look like you could use a little help yourself."

Something stirred in the old bum's eyes, some buried recollection of another life. He leaned in to Freeboard, his jaw jutting forward. "It ain't over," he defied her, "till the fat lady sings."

Stifling a smile of rue and compassion, the realtor looked down into her blue leather purse, plucked out something from her wallet and slid it across the beige table to the bum.

"I think you must have dropped this, Mr. O'Selznick."

It was a one-hundred-dollar bill.

"A C-note!"

Freeboard stood up and she turned to leave.

"Just a second," said the bum.

The realtor looked back at him.

"I charge *two* hundred dollars for interviews."

Freeboard nodded, appraising him fondly, as if she had met a kindred spirit. An image of her alcoholic father flashed to mind, harshly slapping at her six-year-old's face until it purpled. *"You gonna do what I tell you now, bitch?" "No!"* "Attaway, old champ," approved the Realtor. "Go get 'em. Don't ever let the bastards get you down, keep on fighting." Then she turned and prided out into the jostling street where the rumble of trucks, the gasp of buses braking, and the strident honking of horns and the dreams, the hurts, the spites, the fears, the schemes of the hellbent crush of pedestrians rushing for their trains hit her psyche like a wave that washed away from her mind all clouds, all webs, all thoughts that had nattered at its edge, unfocused, and recharged her with the energy that made her Joan Freeboard, child-woman on the make, do or die.

Do or die.

That night in her penthouse on Central Park West, the only sound was the scuffing of soft leather slippers over wide-planked polished oaken floors as the Realtor, in a belted forest-green bathrobe, pensively wandered from room to room mulling over a curious proposition that had walked her way a few days before:

"Did I hear you say twenty *percent?"*

"You did."

"What's the catch?"

"My clients want the best. That's you."

"But you told me nothing's happened there for years."

"Nothing has."

"So then put it on a multiple and lower the price. What's the problem?"

"The problem is the house's reputation. Dark memories die slowly, Mrs. Freeboard."

"Miss."

"Miss. Think it over, would you please?"

"Yeah, I will."

Freeboard drifted to a small, round, white-pine table in the corner of her cherrywood-paneled study. On the table was a map, some printed sheets, a brochure, and several photos of a massive mansion crouched upon an island in the Hudson River. Freeboard slipped her hand into a pocket of her robe, withdrew a lighter and a package of Camel Lites. She lit one, dragged deeply, and picked up a photo, then she exhaled smoke and shook her head. No way, it's a waste of time, she lamented; this screwed-up house is straight out of *Dark Shadows.* Brooding and oblong, made of gray stone, it was gabled and crenelated like an old Scottish castle, like Glamis, and here and there a sinister conical tower rose up like an eruption of evil thought. Freeboard sighed and let the photo flutter back to the table, where it landed with a soft, thin, papery click. Too bad this piece of shit's not in Greenwich, she dismally mused; I could sell it for a fortune in a week. Yet she lingered by the table, picking at the photos, tantalized, drawn by this challenge to her boredom. Only You, Dick Daring, she reflected; right? At the edge of her consciousness she heard the crackle of her answering machine, her recorded announcement, a pause and then a hangup. Harry, she thought. She shook her head. Then her glance shifted over to a black leather folder containing the history of the house. She'd only skimmed it; since her youth she'd been afflicted with a mild dyslexia, a gift of brutal beatings by her alcoholic father, undernourishment, and long and frequent absences from school. Reading was arduous for her, a defeat. An assistant handled writing up most of her contracts. All she knew about the house was what she'd been told: that it was built in 1937 by a doctor who murdered his wife in some horrible fashion and immediately afterwards killed himself.

She picked up the folder. On the cover in large white letters was a word that she could read without strain: "ELSEWHERE." And abruptly she remembered a fragment of her dream: a strange place. Some peril. Someone trying to save her, some luminous being, like an angel, like Clarence in *It's a Wonderful Life.* In the dream he had told her his name, something memorable; now she strained to recall it but couldn't.

The phone and then the click of the answering machine. She tilted her head to the side a bit, listening. Not Harry: Elle Redmund, the wife of James Redmund, celebrated publisher of *Vanities Magazine*: ". . . awfully cheeky of me, really, but this friend of ours has popped into town for the night, and we'd both rather *die* or go to France with Club Med or some such thing than miss out on your fabulous party. Would you mind if we . . . ?"

Freeboard dropped the folder to the table, stubbed out her cigarette, lit another, then returned to her brow-creasing, thoughtful pacing, randomly scuffing from room to room like a chain-smoking wraith condemned to this vigil in a well-appointed, rent-controlled corridor of hell. About her were no photographs, no traces of a personal history, of affection or of unhappy times; but now and then she would pause in front of a painting, a small Monet or a Picasso miniature, not admiring its beauty or its craft but only taking wan comfort in the knowledge of its cost. Then again she would wander and puff and think until at last she grew weary and fell into her downy-soft four-poster bed, where she lay staring up at her mirrored ceiling groping for a way to solve the puzzle of the house. Once she heard an elevator cage clatter open, then a front door key slipping into the lock; Antonia and George, her live-in help, coming back from an evening off. She sighed and turned over. It's a bitch but you can whip it, she brooded. *Think!* She soon fell asleep. And dreamed of her father, drunk and naked, chasing her high school date down the street. Then she dreamed of the angel again. He was winged and tall and magnificent, but his face was an ovoid blank. In the dream she was waiting for a table at the Palm, a narrow little steak house on Manhattan's East Side, and the angel was attentively taking an order from a young and beautiful dark-eyed woman when abruptly he looked up and met Freeboard's gaze and warned, "Take the train. The clams aren't safe." "What the hell is your name?" the puzzled Realtor had shouted at him then and at that she was suddenly awake. She groaned and peered over at her digital clock. It was six A.M. *Forget it. Too early.* She lay back and stared up at the mirrored ceiling. "The clams aren't safe?" she puzzled. What was *that*? Moments later her thoughts curled back to the mansion. The agent in charge of the owners' affairs had explained how she could see it at any time.

She abruptly sat up. Today would be the day.

Comfortable in jeans, western boots and white sweater, Freeboard drove her green Mercedes Cabriolet with the top down across the George Washington Bridge and then north along the Hudson to Craven's Cove, a tiny and sparsely populated village, and from there she took a motor launch across to the island. At the wheel of the boat was its sole crew and owner, a taciturn, slender man in his sixties with brine-wrinkled skin and squinting eyes that were the pale bluish gray of a faded seashell. As they chugged through the mists of the morning river, he squinted at the mansion and asked "You gonna live there?" Freeboard couldn't hear him. There was wind and the engine's whiskey growl. She cupped a hand to her ear, raised her voice, and asked, *"What?"*

"I said, you gonna *live* there?"

For a moment she stared into those faded denim eyes, then glanced up at the stitching on the old salt's nautical cap and the name of the boat: FAR TRAVELER. She turned back to the mansion.

"No."

When they docked, the old ferryman remained on the launch, lighting up a briar pipe while he leaned against a rail and watched Freeboard as she clumped down the dock's old planks and then entered a shadowy grove of great oaks until at last he couldn't see her anymore. She troubled him. He didn't know why.

The Realtor followed a gravel path that snaked through the wood about a tenth of mile and led her directly to the front of the house. Beside the front door she found a Realtor's lockbox, expertly twiddled the combination, extracted a key, and then turned for a look at her wider surroundings. Past the woods she caught a glimpse of a shoreline and beach next to waters breathing placid and shallow and clear, and beyond, in a shimmer of sun and haze, gleamed the jutting and sprawling skyline of Manhattan, looming tall and commanding and implacably unhaunted. She peered up at the mansion's forbidding hulk. *Very good,* she thought, satisfied. *It's not staring back. So far the fucking house has done nothing wrong.*

The river's breath caught a bright green scent from the trees, smelling sweet, and the earth and sky were quiet. Freeboard heard the soft rippling sound of her key slipping over the metal serrations of the door lock. She turned, pushed inward and entered the house.

She was standing in a gracious, vaulted entry hall. Beyond a pair of oak doors that stood open, she beheld a huge Great Room ghostly with furnishings bulging and misshapen under white slipcovers meant to guard them from dust and the beat of the sun. The owner—the heir to the original builder—and his family, a wife and two very young children, had been living in Florence for the past three years, and the house, though available for sale or lease, had during that time remained untenanted. No one would buy it or live there. "Haunted."

With a lazy gait, lips puckered judiciously, Freeboard ambled into the room and then stopped with her hands on her hips and looked around. The room's high ceiling was heavily beamed in the crisscross style of an old Spanish mission, and in the middle of a wall a huge firepit yawned. The Realtor moved forward, her boot heels thudding on the random-width planks of a hickory floor as she prowled through the room pulling covers off the furnishings, and when she'd finished she found herself surprised: filled with groupings of overstuffed sofas and chairs that were upholstered in homey and reassuring paisleys, the room was a warm invitation to life that included a game table, stereo equipment, and an eight-foot Steinway, gleaming and inviting, as down upon all, from the high gabled windows, shafted columns of relentlessly cheerful sunlight like the fiery blessings of a bothersome saint. *So where's Christopher Lee and the freaking Fangettes?* Freeboard glanced to her left and a cozy bar in a fireplaced library bristling with books, and then sauntered past a wide and curving staircase that led up to several bedrooms off a second-floor hall. Then she paused as she noticed that there was an alcove tucked like a secret under the stairs. She walked over and discovered there, lost in shadow, an arched ornamental oaken door that had carved into its center, like an ugly threat, an icily unsettling gargoylish face whose mouth gaped open in a taut and malevolent grin and with eyes bulging wide with rage.

Freeboard stared back and uttered quietly, "Asshole."

She gripped the brass doorknob and attempted to open the door but discovered that she couldn't. It was locked.

Ping.

A faint sound tinged the silence behind her, something like the muted single note of a piano. She turned around slowly and stared at the Steinway, half expecting to see someone sitting at the keys. There were several other wings to the house, she'd been told, including quarters and a separate kitchen for staff. There might have been a caretaker somewhere about. But there was no one there, she saw. She was alone. She walked to the piano and lifted the keyboard cover, and then, leaning over with a grin, began to play "Put on a Happy Face" as she looked all around and then called out loudly, "This is for you, you crazy house!"

Then she stopped and stared pensively.

"But what do we do to make someone come and see you?"

The house did not answer.

Fine. Be that way.

She drove back to Manhattan lost in ponder, gave the car to her doorman, rode up to her apartment, let herself in and went straight to her study, where she sat and began to tug off her boots.

"Evening, Madam."

Antonia, the maid, had come in.

"You are going out for dinner, Missus?"

"No. I'll eat at seven."

"Very good."

"Tell George to fix me a Cajun martini, would you, Tony?"

"Yes, Missus. Something else?"

Freeboard finished tugging off a boot, dropped it, and then scrutinized the housekeeper carefully, frowning. "You look tired. You've got bags. Are you sleeping okay?"

"Not so good."

"Are you worried about something?"

"No, Missus."

"You sure, Tony?"

"Yes. I am sure."

"I think maybe you're working too hard."

The housekeeper diffidently shrugged and looked away.

"You and George take the day off tomorrow, Antonia."

"Oh, no, Missus!"

"*Yes*, Missus. You do what I say. And you know, I don't feel like much dinner. Just a sandwich. Okay? Just whatever. And would you make that martini a double?"

"Very good, Missus. Yes. Right away."

Dainty in her blue-and-white housemaid's uniform, the middle-aged housekeeper padded away. Freeboard stared at her back with concern. She finished pulling off the other boot, let it drop to the floor, then stretched her legs out and wriggled her toes.

My God, does that feel good!

Staring softly into nothingness, she thought of the mansion again. And then stopped. *Yeah, let's give it a rest.* She leaned her head back on the chair and closed her eyes. Then heard the click of the answering machine coming on. The publisher's wife again, Elle Redmund. "Hello, darling, did you get my other message? Well, never mind; it turns out that our visitor isn't coming after all. Thanks anyway, Joanie. We'll see you Friday night."

Another click.

For a time there was silence and shallow breathing. And then suddenly Freeboard's eyes opened wide as, in one of those mysterious events of the spirit wherein the unconscious broods upon data, draws conclusions, then presents them to the mind as inspiration, she experienced a sudden, overwhelming revelation.

There it was! That was it! She knew how to sell the house!

"Your martini, Missus Freeboard."

"Thanks, Tony. Tell George it looks perfect."

"Yes, Missus."

Freeboard took the glass but did not drink. She was plotting.

Not every epiphany originates in grace.

Freeboard's party that Friday was lively and crowded, crammed with playwrights, politicians and corporate executives, models and socialites and Mafiosi, anyone who'd ever bought a property from her. For the space of half an hour the hostess was nowhere to be found, nor was her publisher guest, James Redmund. When Freeboard reappeared among her guests, she seemed pleased.

Step One of her plan had been completed.

On the following Thursday, five days later, the renowned British psychic, Anna Trawley, sat by a fire while she sipped at tea in the den of her Cotswold cottage in England when a message arrived from a total stranger, an American Realtor named Joan Freeboard. Her little face a cameo, delicate and pale, Trawley, in her forties, had a quiet beauty and her small and limpid chestnut eyes glowed faintly with some distant but ineffable sadness on which they seemed constantly inward turned. Beside her on a small, square teakwood table waited mail and a fresh-smelling copy of the *Times,* and on a paneled wall hung a few remembrances: a photo of herself with the Queen; a newspaper headline NOTED PSYCHIC FINDS KILLER; and a photo of a child, a pretty, dimpled young girl who, in the blur of retouching and tinting over the black-and-white photo with pastel colors, seemed lost in some other dimension of time. Beneath an open window lay a plastic Ouija board upon a table with two facing chairs.

"Mum?"

Trawley turned to the girl who had entered, her pretty, young maid, newly hired. "Peta?"

She was holding out a small, round silver tray. Trawley absently stared at a deep white scar tucked into the maid's right eyebrow for a moment, wondering what painful event it commemorated and whether it had happened by chance; then she lowered her gaze to the offered tray. Upon it, in a square dull yellow envelope, lay a cablegram and a message that, by a path at once straight yet labyrinthine—depending on the viewer, man or God—would bond Trawley's destiny forever to Joan Freeboard's.

"Thank you, Peta."

"Yes, mum."

The maid quietly walked out. Trawley picked up the envelope, slipped out its contents and saw that the cable ran on for six pages. She read them and then rested the papers in her lap, put her head back on the chair and closed her eyes. A sudden breeze sprang up from the wooded outdoors that ruffled the white lace curtains of the window, and below them, perhaps pushed by the brief, sharp gust, the coned glass planchette that had rested on the Ouija board slid from the center of the board to the top, and there it rested directly on a word.

The word was *no*.

Chapter Two

"I've been dead for eight months, just in case you hadn't noticed." Tall and Byronic, urbane, aristocratic, Terence Dare swabbed his brush at a yellow on the palette and then dabbed at the canvas propped before him in the sunlit, high-ceilinged, pitched-roof studio of his Fire Island home. "Ever since Robert walked out of my life," he mourned in a rich and cultivated voice. "No, I can't write a word," he sighed. "I've no heart."

"Shit shit shit!" muttered Freeboard. *"Shit!"*

Dare wiped a spatter of red from his finger onto the painter's smock that he wore above a T-shirt and faded black denim jeans and then shifted a hooded blue gaze to the Realtor, who was smoking and pacing back and forth in agitation, the echoing clacks of her spike-heeled shoes on the oaken floor bouncing up to a skylight. She swatted at a haze of grayish smoke in her path.

"It's the cover of *Vanities,* Terry! The *cover!*"

"Let me get this straight," said the world-famous author: "James Redmund repels you, he's a prig and a bore and is also among that elite corps of rectums who are constantly telling us how much they love a challenge, as if living on a spinning rock hurtling through the void dodging asteroids and comets weren't challenge enough, not to mention tornadoes, death and disease as well as Vlad the Impaler and earthquakes and war, but you laid him anyway?"

"I told you, it was business."

"Are you shtupping for the Mafia now, my precious, and no longer, as usual, for all of mankind?"

"Oh, fuck you, Terry."

"Darling, thousands have tried; only hundreds have succeeded."

Looking chic in her navy Armani suit, the Realtor stopped pacing and coughed into her fist. "Gotta quit," she resolved, her eyes smarting and teary. She clattered to a table where she stubbed out her cigarette in a large white seashell ashtray. "Look, I told you, they don't run this kind of stuff. Not normally."

"No, not normally," Dare said inscrutably.

"He's the publisher; he does what he wants."

She kept crushing and tamping the burnt-out butt.

"When and where did you commit this unspeakable act?"

Freeboard flopped down into a chair by a window, crossed her arms and stared sulkily at the author. "Jesus, Terry, you could write it in a week."

"When and where?" Dare persisted.

"At the dinner party Friday. In my bathroom."

"In your *bathroom*?"

She gave a little shrug.

"It's okay. We ran the water real loud."

The author appraised her as if he were measuring the distance to a star. In her small green eyes set close together he could find no trace of blush or guile; their expression was just as he had always observed it to be, which was blank and vaguely expectant. It was as if she were eternally awaiting further comment. Her soul is a wide-open window, he reflected; she's as simple and direct as a shopping cart.

"You could write the fucking thing in an *hour*."

And more tenacious than the grip of a deep tattoo.

"Now let's see if this is right . . ." Dare started expressionlessly.

She looked away and rolled her eyes. "You always do this."

"You've been offered the exclusive listing on Elsewhere," he reviewed, "but the problem, it would seem, is that it's haunted and—"

"It's no such thing! Nothing's happened there in years! I mean it's just that it's got this shitty-creepy reputation."

The winner of a Pulitzer Prize for Literature stared numbly.

"Shitty-creepy?"

"So okay, I'm not a writer."

"You're a criminal. You've lined up Anna Trawley, the world-famous psychic; the renowned Dr. Gabriel Case of NYU, *the* authority in all such matters, smile-smirk; the four of us then spend a few nights in the house, and while Trawley and Case take baths in the vibes and discover nothing ghostly or unusual whatever, I observe, making copious notes, of course, and then I write a little shitty-witty article about it that thoroughly debunks the idea that it's haunted; your pipe-smoking bathroom incubus prints it, the house's reputation is now Caesar's wife and you sell it and get filthier rich than ever. Does that sum it up fairly, my Angel of the Closings?"

"I've been offered a triple commission on this, Terry. That's seven fucking figures."

"Must we really use the eff word so incessantly?"

"We must!"

"Then might we please pronounce it 'fyook' or something, precious? I mean, really."

Aloofly, he turned and examined the painting, a swirling mélange of varied shades of vivid yellow. Freeboard leaped up from her chair and approached him. "You owe me, Terry!"

Dare lifted his brush to paint.

"Now it comes, the deadly rocket attack on my guilt."

"You're *denying* that you owe me?"

"Sigmund Freud would have killed for your gifts."

She planted herself in front of him and folded her arms across her chest. "You're *denying* it?"

He looked down at his bright red Nike tennis shoes and then shook his head and sighed. "No, I owe you," he admitted. "I owe you immensely. You've always been there for me on the Dawn Patrol, all those endless, awful nights when I needed a shoulder that I knew wasn't padded with secret envies and lies and spites." His eye caught a glistening blue on his palette. "You're steadfast and loyal and completely unexpected, my Joan; you're the only living human that I trust. Still, I'll have to disappoint you on this, I'm afraid."

"For godssakes, it's just a magazine article, Terry! You could have a broken heart and still write a freaking *article,* couldn't you!"

He looked up at her with quiet incredulity.

"I mean, it's not like a book or something!"

"No, it's not like a book," he said tonelessly.

"What's that look for?"

"What look?"

"*That* look."

"I am probing for the source of your feral cunning."

"Meaning what? What does *feral* mean?"

"Anything relating to the national government."

Glaring, he turned back to the canvas and painted.

"Oh, was that some kind of faggoty joke?"

"As you like it."

"Come on, Terry, quit kidding around and do the piece."

"I would love to but it's simply not possible."

"Even though this freaking deal means the world to me?"

"Yes."

"And all because of some weight-lifting wannabe model you picked up in the park feeding steroids to the pigeons? I'm not getting this, Terry; I'm not getting this at all."

"My dear Joanie, there is more to this matter than Robert," sighed the author. Freeboard watched him intently, frowning; there was something evasive in his manner and his voice. "In fact, there's a *great* deal more," Dare asserted.

"Yeah, like what?"

"Well, just more."

"What more? Come on, what? Be specific."

"It's just writing itself."

"What about it?"

"I've given it up forever."

Freeboard clutched at her forehead and cried out, *"Fyook!"*

"It's too hard, love," Dare told her, "too many decisions. 'Had a wonderful day,' it says in Oscar Wilde's diary: 'I inserted a comma, removed it, then decided to reinsert it.' Joanie, writing is dross."

"I'm not believing this, Terry!"

"It is mental manual labor. As of now, I consider myself a painter."

Freeboard's frustrated glance darted over to the canvas, swiftly taking in its spiraling yellow meanderings. Her eyes narrowed in dismal surmise.

"What the hell is this supposed to be, Terry?"

"Lemons Resting."

She reached out and grabbed the brush from his hand, looking worried. "Are you dropping LSD again, Terry?"

"Oh, don't be so silly," Dare sniffed.

"No more camels in cheap orange taffeta dresses who swear they're Jehovah's Witnesses sneaking in the house at night to talk about your books?"

"You haven't even a shred of common decency, have you?"

"No, I don't."

"And all of this because I've given up writing?"

"Yeah yeah yeah: first it's Robert and a broken heart and then writing is a pain in the ass and you're Picasso. This is sounding like bullshit to me, Terry. Are you scared? You believe in stupid ghosts, for chrissakes?"

"That's absurd!"

Dare's cheeks glowed pink. He recovered the brush and turned back to his canvas. "Look, the fact of the matter, if you really want to know, is that I simply couldn't bear to go away and leave the dogs."

"Now I *know* this is bullshit."

"It isn't," Dare insisted.

"You'd ruin my life for those two little fucks?"

Dare turned and glared down at her stonily. "Am I to presume that by 'those two little fucks' you are referring to those sweetest, most refined toy poodles, Pompette and Maria-Hidalgo LaBlanche?"

Freeboard glared back, her face inches from his chest.

"So bring them with us."

"I beg your pardon?"

"Bring them with us. Bring the dogs."

"Bring the dogs?"

Something faintly like panic edged his voice.

"Yeah, we'll bring 'em."

"No, it simply wouldn't work."

"It wouldn't work?"

"No, it wouldn't."

"Why not?" Freeboard asked him.

"I don't know."

"You don't know? You're scared shitless, you literary asshole! Do you sleep with a nightlight, you flaming fyook?"

"*Fyook* has never been a noun," Dare said coldly.

"Yes, it is," shot back Freeboard.

"Poor usage. Furthermore, your vile and repellent accusations, Miss Whoever You Are, are absurd if not pathetic."

"Are they true?"

The author flushed.

"Why don't you find some other writer, for heaven's sakes!" he whined. "My God, Joanie, *Vanities* can get you your pick!"

"Well, they picked."

" 'They picked'? What on earth do you mean?"

They were sitting at a window table for two in the Hotel Sherry Netherland bar. It was not quite five o'clock and the tables on either side were still empty. "Hold it," said Freeboard. She was groping through a briefcase. "There's a really spooky picture of the house. Let me find it." Troubled and distracted, the publisher of Vanities *darted an apprehensive glance at the door as he heard another patron coming in from the street. It was no one that he knew, he saw with relief. Nervously tapping the stem of an unlit briar pipe against his teeth, he shifted his fretful gaze back to Freeboard. "Four of us alone in a haunted house," she effused, "and Terry's first magazine piece ever!"*

A waiter placed a chilled Manhattan cocktail softly on the crisp white tablecloth in front of her, and then a glass of chardonnay in front of Redmund. "Chardonnay, sir?"

"Right," murmured Redmund. "Thanks." In his eyes, open wide and faintly bulging, an incipient hysteria quietly lurked. When the waiter had gone

he leaned his head in to Freeboard. "Don't you think we should talk about what happened at the party?"

"Oh, what happened?" Freeboard responded absently, still groping through her purse for the photos. And then abruptly looked up with a stunned realization. "Oh, what happened!" Her hands flew to Redmund's, squeezing them ardently. "Oh, yes, Jim! That's all I want to talk about, think about! Come on, let's get this article out of the way and then we can get back to real life, to us! Do you like it? You'll publish it?"

"It's interesting, Joan," observed Redmund.

Freeboard let go of his hands, leaned back, and then folded her arms and looked away. "Yeah, right."

She knew very well what "interesting" meant.

"But it really isn't right for us," Redmund pleaded. "Joan, look . . . The other night was incredible."

"Sure."

"Just amazing. More exciting than anything I think I've ever known."

"Yeah, me too," Freeboard murmured. She was dully staring at the decorative fountain directly across from the Plaza Hotel.

"But it was wrong, love, we made a mistake," Redmund faltered. "I thought it all over today while I was jogging and . . ."

Freeboard turned to stare at him in blank surmise.

"Well, I could never leave my wife," said the publisher firmly. "I just couldn't. This is taking us nowhere, Joanie. If I didn't tell you now there'd be a lot more pain down the line. I'm sorry. I'm so terribly sorry."

The Realtor continued to stare at him numbly, her eyes growing wider in disbelief.

"You're sorry," she echoed.

He gloomed into his drink.

"Yes, I know; that's a lame word, isn't it—sorry."

Redmund heard a single, stifled sob, looked up and saw Freeboard choking back tears. "Ah, dammit," he fumbled. The Realtor clutched at her linen napkin and held it tightly to her face; she appeared to be weeping into it softly.

"I feel awful . . . horrible," Redmund groped. "Now how do I live in that condo you sold me? I'll be seeing you everywhere . . . in every hallway, every square of parquet."

This seemed to propel the weeping real estate broker to a noticeably higher emotional pitch, although one could not confidently distinguish, with anything approaching absolute certitude, her sudden, soft moan of pain from a desperate attempt to stifle a guffaw. Redmund glanced around to see if anyone was watching them, and then fumbled at emptying his pipe. "Listen, Joanie, that *article; it sounds—well, very challenging. Really. You're certain that Terence would do it?"*

"Redmund won't do it unless you write it," said Freeboard, concluding her account of the meeting.

"You are Liza Doolittle's evil twin."

"Liza Who?"

Dare assessed the avid shine in her eyes, the lower lip jutting out, the dimpled chin tilted upward defiantly. He saw the frightened child inside. "It isn't the money at all, is it Joanie? It's that ravenous tiger burning bright in your soul, that desperate drive to stay ahead, to keep winning, that need to keep proving that you're really okay."

She frowned and looked puzzled. "It isn't the money?"

Abruptly a door from the beach clicked open and into the room bounded two yapping poodles, their claws etching clittering sounds on the floor. They were followed by a clubfooted man in his forties, a houseman Dare had hired years before out of pity.

Freeboard glared at a poodle that had stopped at her feet and was staring at her leg with intense speculation. "Don't even *think* about it," she threatened, "or I'm turning you into a tiny rug."

"Go, Maria! Scott!" Dare warned. "She's a killer! Run! She meant it!" He looked over at the houseman. "Pierre, *sortez les chiens.*"

The houseman nodded and replied. "*Immédiatemont.*" He clapped his hands at the dogs. *"Allez les chiens! Allez sortez! Nous allons dehors!"* The dogs skittered away through an inner door and the houseman followed them, one shoulder low, a shoe clumping.

"This means a whole lot to me, Terry. A lot."

The author turned his leonine head to her and stared. He had bought this very house through Freeboard's offices, it was how he had come to meet her; yet never since that time had she asked him for anything, not even for a copy of one of his books. His celebrity meant nothing to the girl, that he knew; and that, for some reason, she cared for him deeply. He searched her eyes for the secret wounds that he'd learned to detect behind their gleam of self-will.

"A *whole* lot," she repeated.

"And how long would we be there?"

"Five days."

She explained how Dr. Gabriel Case, the psychologist, professor and expert on the subject of hauntings, would precede them to the house with his special equipment and set it all up before they arrived.

Most of their luggage would be sent on ahead, and when Anna Trawley had landed in New York they would all take a limo to Craven's Cove, where the motor launch would carry them across to the island. "Case is making all the arrangements," she finished. "I mean like the phones and utilities and crud."

"How very sporting."

"Yeah, he's neat."

"He's *neat*?"

"Oh, well, at least on the phone. I've never met him."

"You conned him into doing all of this on the *phone*?"

"Come on, Terry, I'm paying him a bundle. Okay?"

"Oh, I see." The author turned stiffly to his painting. "So the fix is in. I should have known."

The Realtor frowned and moved in closer.

"Listen, let's get serious," she said.

"Oh, yes, serious."

"Margoittai is packing all our meals. The whole time we're at the house we'll be eating Four Seasons."

The author's brush stroke froze in midair.

"Ah, Mephistopheles!"

"Is that a yes?"

The year was 1993.

Later on there would be serious doubts about that.

PART TWO

Chapter Three

The carved front door of the mansion burst open as if by the force of a desperate thought. "Holy shit, is this a hurricane or what!" exclaimed Freeboard. Sopping in a glistening yellow sou'wester provided by the captain of the launch *Far Traveler,* she staggered and tumbled into the entry hall with a keening wind at her back. She turned to see Dare rushing up the front stoop, and Trawley, carrying a bag, behind him, slower, deliberate and unhurried. A rain of all the waters of the earth pelted down.

Freeboard cupped a hand to her mouth:

"You okay, Mrs. Trawley?" she squalled.

"Oh, yes, dear!" the psychic called back. "I'm fine!"

A booming thunder gripped the sky by the shoulders and shook it. The sudden storm that had arisen as they crossed had been a terror, buffeting the launch with tempestuous waves. Hurricane warnings had been issued that morning, but the winds had been expected to diminish at landfall. This had not occurred.

Dare entered and dropped a light bag to the floor. "Joan, I owe you a flogging for this," he vowed. "I knew that I never should have done it."

"Well, you did it," Freeboard told him. "Now for shitssakes, watch your mouth around these people, would you, Terry? I had to practically beg them to do this."

"Thank heaven *I* gave you no trouble."

Freeboard lifted off her windjammer hat, and then gestured to the open door, where the psychic seemed to falter as she climbed the front steps. "Terry, give Mrs. Trawley a hand."

"Oh, very well."

Dare giraffed toward the psychic with a limp, loose gait and reached out for her bag. "May I help you?"

"Oh, no thank you. I'm fine. I travel light."

"Yes, of course. Tambourines weigh almost nothing."

"*Jesus,* Terry!"

Trawley entered, swept her hat off and set down her bag. "That's all right," she told Freeboard benignly; "I didn't hear it." In fact, she had heard enough from Dare in the limo, including a request to compare her methods with those of Whoopi Goldberg in the motion picture *Ghost,* in addition to a penetrating follow-up question concerning the cholesterol content of ectoplasm. At each sally, Trawley'd nodded her head and smiled faintly, mutely staring out serenely at the landscape through her window, and the effect of this on Dare had at last begun to show: with every mile that brought him closer to the island and the mansion, his darts at matters psychic or supernatural had grown increasingly frequent and acerbic. "Edgar Cayce reportedly first went into trance," he asserted as the limousine neared Bear Mountain, "as an excuse for not going to school, and when someone claimed a frog that he had kept in his pocket was somehow cured of mononucleosis, why, of course, people tended to sit up and take notice."

Freeboard leaned into the wind and shut the door. In the silence, it was Dare who first noticed the music. "Dearest God, am I in heaven?" he exclaimed. "Cole Porter!" The author's face was aglow with a child's first joy as from behind the stout doors that led into the Great Room drifted a melody played on a piano.

Dare beamed. "My favorite: 'Night and Day'!"

Freeboard moved toward the doors.

"That you in there, Doc?" she called out.

"Miss Freeboard?"

The voice from within was deep and pleasant and oddly unmuffled by the thickness of the doors. Freeboard opened them wide and stepped into the Great Room. All of its lamps were lit and glowing, splashing the wood-paneled walls with life, and in the crackle of the firepit flames leapt cheerily, blithe to the longing in the notes of "Night and Day." Freeboard breathed in the scent of burning pine from the fire. The howlings of the storm were a world away.

"Yeah, we're here!" she called out to the man at the piano. She smiled, moving toward him, while at the same time removing her dripping sou'wester. Behind her strode Dare and, more slowly, Anna Trawley. Freeboard's boots made a squishing sound. They were soaked.

"Ah, yes, there you all are again, safe and sound," said the man at the piano. "I'm so glad. I was worried."

He had strong good looks, Freeboard noticed: long wavy black hair above a chiseled face that seemed torn whole from some mythic quarry. The firelight flickered and danced on his eyes and she saw that they were dark but wasn't sure of their color. She judged him in his forties or perhaps early fifties. He was wearing a short-sleeved khaki shirt and khaki pants.

"This storm is amazing, don't you think?" he exclaimed. "Did you order this weather, Mr. Dare? Are you to blame?"

Dare was noted for his Gothic mystery novels.

"I believe I ordered Chivas," the author said crisply. He and Freeboard had arrived at the piano and stopped while Anna Trawley hung back beside a grouping of furniture that was clustered around the fireplace. She was glancing all around the room with a puzzled and uncertain, tentative air.

"Are you a ghost?"

Dare was speaking to the man at the piano.

Freeboard turned to him, incredulous.

"What crap is this?" she hissed in an irritated undertone.

"That's how they show them on the spook ride at Disneyland," said Dare in a full, firm voice: "A lot of spirits dancing while a big one plays piano."

"I'll strangle your dogs, you little creep!" Freeboard gritted.

Anna Trawley sank down into an overstuffed chair and fixedly stared at the man at the piano. "I'm Gabriel Case," he declared. He stood up. "I'm quite honored that you've come, Mr. Dare. And Mrs. Trawley."

"Oh, please don't stop playing!" Dare insisted.

"Then I won't."

Case sat down and began to play "All Through the Night." Freeboard stood quietly studying him. His eyes, she now saw, were pitch-black, so that even his casual gaze seemed to pierce, and down from his cheekbone almost to his jaw raced a vivid, deep scar that jagged like lightning. Freeboard heard a muted roll of thunder far away; the rain on the windows was patting more softly now, like a melancholy background for the song.

"So, Miss Freeboard," Case continued. His smile now was brilliant. Like a fucking archangel, the Realtor thought. "I'm so glad to meet the face behind the telephone at last," Case said. "And a lovely face at that, if I may say so."

"How long have you been here?" Freeboard asked.

"Seems forever. What's the matter, Miss Freeboard? You're frowning."

"You don't look like your picture," she said. She moved closer, appraising him intently, looking puzzled. She added, "The one on the back of the book."

"Ghosts and Hauntings?"

Freeboard nodded.

"Yes, they wanted something spooky," he told her, "so they posed me in a very strange light."

"Guess they did."

"I've read all of your works, Mr. Dare," Case effused. "All quite wonderful. Really."

"Thank you."

"My absolute favorite was *Gilroy's Confession*." Case lifted his hands from the keys of the piano. He was looking at Freeboard. "There you go again," he said, not unpleasantly. "What's wrong?"

For once again she was frowning.

"This has happened before," she said oddly.

Case leaned in to her as if he hadn't heard. "What was that?"

"I'm having *déjà vu*," she answered.

"This is neither the time nor the place," snapped Dare.

Case chuckled and Freeboard was bewildered as to why.

The author glanced up at a painting high on the wall above the massive fireplace, a life-sized figure of a man in the dress of a bygone time, perhaps the thirties. Though the rest of the painting had a sharp and rich presence, the face of its subject was milky and occluded, presenting a hazy, oval blank.

"Who's this?" Dare asked.

Case looked up. "Dr. Edward Quandt, the original owner."

"Why on earth is his face like that?" Dare wondered.

In the shadows Trawley looked up at the painting.

Case nodded. "Yes, it's strange," he observed. "Very strange."

"It's the haircut."

Case turned and saw Freeboard staring at him thoughtfully. "Yeah, I think that's it," she went on. "That's what's different. It's the haircut."

"Hello?"

Warm and mysterious, a field of dark flowers, the husky voice floated across the room with the breath of some indefinable emotion, like remembrance of a long-lost summer or of grace.

Case stared past the others. His expression had changed.

"Ah, here's Morna," he said very softly.

Her head slightly angled to the side, as if questioning, a lissome young woman was slowly approaching them, moving with a soft and gliding motion like a figure in the corridors of a dream. Her features were rawboned and rugged, imperfect, with protruding high cheekbones and a large jutting jaw, and yet she gave an effect of sensuality and beauty. She wore a paisley-printed purplish taffeta skirt, a white shirt and a silken red string tie. Set deep in the shadowed gold of her skin, her widely spaced pale green eyes were startling. Case stood up slowly and met her gaze.

"Yes," she said, halting before them. "I have come."

Her long black hair cascaded to her shoulders, smelling of hyacinth and morning. For a moment Case continued to stare. "Morna, these are our guests," he said at last. "Miss Freeboard. Mr. Dare."

"How do you do?" said the girl. Her brief glance took them in.

"And Mrs. Trawley," Case added with a gesture toward the psychic. "Mrs. Trawley is clairvoyant, Morna."

The girl turned and fixed her bright green gaze on Trawley. She held it there for seconds. And then she turned back and slightly nodded. "Yes."

"Morna is my housekeeper," Case explained. "No one else lives on the island, as you know; we're quite isolated here. Morna's kindly volunteered to help out."

"Aren't there people in the town across the way?" asked Dare.

A faint, high note of strain tinged his voice.

"Yes, there are," answered Case, "but . . ."

He hesitated, silently searching their faces.

"But what?" Dare demanded a bit too crisply.

Case took the author's sou'wester from his hands. "Well, you're quite soaked through," he said. "We can talk this all over later on; you know, try to get properly acquainted and all. But for now I'm sure you're anxious to get into dry clothes. Morna, kindly show our friends to their rooms, would you please?"

"Your hair was longer in the picture," said Freeboard. "*That's* the difference." Once again she was fixedly staring at Case.

Case turned to her, smiling a little, and he paused. In his eyes some ambiguous emotion lurked, like a wanly affectionate, patient sadness. He held the Realtor's gaze, then spoke quietly. "Yes."

By late that morning, once again the rain had quickened and Freeboard was pacing back and forth in her room. She had a phone at her ear and kept irritably whipping the cord from her path. Again and again she breathed out, "This is nuts!"

In addition to an attic section and a basement, the mansion's rooms were arranged on three levels. The investigators' rooms were all a-row along a hallway on the second floor overlooking the Great Room. Freeboard's suite was the closest to the staircase. Spacious and airy, it had its own fireplace, a high vaulted ceiling and heavy wood beams, but its only two windows were high and narrow, so that both of the bedside lamps

were turned on, pouring light on a green leather Gucci suitcase wide
open and half emptied out atop the bed, an ornately carved, quilt-covered
wooden four-poster. Freeboard hadn't yet bothered to change her clothes
and was still in her stonewashed shirt and jeans. Once arrived in the
room she'd thought hotly, God we're here! We're really doing it! It's
actually happening! We're here! Manically energized and elated, she had
only taken time to tug off her wet boots and pull on a dry pair of fluffy
white woolen socks. She stopped pacing and wriggled her toes in them
now as she listened to the ringing at the end of the line; hypnotically
regular and low, it seemed distant, as if it were ringing in some other
dimension. Freeboard took the phone from her ear and eyed it, frowning
and squinting in consternation. She'd dialed her office and no one had
answered. And then she'd redialed again and again. On this try she had
counted more than fifty rings. She breathed "Christ!" and then clumped
to an antique desk where she slammed the receiver down into its cradle.
"It's freaking *impossible!*" she vehemently murmured. Hands on her hips,
she stared down at the phone, and for a moment the lamplights flickered
and dimmed before surging back up to their former brightness. Freeboard
peered around the room, her eyes slits, as she grittily murmured, "Don't
try that crap on *me!*"

She heard a sound, a deep rapping from the wall beside the mirror.
Expressionless, she shifted her glance to the spot.

Through the wall came the voice of Dare, low and muffled:

"Are you there?"

"No."

"This wall sounds hollow to me."

"No shit."

"Does your room have any windows?"

"What's it to you?"

"I feel smothered. And I keep hearing creaking sounds."

"Stop walking. It's an old wooden floor."

"You have no heart, bitch."

"No."

There came a single loud rap from the other side.

"This wall is *definitely* hollow," worried Dare.

Freeboard curled in her lips. Her eyes narrowed.

"Goddamit, that's *just* what I was afraid of!"

Grimly, the Realtor strode out into the hallway and up to the
door of the room next to hers, where she grasped the doorknob,
threw the door open, walked in and loudly slammed the door shut
behind her. "Listen here, Too Little, Too Latent," she began.

Dare flinched. He'd been standing with his ear to a wall, a round stone paperweight lifted in his hand. He was clad in a full-length white mink dressing gown.

Freeboard strode across the room and confronted him.

"Do you remember why we're here?" she demanded.

Dare looked down at her haughtily. "To break and enter?"

"We are here to clear this fyooking house's fyooking reputation!" Freeboard snatched the heavy paperweight out of Dare's grasp.

"Knock it off with this rapping and shit!" she warned him. "I thought you were a total nonbeliever!"

"So I am. Can't you see that I was teasing you, precious? And of course you took the bait like a well-famished trout."

"Oh, yeah?"

Dare drew himself up imperiously. "Rest your mind," he said. "I *am* doubt." Then he held out his upturned hand and demanded, "Now would you please be so kind as to return my lucky rock?"

Freeboard hefted the weight. "Where do you want it?"

"I've already set up cameras on timers here and there," explained Case as he added more cream to his coffee. "Please don't trip over them," he cautioned with a smile. He was sitting at the end of an oblong table amid the remains of a savory brunch that had included a bacon-and-onion quiche, prawns sautéed in a coconut mustard sauce, varied jams and assorted pastries and breads. Croissant crumbs speckled the white linen tablecloth and no butter knife was unsmeared. At the opposite end of the table sat Dare, with Freeboard at an angle close beside him, while Trawley sat close to Gabriel Case. The psychic had changed into a gauzy turquoise dress and from her hair a scent of jasmine rose. "I've had all the phones turned on and all that," continued Case. "If you'd like to make a note, the number's 914-2121. Awfully easy to remember. In the meantime, as for now there isn't anything for anyone to do except relax and be terribly observant; and, of course, report anything unusual to me."

The drumming of rain on mullioned windows looking out to a wood filled a momentary silence. Then Dare cleared his throat and looked at Case. "Have you ever caught a ghost on film?"

"No, I haven't."

"Well, that's honest," the author admitted. He nodded.

Case sipped at his coffee and then set down his cup. It made a faint little pewtery sound against the saucer. "Mr. Dare," he said, "I do hope you won't take offense but I'm finding the mask a little bit of a distraction."

"Then perhaps you have Attention Deficit Disorder."

Dare wore a Phantom of the Opera mask.

Freeboard reached over and ripped it from his face.

"Thank you," Dare quietly told her.

"You're welcome."

Freeboard folded her arms across her chest, looked away and shook her head with an exasperated sigh. From a pocket Dare produced a transistorized tape recorder. He set it before him on the table.

"Dr. Case, do you mind if I record this?"

"No, of course not. Good idea. Go right ahead."

The author slid a switch on the side of the recorder and a tiny red light flashed on. "There we are," Dare announced. "You may fire when ready, Master Gridley."

Case put his arms on the table, leaning forward. "Do you all know the history of the house?" He scanned their faces.

"No, I don't," said Trawley. Her voice was barely audible. All through the brunch she had hardly said a word, except in answer to a question about her trip and then another concerning a case she'd been involved in, the search for a missing child in Surrey. Mainly, she'd been fixedly staring at Case.

"It was—"

"Built by Dr. Quandt," Dare finished over Case, "in the middle of the thirties for his beautiful wife, whom he came to believe was being grossly unfaithful, resulting in his promptly and savagely offing her."

"I see you've done your homework, Mr. Dare."

The author shrugged. "All I know is what Joanie has told me."

"Yes, Quandt was a violent man," Case confirmed.

"I'm not surprised," answered Dare. "I think surgeons have violent natures, that's the reason they go into that line of work: normal people couldn't slice another person into bits and moments later eat a double Big Mac with fries."

"No, I agree."

"It's rude," added Dare.

"So it is. However, Quandt was not a surgeon," said Case.

"He wasn't?"

"No, Quandt was a noted psychiatrist."

The author turned a frimmled, cool look to the Realtor.

Freeboard stared back at him defiantly. *"So?"*

"Quandt was also maniacally jealous," Case offered. " 'Physician heal thyself' and all that. She was very much younger and he loved her intensely."

Dare turned back to him. "What was her name?"

"Her name was Riga." Case glanced up at Morna, who had entered from the kitchen and was quietly approaching him with a silver coffee server. As she lowered its spout to refill his cup, Case quickly covered it with his hand. "Oh, no, thank you, my dear. I'm fine."

He looked around. "Someone else?"

"Yes, a little here, please," requested Dare.

Morna moved to his end of the table.

"He met Riga at a music hall," Case resumed. "She was a dancer. Her parents were Romanian immigrants, Gypsies. She was only sixteen."

"Yes, that's young," agreed Dare. He moistened the tip of his finger and placed it on top of a large croissant crumb, pressed gently down, and then lifted the fallen crumb into his mouth. Morna was leaning over his cup. "And so how did he kill her?" Dare asked.

"Suffocation."

Dare emitted a yelp.

Morna gasped, her hand clapped over her mouth. Somehow missing Dare's cup, she had poured hot coffee onto his lap.

"Oh, I'm so sorry!"

Dare dabbed at the stain with his napkin.

"It's all right, love. I mean, really. Nothing to it. Not at all."

"You see, Morna?" said Case. "He forgives you."

She turned and met his odd, steady stare in silence; then she turned back away and uttered softly, "I know." While she filled Dare's cup, her green gaze lifted up and for one intense moment met and held Trawley's.

"We're all fine here now, Morna," Case told her.

She nodded and moved off toward the kitchen.

"Getting back to the history of the house," resumed Case. He laid it out briefly: Built in 1937. Then in 1952 the murder of Riga and the death of Quandt himself minutes afterwards, apparently by his own hand. Ownership passed to a son, Regis Quandt, aged twelve when the tragedy occurred, and taken to live with Quandt's brother, Michael. Regis died when he was only twenty, mansion ownership passed to Michael and then finally to Michael's son, Paul Quandt. Meantime, the mansion had been put up for sale, but without success, and in 1954, and over the course of the next twenty years, was leased out any number of times, with the leases always broken through departure or death, including a period late in the fifties when the house had been occupied by a contemplative order of nuns who experienced an outbreak of "possession" hysteria reminiscent of three hundred years before among the nuns at the convent of Loudun in France. The nun in charge was found hanged from a wooden beam. "That was in 1958," said Case. From then on, he explained, the house was unoccupied until 1984, when Paul Quandt, wealthy already from inheritance and now a historian of some note, moved in with his wife and three young children. Like others, they experienced the haunting phenomena, in particular deafening bangings on the outer walls. "And then there were other things . . ." said Case, his voice trailing off. He left it hanging. In 1987, he then recounted, the unnerving manifestations ceased, and so things remained until 1990, when the Quandts moved to Italy, decided they liked it there, and put the island and the mansion up for sale. But the house's reputation had outlived its reign of peace.

"So far," ended Case, "the tragic words of this ghastly gospel."

"So it all goes back to the wife being suffocated," said Dare.

"That's right," agreed Case.

"And so the wife is the ghost, is that the plot? Heavy breathing and moaning in the hallway at night? Perhaps the sound of someone tapping a pipe against his teeth?"

Subtly, Freeboard's middle finger lifted up in Dare's direction.

"I have no information that Quandt smoked a pipe, Mr. Dare," said Case, looking mildly at sea.

"Oh, you're saying that it's Quandt who haunts the place?"

"Perhaps so." Case reached out and plucked a chocolate from a small silver tray. "Most of the victims," he imparted, "have been women."

Dare paled. "Victims? What victims? You mean *dead* people?"

"Quite."

Freeboard sighed and then shifted in her chair.

"Are we going to talk about this forever?"

The Realtor's eyes were glazed over with boredom.

"And of course, all these women died of fright," Dare said tightly.

"Only one. Three were suicides," said Case. "Two went insane."

The author turned his head and stared archly at Freeboard. "Some unscrupulous Realtor, no doubt, kept leasing the place to loonies and chronic depressives."

"Mr. Dare, you sound defensive to me," observed Case. "Is it possible you secretly believe?"

"The suspension of *my* disbelief would require more cables than the Golden Gate Bridge."

"Yeah, Dare *is* doubt," Freeboard murmured, eyes hooded.

"Precisely. But merely for the sake of my article," said Dare, "even if there were such things as ghosts, why on earth don't they beetle on along to their reward instead of drifting and clotting around the old clubhouse making thoroughgoing pains in the ass of themselves?"

Case lifted an eyebrow. "Mrs. Trawley?"

But the psychic mutely demurred, lowering her eyes and shaking her head before again looking up at a sound from Freeboard as the Realtor, with a heavy and impatient sigh, bowed down her head and closed her eyes; she'd awakened at approximately four that morning, after tossing and turning in a restless sleep. Case glanced at her unreadably, then turned to answer Dare. "Well, who knows?" he began. "But assume that when you die you're convinced—as you are, I presume, Mr. Dare—that death is the end of all consciousness. And then you die, but you remain fully conscious, so that the moment immediately after death seems no different from the one that came before. So in that case would it really be so terribly odd if there were some of us who simply didn't notice that we're dead?"

"I would notice," Dare insisted.

"Three months' notice," muttered Freeboard, half awake.

"Joan, I'm marking you absent," said Dare. He reached over and poked her in the side with a finger. Freeboard's head snapped up and her eyes opened wide. "Yeah, what's up?" she said, attempting to sound alert.

"Dr. Case was just implying that ghosts are nonbelievers; a rather nice irony, that, don't you think?"

"Yeah, that's great."

"Yes, I thought you might say that."

"Quit staring."

"I'm not staring."

"Yes, you are, Terry! Quit it!"

"I will."

The author returned his attention to Case.

"And so why wouldn't some sympathetic angel just come and tell these spirits to wake up and smell the coffee?" he asked.

"Good point. Perhaps they have to find it out for themselves."

"I think not knowing that you're dead is shocking ignorance, frankly."

"Maybe ghosts can't let go of their attachments," said Case.

"Lucky rocks," mentioned Freeboard.

Dare ignored it.

Case turned to Trawley and stared at her intently. "I meant mainly *emotional* attachments. Don't you think so, Mrs. Trawley? Or do you?"

Trawley lowered her eyes and shook her head. Softly, barely audibly, she said, "I don't know."

"What precisely *do* you know?" Dare demanded. "What is it, in fact, that you *do,* Mrs. Trawley? You're the quietest person I've ever met. Do you talk to the spirits, at least?"

The noted psychic stood up. "You'll excuse me just a moment?"

"Yes, of course," murmured Case. He looked embarrassed.

"You didn't say she was sensitive, you said *a* sensitive."

"Terry, you're a hemorrhoid," Freeboard told him quietly.

"I'm just going for some water," said the psychic, smiling thinly. She opened a door and disappeared into the kitchen.

"I respect and adore you!" Dare called after her. "I kiss your ectoplasm."

"Shall we leave it at that, Mr. Dare?" Case suggested.

Freeboard glared. " 'I am doubt' could be 'I am dead.' "

In the kitchen, Trawley went to the double sink where Morna was standing washing dishes. "May I have a clean glass?" she asked. "I'd like some water."

Silently, the housekeeper rinsed her hands, dried them, then reached to the cupboard for a glass and began to fill it from the tap.

Trawley was staring at her intently.

"You've been with Dr. Case for many years?"

"Many years."

Morna's voice was colorless and quiet.

She turned off the tap and handed Trawley the glass.

"Such an awfully pleasant atmosphere to work in," said the psychic. "Dr. Case lives near the campus, does he, Morna?"

"Very near."

"And you?"

"Very far."

Morna had returned to the washing of the dishes.

"Oh, well, thank you for the water," Trawley told her.

"Yes."

For a moment Trawley stood there, silently staring, Then abruptly she turned and walked out of the kitchen, quietly closing the door behind her. Hearing the sound, Morna turned and looked after her with unreadable ice-green eyes.

When Trawley retook her seat at the table, Case and Dare were still arguing over ghosts and Freeboard was again half asleep in her chair. "Dr. Case," Dare was saying, "with all due respect to your learning and intelligence, am I gathering correctly that you've actually made up your mind that ghosts in fact exist?"

"Mr. Dare," Case replied, "with all respect to your literary genius, I'm proposing that the mechanistic, clockwork universe of materialistic science is probably the greatest superstition of our age. Do you know what the quantum physicists are telling us? They're saying now that atoms aren't things, they're really 'processes,' and that matter is a kind of illusion; that electrons are capable of moving from place to place without traversing the space in between and that positrons actually are electrons that appear to be traveling backwards in time and that sub-atomic particles can communicate over a distance of trillions of miles without there being any causal connection between them. Do ghosts exist? Are they here with us now? In this room? Right beside you, perhaps? Who can say? But in a world like the one that I've just described, can there really be a place for a thing like surprise?"

As Dare was considering this statement, a soft but distinct, clear rap was heard. All eyes shifted to the center of the oaken table; it was as if it had been struck by an invisible knuckle. For moments no one spoke and the only sound was the patter of the rain on the mullioned windows. Then at last, beneath her breath, Freeboard murmured, "Shit!"

Trawley eyed her with a look of fond indulgence.

Dare cleared his throat and sat up in his chair. His gaze remained fixed on the center of the table as he asked, "Have you ever *seen* a ghost, Dr. Case?"

"Oh, I see them constantly."

Dare looked up and saw that Case was smiling. "Oh, come on now, let's have a straight answer," he chided. "Have you ever seen a ghost?"

"Carl Jung, the great psychiatrist, saw one."

"You jest, sir."

"No, he saw one right beside him in his bed."

"Oh, well, some people will say anything at all to get published."

"Jung suspected that the dead aren't really in a different place at all from the living," Case went on, "but in fact were in some sort of parallel state that coexists alongside our world but remains unseen because it exists at a higher frequency, like the blades of a propeller or a fan."

"You mean the afterlife is just another alternative lifestyle?"

Case smiled, put his head down and shook it. "Mr. Dare!"

"Doggie bow-wow," Freeboard murmured with a soft, lilting men-ace. Then she grimaced, briefly crossing her eyes, while her finger made a rapid slashing move across her throat. Dare shifted hooded eyes to her briefly, then ignored her. "Dr. Case," he said, "assuming the preposterous for a moment, what on earth makes you think that any ghost is going to act up on cue just because we're all here on this mission?"

"Oh, no solid reason, really." Case shrugged. "But I've charted all the really nasty happenings at Elsewhere, and, oddly, as it happens, almost all of them occurred at the same time of year."

"So when is that?" Freeboard asked. She was stifling a yawn.

"Sometime in June. Early June. In fact, right about now."

No one spoke. The only sound was the scraping of Case's spoon against the porcelain bottom of his cup as he stirred his coffee in an absent gesture. Freeboard shot a wary glance to Dare, appraising him, and felt an incipient rush of dismay as she couldn't discern that he was actually breathing. But at last he cleared his throat. "These people that you said went insane," he asked Case without a trace of his customary mocking tone: "Are they living? Is it possible they could be interviewed?"

"Yes, there is one who is still alive—Sara Casey. She's in Bellevue Psychiatric at the moment. The poor woman is completely unbalanced, I'm afraid. She insists that at Elsewhere malevolent entities are living in the spaces in the walls."

The author turned to Freeboard with a bloodless surmise.

"*Hollow* walls?" he intoned.

Case nodded.

Freeboard flipped the Phantom mask at Dare's face.

The brunch ended, Anna Trawley was back in her room. She sat on the edge of the bed in quiet reverie, staring at the silver-framed photo of a dimpled young girl that she held in her lap with still hands. Fleeting shadows of the rain's trickling currents on a window crept weakly down the paleness of her face like dying prayers. At last she propped the photo on a nightstand by her bed. She'd already placed a miniature alarm clock there, a perfect square with sides of smooth shiny brass and red numerals; she had bought it while working in Switzerland during the search for a serial killer. She noted the time: 1:14. Case and Dare were still talking downstairs when she'd left them and Freeboard had gone to her room to rest. She stood up and walked over to a narrow writing desk beneath a rain-spattered gabled window, pulled out the straight-backed wooden chair, sat down, and then reached a pale hand into the drawer of the desk and from within it fetched a silvery ink-fed pen and a diary bound in soft pink leather; in the center of the cover a floral design of lavender blossoms entwined in a circle. Trawley unsheathed the point of the pen, and with slender, short fingers she opened the diary; it was new and emitted a faint, quick whiff of glue and new-made paper. At the top of the blank first page she wrote "Elsewhere" in a large and rounded, elegant script. Her pen made a tiny scratching sound. She turned in her chair to check the clock, and then at the top of the next clean page she recorded the day, the date and the time. Below that she carefully penned an entry:

Finally, I am at Elsewhere. Forbidding from without, within it is warm. And yet something feels broken here, awry, though I haven't any inkling of what it could be. Joan Freeboard, the Realtor, is an original, I am fond of her already; she seems to make me smile inside. And though it might shock him to know it, perhaps, I do find that I like Terence Dare as well; so amusing, so wounded at his core, like the world. Dr. Case, as expected, is quite professorial. He is also quite smashingly handsome. Yet I'm sensing an aura of danger about him, as well as some mystery that he exudes. I felt it when the housekeeper, Morna, appeared. He seemed somehow taken aback. Why was that? And then again when he pointed me out to her and said, "Mrs. Trawley is clairvoyant, Morna." He said it very pointedly, I thought. And then something else: when we arrived he said, "There you all are again." What on earth could he possibly have meant by that? It could be that he misspoke, I suppose; likely so. I feel myself attracted to the man, I must say; I suppose that's why I had to get a closer look at Morna. (I still can't believe I was poking around to find out if the girl was a "live-in." Shameless!) But I find I'm unable to penetrate Case: my impressions are as stones flung and skimming off the surface of a pond in whose depths some Leviathan lurks, some puzzle that has to be solved—and yet mustn't. I see I am wandering, making no sense. The trip has been hard on my bones, so exhausting, and I'm feeling disconnected, as if in a dream. Perhaps a little lie-down will clear away the foggies. Dreams. How I dread them; I always wake up. Who was it in Shakespeare who "cried to dream again"?

Trawley looked up at the rain-streaked window, pensive, her eyes pools of memory and sadness; then abruptly she turned to her left and listened. Immobile, she waited, head tilted to the side. Then it seemed as if a tremor had bolted through the room, the lone strike of an earthquake, faint but sharp. The psychic held still and continued to listen. Then she lowered her head to the diary and wrote:

Perhaps there is something going on here after all. Either that, or I am losing my senses completely. I have just heard the voice of a man speaking Latin. Here. In this room. Not sensed—heard. I can translate the words, but I don't understand them:
*   "I cast you out, unclean spirit. . . ."*

Downstairs in the comfortable, teak-paneled library crammed with books and mementos of travel, Gabriel Case adjusted a television set as Dare watched him from a downy sofa. "Getting nothing but static," murmured Case with annoyance.

There was no picture on the screen, only "snow."

"Try another channel," prompted Dare.

"I've tried them all."

Case flipped through more channels, and then turned off the set. He sat down on the sofa facing Dare. "Perhaps it's the storm," he observed. "At least I hope so. We'd never get a repairman to come over here. Never."

Dare glowered. "I wish you'd try not to say things like that."

"What's the difference? Nothing's happened here in years."

"No one's *been* here in years."

"Quite so. Like a drink? We've got everything." Case gestured toward a built-in bar in the corner made of dark-stained oak that was shiny with wax. Four ornately carved oaken stools stained to match were arranged along the gentle curve of the counter.

Dare shook his head. "Much too early. My God, it's barely three." He checked his watch. "Eight minutes after."

"Would you like to hear the story of Jung and his ghost?"

Case was innocently staring, hands folded on his stomach.

"You have a dangerous and sly sense of humor, Dr. Case."

"The story's fascinating. Don't you want to hear it?"

"I would sooner be in Bosnia-Herzegovina eating sushi with Muslims in an old Russian tank."

Dare stood up. "I must make a few notes. You'll forgive me?"

Without further ado the author strode from the room. Case watched him walk stiffly to the staircase, ascend it, and finally vanish into his room. Case sighed and bent his head and then looked up to his left as a long and jagged fissure in the wall opened up, deep and wide, with a crackling of plaster and wood. Case watched without expression, silent and ummoving, as the massive gap sealed itself up without a trace. Then he lowered his head and gently shook it.

"Bad timing," he murmured.

A tremor shook the room.

"Bloody nuisance as well," Case grumbled. "It's the left hand not knowing the activities of the right."

He waited for another disturbance. But nothing else came.

Not yet.

Chapter Four

"You're all right?" Case asked.

"Yes, I'm fine," Trawley murmured.

"Watch your step there just ahead."

"Oh, yes, thank you."

They had entered by the alcove door beneath the staircase, descending stone steps to a concrete passageway that was narrow and dank and dark. Case shone a powerful flashlight beam on the ground just ahead to illuminate the way.

"There aren't any lights down here?" Trawley asked. Above her dress she wore a thin tan cardigan sweater. "Seems there ought to be," she gently complained.

"They're here. They don't work for some reason."

"No."

"In here. Watch your head, Mrs. Trawley."

"I will."

He led her through a doorway into a small rectangular chamber. "Well, we're here," he announced, and they stopped. He lifted the flashlight beam to a structure, an ornamental gray stone crypt just ahead of them. Carved into the front of it, glaring in fury, was a hideous and gaping demonic face identical to that on the door above.

"This is the heart of the house," Case intoned.

The psychic made no comment. He turned to her.

"That was meant to make you laugh," he said quietly. "It's what they say in haunted house movies."

"I know," Trawley said. "My heart smiled."

"It should do that more often."

Case centered the light beam on the gargoylish face. "Pretty creature," he observed sardonically.

"How hideous. That's where he buried her?"

"Not exactly," answered Case.

"Not exactly?"

"He sealed her up inside while she was still alive."

Trawley winced. "Dear God," she murmured.

"Brutal bastard. Forgive my French."

Trawley moved slowly forward and then lightly brushed a hand along the face of the crypt.

"Can you see?" Case inquired.

"Very well."

He came up beside here.

"Is Quandt in here too?" she asked him.

"Yes," replied Case. "He is here."

"How did he die?"

"Chironex fleckeri."

Trawley stopped feeling at the crypt and turned around to him. She couldn't see him, his face was a darkness.

"That's Latin," she said softly.

"It's the venom of the sea anemone. They discovered a vial of its dregs in his hand. Here. On this spot. The venom paralyzes the vocal cords, and then the respiratory system, and in an hour the victim is dead from suffocation."

Trawley put a hand to her neck. "Oh, how horrible."

"Yes."

"Why would he choose such a painful way to die?"

"God knows."

She stared at his silhouette for a moment, then turned again to look at the crypt. "Bizarre design. You said the house dates from 1937?"

"Yes. But this was here first. Before. There was once another house on this site."

"Is that so?"

"Edward Quandt tore it down and rebuilt."

"But he left this crypt untouched?"

"He did."

"And who was buried here then?"

"Or what."

Once again she turned her head to his voice. She could see him more clearly now, though his eyes were still shadowed and hidden.

"I've found mentions in his diary of something," Case said quietly. "Some overwhelmingly cruel and malevolent . . ." He paused, as though searching for a word; then said ". . . presence."

In the hush that followed, a fragment of plaster broke loose from a wall. It trickled to the floor. Case turned his head to the sound, listening; then after a moment turned back to look at Trawley. "Do you sense something, Anna?" he asked her.

"Why?"

"The way you're staring."

"You seem so familiar to me."

"Really?"

"Yet I know we've never met," Trawley mused.

"Perhaps in some other lifetime," said Case.

"Exactly. But past or future?"

Trawley turned again to look at the crypt, then she shivered and started to button her sweater as she faced around again and looked down. "Let's go back. I've caught a chill," she said.

"Oh, I'm so sorry."

He tilted the flashlight's beam to the ground just ahead, and together they exited the chamber and slowly walked back toward the steps leading up.

"Do you really believe in past lives, Dr. Case?"

"Need we really be so formal?"

"Very well," she said. "Gabriel."

"Good."

"Do you believe?" she repeated.

"I agree with Voltaire."

"Who said what?"

"That the concept of being born twice is really no more surprising than being born once."

She turned her head. His face was still shrouded in darkness, yet now she could see him much better.

"Hey, Terry!"

"You called, my dove?"

"Yeah, come in here a second, wouldjya?"

Freeboard was sitting at a desk in the library working with a small electronic calculator and a stack of recent real estate statistics. She wore thick-lensed reading glasses. Dare was in the Great Room in front of a stereo cabinet reading an album cover as Artie Shaw's "Begin the Beguine" warmed the air. "What is it?" he called out. "Too loud? Do you want me to turn down the music?"

"No, I like it. Just get in here a second, Terry, would you?"

Dare placed the album down and approached. He wore jeans, a camel sweater and new white tennis shoes. He reached the desk and looked down at the Realtor. She continued to work at the calculator.

"You're all fresh-eyed and loathsomely alert," he remarked.

"Took a snooze. God, this Case must be getting to me, Terry. I dreamed I left my body and went traveling."

"To where? Some construction site?"

"Very funny. I dunno. Someplace dark. A dark box."

"Could be worse. So what's up, my dear? What's on your mind?"

"Today a holiday or something, Terry?"

"Why?"

"You tried calling anybody?"

"Don't the phones work?" he asked.

"Yeah, they work," she replied, "but I can't get anyone to answer."

"Don't be silly. How on earth would they know who was calling?"

She looked up at him dismally for a moment, then returned to her work. "You can be such an asshole at times."

"It's a gift."

"I've called the office nine times now," she told him, "and the phone just keeps ringing and ringing. No service, no voice mail, no nothing." She nodded her head toward a telephone receiver that lay on its side atop the desk. "You hear that? Twenty minutes."

Dare picked up the receiver, put it to his ear and heard the distant, steady ringing at the end of the line. He frowned, then put the phone gently back on the desk. "Oh, well, it could be a bomb scare or something."

"Or not. Same thing happens when I try to get an operator. *Shit!*" She ripped off a length of computer tape and crumpled it up in her fist. "Now I've got to do the freaking thing over!"

Dare stood pondering silently with his head down, his hands deep down in the pockets of his jeans. "God, I really miss the dogs," he said wanly.

Freeboard punched at the calculator rapidly.

"Times one-oh-point seven two . . ."

Dare looked up as if in sudden realization and dismay.

"The dogs!" he exclaimed. "I forgot to bring the dogs!"

"No, you brought them," said Freeboard.

Dare frowned, looking puzzled and uncertain. "No, the dogs aren't here. I must have left them behind."

"I could swear that you brought them," Freeboard murmured distractedly as she punched in another set of numbers.

Uneasy, Dare looked down at the telephone receiver. "Begin the Beguine" had just ended, there was silence and the ringing at the end of the line seemed more resonant now, although somehow even farther away. Dare shook his head and bit his lip, then spoke quietly.

"How on earth could I have forgotten the dogs?"

Chapter Five

Trawley sipped tea laced with sugar and milk as she stared out the window almost touching her shoulder where splatters of rain fell in random strikes. "How long is this predicted to last? Have you heard?"

Case followed her gaze and shook his head. "No, I haven't. There's still no reception on radio or television."

"Oh."

"Must be the storm. I'm getting nothing but static."

Trawley turned to study his face. "Me too."

He looked around and met her gaze. They were sitting across from each other at a table in a windowed nook of the breakfast room that was tucked away just off the kitchen. Case gripped the handle of the porcelain teapot. "More?"

The psychic shook her head and said, "No."

He poured for himself and then plucked two sugar cubes from a bowl. They made a crisply papery sound as he unwrapped them. "And so what do you make of all this?"

"Make of what?"

"This whole thing." Case plopped the cubes into the teacup and stirred. "Miss Freeboard seems bored beyond terminal ennui," he went on, "yet she pressed me to take this thing on."

"Oh, well, yes. She did the same thing with me."

"She told me she was doing it as an enormous favor for a friend.

Forgotten his name. Oh, yes, Redmund, I think," recalled Case. "James Redmund."

"Oh."

"Why 'Oh'?"

"Well, Mr. Dare was going on about some friend of Miss Freeboard's for quite a little while in the limo driving up. Said he'd 'seen better faces in a Kuwaiti police lineup.' Could that be the same person, I wonder? Smokes a pipe?"

"I don't know. Miss Freeboard told me that he'd begged her to put this thing together. Did she tell you that, too, by any chance?"

"Not exactly. She said if it turned out that the house is haunted, she could never in good conscience make a sale at *any* price."

"No, of course not," Case agreed with a shake of the head.

Their eyes met earnestly for a moment, and then suddenly they broke into laughter together. "Oh, I suppose we'll get the truth of it one of these days," said Trawley as their chuckling tapered to smiles.

"Yes, I'm sure that we will one day. So we will."

Suddenly the tempo of the rain picked up. Trawley turned to look out but the rain was slashing and the arbor of trees beyond was blurred. "Reminds me of a science fiction story I once read," she mused. "About a planet where it never stopped raining. That could surely put an edge on, couldn't it?"

"Yes."

"Tell me, how did you get into this field?"

"Through death."

She turned her head and found him brooding out the window.

"The death of someone close to me," Case said very softly. "Someone that I loved more than life . . . more than myself. I grew obsessed with somehow proving to myself that she hadn't been utterly extinguished. Dear God, is there any pain of loss more keen than that one? I don't believe that I'd ever felt farther from the sun." He turned and met Trawley's gaze for a moment, and then looked toward the Great Room sadly. "No Cole Porter," he noted. "Too bad. I was getting quite attached to it, really."

He looked down into his teacup. "Oh, I'd always theoretically believed in the soul. Matter cannot reflect upon itself. But my grief needed more than that, it needed evidence."

"And so here you are trying to prove that there are ghosts."

Case looked up into her eyes with a warm, slight smile.

"Do you think I'll succeed, Anna?"

"Yes. I think you will."

Abruptly the rain slackened off to a patter.

"And what of you, Anna?"

"Me?"

"Yes, how did you come by your gift?"

"My gift?" She said it with a trace of bitter irony.

"You said that very oddly," Case observed.

Trawley stared out the window.

"My gift," she said dully.

"Yes, how did you come by it, Anna? By the way, there's an ancient Egyptian version of Genesis in which God says repeatedly to Adam, 'You were once a bright angel,' then describes how he and Eve have been stripped of the faculties of telepathy and knowledge at a distance. Perhaps it was natural to us once. Were you born with it, Anna?"

She turned and stared down at her tea.

"No," she said softly. "I wasn't born with it at all. It came when I'd suffered a severe concussion. I was driving my four-year-old daughter to school. The road was icy. I skid and hit a pole. She was killed."

"Oh, I'm so terribly sorry."

The psychic looked up, staring off with concern.

"Someone's frightened. I'm feeling someone's terror."

"He'll be fine," said Case.

Trawley turned and searched his eyes inscrutably.

"What was that?" she asked.

"Oh, I'm just guessing."

"Guessing what?"

"That you're sensing our esteemed Mr. Dare. I really think he's half frightened to death."

"Yes, that could be."

Case's brow knitted slightly. "He asked me if he'd brought along two little dogs. What a question!"

"Yes, he asked me that, too."

"What did you tell him?"

She looked suddenly blank.

Case waited, and then turned to another subject.

"Have you ever tried reaching your daughter?"

"Yes, I have."

"With success?"

"I don't know. I reached someone."

"You're not sure of it?"

"Dead people lie. They're just people."

He leaned back and pressed his palms against the edge of the table. "How amazing you should say that!" he declared.

"Well, it's true."

"No, I meant it confirms something for me."

"Really."

Case seemed to grow energized; his eyes sparkled. "There's a fascinating book by a Latvian scientist named Raudieve who claimed to hear voices of the dead on a tape recorder. It's called *Breakthrough: Electronic Communication with the Dead.* Do you know of it?"

"I've heard of it."

"Right. The author says more or less the same thing as you: that the dead know no more than when they were alive and gave false and often contradictory answers to his questions."

Trawley nodded.

"The voices were faint," Case went on, "and quite fleeting, almost buried under amplifier noise, and with a strange and unexpected lilting rhythm. Some moaned and said 'Help me' and seemed tormented. Others seemed content, even happy. Raudieve heard one voice that he was able to recognize, an old colleague from medical school. Raudieve asked him to describe his situation in a word or two—the voices are so difficult to hear and detect—and he answered distinctly, 'I'm in class.' Is this striking you as balmy, by the way?"

Trawley gently shook her head but her eyes smiled faintly.

Case went on: "Another time Raudieve asked—of no one in particular, he says—'What is the purpose of your present existence?' and he heard back very clearly, 'Learning to be happy.' What a statement! When I read it I got the strong feeling that what Raudieve was in touch with was precisely the afterlife described by C. S. Lewis in *The Great Divorce,* with the dead being all in the same place, really; it's how they perceive it makes it heaven or hell; and their perception is shaped by how they've lived their earthly lives." He looked down and shook his head. "I don't know. When Raudieve asked where they were, he heard a voice answer clearly, 'Doctor Angels'; then there came another voice that said, 'It's like a hospital.' And then later someone answered, 'Limbo.' "

"It's the Disturbed Ward of a lunatic asylum."

Case glanced up at the psychic. He looked puzzled.

Trawley was staring at him intently.

"And some of the inmates," she finished, "are dangerous."

Case held her gaze without expression, unblinking.

"Yes, no doubt," he said finally.

"No doubt."

"Getting back to Raudieve and the tapes . . ."

"Oh, yes, do."

"He gave up the experiments when the voices grew threatening. But before that he'd asked them, 'Does God exist?' and back came the answer, 'Not in the dream world.' When I read that it chilled me for some reason. Don't know why. Then it suddenly occurred to me that the dream world wasn't there—it was *this* one."

For a time Case probed the psychic's eyes.

She broke the silence.

"Did you ever remarry?" she asked.

Case said, "No."

Bright yellow sunlight shafted through the window.

They turned their heads and stared out at the sky.

"Ah, sun. The storm's broken," said Case.

"So it has."

"The sky's a wonder after rain, don't you think? There really are some very lovely things about this world. Sometimes we tend to grow attached to its griefs."

Trawley turned to him. Color had risen in her face.

"What do you mean?"

Case shrugged and stared down at the table. "I once heard of a woman addicted to surgery. She had endless unneeded operations. Not in a masochistic way, you understand. She'd simply grown attached to the pain. She couldn't bear to be without it for too long. It had become her very reason for existence."

He looked up and met her riveted gaze.

"We'll have a séance later?" he asked her.

Trawley looked flustered and ill at ease.

"Very possibly," she answered him tersely. "We'll see."

Case turned to the window, staring out thoughtfully, and his brow began to wrinkle a little as he nodded and murmured to himself, "Perhaps we should. Yes, maybe this time we should try something new."

Trawley stared. " 'This time,' did you say?"

Case turned to her blankly. "I'm sorry?"

"You said, 'This time.' What did you mean by that?"

Case looked foggy. "I haven't a clue. My mind wandered."

She stared at him steadily. "Yes. That happens to me, too."

"I'm so sorry."

She picked up her teacup.

"So you teach at Columbia," she commented.

"Yes."

"Such a stimulating atmosphere to work in. Do you live near the campus, by chance?"

"No, I commute," said Case. "Why do you ask?"

"Oh, just curious, that's all. No special reason." Trawley sipped at her tea, and as she set down her cup it made a tiny but prolonged faint clattering sound against the brittle porcelain of the saucer. Case darted a glance to the cup, her trembling hands. She lowered them swiftly to her lap and out of sight. After a moment Case lifted his gaze.

"You're still worried about Dare?" he asked quietly.

"Yes," said Trawley. "I'm worried about all of us, really."

"Don't be concerned," Case told her.

"Why not?"

"Nothing ever seems to happen here until dark."

"Boys? Where are you, my babies? Are you here?"

Lost and forlorn, confused, frightened, Dare made his way slowly along a hallway. Setting out to find his dogs, he had entered the hall from which Morna had first been seen to emerge, and in moving from hall to connecting hall he'd soon found himself wandering in a maze and completely unable to retrace his steps.

He opened a door and looked into a bedroom.

"Boys? Are you here? Maria? Pompette?"

Through a window sunlight sifted into the room, thin and filtered through the branches of giant oaks. A narrow beam had found its way unbroken to a bureau. Dare stared; he thought it odd that no dust motes danced within it. The next instant the dust motes appeared in the beam, swirling swiftly in a spiraling Brownian movement. For a moment Dare contemplated this event, then dismissed it and again called out softly, "Here, boys!"

He heard an ominous creaking sound from the hall, like that of a single, tentative footstep, and then the sound of a door closing quietly somewhere. Dare held his breath. He stepped out into the hallway and looked down its length. Nothing. He exhaled, then carefully moved down the hall again. "'Come on, boys! Maria Hidalgo? Pompette?" He made smacking summoning sounds with his lips.

Dare came to another door and stopped, but as he was about to push it open he heard yet another strange sound from somewhere. At first it sounded like the distant buzzing of bees, but then as Dare stood motionless, straining to hear, it became a low murmuring, indistinct and run together, of several men speaking—praying?—in Latin. Confounded, Dare stopped and attentively listened and then saw something moving at the end of the hall, a black shape. He saw it open the door of a room at the end of the hall, walk into it, and close the door behind it. The author's eyes widened. And then suddenly he leaped from his skin with a yelp as from behind him a hand came down on his shoulder. Dare whirled, his heart pounding.

"Oh, there you are," said Gabriel Case. He was standing there, smiling indulgently. "Mr. Dare, I've been searching for you everywhere. Really. Exploring the house, are we?"

"Yes. I mean, no."

The author put a hand to his chest to still his heart.

"My God, I'm awfully glad to see you," he exhaled with relief.

"I had a feeling that that might be the case."

"I got lost."

"Not so difficult to do in this house: it's disordered, no sense to where anything lies or leads. Come along," urged Case, "we're right this way." He opened a door and led Dare into yet another hallway.

"We've been missing you," he said.

"I've been missing a tall brandy-soda. Incidentally, what's that priest doing here?"

"What priest?"

"How would *I* know? Boris Karloff's old chaplain!" Dare expostulated. "I just saw him down the hall back there."

Case halted. "Are you serious?"

"Please don't do that to me, Doctor."

"Call me Gabriel," said Case.

"I said *stop* that!"

"Doctor," Case quietly amended.

"Thank you. I thought I heard this murmuring and mumbling in Latin, then I saw this tall priest walking by. You mean you don't know who he is?"

Case mulled it over, then again began to walk. Dare followed.

"Are you Catholic, Mr. Dare?"

"*Ex*-Catholic."

"Is there actually any such thing?"

"What's your point?"

"We're all alerted to seeing *something* in this house," Case said soothingly. "Our unconscious expectations have been heightened. And you've heard me say some nuns were once exorcised here."

"You're suggesting I've had a papally induced hallucination?"

"I'm suggesting that you're more of a believer than you say, and saw shadows, or, more likely, that you're sending me up. Can you tell me which it is, Mr. Dare?"

"Let's find a drink."

Anna Trawley checked the time, sat down at the desk and then penned a new entry into her diary. She wrote:

It's 5:23 p.m. I am shaken and not certain as to why I had tea with Case. My attraction grows stronger. And yet so does my sense that he is somehow a peril to me, to my soul, to my very life. When I'm near him I tremble. Isn't that absurd? God help me, I simply cannot figure it out. Am I dotty? Yes, of course, that might explain almost everything. How easy to become insane. And yet certain odd puzzles are not of my imagining. He and Morna don't agree on where he lives: one says close to the Columbia campus, and the other—Case himself—says far, far away. It's too bizarre. Perhaps one of them—the girl, I would think—misunderstood me. But that's a minor matter. The main thing is my instincts are crying out danger. And not merely from Case. I continue hearing voices, threatening, angry. I know I'm not imagining them.

They are here.

Chapter Six

Smothering, shrieking in terror, trapped in a narrow dry prison of night, Freeboard wakened abruptly from a brief, light doze and sat up on the bed with a whimpering cry. She put a hand to her forehead. It was chilly and damp. "Shit, that stupid dream *again!*" she muttered. She waited, then at last she swung her legs off the bed, stood up, trudged into the bathroom, turned on a tap and splashed cold water onto her face. Drying off with a towel, she looked in the mirror. Get a hold! she admonished herself. It didn't work. The dream was recurring and always disturbed her, yet she couldn't remember when she'd started to have it. Involuntarily, she shivered. She needed to be out of this room, to be with people. She hurried from the bathroom, picked up a clean ashtray and banged it once sharply against the wall.

"You in there, dickhead?"

Freeboard waited. Nothing. Silence. She put back the ashtray, strode to the door and walked out into the hall. There she looked up and down but saw no one. It's so quiet, she thought. She walked to the railing and glanced down at the Great Room. It was empty and still. The sconce lights were on.

"Terry?"

Freeboard waited. Then she heard something, voices, to her right. They were low and murmury, indistinct. She turned toward the sound. It was coming from the long empty hall that ran past Dare's and Trawley's rooms. At the end was a door. Freeboard stared at it, puzzled, then strode toward it purposefully as she heard the low voices again; they seemed to be coming from that direction. She got to the door and pushed it open, and as she did the voices ceased and there was sudden, deep silence. Freeboard frowned. She was peering down a long windowless corridor at the end of which stood another door. "Terry, you flaming asshole," she called, "is that you screwing around in there?" Freeboard heard a door softly closing behind her. Turning quickly, she saw Trawley coming out of her room. The psychic saw her and approached, looking tense and troubled. "Something in there?" she asked. She was looking past Freeboard into the darkened inner hall.

"No."

Freeboard closed the hall door.

"Joan, I thought I'd take a stroll around the island. Want to come?"

"Yes, I'd like that a lot," said Freeboard. "Yes!"

It would prove to be no ordinary walk on the beach.

"Your health," toasted Case.

"You keep saying that," said Dare.

The author's voice was faintly thickened and slurry.

They were sitting across from one another on the library sofas, close to the crackling of a fire. Case was leaning across a pine coffee table pouring scotch into Dare's tall glass.

"No one's forcing you to drink," Case observed.

"I wasn't bitching, I was merely observing; that's a thing that we painters can do so awfully well."

"Oh, you paint?"

"Must you challenge almost everything I say?"

Slightly inebriated, feeling loose, the author sipped at his glass and savored the scotch. And then the earth seemed to shift in a quick, sharp jolt. Dare lowered his glass and stared.

"I think a sumo wrestler just landed on the island," he intoned. He looked over at Case. "Did you feel that?"

"Feel what?"

"Never mind." Dare kicked off his shoes, swung his long legs around and stretched out full on the sofa. "There. I am invulnerable, I hold back the night. You may now tell me more about Carl Jung's ghost."

"Really?"

"Oh, yes, really, sir. Indeed. My very word."

"Well, it looked like a one-eyed old hag," began Case. "Jung was looking for a place to relax for a time, and a friend of his in London—another doctor, I believe—offered use of his cottage in the country. One beautiful moonlit night with no wind as he lay in bed, Jung said he heard trickling sounds, odd creaks, and then muffled bangings on the outer walls. Then he had the strong feeling that someone was near him and so he opened his eyes and immediately saw, there beside him on the pillow, the hideous face of an elderly woman, her right eye wide open and balefully glaring at him from just a few inches away. The left half of the face, he said, was missing below the eye. Jung leaped up and out of bed, lit a number of candles and spent the rest of the night out of doors on a cot he'd dragged out of the house. Later on he found the cottage that he was vacationing in had long been known to be haunted and was formerly owned by an elderly woman who had died from a cancerous lesion of the eye."

"I had to ask," muttered Dare.

"Yes, there you have it."

Dare reached out, retrieved his glass and sipped. He stared at the fireplace flames as if in a reverie. "I may have had a taste of the supernatural once," he said in a quiet tone. "I was in Budapest doing some research. I knew few people. I was lonely. On the morning of my fortieth birthday I went to the lobby and in my box there was a cablegram, my only mail in several days. It said 'Happy Birthday, dear Terry' and at the bottom it was signed, 'Your brother, Ray.'" Dare paused and looked down into his glass and swirled the scotch. "Oh, yes, I had a brother Raymond," he said after that. "But he died, you see, in infancy. Another brother had sent me the cable. Edward. But how on earth did Edward turn into Ray?"

The author held his glass out to Case.

"May we hear 'To your health' one more time?"

"You need ice?"

"I need warmth, my dear man, I need fire. Just the scotch. The world is quite cold enough for me, thank you."

Case picked up the bottle. Its treasure had dwindled and he poured it all out into the author's glass.

"Forgive me for asking, Mr. Dare—or rather, Terence. You don't mind if I call you that?"

"I'd say about time."

Case set the empty bottle down and leaned back.

"May I ask you a personal question?"

"Has it anything to do with LSD?"

"I don't think so."

"Or priests?"

"Oh, well, possibly priests."

Dare glared. "Henri Bergson thought the principal function of the brain was to filter out most of reality so that we could focus on the tasks of earthly life," he said. "When the filter is weakened by a powerful drug, what we see is not delusion but the truth."

"I haven't followed you," said Case.

"I saw the priest," insisted Dare.

"Oh, I see. No, that's not what I meant."

"Then what is?"

"What sent you away from your church?"

For a moment there was silence. Dare gulped down the scotch and stared into the fire. "All that rot about eternal hell's fires and damnation. Just because I like Mackinaws more than silk blouses, I'm condemned to take baths in jalepeño juice and eat napalm hot fudge sundaes with Son of Sam for all of eternity in some Miltonesque Jack in the Box? Is hell fair?"

"No, no one said that it was fair," said Case quickly.

"Well, it isn't."

"In any case, you're over that now."

"Absolutely. Dead is dead and that's that."

"So there we are. Oh, incidentally—one more thing about that one-eyed old ghost . . ."

Dare lowered his brow into a hand. "Ah, my God!"

"You find this threatening?"

"No, my fingernails *always* look charred. It's some sort of genetic balls-up in my family."

"I see."

Dare looked up and set his glass down on the table.

"You were saying?"

"Well, the ghost spoke to Jung."

"Good *Christ*!"

Case looked slightly bemused, a little grave.

"And what did it say?" Dare asked.

" 'When you have learned to forgive others, Jung, you will finally learn to forgive yourself.' "

Dare paled. He seemed taken aback.

"It really said that?"

Case was staring at him steadily. He shook his head. "No."

"You're a dangerous man, Dr. Case," Dare said softly. "I've said that before. Yes, you are. You're a peril."

Case turned and looked out through a window. The shadows of the trees were beginning to lengthen, and the sound of birds calling were fewer, more muted.

"The sun's lower," he said softly. "I'm impatient for the night."

"Pretty sky," said Trawley.

"It's a sky." Freeboard shrugged.

They had sauntered through the oaks around the house and now were ambling by the evening river's glistening shore where the sun had laid a gold piece on the surface of the waters. Her tanned arms folded across her chest, the Realtor seemed pensive, staring down at the ground.

"Something wrong, Joan?"

"Huh-uh."

"You seem edgy."

"No, I'm fine. I'm just thinking."

"What about?"

At that moment she'd been pondering her dream of the angel, the one with the memorable name unremembered and his cryptic admonition, "The clams aren't safe." Before that she'd been thinking of Amy O'Donnell from the second grade at St. Rose in the Bronx. Her best friend. Dead at nine. Pneumonia. "Nothing special. Business. I dunno." Freeboard shrugged. A moment later she stopped and looked up. She was squinting toward the sun, her browed furrowed.

"You hear that?"

"No, what?"

"Sounds like organ music. Listen."

Trawley followed her gaze, her head bent.

"Yes, I do," she said shortly. "Far away."

"Yeah, I guess there's a skating rink somewhere."

"Perhaps."

Freeboard nodded and the women resumed their walk.

"So there's Manhattan," said Trawley, looking off to the south. "I've never spent any time there to speak of," she mentioned. "Perhaps I should do that before I go home. What do you think? Is it a fascinating city?"

"Fuck it."

"You don't recommend it, then?" Trawley asked earnestly.

Freeboard turned her head to unreadably appraise her. The psychic's expression was somberly questioning, but her eyes seemed faintly amused. "You're okay," Freeboard judged her at last.

"I'm okay?"

"Yeah, that's right. You're okay. You're real."

Both hands in the pockets of her jeans, thumbs hitched, Freeboard turned and frowned down at the ground ahead. "Listen, what's the bottom line?" she asked. "I mean, spookwise."

"Beg your pardon?"

"Hey, look at this," Freeboard said abruptly. She had stopped, staring down at a sand-covered object that looked as if it might have washed up on the shore. She stooped and picked it up.

It was a bottle of champagne.

Freeboard brushed away sand and read the faded, blurred label.

"Veuve Cliquot," she pensively murmured.

Trawley eyed the bottle. She looked troubled.

"Unopened," she observed.

"Yeah, it is."

Freeboard looked up and Trawley followed her gaze to where the shoreline just ahead sharply curved to the right, disappearing from view. The two women stood immobile, blankly staring. A light spring breeze played at Trawley's dress for a moment, furling and flapping it about. Freeboard lowered her hand and the champagne bottle slipped from her fingers down to the silent and watching earth. Then as one the women turned and walked stiffly toward the mansion.

Neither of them uttered a word.

On the library sofa Dare lay somnolent as the women entered the house. Hearing their voices, soft and feathery, drifting in low from the entry hall, he opened a drowsy, bloodshot eye. "I think I'll have another lie-down," he heard Trawley saying; "I'm quite tired for some reason."

"Yeah, me too," answered Freeboard. Then footsteps ascending the stairs, doors softly opening and closing. Dare's eye slid shut and he took a deep breath. And then he opened both eyes and raised his head and listened. A sound. Yes, again! A distant whine and then a yip! And then another! Dare's face was aglow with rapture.

"Boys!"

He had brought them after all!

He would have to go and find them.

"Dr. Case?" he called loudly.

He got up and walked over toward the Great Room.

"Doctor?"

It occurred to him he didn't know which bedroom Case had taken. He hurried to the kitchen, walked in and looked around, calling, "Morna?" But no one was there.

He breathed deeply. He would have to go alone.

Chapter Seven

Uneasy and confused, fatigued, her body heavy, Freeboard lay on her bed staring up at the ceiling. Something was wrong, she knew. What was it? She tightened her hands into fists at her sides, shut her eyes and attempted to shake it off. The middle finger of her hand lifted up. "Haunt *this*!" Abruptly she sat up and swung her legs off the bed. She listened. A piano being played. She smiled. Rachmaninoff's Concerto #2, the second movement, softly reflective and colored with longing. It was the only piece of classical music she could recognize, although she never had learned its name. She had heard it in a movie.

Mesmerized, Freeboard got up from the bed, walked out into the hall and leaned over the balustrade. She saw Case at the piano below. Drawn, she walked slowly down the stairs and through the Great Room, not noticing her sense of anxiety had vanished. When she'd reached the piano, Case looked up. He smiled, then looked down at the keys and stopped playing. "Oh, well, something like that," he said in self-deprecation. He shrugged.

"That's my favorite piece of music," Freeboard told him.

"Oh, really? Well, in that case I'll continue."

"Yeah, you do that."

He lifted his hands and again began to play.

Freeboard looked around her. "Where's Terry?"

"Last I saw him he was stretched out on a couch in the library posing as a very large illuminated manuscript."

"A what?"

"He'd had a number of scotches."

"Yeah, right."

"Did you and Anna enjoy your little walk?"

Freeboard frowned, looking puzzled. "What walk?"

Case stared. A strange sadness had come into his eyes.

He lowered his gaze and shook his head. "Never mind."

"Where are you, boys? Come to me! Come!"

Apprehensive, barely breathing, grasping for courage, Dare picked his way slowly along the hallway deep within the maze of rooms within the house. The hall was interior, there were no windows, and the light from ornamental copper sconces was dim. "Boys? Come on, boys. Where are you?" Dare hiccoughed. He could taste a bit of scotch coming up. He made a face. And then froze as from somewhere behind him he again heard a small creaking sound, slow and careful, like a stealthy footfall. The sconce lights flickered and dimmed. Dare swallowed. Come along now, don't be absurd, he thought. Aloud he said, "I've written this scene a dozen times." He turned his head and peered down the length of the hall. There was nothing. The lights came back up to full brilliance and instantly the author felt the atmosphere change, like the sudden relenting of a powerful gravity, leaving the corridor buoyant and free. Dare exhaled, turned around again and slowly walked on until he arrived at a door at his left. He opened it and looked into a spacious bedroom. "Boys?" He glanced around, then closed the door and moved on. Another door. He opened it and looked in. Another bedroom with a four-poster bed. To his right he saw a makeup table. The room had belonged to a woman.

"Boys?"

No response. Yet he entered and closed the door softly behind him. Something had drawn him. He looked out a window at the pale, thin light of end of day. The branches of the oak trees were gnarled silhouettes, like those used to illustrate a Grimm fairy tale. Dare turned on a lamp on a bedside table where he noticed a large, round porcelain pillbox, white, and decorated with little purple rabbits. He picked it up carefully and opened it. It was a music box. It was playing. Dare stared as the tiny chimes tinkled in the air, a Stephen Foster tune, "Jeannie with the

Light Brown Hair." Who had wound it up? Dare wondered. He gently
closed the lid. It was then that something else began to strike him as
odd. He reached down and rubbed a finger along the table, then held
it to his gaze for examination. The room and its contents were completely
free of dust, and the surface of woods appeared newly waxed. Who was
cleaning the house? Were there unseen staff in a hidden wing? He
thought of his vision, the man in black. LSD or a *truly* silent butler? he
wondered. "Also invisible," he muttered. Then he sniffed. He smelled
perfume in the air, the scent of roses.

"Can I help you?"

Startled, Dare yelped and whirled around.

Morna was staring at him, expressionless.

Her eyes flicked down to the music box.

"Are you looking for something?"

Dare said, "No," but the reply was almost soundless, gasping through
the ice that had formed in his larynx. He cleared his throat with effort
and amended, "I mean, yes. My dogs. Have you seen them?"

"The little ones? No."

He absently nodded. He was staring at her neck.

He looked past her and noticed that the door was still closed. He
stared at her neck again. He was frowning. Then something occurred
to him. "How did you know that my dogs are little?" he asked.
"Have you seen them in the house? Are they here?"

Morna smiled, as if in secret amusement, then without another word
she turned and glided to the door, pulled it open and exited the room.
For a moment Dare stared at the open doorway, and then down at the
music box still in his hand. He gently replaced it on the table, then
walked out into the hall. "Morna?" he began. He had another question
concerning the dogs. But in the hall he saw no one. She was gone.

He was suddenly electrified by a sound. Muted and distant. The
yapping of a dog. Dare beamed and then frowned as he realized that
the bark was of a larger animal. Yet he called again, "Boys? *Men?*"
The yapping continued. Dare began to move toward the sound apprehensively. At the end of the hall he saw a door and as he neared it
the yapping grew louder, more excited, then elided into threatening
growls and barks interlaced with piercing whines, as of fright. Near
the door, Dare stopped as the voice of a man came through from
behind it: "What is it, boy? What?"

So there *was* someone here, thought Dare. There was staff.

He grasped the doorknob and opened the door.

Dare gaped. He was looking at what seemed to be a kitchen.

Trembling, teeth bared, a collie dog was confronting him, alternately whining and growling and barking. At a table sat a man and a woman in their fifties and what looked to be a husky young Catholic priest dressed in cassock and surplice and purple stole, while by a window stood a taller old redheaded priest who gripped a book that was bound in a soft red leather. The man and the woman and the younger priest were staring toward Dare as if in numb apprehension, but the red-headed priest by the window seemed calm as he walked to the table routinely, unhurriedly, to pick up a vial filled with colorless liquid. A woman in a housekeeper's uniform entered the room. She was carrying a steaming pot of coffee. As she moved toward the table she glanced toward the door, dropped the pot and emitted a piercing shriek, and as she did the old priest uncapped the vial, flicked his wrist and shot a sprinkle of its contents at the dumbfounded author, where-upon the people in the kitchen vanished.

Shaken, Dare whirled about and ran for his life.

Anna Trawley was dreaming that Gabriel Case had walked up to her bedside and put out his hand to her. "Come, Anna," he said to her gently. And then she was alone, carrying a candle and walking in the underground passage to the crypt. She knew that she was looking for something but she didn't know what it was. She stopped and raised the candle. The crypt was before her. She listened. A whispering voice. Dr. Case. "Anna," he was saying. "Anna Trawley." Then the huge stone door of the crypt came open and out of it floated an open coffin containing the white-shrouded figure of a person whose face was indiscernible, a blank. "Look, Anna! Look!" the voice of Case again whispered. The face in the coffin began to take form and Anna Trawley was suddenly awake.

Screaming.

Chapter Eight

Case lifted an eyebrow.

"Refresh your drink?" he asked.

"Refresh my *life*," Freeboard muttered.

Broody, quietly on edge, a little drunk, she was slouched in a stool at the library bar as she tamped out her Camel Lite in an ashtray overflowing with a smother of crushed, bent butts. Behind the counter Case picked up a fluted martini pitcher and poured into Freeboard's glass before beginning to prepare another batch.

"That's all of it," he murmured. "I'll have more in just a shake."

Freeboard woozily lifted her glass. *"Salud!"*

They had been at the bar for almost an hour. Freeboard had wanted a drink. She'd had several, and was verging on fluency in several languages theretofore unrecorded by man. In the meantime, their conversation had been casual, much of it centered on questions by Case about "your fascinating friend, Mr. Terence Dare." Now the Realtor observed with fogged, droopy eyes as Case poured Bombay gin atop the ice cubes that he had just dropped into the pitcher. They made a liquidy, crackling sound.

"Doc, are you on the level?"

Case looked up at the Realtor.

"Pardon?"

"I mean spookwise. You're not into this only because of the dinero or you maybe saw *Ghostbusters* twice and got jazzed?"

"I can virtually swear that number two was not the reason," Case averred. "And as far as the dinero goes, you're the only one I know who's ever paid me for this work."

Freeboard fumbled for her cigarette pack on the bar.

"How do you live?"

Case eyed her with a kindly patience.

"The university pays me," he said gently. "I teach."

"Oh, yeah yeah."

"I'm a teacher."

"Hey, I got it, okay? You want to drop it?" Freeboard glared and lit her cigarette with unsteady hands, then set her solid gold lighter on the counter with a thump.

Case lifted the pitcher and topped off her glass.

"Another olive?" he asked her politely.

"You married?"

"Yes, I am."

She looked away and muttered, "Who gives a shit?"

She picked up a book that was resting on the counter, standing it on end as she eyed its cover. *"The Denial of Death,"* she read aloud. "Is this good?"

"Yes, I think so." Case was pouring a martini for himself. "I mean to reread it tonight," he told her. "The author's Ernst Becker."

"Who's in it?"

"It isn't a movie."

She let the book drop.

Case plopped an olive in his glass and took a sip.

"Are you married, Joan?" he asked her.

She looked down, blew out cigarette smoke and shook her head.

"*Never* married?" he persisted.

"Never married."

"Any family?"

"All dead. I was the youngest," Freeboard said. "I'm the last."

"No other relatives?"

She looked down into her drink. "No, no one."

"Mr. Dare is rather close to you, I've noticed."

"He's the only man I know would never hurt me."

"Men have hurt you very often, Joan?"

Dismissively waving her hand, she said, "Ah, fuck it."

She plucked up her martini glass, sipped, and then set down the glass with a bang. Then she snatched at the book and stood it on end. "So what's this all about?" she said.

"You wouldn't like it."

Abruptly she lay the book down, staring off.

"God, I just had that déjà vu feeling again."

"Oh?"

She nodded. "Yeah. Real strong."

Case folded his arms atop the counter, leaning forward.

"Joan, I'd like to hear more about your work. Do you enjoy it?"

"Shit, I love it to pieces."

"How nice."

"I'd rather sell a fucking town house than piss."

"That should settle any lingering ambiguity in the matter."

Freeboard looked out a window. "This place is so isolated."

"Completely."

"I wonder if it's burglarized a lot."

"I don't think so," said Case without expression.

"Well, don't look at me like I'm some kind of retard," she blurted, her droopy eyes narrowing with resentment. "A lot of Navy Seals later on become criminals. Why the fuck do you think Malibu keeps getting ripped off?"

"I'd never thought of that."

"This place would be ripe."

"I see your point."

Freeboard tilted up the book again, narrowly avoiding knocking over her glass. Case grabbed it by the stem before it could fall.

"Hey, man, thanks," said Freeboard slurrily.

"Don't mention it," said Case.

"Good hands."

She looked back at the cover of the book.

"And so what's this about, Doc? Is it good?"

"Well, it deals with our terror of death," answered Case, "and how we avoid it by trying to distract ourselves with sex and money and power."

Freeboard eyed him in blank incomprehension.

"Who needs death for all that?" she said.

"Well, exactly."

She stared at the book.

"I love my life," she murmured.

"So you should," said Case. "Lots of toys."

Freeboard propped an elbow on the bar and then lowered her head into her hand. Case could no longer see her face. "Lots of toys," she said weakly. She nodded. And then, the words muffled and narrow in her throat, she murmured, "Yeah, a whole lot of toys. A whole bunch."

Case stared. "Something wrong?" he asked.

She shook her head.

"Can't you tell me?"

She was silently sobbing into her hand.

Case set down his glass and gripped her forearm very gently.

"Can't you tell me? Please tell me," he said.

"I don't know. Sometimes I cry and don't know why. I don't know. I don't know."

She continued to sob.

"What were you thinking about just now?" Case asked her.

Freeboard shook her head. "I don't know."

He touched a comforting hand to her cheek.

"Then just cry, dear," he said. "It's all right."

He looked up as a troubled Dare entered the room and sped stiffly and immediately to the bar. The author's glance quickly taking in Freeboard's demeanor, he pronounced, "I see the serious drinking flag is flying." He slid onto a stool.

"What's your pleasure, Mr. Dare?" Case inquired.

"A new body," Dare answered, "and a brain that doesn't know who I am."

"I've got martinis all mixed."

"No, no, no!" Dare pointed to the liquor bottles shelved behind Case. "Please just hand me the Chivas and a glass," he requested.

Case reached for the bottle. "You look deathly," he said. "What's the trouble?"

Case set down the bottle and looked solicitous.

"The trouble? Well, I'll tell you the trouble," snapped Dare. About to speak, he caught sudden sight of Freeboard staring at him as she dabbed at her eyes with a tissue. Dare shut his mouth and turned away. He said, "Nothing." He picked up the bottle, poured out two fingers, put it back, and then set his glass down on the bar emphatically. "Nothing's wrong whatsoever. Not a thing."

Anna Trawley now entered the room. Visibly upset, she moved swiftly to the bar and sat beside Dare.

"Hello, Anna. Have a drink?" asked Case.

"Yes, a double," said Trawley tightly.

"Then I gather nothing's wrong," said Case.

"Beg your pardon?" she asked. "I didn't get that."

Case stared at her innocently. "Just a comment."

Dare turned to look at Trawley, examining her drawn and ashen face and then her shaking hands now clasped atop the counter. He looked back into her eyes.

"What did *you* see?" he asked her.

At this Freeboard roused herself.

She said, "What? What do you mean? Who saw what?"

"I saw nothing," said Trawley, staring fixedly ahead.

"I saw less," replied Dare.

"Well, that settles it," said Case. He pulled a bottle off the shelf. "Dry sherry with a twist?" he asked Trawley.

She stared at him oddly.

"Why, yes," she said at last. "Exactly."

She continued to stare.

Case saw Dare gulping down two more fingers of scotch.

"Your health," said Case, looking over at the author.

"It isn't funny," growled Dare.

"I didn't say it was funny."

"It was *nothing*," Dare insisted.

"I know."

"What the fuck are you all *talking* about?" demanded Freeboard. She'd been glaring back and forth, her confusion and irritation mounting. Dare patted her hand. "Never mind."

Case put the sherry in front of Trawley. "I notice you staring," he said to her quietly. "Are you getting any sense of something yet?"

"Nothing new," she said almost inaudibly.

"I didn't get that," said Case.

Her gaze bored into his eyes. "Nothing new," she repeated.

"Oh."

Case glanced to the television set. "Oh, I do wish these TVs and radios would work," he bemoaned. "I'd so love to see the six o'clock news."

"Yes, no doubt," murmured Trawley. "So would I. But I certainly don't want to see myself on it."

"What was that?" asked Case.

She said, "Nothing."

Trawley sipped at her sherry. Her hand was still trembling.

"Speaking of the news," began Case. He turned back to the bar. Dare and Freeboard, he saw, were speaking quietly together. Case cleared his throat, and said, "And now what do we think about President Clinton's handling of foreign policy?"

A sudden hush fell upon the room. Freeboard and Dare had abruptly stopped talking and mutely turned to stare at Case. Their expressions, like Trawley's, were blank and numb. Not a breath, not a thought appeared to stir in the room.

Case looked from face to face, his eyes a question.

At last Dare frowned and asked, "*Whose* handling?"

Case paused, as if waiting for something, and then answered with a tinge of what could have been regret. "Oh, I meant to say President Bush. Awfully sorry. Yes, sorry. I misspoke."

The trio continued to stare, still motionless, and then they all looked down into their drinks. Trawley took a sip of her sherry, then, and turned to look out a window at the blood-red massive ball of the sun slipping low upon the mud-brown waters of the river.

"Nearly dark," she said softly. "Night's coming."

Case didn't move. He was staring at the three of them.

He lowered his head and shook it.

In her room later on Trawley opened her diary, pressed it flat, reviewed her last entry, and then carefully penned her next notation:

Past nine. Dinner over. I continue to be frightened. And what of it? To exist in the limitless dark of this universe, bruised and unknowing whence we came and where we go, to take breath on this hurtling piece of rock in the void—these alone are a terror in themselves, are they not? Fear, if we correctly observe our situation, is our ordinary way, like feeding, like dying. And yet what I'm feeling now is quite totally different; it is a terror of another kind. Not of ghosts. There is something else here that I am sensing, something chillingly alien and implacable; I fear it even more than the world. Case wants a séance tonight. It's so perilous. God help me. I dread what might come through that door!

Chapter Nine

Freeboard was sitting on the edge of her bed and the edge of her mind when she heard the rapping. Pensive and frowning, deeply troubled, her elbows were propped atop her knees while she cupped her face between her hands. Facedown and open on the bed beside her was a copy of the book, *The Denial of Death*. She had been reading it for a time but then her eyes had begun to hurt.

Although not nearly as much as her head.

The knocking again. Two raps. Much louder.

Freeboard didn't bother looking up.

"Knock it off, will ya, Terry? Cut it out!"

She heard her door opening and looked up at Dare.

"It's me," he said tensely.

"How would *you* know?"

Dare came over to the bed and sat beside her.

"Are you sitting on my glasses, Terry?"

"No. Joan, there's something very creepy in our midst."

"Please don't start with me, Terry. I mean it."

"My dear, I'm dead earnest," said Dare. She heard a tremor in his voice and looked up. He was pale and his eyes were tight and blinking. "I haven't been as frightened since I dreamed I was a Zulu trapped in the locker room of Rudyard Kipling's club."

Freeboard searched his eyes and found genuine terror.

She frowned. "You seeing things, Terry?" she asked him.

"Joan, I swear to you, I haven't dropped acid in years!"

He raised his right hand as if taking an oath.

Freeboard pondered.

"It's got residual effects, remember? Remember the giant squids with the ray guns and the letter of reference from Cheech and Chong?"

Dare pushed up the sleeve of his shirt, disclosing a red and vivid welt running up from his inner wrist to his forearm. "Does this look as if I'm seeing things, Joanie? Take a look at this! Look at my arm!"

Freeboard stared mutely at the welt for a moment. She looked up at him quizzically and said, "How'd you do that?"

"I saw a group of people in the back of the house," explained Dare. "Two of them were priests."

"They were *what*?"

"I said *priests!*"

"Oh, for chrissakes, Terry!"

"I mean it! One of them threw something at me! *This* happened!"

Freeboard reached out her hand as if about to touch the welt.

Dare flinched. "No, don't touch it!" he exclaimed.

"Looks like a burn," she said quietly.

"It *is!*"

Freeboard looked up at him. She looked dubious.

"You weren't ironing your scrapbook or anything, were you? I mean, where *are* these priests?"

"I don't know," answered Dare. "They disappeared."

"They ran away?"

"They simply vanished."

Freeboard turned and rolled her eyes. "Yeah, they vanished."

Dare thrust out his arm and showed the welt. *"This didn't!"*

She stared at it soberly. "It could have happened when Morna spilled the coffee on you, Terry."

"Yes, but wouldn't I have known that?"

"Yeah, maybe."

"I've tried to call the boatman to see about getting off the island, but—"

"You turdhead! What happened to 'I am Doubt'?"

"It got mugged in the alley by 'I am burned!' Look, the boatman didn't answer." Dare's manner was earnest and pressing, urgent. "No machine, no nothing," he continued. "I tried to call a helicopter service. No answer. I tried to call Pierre about the dogs. No answer. The *service* doesn't even pick up. You remember how you asked if today was a holiday?"

"Yeah. It's like Manhattan got nuked or something."

"And have you taken a really close look at Morna?"

Freeboard stared at Dare's hands. They were resting on his thighs. "Why, Terry, your hands are shaking!" she marveled.

"All those tiny purple spots on her face and neck?"

"What do you mean?"

"Well, she has them. They're known as *petechiae*. I researched that for *Gilroy's Confession*."

"And so?"

"They're what you see when someone dies from suffocation."

Freeboard stared.

"Oh, Mr. Dare? Miss Freeboard? Are you there?"

Case. He was calling up from the Great Room and his voice had a sinister lilting quality, as if it were coming from a fog-shrouded moor. Dare and Freeboard looked at one another in surmise.

Where had it come from, this fear? How had it jelled?

"Could I speak to you a moment?" Case called up to them again.

"He sounds just like Freddy Krueger," whispered Dare.

"Oh, shut up!"

Dare got up, went out the door and stepped into the hallway. Leaning over the balustrade he looked down and saw Case standing next to a round game table where Anna Trawley already was seated. "Ah, there you are," said Case. "And Miss Freeboard? Is she there?"

"Yeah, I hear you," Freeboard called out from the room. "What's up?" The next moment the Realtor appeared at the balustrade.

"What's harpooning?" she asked without a smile.

"If you'll both come down we can start the séance."

Chapter Ten

"Would you sit here beside me, Mr. Dare?" Trawley asked.

"Why beside you? Do you feel I'm more in need of vibrations?"

"Oh, for shitssakes sit down!" Freeboard told him.

Trawley patted the seat to her left. "Right here."

"Very well," agreed Dare. He sat down.

"And you here on my right, Miss Freeboard," Trawley told her. Freeboard nodded and quickly took her place. Case was already in the chair across from Trawley.

"Thank you," said the psychic. "We can start."

On top of the game table rested a Ouija board with an American-style planchette, a cream-colored, heart-shaped piece of plastic with a circular window set in its center. The room was in darkness except for the fireplace flames and the flickering light on the table from a group of thick candles arranged close by.

Trawley lifted an eyebrow at Dare. "No tape recorder?"

Dare shook his head. His manner brusque, he said, "No. No, I'll remember. No need." The author glanced up to the second-floor landing and a video camera put there by Case. It was aimed at the table. "And it's going on film," Dare noted further.

Trawley nodded. "Very well. Now then, you may have a few misconceptions that I think I should disabuse you of."

Dare murmured, "Of which I should disabuse *you*." Distracted, he was staring at the planchette and was hardly aware that he had spoken. Trawley glanced in his direction "There will not be any floating tambourines, Mr. Dare. No ectoplasm. No ghostly apparitions. No voices. Nothing will possess me or attempt to speak through me. Yet if something is here, it will show us, it will make itself known. My pitiful"—she turned to look at Case—"gift," she finished, "is somehow to focus its energies, that's the best that we can expect. We don't need to have the lights off, incidentally."

"Oh, I know that," said Case. "It's just to put us in the mood."

"Well, we're in it," snapped Dare.

Freeboard folded her arms and looked at Trawley.

"And so what's supposed to happen?" she asked.

"I don't know," said the psychic.

"You don't *know*?"

"No. Perhaps nothing at all will occur."

Trawley held out her hands to either side.

"Now all join hands, would you please?"

They followed her instruction.

"I need you to be quiet and perfectly still," said Trawley. "Try to help me, please. Even if you think this is foolishness, try not to speak and keep your thoughts fixed on me." She closed her eyes. "Think only of me and what I'm trying to do," she said. "Now then, shut your eyes, please."

They obliged, and as they did, a slow creaking sound was heard, as of a shutter or a door coming slightly ajar.

Dare's eyes opened wide.

"Mr. Dare, are your eyes still open?" asked the psychic.

"How on earth did you know that, madam? Are you peeking?"

"I am not. Would you close them, please?"

"I will." Dare shut his eyes.

"And now we wait," uttered Trawley. "Try to help me. And wait. Just wait." Her final words were barely a whisper. She appeared to breathe slowly and deeply for a time. And then again she spoke. It was a quiet question: "Is there anyone here with us?"

They waited. Only the crackling of the fire could be heard.

"Is there anyone here?" the psychic repeated.

Another deep silence ensued. A minute passed.

Dare opened his eyes and was about to comment tartly when the candles and the fireplace flames were snuffed out, as if extinguished by a single massive breath. The Great Room was plunged into absolute darkness and the scent of the river was abruptly in the air. "Oh, well, really," said Dare in a voice that was straining to be blithe: "How utterly banal and degrading. I saw this scene in *The Uninvited*. Is our budget too tight for a fragrance of mimosa, or is *eau de clam chowder* the scent of the day?"

Freeboard shut her eyes, then put her head down and shook it.

From somewhere a keening sound arose, and then a violent banging that kept repeating, insistent, implacable, jarring their souls.

"Domino's Pizza," said Dare. "They're aggressive."

But his voice held the hint of a tremor.

Case stood up and moved deliberately across the room to where a wooden shutter, tossed by a gusting breeze, was crashing against the inner wall. "There's our trouble," said Case. "We may have another storm coming up."

He reached the window, locked it shut and then returned.

He struck a match to relight the thick green candles.

"Oh, can't we have the lights on?" asked Trawley.

"Yes, of course." Case snuffed out the match. He walked over to the wall and flipped a number of switches, turning on all of the sconce lights and lamps. Coming back to the table, he took his chair and remarked, "So it seems it was really Mother Nature, Mr. Dare, and not Mother Trawley who produced the cliché."

"My apologies, madam," Dare told her.

"Now then, may we proceed?" Trawley asked him.

"Your servant."

As the others closed their eyes, Dare goggled. Far across the room he saw the collie dog he believed he had seen in the other wing. It was staring through a partly open door that led to the inner maze of the house. With a yip it scampered back and out of sight.

"Mr. Dare, are your eyes closed?" Trawley asked softly.

"Oh, for God's sakes, *yes*!" Dare irritably answered. He immediately closed them. There followed a silence like that of cathedrals at dawn or in lucid dreams of flying.

"Is there anyone here?" asked Trawley quietly.

More moments passed in silence.

Dare opened his eyes and let go of the hands he'd been gripping. "I don't want to do this anymore," he said tightly.

The others at the table opened their eyes.

"Oh, well, it really doesn't seem to be working, now, does it?" said Trawley. She sounded very matter-of-fact.

"No, it seems not," answered Case. He looked at Freeboard. "Well, so far it seems your clients should be perfectly safe here, Joan."

"I didn't say that I don't sense a presence," said Trawley.

Freeboard looked away and murmured, "Shit."

Case probed Trawley's eyes. "Good or evil?"

She waited before answering: "Dangerous."

Dare made a move to get out of his chair, but Freeboard gripped him by the wrist and tugged him down.

"Let's see what happens, 'I am Doubt,' " she said firmly. "Okay?"

Dare saw the interest in her face and looked appalled.

Case shifted in his chair.

"Well, shall we try something else now, Anna? Something new?"

Trawley stared at him intently for a moment, saying nothing. Then she lowered her gaze to the table and said, "Yes. The Ouija board. Just as you suggested," she added.

Case nodded his head toward the board. "Worth a try."

Dare looked past him to the door where he'd seen the dog.

"Mr. Dare, is that agreeable?" Case asked him.

Dare shifted his glance. "Yes, what's the harm?"

"Did you see something?"

"See something?"

"I saw you looking past me rather oddly."

"No, nothing," Dare said curtly. He looked tense.

"Very well, then, let's begin," said Case. "I'll just observe, if you don't mind. Go ahead. You've all done this before?"

"I know the drill." Freeboard nodded.

"And you, Mr. Dare?"

Dare said, "No. Nor have I bungee-jumped from a bridge in Lahore with a purple sacred cow in my arms."

Trawley instructed him, and moments later all except Case were resting their fingertips on the planchette as it glided slowly around on the board. "That's it," said Trawley. "Get the feel of it a bit."

"Of course it's *you* who'll be actually moving it," Case ruminated. "Your unconscious minds, I mean. On the other hand, I think that if there *were* something to it, it's because the unconscious must in some unknown way form a bridge to the other side: the spirit gives a message to the unconscious, which in turn prompts our fingers to move the planchette. You think that's right, Anna?"

"Possibly. Yes." The psychic nodded.

"Say again why we're doing this," Freeboard asked. She was staring intently at the planchette. Something was pulling her into this process. And somehow unnerving her as well.

"To be sure that the house is safe for your clients," said Case.

He and Trawley shared a look.

"Yeah, that's right," Freeboard grunted.

Dare shook his head and murmured, "Shameless!"

Her gaze still fixed on the roaming planchette, Freeboard murmured, "You're fucking up the spirits here, dickhead."

"Let your hands be at rest now," Trawley advised them. The planchette ceased its motion and the psychic closed her eyes. A deep silence ensued. Trawley lowered her head.

"Is there anyone here?" she asked.

Nothing happened; the planchette stayed at rest. Then as Trawley began to repeat the question, the planchette made a lurching slide to the YES in the upper left corner of the board. Dare stared at the word. "I didn't do that," he said quietly. He shifted his glance to Freeboard. "Did you move it?"

"No, *you* did."

Trawley uttered softly again:

"Who is here?"

The Great Room was still. The air was thick. And waiting.

Trawley's brow began to crease. Vaguely troubled, she again probed the darkness: "Who is here?" she repeated. Almost before she had finished speaking, the planchette lurched downward with vigor to a letter. Trawley opened her eyes in apprehensive surmise.

"U. The letter U," noted Case.

Again the planchette began to move swiftly, carrying their fingers from letter to letter.

"Come on, Terry, you're moving it!" Freeboard accused him.

"I am not!"

Case called out the letters one by one as the planchette moved to Z, and then U, and then R - D - E - R - E - R - H - E - R - E.

And stopped.

"Zurderer here?" Dare wondered.

He was rapt and intent, all cynicism vanished.

"Makes no sense," Freeboard commented, frowning.

As she spoke, the planchette glided up to the NO.

" 'No,' " said Case, looking thoughtful.

Then, "There it goes again," he said abruptly.

The planchette moved to Z and from there to M.

"Z-M," Case murmured. " 'No Z-M.' What on earth could that possibly mean?" he pondered.

"Not Z but M," guessed Dare.

He looked up. "The Z is wrong; it should be M!"

" 'Murderer here'!" exclaimed Freeboard.

The planchette fluttered up to the YES.

"My God, it's Quandt!" Dare breathed.

A shocked hush fell upon them. Trawley lifted her eyes to Case. "Are you Edward Quandt?" she asked the presence.

Somewhere a door creaked slightly open. Freeboard was watching it as it happened: it was the thick carved door that led down to the crypt. She turned to look at Dare as she noticed that his fingers felt icy cold, and as she did the planchette slid upward again. It stopped on the NO. Then rapidly it flew to other letters and numerals. As it did, Case called them out: "M - O - N - E - O - F - U."

Her eyes on the board, Trawley paled.

" 'Murderer one of you,' " she said softly.

For a moment no one spoke. Then Freeboard erupted, "I'm getting freaked! Take your hand off it, Terry!"

"I'm not moving it," said Dare.

She looked angry. *"I said, take off your hand!"*

Dare caught a glimpse of Trawley and was taken aback to see tears in her eyes. Then he noticed Case staring at the psychic with compassion; he was shaking his head and seemed to be mouthing the words, "No, Anna. No. Not you." What the *hell* was this about? the author wondered. He lifted his fingers from the planchette.

"Tell us who is the person who is communicating," said Trawley in a husky, low voice. "Who are you? What is your name?"

They waited but the planchette did not move. Freeboard turned to Dare with a knowing and accusatory smile. "Ah-*huh*!" she said, nodding her head. Then abruptly she turned her head back to the board as the planchette moved rapidly under their fingers.

Case called off the letters. "A . . ." he began.

On the next one, Freeboard joined him, chiming in, "Ce."

Case looked up at her and smiled. Then he leaned back and

watched with what looked like satisfaction as the Realtor alone went on calling out the letters:

"Ce . . . Ee . . . P . . ." The planchette hesitated. "T."

Then the movement ceased.

" 'Accept,' " said Dare with a frown. "It spells 'accept.' "

"So what's *that* supposed to mean?" puzzled Freeboard. " 'Accept.' Accept what?"

"Or who?" mentioned Dare.

The planchette was moving again, swinging wildly back and forth between the letters G and O.

"G - O -G - O," murmured Dare.

Trawley winced and put her head into her hand. It was as if she'd been stricken by a sudden stab of migraine. As she lifted her hand from the plastic planchette, it flew off the board and rattled onto the floor, where after brief motion it at last lay still.

Case put a hand on Trawley's arm. He looked concerned.

"What is it? What's wrong?" he asked.

"I have to stop. An awful stabbing in my head."

"Oh, I'm so sorry," said Case.

Frowning, Freeboard stared at the Ouija board. " 'Go.' 'Accept,' " she wondered aloud. "What in shit could that mean?"

"What did you *mean* it to mean?" Dare said coolly.

"And what the hell does *that* mean?"

"Oh, well, clearly you were moving it, Joan."

"Bull-*shit*!"

"You're suggesting Mrs. Trawley was moving it? Bizarre!"

Freeboard stood up and strode away from the table.

"I've had it, guys. Really. Adios."

"Where are you going, love?" Dare called after her.

"I don't know," she replied. "I don't care."

She was headed for the foyer.

"Maybe for a walk," she called back. "I need air."

The clacking of her heels on the floor receded. The front door opened and closed. She was gone. Case turned back to Trawley. She had both elbows propped on the table now, her head cradled down into her hands.

"How's the head?" Case asked with concern.

"Getting better."

Dare's glance shifted back and forth between them.

"Are we finished?" he asked stiffly.

"Yes, I think so," said Case.

Dare stood up and addressed them both. "Let me thank you for these thoroughly exhilarating moments. Never have I felt quite so glad to be alive since Evel Knievel invited me to join him in leaping a chasm in Ulan Bator. You'll excuse me? I'm finding that I need to make a call." The author turned on his heel and strode toward the staircase. Case watched his quick footsteps ascending the steps, saw him walk down the hall and disappear into his room.

Case dropped his glance to Trawley.

"Shall I ask Morna to bring you some aspirin?"

Trawley said, "No." It was barely audible.

"Been a bit of a bust tonight, hasn't it?" said Case.

Trawley nodded her head. Case thoughtfully appraised her in silence for a time and then he reached out his hand and touched it to her arm.

"Did you move the planchette?" he asked her quietly.

She dropped her arms to the table, lifted her head and stared at him blankly. "What?"

"I mean, unconsciously," he said to her gently. "Do you think you caused your daughter Bethie's death? That you're the murderer?"

Her look was incredulous.

"I really don't know what to say," she responded.

"When your daughter Bethie died—" Case began.

But she cut him off.

"I never told you that my daughter's name was Bethie."

Head down, hands deep in the pockets of her jeans, Freeboard trudged along the shoreline, lost in thought. There was an aching and a churning deep inside her, a sense of displacement, of loss, of fear, and of an answer that kept voicelessly shouting its name. *Case. That freaking Case and his freaking martinis.* That's what had started it, she brooded. *And then reading that goddam freaking book.*

Abruptly she stopped in her tracks and looked up.

Something was wrong, she felt. What was it?

The silence, she suddenly realized. No sounds. Not of the river nor of birds nor any life. She could hear herself breathing, hear the beat of her pulse.

This is weird!

Freeboard looked toward the village on the opposite shore. There wasn't any fog and the night was clear. Shouldn't there be lights? she wondered dimly. When she turned her gaze south toward Manhattan she blinked. And then suddenly her eyes were wide. She gaped numbly. She took a step backward, bewildered, frightened, and then cried out in outraged incredulity, *"What?"*

She turned and ran back toward the house.

Chapter Eleven

Breathless, Freeboard burst into the entry hall, closed the door with a bang and fell against it. She looked up at a sconce and then into the Great Room as all the mansion's lights began to flicker down to dimness. "Terry?" she called quietly. She waited. No response. Cautiously she moved into the Great Room. "Terry?" she called out more loudly.

She glanced all around.

"Dr. Case? Anna?"

The silence grew stranger. Nothing moved. Freeboard walked to the library, scanned it quickly, and then rapidly moved to behind the bar, where she poured a few fingers of rye into a glass, gulped it, and then stood there, trying to collect herself. Then her eyes grew wide and she froze as she heard a sound like rusted hinges, and then of heavy stone grinding slowly over stone. It seemed to be coming from beneath her. Freeboard darted a numb look into the Great Room and the door beneath the staircase leading to the crypt.

Shit!

It was still unlocked and ajar.

Freeboard set down her glass and strode out of the library, calling out, "Terry? Terry, where the fuck are you?"

She looked up at the door to his room.

"You up there? Terry? Dr. Case?"

She went to the stairs and quickly ascended them and then walked to the door of Dare's room. She knocked and called, "Terry?" but immediately burst into the room without waiting for an answer.

Dare was packing a suitcase that lay on the bed.

"Do come in," he said tartly. He didn't look up.

Freeboard flung the door loudly shut behind her.

"I'm beginning to think that you're right!" she said tremulously. She swooped to the bed, sat down and watched him arranging a shirt in the bag. "I'm beginning to think there *are* ghosts," she admitted. Dare threw his hands into the air and quickly turned to her, squalling, "But I don't *want* to be right about that!"

"I'm getting freaked, Terry. Really."

Freeboard held up her hands to her own inspection.

"Look at this! I mean, *look* at this! *My* hands are shaking!"

Dare looked down and saw the trembling, then said softly, "Oh, my dear!" He dropped the lid on the suitcase and sat down beside her. Taking hold of her hands, he tightly clasped them in his own.

"Why, my dear, dear Joan," he said to her worriedly.

He looked into her eyes.

"Yes, you truly are frightened. Terribly."

She glanced at the telephone receiver; it was lying on its side on a bedstand. She could hear the dull ringing at the other end.

"Is that the boat you're calling, Terry?"

"Trying. Tell me, precious, what has happened? Tell me all."

"Take a look out the window."

"There aren't any."

"Right. Holy shit, Terry!"

"What, Joan? What is it?"

She bent and put a hand to her chest, as if trying to catch her breath. "I went outside," she told him haltingly. "The sky's clear, there's a moon, big stars. But there isn't any city there, Terry; there's no skyline of Manhattan—no lights, no planes, no nothing!" She looked up into his eyes. "God, I'm really getting scared, Terry. What's going on with this place? I wish—"

She halted. Something was different. Her glance flicked over to the telephone receiver. Dare said, "What?" Then he followed her gaze.

"The ringing," said Freeboard. "It stopped."

The silence that had settled on the room was profound. It spoke of finality, of a chapter that was ending. And a new one, something alien, about to begin. Dare stood up, reached over, picked up the receiver and slowly put it up to his ear. Then he quietly placed it back down on its cradle.

"It's dead," he said dully.

The next moment the lights in the room dimmed down and from somewhere in the house came a jarring sound, like the muffled blow of a giant sledgehammer wrapped in velvet striking a wall. Freeboard turned a frozen look to Dare. "Terry?" He sat down beside her as another blow came, and then another and another, growing louder, coming closer to the room.

"God, what is it, Terry? What?"

"I don't know."

Freeboard gasped. Her eyes widened.

"It's coming up the steps!"

"Is the door locked?"

She shook her head and said, "No! It doesn't lock!"

"Oh, my Christ!" uttered Dare.

Freeboard clutched him with both her arms.

"Jesus, Terry, hold on to me! Hold me! I'm scared!"

He glimpsed the child's fear in her eyes, the helplessness. He took hold of her and held her tightly. "Don't be frightened," he said into her ear. "It's all right!" And she might have believed it had she not felt the furious racing of his heart.

They gaped at the door.

The poundings were picking up speed, throbbing closer.

"It's out in the hall!" whimpered Freeboard. "It's coming!"

"Shh, shh, Joanie!" Dare hissed in her ear. "It may not know that we're in here! Don't move!" he ordered. "Don't make a sound!"

Dare thought of every ghost story ever written, of every imaginable malevolence conceived by every fantasist who ever had lived. Malevolence? No, that wasn't what he felt was coming toward them; it was hatred, an implacable, terrifying fury.

Her eyes wide with fright, Freeboard gasped.

"Oh, my Christ!"

The poundings had stopped in front of the door.

God in heaven! thought Dare. Let me faint! Please let me faint!

A flow of cold energy, sickening, enraged, flowed into the room in sheets, in waves. Then the presence, the stillness, at the door grew thicker. Moments later there were tiny creaking sounds, tiny thumps, like fingers feeling at the door frame, as if they were seeking an entry point. Freeboard jammed a knuckle of her hand into her mouth in an effort to stifle another whimper. There were tears in her eyes. Then the probings ceased and from the hall they heard only a threatening silence. And then they were gasping, crying aloud, at a deafening crash against the door. And then another and another, relentless, unceasing, a battering ram made of murderous thoughts.

"Dr. Caaaaase!"

It was Freeboard. Terrified. Shrieking.

Abruptly the pummeling came to an end and Freeboard's cry bled into silence and the frigid and weightless air of the room. Dare felt her trembling uncontrollably. "It's all right!" he whispered in her ear, then put a comforting hand against her cheek. *What's the meaning of this ludicrous courage?* he marveled. It would never have occurred to him the answer was love. He listened. A sound. A faint squeaking of metal. He looked and then gasped: the doorknob was turning! Dare quickly put his hand over Freeboard's eyes and tried to remember the Act of Contrition. Then the turning stopped and reversed itself, easing back to its original position. The next instant the poundings resumed, but more softly, the hammerings more muffled and pneumatic. Throbbing like a heartbeat, they were moving away, growing fainter and fainter, more distant. Dare exhaled in relief and took his hand from Freeboard's eyes. They were wide. "What's happening?" she whispered in terror. "It's going away," he whispered back. And then suddenly the pounding started up in full force again, deafening, returning to the door with savage fury. Freeboard gaped and her lips were moving but her words were completely inaudible as a strident keening filled the hall and the door began to buckle and bow in its center, bulging and creaking and straining inward as if bent by an angry and unthinkable energy furiously attempting to break into the room. Freeboard's mouth was wide in a scream of terror that not even Dare was able to hear. And then he was gaping at something, astounded, for though the door was still closed he could see two figures who were standing in the hall directly in front of it as if they were about to enter: motionless and silent, staring into the room, they were the priests he thought he'd seen in the other wing. The taller one, older, with a freckled face, held a book that was bound in bright red leather. With the vision the poundings grew faster, more violent; then abruptly the energy seemed to relent and it ebbed to a muffled, steady pulsing as the door creaked back to its original shape. Freeboard cupped a hand to her mouth and emitted a stifled sob. The soft poundings receded, moving slowly down the hall, growing fainter and fainter until at last they were gone.

Freeboard took the hand from her mouth. "Jesus, Terry, I want to get out of this place!" she whispered hoarsely.

"Me too."

"You think it's gone?"

Dare shook his head. "I don't know."

He started to get up to go to the door but the Realtor quickly tugged him back down. "No! Don't open it yet! I don't trust it!"

"Yes, you're right," he whispered back.

They waited. And then voices. From below. Trawley and Case.

Dare and Freeboard leaped up and moved swiftly to the door, opened it and rushed out into the hallway. Below them, Case and

Trawley were ambling into the Great Room, quietly chatting. Trawley laughed. Freeboard called down to them loudly, "Hey!"

Case and Trawley looked up. Dare and Freeboard were hustling down the stairs, rushing up to them. "My God, am I glad to see you guys!" exclaimed Freeboard. She was breathless. "Where in freak have you been?" she exclaimed.

"Why, I was just showing Anna the rest of the house," replied Case. "Is something wrong? Have you seen something? Tell me." He fumbled at his pockets, as if searching for a notepad and pen. He examined their faces. "Yes, I see something's happened," he said.

"No shit! Listen, don't ever leave us like that!" Freeboard told him.

"You're so pale, dear," the psychic observed. "And you too, Mr. Dare."

"I'm in tatters," Dare declared. "Undone."

"Well, what was it?" asked Case. "What did you see?"

"I don't know," Freeboard answered. With a knuckle, she brushed away a tear from her eye. "There was something. It came down the hall. It was trying to get in, it almost bent in the door!"

"What door?" asked Case.

"To my room," said Dare.

"First we heard this loud sound," recounted Freeboard. "Like a sledgehammer pounding on the walls. The whole house shook, it filled up your brain! And then it—"

"Excuse me," said Case, looking past her. "Oh, Morna, dear?"

Dare and Freeboard turned and saw the housekeeper standing close by. Where had she come from? wondered Dare.

Morna's eyes were on Case as she answered, "Yes?"

"Have you been in the house this past hour?"

"Of course."

"Then you heard it," said Freeboard.

"Heard what, Miss?"

"Heard *what*?" Freeboard giggled.

"You heard nothing unusual, Morna?" Case asked. He was frowning and seemed dubious and uncertain.

"No, nothing at all," Morna answered serenely.

"It was shaking the *house*!" Freeboard blurted incredulously.

"Yes, *exactly*!" added Dare. "It was deafening!"

Morna gently shook her head and said softly, "I heard nothing."

"Oh, well, shit!" muttered Freeboard. "So I'm looney toons."

"But *I* heard it *too*," Dare exploded.

"Tell me, Morna, where were you?" Case asked, his frown deeper. "I mean, just this past hour," he added.

"In the kitchen."

"This is crazy!" blurted Freeboard. She threw up her arms.

"Will there be something further?" asked Morna.

"You're very sure, Morna?" Case persisted.

"I am. Is that all, please? I can go?"

Case held her gaze with some mysterious emotion in his eyes. It was something like longing. Or grief. Then after moments he said softly, "You may go. And thank you. Thank you more than I can say."

"Yeah, me too. Thanks a bunch," grumbled Freeboard.

"Then good night," Morna told them. She held Case's gaze for another long moment, and then turned and glided slowly toward the hall at the end of the room, the one from which she first had appeared. Freeboard watched her, nonplussed. "Good *night*?"

"There's no question of what we saw and heard," averred Dare. "Oh, well, *heard,* at least."

"You saw something?" Case raised an eyebrow.

"No, not really." Dare backed off it. "I'm afraid I misspoke."

"Oh, well, screw it. Doc, I want to get out of here," said Freeboard. "Like tomorrow. First thing. If it means I have to *swim* back, I'm outta here. Really!"

"Yes, ditto, as Joe Pendleton would say," agreed Dare.

Case looked puzzled. "Joe Pendleton?"

"The boxer in *Here Comes Mr. Jordan,*" Dare told him.

"Ditto ditto," said Freeboard. "I want out."

"Yes, of course," replied Case. He seemed thoughtful, staring down at the floor as in an absent gesture he gently stroked and tugged at his lips. He shook his head. "In the meantime, we seem to have a mystery on our hands. But I think that perhaps we can solve it."

"How's that?" demanded Dare.

Case gestured toward the second-floor hallway.

"There's a camera been running up there through the séance, and another at the end of the hall. If there was anything there, it would appear on the film or on the sound track, in which case we'll have learned what we set out to find and Mr. Dare can write a mesmerizing article about it. On the other hand, if nothing turns up on the film— no hammering sounds, no ghosts . . ." Case shrugged and let it trail off. Then he turned to look at Freeboard.

"Would that ease your mind?" he asked.

Freeboard set her jaw firmly. "It's there."

*   *   *

"Note the time code at the bottom right corner of the screen," said Case. He pointed to the spot with his finger. "As you see it reads eleven thirty-three P.M."

He was standing by the library television set and on the screen was a view of the empty Great Room. Trawley, Dare and Freeboard watched from a sofa close to the warmth of the fireplace flames. "As you can see," continued Case, "there's nothing there. Nothing visible. No sound of any kind. No poundings. Neither camera turned up anything at all."

Dare looked flummoxed.

"Oh, well, the microphones must have malfunctioned."

"No, they didn't," said Case. "Not this one, at least. Here, watch."

Within moments Case and Trawley appeared on the monitor screen as they entered the Great Room from a hall. Their footsteps, their quiet conversation, were fully and crisply audible.

Freeboard stared at the screen and shook her head.

"That's just plain crazy," she murmured. "It's nuts."

"But no poundings and no ghosts," reminded Case.

"But I tell you we heard it!" Dare fumed. "There's no question, it was absolutely there!" His cheeks had reddened.

"Yes, it's certainly a puzzle," Case agreed. "No doubt of that." Working buttons on the video camera he'd connected to the television monitor, he was rapidly rewinding the tape. "But now here's an even deeper one," he told them. He was shaking his head. "I just don't understand it," he said. "Not at all." Then at last he said, "There. There's the spot. Now look at this. It's from when we did the séance." Case touched a little button and the tape ran forward. Once again the Great Room was projected on the screen. Near its center was the game table, with the Ouija board resting atop it.

The time code read 10:30 P.M.

Freeboard gaped. "Hey, where are we? What's going on?"

The planchette atop the Ouija board was in motion, desultorily gliding from letter to letter. But no one was seated at the table. There was no one to be seen in the room, in fact, except, for a moment, a large collie dog who appeared at the entrance to a hallway and then hastily scurried away and out of view. Dare stared at the screen, his face blanching, and Trawley was mutely shaking her head. "The date's wrong," the psychic murmured. She was staring at the date just below the time code. "It says 1998."

"We're not on the film," said Freeboard dully.

She was staring at the screen, uncomprehending and lost.

Dare leaped to his feet. "Oh, well, for godssakes, this is ludicrous! Really! It's mad! It's clearly some sort of absurd mistake!" He looked over at Freeboard. The Realtor had jumped up with a wince of pain and began to move quickly away from the fireplace.

"Holy shit, I'm burning up!" she grimaced.

And then Trawley leaped up, and then Dare. "Where's this god-awful heat coming from?" he complained. He followed Freeboard and Trawley into the Great Room. Of them all, only Case seemed completely unaffected. He came to the library door and watched calmly, although not without a look of great interest and concern.

"Dear God!" Trawley cried.

With a look of surprise, she staggered backward a step, as if shoved by an invisible assailant. And then surprise was transmuted into gaping fear as she staggered yet another step back, and then another. "Someone's pushing me!" she gasped. Another shove. "Oh, my God!" she started crying; "Oh, my God!"

And now the sound of a blow against the mansion's outer wall.

"Oh, my Christ!" breathed Dare in terror. "Oh, my Christ!"

"I'm burning up, Terry!" cried Freeboard. "I'm burning!"

The pounding at the outer walls continued, thunderous, painful, penetrating bone. Lamps and tables began tipping over, scraping, sliding, hurtling through the room while huge paintings were ripped by a force from the walls and sent flying, spinning through the air of the Great Room as agony and madness descended upon it, on the house, on their bewildered, burning souls. "Someone tell me what's happening!" Freeboard screamed, hands pressed against her ears and the torment of the poundings, and suddenly Trawley was shrieking in pain as a bloodless furrow slashed down her cheek, as if plowed by an invisible white-hot prong. A ritual chanting in Latin began, nightmarish, reverberant, and low, as if murmured by a hundred hostile voices, and then Freeboard was lifted by an unseen force and sent hurtling, shrieking, across the room to slam into a wall with a sickening final thud and crunch of shattered bone. Dare and Trawley couldn't see anymore, all their blood had rushed up into their brains as now they too were seized by the force and carried up swiftly, spinning, toward the ceiling, spread-eagled, eyes bulging in terror, screaming, until they had slammed into the mansion roof and then plunged to the floor like crumpled hopes.

It was not a dream. It was real.

PART THREE: DÉJÀ VU

Chapter Twelve

The carved front door of the mansion burst open as if by the force of a desperate thought. "Holy shit, is this a hurricane or what!" exclaimed Freeboard. Sopping in a glistening yellow sou'wester, she staggered and tumbled into the entry hall with a keening wind at her back. She turned to see Dare rushing up the front stoop, and Trawley, carrying a bag, behind him, slower, deliberate and unhurried. A rain of all the waters of the earth was pelting down.

Freeboard cupped a hand to her mouth:

"You okay, Mrs. Trawley?" she squalled.

"Oh, yes, dear!" the psychic called back. "I'm fine!"

A booming thunder gripped the sky by the shoulders and shook it. Dare entered and dropped a light bag to the floor. "Joan, I owe you a flogging for this," he complained. "I knew that I never should have done it."

"Well, you did it," Freeboard told him. "Now for shitssakes, watch your mouth, would you, Terry? I had to practically beg these two people to do this."

She removed her yellow windjammer hat and then gestured to the open door, where the psychic seemed to falter as she climbed the front steps. "Terry, give Mrs. Trawley a hand," ordered Freeboard. Dare snailed toward the psychic unhurriedly and reached for her bag with a drooping hand. "May I help you?"

"Oh, no thank you. I'm fine. I travel light."

"Yes, of course. Tambourines weigh almost nothing."

"*Jesus,* Terry!"

Trawley entered, took off her hat and set down her bag. "That's all right," she told Freeboard with a smile; "I didn't hear it."

Freeboard leaned into the wind and shut the door. In the silence, it was Dare who first noticed the music. "Dearest God, am I in heaven?" he exclaimed. "Cole Porter!" The author's face was alight with a child's pure bliss as from behind the stout doors that led into the Great Room drifted a melody played on a piano.

Dare stared. "My favorite: 'Night and Day'!"

Freeboard moved toward the doors.

"That you in there, Doc?" she called out.

"Miss Freeboard?"

The voice from within was deep and pleasant and oddly unmuffled by the thickness of the doors. Freeboard opened them wide and stepped into the Great Room. All of its lamps were lit and glowing, splashing the wood-paneled walls with life, and in the crackle of the firepit flames leapt cheerily, blithe to the longing in the strains of "Night and Day." Freeboard breathed in the scent of burning pine from the fire. The sounds of the storm were distant.

"Yeah, we're here!" she called out. She smiled, moving toward the piano, while at the same time removing her dripping sou'wester. Behind her came Dare and, more slowly, Anna Trawley. Freeboard's boots made a squishing sound. They were soaked.

"Ah, yes, there you all are again, safe and sound," said Gabriel Case. "I'm so glad. I was worried."

He had strong good looks, Freeboard noticed. The firelight flickered and danced on his eyes. She saw that they were dark but wasn't sure of their color.

"This storm is amazing, don't you think?" he exclaimed. "Did you order this weather, Mr. Dare?"

"I ordered Chivas."

Dare and Freeboard had arrived at the piano and stopped. Anna Trawley hung back beside a grouping of furniture that was clustered around the fireplace. She was glancing all around the room with a vaguely uncertain and tentative air.

"Are you a ghost?" said Dare to Case.

Freeboard turned to him, incredulous, her eyes flaring.

"What crap is this?" she hissed in a seething undertone.

"That's how they show them on the spook ride at Disneyland," said Dare, not lowering his voice: "a lot of spirits dancing while a big one plays piano."

Abruptly Freeboard put a hand to her forehead. "This has happened before," she said, frowning.

Case raised an eyebrow. "What was that?"

"I'm having déjà vu," Freeboard answered, troubled.

"This is neither the time nor the place," snapped Dare.

Freeboard put her hand down and looked at him oddly.

"Jesus, Terry. I knew you were going to say that."

"How could you?"

"And I knew what Dr. Case was going to say."

"That's incredible," said Case. He lifted his hands from the keyboard. "Déjà vu reflects backward, not forward," he said. He turned his head slightly and looked past Freeboard. "Ah, here—"

"Comes Morna."

Dare and Freeboard had said it together with Case.

Case stared. He glanced to Morna for a moment—she was standing close by—and then stood up, looking mildly puzzled.

"How on earth could you have known Morna's name?"

"I don't know," said Dare. He looked perplexed.

"It's all happened before."

At the quiet voice, they all turned and saw Trawley in a chair by the fireplace. Her haunted stare was on Case.

"You too?" Dare asked her.

The psychic turned to him and nodded. "Yes."

Freeboard lowered her head into a hand.

"Hey, wait a minute, guys. I'm getting weirded out."

"Yes, it truly is amazing," said Case. "Awfully strange." He continued to stand behind the piano, but his arms were now folded across his chest. He seemed somehow not a part of the group, but an observer, detached, as if watching the unfolding of a play.

Freeboard put a hand to her head, walked sluggishly over to a sofa and sat on the back of it. "I've got to sit down," she said weakly. "I'm feeling so tired all of a sudden."

"Now that you mention it," said Dare, "ditto." He headed for the furniture grouping. "What is it?" he wondered aloud. "I feel utterly drained for some reason. And I'm feeling disconnected from things."

Freeboard nodded. "Yeah, me too," she said softly.

Dare sat down on the sofa behind her.

"What is it, Joanie? What could it be?"

"I don't know." Abruptly Freeboard winced, as in pain. "Jesuspeezus, my head!" she complained.

"Is this house playing tricks with us already, Dr. Case?" Dare asked. "I mean, presuming there are tricks to be played."

Inscrutable, Case glanced over at Trawley and asked, "What's your read on all this, Anna? What do you think? Are you having the same reaction?"

Trawley nodded.

Case unfolded his arms and scratched his head.

"Well, this is all too bizarre," he said.

"You mean it's creepy," said Freeboard.

"It's so hard to accept that you knew Morna's name," pondered Case.

Dare looked up. "What did you say?"

"Accept."

And now Freeboard was staring at Case intently, her eyes growing wide with some jarring realization.

"Accept," Dare murmured to himself.

The quiet word was affecting him strangely. Why?

"Just so baffling," said Case: "Three people with the same déjà vu; with jamais vu, in fact."

Freeboard rose from the back of the sofa, perplexity and nascent alarm in her eyes. "Hey, wait a second! What the fuck is going on here?" she demanded. Her tone was belligerent and angry.

"Yes, we're trying to figure that out," Case said blandly.

Freeboard strode up to him, stopped and examined his face.

"You're not Gabriel Case!" she declared.

Dare turned to her, taken aback.

"What on earth are you saying, Joanie?"

"I'm saying this guy is a fake! He's not Case!"

Dare looked at Case and became more confused, for he read his expression as fond, perhaps pitying.

"Are you bleeding mad, Joan?" he exclaimed.

Freeboard whirled on him.

"Terry, I've seen pictures of the man! I've talked to him!"

"Then why didn't you say so in the first place?"

"Who gives a shit, Terry! Who cares! All I know is, this man isn't Dr. Case!"

"Yes, it is!" insisted Dare.

"It is not!"

"It is! He looks *exactly* the same as every other time before: the same scar, the same—!"

The author abruptly broke off as the meaning of his words began to register upon him. "What on earth?" he whispered, shaken.

"Terry, what is it?" asked Freeboard tremulously.

She'd seen the look on Dare's face and felt a dread.

"What in God's name is happening to us?" breathed Trawley.

Stunned, Dare slowly stood up.

"This keeps happening again and again," he said numbly.

Freeboard walked over to Dare, her face ashen.

"What is it? What's wrong with us, Terry? *Tell* me!"

But the author was staring at Case, transfixed.

"Who are you?" he asked him in a weak, dead voice.

Freeboard and Trawley turned their heads to look at Case.

"Yes, who are you?" the psychic repeated dully.

Case scrutinized each of their faces intently. "Come with me," he said gravely. "I have something to show you. I think that perhaps you're now ready. Will you come? We'll just go for a pleasant little walk on the beach."

The trio stood motionless and silent. Something submissive had entered their beings. Their eyes and their postures had changed. They looked crumpled.

Case turned a kindly look to Freeboard.

"You seem tired, Joan," he said to her gently. "Are you tired?"

She shook her head mutely.

"Then come," said Case. "Let's go."

Staring and moving as if in a reverie, the trio followed Case outside. It was dawn but a heavy fog enshrouded them. Another storm was on the way: swift gray clouds scudded low above the river, and far to the north they could see dim lightning flashes, brief bright souls in the dark. Case escorted them in silence through the grove of oaks and to the path along the river where Trawley and Freeboard once ventured but then mysteriously had stopped. And now, as they neared the sharp bend in the shoreline, it was Dare who first halted, staring quietly ahead. The others stopped with him, uncertain, apprehensive. A gusting breeze ruffled Trawley's dress.

"Do you wish to continue?" Case asked softly.

No one answered. No one moved. Then at last it was Freeboard who broke away from them and strode toward the curve in the shoreline. One by one, then, slightly faltering, the psychic and the author followed. Apprehensive but satisfied, Case stayed behind. He looked to his right. Then he walked to a marshy, reeded area, where he parted a clump of brush and stared sadly at the tiny, sun-bleached skeletons of what appeared to have been two dogs. He looked up at a sound from around the bend. A horrified shriek. Freeboard. Case sighed and looked regretful, shaking his head. He hastened to catch up with the others.

Around the bend Anna Trawley had fainted. Their eyes wet with tears, Dare and Freeboard helped her up, and then together, legs trembling, they walked toward the shore where they stood and stared mutely at the rusted wreckage of a capsized motor launch whose name, though blistered and faded, could be read: *Far Traveler*.

A tiny sob escaped Trawley.

"We're all dead," said Freeboard numbly.

Dare nodded his head, looking dazed.

He said, "We died in the storm coming over."

"That's correct."

They turned and saw Case coming toward them. When a few yards away, he stopped and surveyed them, and then said to them: "*You* were the ghosts haunting Elsewhere."

With a whimper, Trawley slumped and fell back against the wreckage. Dare reached out a trembling hand to Freeboard.

"Hold my hand, love," he said, his voice quavering slightly.

Freeboard took his hand and gripped it firmly.

"It's okay. I'm with you, Terry," she said.

"And I with you."

Case appraised them for a moment, then spoke. "I never quite completed my history of the house," he began. "I don't suppose you'd like to hear it."

"Oh, now, stop that," snapped Dare, recovering. "Bad enough to be dead without having to stand in the damp and hear tired old rhetorical devices. Could we simply go on with it, please?"

Case smiled. "For the longest time—years after their death—Edward and Riga Quandt haunted the mansion, frightening and unbalancing the tenants, even killing a few, by the force of their hatred and rage at one another. But by the middle of the eighties they had made their peace, accepted their deaths and decided to move on. But then four years ago, *you* came. You and the launch captain died coming over. The captain moved on. You three didn't. Or, to be more precise—you *wouldn't*; you refused to accept that you were dead."

"Yes, I know that now," Dare sighed. "I understand. I see everything clearly now. Very clearly."

"In that case you can explain why you refused to accept your death," Case challenged. "Can you do that, Mr. Dare?"

"Yes, of course. I was terrified that death meant damnation."

Case nodded. "Quite so. And you, Anna? Can you see what held you back?"

"Only dimly, I'm afraid."

"You'd grown addicted to your grief for your daughter."

"Oh, dear God!"

"Strange attachments that we make, don't you think?"

Trawley shook her head. "Could that really be so?"

"Am I some kind of orphan here?" Freeboard said testily.

"Oh, Joan," said Case.

"Oh, yeah, 'Joan.' Cheezus-peezus," she grumbled.

"You were terrified of dying," Case told her.

"Shit, so's everyone. Come on, now. What else?"

"You couldn't bear to let go of your toys," Case said gently.

Dare turned to her loftily and sniffed, "So immature."

Freeboard glared.

"And what now?" Trawley asked. "Do we leave here?"

"That's entirely up to you," replied Case. "You may choose to cross over or choose to stay. In the meantime, my assignment here is mercifully finished."

Freeboard wrinkled up her nose. "Your assignment?"

"Yes, Morna and I—we were sent here to lead you to discover the truth. Each time in the past that you almost confronted it, you'd reject it and then start the whole cycle all over, reliving again and again your first arrival here at the mansion; all but the shipwreck, of course; you blocked that out, just like everything else that would bare your delusion. That's why you had no memory of your walk on the beach, Joan, because you knew around the next bend was *Far Traveler*. Incidentally, you've been acting out this fantasy for years, dear hearts, even *after* we arrived here to help. Stubborn sorts!"

Trawley gasped and put a hand to her cheek.

"And so that's why you seemed so familiar to me."

"Yes."

Trawley sighed. "So it was not another lifetime."

"No, Anna," said Case.

"I'm crushed."

Dare turned to Freeboard and spoke to her quietly. "Isn't it hysterical? You couldn't sell the house because you were haunting it." Freeboard lowered her head into a hand. "Honest to God, if you weren't dead already . . ." she murmured.

"Speaking of which," spoke up Trawley. "We were eating and drinking and all that sort of thing. Have we got new bodies?"

"Heavens no," replied Case. "It's all an illusion, my dear, nothing more. You've all been creating your own reality. The island and the mansion are solid, they are here, but you've all reconstructed them to fit your delusion."

"We're not solid?" the psychic persisted.

"You are not."

"Not even astral sort of somethings or other?"

"Give it up," Dare advised her.

"Get a life," added Freeboard in an undertone.

Dare turned to her and nodded approbation.

Case lifted his chin. "Now then, what have you decided?" he asked. "I must say, if nothing else, I do hope that if you cling to the earth you'll at least have some pity on those poor, abused people who've been trying for so long to live peacefully at Elsewhere. You know; Paul Quandt and his family, poor darlings. You've given them a devil of a time. No pun intended."

"What on earth do you mean?" asked Dare.

"You had them terrified out of their wits! You remember all that burning and flinging about and those nightmarish poundings that so frightened you all? Don't you know what was causing all that?"

"I can hardly wait to hear," Dare said dryly.

"The Quandts brought in *Jesuit priests to drive you out!*"

The author turned to Freeboard with a smirk of satisfaction.

"Did you hear that?"

"Oh, be quiet, Terry."

"Priests!"

"Shut—*up!*"

They heard someone clear his throat. It was Case.

"And so what's it to be?" he asked. "A change of frequency? I certainly hope so. I must say, I've grown fond of you all. Very fond."

Freeboard looked down and shook her head, uncertain.

"Boy, I really don't know," she said.

Case looked at her with fondness.

"I must say, I would miss you, Joan."

She looked up in surprise and said, "*Me?*"

"There'd be no more loneliness there. No more tears."

Freeboard's eyes began to fill.

"That's the deal?" she asked.

"That's the deal."

"This world was never meant to be a home to us, Joan," said Case. "This world is a one-night stand."

Abruptly Freeboard's eyes lit up in surmise. "Hey, it's you! You're the angel in my dream! Gabriel! 'The clams aren't safe'; that meant the river!"

"Well, I know what *I'm* doing," said Dare.

Freeboard turned to him and lifted an eyebrow. "You're going?"

"Yes!" exclaimed Dare. "I'm off!" The author threw a kiss in the direction of the river. "*Adieu*, space-time!" he called out. "Be good!"

He was beginning to disappear.

"Hey, wait for me!" Freeboard shouted.

She, too, was beginning to vanish.

"*Adieu,* sucky speed-reading critics and reviewers!"

Dare was almost invisible.

"Hey, slow down a second, will you?" Freeboard nattered.

"Oh, well, of course, I'm at a *much* higher frequency, Joanie."

The next moment they were gone. But a raucous cry of pique and frustration was heard, then a slap, and then the voice of Dare complaining: "No hitting in the afterlife, Joanie!"

Case and Trawley remained, and they looked at one another and smiled as they heard a dim yapping, as of two little dogs.

"Oh, my heart! Can it be?" came a waning cry from Dare.

And then Freeboard. "Can you puke in the afterlife?"

"Boys!"

Dare's voice, intermingled with the dogs' faint yapping, held a joy that he'd never felt or known.

In this life.

The sounds faded away.

"Well, Anna, and what about you?" Case asked her. "Are you coming? Bethie's waiting, you know."

Trawley frowned. "What's become of Dr. Case?" she asked. "I mean, the real one. Did you off him or something?"

"No, Anna. Dr. Case is alive, poor soul. When he heard that you three had died, he simply left and went back to his teaching."

"Oh."

Case took a step toward her. "Now then, shall we go together?"

Trawley stuck her hand out in front of her, halting him.

"No, not yet," she said. "First I want to know who you are."

"Would you believe that I'm a being of light?"

"Try again."

"Now *I'm* crushed," Case replied. "What's the difference *who* I am?"

"A very large one. Knowing where you came from might give me some clue as to where you might take me, if you get my drift. In this circumstance, I'd have to say that character matters."

"There isn't any smoke or mirrors, Anna. You can trust me."

"It's the smoke part that worries me," she said.

"You're not serious, Anna. Oh, come, now!"

"Well, you're certainly not an angel, now, are you? You deceived us. You pretended to be Gabriel Case."

"But of course. It's as you said, Anna—'Dead people lie.'"

He smiled that brilliant archangel smile.

Trawley's laugh was full and rich, free of burden, overflowing.
Case started forward, his arms held out to her.
"And now shall we go elsewhere, my lovely?"
She jabbed a fist high into the air and cried, *"Yes!"*
Then rushed forward to meet him with open arms.

E PILOGUE: 1997

The waking sun strewed shuttered gold upon the blue-gray waters of the silent river and the island air was filled with peace. Inside, in the echoing mansion Great Room, laughing young children were chasing one another while their parents, Paul and Christine Quandt, were in the library wrapping up some interesting business with a pair of tired Jesuit priests. One of them—husky, very young, inscrutable—stood with his hands in the pockets of his coat as he watched an older, taller priest tuck a book of prayers bound in bright red leather into a briefcase, snap it shut, and then scratch his nose with a freckled finger. "There, that's that," he sighed. "We're done."

He reached up and ran a hand through his thinning red hair.

Christine Quandt glanced into the Great Room.

"Oh, well, the kids are feeling good about the place," she noted.

The old priest followed her gaze. "Bless their hearts."

He picked up the briefcase.

A somber Paul Quandt was seated at the bar in a short-sleeved blue denim shirt and jeans. He shook his head. "I can't believe all this business started up again, Father."

"You moved back in when?" the priest asked him.

"May second. We'd been living in Europe. We'd taken the house off the market after that poor woman died, that Realtor. My God, what a shock to come back to all this!"

He took a sip from a large white mug of coffee.

The red-haired Jesuit glanced to his companion, who'd continued to silently watch and wait. The young priest somberly and knowingly nodded and then fixed an unreadable gaze on Paul Quandt.

"Oh, well, yes, I can imagine," said the redheaded priest.

He moved toward the bar.

"Well, all right. And now let's hope that's the end of it," he offered.

"Really," Mrs. Quandt said dryly, nodding.

"I'll be waiting outside," the younger priest told the other with a move of his head. "I need a smoke."

"All right, Regis. Be right with you," the older man answered.

The young priest started away.

Paul Quandt called out to him.

"Thanks for everything, Father!"

"Me too!" his wife added.

The priest raised his hand in acknowledgment.

He kept walking and didn't look back.

"Good fellow," said the older priest, looking after him.

"So young," murmured Christine Quandt. She watched the young priest go out the door. "Looks barely twenty."

"Yes, I know," said the older man. "My assistant took suddenly ill; they found Regis at the very last minute for me."

"Oh, you just met at the house?"

"Yes, that's right." Something occurred to him. "Wasn't that the name of the boy who died? Your cousin? Edward Quandt's son?"

"Yes, it was," confirmed the wife.

"Lovely name."

The priest held out his hand.

"You won't stay for some brunch?" she asked.

"Thank you, no. I've got a mass at eleven. In the meantime, God bless," he said. "You're nice people." The priest took her hand. "Oh, would you please call the boatman?" he asked in an afterthought.

Paul Quandt got off the stool and shook his head.

"Already done it. Thanks again for the exorcism, Father."

"Well, let's hope that it gives you some peace."

Quandt nodded. "Amen."

"That's *my* line," said the priest.

The Quandts smiled. Then they noticed that the Jesuit was staring at something, a large oil painting above the fireplace of a man and a younger woman.

"Are these your famous aunt and uncle?"

Quandt said, "Yes."

The priest nodded, then said softly, "I know their story."

He slowly walked over to the painting, staring up.

"Tragic history: a murder and a suicide," he grieved.

"No," said Quandt quietly behind him.

The Jesuit turned around to him quizzically.

"No suicide," said Quandt.

"No suicide?"

Quandt came over and stood beside him, the porcelain coffee mug still in his grip. "No. No suicide, Father. Two murders."

"What?"

Quandt looked up at the man in the painting.

"Well, the truth of the matter, Father, is that Auntie apparently was cheating on Uncle and wanted him out of the way so badly that she put a deadly slow-acting poison in his drink. While he was dying, Uncle Edward found the vial that the poison had come in, and he sealed up Auntie alive in the crypt and then died himself right there on the spot."

"By the crypt?"

"By the crypt."

"How awful," said the priest.

"Not quite *Romeo and Juliet*," said Quandt.

His wife came up beside them. "Just misses."

The old priest took a final look at the painting, and then turned away to leave. "Well, I'll pray for them both."

"Thanks, Father," Paul Quandt told him. "I'd really like to imagine that they're at peace."

"Well, good-bye again."

The priest gave a wave.

"Bye, Father."

As the red-haired Jesuit left the room, a large collie dog came bounding up to him, and then followed him toward the door.

"Hello, boy," the priest greeted him.

"Oh, now, leave the good Father alone," Christine Quandt called out. "Come on, Tommy! Come on back here, you nutcase!"

The priest, still walking, looked over his shoulder. "No no no, I like dogs!" he called back. Then he turned and looked down at the collie. "Come on, Tommy! Good boy!"

The dog barked and leaped up at him playfully, following.

"Yes, I had a good doggie like you when I was little," said the priest. "Oh, yes, Tommy. Good boy. Good boy."

They had reached the entry hall. The priest opened the door and they went out. Paul Quandt put his arm around his wife's waist and together they looked up at the painting again. Riga Quandt had rugged, imperfect features that nevertheless were intensely sensual and gave an impression of beauty. Her star-crossed husband, Edward Quandt, had dark good looks, a chiseled face, and a vivid scar that jagged like lightning from his cheekbone down to the base of his jaw.

They were the faces of Morna and of Gabriel Case.

★   ★   ★

The two priests and the dog were approaching the dock where the motor launch would soon pick them up. They could see it starting toward them from the opposite shore. The older priest picked up a stick and threw it. "Go, Tommy! Go!" he commanded. "Fetch!"

The dog took off with a bark and a bound.

The freckled old Jesuit glanced at the sky.

"Clearing up. Looks as if it's going to be a nice day."

They walked onto the dock and to its end, their steps thudding hollow on the dry old planks.

"I'm so glad you were able to fill in," said the older priest. "You're at Fordham, you said?"

"Yes, at Fordham."

"You know Father Bermingham there?"

The stolid priest shook his head.

"The directions were good, by the way? You found the village and the dock with no trouble?"

"No trouble. The launch was there waiting for me."

"Good. And so what do you think, young Regis? Tell me. Do you think we accomplished something? You believe the house is haunted?"

The other shook his head. "Beats me."

The old priest stared at him. "You look so young."

"I know."

The old man stared down at the sparkling waters where some blueness of the sky was beginning to reflect. "What a terrifying mystery the world presents to us, Regis. We know so little of the way things really are; of what *we* are, finally."

"True."

"A neutrino has no mass nor electrical charge and can pass through the planet in the twinkling of an eye. It's a ghost. And yet it's real, we know it's there, it exists. Ghosts are everywhere, I think; they're right beside us . . . lost souls . . . the unquiet dead. You know I wonder if . . ."

Turning to the Jesuit beside him, he broke off and looked puzzled, then taken aback. He looked around and behind him, frowning in bewilderment. He said, "Regis?"

There was nobody there.

Copyright Notices

NATIONWIDE PRAISE FOR
999

"Dazzling . . . a devilishly good deal." —*Boston Herald*

"A new benchmark of excellence."
—*Publishers Weekly* (starred review)

"Proof positive that the horror genre is alive and well."
—*Denver Post*

"Anyone unable to find something to raise the hair on the nape of the neck in *999* is likely in need of resuscitation paddles."
—SFSite.com

"It will certainly be around for decades." —*Kirkus Reviews*

"One of the best anthologies of horror and suspense of all time."
—*Rocky Mountain News*

"For horror fans, *999* is a romp in paradise." —Associated Press

"Here comes horror utopia. . . . A surefire fan pleaser." —*Booklist*

"Chock-full of excellent fiction showcasing the breadth of writing that exists in the horror field." —*Cinescape*

"An extraordinary anthology." —*Interzone*